THE CRAB APPLE CREEK ANTHOLOGY

Set 1 – The Crab Apple Series
Safe in Crab Apple Creek
Return to Crab Apple Creek
The Other Crab Apple Creek

Set 2 – The Legend of The Crystal Caves

The Crystal Dragon

The
Other
Crab Apple Creek

Dr. KARMLE L. CONRAD

The Other Crab Apple Creek

By

Dr. Karmle L. Conrad

DEDICATION

"For all the Dreamers…Always believe in Your Magic."

~Karmle L. Conrad

ACKNOWLEDGEMENTS

Thanks to my Katelyn Lee for your inspiration. Keep living your life to the fullest…follow your dreams. I love ya' to the moon and back infinity googlie!

Thanks for your support my Sammi – your dedication to my work keeps me going! Bless your little ol' pea-pickin' heart!

Map by Jay Mooers - www.edenparktales.com

CHAPTER 1

I t happened again. The dream. This time there was more detail. And, this time it woke Katelyn up from a sound sleep. She woke up trembling and scared. At first, she didn't know where she was. She was about to scream when she felt her bed beneath her and realized she was about to throw her pillow at something horrible. She turned the light on as fast as she could and saw that she was in her room. She took a deep breath, dropped the pillow, and shivered. She was cold! She wrapped herself in her robe she found at the foot of the bed and sat there trying to figure out what had just happened.

She had fallen asleep around eleven or so. It was Tuesday last night. She hadn't had any alcohol with dinner. Dinner was around seven. Nothing out of the ordinary. She didn't do street drugs so that didn't count. What the hell was that dark, disgusting thing that had tried to grab her? It was just a dream but, what the fuck? This was the fifth time she'd had it in the last couple of months. And, this time, it was worse than the last.

Katelyn got out of bed and turned on every light in her little cottage. She made herself a cup of soothing tea from the blends she had and sat down at the table. Time to figure this thing out.

It started the way it always did. She had had a busy day and was ready for bed. She fell asleep without any worries. Somewhere in the night, she found herself in a dark place. A place with little light. The air was gray and black and the place was not familiar to her. It seemed to be a bad place. Maybe like hell. She tried to walk out of the darkness but no mater which way she went, she always stayed in the darkness.

The first few dreams ended here and she would wake up feeling a bit scared until she realized she was in her own bed. She would then shake it off and go back to sleep. The dream never came back the same night. The last two times the dream had gotten worse like tonight. She was being chased by a

1

demon. He was all red with bright yellow eyes oozing blood and he smelled so bad she threw up in her dream. The demon laughed at her and kept chasing her telling her she was his. She screamed so loud tonight that she woke herself up. Oh my God! What the fuck was that all about? She ran to her room to make sure she hadn't barfed all over her bed and the floor. She saw that she hadn't. Good.

Katelyn went back to the table and made another cup of tea. She looked at her hands because the tea cup was shaking and realized that she was still trembling from the dream. She remembered she had a quartz crystal her friend Kendra had given her years ago before she left for college. Kendra had told her to keep it with her, in her pocket, at all times. Katelyn had forgotten to do this a long time ago. She grabbed the crystal off the window sill and held onto it. She immediately felt a warmth come over her and she calmed right down. She knew a little about Magic having grown up in The Creek, but she had never felt it, experienced it, until now with the crystal. Crab Apple Creek was surely a place where Magic lived.

She felt better like someone was protecting her. Or something was protecting her. She finally began to feel sleepy so she went back to her bedroom and crawled into bed. She looked at the clock and saw that the time of the dream night terror was the same as all the other times. It was a bit past three in the morning. She left the light on and fell into a deep sleep.

Katelyn woke up when her phone played her alarm song. She stretched then remembered the night terror. She felt something poking her arm and saw that her crystal was lying under her.

She grabbed it, got out of bed and got ready for work. Not sure why, but she felt protected from the demons in that dream as long as she held onto the crystal.

The next few nights were quiet. No night terrors.

It had been a long day in the design studio for Katelyn. She loved her work and had three major projects going at the same time. Designing dream home interiors that made her client's dreams come true was her passion. As soon as she stepped outside, she was reminded what Alabama was like in the summer. Sizzlin' hot and humid. Thank God for remote start. At least her SUV was getting cool inside. She set her portfolio in the back and hopped in the driver's seat and closed the door as quickly as she could. She removed the sun screen from the windshield and realized it was later than she thought. The sun was getting ready to set which meant it was close to nine o'clock. She was exhausted. Good thing it was Friday and she could sleep in tomorrow morning.

As she headed out, she decided to get take-out for supper as it was so late. Her favorite food was anything southern as long as it came with cornbread and honey. She got home close to ten o'clock as she lived a ways outside of Montgomery in a little tiny community near the Wetumpka Impact Crater site known by the locals as The Crystal Village on account of all the shocked quartz crystals found in the crater. It didn't even have a post office, but was well-known as a place were creative folks liked to live. There was always music, theatrical productions, art shows and more going on in the village. Katelyn felt right at home here. It was a bit like The Creek in that it held some Magic as well.

Just as she was unlocking her door, a shadow flew over her. She looked up into the clear evening sky and saw a huge shape fly by. Oh well, it was probably an eagle or something. It looked like one of its tail feathers was broken or something as it was hanging down off the back of the bird. Those eagles were huge and there were a lot of them in the area. Beautiful and majestic to watch.

She settled into her supper and soon fell asleep. It happened again. But this time she could have sworn it was real. She found herself back home in The Creek. It was a sunny summer day with a light breeze. She had just walked into The Bend in The Road Country Store and saw Ted and Michael up in the dining area. The Store was a gathering place for everyone and Ted was known for his creative meals and such.

"Hey Ted, Michael," she called out as she walked towards them.

"Katelyn," they both hollered out as they rushed to grab her into a big hug. "It's great to see you after so many years. What brings you home?" Ted said.

"My stars, child, it's been forever. You okay?" Michael asked.

"Yes. Yes, I'm okay. Just felt it was time to come home," Katelyn replied.

Ted and Michael looked at each other and smiled.

"Whatever the reason or reasons, we're thrilled you're here. How long are ya' plannin' on stayin'?" Ted asked as they settled at the dining room table.

"Well, I'm here for good," Katelyn began.

"Yahoo!" Michael hollered. "This is some of the best news I've heard in a long while."

She looked at them both, then the tears started to fall.

"Oh, darlin', what's the matter?" Ted asked as he went over to her and put his arms around her.

"Nothin', I think," Katelyn replied. "It's just been so long since I was home that I didn't expect to feel this way. I guess I missed home more than I thought."

"That happens for sure, Miss Katie," Michael said. "Well, I do believe you've lost way too much weight since you were last here. Ted, time to feed this child."

Katelyn laughed through her tears as she gave Ted a hug before he took off for the kitchen. "I'm not even gonna' begin to ask what y'all have

3

cookin' back there. I know better than that. You always seem to know just what a body needs."

"Yes, we do," Michael said as Ted came through the kitchen door with a loaded tray of food.

"Since it's in the middle of the mornin', I brough a little bit of breakfast and lunch. Help yourself," Ted said.

"Oh, my stars, this is what I think I missed the most. Or, maybe in my top five things I missed the most," Katelyn said as she started to sample a bit of everything. "There's no way I'm gonna' eat all this, so help me out boys."

"Of course," Ted and Michael said at the same time. They all laughed then spent the next while eating and talking about the food, The Creek, and Katelyn's work.

Ted and Michael brought Katelyn up-to-date on Emily and Ethan, Matthews and Jenna, Miss Cora, Kendra, the battle in the Sacred Rock Meadow, Jay's passing, the fight to keep The Magic in the Creek up at the Holler, and all the little details she had missed.

"My family kept me in-the-loop with most of this stuff. But, not so much about Jordan Jackson's new farm and those crystals. They sound amazin'. I wonder if he'll allow me to stop by and take a look at them? I lived in The Crystal Village in Alabama for the past few years and Jordan's crystals sound like some of the ones I've seen back there."

"I'm sure he would. He such a great guy. And, now, a part of The Creek family forever," Michael said.

"Great. I'll get a hold of him in a few days. I've still gotta' get home. No one knows I'm back except the two of you. Please don't tell anyone. I want to surprise the folks."

"We will keep your secret," Michael said as he looked straight at Ted.

"Who me? Tell on a secret?" Ted laughed. "I promise, Miss Katie, not a word until I hear it from someone else that you're home."

"Okay. Thanks. Well, now that I've been stuffed like a Thanksgiving turkey, I'm gonna' head home."

"Miss Katie, take the leftovers for a snack later or whatever," Ted said as he boxed them up for her.

"Now, Ted, my folks are gonna' love you for this. Bless your little ol' pea-pickin' hearts," Katelyn said as she took the bag from Ted and they headed to the door.

"Thanks guys. It's so great to be back home in The Creek," Katelyn said as they hugged.

"See ya' soon," Michael said as she walked out the door.

When Katelyn woke up a few hours later, she was surprised to find she was still in her cottage in Alabama. She was so sure she had returned home to The Creek. She could still taste the food she had eaten with Michael and

Ted. She was bewildered and confused that she was still in her place in The Crystal Village. That was no ordinary dream. Something was going on here. As she got up, she looked at the clock on her phone and was surprised to see it showed eleven o'clock.

No way! She knew she was tired, but she hadn't slept that late since her college days at Brenau University, where she earned her Bachelor's Degree in Interior Design with a minor concentration in business management. Those four years had been fun and exhausting. Her mind wandered back to some of those happy memories for a bit.

She moved right into her Master's program in Architectural and Interior Design, finishing in less than the usual two years. She was on a mission. Her plan was to be hired by a big design firm to get a few years of experience then open her own business. She was hired as soon as she finished her Bachelor's degree by the leading design firm in Montgomery, Alabama. The Lloyd and Johnson Design Firm was known for their high-end clientele and their out-of-the-box designers, both structural and interior designs. They were in great demand all over the Southern U.S. and even had clients around the globe. They only hired the best designers and they had been watching Katelyn's progress throughout her college days. They had been told about her from one of their designers who had met Katelyn at a design convention during Katelyn's junior year. The designer and Katelyn had stayed in touch and when the designer from Lloyd and Johnson asked for Katelyn's portfolio in the last couple of months of her senior year, she gladly shared it. She was offered the job the day after she graduated. She told the firm she was going right into her Master's degree and they said they supported her and would work around her schedule. It was a match made in heaven for sure. Katelyn had just finished her fifth year with them when the dreams about returning home started.

This one this morning was another in a series that had started out just like any other dream except she remembered every one and all the details. The first few had been simple. But the one this morning was in great detail and she knew something was up because she could still taste the food she had eaten in the dream.

She may not have had any other worldly or magical experiences growing up but she knew about The Magic and this dream was, for sure, something different. She wouldn't be surprised if Magic had something to do with it.

She got out of bed, showered and ate lunch. She jotted notes about the dream down in her journal, which she kept next to her bed for just this reason.

It was Saturday and she was meeting her best friend Sami at three. They were headed to a local fair that always had great events and stuff. People from all over the south came by each year. This was the first fair of the spring and summer seasons. The dream kept nudging into her thoughts as she went about her day and was still there when she met Sami and they headed out to the fairgrounds.

"Hey girl what's new?" Sami asked as they jumped into Katelyn's SUV.

"Not much. How about you?" Katelyn replied.

"Same thing. I've been thinkin' about changing my life and getting my Master's degree. All online of course."

"Really? That's awesome! What area?"

"Well, that's what I'm having a bit of trouble settling on. Can't decide between, civil engineering, architectural design, or something between the two? What do ya' think?"

"Holy shit, girl, that's a wide bunch of space between the two! You do love architecture since you're always drawing some kind of building. I love the designs you come up with. They are so different than most almost as if they have an other-worldly aspect about them?"

"What? Like Disney stuff?"

"Noooooooo. So far removed from Disney. They have a feel of their own. A few have reminded me of Star Wars stuff a little, but very different in the end. Where do you get these ideas anyways?"

"I don't know. They just come to me. So, I guess the civil engineering thing is a no," Sami laughed.

"Yeah...a no for sure! Have you checked out different schools with all online programs yet?"

"Funny you should ask. I have and I like what two of them have to offer. I guess I'll do the FAFSA thing and then decide on the school. This was really easy. I should have brought this up before."

"I am a firm believer of things happening just like they're supposed to. You were supposed to talk about this right now."

"I agree. So, now that that's taken care of, let's talk about the fair. I have a few artists I want to go to and, of course, the music at the end of the day. I love to hear the kids singin' and all."

"I agree. I have a few artists I want to visit, too, so I guess we're gonna' have a blast," Katelyn replied.

"We should be there in about ten minutes. I can't wait to see the art work from the shocked crystals from the meteorite. Those are really amazing," Sami added.

"Yes, they are and that's one of my picks as well. Look, seems like a lot of people want to see stuff. How about we park in the field behind the fairgrounds like last year? I'll turn down this dirt road and we should be there soon," Katelyn offered.

"Okay. Be careful of the ruts and stuff," Sami said as they bounced along.

They found a place to park rather close to the fairgrounds and were inside a few minutes later.

The place was really busy and full of people.

"First things first," Sami said. "Fair Food!"

Katelyn laughed as they headed for the fried dough booth. They both bought fried dough nuggets. Katelyn had powdered sugar on hers and Sami had chocolate drizzled over hers. They found a spot under an old oak tree and proceeded to laugh as they got powdered sugar all over the place. Folks nearby were doin' the same thing so they all laughed and talked for a bit as they enjoyed their treats.

"Well, we'll be on our way. Take care y'all," Sami said as she and Katelyn left.

Folks replied in kind and the girls spent the next few hours visiting their favorite artists and looking at all the fair had to offer.

Just a bit before the singing was to start, they found the shocked crystal artists' booths. The booths faced the west and the sun was at an angle that made the crystals shine so bright you had to shade your eyes just to look at some of them.

Katelyn was drawn to a stone that was set off by itself, not as a piece of jewelry or anything. It just sat there on a shell and shone brilliantly. The colors were every shade of the rainbow. It was about the size of a small potato.

"May I pick this up?" Katelyn asked the artist.

"Why, yes, darlin'. It seems to be shinin' just for you." The artist replied.

As soon as Katelyn touched it, a shock of electricity zinged up her arm to her head. It looked like she had a halo around her head.

"What the hell was that?" Sami whispered. "Ya' got a halo around your head!"

The artist was just staring at Katelyn. "I've never seen anything like that before. They say some crystals are made for special people. I guess this one's made for you."

Katelyn just starred at the artist and Sami.

"Say somethin' Katie," Sami said.

Katelyn blinked her eyes at Sami and became aware of her surroundings again.

"Oh, I, ah, yeah, this is some crystal," Katelyn muttered.

Sami took a picture of Katelyn just then.

"Miss, I guess you better keep that crystal. It hasn't shone like that for anybody else ever. I found it over along the Wetumpka Impact Crater trail a few months ago. It was just sitting on the ground like someone had set it there. I picked it up and have been showing it ever since. This is the only time any of this has happened. Ya' know you're all aglow like you were surrounded by an ethereal light," the artist pointed out to Katelyn. "Here, look at yourself."

The artist handed a mirror to Katelyn and when she looked into it, she was shocked to see herself all aglow with the crystal in her hand sending shooting beams of light all over the place. Others had gathered to look at her and the crystal. A quietness filled the air around them for the longest time.

Katelyn finally looked up from the crystal and noticed Sami, the artist, and all the people just staring and watching her. She took a deep breath and stood tall.

The crystal was very warm in her hand and she could have sworn it was vibrating and humming ever so quietly.

"Well, I've never seen anything like this before," Katelyn said as she looked around at folks.

People started talking all at once about the crystal and Katelyn.

"Sure is shinin' bright."

"Would ya' look at that?"

"She's all aglow like the stone."

"Must be somethin' special about that rock."

"Bet it's from the meteorite crater. Those stones are always different."

Folks finally began to wonder off and Katelyn and Sami looked at each other.

"What the hell was that?" Sami asked.

"Beats me. I just picked it up and it began to glow really bright and send energy up my arm like electricity. You know anything about this?" Katelyn asked the artist.

"Well, I do know quartz crystals have energy and some folks I've known have shared stories about how they felt a zing from a crystal or two. I've never seen one glow like this one. And, it isn't just from the sun. You're blocking the sun and it's still glowing. And, you're still glowing. I'll bet ya' it's got to do with your energy and the crystal's bein' in sync."

"I've heard about that before," Katelyn said as she looked at the crystal. She set it back down on the shell and it slowly stopped glowing and the halo around her went away as well.

"Well, I guess this should be goin' with you," the artist said as she placed the crystal in a cloth sack and handed it to Katelyn.

"Okay. How much please?" Katelyn asked as she reached for her cash.

"Oh no. This is a special crystal. It belongs with you. I've just been the caretaker until it found you," the artist stated.

"Really? Well, then thank you and bless your heart for such generosity," Katelyn said.

"My pleasure. Love when stuff like this happens. I love Magic."

Katelyn smiled as she said, "And so do I."

Sami was speechless as she and Katelyn moved along. They visited more artists and Sami bought a few things she liked.

They watched the kids creating artwork by using their hands as paintbrushes. The clothes line art was beautiful.

They stopped at the create-your-own-fan table and made their own fans from paper, glitter, markers and such. They were sparklin' a bit when they finished. And, as they waved their fans as they walked along, they left a little trail of sparkle along the way just like everyone else who had been creative at one of the arts and crafts tables.

They grabbed some supper and settled on a bit of the lawn near the stage area as the evening's musical entertainment was getting set up.

Magic? Really?" Sami said as they finished with their supper.

"Yeah. Magic. It's real. Why? Don't you believe in magic?" Katelyn asked.

"Well. I don't really know. Of course, I've heard about magic. All the stuff on TV seems so dramatic so I know that's not real. And, I've heard people talkin' about magic all my life. But, to really see it as real, as it's really happening, I don't know what to think. You ever see it before?"

"I grew up in Crab Apple Creek as you know. That place is loaded with Magic. I've seen what it can do, but I've never seen it happening like today. I'm still buzzing from the energy zing I felt when I picked up the crystal. It shot up my arm right into my head like I was electrocuted. But I wasn't. It didn't hurt. It was warm and kept zinging along and I felt like it was humming or something. I forgot where I was for a bit. I'm still a bit fuzzy from the whole thing. Wonder if that's because I'm holding the crystal in my hand. I think I'll put in in my backpack and see if the fuzzy feeling goes away."

Katelyn placed the crystal in its cloth sack into her backpack and sat there for a minute.

"It seems to be settling down. I don't feel so fuzzy anymore. My mind is definitely clearer and I don't hear the humming anymore. I guess we know that if I hold it then the hummin' and glowin' will happen."

"This is wild. Really cool though," Sami said as she looked at Katelyn. "Yup, you're not glowing anymore either."

"Well, good thing. I don't want to call attention to us for sure," Katelyn said as one of the bands took to the stage and the music started up.

The bands were local groups and they were really good. When the second half began, local kids' choirs came onstage and the bands and kids played and sang some of the old songs of the South along with a few current tunes. Folks got up and danced along with the bands.

As the last song seemed to fade away, one of the singers came up to the mic.

"Folks, we kindly thank ya' for your support. Love to see y'all singin' along and dancin'. We're gonna' close out the fair with everyone's favorite. Let's go boys," the leader said as the band struck up the first few cords of *Sweet Home Alabama*. The crowd went wild. Folks were hollering, singing, and dancing and kept the band going, making them play the song three times through.

As the music faded away, folks hollered and cheered for the longest time. Finally, things quieted down and the fair came to an end. It was close to ten o'clock when Katelyn and Sami finally made it to the SUV. They had made a couple of stops along the way for popcorn and drinks, of course. Good thing they had taken Katelyn's SUV. It was pretty much filled by the time they got everything loaded.

"And, this is why you drive when we go out and about," Sami said as she got in. "My car would definitely not hold half of this stuff."

"I keep tellin' you to get an SUV," Katelyn said in a know-it-all manner that made them both laugh.

"I've been thinkin' about that for a bit now. We'll talk more before I make up my mind."

"Yes! It's about time girl," Katelyn hollered as they waited in line to leave the field. Seems a few folks knew about their secret parking place. Not many though. They were on the road home just ten minutes later.

They unloaded the car and went inside to freshen up and decided to sit and talk for a bit. Katelyn had told Sami about the dreams about going home since they started and wanted to tell Sami about the one from last night.

"So, I had another goin'-home dream last night," Katelyn started. "But, this time, it was real. So real that when I found myself waking up, I wasn't sure about where I was. I should have been home in The Creek but I was here. And, I could still taste the food I had eaten with Ted and Michael."

"Whoa! What? Really? That's never happened before. Give me the details," Sami said as she got more comfy on the couch.

Katelyn told her everything and Sami just sat there real quiet for a bit.

"I don't even know where to start. I agree that it was more than just a dream for sure," Sami said as she gave more thought to what she had just heard.

"And, I know you've had premonitions all your life, Now," Sami said as Katelyn started shakin' her head. "You don't have to call them that, but that's exactly what they are. You dream of stuff happening and then it happens."

"Don't label me like that. It's just a coincidence. That's all," Katelyn said.

"And you tell me you know about Magic and come from The Creek where Magic seems to be the norm. How do you explain that?"

Katelyn just looked at Sami with a scowl on her face.

"See? You can't explain that away. And, ya 'know why? Cause it's true!"

"Ya know, you're a real pain in my ass sometimes," Katelyn said pointing at Sami.

"Much obliged, Ma'am," Sami said as she laughed at Katelyn. "When ya' gonna' admit that you're Gifted with premonition abilities? It's not like it's gonna' go away just 'cause you refuse to say it out loud. Well? Ya' have an answer for that?" Sami kept poking at Katelyn, hoping to get her to accept the fact that she had premonitions and was Gifted with The Magic of The Creek.

"Do I need to mention the time you dreamed about that guy in your senior year who kept askin' you out and you kept refusing 'cause you felt' he was really gay and was tryin' to hide it? And, what happened when you said no? He finally admitted he was gay and felt a whole lot better about it. And, what about the time we were driving along and who got a real bad feeling about the train tracks ahead and refused to cross them? You wouldn't budge no matter what I said. You kept tellin' me you had a bad feelin' about those tracks. You finally turned around and we went another way about five miles out of our way. And, then we both saw the news flash about the train jumpin' the tracks at that exact crossing on our newsfeeds at the same time. Thing is, we would have been crossing the tracks at the exact same minute the train jumped the tracks, killin' both of us. As it was, three people in a pick-up truck died as they were crossing the tracks when the train thing happened. Do I need to go on?"

"No. Please. I feel bad that those people died. I know I couldn't have stopped them, but I still feel bad about it and all," Katelyn said.

"I know you do," Sami replied softly. "Katelyn, my MeeMaw has premonitions. She says a lot of folks, especially women, tend to have premonitions. It's okay."

"But what am I supposed to do about them?"

"That I don't know. Maybe just be aware that you have them and if they involve you, keep track of them. Pay attention to them just like you did with the train thing."

"Well, I guess I can do that. It's just that the dream last night was more than a dream. I swear I'm supposed to pay attention to it. Something is comin' from it."

"I agree with that for sure. Maybe you're supposed to think about going back home to live. Permanently," Sami offered.

"Oh, Sami, that's what I've been thinkin' it means, too. But how do I know for sure? I'd need a job and all and there isn't much in The Creek and

Pine Ridge. I don't even wanna' think about drivin' to Boone every day. So much to think about," Katelyn said.

"Now, Katie, just slow down. No one said you had to move today or ever. It was just a thought. How about you keep detailed notes when the dream comes again and anything that seems to be connected to the dream. Then we'll talk about it and try to see where it may lead us."

"I do like the way you calm me down and keep me on track," Katelyn replied.

"Okay then. Well, I guess I'm headin' home. It's already goin' on midnight."

"Wow! Didn't know we had talked so long. I do love you, my Sami. Thanks for listenin' and bein' a great friend," Katelyn said as they hugged.

"Later gator," Sami said as she left.

Katelyn watched as Sami drove away then turned off the outside lights and settled the place before she climbed into bed. It had been a great day for sure even with starting at eleven in the morning. The fair had been fun and that crystal thing was so amazing. She was thinking about that crystal setting on her bedside table as she fell into a deep sleep.

She slept without remembering her dreams that night.

CHAPTER 2

May moved along into June and the going home dreams kept coming. It wasn't until mid-June that more was added to the dream thing. And, so, the dream continued that night.

Katelyn had just left the store when she heard her name called out. She looked around and found Kendra waving at her from her house across the road.

"Hey, Katie girl," Kendra said as Katelyn walked across the lawn.

"Hey, yourself," Katelyn said as they hugged.

"What brings you back to The Creek?" Kendra asked as they settled on the porch.

"Well, I guess it's time to come home. For good." Katelyn explained. "I've been havin' these dreams that started out as little dreams but got to be way too real to be just dreams. They kept coming every night then for the last couple of weeks. They've been showin' up during the day right in the middle of whatever I was doin'. I finally realized I was supposed to come home. So, here I am."

"Amazin' how that happens," Kendra replied.

Katelyn took a long hard look at Kendra then said, "So, you knew I was havin' those dreams and that I'd be comin' home, didn't you? It's all about The Magic, isn't it?"

Kendra replied very softly, "Yes, Katie girl, it is. So glad you finally paid attention."

Katelyn sat there real quiet for a while.

"Does that mean I can feel The Magic, too?"

"What do you think?" Kendra asked.

13

"Well, I'm not so sure. My BFF Sami and I were at a local spring fair and I stopped to look as some of the shocked crystals gathered from the We-tumpka Crater site. One of them was glowin' like crazy. I asked if I could hold it 'cause that seemed the right thing to do. The artist said I could. When I picked it up, a zing of electricity went up my arm and into my head. I felt like I was someplace else for the longest time. Sami nudged me and brought me back and said my head was glowin' like the crystal. I looked at the crystal and it was shooting beams of colored light everywhere. Folks stopped and watched and commented on the whole thing. They finally left and I set the crystal back down on its shell. Then the buzzing and glowing kinda' stopped. I guess that's the only Magic I've ever felt or been a part of."

"Yup, sure sounds like The Magic was callin' out to you," Kendra said.

"I'm a bit confused about being back. I need to find work and I know there isn't a need for interior design work around here or in Pine Ridge. I'll have to start lookin' soon though. My savings won't last through the winter. I need to find a place to live as well. My folks always said I could move back to the farm, but I know I need my own space. Any ideas?"

"Yup. You're welcome to stay at one of my two houses here. They're both empty right now. Let's say rent is a hundred dollars a month, including utilities and Wi-Fi. Sound good?"

"You kidding? Of course, that sounds great! I'll move in right now if that's okay with you?"

"Sure is. Need some help?"

"Yes, I do. I'll drive the car right over. Wait. First, I have to decide which house. Let's go look at them," Katelyn said as she ran over to the house to the north of Kendra's. "Can we look inside please? I need to see how the light lays in each room."

"Of course," Kendra said as they looked over the house to the north then the house to the south.

"I like the way everything fits in the house to the south. I choose that one," Katelyn decided.

"Okay. Here's the key. Drive on over and we'll get you settled," Kendra said.

Katelyn didn't remember anything more of the dream when she woke up that morning in mid-June. She sat quiet a bit and pondered on the dream and finally realized she was supposed to move back to The Creek as soon as possible. She couldn't tell exactly why; she just knew in her gut that this was the thing to do.

She called Sami and asked her to come over after work that night.

Sami arrived with dinner and they sat at the kitchen table talking over their day and all.

"So, what's goin' on, Katie?" Sami asked as they finished.

"Sami, you know all about those goin'-home dreams and all," Katelyn stated.

"Yes, I do. Have you decided what they might mean?" Sami asked

"Yes. I've decided I need to move back to The Creek," Katelyn said rather quietly.

"Well, it's about time you figured it out," Sami said with a smile.

"You're not upset?" Katelyn asked looking right at Sami.

"Upset? No. I know things move along and I'm gonna' miss you like you can't believe. But I've got some news for you, too."

"What? Spill," Katelyn said.

"Well, seems the bosses like the work I've been doin' and the fact that I'm goin' back to school. So, they've put me in charge of the structural designs for a major hotel corporation that's ready to reinvent itself. It means I'll be on the road a lot from Maine to Florida for the next few years."

"Oh my God! That's so awesome!" Katelyn said as she ran around the table to hug Sami.

"So, you see, I would be away a lot and we'd miss each other anyway," Sami surmised.

"Yeah, you're right. This is great how this is all workin' out. When do you start?"

"Monday. I start sittin' in on video meetings to meet the owners of the corporation and then meet with the managers of each line of hotels. Their hotels are designed to fit into the local landscape and area cultures. So, I'll have a lot of work to do before any physical construction begins. I think I'll start traveling in mid-summer beginning in Maine then moving throughout the Northeast. Boone is on the list," Sami said with a big smile.

"That's awesome," Katelyn hollered out. "So, you can stay with me every time you need to be in the area."

"That's exactly what came to mind when you said you were goin' back home," Sami replied.

"I guess things do work out just fine if we let them," Katelyn said.

"I guess they do," Sami replied.

They spent the rest of the evening talking and planning.

Just before Sami left, she asked Katelyn, "When do you think you'll be leaving?"

"Well, I just finished that big project you know about and the smaller one will be completed by the end of the week. That leaves the middle one. I think I can finish that in about ten days. So, I was thinking of giving my notice tomorrow effective the end of June. That will give them more than two weeks to figure things out. Does that sound okay?"

"Yes, it does. It sounds fair and professional," Sami agreed.

"Okay, then. I guess I'm headin' back home. I think I'll call my folks now and tell them. It's not too late," Katelyn said.

"I'm sure they're gonna' be thrilled. I love your folks even though I've only met them through the internet."

"Well, now, you'll be able to meet them in person," Katelyn said.

Sami left and Katelyn called her folks. They were thrilled and happy that she was coming home.

The next two weeks flew by so fast Katelyn wasn't sure what she was doing. Her last day at work was fun. The firm decided to have a party for her all afternoon. Some of her past clients came by to wish her well and said they would be in touch once she got settled in back home. She had moved all her office stuff home the day before. The firm gave her a great gift in that it was a set of artist brushes in every size and texture you could imagine. And, a bonus that equaled two month's pay. Others gave her fun gifts and gift cards to Starbucks as they knew she loved the specialty coffees and all. She said her final fair well and left with tears gently rolling down her cheeks.

She had given notice to her landlady the morning after she and Sami had talked. She was ready to have to pay an extra month's rent for giving such short notice. Thing was, the landlady said, there was no need as she had a client ready to move in as soon as she had the place cleaned and painted. And, she gave Katelyn her security deposit and last month's rent back. The landlady said there was no need to keep the last month's rent as Katelyn had already paid for this month. And, there wasn't any damage to the cottage.

Katelyn had shipped a lot of her stuff home during the week. It would arrive at her folk's farm early the next week. Sami came over that Friday evening and they had a celebration of their own.

"So, Katie girl, I got a huge raise with the project management thing. As the designer and project manager, my salary changed from $60 thousand to $110 thousand and an SUV I can use for personal needs as well as work needs. Can you believe that?"

"Holy shit! That's fantastic!"

"And, when I travel, I use the company's credit card and I get an SUV and hotel suite as well."

"Whoa! That's the best thing you could have told me. I won't worry about you so much now."

"Yeah, I know. I won't be worrying so much either. My student loans will be on hold as of September as long as I'm in grad school. I'm gonna' pay my current student loan way down with the bonus I got for takin' the job"

"Now that's a great idea. Remember to keep a bit for yourself."

"Oh, I am. I know you're leavin' in the mornin' and I'm sad about that. I know things change for the better and we leave a great life behind. But it doesn't make it easier to say good-bye."

"I know. I was thinking the same thing driving home today. I'm sad to leave Alabama and you, but I'm happy to be goin' back to The Creek. The fact that you'll be along really makes it a lot easier to handle."

"Same here. So, I guess it's time to get goin'. You have a long drive ahead of you. Glad you're gonna' take it easy gettin' home. Take lots of breaks and enjoy the view."

They walked out to Sami's car and just stood there. They were both crying as they hugged again.

"Love you always and forever," Sami said.

"Love you always and forever," Katelyn replied.

Sami drove away and Katelyn went inside and cried for a bit. She was sad and excited. She didn't remember falling asleep but she did remember being woken up by a really gross odor. She flipped on her bedside light and saw a monster leaning over her. She immediately grabbed the shocked quartz crystal she had hidden under the covers. The minute she brought it into the light, she heard a horrible scream and the monster exploded and vanished into thin air.

Katelyn sat there scared and relieved. What the hell!? She didn't realize she was holding the crystal until her hand began to feel hot. She looked down and saw the crystal was glowing bright blue and vibrating. She focused on the crystal and slowed her breathing and was soon calmed down. She lay back down leaving the light on and slept until her six o'clock alarm woke her. She laughed as she heard the music. It was '*This Girl is on Fire.*' How appropriate after what had happened in the night.

Those damn night terrors. Katelyn wasn't sure why they were happening. She would have to talk to Kendra when she got to The Creek. Kendra knew a lot about The Magic and maybe she could help her figure them out. In the meantime, she would make sure she had that shocked crystal on her body from right now until she got back home.

She showered, packed her last few things, and was out the door by seven. The landlady came over and gave her a package.

"Now Katie, you be careful out there. I made ya' some cornbread just now and there's butter and honey for it along with napkins and such. I'm gonna' miss you. You keep in touch now, ya' hear?"

"Oh my, Miss Bonnie. Thanks so much for this treat. I'm gonna' eat it in just a bit while it's still warm. And thanks for being such a great friend," Katelyn said as she kissed Miss Bonnie on the cheek.

"Let me know you got back safely."

"I will Miss Bonnie. And, if I may say, bless your heart for everything."

Katelyn waived to Miss Bonnie as she drove away. She stopped a few minutes down the road to get a coffee using one of her gift cards and sat in her

SUV enjoying the warm cornbread with the fixins' from Miss Bonnie. Boy, that woman really knew how to make cornbread.

Katelyn was on the road a bit later. She drove to Atlanta, GA along Rte 85 and right into South Carolina. The traffic had been heavy all along the way and it had taken her more than ten hours of stop-n-go and slow-moving traffic to get just to the other side of Greenville, SC.

It would have usually only taken about 4 hours, but she made a few stops to look around, too. It was around six o'clock and she was hungry and tired. She googled to look for hotels and chose the Holiday Inn Express cause it had a hot tub, free breakfast and available rooms. She booked her room right then and there online and arrived a little bit later. The hotel was just a few minutes off the highway along what looked like the old main street of the town. She checked in and was in her room right quick.

Katelyn went back down to the front desk to inquire about places to eat. She explained she preferred a local place, not one of the cookie-cutter restaurants.

"Well, then, I'd suggest the diner just down the way. If ya' take a left at the second set of stop signs, you'll see it about three blocks down on your right. It's been run by the same family for over a hundred years. It's called Old MacDonald's Kitchen. And, yes, the MacDonald's still own and run it. Great cornbread, by the way."

"Great. I love cornbread. Thanks for the info. I'll check in with you when I get back." Katelyn said.

She had a bit of a wait when she got to the diner. It did look like a popular place for sure. Once she was seated at a table for two, she began to look around and was intrigued by all the paraphernalia about extra-terrestrials and magic on the walls. There were pictures of celebrities and past presidents with the owners as well. There was even a picture of Elvis Presley with the wait staff from the late 1950's. She placed her order and kept looking around. The noise in the place seemed to dim as she focused on a picture of the area outside of the diner. It looked a bit like it did when she walked in the door, but something was very different.

As she continued to focus on the picture, she felt as if she were being pulled into the picture and found herself outside the diner looking all around. The diner looked really old and it had a closed sign on it. The area around the diner hadn't been tended to and the lawn was all weeds and the bushes were out-of-control and as high as the diner. The parking area was now a tangle of weeds and fallen-down trees. It had a sad and lonely feel to it. She watched as a man approached her dressed in a suit and tie, carrying a briefcase.

"Howdy, Miss," he said, tipping his hat.

"Hello," Katelyn replied.

"So, you're interested in buying the place I gather, from our phone call. This place hasn't been open in over forty years. The owners, the MacDonald family, closed it when no one wanted to take over from the current generation. That'd be three generations back. Some where's in the 2030's, I think. They still own all the land, about forty acres but don't want to tear down the diner just yet. They're hopin' the new owner will rebuild the diner and open for business."

Katelyn just starred at the man. She could have sworn she was outside the diner talkin' to him. But, how could that be? She was sitting inside, looking at a picture, waiting for her supper.

The man smiled at Katelyn. "Well, do ya' have any more questions? If not, they accept your offer and we can get movin' along with the paperwork and get this property into your name. They're thrilled that you remember stopping in here back in 2016 for supper one night. That's why they finally accepted an offer. They've had lots of other offers, but those folks wanted to tear down the diner and build condos instead. The owners refused to sell to them They wanted someone who would carry on the tradition and respect the land."

Katelyn cleared her throat to speak when she heard, "Here ya' are, honey. Fried chicken, mashed taters and gravy and cornbread, of course. That's our signature dish.," the waitress was saying as she set Katelyn's supper on the table. "Anythin' else ya' need, sugar?"

Katelyn turned away from the picture and saw that she was in the diner again.

"Ah, no thanks. This looks fabulous," Katelyn managed to say before the waitress caught on that she wasn't really in the moment.

"You been lookin' at that there picture, haven't ya?"

"Yes. How can you tell?"

"Cause you're the third person, in all the years I been workin' here, and that's a lotta years, that's been taken into the picture. You must be one of the special ones," the waitress explained in a hushed voice.

"You know what just happened?" Katelyn replied.

"Yes. It happened to my Mama years ago and she was special with The Magic and all. You must be, too. She said only real special folks connected with The Magic are taken into the picture"

"Well, that explains a lot. I'm kinda' new at this Magic stuff," Katelyn explained very quietly.

"Well, don't try to fight it. Won't work. Now, how about you dig in? Let me now if ya' need anything else," she said as she walked away with a wink to Katelyn.

Katelyn just shook her head and started in on her supper. It was fabulous. The cornbread did not disappoint, either. She would think about the picture later.

As she finished, the waitress returned and smiled at her. "I guess you were hungry."

"I do believe I was. Been travelin' in this holiday traffic and it was time to stop for the night. Thanks to the chef and y'all. This was some of the tastiest fried chicken I've had in a right long time. And, the cornbread was top notch."

"So glad you enjoyed. I'll be sure to pass along your message. Desert?"

"I don't think I have any room," Katelyn laughed.

"How's about I send some apple pie along with ya' for later? Makes a great late-night snack."

"Great idea. Thanks."

The waitress left the check and when she returned with the pie all packed up ready to go, Katelyn paid in cash with a hefty tip included.

"Thanks so much. Now, don't ignore your Gifts. You'll be just fine," she said as Katelyn got up to leave.

"Thanks," Katelyn smiled as she left the diner. She took a long look around the outside of the place as she stood by her car. It was, for sure, the same land that was in that picture. This Magic stuff was getting really weird. She wasn't trying to fight it. She was just surprised at all the ways it was involving her. She gave herself a shake and turned to look at the diner. The waitress was smiling at her from the door. She smiled and waved at the waitress and the waitress vanished into thin air. Holy shit! She just vanished like that! Katelyn got into her car feeling like there was Magic right in her face. She laughed a bit and set out for the hotel.

She stopped at the front desk to thank the clerk for her suggestion and was in her room a few minutes later. It was around nine o'clock and Katelyn was tired. She turned on the TV and found an episode of '*Ancient Aliens*' to watch.

She warmed up the pie and devoured it. It was heavenly. A bit later she drifted off to sleep, holding the crater crystal for protection.

The Dark tried hard to wake her up and take her for their own but the crater crystal surrounded Katelyn in a protection grid. The Dark could never break a crystal protection grid no matter how hard it tried. In all creation since the beginning of existence, The Dark would never be able to destroy the protection of the crystals. Never. This made The Dark very angry. It had to keep Katelyn from growing her Gifts no matter what. It would get to her the next time she fell asleep.

Katelyn woke up and was on the road around six after a quick breakfast at the hotel. She was excited to be going home now that it was just a few hours away. She took Rte 26 north to Spartanburg where she changed over to Rte 74 east. This would take her to Rte 221 next to Boone and she would take the back roads through Boone up into The Creek. There was a bit more traffic than usual and the trip took about four hours. The drive was beautiful and she only made one quick pit stop before driving into The Creek.

It looked just the same. She stopped at The Store as planned.

She walked into the store and saw Ted and Michael up in the dining area.

"Hey Ted, Michael," she called out as she walked towards them.

"Katelyn," they both hollered out as they rushed to grab her into a big hug. "It's great to see you after so many years. What brings you home?" Ted said.

"My stars, child, it's been forever. You okay?" Michael asked.

"Yes. Yes, I'm okay. Just felt it was time to come home," Katelyn replied.

Ted and Michael looked at each other and smiled.

"Whatever the reason or reasons, we're thrilled you're here. How long are ya' planning on stayin'?" Ted asked as they settled at the dining room table.

"Well, I'm here for good," Katelyn began.

"Yahoo!" Michael hollered. "This is some of the best news I've heard in a long while."

She looked at them both, then the tears started to fall.

"Oh, darlin', what's the matter?" Ted asked as he went over to her and put his arms around her.

"Nothin', I think," Katelyn replied. "It's just been so long since I was home that I didn't expect to feel this way. I guess I missed home more than I thought."

"That happens for sure, Miss Katie," Michael said. "Well, I do believe you've lost way too much weight since you were last here. Ted, time to feed this child."

Katelyn laughed through her tears as she gave Ted a hug before he took off for the kitchen. "I'm not even gonna' begin to ask what y'all have cookin' back there. I know better than that. You always seem to know just what a body needs."

"Yes, we do," Michael said as Ted came through the kitchen door with a loaded tray of food.

"Since it's in the middle of the mornin', I brough a little bit of breakfast and lunch. Help yourself," Ted said.

"Oh, my stars, this is what I think I missed the most. Or, maybe in my top five things I missed the most," Katelyn said as she started to sample a bit of everything. "There's no way I'm gonna' eat all this, so help me out boys."

"Of course," Ted and Michael said at the same time. They all laughed then spent the next while eating and talking about the food, The Creek, and Katelyn's work.

Ted and Michael brought Katelyn up-to-date on Emily and Ethan, Matthews and Jenna, Miss Cora, Kendra, the battle in the Sacred Rock Meadow, Jay's passing, the fight to keep The Magic in The Creek up at the Holler, and all the little details she had missed.

"My family kept me in-the-loop with most of this stuff. But, not so much about Jordan Jackson's new farm and those crystals. They sound amazin'. I wonder if he'll allow me to stop by and take a look at them? I lived in The Crystal Village in Alabama for the past few years and Jordan's crystals sound like some of the ones I've seen back there."

"I'm sure he would. He such a great guy. And, now, a part of The Creek family for sure."

"Great. I'll get a hold of him in a few days. I've still gotta' get home. No one knows I'm back except the two of you and my folks. And, I swore them to secrecy. Please don't tell anyone. I want to surprise them."

"We will keep your secret," Michael said as he looked straight at Ted.

"Who me? Tell on a secret?" Ted laughed. "I promise, Miss Katie, not a word until I hear it from someone else that you're home."

"Okay. Thanks. Well, now that I've been stuffed like a Thanksgiving turkey, I'm gonna' head home."

"Miss Katie, take the leftovers for a snack later or whatever," Ted said as he boxed them up for her.

"Now, Ted, I appreciate your generosity," Katelyn said as she took the bag from Ted and they headed to the door.

"Thanks guys. It's so great to be back home in The Creek. Bless your little ol' pea-pickin' hearts," Katelyn said as they hugged.

"See ya' soon," Michael said as she walked out the door.

Katelyn suddenly realized she was actually living the dreams she had been having about returning to The Creek. This was really weird. She didn't have much time to ponder this as she heard her name hollered out. She looked around and found Kendra waving at her from her porch across the road. Exactly like in the dreams.

"Hey, Katie girl," Kendra said as Katelyn walked across the lawn.

"Hey, yourself," Katelyn said as they hugged.

"What brings you back to The Creek?" Kendra asked as they settled on the porch.

"Well, I guess it's time to come home. For good." Katelyn explained. "I've been havin' these dreams that started out as little dreams but got to be way too real to be just dreams. They kept coming every night then for the last couple of weeks, they've been showin' up during the day right in the middle of whatever I was doin'. I finally realized I was supposed to come home. So, here I am."

"Amazing how that happens," Kendra replied.

Katelyn took a long hard look at Kendra then said, "So, you knew I was havin' those dreams and that I'd be comin' home, didn't you? It's all about The Magic, isn't it?"

Kendra replied very softly, "Yes, Katie girl, it is. So glad you finally paid attention."

Katelyn sat there real quiet for a while.

"Does that mean I can feel The Magic, too?"

"What do you think?" Kendra asked.

"Well, I'm not so sure. My BFF Sami and I were at a local spring fair and I stopped to look as some of the shocked crystals gathered from the Wetumpka Crater site. One of them was glowin' like crazy. I asked if I could hold it 'cause that seemed the right thing to do. The artist said I could.

"When I picked it up, a zing of electricity went up my arm and into my head. I felt like I was someplace else for the longest time. Sami nudged me and brought me back and said my head was glowin like the crystal. I looked at the crystal and it was shooting beams of colored light everywhere. Folks stopped and watched and commented on the whole thing. They finally left and I set the crystal back down on its shell. Then the buzzing and glowing kinda' stopped. I guess that's the only Magic I've ever felt or been a part of."

"Yup, sure sounds like The Magic was callin' out to you," Kendra said.

"I'm a bit confused about being back. I need to find work and I know there isn't a need for interior design work around here or in Pine Ridge. I'll have to start lookin' soon though. My savings won't last through the winter. I need to find a place to live as well. My folks said I could move back to the farm, but I know I need my own space. Any ideas?"

"Yup. You're welcome to stay at one of my two houses here. They're both empty right now. Let's say rent is a hundred dollars a month, including utilities and Wi-Fi. Sound good?"

"You kidding? Of course, that sounds great! I'll move in right now if that's okay with you?"

"Sure is. Need some help?"

"Yes, I do. I'll drive the car right over. Wait. First, I have to decide which house. Let's go look at them," Katelyn said as she ran over to the house to the north of Kendra's. "Can we look inside please? I need to see how the light lays in each room."

"Of course," Kendra said as they looked over the house to the north then the house to the south.

"I like the way everything fits in the house to the south. I choose that one," Katelyn decided.

"Okay. Here's the key. Drive on over and we'll get you settled," Kendra said.

It didn't take long to get Katelyn's stuff into her new house.

"Thanks so much, Kendra. I really appreciate all of this," Katelyn said when they finished.

"Of course. Let me know if I can help you with anything else, like The Magic stuff," Kendra said with a wink.

"As if you didn't know. I'll come by in a few days. I need to get to my folks right now and tell them about all of this."

"Alright. Enjoy the place," Kendra said as she let herself out.

Katelyn looked around for a few minutes. She thought about how she was living the dream in reality. This was gonna' take some time to think out. She set out for her childhood home. It was a ways northeast of The Creek proper. It was a 140-acre farm that had been in the family for the past two hundred years. Her folks had changed it from a cow, pig and chicken farm to a berry farm when they took it over about thirty years ago. Katelyn's twin brothers had stayed and learned how to run the farm after college. They took care of it right alongside their folks. The boys had been named Nathan and Jeremy. They were identical twins as well. Nathan had bought about twenty acres right next to the family farm on the east side and Jeremy had bought twenty-five acres that bordered the family farm on the north side. His land bordered the national forest as well. Both boys were thinking about building their own homes but hadn't told anyone yet, just each other. When they heard their sister was coming home to stay, they both had the same idea at the same time. They would ask her to design their homes for them. After all, she knew them better than most.

Katelyn parked next to the barn and was walking around to the back of the farmhouse when her dad caught sight of her.

"Katelyn," he hollered for all the world to hear. He ran over to her and scooped her up into a big bear hug. Her dad, not a heavy man, was built strong and gave bear hugs like no one else.

Katelyn's mom heard her husband holler and came running out of the house and grabbed onto the two of them.

The both started asking Katelyn questions at the same time.

Katelyn pulled back and said, laughing "Now, you two, one at a time, please."

Her mom and dad looked at each other and then started laughing as well.

Finally, her mom said, "Well, we knew you'd be home today, just not what time. You must be hungry."

"Nope. I stopped at the store and Ted and Michael stuffed me like a Thanksgiving turkey. There are leftovers in my car. Enough to feed everyone. Where are my brothers?"

"They're out in the blueberry patch. I want you all to myself before they get here. I'll never get a word in edgewise when they show up," her mom said.

"Okay I'll get the food and be right in. Dad, how about you help me?"

"Sure thing. Lead the way," her dad replied. "Nice car, girl. Real nice."

"I bought it about two years ago. It has everything except a sun roof. Don't like those," Katelyn explained as they took stuff from the backseat and walked into the house.

Katelyn and Joe handed the food to her mom.

"Look, Joe, there's enough to feed a small army here," she said as she unpacked everything. "Come make yourself a plate. It's lunch time anyway."

"Good idea. I suspect the boys will be here in a minute," Joe said as he loaded his plate and put it in the microwave.

Jackie, Katelyn's mom, did the same thing just before the boys walked in.

"Katelyn!" they both hollered when they saw her. The grabbed onto her and wouldn't let go for the longest time.

"Didn't know you were comin' for a visit," Nathan said as he spied the food.

"It's not a visit. I'm here for good," Katelyn said as Jeremy let her go.

"Really? For good? Hot damn!" he said. Then he saw the food. "Hey, Nate, leave some for me."

"No way! This is from The Store and I'm eatin' it all," Nate said as Jeremy pushed him aside.

"I swear, bro, I'll take it off your plate if I have to," Jeremy replied as he tried to take his brother's plate from him. They went at it for a few minutes all in fun.

Finally, Nathan put his plate in the microwave and Jeremy fixed one for himself.

They gathered at the kitchen table and the questions began.

"Before y'all get crazy with these questions, let me explain a few things. Kendra has set me up with one of her houses for little rent until I find a place for myself. Now, mom, I know I can stay here but I have a business to get started and I need a lot of space and time for me."

"I told her that. But you know your mom," Joe said nodding his head at Jackie.

"I know, Katie bug, but this is your home whenever ya' need it. I'll still be cookin' and such for ya' anyways," Jackie said with a wink towards Katelyn.

"I know, mom, and I love ya' for it always and forever. I'll always take the cornbread you make special for me," Katelyn smiled at her mom.

"Now, how about dinner here tonight? I've got your favorites ready to go," Jackie offered.

"Deal! Usual time?" Katelyn replied.

"Yup!" they all said at the same time.

They ate lunch and talked for quite a spell.

"Time to get back to the blueberries. Looks like a bumper crop this year, dad, with all the sunshine and rain at night. Should be ready to pick right after the fourth."

"The fourth? That's right, Katie. It's tomorrow. Gonna' be great as always," her dad said.

"Yes sir. And, I can't wait for all the fun!"

"Later," the boys said as they left.

"I need to get back to my little house to unpack. I've got a bunch of stuff coming Tuesday so I'll be over late morning and all."

"Okay, honey. Thanks for lunch. Love Ted and Michael. See ya' for supper" Joe said as he gave her another hug and went back outside.

Jackie looked at Katelyn for a long moment. "There's Magic goin' on, isn't there, Katie bug?"

"Yes, I do believe there is. Gonna' talk with Kendra about it."

"How about Miss Cora, too?"

"Yes, great idea, mom. Why? What do you know about The Magic?"

"My sweet Katie bug, I know a lot. We'll talk more later. Just know I've been waitin' for you to feel The Magic since you were born. It's all good."

"I believe ya' mom. I really do," Katelyn said as she hugged her mom.

They walked out to her SUV, chatted for a minute, then Katelyn was on her way.

So, what did her mom know about The Magic? This was gonna' be an interesting time in The Creek for sure.

CHAPTER 3

Katelyn had a lot of unpacking to do. But first, time to party. The next day was July 4th and there was a lot of celebrating to do in The Creek. Monday morning brought the usual pancake breakfast held at The Store and the afternoon was filled with visiting and games for everyone. The big picnic bar-be-que would start around four and the whole Creek and their neighbors turned out for that. The Kirkland's always hosted the picnic and bar-be-que at their tree farm and nursery. They had plenty of space for this huge gathering.

Katelyn and her family showed up just before four and found a spot under a big old shade tree. They set up their table and chairs and got their drinks and such out. Jackie and Joe took their dishes over to the food area.

"Hi Jackie, Joe. Thanks for coming over. We can put those things in the coolers in the barn just over there. I see ya' made your special potato salad Jackie," Scott Kirkland said.

"Just like always, Scott. Wouldn't want to disappoint anyone," Jackie replied.

Joe and Jackie put their dishes in the barn and stopped and visited on their way back to their spot.

As they got close, they saw Ethan and Emily setting up next to them. Ethan was introducing Emily to Katelyn.

"Emily, this here's Katelyn. We kinda' grew up together, although she's a bit younger than the rest of us."

"Nice to meet ya', Katelyn," Emily said as they shook hands.

"Same here," Katelyn returned with a smile.

"What brings ya' home Katelyn? Vacation?" Ethan asked.

"Not really, Ethan. I'm home for good. Time to settle down and this is where I want to be."

"Well, that's fantastic news. I bet your folks are thrilled to have you home."

"They are. Although I'm not livin' at the house. Kendra's renting me one of her houses for now. The one to the south of hers. It's beautiful and has just the right light for my work."

"That's right. You're an interior designer, aren't ya'?" Ethan asked.

"Yes, I am. And, Ethan, if I may put a bug in your ear. If ya' know of anyone looking for a designer, I'd be much obliged. I need to get to work and don't even know what's available. I'm sure nothin' in The Creek. But, maybe somethin' in Pine Ridge. I'd rather not travel to Boone every day, if ya' know what I mean." Katelyn said with a laugh.

"I know exactly what you mean. Let me think about this and talk with Ian. Maybe we can come up with somethin' for ya' to think about."

"That would be fantastic. Thanks. Here come the folks," Katelyn replied as her mom and dad joined the group.

"Hi Ethan, Emily," they said at the same time.

"Hi Joe and Jackie. Looks like we're gonna' be neighbors for the rest of the day," Ethan said as they all sat down to talk for a bit.

Katelyn began looking around and caught site of an old childhood friend.

"Hey, Finn," Katelyn said as she ran over to him.

"Katie girl," Finn hollered as he scooped her up and swung her around. "God, it's great to see ya'. Didn't know you were comin' home for a visit."

"I'm home for good, Finn."

"Yahoo! Now that's some of the best news I've heard in a long time," Finn said smiling at Katelyn.

"Why, thank you kindly, sir, for such kind words," Katelyn replied blushing.

"Katie girl, what 'cha all blushing for? Ya' know we always had a special friendship since we were little kids. I've got so much to tell ya' about. Can't wait to get together for a long visit."

"I would love that, Finn. I, ah, I don't even know what to say about Jay and all. Makes me cry every time I think about him," Katie said softly as tears rolled down her cheeks.

"Oh, Katie girl, I know," Finn said as he gathered her in a gentle hug. "I still have horrible moments of that time and all. But, my folks and I, and The Creek, are helping us all move along."

"That's good to hear. Ya' know, I'm here for ya' anytime, anyplace, any reason. Just for anything."

"Thanks, Katie girl. I'm gonna' take ya' up on that for sure. Now, let's wander around and visit a bit before the eatin' begins," Finn said as they went back to Katie's family to say hello before moving around the place.

A whole lot of visiting and catching up went on for a long while. Then Scott called for everyone's attention for the blessing.

The Chiefs gave the blessing as always and the party really got going.

Groans of ecstasy were heard as folks bit into their favorite foods again and again. Katelyn and her brothers were on their way back for seconds when they were joined by Laine and Mo.

"Hey, Katelyn, heard the rumor you were back home. Great to see ya'," Mo said as they bumped shoulders.

"Great to see you and Laine, of course. We do have some history together, don't we?" Katelyn said as she looked at Laine and Mo and began to laugh.

"We most certainly do," Laine replied with a conspiratory wink. This got them all laughing and talking as they got more food and returned to their picnic spots.

"We'll catch up in a few days, girl," Mo said as they went off to their picnic spot.

"Yes, we will. I'll stop by one evenin' soon, for the usual chat," Katelyn said.

Nathan looked at his sister before saying, "Usual chat? What's that all about?"

"Girl talk, little brother. Strictly girl talk," Katelyn said with a smile on her face.

"Yeah, right," Jeremy added looking at Katelyn then Nathan. "We know better."

"Then what are ya' askin' for?" Katelyn replied with sass.

Joe and Jackie just laughed and shook their heads as they always did when their kids were teasing each other.

Folks ate and visited and ate some more. A few jugs were making their way around the crowd.

"Looks like the boys are here." Jeremy said as he took a swig from a jug and passed it to his dad before his brother could get a hold of it.

Joe took a swig and replied, "Good stuff like always," as he handed the jug to Nathan.

Nathen took a pull and smiled. "Yup."

Jackie and Katelyn just laughed at their guys.

Bubba and Earl happened to walk by at this exact time and saw one of their jugs being enjoyed.

"Hey Joe. How's the shine?" Bubba asked.

"First rate for sure," Joe replied as he handed the jug to Earl.

"Looks like it could use some fillin' up. I'll see to that," Earl said as he smiled at the men.

"Always excellent. Thanks for bringin' it along," Jeremy said with a nod to Bubba and Earl.

"Glad to oblige. Wouldn't be a real gatherin' without it," Bubba replied as he and Earl went on their way.

One of the most anticipated events at the Kirkland's was the Bluegrass play-off. It was more of a fun thing than a competition. A number of local musicians would gather in the late afternoon and begin to play. One would start, another would take over and, before long, they were challenging each other using the old songs from the Blue Ridge. This went on for about an hour or so until only two musicians were left. They took a short break then the dueling banjos or fiddles or whatever instruments the musicians chose began.

This year it was fiddles. The fiddlers were known to all and folks had a blast cheerin' them on. They played a number of songs but the last one was the one that found the winner It was Charlie Daniel's, '*The Devil Went Down to Georgia.*' Clyde and Ben were two of the best fiddlers in all of the Blue Ridge. Clyde was older by about three months and the two of them played on this by saying Clyde was getting on in years and probably wouldn't be able to keep up with Ben. The challenge took on a new dimension when Clyde started playing his fiddle above his head. Ben had to follow. He did just fine. Then Ben changed hands and Clyde followed. It was when Clyde started to dance that Ben finally gave in. He bowed to Clyde to show he deemed him the winner and the crowd went wild. They both finished the song in a grand flourish. Clyde was announced as the winner and his name would be engraved on the trophy which would be on display in The Store.

"Folks, we're gonna' take a short break before we begin the storytelling. So, help yourselves to whatever and we'll see ya' back here in a bit," Scott said.

Ethan signaled to Ian to follow him and they walked a ways from the gathering to a more private place.

"What's up Ethan?" Ian began.

"Well, I think we've found a solution we never even thought of or dreamed of for your end of the business." Ethan replied.

"What's that?"

"Katelyn MacDonald has come back to The Creek to live permanently," Ethan informed Ian.

"Great news! She's always been one of our favorites with her artistry and imagination. How can she help us out?"

"She's an interior designer brother. I think she might be a great addition to Soaring Mountain Builders."

"Wow! I would have never thought of her. Have you seen any of her designs yet?"

"I did a quick google search right after I saw her today. Look. What do you think?"

Ian spent a few minutes looking through the stuff Ethan had found about Katelyn on the web and on the Lloyd and Johnson website.

"I like what I'm seeing. Can we set up a meeting with her right away?"

"I already have. I suggested she bring her portfolio over soon. Is tomorrow soon enough?"

"Damn straight it is. How about ten o'clock? That'll give us time to get the day goin'."

"Agreed. I'll go find her and set it up."

"I'm excited about this. It would open the business up and free me from some of the interior design work. Great thinkin' bro."

"That's exactly what we were talkin' about the other day. Love how all this stuff works out," Ethan said as he went over to talk with Katelyn.

"Later genius," Ian said as he rejoined his family.

Katelyn saw Ethan headed her way and got up to greet him.

"Hey, Ethan," she said.

"Hey everyone," Ethan replied and was greeted in kind.

"I wonder if I could speak with Katelyn for a minute? I promise not to keep her too long."

Katelyn put her hands up to silence her family. "Of course."

Katelyn and Ethan walked over by the barn.

"Katelyn, I spoke with Ian about the following idea. It concerns you. We've been getting wicked busy with new builds and remodels and add-ons ever since we finished Jordan Jackson's place. We're finishing up on Matthews' place right now and we have enough work to keep us busy for the next few years. We have plenty of great carpenters and all. Only one problem with all this work. Ian can't keep up with the design demands. So, after you and I chatted a while ago, I found him and suggested you come talk to us tomorrow about the possibility of joining Soaring Mountain Builders as a design consultant. What do ya' think?"

Katelyn just stared at Ethan for the longest time then said, "Of course! Of course, I'll come over tomorrow with my portfolio and answer all the questions you can think of. Oh my God, this is awesome. Not even home more than a day and things are working out."

"We looked up some of your work on the internet and on the Lloyd and Johnson web site. I'm totally impressed with everything I've seen so far. You are quite the surprise, Katie girl."

"Oh, my stars! Thanks so much for the kind words. I love to design for folks to help bring their dreams to life. I won't sleep a wink tonight just thinkin' about tomorrow. Oh, what time Ethan?"

"Oh yeah. How about around ten o'clock? If you have anything digital, bring that along as well. Now, don't spend the night creating anything. This is The Creek and we both know somethin' other than human is at work here. The Magic. Let's just let it do its work."

"Wow! I agree about The Magic for sure. I am so grateful, Ethan. I'll see ya' tomorrow mornin." Katelyn said as they both headed back to their groups as the storytelling was about to begin.

Jackie looked at Katelyn as she sat down. "Hey Katie bug, what was that all about? You look like you just won the lottery."

"Oh, no, mom. Better than that. Ethan and Ian want to talk to me about the possibility of joining Soaring Mountain Builders as their design consultant."

"Fantastic!" Jeremy said.

"You've always loved to draw stuff," Nathan added.

"And, you're home. Can't wait to hear how it all goes. When do you meet with them?" her dad asked.

"Tomorrow morning at ten o'clock," Katie answered.

"This is so great," Jackie stared to say when Scott walked over by the fire to get everyone's attention.

Folks settled as Scott began the storytelling part of the evening.

"Glad to see y'all are comfy and cozy. Time for a bit of yarn weaving. Tonight, we've got a special someone with us. He's usually busy gettin' his next book ready. But I was able to convince him to be here tonight. Folks, I give you our very own Ben Wilkinson."

Folks hollered and applauded as Ben came up to the fire.

"It's great to be here with y'all tonight. By the way, I do believe Scott and his boys actually threatened to hog tie me and drag me over if I didn't agree right then and there the other night. So, here I am."

Ben bowed to the hoots and laughter from the crowd.

"Tell us a good one, Ben."

Ben smiled and saluted in the direction of the request.

"Well," Ben began, "most of you know my story. I was born and raised here like most of y'all. After college I started to hike the Appalachian trail, beginning in Georgia right up through Maine. Took me a few years and gave me an endless supply of stories to tell. Y'all have seen my fiction books based on Appalachian history and such. Well, there are a few stories I won't be writing up in a book and it's one of those stories I'm gonna' share with y'all tonight. So, get comfy, for I've got a tale to tell."

A chair found its way to the fire and Ben sat down.

"Much obliged. I do believe these weary bones of mine need a rest."

Folks smiled and a bit of laughter could be heard throughout the crowd.

"It was many, many years ago. I do believe it was from a time long gone by. There was this old woman who lived in the mountains near the Georgia-Tennessee border. Now, old could mean she was nigh onto eighty or it could mean she was in her forty's. No tellin' how old some folks are by just lookin' at 'em. Folks in the area say she was always there. It seemed she never died and no one could tell ya' just when she was born. She was known as the old, wise woman who lived by herself away from folks. She wasn't really antisocial just liked being alone most of the time. Folks told me she knew a lot about herbs and the locals would go to her if they needed somethin' for any kind of ailment. You could say she was a medicine woman of sorts. She would readily help anyone who asked. Folks paid her in cash, helped out with her house keepin' it all good and safe, and whatever else she needed done around her place. She had a huge truck garden and folks visited her during the seasons for her vegetables, herbs and the like. No one really knew if she had kin. She had a few Magical powers, if truth be told. She could tell ya' when a big storm was coming. It was as if she could talk to the sky. She would warn folks when strangers were gonna' appear. Good ones and bad ones. They tolerated the good guys. They drove the bad ones away. The old woman needed to be protected from any evil thing or person.

"It was agreed by the locals that I was a good guy and I was invited to stay as long as I wanted to as long as I didn't ask too many questions about any one thing, including the old woman. I just listened to what anyone had to say and that's how I learned of a peculiar thing that took place every full moon. No one person told me the whole story, but enough folks gave me bits of it and I wove them together to get a pretty clear picture of this ceremony thing.

"Seems these folks were a very religious group. The area was first settled by the Spanish, then the British and French. The native peoples had lived there for thousands of years before the Spanish laid claim. So, the area was a mishmash of many cultures. The folks I met were either strong Christians or not. No matter, they were all accepted by one another 'cause they were born and raised there.

"Seems there was a lot of quiet talk about Magic being a regular part of the place. And, that's where the ceremony thing comes in. About a week after I got there, they invited me to a gatherin' for supper. It was someone's birthday and they thought I'd enjoy myself which I did for sure. They have a few folks down there that must be related to Bubba and Earl. Their shine is about as good as ours. Jugs were being passed and food was aplenty. I felt right at home when they bar-be-queued a pig just like we do. All day long. It was a great reminder of The Creek."

Folks commented on this for a bit, then Ben continued.

"Seems the more the jug was passed, the better the stories got. I wasn't drinking much of the shine although I pretend to be. I didn't want to insult the boys. One of them got around to the full moon story and I sat and listened real quiet-like. This is what I heard.

"Every full moon was a special night. There were, are, those that choose to acknowledge the gods and goddesses of the earth, sky, water, and air. They respect those that think other ways but know that their way is the real way. On the full moon nights, there is always someone who holds the sacred fire ceremony in a special grove deep in the mountains. Some of the folks let it slip that it was the old woman who danced the full-moon dance. They said no one had ever seen her do it. They had been told for generations that her kind had always protected the old ways of Magic and performed the necessary ceremonies for hundreds of years. I thought that mighty interestin' 'cause it was only a night away from a full moon. The party finally settled down and we all went our own ways home.

"The next day, while I was hiking a local trail, the old woman crossed my path. I knew I wasn't anywhere near her place and was only a bit surprised to see her. She looked long and hard at me then motioned that I should follow her. It was the good part of an hour before we stopped.

"She said to me, 'Ben, I appreciate you leavin' me alone. Yes, I know your name 'cause some of the folks told me about you. I would like to invite ya' to my place for a sit."

"I smiled at the old woman and said, 'I'd be mighty honored to sit with you for a spell.'

"Good. Follow me,' she ordered and we were at her house just a few minutes later.

"She got us drinks of some kind of herbal tea and we sat on her porch lookin' out over her gardens and the mountains.

"I know ya' know about Magic. I can tell and they told me you was comin','" she said.

"Who told you I was comin'?" I asked.

"They did. The ones who watch this place and protect it just like your place in The Creek.'

"I stared at her for a minute. 'How do you know about The Creek?'

"She smiled and filled my glass with more tea and said, 'I know about The Magic all over these Appalachia Mountains. And you know I do.'

"I looked at her and she began to seem to get a little fuzzy. I shook my head to clear it and she still looked fuzzy. It was getting towards sundown and I needed to get back to my place. I tried to stand up and found my legs would not cooperate.

"Don't' worry. You'll be good to go in a few minutes. It's a full moon and there are things to be done. You need to be a part of these things this time."

"I just looked at her. She was smilin' and rockin' away. A little bit later, she told me to stand up. I tried and found I could. My head was still fuzzy and I couldn't really concentrate on anything. She got up and told me to follow her inside. We needed to eat before we set out.

"A bit later we were on a trail, heading into the mountain. Just as the sun settled below the horizon, we came to a clearing and I saw a rock formation in the center of the clearing. I just stood there. The old woman told me to follow her and she took me to a place where I could sit on some boulders that looked like chairs. As I sat down, I felt like I was higher than a kite. Everything was soft and glowin' and I began to see other shapes enter the clearing. I wondered if this is how people felt when they dropped acid. LSD. I couldn't clear my head so I just watched.

"As the full moon rose, the old woman entered the center of the clearing by herself and as I watched, she changed. She became really young and her clothes changed to a flowing gossamer dress-thing. She began to chant and raised her arms and head to acknowledge the moon.

"Now, I know this sounds strange but I'm tellin' ya' the truth. And this is only the beginning. As she chanted along, I saw a shooting star fly overhead. It looked like it was real close but ya' know how that is. Then I saw another one and another one. Then I heard this humming sound. And, all of a sudden, there were three small spaceships just over our heads. They were all silvery-white and shiny and they just hovered there not making a sound. I kept thinkin' whatever that tea stuff was, this was a great hallucination for sure. I wasn't gonna' try to get out of it. I decided to just watch and listen. I swear this is the God's truth."

Folks commented and teased Ben for just a minute.

"Well, as I said, I just sat there and watched. I can't rightly tell ya' how long those ships just hovered there but it was quite some time. It seemed like a long while. The old woman stepped aside from the center and a light beamed down from all three ships and beings emerged from the light. They were dressed just like the old woman and looked like her. They all chanted a beautiful song. Then other shapes came into the circle and joined in. It was the most beautiful music I think I've ever heard. Almost like a church choir kinda' thing. It eventually ended. The other shapes bowed to the old woman who looked really young then left the clearing to vanish into thin air. The beings from the three ships were returned to their ships by the same light beam. The ships flashed a colorful salute then they just vanished into the night sky.

"The old woman was still young and she walked over to me and said, 'You have been granted this special experience because the Others know who you are and know you will keep The Magic safe. We will go home now.'

"Right before my eyes she changed back to the old woman in her everyday clothes. She began walking out of the clearing and I followed her. As soon as we got to her house, my head cleared and I was back to being me. She sat me down and gave me a bottle of water saying, 'Don't worry. I didn't put anything in the water. Drink.'

"I took the water and drank a lot of it before I said, "Did I really see everything I think I saw out there?"

"What did ya' see?"

"You changed to young and others were in the clearing. Then the three spaceships came and beings came to the earth and y'all sang a most beautiful song.After the song ended, everything changed back to the way it was before we entered the clearing."

"'Yup. You saw the real thing.' she replied. 'It all happened just like you think it did. Wonder why you were privileged to be there?'

"Yeah. Why me?"

"Cause you know about The Magic and you'll honor it. You can tell everyone you know about tonight. This place is protected just like the Applewood Grove back home. Magic is everywhere,' she explained with a smile.

"As I was about to say something, she winked her eye and the next thing I knew it was the next morning and I was waking up in my bed. I sat up and thought about what had happened or what I thought had happened. I was just about to chalk it up to too much shine when I noticed somethin' shiny on the bedside table. It was a crystal. The old woman had given it to me as we left the clearing. The whole thing had been real. Very real. I left the area that day and continued my hike. I had a lot to think about as I headed north. And, that's all I have to tell ya' about tonight. God's honest truth."

Folks got on their feet and applauded Ben for quite some time before settling down.

Scott shook hands with Ben and said, "Now, Ben, we are reminded why your stories are so popular with the world. Thanks for bein' here with us all tonight."

Ben nodded his head and headed back to his group.

"Folks, we have one more storyteller for ya' before it's time for the fireworks. It's our own Miss Sissy Travis." Ben stepped aside as Miss Sissy came forward.

Sissy Travis was born and raised in The Creek. She was respected and followed the old ways that they used to protect The Creek, but she used modern technology in her everyday life as well. Sissy was a legal consultant in the corporate business profession. Most of her work was done from home. When she did have to travel for court dates, she drove if local or flew out if called for. She was extremely well paid as she was an expert in her field. She could always be seen walking along the road with her dog Manfred every day as she took a break from legal issues.

Folks greeted her with applause and cheers. She was known for her colorful storytelling.

"Hey, y'all. Good to see everyone," Sissy waved to the crowd.

"Hey, Sissy."

"Great to see ya' again."

"Love your stories"

"Thanks everyone. So, when Scott asked me to share a story, I knew right away the one I was gonna' tell ya'. It's about my dog Manfred."

"What's that crazy dog been up to now?"

Folks laughed as Sissy began her story.

"Well, as I can tell from some of ya,' y'all know my dog Manfred. I found him, or rather he found me, one spring day about four years ago. You could tell he was just past his puppy stage. He looked a mess and was hungry. So, of course, I took him in, cleaned him up and fed him and he's been with me ever since."

"How'd he get his name?" a voice in the crowd asked.

"Well, he didn't have a collar or anything so I started calling him Dawg. But that didn't feel right. So, I tried a few names and when I got to Manfred, his ears perked up and he started wagging his tail. So, that's the name he chose. Manfred was a name I heard once in my travels and I liked the way it was said, so I thought to myself that I'd remember it and use it when the right time came. It did and I did and that's how my Manfred got his name."

Folks laughed and talked a bit and the story moved on.

"So, when Manfred was celebrating his first anniversary with me, I was celebrating a victory for the company that had hired me. They won their court case using my information. They were a multi-million-dollar international corporation and they showed their appreciation with a surprise bonus that still keeps me goin' four years later. I was so excited that I was hollerin' and laughin' and cryin' all at the same time. I was tellin' Manfred all about how I won the argument for them and he just sat there and paid attention waggin' his tail and all. I was so happy that I flipped on the computer and opened up an app that played Broadway show tunes. I especially like the older ones from the mid-1900's and all. I was singin' along and all of a sudden Manfred started to howl a bit. As the music kept goin' and I kept singin', he got louder and stronger in his singin'. It was a mix between a beagle and a hound dog howl. Now, Manfred's a mutt for sure, so I wasn't too surprised that he'd had a special kinda' voice. When I stopped, he stopped. I took a drink of my soda and started singin' again. Manfred got a drink of his water and started right up with me."

Folks were laughing and carrying on some.

"Seems this dog was a special kinda' mutt. A talented dog for sure. When I started to sing one of the ballads from the Molly Brown show, he lamented right along with me. I had to stop 'cause I was laughin' so hard at his singin'. He looked mournful and soulful as he sang. This time when I stopped, he didn't. He finished the song and smiled at me as if to say, 'And you thought you had a great voice!' Well, I just sat down and stared at him. He came over and put his paw on my hand and we sat for a minute. I got up and fixed a treat for him knowin' he must be hungry after all that singin'. He ate and drank then lay down an took a long nap. I figured it must have been a once-in-a- lifetime thing. But, no! The next time I played show tunes, Manfred sang along just like the first time."

"Maybe ya' can get him a job on Broadway and retire from your work," Bubba hollered out.

This brought a round of laughter and more wise ass comments from the crowd. It was a bit before they all settled down and Sissy moved along with her story.

"Now, mind ya,' I think it's a hoot that Manfred likes to sing show tunes. Can't rightly say I know of anyone else with a singin' dog. It was a few months later, in the late fall, that I was surprised again. This time when Manfred and I were singin' songs from White Christmas, my cat started to yowl along. I looked at her and she just kept it up. No kiddin'. It didn't sound like someone was cryin' at all like some cats do. It was just Miss Meow singin' in her own sweet way with us. I stopped the music and looked at her. She gave me the 'look' as if to say 'Get the music back on. Now!' So, I did and those two joined in. Ever since, those two sing along whenever I play show tunes. I tried rock-n-roll and country but they wouldn't have it. Just the show tunes. Here, let me show ya'," Sissy said as she went and got Manfred.

She tuned into some show tunes on her phone and began to sing along. Manfred took one look at her and then joined in. Miss Sissy had a beautiful voice and it was a treat to hear her singin'. It was hilarious to hear Manfred join in. The crowd began singin' along with the two of them and before long, other critters in the forest joined in.

Sissy finally finished the last show tune and Manfred wandered back to get a drink.

"Well, folks, that's just how it is with Manfred and me. Thanks for listenin' and singin' along." Miss Sissy said as she finished up.

Folks stood and applauded and laughed for the longest time before settling back down.

"Now that was a great story and performance and we kindly thank ya', Miss Sissy. Folks, if ya' got a minute, take a look over head," Scott offered.

The fireworks began and went on for a while ending in a blast that showed the flag and what looked like shooting stars all around it. Miss Cora saw a shooting star that was bigger than the rest and knew right away it was one of the ET's ships that looked over The Creek. She smiled and waved and the shooting star shot off in a glory of color. Folks applauded this last bit of fireworks.

"My family and I want to thank y'all for comin' by as always. The wagons will take ya' back to your cars. Be safe and we'll see y'all soon. Good night and Happy 4th," Scott said.

Folks gathered their things and began to wander over to the wagons and before long, the meadow was cleared and folks were on their way home.

Katelyn had come over with Kendra and Ted and Michael. They all piled into Ted's truck and were back home just a few minutes later.

"This sure was a great 4th of July gatherin,'" Katelyn said as she yawned and gathered her things from the bed of the truck.

"It sure was special hearin' Miss Sissy's Manfred singin' along, that's some crazy dog," Michael said.

"Ya' never know about animals. They sure do surprise us," Ted added as he and Michael headed towards their back door. "Night ladies. Sleep well."

"Thanks guys. We will. Sweet dreams," Kendra said as she and Katelyn headed across the road for their homes.

"See ya' tomorrow, Kendra. I think I have just enough energy to drop into bed," Katelyn said as she went to her front door.

"Night. Keep the crystal next to you," Kendra as she stepped into her house.

The last thing Katelyn remembered before she fell into a deep sleep was that she was holding her shocked crystal real tight.

The Creek slept deeply that night.

CHAPTER 4

Tuesday morning found Katelyn gathering her portfolio and resume for her meeting with Ethan and Ian. She had slept so soundly last night that it took her a minute before she remembered she had the interview today.

She lay there waking up remembering the gathering at the Kirkland's Farm. She had reconnected with lots of folks and they shared stories from the past and present. One of the best things about yesterday, besides the interview and all, was meeting up with Finn again. They had grown up together with everyone else in The Creek and the fact that they were a few years apart in age didn't matter a bit. He sure was a fine-looking specimen of a man. She was sad that Jay had died and she wasn't here to be able to support his family and The Creek. She would think about making something special to remember Jay by and give it to The Creek as a way of grieving and showing her love for Jay and the family.

She rolled over and crawled out of bed. It sure was a bright, sunny day. Time to shower, eat and gather her thoughts before the meeting.

Ethan and Ian had been at the shop since six. This was a crazy, busy time for them. They were finishing up the final stuff at Matthews' place and would be starting on Jenna's studio next. It was just a ways behind the barn on Matthews' land. Seems the two of them were a set match.

Jordan Jackson found himself with deliveries for The Creek that Tuesday. He always liked it when he got The Creek on his list. It would be the last of the morning deliveries around ten o'clock. He had called The Store and asked Ted to set aside an everything bagel for him. He was treating himself to a late morning breakfast bagel today. He had left the farm around five to get to the UPS distribution center in Boone a half hour later so he could load up and get busy delivering his stuff. He would finish his ten-hour day around seven tonight. He had opted for four, ten-hour days ever since he moved to The Creek. He liked having three days off in the week. He had a lot of work to do on his farm. One of those things was creating just the right name for the farm. Since he had found those amazing crystals, he was thinking the word crystal would be in the name. Maybe. Maybe not. No hurry. He knew the name would show itself when the time was right.

Ethan had mentioned the return of one of The Creek's own, Katelyn MacDonald, and that she had found an amazing crystal of her own. Ethan said he would connect the two in a few days or so as Katelyn wanted to come look at Jordan's crystals. Jordan was excited to see Katelyn's shocked crystal as well.

Kendra and Miss Cora were getting together so Kendra could show Miss Cora some of the new stuff she could do on her laptop. Miss Cora had been gifted a laptop by the ETs that looked over The Creek. In one of the many attempts to take The Magic from The Creek, The Dark had destroyed Kendra's home and the two houses she owned next to hers. The ETs had immediately replaced these homes with bigger and better ones and filled the insides with everything a body could think of. Miss Cora had visited Kendra and saw her new computer. Kendra showed Miss Cora how to use it and Miss Cora was so excited about email, that she said she would appreciate it if Kendra would help her find one. Right in front of them, a new laptop appeared with a red ribbon on it and a note from the ETs showing their appreciation for all Miss Cora does in keeping The Creek folks safe and all. Miss Cora had been using hers since day one and loved emailing everyone. And, The Creek loved sending emails to Miss Cora. Kendra was going to show Miss Cora how to use dictionaries and information apps today.

The rest of The Creek was busy with their own chores and such. The Store was humming with folks gathering for coffee, breakfast and to share news of the day. Talk of the celebration could be heard in most conversations. Ted and Michael were creating a little something special for Katelyn, Ethan, and Ian. They knew that Katelyn would be asked to join the Soaring Mountain Builders and that she would accept. Ted told Ethan to bring everyone in for a celebratory lunch today. Ted and Michael knew that The Creek Magic was at work here. And they suspected that something was beginning to brew that would include Katelyn.

Katelyn arrived at the shop just a bit before ten. She never liked being late so she usually arrived a couple of minutes early. She was nervous for sure but not as much as she would be for people she didn't know.

Ethan saw her from the window and opened the door for her. "Hey Katelyn, welcome to Soaring Mountain Builders."

"Hey Ethan, Hey, Ian. Thanks for askin' me over. This is a great work space. Love the wrap-around architect tables."

"Hey, Katelyn. I demanded that Ethan build them 'cause I knew what I needed. He wasn't so sure but did it anyway. Now, he tries to take over at least half of them when I'm not lookin'," Ian said.

Ethan laughed at Ian. "Well, little brother, they did turn out to be a great idea. I may just have to build a few in the barn as well."

"Good. Then you can leave mine alone," Ian laughed at Ethan.

"How do you guys ever get anything done around here with all this teasing going on?" Katelyn asked as she laughed with the guys.

"Oh, we manage," Ethan said. "So, Katelyn, thanks for comin' over, Let's set up your portfolio here on this empty table and we'll take a look."

"Okay. I have my thumb drive with the portfolio on it as well. Where can I get it set up?"

Ethan pushed a button and the walls behind the tables opened and full screens moved a bit forward.

"Whoa! Now that's totally awesome!" Katelyn exclaimed. She handed Ethan the thumb drive and, in a few seconds, her portfolio was alive.

"Let me walk you through some of my projects," Katelyn suggested as she took the remote laser pointer from Ethan.

Ian laughed as he looked at Ethan and Katelyn. "I like a woman who takes charge especially from my brother."

Ethan looked at Ian as he said, "Ian, you can be replaced."

"Nah, not really," Ian made a face at Ethan.

"You boys ready?" Katelyn asked as she laughed at their antics.

"Yes, Ma'am, we are," Ian said as he and Ethan took seats to watch Katelyn's presentation. It took the better part of an hour.

Katelyn finished with this: "I love to design things for people just like I told Ethan yesterday. I feel honored and privileged to be a part of making their dream home come true."

She took a little bow and clicked on the last picture in her portfolio. It was of her at work at an architect's table showing design work with the Soaring Mountain Builders logo at the top of her design.

Ethan and Ian jumped up and applauded and hugged her.

"Katelyn, that was fantastic," Ian and Ethan said at the same time.

"Thanks guys. I hope you'll give some serious thought to your idea about me joining the company. I'd love to work with everyone."

Ethan and Ian looked at Katelyn and winked at each other.

Ethan began with, "Katelyn, just one more thing to discuss. Salary. Any ideas about how much you'd like to be paid?"

Katelyn knew this question was coming and she had thought long and hard about the answer.

"Ethan. Ian. I do believe something in the $80 - $90 thousand range would be acceptable.

Ian looked at Ethan. "Since she'll be my responsibility, I feel that that range is out of the question."

Katelyn looked at Ian and her smile disappeared.

"I was thinking more like $125 thousand to start with an appropriate raise after six months and all the benefits as well," Ian said with a smirk on his face.

Katelyn just stared at the guys. "Holy shit! Really?"

"Holy shit! Yes," Ethan and Ian replied.

"Oh, sorry guys. You took me by surprise. I accept!" Katelyn said.

"Great! So glad you came home. We really have a ton of work with our current projects and now we can take on a growing list of others. We'll add tables to this room. Ian and I have worked out an expansion of this shop to include a work area for you and an office of course. All the bells and whistles will be added. We've already ordered all the computer and other digital stuff you're going to need. It should be here later this week. I've hand-picked a crew to get started on the expansion and have already gotten the okay from the building inspector. He was by this morning looking over the plans Ian and I finalized."

"Wow! You guys don't waste a minute. When do I start?" Katelyn asked.

"Well, how about this afternoon? You and I can go over some of the basics around here than the rest of the week you can come in for a few hours each day until we get your area all set. We should be ready to go full force by next Monday. We'll discuss hours and all later today," Ian offered.

"I agree. This is so fantastic and all. I sure do appreciate your confidence in me and I'll do my best, as always," Katelyn said.

"Okay, so now since it's almost noon, how about we take you over to The Store for lunch? On us of course. We need to keep you well fortified for all the work that's about to come your way," Ethan suggested.

"I love the idea," Katelyn said as she gathered her things.

"Let's just leave them here. You're coming back to work this afternoon. Remember?" Ian said trying to sound firm.

"Sure. And, Ian, it didn't work. You couldn't sound gruff if you tried," Katelyn said laughing as the three of them piled into Ethan's truck.

They arrived at The Store a few minutes later and when they walked in, Ted and Michael hollered, "Congratulations Katelyn. Welcome aboard!"

They had a party of sorts set up and just a short time later Katelyn's folks joined them. Others wandered in including Kendra and Miss Cora.

They spent about two hours at this impromptu party before it was time to get back to work.

On the way back to the shop, Katelyn got a surprise call from Sami.

"Hey Sami. Great timing. How are ya?" Katelyn asked as she answered the phone.

"I'm great. Just wondered how the bar-be-que was yesterday," Sami replied.

"It was awesome as always. I can't talk much now 'cause I'm with my new boss partners," Katelyn said.

"What? A job already?"

"Yup. It's with my growing-up friends. I'm the new designer for Soaring Mountain Builders," Katelyn told Sami.

"And we're mighty glad she agreed to join us," Ethan hollered.

Katelyn was laughing as she said, "Sami, that was Ethan. He and his brother Ian, the architect extraordinaire, created the company and they design and build the most amazin' homes. Check them out on line."

"I will. Congrats girl. And thanks for hiring one of the best designers I know and love. Now, I won't worry about you so much," Sami said.

"Thank, Sami. How about I call you tonight and give you all the details?" Katelyn suggested.

"It's a date. Later. Love ya'," Sami said as they ended the call.

"Sounds like your Sami is a keeper," Ethan said as they drove down the drive.

"She sure is. My BFF for real," Katelyn said as they walked over towards the shop.

Ethan motioned them to follow him and they went around the east side of the building and found the work crew digging a foundation for the expansion.

"We're adding a basement to this part of the shop. Mostly for storage and whatever," Ethan explained as they watched the backhoe scoop up the earth. "Should be ready for the foundation forms tomorrow."

"It sure will, boss," the foreman said. "Welcome aboard Katelyn. Nice to have you here."

"Thanks. It's Dan, right? I met you last night," Katelyn replied.

"Yup. We'll be workin' alongside each other before you know it," Dan replied and got back to work.

"You guys really don't mess around, do you?" Katelyn said as they settled down to their work inside.

Ian began showing Katelyn the basics of the space and how it was used. He had her fill out the necessary new hire paperwork and he scanned it to their accounting firm to be processed.

"Oh, Katelyn, there's a sign on bonus you'll be receiving on Friday with your first paycheck coming along next week. Let me know if you need anything before then. We can work something out," Ian said.

"Wow! A sign-on bonus. So generous of you guys. Ian, I'm all set financially. I've been frugal with my funds since my first day of work with Lloyd and Johnson. I have enough to tide me through for quite some time as I didn't know when I'd find work. I do appreciate your generosity and kindness."

"We take care of our own, Ethan and me," Ian replied.

"I'm much obliged," Katelyn said with a nod of her head.

"Now, let's get back to work."

They worked until the shadows began to get long coming through the windows.

"Oh shit!" Ian said as he looked up from their work and realized it was going on seven o'clock. "I didn't mean to keep you so long. So sorry Katelyn."

"No worries, Ian, this has been fun. These houses are amazin' and being a part of them is a dream come true. I do believe I'm quite hungry though. I'll grab something from The Store on my way home."

"Thanks. How about you come in tomorrow whenever you get to it and we'll keep goin'?"

"Sounds good to me. Thanks, Ian. See you tomorrow," Katelyn said as she left the shop.

Ethan saw her driving away and jumped on his brother.

"Ian! I can't believe you kept her so late," Ethan started.

"Ethan, we lost track of time. I apologized and Katelyn was okay with it. We really did have fun this afternoon. I told her to come in whenever she got around to it tomorrow."

"Really? She liked it here?" Ethan asked.

"Yes, she did and I am so excited to be working with her. She had some great ideas for two of the new builds. This is one of the best ideas you've ever had."

"I'm so relieved. I didn't want to turn down any of the work but knew we couldn't take it on with just you. I love the way The Magic works around here. I really do."

"Me, too, brother. Me, too. But it is time to get home. My family is gonna' be thrilled about Katelyn. With her here, I can get home earlier than dark this summer," Ian said as he grabbed his keys and headed out the door.

"See ya' later," Ethan replied.

Katelyn stopped at The Store for take-out and was in her kitchen a short time later. She called Sami to bring her up-to-date on all that had happened in the few hours since she returned home.

"Geez-oh-Pete, Katie. This is all so awesome!" Sami said after Katelyn finished.

"And, my salary is like yours. They're paying me $125 thousand and all the benefits as of today!"

"Holy shit! That's totally cool! I'm so happy for you. This has happened so fast ya' gotta' believe in The Magic for sure."

"And, I do! That crystal from the fair has protected me from those night terrors ever since I started to keep it next to me when I sleep. I mean in the bed next to me. The last terror was really bad."

"Tell me about it," Sami said.

Katelyn told her about that last night terror and how as soon as she held the crystal up against the monster, everything exploded and she was safe.

"Jesus! That's some crystal. I guess it really was meant to be with you. Good thing we went to that fair and all," Sami commented when Katelyn was done.

"I know. I am so lucky," Katelyn.

"Katie, I don't think luck has anything to do with all this. I think you're following some kind of blueprint that the Universe has for you," Sami said.

"Sami, you're right. That's exactly what's happening here. I'll pay close attention to whatever comes next. How's your new adventure? Been travelin' much yet?"

"Katie, it's only been a few days. But, yes, I am set to start in Maine next week. I'll keep you posted as I get closer to Boone. Looks like I'm gonna' be spending two or three days at each property to get an idea of the realistic look rather than the digital look. They gave me a Panasonic bridge digital camera. I've been learning how to use it. It's so fuckin' cool! Anyway, there are about eight properties before Boone, but my boss said I may be hopping around for a bit so I could be in Boone sooner."

"I love how all this is coming along. Can't wait to see you," Katelyn said.

"Me, too," Sami replied. "I gotta' get goin'. I've got a few things to do before tomorrow. Let's talk again in a few days and you can tell me all about your new job and I'll tell you all about my latest adventure."

"Love the idea. Love you forever and always," Katelyn told Sami.

"Love you forever and always," Sami answered as they hung up.

Katelyn finished her supper and called her folks. They had a short chat about Katelyn's new job with the promise to get together over the weekend.

Katelyn began to get sleepy a while later so she grabbed her crystal and fell sound asleep. She dreamed about crystals and caves and some big bird during the night.

The Creek slept. Most of The Creek. Miss Cora was awake late into the night as she began to have a feeling something was beginning to brew.

CHAPTER 5

than had called Katelyn first thing Wednesday morning to tell her to wear outdoor clothes as they would be visiting worksites. She told him she had a pair of old work boots as he wanted to make sure her feet were protected.

Katelyn arrived around nine and Ian just smiled at her.

"Couldn't stay away, huh?"

"Nope. I love this stuff," Katie said back smiling from ear to ear.

"Nice boots," Ethan said.

"They're old but still work. I'll be getting a new pair real soon," she laughed back at Ethan.

"Good. Gotta' stay safe on the sites," Ethan replied.

"We're gonna' start at Matthews' place just down the road. We want you to see how one of the projects I was showin' you yesterday has developed. It's almost finished. Just a few minor details to complete," Ian explained.

"Great. Let's get goin' then," Katelyn said as she held the door open for the guys.

"I love this girl, already," Ethan said as they piled into the truck and arrived at Matthews' a few minutes later.

Katelyn remembered how the place looked when she was growing up. This place was totally different and still the same. The farmhouse was new but it still held the charm of the old house. The barn was the same although it had had some perking up done. There were no utility lines to be seen anywhere.

"Underground utilities?" Katelyn asked as they began the walk around.

"Yes. In all our builds, utilities are underground. It costs a bit extra, but the benefits out way the costs," Ian answered.

"I agree. And, it makes the property look clean as well."

"Katelyn, I do believe you've done this a few times before," Ethan said with a smirk.

"Just a few, Mr. Ethan. Just a few," Katelyn answered with a smirk.

"Wise ass for sure," Ethan laughed.

"Why, yes, I am and thanks for noticin'," Katelyn replied.

Just then Matthews walked out from the back-porch entrance. The porch was a wrap-around. It was magnificent.

"Hey guys, oh, and, Katelyn. So, you took the plunge and joined the team? You're a brave girl," Matthews said.

"Another wise ass," Ethan commented.

"One of the best," Matthews said with a bow.

"Matthews, we're showin' Katelyn some of our projects, starting with yours. Any chance we can get inside for a bit?"

"Of course. The doors open when you're ready. Jenna left a while ago. Something about the light and shadows over by Emily's place," Matthews replied.

"Great. Thanks," Ian said as Matthews went into the barn.

Ethan, Ian, and Katelyn spent a couple of hours inside the barn then inside the house.

"Everything looks good here, Ian," Ethan said about the barn. "The other cross beams are due to be delivered this week and the crew can get them in place."

"Is the barn safe without them?" Katelyn asked as they stood in Matthews' kitchen.

"Great question, Katelyn. Yes, it is. The original cross beams are solid oak and were tested for strength before we got started. None of them needed to be replaced. Ian drew up the sketch you're looking at and suggested to Matthews that we add the other five to be placed for future support and aesthetics. The crew will use a fork lift to get the beams in place so they can be secured with cross sectional steal supports. Kinda' like an ankle wrap for wood."

"This is incredible. I guess that's why y'all are sought after so much. You think of stuff way into the future, not just the present. And, I've always been a supporter of saving the old designs as much as possible if that's what the client wants. It looks like Matthews thinks that way, too."

"You've got us figured out in less than a day. Ian, we better be careful around her. She may come up with stuff we haven't even thought of," Ethan said.

"You're right Ethan. She could be trouble," Ian said with a wink.

"Oh, boys, there's no doubt about it, I AM trouble," Katelyn said laughing. "Let's take a look at the rest of the house. I remember this place from when I was a kid. Most of us in The Creek have been inside the old farmhouse playing with the kids that used to live here. I'd like to see if I recognize any of the designs from the old farmhouse."

"Sure thing. Let's get goin'. We'll start in the living room. As we all remember, it was a small room. We opened it up to join the library and the small study. Now it's big enough to hold a lot of people. We left the wall between the study and the kitchen intact as it's only a short full wall. It gives the feel of separation without blocking the rest of the great room. We turned the mud room into a pantry and in adding the full wrap-around porch, we were able to create a mud room off the back entrance."

Katelyn looked around the new great room and suddenly stopped in her tracks.

"Oh, my God! You guys kept the original staircase in the back of the kitchen although I think you widened it a couple of feet. And, look, the marks where the family measured the children are still there. Or, wait. It's the measurement marks but you guys must have photographed them then laminated them and set then into the wall. Oh, how wicked cool is that?! Does the family know you did that?"

"Yes, they do," Ian replied. "We had them here a couple of weeks ago to take a look over the farmhouse and all. They were so shocked to see we preserved the barn almost one-hundred percent in its original form and style. They left some of the farm equipment here for Matthews to use. They were in tears lookin' at it though. They said it looked like they had stepped back a lifetime ago when they walked into the barn. They were really quiet for the longest time. Tears were flowing quite freely all around. Us, too."

Ethan added, "When we got into the house they went right to the old staircase and saw their marks. We made sure their names were next to the marks. They talked about how they remembered each time they were measured by their grandparents. More tears, of course. They spent a long time going from room-to-room looking at the work we did and remembering their childhood here. We kept a lot of the old wood and worked it into the new walls and such. It was a special day for sure. We took lots of pictures of them in every room and space. They loved how we opened the rooms to create the great room and kept some of the old bookcase shelves for the bookcase inset in the wall over there. We framed some of those pictures for Matthews and he has them ready to hang up all over the house. "

Ian broke in with, "One of the coolest things we discovered was when we were tearing down walls and running the new electrical lines was in the master bedroom. It was a small room so, we tore down the wall in the adjoining room to the south and found some old maps of The Creek. It looked like someone had purposely put them there to hide them from someone or something. We asked Miss Cora to take a look at them after we placed them in plastic to preserve them. She's comin' over tomorrow to take a look and tell us what she thinks about them."

"Probably has something to do with The Magic," Katelyn thought. Thing is, she said it out loud.

"Oh, sorry, guys. Just thinking out loud, I guess," Katelyn said not sure how the guys would take it.

"Well, now, Katie, if I may call you Katie," Ian asked.

"Why, yes you may, Ian. Thanks for askin'. I only let special friends call me Katie, as you are well aware of."

"Yes. I know," Ian replied. "Well, anyway, that's just what Ethan and I were wonderin' about, too. So, we thought Miss Cora would be the one to ask about it."

"This place is so amazing. Not just the work you all did; the craftsmanship is beyond magnificent. It's that you kept the old with the new as if this is how it should have always been."

"Matthews invited the O'Connell's to come by anytime they wanted. Just stop in and wander around the land if they wanted to. He told them to let him know when they'd be around and he'd make sure the house was open for them."

"This new chapter of my life is going to be, has already been, indescribable. Thanks for inviting me to join y'all."

"We're excited to have you, Katie," Ethan replied.

They looked over the rest of the house then they took her down to the brook to show her the little faerie house.

"This is wicked cool! A faerie house. That is what this is, right?"

"Yes, it is. But how did you know that?" Ethan asked.

"Really Ethan? I grew up in the middle of some of the most powerful Magic on the planet. How would I NOT know it was a faerie house?"

Ethan and Ian just stood there and laughed.

"Oh, yeah, Ethan. She's the right person to join our team," Ian said as he slapped Ethan on the back.

They walked back to the barn along the trench in the tractor path.

"What the fuck happened here?" Katelyn yelled.

"An earthquake is what happened here," Ethan said.

"No way. We don't usually have earthquakes around here," Katelyn replied.

"Well, we did this time," Ian said without looking right at Katie.

"Alright guys, what gives? Did Magic have something to do with this?"

"Well, it was evil that did this tryin' to take The Magic from The Creek," Ethan explained.

"My mom told me somethin' happened up at The Holler. Was this part of it?"

"Yup. Happened a bit before The Holler thing, tryin' to scare Matthews off the land. Didn't work. Obviously," Ian explained.

"A whole lot more has happened than that thing at The Holler. I gotta' get caught up on things right away," Katelyn said as they walked back to see Matthews with Jenna in the driveway.

"Hey Jenna," Ethan called out.

"How are ya, Jenna?" Ian asked as they met up.

"Katelyn, you remember Jenna, don't ya?"

"Of course, I do. You used to babysit Finn and Jay and a few others around here. So glad you survived those rascals," Katelyn said laughing.

"I'm glad I survived them as well. Nice to see you again. I hear you've come home for good," Jenna said.

"Yup. I'm happy, too," Katelyn replied.

"Katelyn, how about we get together soon and talk design and artwork and stuff? I think we'll have a lot in common. Ethan and Ian are building my art studio just behind the barn. I'm sure you saw where it's gonna' be when you went down to the faerie house."

"I sure did. I looked at the blueprints earlier and it looks perfect for you," Katelyn said. "I'd love to get together with you. How about Saturday morning?"

"Great. How about you come over here around nine?"

"It's a deal," Katelyn replied.

"Oh, no! I think we've created a monster with the two of them," Ethan said as he poked fun at the girls.

They all laughed and talked for a bit longer before Ethan, Ian and Katelyn went on their way. The stopped off at Jordan's place next to have a look at his barn as well. It had not been completed before winter and the work crews were busy getting it finished up.

Jordan happened to be home when they arrived. He was delivering in The Creek that late morning and had stopped off at home for lunch.

"Hey Ethan. Ian. Nice to see you in the middle of the day," Jordan said as they shook hands.

"Jordan, this here is Katelyn. She grew up here and has come home to stay. She's an interior designer with a bit of architect mixed in. She's joined Soaring Mountain. Katelyn, this here's Jordan Jackson. He's got the super special crystals I told you about."

"Hey, Katelyn. Nice to meet ya'," Jordan said as they shook hands. The minute their hands touched, you could see electricity shoot out around everyone.

"Holy shit! Not again!" Katelyn hollered as the zing shot through her. Ethan and Ian just stared at them.

"I do believe somethin' is about to happen around here. Again," Ethan stated matter-of-factly.

"What the hell?" Jordan yelled as the zing shot through him.

Ian shook his head as he said, "I do believe The Magic is alive and well in The Creek, as always."

They all stood there completely silent for the longest time. Then everyone began to speak at once.

"What do ya' mean not again?" Ethan asked Katelyn.

"How'd that happen?" Ian asked.

"What the hell is going on?" Jordan asked.

"There's got to be Magic right here on your farm, Jordan," Katelyn said.

"That was one hell of a jolt. Except, I don't feel any pain or anything like that," Jordan said as they stood apart.

"It didn't hurt me either," Katelyn said.

"Katelyn, what did you mean when you said not again?" Jordan asked her.

"Oh. That. Well, when I was at a fair back in Alabama, right before I moved home, my BFF Sami and I stopped at an artist's booth to look at her work with the shocked crystals from the Wetumpka Meteorite Impact Crater. They are magnificent! Well, I was drawn to one sitting by itself and asked if I could hold it. The artist said I could and when I picked it up, I felt the same kind of electrical zing we just felt. Although that zing went to my head and had me glowin' as long as I held the crystal. The artist said the crystal must have been lookin' for me and gave me the crystal as a gift. I keep it in a cloth bag on me at all times. I have it now. Look," Katelyn said as she showed them the crystal she had in her satchel. She held it in the cloth so she wouldn't be zinged again.

"That's absolutely beautiful. And so small. Come look at this one," Jordan said as they went around to the front porch and showed the huge crystal by the front door to Katelyn.

"Wow! That thig is huge! Beautiful. It almost sounds like it's humming. Listen," Katelyn said as they all stopped talking and leaned into the crystal to hear it.

They listened for a minute or two then stood up.

"I've heard it hum like that when the sun hits it at sundown but never in the day time. Must be you and your crystal, Katelyn," Jordan surmised.

"Bet Katelyn has somethin' to do with all this crystal stuff," Ian added.

"Could be why she was 'sent' home by The Magic," Ethan offered.

"Well, this sure has been an unbelievable mornin' guys," Katelyn said as she put her crystal back into her satchel.

"Katelyn, how about you stop by any evening or any time on the weekend and I'll show you the other two crystals I have inside and where I found them?" Jordan offered.

"It's a deal," Katelyn said. "Give me your cell and I'll give a call."

Jordan and Katelyn exchanged numbers as they all walked back to Ethan's truck.

"Time for me to get to The Store with their deliveries. Later," Jordan said as he got into his truck and drove off.

"Well, this sure has been a surprising day," Ethan said as they watched Jordan drive off.

"Sure has," Ian and Katelyn said at the same time. Then laughed.

"Time for food. How about we get take out from The Store and get back to the shop to look over some of the blueprints for the next couple of projects?" Ethan offered.

"Fine by me," Katelyn replied. "I'm so hungry, all of a sudden, I think I could eat a cow!"

They grabbed food at The Store and were back in the shop for the rest of the afternoon.

They all stopped at the same time and stretched in unison.

"Well, I guess we all know it's time to call it quits," Katelyn said as she yawned.

"I agree," Ian said as he yawned as well.

"Don't get me started," Ethan added as he started to yawn.

"Guess all that fresh air has done me in," Katelyn said as she gathered her things.

"It's quitin' time, folks," Ethan proclaimed. "It seems a few hours a day has already turned into two full days for you, Katie. How about you come in around noon tomorrow. No earlier, hear?"

"I hear ya', boss. Noon," Katelyn said as she saluted Ethan. "I gotta' say I sure do love workin' with you two. This has been a great beginning. Later."

They waved at Katelyn as she walked out the door.

"Brother, I do believe Magic is alive and well here in The Creek as usual," Ethan said.

"I do believe it is. And, somethin' is brewin' for sure," Ian added softly.

"It is brother. It for sure is," Ethan added just as softly. "And, it has somethin' to do with our Katie."

"Oh, I know that for sure. Wonder what Miss Cora has to say about all this?"

"I'm sure she'll let us know when the time is right. Time for you to get home. Hug that beautiful wife of yours and my niece and nephew."

"I will. Goodnight," Ian said as he left.

Ethan had a lot to tell Emily tonight. He closed the shop and set out for Emily's Meadow to tell her everything and get her take on the whole of it.

Matthews and Jenna were settling in after a light supper. They had been living at Matthews for the past month since the house was ready. Well, not really living together. Jenna just spent a lot of nights there. She still had her place where she did her work both on computer and free hand drawing and painting. Although she and Matthews hadn't made any formal decision about being together for life, it was moving in that direction. Afterall, Matthews was building Jenna her artist studio on his land in the meadow a ways behind the barn. That meadow faced south and the light would be perfect for Jenna.

The had just moved into the great room and settled on the couch when Jenna looked at Matthews with longing in her eyes.

He picked up on it and moved over to her and ran his hand along her breast.

"Oh, G-man, I like the way you think," Jenna said as she raised her arms so he could stroke her better.

"And I like the way you move," Matthews replied.

Their love making had been getting better and better ever since that first time a few months ago when Jenna had visited Matthews in his house next to Kendra's. The earth moved that night.

It looked to be headed in that same direction now. It was still light out, but the great room looked out of the back of the house and the house had been set a ways back from the original one. It was much closer to the barn for easier access and all.

Matthews raised the remote and locked the house up. He slowly removed Jenna's shirt and looked at her breasts. They were bulging out of the tiny bra she had on.

"I do believe you dressed just for this occasion," Matthews said as he leaned towards her.

"I did indeed," Jenna replied as she moved into Matthews.

He took her breasts in his hands and began stroking them and lightly flicking her nipples.

Jenna moaned and released the front snap on her bra. It fell away as she laid against Matthews, pushing him down so her breasts were above his mouth.

As he reached for her, she placed her breast against his mouth and he opened and began sucking her. Jenna moaned and he sucked harder. His other hand went for her shorts and he unzipped them and pushed them down far enough to get to her hot spot. He found it and began to rub her to bring her to a climax.

Jenna managed to kick her clothes off so she was fully naked for Matthews. He brought her close to her first climax then he laid her down on the floor on the big rug. She watched him undress and she grabbed his dick when he crawled over her. He let her stroke and play with him until he was close to exploding. He slid down her belly with his tongue, found her clit and started to flick it. He pushed his fingers into her and she erupted into a hot climax. She was bucking and moaning as he brought her to her full ecstasy. He released her and let her calm down for a bit.

She let him know she was ready when she rolled onto him and began pushing against his hard dick. He grabbed her breasts and pulled her to his mouth sucking on one then the other. She kept rockin' him until he couldn't take it anymore. He flipped her over again and this time he stroked her clit as he began to enter her. She began to push against him and he knew that was her way of telling him to push harder and faster.

She wrapped her legs around his ass as he pushed harder and faster bringing her, at last, to utopia. As soon as she began to climax, she pushed harder and faster against him and brought him with her on that ride through the universe. They soared for a long while before they started to settle down. Then they slept.

It was just beginning to get a bit shadowy when they woke up.

"Holy cow, dude. That was some awesome love makin'," Jenna whispered as she kissed him.

"No kidding, Miss Jenna. I do believe I heard the angels singin'," Matthews replied as he kissed her back.

"We could keep goin', ya know," Jenna suggested.

"Yes, we most definitely could. Just one thing. I'm starving. You make me hungry for more than just you," Matthews said as they got up and found their clothes.

"I agree, sir," Jenna said as they raided the frig. "Would you be available in a little while, sir?"

"I would, indeed, Ma'am. Upstairs good for you?"

"Why, yes, it is."

"See you soon, then," Jenna said laughing.

"It's a date," Matthews replied laughing as well.

The spent the evening eating and talking about The Creek.

"I like that, Katelyn. Seems she's good at her design work. I googled her and looked at some of the designs she's done. I think I might have some free-lance work for her. Remember that client I told you about down in Pine Ridge?"

"Oh, yeah. The one that likes the history of the Blue Ridge and wants to incorporate it into his home. You're creating a wall mural for him in his basement entertainment room. What'd ya have in mind for Katelyn?"

"I think I'll tell her about his ideas and see if she might be interested in talkin' to him. If she is, then I'll tell him about her and if he's interested, we can get together at his place to see how things go."

"Okay. I've already run a check on him, but I'll do another one just to be careful."

"Good idea Matthews."

"There's somethin' about that Katelyn I like. And, when I have hunches like this one, I've learned to listen to them."

She gathered their supper things and cleaned up while Matthews started the security check on the Pine Ridge client. The rest of the evening found them talking about the art studio, the barn and the faerie house. Sunset came around nine o'clock and just at that moment, they looked out towards the faerie house from their second-floor bedroom and saw the twinkling lights they had first seen when they had their first date back before Christmas.

"Guess The Magic is glad we're here," Matthews said as he put his arm around Jenna.

She lay her head on his shoulder as they kept watching the light show. "Guess it is, Matthews. Glad to have your blessings little faerie folk," Jenna offered.

They must have heard her and Matthews because all of a sudden, the light show turned all the colors of the rainbow and twinkled very brightly for a few seconds, then was gone.

They spent the night making slow, delicious love.

Ethan found Emily rounding up the chickens with the help of Trouble. Trouble was the mutt that had wandered into the meadow one day last year right after the build was completed. Emily says he found them. Either way, his name was well suited for him. He did know how to help with the chickens and the two of them had them in their outdoor coop in quick time.

"Thanks, Trouble," Emily said as she ruffled his ears and gave him a treat.

Ethan came around the corner and Trouble bound up to him.

"Hi, boy. Nice to see you, too," Ethan said as he gave him a head rub.

"Nice to see you, too," Ethan said as he grabbed Emily and kissed her soundly.

"Nice, indeed," Emily said as they parted. "How was your day with Katelyn?"

"It was awesome. Katie is just what we need. Love how that all works out," Ethan said as the three of them walked into the mudroom from the back porch. "Something smells delicious."

"I made you that spaghetti and meatballs you love so much. I knew you would have a very busy day and be hungry come supper time."

"I couldn't ask for more," Ethan said as he kissed the top of her head.

"Set the table while I get the garlic bread and set dinner on the table."

They sat down and spent a good amount of time eating and getting caught up on the day's events.

"How was Katelyn's first field day?" Emily asked as they finished and sat relaxing in the living room.

"Well, let me tell ya'," Ethan began. "She's a real trooper. She kept up with us all day. Somethin' happened at Jordan's and I want to get your take on it. I introduced the two of them to each other and when they shook hands, we all saw electricity shoot out of their hands. It was wild."

"Really? Tell me more," Emily said.

"Okay. Well, as soon as they let go, the energy thing stopped. Jordan was really surprised but Katelyn didn't seem as surprised. She looked at us then told us that a similar thing had happened at a fair she and her BFF Sami went to just before she left Alabama. She and Sami were lookin' at the shocked crystals collection one of the artisans had on display. Katie says one of them was calling to her and she asked if she could hold it. The artist gave it to her and when it was in her hand, she felt an electrical zing go up her arm into her head. She told us that Sami and the artist were just lookin' at her and when she asked why, she says Sami said she was glowin'. Katie then told us that she felt like she wasn't really there, at the fair. She felt real fuzzy the whole time she was holding the crystal. The artist insisted she keep it and wouldn't let Katie pay for it. As soon as the artist put in into a cloth sack, the fuzziness went away and she stopped glowin.'"

"Well, that's a lot of Magic there," Emily said with a smile on her face.

"And, Katie told Ian and I that she keeps the crystal on her body at all times to protect her from evil night terrors and dreams."

Ethan looked at Emily and Emily was smiling and kinda' gazing off into space.

"Oh, oh. I know that look," Ethan said. "It's Katie. She's got somethin' to do with The Magic around here. Emily?"

Emily shook her head and replied, "I'd say she does. Where did her shocked crystal come from? Do ya' know?"

"Yes. She said it was from the Wetumpka Meteorite Impact Crater just north of Montgomery, Alabama. Why? Does it make a difference?"

"Yes, it does. Each crystal has special powers from the place they are found. I'd say that meteorite has some powerful Magic in it."

"Well, now, that's somethin' to think about."

"Yes, it is. I'll give Miss Cora a call and tell her about this and see what she has to say. I'd say somethin' is about to get started around here that is linked to Katelyn. That's probably the big reason she felt the need to come home."

Ethan leaned into Emily as he said," I do believe you are right about that. Just now, though, I feel the need to get real cozy with you."

Emily laughed softly as Ethan unbuttoned her blouse and stroked her breast. They spent the rest of the evening making slow, sweet love.

CHAPTER 6

hursday found everyone in The Creek going about their business as usual. It was after supper when Katelyn decided to visit Kendra. She could see her on her front porch so she walked over. She wanted to talk to her about those night terrors she'd been having and how the crystal kept them away.

"Hey, Kendra," Katelyn said as she stepped onto the porch.

"Hey, yourself. Have a seat," Kendra replied. "What brings you here on this gorgeous summer evening?"

"Well, I wanted to talk to you about some stuff that has been happening to me. I'm sure it has to do with Magic."

"Okay. Can I get you somethin' to drink?"

"Nope. All set," Katelyn said as she showed Kendra her iced tea.

"Okay then. Start talkin' girl," Kendra said.

"Well, I've been having these horrible night terrors for the last few months right before I felt the need to come home. They've stopped since I got the shocked crystal and keep it on me all the time." Katelyn showed it to Kendra.

"That is one powerful crystal," Kendra said.

"Yes, it is. And, I don't understand much about it. I know it has to do with The Magic here and all over the place. Just don't know why it found me."

"We'll figure it out as we go," Kendra replied as she motioned for Katelyn to keep telling her story.

"The dreams, or I guess I should say night terrors, started about four months ago. They were kinda' not specific at first. I knew they were bad but couldn't describe any details after I woke up. They would wake me up in the middle of the night usually around three o'clock. Then, one night about a month ago, it was bad. The monster was gross. He looked like he was oozing blood and smelled like rotted skin. I threw up in my dream. I woke up screamin' 'cause, in my dream, this monster was chasing me, trying to grab me.

"I got out of bed, turned on every light in the cottage and made some chamomile tea. I sat at the kitchen table for the longest time before I began to calm down. I suddenly remembered the crystal you had given me years ago. I don't know why, but I grabbed it off the window sill. I went back to bed with all the lights on, holding onto that crystal for dear life. I didn't have any more night terrors as long as I held onto that crystal.

"The last night terror, just before I left Alabama, was horrible as well. I woke up 'cause it smelled really gross. I flipped on the light and found a monster leaning right over me. I grabbed the shocked crystal I had under my covers and brought it into the light. As soon as I showed it to the monster, he screamed and blew up into a zillion pieces. I was really scared and relieved that the monster had blown up. I felt somethin' hot in my hand and looked down and found the crystal glowin' like crazy and vibrating. I focused on the crystal and my breathing slowed and I felt better. Now, I keep that crystal on me all the time."

Kendra took a moment before she responded to all that Katelyn had told her. It almost looked like she was having a conversation with someone you couldn't see.

She turned to Katelyn with a smile and said, "Katelyn, those night terrors are horrible. They usually happen to people who are wakin' up to Gifts from the Universe."

She watched Katelyn as she thought about what Kendra had just said.

"What? Really? Me?"

"Yup. You."

"No way, Kendra."

"Yes. Every way, Katelyn. Take a minute to take it all in."

They sat there quiet-like while Katelyn thought about everything.

Katelyn took a deep breath and asked, "So, does this mean the bad guys are gonna' keep tryin' to kill me?"

"Nope. Not at all. First, do you accept the reality that you're a part of The Magic and have been given special Gifts to communicate with the Spirts on The Other Side?"

"Give me another minute. You mean ghosts, right?"

"Yes, ghosts."

"Okay. I do believe we live after we die. Well, our soul does. Is that what spirits are? Our souls?"

"Yes. Same thing."

"Okay, explain how all that works. In a body and then a spirit thing, please."

"With pleasure. We know that you know about The Magic in The Creek. Good. So, here goes. We are a beautiful bright energy before we come down into the physical body. We sit in counsel with our Guides and Master Teachers to discuss what we want to experience in the human body. What kind of lessons do we want to learn during our time as a human being? Once we're here, we go along growing up and living our lives. Some of us agree to be Gifted and some of us do not. When we leave the earth body after it dies, we go back into The Light and sit with our Guides and Master Teachers to talk about the experience. Ya' with me so far?"

"Yes. I do believe all of this, but I appreciate the way you've given me more details and all."

"Good. There is a law of physics that states that energy can neither be created nor destroyed. It can only change shape. Like liquid water changes into ice and vapor or fog. It's still water. And, just like that, our energy can't be destroyed nor can anymore be created. We just change shape We change the container we live in. In the physical body or as a pure white energy form."

"Okay. I got that. Really cool, by the way. So, why all those night terrors? Do they have anything to do with all of this stuff?"

"Yes, they do. There are forces in all the universes and beyond. Two of them. There is The White Light and The Dark Force. I see you understand these well. So, when a human person who decided to be Gifted before becoming human, begins to wake up or become aware of their Gifts, The Dark Force tries really hard to scare that person, you this time, into not accepting your Gifts and choosing not to walk in The Light. Once we are aware that we can connect with The Other Side, we need to choose to walk in The White Light or join The Dark Force."

"Got it. So how do I make the choice? No, how do I tell whomever my choice?"

"Well, first, let me give you a bit more information. The Dark Force is always tryin' to keep The White Light from being strong. The more damage the Dark Force can do, the better for it as it wants to control all the universes throughout the dimensions. I'll explain more about the dimensions thing much later. The Dark Force wants to control all mankind. Thing is, mankind can choose for itself whether it wants to be with The White Light or The Dark Force. This makes The Dark really angry. So, when someone begins to wake up to their Gifts, The Dark tries really hard to make you NOT choose to walk in The White Light to gain more control over mankind. That's what all those night terrors are about. To scare you into *Not* using your Gifts and *Not* walking in The White Light."

"Holy fuck! That's a lot of stuff goin' on," Katelyn exclaimed.

61

"It sure is," Kendra replied. "Ya' need a minute?"

'No. I really do understand and it makes pure sense to me. It's almost as if I've always known about this. Can't explain how but it does."

"That happens sometimes. So, to answer your questions about how you choose which way to go. Have you made a choice, Katelyn?'

"Yes. I choose to walk in The White Light. How do I make that happen?"

"So happy with your choice. There are three things you need to say to seal the deal. Let me tell you what they are then you can repeat them and be safe in The White Light."

Kendra told Katelyn what to say and she repeated these special words as Kendra said them. As soon as Katelyn said the last words, she felt a wave of energy flow through her that made her a bit light headed.

"Whoa! What a rush! That's so cool," Katelyn said.

"It is indeed. Welcome home Miss Katelyn," Kendra said as she walked over to hug her.

"Oh my God, I feel so happy. It's as if the weight of the World has been lifted off my shoulders."

"It's the negative energy of The Dark that has been pushed away from you. The Dark can never get to you again. You'll be aware of it, but it can't bother you mind, body and soul. No more night terrors. Some people suffer depression and physical pain as The Dark tries to control them and keep them from walking in The Light. They feel free and relieved when they make the choice like you've just done.

"Now. Let's get started on how you use those Gifts. Yes, there's always more than one. But you usually only start with one at a time. I suggest you tell your Guides and all that they can't bother you when you sleep and when you're driving. Trust me on this. You decide when you connect with The Other Side."

"Okay then. Just like Kendra said. Don't bother me when I'm sleeping and when I'm driving. Next"

"Movin' right along," Kendra said with a laugh. "Now, you can choose to learn about your Gifts all at once. Kinda' like jumpin' off a cliff or a little at a time. Whatever suites you."

"Okay. I choose to learn about my Gifts not all at once but at a medium pace. If I need some down time, I'll let ya' know and y'all need to respect that," Katelyn said.

Kendra laughed as she said, "Katie, I think ya' got the hang of this thing. Welcome home."

"Thanks, Kendra. It feels all so right and like I've done all this before."

"It's because you have. We come to the earth plane many times as we learn to become benevolent and understanding of all life in the universes and beyond. You may even see something that you've never seen before and know all about it. That's past life experiences being brough to your conscious mind at the current time."

"Well, that explains a lot," Katelyn said as she took a minute to look around. "Hey, Kendra. It feels like we've been here for a long time, but the sun is just starting to touch the top of the trees. I swear we've been here for the longest time."

"That's how all this happens sometimes. Time kinda' stops or slows down when we learn about The Magic and when we connect with it. Sometimes, we dream of being somewhere for days or months or longer and then wake up and find it was just a dream. I think you know what I mean."

"Why, yes, I do. And, you know it," Katelyn laughed as she pointed her finger at Kendra.

"I thought you might catch on real quick and you have. One more thing before we stop for the night. Every day and whenever you feel like The Dark is tryin' to hurt you and anyone with you, all you have to do is say these six words: *White Light surround and protect me.* I do this every morning when I wake up. Out loud or in your head. Either way works. Remember this. Now, time to stop. The physical body can only take so much at one time. How about some desert and a cold drink?"

"Sounds good to me," Katelyn said as she followed Kendra into the kitchen. They talked for a while then Katelyn wandered back home.

The sun was shooting sunbeams of color everywhere as Katelyn stood on her porch watching the sun set. Absolutely magnificent light show.

Katelyn slept that night like she hadn't slept in a long time. Deep and restful with no bad dreams.

Friday found everyone finishing up their week's work and planning for a fun weekend. Ted was creating new food combos and Michael was his test taster. Some recipes were good, others, well, let's just say they would never be used again.

Bubba and Earl were enjoying watching their new cabins being built. Ethan had said he would keep them secret and he was. Earl had commented on the realization that those cabins were more like full homes. Small, yes. But fully insulated and they had electricity and heat from the geothermal springs up the mountain. Some of those streams ran underground right near the cabins and Ian and Ethan had worked with a specialist, that could be trusted, and they tapped into the flow of energy to produce electricity for the boys. The structures were now weather tight and the inside work was under way. The outsides looked like log cabins, but with all the latest in weather tight technology.

"Bubba, I think it's time to leave a little somethin' for Miss Emily. She doesn't really drink the shine, so how's about we take some of those special azaleas for her gardens around her porch?"

"That's a great idea. Let's go get 'em now and we can drive them over this evenin'," Bubba suggested.

The boys spent the afternoon digging and preparing those bushes for transport to Emily's Meadow.

Laine and Mo were kept busy tending their truck garden and their special herbs. The marijuana was coming along beautifully. The new strains they had created looked to be growing like crazy. Folks stopped by for the veggies at the stand by the road and the girls kept it well supplied.

Emily's Meadow was running well. The horses were enjoyed by many and Mr. Jonah was a master at taking care of them. The chickens were producing more eggs than Emily could use so she sold the extras to Ted and Michael. The locals loved the whole thing.

Ethan was working with inspectors at a number of their job sites. Ian and Katelyn were busy in the shop. The extension was weather tight and the outside was being finished today. The electrical and rough plumbing was being run inside. Roofing was being done as well. The place was noisy and busy.

Kendra was busy with a few new real estate customers looking for land between Pine Ridge and The Creek.

Matthews was running security checks on anyone that worked in and around The Creek. He heard his computer signal that meant something had come back that was a potential problem. He pulled the report off the printer and sat down to have a look.

It seems there was a person of interest living in the Pine Ridge area that had a record for causing trouble along political lines. His name was Roy Adams. He had moved to Pine Ridge just six months ago.

Matthews had a bad feeling in his gut. He called Jenna.

"Hey, Jenna," Matthews said when she answered her phone.

"Hey G-man. What's up?"

"What's the name of the client you're doing the mural for that lives in the Pine Ridge area?"

"Roy Adams. Why?"

"I got a security alarm on him today. Seems he's caused some trouble in the past. Nothing in the past year though."

"What kind of trouble?"

"Political rally stuff. Part of the crowds that protest that climate change is a conspiracy. Stuff like that. Have you had any problems with him?"

"Nope. I haven't even met him in person. Just through web meetings. He asked for a mural that showed dinosaurs in their natural setting for his basement entertainment area. I just sent him the preliminary sketch. Should I withdraw the contract?"

"No. Just keep an eye on him and if he starts to do anything strange, hit the emergency button on your phone. I don't think he'll be a problem as there are no political rallies or anything like that in the area."

"Okay. Thanks for the head's up, G-man. Love it when you protect me."

"Love protecting you. Bye."

They hung up and Jenna made a note in her sketch book.

Miss Cora was working in her gardens. The herbs were looking good and the flowers were in bloom all over the place. She took a minute to listen to the air. She felt a little ruffle in the energy flow so she went and sat on her porch and tuned into the mountain for a bit.

As she came back to present day, she knew something very different from the things in the recent past was beginning to take root. It seems that The Magic in The Creek was about to involve a few folks as it continued to keep its secrets from the world-at-large and protect The Creek.

Friday evening found folks bar-be-queing, swimming and just plain relaxing and the night came on soft and gentle.

Saturday morning Katelyn called Jenna and they decided to meet at Jenna's current studio. Katelyn brought her sketch pad and supplies just in case they decided to be creative.

"Hey, Jenna," Katelyn said as Jenna came through the door.

"Hey, Katelyn. Glad we could get together," Jenna replied. "Let's set up in my studio upstairs. The light is perfect this morning."

Katelyn looked around at Jenna's sketches and drawings.

"These are great. Working on anything right now?" Katelyn asked.

"Yup. That one of the dinosaurs. I have a client that wants his basement entertainment room to be a mural of dinosaurs in their natural habitat. That's one reason I wanted us to get together. I think you could help me out with this guy. He likes archeology. Got his Master's in it. I looked him up and he's written a few books on dinosaurs. Not academic textbooks. More like informational ones. He keeps askin' about my ideas about finishing his space to add light and texture to blend with the mural."

"Okay. Do you have any photos of the space?"

"Yes, I do. He sent some the other day. I printed them out," Jenna said as she handed them to Katelyn.

Katelyn got a quick twitch in her gut when she looked at the pictures.

"Did you do a history check on this property?"

"Why do you ask? I usually don't if it's just for interior work. You pickin' up on somethin'?" Jenna asked as she stood next to Katelyn looking at the photos.

"Not sure. It just seems there's somethin' about this place. Let's do a google search of the address and see if any stuff shows up. Weird stuff."

They spent quite a bit of the morning looking at stories about the property. Nothing really horrible happened there. It had had a lot of owners over the past sixty-five years. One old couple died there but it was determined to be natural causes.

"I just got an idea. Let's look at the land history. We can use the address or look at the history of the area and see how it's changed over time," Katelyn said.

They found that the land had been part of the Catawba territory for thousands of years and that it was given to early settlers as a gift for defending the area. It had never been settled in a treaty. It was some of the land that had been stolen from the Catawba by the European settlers.

"Well, that explains the weird feelin' I got when I looked at the photos. Part of it, anyway. There's somethin' else here. Could be the centuries of sorrow coming through the earth."

"Probably. So, do ya' want to take a look at the place and decide if you want to design the place? Hefty commission, of course."

"Sure. It'll be a fun side job. When?"

"I'll contact the owner today and see if a week night will work. Seven o'clock sound good?"

"Sure. Now, let's take a look at your sketches of the dinosaur thing. I may be able to get an idea from them and the way you describe the place and the person."

They spent a few hours creating ideas and having fun. Katelyn left around lunch time and spent the rest of the day doing her own chores.

Later that afternoon, Jordan Jackson called and asked if she wanted to come by Sunday afternoon for a visit. They agreed on early afternoon. Katelyn was excited about looking at Jordan's crystals and seeing where they came from. This was gonna' be a fun afternoon.

She was on the porch most of the evening saying "Hey' to those who were at The Store and folks who were out walking. She fell asleep and dreamed of dinosaurs that night.

The Creek was peaceful all night.

CHAPTER 7

S unday found her sleeping in late. She laughed when she looked at her phone and saw it was close to ten. She had had a very busy and exciting week and needed the extra sleep for sure. She faintly remembered dreaming of dinosaurs in the night. Real ones and cartoons ones from her childhood. She smiled and went about her morning.

She was at Jordan's place right on time. She parked out near the barn and was met by Jordan as she approached the back-porch door.

"Hey, Katelyn. Welcome to the farm," Jordan said.

"Hey, Jordan. This place is beautiful. You can tell it's an Ethan and Ian build with the wrap-around porch and all. Those guys sure do know how to create cool stuff."

"Yes, they do. I love this place. The barn's comin' along. I haven't come up with a name for the farm yet. Still workin' on it. Come on in and get cooled off. It is the middle of the summer after all."

He got them sodas and they talked in the kitchen for a few minutes.

"Follow me. I wanna' show ya' the crystal I found out back. It was the first one I found just when they were excavating the foundations and all. It was just lying there on a pile of earth like someone had set it there for me to find."

Jordan brought Katelyn to the fireplace so she could see the crystal on the mantle.

She was mesmerized by it. It began to glow a bit and change colors.

"Whoa! It has never done that before. Gotta' be you. You must have some Magic in ya'," Jordan said as he watched the crystal and Katelyn.

Katelyn finally looked at Jordan and the crystal stopped glowing. "How'd that happen? And why?" Katelyn said to no one in particular.

"Beats me. This is really cool. I'll bet Miss Cora will have plenty to say about this," Jordan said as he sat down.

Katelyn turned from the fireplace and just looked at Jordan for the longest time.

"Somethin' wrong, Katelyn?" Jordan asked.

"Oh, no. Sorry to stare at you. You just seem to remind me of someone I know. It's as if I've met you before. Ya' know, like that déjà vu feelin'," Katelyn said.

"I had that same feelin' when we first met. Nothin' real strong. Just a knowin' kinda' thing. Can't explain it," Jordan offered.

"Well, stuff happens just like it's supposed to. I believe in that," Katelyn said.

"I'm beginin to understand that the longer I live in The Creek. How about we wander outside and I'll show you where I found the crystal that's on the front porch.?"

"Great. Let's go," Katelyn said as they went through the kitchen and out the door.

"We'll go through the barn. It's safe and all. I checked with Ethan about bein' inside and he said it would be okay if we didn't move anything around," Jordan explained as they entered the barn.

"This is huge! I love the smell of new wood. Looks like you're gonna' have a loft apartment or somethin'," Katelyn said as she looked over the barn.

"That is correct Katelyn. Good catch. It will be a one bedroom with a small kitchen and full bath. Not sure why but it came to me when Ian and I were talkin' about what I would want the barn for. I told him planting and all but then the apartment idea came up and so we worked on ideas and settled on this loft idea. It has barn access and outside access as well.

"It's a grand idea. Ya' gonna' have any animals?"

"Not too sure about that yet. Gotta' let that idea rest a bit," Jordan said as they walked out the backside of the barn.

"You have a lot of land here," Katelyn said as they walked a ways over the field towards the cave entrance. Jordan wasn't going to tell Katelyn about the cave yet. He instinctively knew it wasn't the right time.

A bit later he came to a stop close to the entrance to the cave although you couldn't see it if you didn't know it was there.

"This is where I found the second crystal. The one on the front porch. I was lookin' out the kitchen window late one evening and I saw somethin' shining out here. I grabbed my jacket and walked over to this spot and there it was. Just sittin' there like the first one. It's somewhat bigger so I got the wagon and loaded it up. I was gonna' leave it by the back door then just knew it had to be on the front porch just where it is.

"The sun began setting a few minutes later and that crystal lit up like a lighthouse. It shot beams of light so bright ya' couldn't look straight at it. Once the sun changed angles and got below the tree line, it slowly dimmed and finally there wasn't any more light comin' from it. Folks come by most evenings just to watch it light up. It sure is magical. Miss Cora says it's supposed to be on the front porch. That The Magic in The Creek is in charge and she's learned to follow its lead."

"Oh, I do believe that. Miss Cora's been right about everything that's got to do with special happenings around here. The super natural ones with Magic and all," Katelyn said. "Do you think the other ones were dug up when they were excavating for your house and all?"

"I thought about that," Jordan began as he looked off over the hill. "I thought they might have been but then I really don't know."

Katelyn watched Jordan as he looked past the hill and seemed to become lost in thought. She saw his face change a bit and his eyes grow dark. He looked like a different person. A person she was familiar with but she knew no one who looked like that. This whole thing was really strange. Katelyn didn't feel scared or anything like that. It was as if a moment in time had changed and they were somewhere else.

Jordan came back to himself and looked at Katelyn. "Ya' ever feel like you've been someplace before and know you haven't? That's how I feel about this farm. I'd never been here, didn't even know it existed, before Kendra showed it to me but I knew it the minute I walked on this earth. It feels like it's always been with me and I've always known it."

"I know just what you mean. I get that feelin' about people sometimes," Katelyn said.

They stood there next to each other and looked over the land for the longest time. Just as they were about to turn around and head back to the house, they both saw a flash just to the left and beyond the rise in the hill.

"You see that?" Katelyn said.

"Here we go again. Let's go find out what it is," Jordan said as they set out across the field.

It took a good ten minutes to get to the spot where the shiny thing was.

"Holy shit! This is truly unbelievable!" Jordan said as he and Katelyn looked at the twin crystals in front of them.

"Ditto! They're beautiful! Purple and pink with tons of yellow tipped spikes," Katelyn said as they kept looking at them.

"Looks like they belong to each other," Jordan said.

"Should we pick them up? Doesn't look like they were dug up and anything."

Then they both said at the same time, "Looks like someone just set them down for us to find."

They looked at each other and laughed.

"I'm at a loss for words here," Katelyn said.

"Me, too," Jordan agreed. "I wonder if they're for us? How do we find out?"

"Well, since Magic is very much alive here, how about we just ask the universe?"

"Okay. Sounds like a good plan. You ask," Jordan said.

"Okay. Ah, universe, are we supposed to pick these up and take them with us? Are these gifts from Mother Earth?"

They both stood quiet and all of a sudden, an eagle flew at them, circled them, then flew off towards the barn.

"I'll take that as a big yes. Thank you for these gifts," Katelyn offered as she bent down and picked up the one on the right.

"Yes, thank you for these gifts," Jordan said as he bent down and picked up the one on the left.

They were identical as if they had been made especially for the two of them.

"The spikes don't hurt," Katelyn said as she turned the crystal over in her hands.

"Same here," Jordan said as he did the same thing. "They do seem to be exactly the same."

"I agree. Now what?" Katelyn asked as they stood there dumbfounded.

"Well, let's get on back to the house. I usually rinse them off outside. Then we can take them in and I don't know what," Jordan suggested.

"Okay. Sounds good," Katelyn said and they began the walk back to the house.

Just as they came around the rise in the hill, the eagle flew out of the barn, circled them, cried out, and returned to the barn.

"Now, that's just wicked cool," Katelyn said.

Jordan just laughed as they watched the eagle fly in and out of the barn and around it a few times. It eventually flew into the barn but they didn't see it come out. When the entered the barn to walk through, they saw the eagle perched on one of the main cross beams in the middle of the roof.

"Now that's just wicked what?" Jordan asked.

"Ah, wicked, wicked," Katelyn said.

They walked through the barn and rinsed the crystals off outside the back porch. They were shinning even brighter than before.

They went inside and set them on the island counter. They were beautiful.

Neither of them knew what to say so they sat there in silence for the longest time.

Finally, Katelyn offered, "Well, this has been a great day. So glad I came over."

"Really? Is that all ya' got?" Jordan said laughing. "I don't know what to say either."

"Yup. That's it. Except, got any snacks around here? I'm starving. How long were we out there?"

Jordan looked at his watch and shook his head. "I know it seemed like a long time but it was only forty-five minutes total."

"No way! It seemed like hours. Gotta' be The Magic. I think I'm on overload here."

"I agree. Food and drinks comin' up. That should help us," Jordan said as he moved around the kitchen and brought out chips, salsa, cheese, grapes and a couple of beers.

"Good spread. Let's heat up the chips and cheese," Katelyn said as she set up the plate and found the microwave.

They spent quite a while eating and talking about what had just happened.

"I think you've got the right idea about talkin' to Miss Cora as soon as we can. Maybe we should go down to The Store and see if she's there? She usually knows when Magic is happenin' around here."

"Good idea. And, we could get some supper as well. It is after six anyway."

"Really? Okay. I'll take my crystal for a ride and see ya' there in a few," Katelyn said as she picked up the crystal and headed out the back door.

She was at The Store in just a few minutes and Jordan followed right along.

As soon as Katelyn walked in, she heard, "Hi Miss Katelyn."

It was Miss Cora. She was sitting at the dining room table.

"I knew you'd be here. I told Jordan so. You always know when Magic is about," Katelyn said as she kissed her cheek.

Katelyn set the crystal down in front of her place at the table and Miss Cora looked at it for a minute.

Jordan came in just then and placed his on the table in front of his place.

"Well, now, would ya' look at that?" Miss Cora said as she looked the crystals. "They're identical."

Katelyn and Jordan nodded their heads in agreement.

"Twin crystals, Miss Cora," Katelyn said.

"They showed themselves the same way as the others, Miss Cora," Jordan added.

"Well, I do believe Mother Earth really likes the work you've done on that land Jordan. As for you, Katelyn, I guess she's welcomin' ya home. And, it's a splendid welcome home gift like no other."

"I knew you'd know what was goin' on here," Katelyn said sitting back in her chair.

"I'm learning all the time and glad to be here," Jordan said as he relaxed a bit.

"I'll keep thinkin' on these and let ya' know if I come up with anythin' else. Now, Ted, how about some supper over here?" Miss Cora said.

"Yes, Ma'am. What can I get for y'all tonight?"

They placed their orders and continued talking about the crystals.

"I can't wait to see what happens when the sun shines on them directly. They were a bit covered by the dirt and all out there," Jordan said.

"Let's take them outside and see what happens," Miss Cora suggested.

They placed the crystals on the planter in front of The Store in the direct sunlight. They shone beautifully, throwing little sunbeams all around.

Folks came over and looked at them.

"More crystals, Jordan?" Hal asked when he saw them.

"Yeah. Around the back of the rise in the hill." Jordan answered.

Hal looked at Katelyn and pointed to the crystals. "You there when this happened?"

"Yup, Hal, I was. I was given a crystal back in Alabama just before I left so Jordan and I were comparing them. These are a lot bigger than mine," Katelyn said.

"Must be some Magic goin' on here. Seems whenever crystals start to appear some Magic is makin' that happen," Hal continued.

"You're right about that, Hal," Miss Cora agreed. "Hal, ya' got your crystal in the truck? Bring it out for Katelyn to see."

Hal got his crystal from the struck and showed it to Katelyn.

"Holy, ah, cow! Hal. That's amazing. Where'd that come from?" Katelyn asked.

"Well, Katelyn, it has to do with the thing up that happened up in The Holler this past spring," Hal said rather hesitantly.

"My folks told me a bit about that and Kendra filled in the rest. I know there were three crystals that helped keep The Magic here. This is stunning." Katelyn said.

"It sure is. Maybe the Chief and Jenna will show you theirs sometime," Miss Cora said.

"I hope so. There seems to be somethin' about crystals and The Magic here in The Creek," Katelyn offered.

"Maybe it has somethin' to do with those crystal caves up north of Emily's Meadow," Michael added.

"It could, Michael. It could," Miss Cora started but was interrupted by Ted calling them all to supper.

"I think I might need a triangle or dinner bell to get y'all in here," Ted said as they returned to the table.

"No need for that. We love your cookin' and wouldn't miss it for anything," Katelyn said as they settled around the table.

Supper was a fun time. Folks came by and stopped to say 'Hey' and news was shared.

As their visit ended, Miss Cora was the first to leave.

"Now, y'all take care," Miss Cora said as she headed home

They wished her well.

Katelyn stood up, gathered her things and her crystal. "Time for me to head home, too. It's been an amazin' day and I have to be ready for work tomorrow."

"That's right. You're now with Ethan and the gang. Like it?" Michael asked.

"I do. It's really great learning the hands-on construction side of things and designing for those two. They are some special people." Katelyn replied.

"Yes, they are," Ted said.

"Later, y'all," Katelyn said as she left.

Jordan soon followed and decided to check the barn when he got home before he went inside. He couldn't believe what he found. The eagle was still there. It was a female as the tail feathers were full white which meant it was at least five years old. As he stood there, another eagle, a male, flew in and perched next to her. Then, two little eaglets came out from under the female's wings. The male and female looked at Jordan and nodded their heads as if to say they planned to stay here. He just nodded back, not quite knowing just what to do. He went into the house smiling though. Twin crystals and a family of eagles all in one day. He was gonna' for sure check the barn tomorrow morning to see if they were still there.

Katelyn had left her SUV in her driveway when she came back from Jordan's so she just had to walk across the road to be home. She set the crystal on the porch railing to catch the sun's rays as she went inside to get things ready for Monday.

When she went back out onto the porch, the crystal was still shining bright as could be. She sat down in the rocking chair and thought she heard something humming. She smiled and leaned over towards the crystal. It was the crystal. She ran inside and got the shocked crystal and set it next to the new one. They both were shining brilliantly and both were humming as if they were having a conversation between the two of them.

Katelyn sat back in her rocker, closed her eyes, and just listened. She became very relaxed and images started to form in her head. She saw a place that looked kinda' like The Creek on account of the real creek was just where it is now but everything else was gone. It was as if the place hadn't even been built on. It was all forest and such. It was truly beautiful and restful. She just sat there in that other world for quite some spell.

She realized the humming had stopped and opened her eyes to see it was going on sundown. She realized she must have been sitting there for a good two hours. She felt very relaxed. She remembered the dream thing or whatever it was. The place had been beautiful.

Katelyn got up, stretched, gathered the crystals, and went inside. It had been some kind of a day.

It must have been nigh onto midnight. Kendra couldn't sleep so she got up, grabbed a blanket and stepped out onto her front porch. The Store was all quiet. Looked like everyone was settled for the night in The Creek. The stars were putting on a fantastic show for all to see. Kendra even saw a shooting star while she was looking about. The big dipper was clear as a bell tonight she thought as she looked across the sky, hoping to see another shooting star.

Just as she was about to go inside, she caught a movement over the trees back of The Store. She focused on it and saw it again. It was flying just above the trees and it was big. I mean really big. It circled behind The Store and flew right over her and then headed down the Pine Ridge Road out of sight. It was huge. Really huge. Couldn't quite see the color but it was mostly dark.

Kendra thought about all the flying critters she knew about in The Creek. It wasn't a turkey or turkey buzzard. They roost at sundown. Hawks usually aren't even close to being that big. Now, some owls can be really big and they hunt at night. If that had been any kinda' owl, it must have been taking steroids or something 'cause it was the biggest one she'd ever seen.

She began to feel sleepy and yawned on her way back to bed. Her last thought was of the huge flying creature. She finally fell into a deep sleep.

The Creek slept peacefully that night.

CHAPTER 8

Monday morning Jordan was in the barn even before the work crew showed up. It was before six. He found the eagle family on the beams just like yesterday. As he stood there, the male flew off and came back with sticks and leaves. He went into the eaves off the center of the barn where the main cross beam and others meet. He dropped the sticks and flew off. A minute later, he returned with more sticks and such. He was building their nest in Jordan's barn. How cool was this? Jordan would have to tell Katelyn as soon as he got a chance. He bowed to the eagles and went inside to finish getting ready for work.

Katelyn woke up ready to go. She got her day underway and headed out to Ethan's.

She was going to be working with Ian on a new client's build today as they started to learn just what the client wanted for the inside of their new home. This was the first project Katelyn would be undertaking with Ian and she was very excited.

Sami was in Kennebunkport, Maine. The property needed a great deal of work. She was meeting with the owners via a video conference including Lloyd and Johnson's owners. They would discuss the depth of the renovation as far as construction costs and such. Sami would offer her ideas for the new look of the property. It was located a few blocks from the ocean just off the old main road. Sami was incorporating an ocean theme as well as including the early history of the area.

Roy Adams was busy in his basement. Jenna and Katelyn were coming by Tuesday evening to talk about how he wanted the space to look. Just as he was starting to climb the stairs to return to the kitchen, he felt a hand on his shoulder. He turned and was shocked to see a man standing there. He looked just like any other man does.

"How'd you get in here? Who are you?" Roy demanded as he inched up the stairs.

"No worries. You are not in danger. I'm just here to help you with your project," the man said as he followed Roy up the stairs.

"Get out," Roy hollered as he ran up the stairs and slammed the door. He dialed 911 and was asking for help when the man appeared on the opposite side of the kitchen away from the basement door.

Roy's phone was whisked across the room, landing on the floor in a million pieces.

"Who the hell are you?" Roy hollered.

"Now, Roy, I'm surprised at you not remembering our deal. You asked for help in buying this place and we gave it to you."

"What? I got a mortgage through a mortgage company who sold it to the bank," Roy replied.

"Yes, that's how things seemed to work. You had a bit of a problem with your credit at first. Remember?"

"So what? It was cleared up by the agent at the mortgage company," Roy said.

The man changed shape right in front of him and became that exact agent.

Roy didn't know what to do.

"Who the hell are you?"

"I'm the agent that cleared up the credit problem. I asked if you wanted the help and you said yes. Then I told you that you may have to pay extra for the help and you signed this paper in agreement."

"Yes, I did. The cost was included in the mortgage fee," Roy said.

"No, Roy. It wasn't that kind of fee. You never read the paper. You just signed it. You see, you signed an agreement to give your soul to The Dark. I believe you folks here call it the devil. Am I making this clear?"

"What? That kind of thing only happens in stories and the movies," Roy replied.

"No, Roy. Evil, The Dark, is very real and we own you now," the agent replied.

"No, you don't. I don't believe in you," Roy hollered.

"Really? Try this," the agent said as he made poisonous snakes appear all over the floor.

Roy screamed and tried to run. He was frozen in place. He watched as several of the snakes bit into his legs. The pain was excruciating. He screamed and screamed.

"Make them go away," Roy begged.

"You ready to believe?" the agent asked.

"Sure. Whatever. Just make this all stop," Roy yelled.

In an instance the snakes were gone and Roy was back to himself.

"What do you want?" Roy asked as he fell against the counter.

"You."

"Me? What for?"

"We have a job for you that involves the artist and her friend. Her friend is a White Lighter and we need her destroyed. Now. Tomorrow when they come here."

"How do you know about that?"

"The Dark knows about everything."

"I can't kill someone."

"You just need to get her into the basement. We'll do the rest."

"Okay. Whatever you say. Just keep those snakes away from me."

The agent vanished right in front of him. Roy didn't know what to do. He looked for his phone then remembered it had been smashed. He found it all in one piece on the counter. He grabbed it to call Jenna and cancel the contract. As soon as he touched the phone, it turned into a snake and almost bit him. Shit! They had control of his phone.

Roy sat there for the longest time. Every time he came up with a way to contact Jenna, a snake would appear. He finally gave up trying and just sat there in despair for the longest time.

Evil was real. It never came to his thoughts to ask for help from the good guys. Roy had been raised in a strong Christian home. He believed in his God right up until his grandparents had died within two weeks of each other. How could a loving God let that happen? He needed his grandparents and God took them from him. He was angry with God and refused to believe in God ever since.

All he had to do to get the evil to go away was reach out to his God. He never even thought to do just that.

As Katelyn was working in the main part of the work shop Monday morning, she heard the door close and looked up to see Finn walking in.

"Hey, Finn. What 'cha doin' here?" Katelyn asked as he walked over to her.

"I work here Katelyn. I'm one of the energy specialists," Finn said as they hugged.

"Really? Oh, that's right. My folks said somethin' about you finishing your Masters and all and it had to do with energy stuff."

"That's right. So, Ethan told me they hired you as their new designer. Who would have thought we'd be doin' all this when we were kids?"

"Really! I've always loved to draw stuff. But, you, Jay and the other guys around here were always getting' into some kinda' trouble or other. None of you had a serious bone about life in your bodies for the longest time," Katelyn said laughing.

"Now, Katie, I don't remember it exactly all that way. We did have us a real good time most times, though," Finn said laughing along with Katelyn.

Katelyn stopped laughing and looked right at Finn, "I, I just don't know what to say about our Jay. I miss him terrible but I'm sure it's nothin' like you and your folks."

Katelyn began to cry. Finn grabbed her into a strong hug as tears ran down his face, too.

"Katie girl, there are no words," Finn whispered.

They stood there for a long while before separating. Katelyn reached for tissues and shared some with Finn.

"Sorry, Finn. The sadness just takes hold sometimes and I find myself cryin' like a baby," Katelyn said as she tried to smile a bit.

"Same here. My folks and I will be talkin' about whatever and Mom will tear up and then all of us will be cryin' and smilin' at the same time. We've gotten used to that happenin' so we aren't upset when it happens to y'all. It really shows us how much Jay meant to everyone. He sure knew how to get us into trouble though."

Katelyn nodded her head as she smiled, "Yes, he did, and rarely got the blame if I remember right."

Finn laughed out loud saying, "That's for sure. I think I was grounded half my high school life 'cause of his antics."

Finn looked across the room and saw Jay's spirit laughing and pointing at him. And Finn smiled and nodded his head at Jay.

"Ya' see somethin', Finn?" Katelyn asked as she watched Finn.

"Katie, sometimes I swear I can see a bit of Jay's Spirit. Whether it's real or not it brings comfort to me knowin' he's still around me."

"I do believe you, Finn. I know Spirits exist for sure."

"Really? You've seen some?"

"Well, let's just say I've seen wavy air that sometimes has a shape. And, since we were born and raised in The Creek, I accept it as real because of The Magic and all. No other way to explain it."

Finn put his hand on Katelyn's shoulder as he said, "I do believe you got that right Katie. Magic is all over the place."

They stood there for a couple of seconds just lookin' at each other. Katelyn felt pulled to Finn for some reason.

"Well, what do ya' need in here or is this where you work, too?" Katelyn asked as she stepped back and looked around the place.

"Well, ya' know about all that buildin' goin on here? Ian tells me it's gonna' be your office, my office and drawing table space and this area will become more of an 'official' space to show clients their designs and all."

"That's what I was told, too."

"So, until the new space is completed, I use the table next to yours for my work. Ian bought some rolling cabinet drawers for me to store my stuff. I see you have a few, too."

"Yup. Guess we'll be workin' together than. I do like this arrangement. Gonna' be fun and I will not be takin' the blame for your shenanigans mister," Katelyn warned with a laugh.

"Like that's ever gonna' happen. You'll always be blamed," Finn said laughing at Katelyn as he walked over to his table.

"Jay, I do hope you can hear me. I'm gonna' need your help with this guy," Katelyn said looking into the space around the room.

A square edge went flying off her table landing half-way across the room on the floor. They both laughed.

"I guess you got your answer," Finn said giving a look at Jay as he was standing right next to Katelyn's table.

"Why, bless your little ol' pea pickin' heart, Jay. Love ya," Katelyn said bowing at her table.

"Okay. The challenge is on," Finn said.

"Accepted," Katelyn said as they shook hands and laughed.

That's how Ethan and Ian found them as they walked into the room.

"Oh no, Ian. I think we're gonna' have to keep an eye on these two. Looks like trouble is brewin'," Ethan said as he picked up the square edge off the floor half way across the room.

"Not me," Katelyn and Finn said at the same time.

"Well, then, it only makes sense that it must have been Jay's ghost. That's what you're gonna' try to make me believe, right?" Ethan asked.

Katelyn and Finn just looked at each other and burst out laughing.

"I don't even want to know," Ian said laughing and shaking his head. "Well, now, how about we look over the rough sketches for that new project down the road from Jordan's place? It's down the dirt road to the east a few miles or so. I do believe there may be a flow line from some of the hot springs way up in the mountain past Laine and Mo's place. Finn, have you had time to check on that?"

"Yes, I have and there are two flows goin' right through that property far enough away from where the buildings will be."

"Great. I had a look out there last week and I think I found a good spot for the house. It's gonna' be set way back from the road. They want a barn. Not a big one like Jordan's but a barn none-the-less. And, they want a green-house set-up. Katelyn, can you work on that? Have you seen Laine and Mo's greenhouses? They have some high-tech heating systems in place that use sunlight. And, they created a special kinda' solar panel made of glass. I was thinking somethin' about half the size."

"Sure. I'll give Laine a call and set up a time to go over and have a look. We're gonna' get together this week anyway. Maybe I can combine the two visits."

"I like the way you think," Ethan replied.

They spent quite a while brainstorming about the project keeping the client's requests in place. It was lunchtime when they called it quits.

"Lunch everyone. I'm starvin,'" Ian said as he laid his laptop down.

"Me, too. Let's eat," Katelyn said as she got her lunch from the frig and popped it into the microwave.

"That smells delicious," Finn said.

"Mom went to cookin' up a storm yesterday and sent down a week's worth of food with Nathan last evenin'. And, none for you, Mr. Finn," Katelyn said as she took her food out and set it on the counter near the frig. She grabbed a stool and sat down. "What'd you bring? I'm sure your mama's been takin' real good care of you."

Ethan and Ian laughed as they prepared their lunch.

"Yes, Katie, she always does," Finn said as he heated his lunch.

The four of them had a pleasant lunch chatting about The Creek and their growin' up days and all.

They parted ways a bit later. Ethan going to one of the work sites and the others working together to further the client's dreams for their new home.

Emily was working around the farm when she felt the slightest hint of a breeze. Thing was, there wasn't any breeze blowing. She stood very still and focused on the sensation. She felt a quick rise of adrenalin and opened her eyes to see a vision in the air. It was of a place that she felt familiar with. For just the quickest half-second, she thought she saw someone she knew in the far distance of the vision. A familiar shape. The vision was gone as quickly as it had come. There weren't any bad or scary feelings with this vision. It was more of an informational vision was the only way Emily could describe it. She looked down at Trouble and he was staring off into the distance as well.

She gave him a pat on the head saying, "Well, Trouble, I guess we saw the same thing."

He looked up at her and gave a soft, "Woof."

She smiled at him and they went about their day.

The rest of the day found folks taking care of their work. Evening came and went as usual.

Nightfall found The Creek at peace.

CHAPTER 9

uesday dawned beautifully. The day was a busy one for most. Jenna went over to Katelyn's around six that evening and they headed out to Roy Adam's' house for a look at the basement area that needed a new design. Jenna had preliminary-colored sketches of the mural to show Roy for his approval. They chatted about the weekend arriving at Roy's right on schedule.

Katelyn got a strong feeling in her gut and it wasn't a pleasant one. She looked at Jenna at the same time Jenna looked over at her.

"What's goin' on, Katelyn? You don't look so good," Jenna asked.

"I just got a horrible feelin' in my gut. Somethin's not right here," Katelyn answered.

"Like what?"

"Not really sure, but I've learned to listen to those hunches and I'm tellin' ya' somethin' just isn't right here."

"Okay. Now what?"

"Well, let's meet the guy and see what happens. I have both my crystals. The small one in my pocket and the shocked crystal in my briefcase. If anything gets really weird, I'm gonna' run like crazy."

"Okay. Sounds good to me. Let's go," Jenna said.

They got out of Jenna's car and grabbed their stuff. They were met at the door by Roy.

"Good evening, ladies. Please do come in," Roy said.

Katelyn and Jenna walked through the door and both got the shivers.

"Nice to meet you in person," Roy said as he reached out to shake their hands.

Neither of them extended their hands to Roy.

"Oh, sorry. I see you've got your hands full," Roy offered.

"Sorry about that. Let's set up in the kitchen and I'll show you my preliminary sketches for the mural," Jenna suggested.

"Ah, Okay. Let's take a look," Roy replied as he cleared the table.

They looked over the sketches and Roy was thrilled with the work.

"Jenna, this looks perfect. Just like I envisioned it would. Your work is exceptional," Roy said.

"Thanks, Roy. So glad you approve," Jenna said with a quick look at Katelyn.

Katelyn was tuned into the energy in the place. It wasn't good. As a matter of fact, it was really bad. Kendra said she couldn't be harmed as a White Lighter but this amount of energy was so much more than she had ever dealt with. She didn't like what she was feeling. She decided it was time to leave.

Before she could say anything, Roy stood up and suggested they go down to the basement and take a look around.

"Well, let's take a look at the downstairs space and Katelyn, you can tell me what you think," Roy said as he tried to steer the girls to the basement door. Jenna picked up on some of the bad vibes as she got close to the door.

"Jenna, I do believe we need to leave," Katelyn said as she grabbed her briefcase and grabbed the shocked crystal from inside.

"No, you don't," Roy said. "You need to look at the space."

"Roy, we need to leave right now," Katelyn said. He had pushed her close to the opened basement door and was now trying to push her down the stairs.

"Jenna, get outta' here now," Katelyn yelled as she saw a monster at the bottom of the stairs.

Jenna grabbed her things and ran out the door.

The monster at the bottom of the stairs yelled at Katelyn, "You're mine now so don't try to fight it. Push her down here," the evil energy yelled.

"No, I'm not. I walk in The White Light. The God Light. The Universal Light," Katelyn yelled back pushing against Roy to set him off balance.

The monster screamed as if he had been pierced through the heart.

Roy tried again to push Katelyn down the stairs. She raised the crystal in her hand and hit Roy with it. He fell away screaming.

Katelyn raised the crystal in front of her pointing it at the monster.

"I call upon the White Light to surround and protect me," Katelyn hollered. The monster screamed again, this time shooting red flaming arrows at Katelyn.

They bounced off her protective field and fizzled and died.

This made the monster even more angry. He started to throw fire balls at Katelyn.

Katelyn yelled out loud, "I call upon my Guardians and Protectors to banish this monster from this place."

In an instant the monster was taken by a tornado of energy and disappeared.

Katelyn stepped away from the basement door and looked at Roy.

He tried to stand up but was held down by an invisible force. He started to beg for his life. Then he was screaming as if he was being tortured. In an instant he was gone. Completely vanished.

Katelyn grabbed her stuff and ran from the place. As soon as she was outside, she fell to the ground. Jenna ran to her.

"Oh my God! What the hell was that? Are you okay?"

"I need some water. In the car."

Jenna ran and was right back with the water. Katelyn drank it down. Then just sat there.

"Holy shit, Katelyn! What the hell is goin' on here?" Jenna demanded.

"Jenna, ya' remember when I said I had a bad feelin' about this place?"

"Yeah."

"Well, I was right. That Roy was bein' controlled by the bad guys. Evil. The Dark Force."

"Jesus fucking Christ! I've known about evil but never saw it in action I guess," Jenna replied as she sat down next to Katelyn.

"Well, I've never seen it like this before either. Kendra's been teaching me some stuff about it. Good thing 'cause that's what I used to protect us."

Jenna and Katelyn just stared at each other for a few minutes.

"Where's Roy?" Jenna asked as they stood up.

"Gone. He was taken by the Dark Force. I suspect he sold his soul at some point and The Dark Force called in his marker."

"This is just too much to take in all at once," Jenna replied as they got into her car.

"I agree. And, I can't believe I'm sayin' this, but I'm starvin'. How about we go to the diner in Pine Ridge and have supper? I love that place and haven't been there in years,' Katelyn suggested.

"Great idea. I love that place, too. And, I haven't been there in a few weeks," Jenna said laughing.

"Their cheesy fries are heavenly," Katelyn added.

"Let's eat first then on the way home we can think about the Roy thing. I'm not gonna' get paid for all the work I've done and that's a hefty loss," Jenna said.

"Okay. Eat first. Business later," Katelyn said as they drove off.

Katelyn knew she and Jenna were in shock mind, body, and souls. She called upon the White Light to keep surrounding and protecting them. She asked her Guardians if they could send some healing energy to both of them.

"I feel a bit better," they both said at the same time.

They looked at each other and smiled.

The diner was a blast. They ordered their food and began to tell stories of when they were teenagers and all and how they would wander off to the diner whenever they could.

Some of their long-time friends came in and they all sat near each other telling their stories. It wasn't long before the diner was full of friends, memories and great diner food.

It was nigh onto nine o'clock when the group split up with promises of getting together soon for a bar-be-que.

Katelyn and Jenna agreed to go right to Kendra and tell her what had happened with Roy. They pulled into Katelyn's driveway, got their things and set them on Katelyn's porch. They walked over to Kendra's calling her name. She met them on the porch.

"Hey, girls, what's goin' on?" Kendra asked as she looked at them. They didn't look too good.

"Well," Jenna started out, "We need to tell ya' what happened at my client's house this evenin'."

She and Katelyn took turns telling Kendra about the evil monster.

"Oh my God, Katelyn! I'm so sorry that happened to the both of you. Good job on calling on your Guardians for help. How are you doin 'now?"

"Well, we decided to go to the diner in Pine Ridge for some supper. I called on the Other Side for healing energy which we both felt at the same time. We felt better instantly."

"Good," Kendra said.

"The diner was a great idea. A bunch of the kids we grew up with came in and we all sat around eatin' and talkin' for the longest time," Katelyn said.

"It was great. It really helped me feel better. But I'm still unsettled with the whole evil thing," Jenna added.

"I expect you are," Kendra said. "How about I give you both some Reiki right now?"

"Reiki? What's that?" Jenna asked.

"It's a kind of healing energy that is only positive energy. It'll help clear the unsettled energy you're feelin' and balance everything back into place. I love it," Katelyn told Jenna.

"Okay. Bring it on," Jenna said.

"Okay. Just sit there and relax. Close your eyes if you want. I'll be standing behind the two of you for a few minutes," Kendra said as she moved into place.

Kendra began channeling the Reiki and the girls relaxed.

A few minutes later Kendra said, "All set. How do you feel?"

"I do feel a lot better. Not so scared anymore," Jenna said as she opened her eyes.

"Me, too. So much better," Katelyn said.

"Good. Now, I would like to offer to teach you both Reiki so you can take care of yourselves."

"Oh, I like that idea," Jenna said. "How about you, Katie?"

"Yes, definitely. When?" Katelyn asked.

"How about Thursday evening after supper? Come on over and I'll teach you what you need for level I Reiki and attune you as healers."

"Deal," Jenna said.

"Agreed," Katelyn said.

They talked for a few minutes more than Katelyn and Jenna went home.

Kendra sat in the house for the longest time. She was thinking how The Dark was going after Katelyn. She wondered what the connection was with Katelyn and The Creek. Time would tell.

The Creek slept.

CHAPTER 10

Thursday evening Jenna and Katelyn were taught about Reiki and attuned as Level I Healers. They spent the next few days thinking about this and practiced on themselves a few times.

Saturday morning Sami and Katelyn video chatted for a long time.

"Hey, Katie girl. How are ya?" Sami said when they connected.

"Great! How about you, my Sami?"

"The same. I gotta' tell ya' about the stuff goin' on here. Ya' know I'm in Maine, right? Yeah, well, when the construction foreman and I were going through the basement of the current hotel Thursday, we found the hallway to the old part. It was all made from boulders. Really cool. We found a room totally by chance. We saw a few large rocks on the floor and looked at the wall where they had fallen from. The contractor and I looked at each other then back at the wall. There seemed to be an indentation behind where the rocks had been. I gave the stone wall a little push and it caved in. We were both really surprised. There weren't any rooms on the floor plan.

"Joel, the contractor, pushed a bit more and the wall fell away so we could move just a bit into the space. It had a table and chairs and a few old cots. I was gonna' walk further into the space but Joel stopped me. He said he wanted his engineers to look the space over to make sure it was solid. He called them and they came right down. The spent about a half hour tapping on the ceiling and the other walls. None of them came apart so they said we could keep exploring. All except a small part of the wall at the back of the space. When one of the engineers knocked on the wall it sounded almost hollow. She used one of her heat sensitive gadgets and it showed a hollow space beyond the wall. The two of them pushed on the wall and it started to move on one side. They figured it might be a door so they used some tools to push on the side that was moving. Sure enough. A door was on the other side of the fake wall. Joel and I kept lookin' at the stuff in the room. There were a few papers on the table. It took only a few minutes to figure out they were maps showing how to get to Canada. We didn't touch them just moved them a little bit with our pens. I looked right at Joel and said, "I think this might be part of the Underground Railroad. Ya' know, the escape route for slaves to get to Canada?"

"Well, Joel was really surprised. He agreed with me and said we would have to get the local historical society down here and an archeologist from Portland. The engineers had been gone for some time. We heard them coming into the room and they were smilin' like crazy.

"They told us they had found a set of two tunnels that ran west then turned north. They didn't follow them all the way because they just kept goin'. We were all so excited. Joel called his archeology friend from the University of Maine and the engineers contacted the local historical society person. They all agreed to come over first thing Friday morning.

"We took them down to the room and they were almost cryin' they were so happy. The archeologist wasn't too happy about us walking into the room. I told him I had taken a million pictures of the place before Joel and I even set one foot into the place and we had left everything just as we found it. I did tell him we had moved the map around by using the top end of a pen. He was okay with that and thrilled I had taken the pictures which I assured him I would send along right soon. He and the historical society lady wanted to walk the tunnels but our engineers said they needed to do more testing to make sure they wouldn't cave in. The archeologist agreed and they're gonna' get together on Monday morning with their crews and all.

"This is so exciting. I knew there were Underground Railroad places in Portland but didn't expect to find any here. Most folks were shipped to Portland, met by abolitionists who did a bit of changing their appearance right at the dock 'cause bounty hunters, for lack of a better phrase, were always lookin' for escaped slaves. The Fugitive Slave Act, enacted by Congress, stated that slaves could be returned to their owners if caught in other states besides the one they had lived in and escaped from. That's why most slaves made their way to Canada. There weren't any extradition-type laws about slaves in Canada. A person was truly free once they reached Canada."

"Oh my God, Sami! This is really wicked cool. Have ya' thought about including the Underground Railroad with the interior design concept?"

"You sure know me well. I was tossin' ideas around with the property owners about creating a mural of photographs, news stories and other stuff folks may have to show respect for the whole slavery thing and the Underground Railroad. They liked it and said to go ahead and create something and show them what I come up with."

"I can see ya' now, workin' your tail off designin' the new look for the hotel and spending every minute you can researching and creating that mural."

"Oh, yeah. Indeed, I will be," Sami said with a laugh.

"Hey, Sami, I just got a great idea. What if you incorporated the whole slavery Underground Railroad thing for all the properties that may have a history like this place?"

"Holy shit! Katelyn, that's genius! I knew there was a reason I liked you," Sami yelled jumping all over the room.

"Ah, earth to Sami. Oh, Sami, come back to your laptop," Katelyn said laughing.

Sami plopped herself down in her chair and laughed with Katelyn.

"Oh, Katie girl, I absolutely love my job!"

"Oh, Sami girl, I absolutely love my job, too."

They spent another hour talking and brainstorm and Katelyn told Sami about her job and the crystals she and Jordan found and becoming a Reiki healer. They finally ended the chat with the promise of talking again in a few days.

Sunday found Finn at The Store just as Katelyn walked in. She was looking for chocolate chips to make cookies.

"Hey, Katelyn," Finn said walking over to her. "What are ya' up to?"

"Hey, Finn. Lookin' for chocolate chips. I feel like makin' cookies."

"Really? Ya' any good at it?" Finn asked with a smirk on his face.

"Why, yes, Finn. I am. But ya' know that. I do believe you are tryin' to get an invite over to my place so you can sample the cookies." Katelyn said poking him in the arm.

"Hey Katie" Ted said giving Katelyn a little hug. "Finn is a cookie monster for sure. I found ya' some chips in the kitchen. One bag enough?"

"Yes, Ted. I am obliged for your kindness," Katelyn said as she paid Michael. She looked over at Finn and laughed out loud at the puppy dog look on his face.

"Alright, Finn, you can come along. I'm gonna' regret this 'cause you're gonna' eat all my cookies." Katelyn said as she headed out the door with Finn following close behind. Ted and Michael just laughed at the two of them.

"So, Katie girl, how do ya' like your job?" Finn said as he stood next to her while she made the cookie dough.

"Hands off, mister. No chips for you," she said as she whacked his hand with the wooden spoon.

"Hey, watch it. I need that hand to steal cookies," Finn said as he nudged her sideways.

"Move aside dude. I need another wooden spoon. This one is contaminated with your cooties," Katelyn said as she pushed Finn a bit to grab another spoon.

They had fun mixing and placing the cookies on the baking sheets. Finn even got to sample the dough.

As Katelyn was taking the cookies out of the oven, Finn pretended to be ready to snatch them away from her.

"Just one question for you Finn."

"What's that?"

"You enjoy life?"

"Why, yes I do especially right this minute."

"Then I strongly suggest you move away or this will be your last minute to enjoy," Katelyn said as she set the baking sheets on the stove top.

Finn just laughed and grabbed Katelyn as soon as she had set the baking sheets down.

"Now I've got you as my prisoner," Finn said as he held her close and looked down at her. "I'm not gonna' even consider letting ya' go until you promise I can have a cookie or four."

"And, if I don't'?" Katelyn replied.

"Then you'll be my slave forever," Finn said as he looked her right in the eyes. He felt his heart begin to race. She was beautiful. Wait, what was happening here? He was getting a bit lightheaded just looking at her.

Katelyn felt the same thing and she couldn't take her eyes of Finn. They stood there looking at each other for what seemed like forever. Then, Finn lowered his head a bit towards her and Katelyn raised her head towards Finn.

Their lips were only a breath apart. Then it happened. They both moved into each other at the same time and their lips met. It was a sweet soft kiss for a minute, then Finn deepened it and Katelyn responded. Both felt like they were spinning out of control

Finn broke the kiss a half-second before Katelyn.

They just stood there, not knowing what to do.

"Well, I do believe we can blame this on the cookies. They must be sendin' a secret vapor into the air," Katelyn said smiling at Finn.

"Yes," Finn said, as he held onto Katelyn. "I do agree."

"Time for cookies," Katelyn said as she turned towards the counter.

"I know they're not as sweet as you, Katie girl," Finn said softly as he devoured a whole one and groaned.

"Really, Finn? The whole thing?" Katelyn said as she bit into one.

"Yup. The whole thing just to make sure they're okay," Finn said as he took another one.

"I'll get us somethin' to drink. Water okay with you?"

"What? No ice-cold milk?"

"No milk. I don't drink milk. Water will have to do," Katelyn replied as she handed a bottle of water to Finn.

They ate cookies and drank their water for a few minutes without talking.

Then Finn said, "Katelyn, I liked kissing you. It was really sweet."

"Finn, I liked kissing you as well. It was great. Wanna' try it again just to make sure it was for real?" Katelyn said as she stood in front of Finn.

"Why, Miss Katie, I do believe I like the way you think," Finn said as he gathered her in his arms and set about kissing her.

This time it was quite passionate. They kissed for quite some time and their hands explored each other a bit.

They separated and looked at each other.

"Finn, I gotta' confess. I've always wanted you to do that," Katelyn said blushing a bit.

"Why, Katie, don't blush. I've wanted to kiss you for as long as I can remember. I know you're a few years older than me and when we were kids, I always had a crush on you. It never went away. I still do," Finn said laughing softly as he touched Katie's cheek.

"I've always had a crush on you and it never went away either. So glad I came home."

"You have no idea how happy I am that you're home. So, does this mean we're goin' steady?" Finn asked.

"I guess it does," Katelyn replied.

"Okay, then, more cookies," Finn said as he reached around her and grabbed a couple more.

"Hey, save a few for tomorrow will ya? I was gonna' bring them to work," Katelyn said shaking her finger at Finn.

"You've got more to bake. Get busy," Finn said.

They spent the next while baking and teasing each other before Finn left. He had to get home. His folks had some work for him to do around the place.

"Later, Katie girl," Finn said as they kissed again.

"Later, Finn," Katie said as Finn finally left.

Katelyn went back into the kitchen to clean up. She was amazed at what had just happened. She would be smiling for quite some time for sure.

The next week went by so fast. Katelyn was loving her job. Especially since Finn was around some of the time. Ethan and Ian were amazing at getting folks to open up to them about their wishes and dreams then making them come to life in their sketches and digital creations. Katie was learning how to use their design software right along with Ian and she couldn't have even imagined all this when she was in college.

Sami was going strong as well. She took Katie's idea of incorporating the Underground Railroad history into the properties she was responsible for and found out that most of them had a connection with the anti-slavery movement of that time period. She put together a slide show of her proposal for Lloyd and Johnson and they loved it. They gave her the go ahead to work it into the other properties as she saw fit. They were thrilled with her. The Kennebunkport property managers were overwhelmed with the find of the hide-away room and tunnels. The local historical society and the group of archeologists from the University of Maine were beyond thrilled. News of the find go out to the media and Sami had not had a moment to herself since. Every day she went to the hotel, news reporters and cameras were waiting for her. The local news had spread across the globe and everyone was fascinated with the find. This find brought the whole slave period in the United States back to life in a big way. The South was being looked at in a new light as historians and locals alike began to look into the history of slavery in every state and town across the country. Descendants of those slaves were looking into their own family histories to make the connections and find out if any of their ancestors had been passengers of the Underground Railroad System.

Katelyn told her family and others in The Creek about Sami's find and they were all talking about it as well. Kendra was working on a few real estate projects in the Pine Ridge area. Jenna had her projects to work on as well. Matthews was busy keeping The Creek safe. Ethan and Ian were wicked busy with new customers now that they had Katelyn on board.

Finn and his family were still grieving for Jay. Jay would show himself to them as a ghost from time to time to help them along. Diane was busy increasing the energy of her Gifts. She and Miss Cora would meet up every week for tea and practice using their Gifts. Hank was busy with his work. Now that his family knew he was a White Light Paladin, they better understood him and his commitment to keeping folks safe from The Dark Force.

Emily and Kendra both felt the shift in the energy in The Creek at about the same time. It was a small shift and they knew it was just a signal that more was to come. Not yet though. Not for quite a while. And, they knew Katelyn was a big part of whatever was going to take place. They would both make sure she was ready by teaching her about The Magic and how to use its special powers.

Saturday morning was beautiful. It was late July and summer was in full swing. Katelyn's family was having a family bar-be-que Saturday evening and had invited a few friends over. Katelyn was going to make some cookies to bring along. She got right out of bed and got busy with her chores.

Around mid-morning, she got a call from Jordan.

"Hey, Jordan," Katelyn said as she answered her phone. She put it on speaker so she could keep folding her laundry.

"Hey, Katelyn," Jordan replied. "Just wonderin' what your plans for today are? I wanted to invite you over to take a look at the barn and the eagle's nest."

"That sounds fantastic. I've got the whole afternoon free. How does one o'clock sound?"

"Great. I'll see ya' then."

"Thanks for the invite, Jordan. I love the whole thing that's happenin' at your farm."

"Me, too. Later," Jordan said as they ended the call.

Katelyn got busy making the cookies so she wouldn't have to hurry away from Jordan's place later. She had a feeling that something was gonna' happen out there. It was a good feeling for sure.

Jordan was outside when she got there.

"Hey," they both said at the same time.

"Let's go right into the barn. The eagles are okay with everyone comin' and goin'," Jordan said as they walked over to the barn.

"Ethan said they had gotten a lot of work done on your barn. This is fantastic'," Katelyn said as she looked over the outside.

"Yeah. The outside is now all finished and the barn is weather tight. They're workin' on the apartment and the inside at the same time."

They walked into the barn and Katelyn spent some time looking over everything.

"Katelyn, look," Jordan said as they walked into the center of the floor. He pointed up at the space where the eagles had built their nest.

"Wow! That thing is huge!" Katelyn exclaimed as she looked up at the nest.

"And, that's only about a third of it. I had to get a ladder to climb up to the rafter level over on this side to get a better look. The eagles were watching me real close so I climbed really slowly and just stood there takin' pictures with my professional camera. I have the prints in the kitchen."

"This is amazing. What does Ethan say about it? Has it ever happened in other barns they were building?"

"Well, Ian did say that a family of owls had taken up residence in Matthews' barn but that was to be expected. They love to roost in safe places."

"I get that. I'll have to take a look the next time I'm over there. This truly is special," Katelyn said as one of the eaglets looked over the side.

"I guess we got their attention," Katelyn said as she pointed at the bird.

"I guess we did. Maybe we should leave them alone. I wouldn't want to interfere with their habits and all," Jordan said.

"Agreed," Katelyn replied as they left the barn.

"Come on into the kitchen and take a look at the pictures. I did a pretty decent job at being a photographer if I do say so myself," Jordan offered as they walked over to the house.

They spent a good part of the afternoon looking at the phots and talking about the eagles and their crystals. It was about four o'clock when Katelyn looked at her phone.

"Jordan, this had been a great afternoon. Thanks for inviting me over to get caught up with the eagle family," Katelyn said.

"My pleasure. Anytime you feel like walkin' around the place, feel free. I don't need to be here. There's a key to the back porch door just under the rock to the left of the door in the garden. Thanks for the cookies. Your family's gonna' love 'em for sure."

"Oh, your entirely welcome and thanks for the open invite. I'll be takin' you up on it right soon. There's somethin' about this place that draws me here."

"I know that feelin.' I felt the same thing when Kendra showed me the place for the first time like I told you before. It has an energy of its own. I keep thinkin' about how I know you so well without ever having met you before. There must be some special energy goin' around for that, too."

"I feel the same way. I bet we knew each other in another life time. I've been learning a lot of stuff from Kendra and Emily and they say we probably met in a prior life. I think I believe in that thought as nothin' else can explain all this."

"I do believe you may have somethin' there, Katie. I'm gonna' think about it for a bit," Jordan said as Katelyn prepared to leave.

Jordan walked her out to her SUV.

"Thanks, again, Jordan," Katelyn said as she got in.

"Any time Katelyn," Jordan replied as Katelyn pulled away.

Jordan spent the rest of the day going about his chores but the idea that he and Katelyn had met in a prior life was with him all evening.

Katelyn and her family had a great time at the bar-be-que. Family and friends came by. Stories were told and everyone was teased about one thing or another. Folks stayed until late into the night. Katelyn was the last to leave around eleven o'clock. She promised she'd be by the next weekend. She fell right to sleep but her sleep was a bit restless as she dreamed about crystals and eagles and places she had never been to before. It was about four in the morning before she fell into a deep, deep sleep.

The rest of The Creek slept peacefully that night.

CHAPTER 11

I t was a typical summer Sunday in The Creek. Katelyn woke up late, again. She seemed to be a bit tired. She remembered the dreams and chalked the being tired up to the weird dreams and all that food and fun at her family's party the night before.

Monday was a regular Monday. Everyone was back to their usual routines. Tuesday morning found Katelyn thinking about Jordan's farm as she woke up. When she got to work, Ian was waiting for her.

"Hey, Katelyn," Ian said as she walked into the shop.

"Hey, Ian," Katelyn replied as she put her things away.

"Don't get too comfy. I need you to go with me to Jordan's place. I'd like your thoughts on the apartment. It needs somethin' to perk it up."

"Great. I'll show you the eagle's nest while we're there."

"Ethan mentioned the eagles that had taken up residency in the barn rafters. I can't wait to see them. Let's go."

A few minutes later found Katelyn pointing to the eagle's nest in Jordan's barn.

"Holy shit! That thing's huge" Ian said as he stared at the nest.

"And that's only about a third of it. Jordan had to climb the extension ladder to get a better look. He's got pictures inside."

"This is amazing. I gotta' get a hold of those pictures. Has anyone contacted the Audubon Society about this yet?"

"I asked Jordan that same question. He said he didn't want to because he didn't want a bunch of strangers botherin' the eagles. I agree."

"I never thought about that. And, I agree, too, now that you mention it. Let's keep it for ourselves."

"Deal," Katelyn said as they shook hands.

"Let's take a look at the apartment. I think the inside staircase is ready to use," Ian said as he called out to the foreman and got the okay.

As they were climbing the stairs, Katelyn looked over at the eagle's nest. The inside wall of the staircase had not been built yet so you could get a good look at the nest.

"Ian," Katelyn whispered and pointed.

They both watched as the eagles went about their business. The eaglets were getting big and Katelyn wondered if they were ready to learn to fly.

Katelyn and Ian went on up to the apartment. The crew was working on running the rough electric and plumbing so they stayed out of their way as much as possible.

"Well, Katelyn, that was some view of the eagles. Really cool," Ian said.

"I never thought I'd see them that closely. Really cool for sure," Katelyn replied.

"So, here's what I'd like your thoughts on," Ian said as he showed Katelyn around the space and explained what he had design questions about.

They spent about two hours brainstorming ideas and looking through online images of ideas they thought might work.

"Okay. I do believe we have a plan. Nice work Katie," Ian said as he patted her on the back.

"Likewise," Katelyn said as she patted Ian on the back.

"I really like the way we kept coming up with ideas, throwing them out, and coming up with more ideas. I like the way you think. Ethan was sure right about you and your gifts and all about design stuff."

"Why thanks, Ian. I love the way we work together as well. It really has been fun this morning. Only one thing," Katelyn said looking seriously at Ian.

"What? What's wrong?" Ian asked.

"I'm starvin'. All this work has made me really hungry," Katelyn said as she laughed at the look on Ian's face.

"Funny. Really funny, Katelyn." Ian replied as he laughed as well. "Let's get back to the shop and lunch."

"Agreed," Katelyn said as they left the barn.

A short time later found them in the shop eating lunch. Ethan and Finn walked in and joined them. They all brought each other up-to-date on their mornings and set about the afternoon with lots to do.

One thing that Katelyn had to do was return to Jordan's place and get a few more measurements of the staircase. She had voiced the idea of including enclosed shelves on the inside of the staircase and Ian had agreed. They had the design all set and just needed a few measurements.

It was about four o'clock when Katelyn finished taking the needed measurements and was throwing her stuff into her SUV. All of a sudden, she had a strong, overwhelming feeling to go walk out into the field where she and Jordan had found the twin crystals. She tried to ignore it but the feeling grew stronger and stronger. She had been learning to listen to those gut hunches so, she changed into her work boots and set out for the field.

She felt like she was being pulled by an invisible cord toward the place where the crystals had been found. When she got there, she didn't find any crystals but she felt compelled to walk a bit to the right, heading west. She felt like the cord had just let go of her as she walked past a bunch of bushes. She looked around and didn't see anything special. So, she turned to head back to the house when the cord grabbed at her again.

It made her turn to look at the bushes again. She looked again and still didn't see anything special. She thought she heard a voice tell her to move the branches of the bushes around. She did. Then she saw it. It was an opening in the hill. She took a step toward it to get a better look and when she did, she saw it was a cave entrance. She'd brought her backpack with outdoor equipment with her. She grabbed the LED flashlight and shown it into the cave. There was plenty of room to walk, although she would have to hunch over a bit at the entrance.

Curiosity got the better of her and she stepped into the cave and began walking along. Just a short distance along the way the cave turned and she followed the turn to find herself at the opening of a big room. She took a step into the room and it lit up like the sun was inside. There were crystals everywhere. She stood there in awe. She instinctively knew the crystals Jordan had found and the twin crystals they had found had come from this cave. She just stood there for the longest time in wonder.

After a bit she walked a few steps into the room and felt a wave of energy go through her. She could see the wave as she got to it, then it went through her as she walked a few more steps into the room. It was a weird feeling. She turned all around just looking at all the crystals. She didn't know how long she had been there but felt it was time to leave.

She retraced her steps but didn't feel the energy wave this time. As she was about to leave the big room, she felt something fall against her leg. She looked down and it was a red crystal about the size of an egg. It was glowing like crazy. She thought she heard someone tell her to pick it up. It was for her. She bent down and took a hold of it and a jolt of energy shot through her just like when she held the shocked crystal in Alabama. It only lasted a second then calmed down. She said a quiet thank you to Mother Earth for the crystal and the cave and left the big room. As she walked through the lower part to the entrance, she though she saw something fly by.

She walked out into the field and saw the shape of a big bird flying off over the meadow. It was really big. Really big. Not sure what it was but it was really big. She felt the crystal vibrating in her hand and looked at it. It was glowing again. No zing this time.

She stood in the field for a while thinking about the cave. It was…she didn't know any words to explain what she had just experienced. Really. She felt a bit unbalanced so she called upon the Reiki energy and grounded herself. She felt much better after she finished.

She walked back to her SUV, drank a bottle of water, placed the crystal on the seat and turned on the AC. She sat there for a minute then realized it was past six o'clock. She texted Ian the measurements and headed for home. She decided to stop off at The Store for something for supper.

"Hey Ted, Michael," she said as she walked in.

"Hey, Katelyn" they replied.

"Gonna' grab somethin' for supper," she told them.

"Okay. You know what to do," Ted said.

She placed her order and walked around a bit. Things looked a little bit different from the other day but that's probably 'cause the guys were always trying out new stuff.

Ted came over with her dinner. "There ya' go, Katelyn," he said as he handed it to her.

"Thanks, Ted. See ya' later," Katelyn said as she went over to pay Michael.

"Have a good evenin', Michael," Katelyn said as she left.

As soon as she got home, she sat down and began to eat. She was really hungry as if she had been crazy busy all day. She fell asleep a little while later, fully exhausted from she didn't know what.

And she slept.

She was up and gone early the next morning. She arrived at work just as Ian was coming out of the shop door.

"Oh, Hey, Katelyn. Great timing," Ian stated with. "How about you just put your stuff away and follow me? We need to get to Jordan Jackson's place and look over the apartment for some design ideas."

"Hey, Ian. You're kidding, right? We did all that yesterday. We were there for a couple of hours."

"Katelyn, no we weren't."

"Sure we were. We talked about making shelves along the inside staircase for more storage areas."

"That is a great idea. But, Katie, we didn't go over to Jordan's yesterday. You feelin' alright?" Ian asked concerned.

Katelyn took a quick breath. As she was talking with Ian, she noticed a few changes in the place. She began to get the feeling that something was a bit off.

"Yeah, I'm good. Maybe I just dreamed all that stuff."

"I've done just that. Dreamed something so strong I was sure I had done it after I woke up. It's a weird feeling."

"Sure is," Katelyn replied not too sure about all this.

"Let's go over there and you can tell me what was in your dream. Probably all good stuff we can use."

"That's a great idea. I'll be right out." Katelyn replied as Ian went outside.

Something wasn't right here. It started yesterday when she was in The Store. Some of the stuff the guys had on the shelves had never been there before. And now this. Something wasn't right.

She took a deep breath and headed out to meet up with Ian.

They were at Jordan's place a few minutes later. Everything looked the same. Jordan was just about to leave for work. He had The Creek route today and didn't need to leave early.

"Hey, Katie, Ian," Jordan said as he joined them in the barn.

They all looked up at the eagle's nest at the same time.

"That is really cool," Ian said in disbelief. "Ethan told me about the nest, but until ya' see it, it doesn't sound like it would be anythin' so spectacular. That thing is huge!"

Katelyn and Jordan laughed at Ian's remarks.

"It certainly is. So cool," Katelyn replied.

"I'm so over-the-moon that the eagles decided to make their home in my barn," Jordan added.

Katelyn was puzzled. Ian had seen the nest yesterday. She was sure they had been here. She got the shivers for a second. Something was definitely off here.

They chatted for a minute then Jordan took off for work.

As Ian and Katelyn climbed the inner-barn staircase, Katelyn pointed out the shelving idea to Ian.

"This is a great idea. Take some measurements later on and send them to me. I'll sketch somethin' up and we can look it over at lunch."

"Ian, I texted you the measurements yesterday. Look, here they are," Katelyn said as she looked over her phone texts for the one she had sent Ian yesterday with the measurements.

She kept looking and looking but couldn't find them.

"I sent them yesterday. I know I did," Katelyn said in a frustrated voice.

"No problem, Katie. Take it easy. It was probable part of that dream thing you had. Can you remember any of them? We can check them out right now."

"Sure," Katelyn said as she handed the measuring tape to Ian and he began taking measurements.

Katelyn told him the numbers she had got for all the spaces yesterday and they were exactly the same as the ones Ian got just then.

"That's really peculiar, Katelyn. My numbers are exactly the same as the ones you said you got yesterday."

"I know. I told you I had already done this. This is really strange. Maybe it's 'cause you were in my dream and you dreamed this part, too. I know weird stuff can happen when we dream. That's all I've got," Katelyn said confused.

"Maybe. I don't always remember my dreams. This is really weird for sure. Let's just say it has to do with The Magic in The Creek. That's all I got," Ian replied.

"Good thinkin'. It's The Magic. Okay. I can live with that," Katelyn said as they went on up into the apartment.

"Now, tell me about the thoughts we had in your dream and let's see if they're gonna' work out for real," Ian said as they started to look around.

The space looked exactly the same as yesterday. Katelyn told Ian about the ideas they had come up with the day before and he agreed that they were perfect for the space.

"I especially like the idea of radiant floor heat from the solar panels on the roof."

"Oh, Finn said I should go look at the panels on Laine and Mo's greenhouses. They seem to look just like the glass panels but have some kinda' technology that does the same thing as those big black solar panels. Is Finn suggesting they be placed here?"

"Yes. We're gonna' use the same glass panels on Jordan's barn roof as sort of a trial thing. If they work as well as the sisters say they do, he's gonna' have us place them on the house roof. He already has thermal heat from one of the hot spring's streams from up in the mountain. We found a few of them when we were doing the thermal imaging of the property before we began excavation. That's how we found those other ones that we're gonna' tap into for the build down toward Pine Ridge a ways off the Pine Ridge Road. Kinda' south of here about five miles or so away."

"I heard Ethan and Finn talkin' about that build. It's gonna' be so cool with the thermal and solar energy sources. They said the owners would be completely off the energy grid. I like that idea."

"So do I. If this works, one of the next projects is gonna' be a new home for my family. I own about ten acres the other side of Matthew's and the

Two Moon Stables. I've left it alone ever since I bought it. But now my wife and I are beginin' to think about building our dream home on it."

"Oh, Ian, that's really wonderful! I hope I get to consult for you," Katelyn said.

"Of course. Wouldn't have it any other way. I'm sure a lot of folks will share their ideas with us once word gets out. Just not yet, though. We need time to think for ourselves."

"Deal. I won't tell anyone," Katelyn said with a smile.

They finished at the barn and headed back to the shop.

The afternoon found everyone at the shop busy. Ethan had been out all day and when he finally showed up late in the afternoon he headed right into his office and got busy. Katelyn and Ian called it quits later than usual.

As Katelyn was gathering her things to leave, she stopped by Ethan's office. The door was open and Ethan was busy with some plans. She knocked on the door.

Ethan looked up, smiled, and said, "Katelyn. Come on in."

"Hey, Ethan. You've been super busy all day. What gives?"

"Oh, sorry. I'm just getting the permits for the new group of builds ready. These builds keep me busy. Now we have five approved and one wait-ing for Kendra to give her okay for the sixth one. The new owners are waiting to sign papers later this week. Things are crazy right now and, ya' now me, I love it all."

"I know ya' do. I was just wonderin' if you and Emily had plans for the weekend? I kinda' want to talk to her about stuff and don't want to interfere with you two."

"Ah, Katie, of course we don't have plans. Why would we? Her build has been done for a long while now."

"Well, ya know, with the two of you getting' along so well. I thought ya' might be busy. That's all."

"Katelyn. That's sweet of you to think about us like that. But, we're just good friends. Nothin' more," Ethan said looking straight at Katelyn.

"You're teasin' me, right? You two are amazin' together," Katelyn replied.

"I think that's sweet of you, Katie. But we're nothin' more than good friends. Why don't ya' give Emily a call so the two of you can get together? I'm sure she'd love that."

Katelyn was beyond surprised. She tried to hide her disbelief. "Ah, good idea. Sorry, just thought the two of you had somethin' special there."

"Nope."

"Okay, then. I guess I'm more tired than I thought. I slept dead to the world last night. I guess I've got that deep sleep hangover thing goin' on."

100

"Most likely. I hate that. It bothers me all day and makes me work even harder just to think about regular stuff. Have a yummy supper and rest easy tonight."

"Good advice, boss man. I have leftovers from The Store. Always a good thing. See ya' tomorrow," Katelyn said as she turned away more confused than ever.

Katelyn sat in her SUV for a few minutes trying to get a grip on herself. Now she knew for sure something was wrong. Ethan and Emily had been a hot item ever since Emily had come to The Creek over a year ago. Most things looked the same, but something was really wrong here. She set out for home after a few more minutes of trying to pull herself together.

As soon as she pulled into her driveway, she saw the truck in the driveway of the house on the other side of Kendra's place. It wasn't there yesterday. She saw Kendra on the front porch and called out to her as she closed her car door.

"Hey, Kendra," Katelyn said as she walked over.

"Hey, Katelyn. How was your day?" Kendra replied.

"Busy and fun. I love workin' with those guys."

"It shows."

"Ah, Kendra, have you rented out the other house?"

"Now, Katelyn, have you had a stroke or somethin'? That house has been rented for the past two months to the energy resources guy from the power company outta' Boone. He's checking out the grid sources and how they support the electrical needs of the area. You know that."

"Oh, yeah. Did he get a new truck or somethin'? It looks different," Katelyn said to try to cover her amazement. Yesterday, no one lived there. No one had lived there since Matthews had moved into his new house. She knew that as fact and wouldn't think otherwise.

"Good eye, girl. He was using his own until the company gave him one. His is dark blue and that one is white with the company logo on it. He parked his around back so you can't see it from the road. Safer there he says."

"Now that's good thinkin' on his part. I guess I really am more tired than I thought. Gonna' get some supper and call it quits early tonight. Thanks.

"Rest easy, Katie girl. Stuff happens," Kendra replied with a little smile on her face.

Okay, so, the truck could be explained but no one had lived in that house yesterday. And what about all of the other stuff? Things just weren't the same as they had been yesterday. She knew she wasn't seeing things.

Katelyn thought about this for a few minutes. She decided to be extra careful when going about The Creek and all and talking with folks. She would call Emily in a day or so and get together with her. Maybe she could tell

Katelyn what was going on around here. Something was really wrong. Well, not really wrong. But, definitely different.

Evening melted into night and the sky was filled, once again, with millions of stars.

The Creek slept and so did their Katie girl.

CHAPTER 12

reg Jones. That was his name. He was the electric grid resources guy that had rented Kendra's other house a couple of months ago. Well, more like six weeks ago. I guess it doesn't really matter when. Or, maybe it does. He was a respectful guy with a sense of humor. He kept mainly to himself. He was pleasant when he was around others. He worked long hours though. Seems he was gone from sun-up to nightfall. He was somewhere in his mid-thirty's it seemed. He liked music 'cause you could hear it coming from his truck when he was driving around.

Greg liked to eat. He was forever getting food from The Store. Most nights he could be seen in The Store having supper or taking it home. Ted and Michael said he didn't talk much about himself more than to talk about his work. Seems he liked history some. He was always asking about the history of The Creek. Folks were glad to answer his questions and fill him in on the happenings all around.

It was just about the time that Katelyn was asking about his truck that Kendra decided to look into his background. She couldn't find much on him except that he worked for the electric company and had lived in the Montgomery, Alabama area. She wondered if Katelyn had ever run across him. Probably not. Montgomery was a big city and most folks only knew their kin, the folks that lived near them, and the folks they worked with. She'd ask Katelyn the next time she saw her. Strange though, Kendra kept thinking. There was something about him that made her pause and think and that usually meant that there was some kinda' connection with The Magic in The Creek. She couldn't say whether it was good or bad yet. But she'd keep an eye on him anyway. Kendra was right to keep an eye on him. He was almost too nice to be true.

Greg had heard that Ethan and Ian had created a new build that would be off the grid. That meant that the homeowners would not be connected to the electrical grid. Greg decided to check out the project. He drove down the dirt road to the build site the day after Kendra and Katelyn were talking about his new truck. That would have made it Thursday morning. He went over around six o'clock 'cause he thought no one would be around to ask questions. Boy, was he surprised to find Ethan and Kendra already there.

He got out of the company truck and walked over to them.

"Hey, Kendra," Greg said.

"Hey, Greg. This here's Ethan Sutherland, owner of the building company that's doin' the work here."

"Ethan," Greg said as they shook hands.

"Greg. What can I do for you?" Ethan asked.

"I heard about all the amazin' homes you build and thought I'd come take a look for myself."

"Well, Greg, no offense, but these builds are on private land and the owners need to give the okay for people outside the work group to stop by."

"Oh, okay. I didn't know that. I did hear how you're gonna' use solar and thermal energy to power the place. That right?"

"Well, now, Greg, that information is private and only for the homeowners to know about. I'm gonna' have to ask you to move on now," Ethan said as he moved Greg back towards his truck.

"Oh, sorry. Didn't mean to cause any concern. I'll be on my way," Greg said as he climbed into his truck.

"Thanks for understandin'," Kendra said.

Greg drove off and Kendra and Ethan looked at each other.

"You get the feelin' he was here for some other reason?" Ethan asked Kendra.

"Sure did. I do think it had to do with bein' off the grid but not for the electric company's concern. Somethin' else."

"Me, too. Somethin' about that guy. Oh, shit! Does that mean there's gonna' be trouble?"

"Probably. You know how The Dark is always tryin' to take over around here. But I hope not," Kendra said as they went back to work.

Greg went on to his own work. He was gonna' call a meeting for tonight. He and his kind had a lot to talk about.

It was a busy day all over the Blue Ridge. Visitors were hiking the trails. The locals were working and tending their land. Bubba and Earl were busy with their new cabins that Emily had built for them. They were thrilled with all the new stuff they had inside. Heat from the thermal springs and electricity from the solar panels Laine and Mo had given them.

Katelyn was set to go over to Laine and Mo's this afternoon to have a look at their greenhouses and solar panel set-up. She hadn't had much time to visit since she returned to The Creek and was looking forward to the visit.

Late afternoon found her makin' her way down the driveway. Laine saw her and shouted out to Mo. As soon as Katelyn was out of the car, the two of them grabbed her and hugged her for the longest time.

"God! I've missed ya', Katie girl," Laine said laughing and crying altogether.

"Me, too," Mo added.

"Me, three," Katelyn replied.

"I couldn't believe my eyes when I saw you comin' outta' The Store just when you got here. I ran home to tell Mo and she jumped all around like me," Laine said as they walked over to the picnic table and sat down.

"I thought I caught a glimpse of you as I was headin' over to Kendra's. I figured you were busy and we'd see each other at the bar-be-que," Katelyn said.

"Which we did, but we couldn't say much and all ya' know with all the folks around. Now we can," Mo added.

"So much to tell for sure. Where do we start?" Katelyn asked.

"Well, first, let me get the pitcher of iced tea and all," Mo said as she ran into the house. She was back right away with tea and more.

Once they all got settled Katelyn told them about her life in Alabama and then when she was finished, she showed them her shocked crystal.

"What a beauty!" Laine exclaimed as she looked the crystal over thoroughly. She didn't pick it up cause she knew only the owner was supposed to touch their crystal.

"Wow! Look at that thing. It's shinin' like a lighthouse!" Mo added.

"Yes, it is. It does that whenever it's in the open air. It's kinda' hummin', too. Can ya' hear it?" Katelyn asked.

The girls sat real quiet and heard the humming.

"Yup, we can. How cool is that? I guess that crystal is very happy to be with you, Katie girl," Laine said rather quietly.

"Guess so," Katelyn replied just as quietly.

They sat there for a bit just enjoying the crystal and the day.

After a bit, Katelyn asked, "Well, what's new with you two?"

"Well, we sort of designed those solar panels Ethan wants you to see and a new strain of marijuana that grows faster and bigger with less bug problems. I think those solar panels have a lot to do with it," Laine said.

"And, I think the new food formula I created has a lot to do with it, too. All organic so it doesn't harm those that use the stuff," Mo added.

"You two are such geniuses. I am overwhelmed at all you do," Katelyn said.

"Why, thank ya, ma'am," Laine said with a bow.

"Wise ass," Katelyn said laughing along with Mo.

"Let's take a look at those solar panels," Mo said as they walked back to the special greenhouse made just for the herbal plants.

Laine explained how she and Mo had dreamed up the clear solar panels one night. She said it seemed to come outta' nowhere. Poof! They had the idea and within a couple of days they had their first prototypes in place. After a couple of weeks and a few tweaks, they had a final product in place across the whole roof and their energy bank was working at full capacity.

"This is absolutely amazing! Don't know any other way to say it. You two really are geniuses. I can see why Ethan is so excited to use your creations on his builds," Katelyn said as Laine and Mo finished with their story.

"We're happy to give him whatever he needs. We filed and got a patent and it got approved just a few days ago. We've had industry experts ask for the details and we said no. We aren't gonna' share our idea with anyone. We're thinkin' of selling application access to a few companies for a few million each. We're still figurin' out how much money these corporations would save using our technology and so far, Mo, you tell her," Laine said.

"Well, so far, we've calculated about seventeen million for one of the smaller solar panel supply companies," Mo said laughing.

Katelyn and Laine laughed along with her.

"So, guess that means you're not gonna' give any access rights to anyone 'cause no one could afford to pay you," Katelyn said as they kept laughing.

"So right, Katie girl," Laine agreed. "So, we are putting a business proposal together between Ethan and us so he has the legal use of our panels as long as we get a share of the profits from the build. Nothing huge, just somethin' that keeps everything business-like and legal."

"That's a great idea, my friends. So cool," Katelyn said as they walked back to the picnic table.

"We've had a few folks stop by trying to get a look at things and we had to insist they leave the property. Ethan is building a gate for us to place at the road end of the property road. It's gonna' look real county-like but be high-tech. It's gonna' be part of the security system we have in place here and be locked at all times. The only way to open the gate will be with the pass code that we have and Ethan, will have, too. There's gonna' be a camera installed in a special place so we can see who's in the vehicles that want to come down the road. It's so cool. It's gonna' show us the people's faces up real close. And, that's all the people in the vehicle. If we know someone's comin' by, we'll keep an eye out for them and buzz them through of course," Mo explained.

"I love that idea. Ethan can make anything look just like it's a part of the place and non-high tech. I love the way that guy thinks for sure.," Katelyn said.

"Well now, it's about time for supper. Let's go onside and see what we can come up with. You joinin' us, Katelyn?" Laine asked.

"Yes, I am," Katelyn replied as they got up and headed into the house. "God! It smells so good in here. You been cookin' all day?" Katelyn said.

"Well, we knew you were headed our way and decided to put some bar-be-que in the crockpot with some chicken and all. We know how much you love bar-be-que," Mo said.

"Why, yes I do. Don't tell me you made homemade cornbread, too?" Katelyn said surprised.

"Of course, Katie girl. Nothin's too good for our Katie girl," Laine said as she brought the hot pan of cornbread to the table along with butter and honey.

"You two are the best forever and ever," Katelyn said as they sat down and enjoyed the feast.

After supper, they sat on the porch and watched the evening go by.

"We have some special brownies for dessert," Mo said as she handed one to each of them.

"This is just too good to be true. You really are spoilin' me my friends," Katelyn said as she bit into the special brownies.

They spent the next couple of hours enjoying the brownies and the way they made the evening so beautiful as it changed from the gloaming to nightshade.

It was near ten o'clock when Katelyn looked at her phone.

"Wow! This has been a super day with y'all. But it's getting on late and I better be headed home," Katelyn said as she stretched and yawned."

"It is," Laine said as she stood up. Mo joined her.

They walked Katelyn over to her SUV.

"Thanks for this special day. It's always great to hang out with you two. I love ya' always," Katelyn said as she got ready to drive away.

"We love ya, too, our Katie girl," Mo and Laine said together.

They waved to each other as Katelyn drove down the road. Once she was on the highway, she was home in what seemed like no time at all. She did a quick tooth brushing and wash up and was in bed right quick.

She dreamed that night of a battle in The Creek. Something about The Dark trying to take The Magic and she had something to do with it and all. The dream was vivid but when she woke up the next morning, she could only remember whispers of it. Nothing solid. Just hints of what it had been about. She'd talk to Emily about it when she saw her next time.

The next couple of weeks found Ethan, Ian and Katelyn very busy with the six new projects. Finn was busy with the same so they often gathered in the office working on the design ideas that included energy sources. It all depended on where the build was located and thermal and solar source availability along with the wishes of the clients. Lots to be considered and worked on.

The Creek was moving along through the summer as always. Beautiful days and warm nights. Visitors and locals enjoying the gifts of the Blue Ridge.

You would think it was all going along just fine. Just one thing, though. There was a ripple of unease felt by those folks tuned into The Magic. Something was a drift and Kendra, Emily and Miss Cora picked up on it right away.

CHAPTER 13

Yes. Greg knew Katelyn and Sami quite well. No. Katelyn didn't even know Greg existed. No. Sami didn't know Greg existed, either. Greg knew all about Katelyn. He had been tracking her ever since her move to the Montgomery, Alabama area. And, since Sami was Katelyn's best friend, Greg got to know a lot about her as well.

Greg was known as an electrical energy expert. This time. On the earth plane. Truth is Greg belonged to a group of bad-guy shape-shifters. ETs that worked for The Dark Force. They were known as the Infiltrator Squad. They could shape-shift into any entity in all the universes and do the bidding of The Dark Fore, which was to destroy The White Lighters and take over The Magic. Greg's usual job as a Dark Force ET was to find humans that were Gifted and hadn't made the decision to walk in The White Light yet. His specialty was to scare the life out of them so they wouldn't walk with The White Light. That way The Dark Force could control them and keep negative chaos in force in the earth-plane dimensions.

Greg thought he was doing a good job keeping Katelyn from becoming aware of her Gifts while she was in Alabama. She hadn't really been aware of them until she started working for the design firm. That's when her visions became strong and real. She suspected she had a Gift 'cause a lot of folks that were born and raised in The Creek were Gifted in some way or another. She just never thought she was one of the strong ones until she started having those dreams of her going back home that were so real, she could taste the food at The Store and all.

That's when Greg's job changed. He was told to stop her whatever it took. Thing was, The White Light had Katelyn surrounded and protected so well that The Dark Force couldn't get to her. She didn't know this. She wasn't even aware of all of her Gifts yet. That would come when she returned home to stay.

So, The Dark Force made some changes to Greg's operation. They moved him to The Creek and he rented the house on the other side of Kendra's. He was gone for most of the sunlight hours, supposedly working for the local electric company. He was not working for the local electric company. He was gathering his forces for an attack on The Creek to wipe out all the White Lighters and take The Magic for The Dark Force.

The first six weeks found Greg minding his own business. The first ripple came when he visited one of Ethan's new work sites a few miles from Jordan Jackson's place. He thought he could get in and gone before the work crews showed up but he was very wrong. Kendra and Ethan were already there so he had to make up an excuse for showing up. His excuse didn't really work as he was almost physically pushed off the property by Ethan. No problem. He would take his next step towards fulfilling the ultimate goal The Dark had planned.

The day after he was escorted off Ethan's build looked to be just another regular day in The Creek. Jordan had a couple of extra stops for the company and he would make them his last three stops as two of them were in The Creek. His supervisor told him to keep the company truck overnight so Jordan wouldn't have to drive all the way back to Boone and then home again late in the evening.

Jordan made his first extra big delivery in Pine Ridge. The local feed and grain had ordered extra manure and mulch products for the mid-summer rush. The owners sent a couple of folks to help Jordan and they finished what would have been a long hour and some job in just an hour. Jordan thanked them and was on his way to the second extra stop.

He pulled into the Soaring Mountain Builders yard, turned the truck around and backed up to the shop garage doors.

"Hey Jordan," Ian hollered out as Jordan jumped down from the truck.

"Hey, Ian. I got your new office furniture and stuff here. Where do ya' want it?" Jordan answered as the two men met at the back of Jordan's delivery truck.

Jordan opened the door and waved at all the stuff inside.

"Most of it's for you guys. Some is for The Store, too."

"Holy shit! That's a lot of stuff. Didn't think it would all arrive at the same time," Ian exclaimed. "Hey Joe, Tim. Come on over here and help us please."

The guys walked over and commenced to give Ian a hard time.

"What? You want us to unload all this stuff?" Tim said with a sassy look on his face.

"Do we look like furniture movers?" Joe added with a laugh.

"Do you two enjoy regular paychecks?" Ian countered.

Jordan just stood there laughing at the three of them. "I like this job. Free entertainment along with free help."

"Let's take a look at your invoice list Jordan and compare it to the original before we move anything," Ian suggested.

"Okay," Jordan said as they got to work comparing the two lists.

"They look identical. Now, let's see if all the stuff on your list is in the truck. Ready guys? We can store this stuff to the right side of the garage space from back to front. We'll unpack and look it over once the addition is ready." Ian said.

The four of them spent a bit more than an hour unloading and checking off the items then putting them in the garage.

It was close to seven o'clock when they finished.

"Joe, Tim, thanks for the extra help. Sorry it kept you so long. You'll get extra pay for helpin' out here. Now, go home. See you tomorrow," Ian said.

Joe and Tim offered their good-byes and drove away.

"That's real nice of you, Ian, payin' them extra for helpin' out. This is a lot of stuff. I suspect it's for Finn and Katelyn's new space?" Jordan asked as he closed the back of the truck and they walked to the front.

"Yes, it is, Jordan. Can't wait for them to see it. It's top of the line for sure. Those two are very special at what they do and Ethan and I wanted to do somethin' to show them how much we appreciate them," Ian replied.

"Well now, you guys are somethin' for sure. Gotta' get this last delivery made to The Store, pick up some supper and head home. It's been a fourteen-hour day today. Take care," Jordan said as he got into the driver's seat and closed the door.

"Thanks, Jordan. Come on by in a couple of weeks to look at the new space and all. Later," Ian replied.

Jordan drove off to make his last delivery to The Store.

"Hey Ted, Michael. I've got your goods here. Want me to bring them in the ramp entrance?" Jordan asked as Ted and Michael stepped through the front door.

"That's a great idea," Michael said. "So glad we kept the ramp in place after Finn didn't need it anymore. It sure has come in handy and some of the folks that have a bit of a problem using the stairs love it."

"Glad we kept it, too. It's easier for Jordan and the others to get the stuff inside." Ted added.

"Here we go then," Jordan said as he pushed the first load up the ramp and into The Store. He made a few more trips then was finally done with his deliveries. He closed up the truck and moved it away so others could use the ramp if need be.

Jordan walked in through the front door and headed to the dining room.

"Ted, I need me some supper and your signature on this delivery slip," Jordan said as he handed the digital pad to Ted.

Ted signed and gave it back to Jordan as he answered, "Well, Jordan, seems tonight was a great night to visit us so we have a just a few things left. Look over the chalk board and let me know your choice."

Jordan gave Ted his order and sat down at the table for a rest. He grabbed an iced tea from the cooler and relaxed while Ted prepared his supper.

"Hey Jordan," Hal offered as he stepped into the dining room.

"Hey, Hal. How are ya'? Haven't' seen ya' for a while and some," Jordan answered.

Hal sat down across from Jordan and they commenced to talking for a bit.

Ted came out from the kitchen with Jordan's dinner.

"Hey, Ted, got anythin' left?" Hal asked.

"Sure do. Barbe-que chicken sandwich with all the fixin's Hal. Just the way you like it," Ted replied.

"That's exactly what I as thinkin'," Hal replied. "Well, Jordan, I better let 'cha go before your dinner gets cold. Enjoy."

"Thanks, Hal. Enjoy yours as well," Jordan replied as he walked to the front to pay Michael.

"See y'all later," Jordan said as he left.

He got into his truck, set his food on the passenger seat and proceeded to set off down the Pine Ridge Road to his farm just a few miles away. He was tired for sure.

Just as he rounded the first curve a bit from The Store, his truck was rammed on the driver's side with such a violent force that it was sent through the woods off the side of the road. It smashed into small trees ripping them from the ground as it rolled over a couple of times before it came to an abrupt stop against a large boulder. Jordan was strapped into his seat and dangled as the truck rolled over and over and was struck on the head by a large rock that materialized inside the truck. He lost consciousness before the truck struck the boulder. It was on its side and Jordan was hanging from his seatbelt.

The noise of the crash was heard back at The Store and folks jumped into their trucks and found Jordan a few minutes later. They called for rescue help and tried to get to him. As soon as the rescue teams showed up, they started to clear the way into the woods with the help of the locals. When they got to the truck, they hollered for the Jaws-of-Life. No one could even get into the cab to get to Jordan. It took the crew about ten minutes to open the cab using the jaws and ripping the windshield out of the way.

They stabilized Jordan while he hung from the seatbelt before they cut the seatbelt away. As he was taken out of the truck, he moaned a few times. He was taken to the road in a rescue basket and placed on the rescue stretcher. The paramedics got busy evaluating him pulling tree stuff and glass out of his face. They tried to talk with him, but he remained unconscious the whole time. He looked to have a broken arm and leg and multiple cuts on his face and head. They wouldn't know about any spinal injuries until he was scanned at the emergency room in Boone. They got two IVs going and had him on oxygen as well. It took about twenty minutes to get all this done before the rescue crew loaded him into the rig and set out for the medical center in Boone, sirens blaring and lights flashing.

Word got around in lightning speed and folks got to The Store right quick.

"Now, everyone, settle down," Michael started. "We gave the rescue folks our phone numbers and all so they can contact us about Jordan. Nor sure who his emergency contact people are. The paramedics said they might have that information on file at the medical center. Katelyn and Kendra are on their way there now and will let us know what's happening. In the meantime, let's all try to settle down."

"The sheriff's department is goin' over the truck and getting Jordan's stuff out of it. They contacted the UPS company and their folks are on their way over as well. The whole driver's side is bashed in like a tank hit it or somethin'. I looked around while they were working on Jordan, walked along the road in both directions and across from the site and I couldn't find any tire marks or messed up road where another vehicle could have been sittin'. There aren't any tire marks like someone gunned it to hit Jordan either or tried to slow down. There just isn't any sign of another vehicle anywhere," Hal explained to everyone.

Folks thought about all this for a few minutes.

"Well, now," Miss Cora began, "I do believe somethin's amiss here. Just doesn't make sense and all. Our Jordan's a great guy and would help anyone out in a heartbeat. I need some thinkin' time and a cup of tea, please, Ted."

Yes, Ma'am, Miss Cora," Ted replied.

Folks gathered around the dining area, getting coffee and tea and such while Miss Cora sat quiet.

Jordan was a whole other thing. Just a second before he was hit, he thought he saw a familiar face laughing at him outside his window. Then Wham! He found himself sliding off the road and beginning to roll through the trees. He felt something hit the side of his head and saw a bright flash for a second. Then nothing. The next thing he knew he was in a real old place, a real old time, and he was dressed in strange clothes. He was old, really old and folks kept smiling at him. He could smell the earth and then something hot like something boiling on a stove. He looked around and saw a fire with a pot hanging over it with vapors coming out of it. That must be what he was smelling.

The place seemed somewhat familiar, like he knew the place. Like he had lived there before. He saw himself mixing some powders and giving them to a woman near the door of the house-like thing he was in. She seemed familiar as well. He suddenly felt a great deal of pain and moaned a few times. The vision fogged over and he thought he could hear someone calling his name. Then the vision came back into focus.

He kept mixing powders and some kind of liquids for the longest time. Then he felt real tired and the vision fogged over once again and he thought he fell asleep. It must have been a long sleep, 'cause the next time he started to see things, he was suddenly aware that that familiar face he had thought he had seen just before the truck was hit, was in front of him, laughing like crazy.

"You're gonna' die now. It was so much fun making your truck roll over and over and watching your life start to ebb away while you hung from your seat. You disgust us with your crystals and all. We rule the universes and you are no more than a pesky insect that needs to be crushed. Die!"

Jordan felt a hot searing pain push through his chest and tried to call for help, but he couldn't breathe let alone call out for help. He didn't want to die. He tried with all his might to fight against that voice. He knew it was evil. Just as he struggled to take what would be his last breath, he saw flickering lights come out of nowhere and surround him. The pain in his chest was gone and he could breathe again.

That horrible voice screamed out, "You can't have him. He's mine!" Then there was a flash of red lightening and the voice and face were gone. He could breathe again. He slipped into another sleep time and didn't wake up for real for another twelve hours.

Katelyn and Kendra arrived at the medical center in Boone and ran into the emergency department. The gave their names and information to the registration clerk who called the trauma center and was told Jordan had been taken into emergency surgery the minute he arrived. The registration clerk said she would check to see if anyone could talk to them about Jordan because he had rights about who was told about his condition.

About a half-hour later, a man in scrubs found them and asked them to follow him.

He explained he was the trauma doctor that assessed Jordan when he arrived and told them he was in surgery. He would be there for a long while because of the injuries he had suffered.

They were in the family room. This was a private place where the doctors could tell families about their loved-one.

"Please, sit down. I have a lot to tell you. I'm Dr. Arron Beckwith, one of the trauma doctors here at the medical center. I specialize in motor vehicle accidents. We looked at Jordan's emergency contact information and he listed you, Kendra. So glad you drove over."

"Wow. I didn't know he had listed me. That's good. This here is Katelyn MacDonald, a friend of ours. Does she need to leave while you talk to me?"

"That's up to you as Jordan can't make that decision right now."

"Okay, then. She stays. What's goin' on?"

"Okay. Here we go. As you know from the accident scene, the paramedics thought he might have a fractured leg and arm. The left leg is fractured in the upper area. The thigh area. It's a clean break that didn't break through the skin and pretty much stayed in place. The surgeons have set that fracture. He was bleeding into his gut. His spleen was removed and that stopped the internal bleeding for the most part. Right now, they are looking around to find another area that's bleeding a little bit. Now don't worry. This is what a trauma surgery team specializes in. Neither arm is broken. His left shoulder was dislocated and that's been put back into place. He has a lot of cuts to his face, neck, hand, and head. He has three teams workin' on him in surgery right now. A team of reconstructive surgeons, plastic surgery types, are taking care of the facial and neck lacerations. Some of them need some special attention."

"Did he wake up at all?" Katelyn asked.

"No, Katelyn, he did not. That's not surprising though. We found an area on the right side of his head above his ear that was bleeding a lot. Looks like he was struck with somethin' hard, maybe a rock. Don't know how a rock got into his truck. The paramedics said all the windows were closed. There's a great deal of mystery surrounding this accident. We figure he's gonna' be unconscious for a day or two as he suffered a concussion from that head injury and then he'll be under anesthesia for at least another two hours while all the teams repair him. Anesthesia and concussions don't mix well and we know that so we're very careful with the medicines we use in surgery and afterwards. Hang on a second, that's my pager."

Dr. Beckwith got on the phone for a few minutes then hung up.

"Looks like they found that other bleeder. It was a nick in one of the lobes of his liver. The liver is amazing. It can seal off small bleeds all by itself and that's just what it has done. The surgeons put a special kind of glue over the spot just to be sure. Jordan's had two units of blood so far and he's about to get another one. That's due to blood loss from the spleen injury. The reconstructive surgeons need about another hour for their work and then the trauma surgery team will get a full body scan when these surgeons are finished. Do you have any questions?"

"Yes," Kendra said. "Would you please have someone tell him The Creek is sending lots of healing energy his way? Right now, while he's in surgery? I know people can hear things even if they are unconscious. Please?"

"It's very important that he knows we are here for him," Katelyn added.

"I believe that, too. Sure," Dr. Beckwith said as he called the surgical suite and gave them instructions to tell Jordan the message. He turned and smiled as he hung up the phone.

"I could hear the anesthesiologist givin' your message to Jordan."

Katelyn and Kendra smiled.

Dr. Beckwith left with the promise of keeping them informed by himself or someone from the surgical teams as soon as more information was available.

"Kendra," Katelyn started.

Kendra put up her hand before Katelyn could continue. "Yes, Katelyn, you got this one right."

"I knew it. The Dark caused that accident. Fuckin' assholes!"

"Agreed!" Kendra said as she put an arm around Katelyn's shoulders. "Let's call The Store and give everyone the news and start a Reiki healing circle."

Katelyn nodded her head and a moment later they had The Store on speaker phone and told them everything they had learned about Jordan. It took a while to answer everyone's questions. Then, Kendra asked about the Reiki healing circle.

Emily replied with, "Done. I got one started here, then went online and sent the request across the globe. Sending it to you two as well."

"Thanks, I wondered why I wasn't a puddle on the floor yet," Katelyn said with a little catch in her voice.

"Ladies, Miss Cora here. I love this whole speaker thing and the cell phones and all. I've been giving some thought to this whole thing and I say The Dark is behind it all."

Folks in The Store who could hear Miss Cora nodded their heads in agreement.

"So do we, Miss Cora," Katelyn agreed.

"How ya' doin' there, Miss Katelyn? This is some way to learn about The Magic and all. So sorry ya' had to experience this and that nasty business with Jenna."

"Oh, Miss Cora, thanks for thinkin of me. It has been crazy for sure. But, I'm alright, really, with the Reiki y'all sent. Makes a big difference."

"Good to hear. Kendra, anything come to mind yet?"

"No, Miss Cora, nothin' more than what you suspect. We'll have to think about the why of this a bit later. Just now, we need to concentrate on Jordan. Could someone go out to the farm and make sure it's all okay? Especially the stuff in the barn?"

"Sure thing, Kendra," Ethan said. "I'll head over now. Jonah, how about you come with me, if you would please? I'd appreciate your company just now."

"Of course, Ethan," Jonah agreed as they left The Store.

"Well, folks, that's all for now. We'll keep in touch and let ya' know when Jordan's out of surgery," Kendra offered.

"Okay. Thanks," they all said.

Kendra and Katelyn just stood there looking at each other as they started to cry. They held onto each other for quite a bit before they settled on the couch. They could feel the Reiki energy surrounding them and helping them to stay calm and balanced. Katelyn could feel the vibration and heat from her crystal she had in her pocket. It was reassuring and soothing.

The folks in The Store stayed there for quite a while longer figuring out how to take care of Jordan's farm while he was in the hospital. They set up a schedule for folks to take turns staying there during the night just to make sure nothing bad happened.

"So, our Katelyn is with The Magic Miss Cora?" Hal asked quietly.

"Yes, Hal, she is. Makes a body wonder if everyone around here has some connection with The Magic and all."

"Yup, it does make one wonder," Hal answered as others nodded their heads.

"Well, thanks for takin' care of Jordan's place. I'm gonna' stay here for a while. Go about your evenin' if ya' need to or visit here. Either way, we're all gonna' be thinkin' about Jordan," Miss Cora said as she sat quietly with her tea.

Folks came and went all evenin' to check on Jordan and the girls.

Jordan was in the recovery room. He was still unconscious but was holding on just fine. He became aware of a bright light in front of him. It changed to a soft blue color then a soft purple color. He liked the colors. They reminded him of his crystals.

He wasn't sure what made him try to move, but when he did, it hurt like hell. He tried to holler but something was in his mouth. He began to fight for air when he heard a woman's voice.

"Well, Jordan, looks like you're tryin' to wake up. Calm down. You're in the medical center in Boone. You had a bad accident and have been in the operating room for quite a while We put a breathing tube in your lungs to help you out. Try not to fight against it. Try to go with it. That's better. Now, when you wake up again, maybe we can take it out. Squeeze my hand if you can feel it and understand.

Jordan squeezed her hand, blinked his eyes a bit and fell back into unconsciousness. The nurse paged the surgeons and let them know he had woken up fighting the ventilator and understood her by squeezing her hand. This was more than any of them expected from Jordan. He was a major trauma case that usually didn't regain consciousness for a few days.

Dr. Beckwith went to Kendra and Katelyn and told them the good news. They called The Store and told everyone there. Folks finally began to calm down and head home. Miss Cora stayed for a bit with Emily and a few others to talk about things. Greg was pissed. He had planned that accident to make sure Jordan Jackson died. He almost did. But those White Lighters kept him alive. He had tried to kill him during surgery but someone in the operating room picked up on his energy and shoved him out of the area and surrounded the whole team with a protection grid. He knew The Magic in The Creek was strong but didn't think it went outside The Creek. This changed things. He would have to meet with his own kind now to come up with a new plan of attack.

CHAPTER 14

G reg got the word out. He called a meeting for late that night. It was nigh onto midnight when others began to arrive at the house one of his group had taken over. It was just west of Boone proper and had been abandon for years. It was a mess. Perfect for Greg's kind to use without any interference from the locals. Thing was, it was down a long dirt drive mostly hidden by trees and such.

As soon as everyone was in place, he began.

"Well, looks like our work just got harder. Those folks in The Creek have some protective powers. Looks like Jordan's become aware of his powers and has been learning about them a bit from Kendra secretly. We need to work on how we're gonna' kill him and take his powers for The Dark. Afterall, that's what The Dark hired us to do. Right?

Everyone agreed.

"Ah, Greg, can we morph back into our own selves? This human form is a lot to deal with," one of the others asked.

"Sure," Greg replied as he changed back into his ET self.

Others morphed back into their original selves in no time.

They were ugly as hell. The all stood about seven feet tall with a pot belly. They were the color of brown diarrhea and pea soup mixed into swirls. They had wrinkles on their torsos in distinct patterns for each ET. The torso had antennae-like things that would appear and disappear at will. Their arms and legs were wrinkled as well. The arms had three finger-like digits about six inches long with suction cups on the tips. The legs had rectangle-shaped feet with no toes.

Their heads were oblong from top to neck, if you could call that thing under their heads a neck. It was more like a roll of fat and skin that the head sat on. The faces were strange looking. They had three eyes with one in the middle at the top of the forehead area. A second and third eye each at the sides of the head about half way down just a bit off from the front of the face. Kinda' like in the front of the human ear area on the sides. All of the eyes worked separately from each other.

Their round nose was set into the face as if it had been punched in. Their mouths were the shape of an upside-down triangle set at the very bottom of the face in what would be the human chin area. When they talked, the triangle protruded from the face into a tube thing and the edges of the triangle bulged out and turned black.

They had a tongue that split into two when it came out of the mouth. Each piece went its own way.

"Well, Greg," one of them started laughing, "why this Jordan human? What's so special about him other than he has some of The Magic we want?"

"Well, dude," Greg answered, laughing as well because the ETs were using human names and words to talk with each other and they found the human language ridiculous, "The Dark thinks he is connected to something really powerful: Old Magic. Magic from the beginning of Magic. Its power is immeasurable and the strongest in all the galaxies. It would make The Dark so powerful that no White Lighter could survive. That's why."

"Is Jordan connected to this power? Does he even know about it?" another ET asked.

"No. Not yet. The Dark thinks he doesn't know about it 'cause he's the newest member of The Creek. The Dark hasn't gotten that powerful Magic from anyone else so he figures this Jordan guy probably has it. We all know how strong that Magic is. But, it's not necessarily Jordan that we want. We want The Magic The Dark thinks is near him somewhere. So, let's get started and figure out a way to end this Jordan guy and take his Magic and The Magic from the land or wherever it is and find the all-powerful Old Magic, too."

They talked well into the night but did not have a solid plan. One of the newer ETs asked Greg how things had been done in past battles. Greg explained it like this.

"Well, young one, there have been a number of times The Dark has had to destroy planets and such to keep its own power from being taken by The White Light. Battles throughout the universes and galaxies have been fought so The Dark could take The Magic and become all powerful.

"When this planet was in one of its early changing stages, very early on in its formation, it was a massive continent called Pangea. The Magic of the planet was held in mountains that had been formed over millennia through volcanic eruptions and ice ages. The Magic was the most powerful in the galaxy and when The Dark found this planet, it tried to take The Magic for itself. No matter what it did, The Magic was held protected in those mountains. So,

The Dark decided to break up the continent hoping to grab The Magic as it was exposed.

"Pangea was ripped apart and The Magic was held in those mountains no matter what The Dark did. The mountain range that had been Pangea broke apart into several ranges settling around the globe. The Appalachian Mountains are the oldest on this part of the old Pangea and hold powerful magic that has grown stronger and stronger. The Dark still wants this Magic for itself.

"Other times since Pangea include the eruption of Mount Vesuvius. It held powerful Magic as well and the local humans were there to protect it. The Dark tried and tried to take that Magic over time but it just couldn't break the hold that mountain had on the Magic. The Dark kept trying to get the Magic in all the mountain ranges across the planet but failed every time. The Dark lay quiet for the longest time. The Dark decided to blow up Mount Vesuvius and take that powerful Magic. The earth and people were destroyed in Pompeii but The Magic was protected."

"It wasn't until the humans had gotten around to discovering steam energy and such that The Dark decided to try again in a big way. It had been messing with the humans for a long time by making them distrust each other and fight about it. There had been many wars and now The Dark decided to escalate things. He put the thought about a pure human race into the heads of several men but only one took the bait. Adolf Hitler agreed to work for The Dark in exchange for ruling the world. The Dark helped him to gather many men and women to work with him to take over the world starting in the countries around him and then expanding around the globe. That was his plan.

"He did get really far. He decided the Jewish peoples were a threat to him and ordered all of them killed because he believed they held a lot of The Magic. It was a great time. So many humans were killed and Hitler went on to take control of a large part of the area known as Europe. But he was stopped. The Light fought hard to defeat The Dark and The Light eventually won. Unfortunately, The Magic was never taken by The Dark.

"The Dark kept the wars going and, from time-to-time, it tried to cause more volcanoes to explode to release the Magic they held. The Dark did make some of those volcanoes explode, but if there was any Magic hidden in them, The Light protected it and The Dark got nothing."

"Well, what about now? Are we supposed to get The Magic in The Creek as well as the Old Magic?" one of the older ETs asked.

"As a matter of fact, yes!" Greg answered.

"How we gonna' do that?" they all asked at the same time.

"Well, that's what we're all here for. To think up a way to make that happen. The accident didn't work. It would have been the easiest thing because I could have grabbed The Magic the instant he died. But that damn White Light protected him. I tried to kill him in the operating room, but some of the people in there picked up on my energy and blocked it. He's now surrounded by The White Light and Reiki energy is healing him so I can't get to him for the time being. I was thinking of us working on a plan to take him down on his farm as soon as he can walk alone. He likes to walk the field and all."

"That's a good idea," the older ET said.

"So, now we need to think about how to make this happen," Greg said.

They talked for a bit longer before one of the ETs noticed the sky beginning to lighten.

"It's time we morphed back and got busy as humans again," Greg ordered.

In an instant, they were all human again.

"Keep thinking up ideas and send them along as we always do. We still have our powers even in this form," Greg ordered them.

They all left as the sun peeked over the horizon. The Dark was not happy. Greg's ETs had done exactly what The Dark had ordered so it couldn't find fault with them. The Dark decided to do some damage to the Blue Ridge and gather what Magic it could. Later that day it set up severe storms to wreak havoc over the whole of the Blue Ridge mountains.

Kendra and Emily didn't sleep well that night. Kendra called Emily first thing the next morning.

"Hey, Kendra, you feel it, too?" was the way Emily answered the phone.

"Sure do. Not good, either,' Kendra replied.

"Come on over. I'll fix us some breakfast."

"Great idea. I'll be right over," Kendra said as she walked out to her SUV and drove away. She was at Emily's in short time.

"Jesus, it smells fabulous in here," Kendra said as she set her things down and walked over to Emily. "Looks yummy!"

"Why, thanks so much, Miss Kendra. How about you get the coffee stuff and pour us a mug full while I set the food on the table?"

"Done," Kendra said as they met at the table and started in on a real country breakfast. "It's been a long time since I had a real farmer's breakfast. This is Fabulous!"

"Me, too. That's why I decided to make all this stuff. I woke up earlier than usual with all this weird stuff and that energy shift thing goin' on. So, I knew you must be feelin' it as well and you know the rest."

"Yup, I agree. I think we'll be seein' Miss Cora any minute now," Kendra said as they heard someone walkin' along the porch towards the kitchen door.

"You got that right," Miss Cora said laughing as she walked into the kitchen and sat down at the table. "I see you're already for me."

"Yes, Ma'am, we are. Help yourself," Emily offered as she poured Miss Cora her cup of tea.

"Much obliged Emily," Miss Kendra said.

They enjoyed their breakfast talking about The Creek, the summer people, the folks all around and the usual things spoken about when visiting with close friends.

Once breakfast was cleared, they got down to the business at hand.

"Well, seems the three of us had a restless night. I was thinkin' it was 'cause of Jordan but I think there's somethin' else goin' on here," Emily offered.

"I agree," Kendra added. "When I did dose off, I had some weird dreams. No, they weren't visions. They were dreams. Bits and pieces of life here in The Creek, old dreams, news stories, and such."

"Me, too," Miss Cora agreed. "It was a mish-mash of stuff as if my mind couldn't decide on what to tell me. Not much sleep either."

Ethan showed up just then and was welcomed in.

"Hey, ladies," he said as he took his hat off. "I figured the three of you'd be here so I took a chance and wandered over."

"Ya' look like ya' got somethin' to say, Ethan. Tell us about it," Miss Cora said as Ethen sat down at the table and Emily brought him a mug of coffee.

"Thanks, Em," Ethan started. "Well, Katelyn talked to the hospital early this mornin' and Jordan's comin' along. She said they were gonna' remove the breathin' tube as he was awake and not happy with the thing."

"That's a good sign," Miss Cora said.

"Thought you'd all want to know about that. Well, when Jonah and I went over to the farm just after the accident, we found most things good. The eagles were flyin' around as if they were lookin' for somethin'. I thought maybe they were lookin' for Jordan, so I asked Jonah what we should do. He said we should talk to the eagles and tell them Jordan was okay. So, I agreed with Jonah and he stood really quiet in the middle of the barn as if he were sending thoughts out to the eagles. All of a sudden, they all returned to the barn and perched on the main cross beam. All of them. The little ones were flyin' too. A bit off balance but they seemed to be getting the hang of it.

"Anyways, once they settled Jonah looked right at the male and quietly said, 'Jordan's alright. He was hurt really bad, but we got to him and he's gonna' be away for a bit. He'll be back in a week or so. Just wanted to let ya' know in case you was worried about him. Ya' seem to be agitated some with all this flyin' in and outta' the barn. So, The Magic here is protectin' him and we folks are takin' care of the farm and all. He'll have lots of folks around him once he gets home to help and all.' We stood real quiet for a bit watching the eagles when, all of a sudden, the male, then the female, flew over us and each one dropped a tail feather at our feet. Now, Jonah knows ya' don't touch an eagle feather unless you're a chief or shaman. So, he called the chiefs and they came right over.

"Both of them looked at the feathers and then offered prayers of thanks in their own languages to the eagles. When they were finished, a beam of sunlight, or what we thought was sunlight, shown on the feathers. As we looked at that beam of light, we realized it wasn't comin' from the sun. It was from a crystal set up high on one of the smaller cross beams in a corner of the barn. How it got up there nobody knows. Don't even try to figure this one out. So, the chiefs bowed to the eagles and then reached down and picked up the feathers. They offered thanks again in English and the eagles bobbed their heads at us. All four of them.

"The chiefs turned to Jonah and placed the feathers in his hands. He was real surprised.

"Chief Running Bear said, 'These are for Jordan. Would you see that he gets them real soon? They should be placed with some sage and lavender in a clear vase. That's the message I'm getting from the eagles and the Great Spirit. This is a sacred moment.'

"Chief Soaring Eagle added, 'The presentation of eagle feathers is a sacred moment. Only those that the Great Spirit is connected to and protects are given this gift. Jordan must be real special for the eagles and the Great Spirit to give this gift. I am honored to be a part of this.' He bowed to the eagles, raised his hands above his head, then bowed to the four directions. Chief Running Bear did the same. Jonah and I were speechless. The energy was so strong and protective and positive and, oh, I don't really know how to explain it. It was beyond incredible."

"Did Jonah take the feathers and all over to Jordan yet?" Miss Cora asked.

"Yes, Miss Cora. Last evenin'. He was in and out of consciousness. The nurse wasn't gonna' let Jonah in, but, all of a sudden, she looked at him and the feathers and showed him to Jordan's room. Jonah says he placed the vase next to the bed and he swears he heard a humming sound comin' from the vase. He told Jordan he was there and had brought him a gift from the eagles. Jordan tried to open his eyes then calmed down again. Jonah thanked the nurse and left."

They all sat there for a minute in their own thoughts.

"Well, I need to be getting along. Lots of inspections today. Thanks for the coffee, Emily," Ethan said as he stood up.

"Thanks for tellin' us about Jonah and all. That's real special Magic for sure," Miss Cora said.

Ethan left and the three talked about this news. It was great news for sure. But it also explained some of the change in the energy in The Creek they had been feeling throughout the night.

"So, that does help explain why the energy is changing. Seems the eagles are workin' at protecting Jordan and The Creek, too. And, that The Dark is tryin' to get at The Magic, again."

"I agree, Miss Cora," Emily and Kendra said at the same time.

"I don't think it's all about Jordan but he's part of a bigger thing. I'm thinkin' that some other folks that have a closeness with the land are gonna' be bothered. We better think about this for a bit."

They spent about an hour making a list of the folks in The Creek that had a strong connection with the land. It included Matthews and Jenna, Hal, Finn and his family, Katelyn's family, Bubba and Earl, and Mo and Laine.

"Now, how do we help protect them?" Emily started.

"I was just thinkin' about that," Kendra answered.

All of a sudden, the digital alert sounded on Emily's phone. She grabbed the phone and starred at it.

"Well, what's that all about?" Miss Cora asked.

"I don't really understand this. I have the weather alert set to go off if any type of bad weather is forecast for The Creek. It has never gone off before."

"Is it for all bad weather?" Kendra asked.

"Yes, year-round. It shows a line of severe thunderstorms are forecast to hit the area beginning around mid-afternoon, say three o'clock and keep going throughout the night. This is really strange. We rarely get severe storms around here. We do get some good old-fashioned thunderstorms sometimes, usually in the spring. But it's the middle of the summer. And, are ya' ready for this? They're forecasting a strong likelihood of tornados here."

"What? Now that's just plain strange," Miss Cora said as she walked out onto the front porch and looked westward. The sky was pure blue with only a wisp of a cloud drifting by.

"And," Emily added, "Looks like this warning is for all of the Blue Ridge. All of it. Tennessee and everywhere in the Blue Ridge."

"Now, that's just wrong. I'm thinkin' The Dark has somethin' to do with this. This has never happened before in all of the Blue Ridge at the same time. We better get prepared and let folks know about this," Miss Cora said.

They returned to the kitchen table and created a plan. Then they set about calling folks, starting with The Store.

"Hey, Emily," Michael answered the phone.

"Hey, Michael. Miss Cora and Kendra and I have come across some severe weather warnings for the area. Have you seen them yet?"

Just then, Ted came running from the kitchen waving his phone and yelling at Michael. "Michael, looks like we're gonna' have some bad weather this afternoon. Tornados and all. We just don't have this kinda' weather here."

"Ted, Emily just called to tell us about it. Keep talkin' Emily," Michael said as he shushed Ted.

'Hey, Ted. We were just talking about stuff and the weather alert on my phone went off. I couldn't believe it either, Ted. We got a plan and a phone tree thing goin'. Kendra and Miss Cora are callin' folks and warning them to get ready and all. If y'all would put a notice on the door and such and send a Creek-wide email out, we think that would get to folks in time to protect them and all. I'm sure once they hear about this, they're gonna' get a hold of friends and family all over the Blue Ridge to warn them of the bad weather. Not everyone listens to the radio and such."

"Great plan, ladies," Ted said. "How about we tell folks if they don't have a basement or root cellar they can come here? We have a basement the size of the whole place so we can take in lots of folks."

"Great idea, Ted. Hold on while I tell Kendra and Miss Cora."

"Okay, they're getting the word out. Thanks for takin' folks in. You two are mighty special,' Kendra added.

"Well, ya' know Miss Kendra, we gotta' take care of each other. That's how most of us think," Michael said.

"I know and that's one of the things that makes The Creek so special," Kendra added,

"Okay. Get busy boys. We'll keep goin' here," Miss Cora said.

It took just a few minutes to get the message about the bad weather out to all of The Creek.

The Dark was not happy with this. It had planned on the element of surprise to destroy as much of the Blue Ridge as possible and snatch The Magic that would surely be exposed as the earth was destroyed. The Dark still had the element of surprise in knowing just when and where the damage would be done. Who said you needed a thunderstorm for a tornado to appear? The weather would be under the control of The Dark. Or so it thought.

Weather alerts were sent out across the land by all kinds of weather systems. Radio, local television, smart phones and word-of-mouth were kept busy. The National Weather Service, known as the NWS, sent out a severe thunderstorm warning and a tornado watch for the whole of the Blue Ridge around one o'clock. Media folks were saying they had never seen anything like this before.

It was late July and the Blue Ridge was chocked full of visitors. Hundreds of thousands of people were camping, hiking, day-tripping and such. Summer camps were full of kids of all ages. Thanks to the NWS, folks were getting ready for the possibility of bad weather. Some of the long-time residents of the Blue Ridge didn't take the warnings seriously. They'd been around a long time and figured they knew better.

That's just what The Dark was counting on.

The first tornado hit a small tiny town in Tennessee, Tellico Plains. The Dark decided to obliterate the town just 'cause it could. At two o'clock a tornado formed out of a somewhat cloudy sky that normally wouldn't even support one rain drop. It touched down on the southern edge of the tiny town and proceeded to destroy every building in the village. Nothing was left standing. Anyone in the immediate area was killed. The tornado took out a few farms northeast of the town before dissipating back into a clear blue sky.

Of the approximately 880 people of Tellico Plains, only 200 were left alive. And, a few hundred more visitors in the area were killed as well.

The NWS didn't even have time to activate the tornado warning system. It was horrible! There was debris and dead bodies everywhere. The county sent in police and fire to get a grip on the situation. Police asked for national guard help, sending pictures of the damage to state officials. Volunteer fire fighters showed up from neighboring towns to help as well.

The Dark was ecstatic about all the people it had killed.! It had taken a tiny bit of Magic before it was blocked by The White Light. The Dark wanted all The Magic. It was pissed. Time to strike again.

This time The Dark sent a severe thunderstorm to the towns of Thomas and Davis in West Virginia. They were close neighbors that had been founded when coal mining got started in the area. The sky began to darken around two-thirty and within ten minutes the rain came pouring down. Then the wind whipped up blowing anything that wasn't tied down all over the place. As the sky turned pitch black, the lightning came forth. It struck trees, splitting them in half and blowing others to smithereens, causing debris to break windows. Lightning struck buildings, starting fires. The thunder was so loud you couldn't hear a thing. Many folks had gone underground thanks to the warnings. A few were caught outside and The Dark had fun with them. First, it caused downpours, then the wind came so strong, they couldn't stand up. They were blown down, some were injured while others were blown onto fences with spikes, killing them instantly. Some were taken into the air and thrown against brick buildings, killing them as well.

The Dark targeted some folks that were inside watching the storm through their windows. It sent lightning into one home, killing the whole family. Lightning kept striking, blowing up buildings and destroying cars and trucks. When most of the two towns were destroyed, The Dark stopped the storm and watched as people found their loved ones dead and most everything else destroyed. It took more Magic, a tiny bit again, as The White Light protected most of The Magic.

The White Light Paladins gathered as they saw what The Dark was doing to the earth people and the earth. They immediately set up a protective grid around all of the Blue Ridge to stop The Dark from taking any more Magic and destroying any more people.

The Dark targeted the town of Boone next as it was next to The Creek. At the same time as it started wreaking havoc in Boone, it hit Snow Creek, VA, Greenville, SC, Dawsonville, GA, Walkersville, MD, and Blue Ridge Summit, PA. It sent tornado after tornado to all these places and more, coming one after the other at the same time it sent an F5 to Boone.

Weather alarms were going off all over the Blue Ridge. Folks were running for cover. Most made it into shelters before the storms and tornados hit. Some of the older folks in the Boone area couldn't believe their eyes when they looked out at the darkening sky that was turning all different kinda' colors. They had never seen anything like it before. Some made it into shelter and some did not. The White Light protected those that were left outside. It lifted them up and took them to a place of calm and quiet in a different dimension to wait for the storms to pass. They didn't know where they were and what was happening to them. Some thought they had died and gone into heaven. They just sat there, not knowing what to do.

Meanwhile, the skies around Boone kept turning colors as the F5 tornado started to form. It came from the sky on the southwestern edge of town as a thin little vortex. The minute it touched down, it grew so fast, the weather folks didn't know what to think. It was at least a mile wide in a wedge shape and it was ripping up everything in its path. It had just reached the edge of town when it stopped moving. The Dark sent more energy to it but it wouldn't budge. All the folks watching this on weather radar screens had never seen a tornado stop dead in its tracks and stay alive. It was as if it had hit a wall or something.

The Dark was angry. It threw more energy at the tornado, but the White Light held its ground. As the battle between The Dark and The Light carried on, The Dark decided to strike The Creek. All of a sudden, the F5 in Boone dissipated and disappeared. The sky returned to blue and you couldn't tell a massive storm had been there a minute before. The only sign that anything might have happened was a long stretch of ground, a field, was torn up for about a half-mile. That's all.

The Creek saw the sky darken and knew the storm had arrived. Emily, Miss Cora and Kendra were at The Store in the basement with most of the folks in The Creek. They felt a sudden shift in energy and knew The Dark had arrived. Outside, The Dark started by sending lightening all over the Blue Ridge. Every state had lightning strikes and fires going. Lightening set many parts of the forest on fire as well throughout the Appalachia's. Emergency services decided to hunker down until the worst was over before going out to help.

The White Light Paladins had surrounded The Creek with a special protection grid. The Dark found out about this protection grid when it sent lightning to hit The Store and it was stopped in mid-air. The Dark sent another bolt, stronger this time, and it was stopped in mid-air, too. The Dark got angry and sent one tornado after another and they were all stopped in mid-air as well. They just hung there, twirling in place.

This made The Dark wicked angry. It howled and that howl was heard by everyone in The Creek, no matter where they were. Ethan looked at Ian and Finn. They were in their basement under the shop.

"What the hell was that?" Ian and Finn said at the same time.

"I don't rightly know," Ethan replied as another howl was heard.

"It doesn't sound like a wolf. Too loud and deep a growl. It doesn't sound like a tree hit by lightning, either. Ya' know how that can sound."

"I don't rightly know, but, damn, there it goes again. Good thing we're down here," Ethan said. They sat there listening to the wind and the howling.

Emily, Kendra, and Miss Cora knew what that sound was. Katelyn looked at the three of them saying, "It's not good, is it?"

Kendra put an arm around Katelyn. "No, it's not. It's The Dark. Seems like The White Light is protecting The Creek and the Dark is angry about it. Listen to that howlin'."

Kendra had been talking so only Katelyn could hear her. "Let's keep real quiet about this. Don't want to scare anyone."

"I agree. Is there anything we can do to help The White Light?" Katelyn asked as another howl physically hit The Store.

"Yes," Miss Cora answered. "Those of us with Gifts can send positive energy to the Universe to help it fight The Dark. Just set up a mantra and keep repeating it as long as you feel it's needed."

"Done," Katelyn said as she closed her eyes and began chanting, sending positive energy to the Universe. Some of the other folks saw what she was doing and joined in.

Now that the Dark had shown its hand in trying to destroy people and the earth to steal The Magic in the Blue Ridge, The White Light got busy blocking The Dark's efforts.

The first thing The White Light did was to set up a reflective kind of energy everywhere The Dark was causing problems. It acted like a mirror of sorts. Whenever The Dark sent a storm to an area, The White Light set up the reflective mirror energy grid and the storm blew back into The Dark, destroying a bit of The Dark and blocking it from taking any Magic.

The first few times this happened, The Dark didn't know what was happening. It was pissed at losing its power. It didn't figure anything out until it was ready to strike Knoxville, TN. It decided to throw another F5 tornado, this time directly at the city, but it never got there. Instead, the energy that formed the tornado was thrown back at The Dark and it lost a lot of its power this time. Thing is, once The Dark loses power to The White Light, it can never get it back.

When this happened in Knoxville, The Dark screamed out so strongly, that windows were shattered across a hundred-mile-wide radius. The Dark knew it was defeated and finally gave up. It couldn't afford to lose any more power to The White Light. It gathered all the storms back into itself and left the earth plane…for a while. It would be back.

The folks in The Store basement felt the quiet come upon them. Ted took a look out from the top of the stairs. The sun was shining like it was just another summer day. He told the others and they all came upstairs and went outside to have a look.

The sky was perfectly blue. The sun was shining like always. Nothing looked damaged. As folks looked around, they all came to a stop as they looked across the way. In the meadow just as the road heads down to Pine Ridge, was a welcome sign. It read: Grandaddy Mimm's Moonshine Distillery, Blairsville, GA. It was standing right up like it had been placed there. It was a bit worn just like a good ole' sign should be.

Miss Cora was laughing along with most everyone else.

Hal offered, "Well, looks like we got us a new sign. Wonder what Bubba and Earl are gonna' think about this?"

Folks laughed even more, thinkin' about Bubba and Earl seein' the sign and all.

"I don't think they'll be worried. Probably laugh like the rest of us. Wonder how that thing got here?" Sally Mae said.

"Probably came along with the tornados and all. Strange stuff like that happens." Hal offered.

"Well, I think I'm gonna' take a few pictures and give Grandaddy Mimm's place a call. They're probably wonderin' what happened to their sign," Michael said laughing the whole time.

Everyone agreed and couldn't wait to hear the phone call. They all gathered on the porch and waited for Michael to come back out.

"Okay. Got the number right here. Let's see if anyone answers."

Michael dialed and waited while the phone rang. It was answered right away.

"Grandaddy Mimm's. How can we help ya?" A woman answered.

"Howdy. My name's Michael and I live in Crab Apple Creek, North Carolina. We've had some crazy weather today and when we came up from the basement, we found somethin' that might just belong to y'all."

"Well, hey Michael. This here is Laura Ann. We've had some crazy weather as well. Folks around here are cleaning up right now. So, what do ya' think you have that might belong to us here at Grandaddy Mimm's?"

"Well, how about I send y'all a picture. It speaks quite well on its own."

"Sure thing. This here is my cell number so send it along."

"Here ya' go," Michael said as he sent the pictures he had taken. One was with everyone gathered around the sign.

"Well, holy cow," Laura Ann said laughing and calling out to some folks in her place. "I do believe that does belong here. Look Joey, it's our sign. Did ya' look outside yet?"

"Not yet. Just heading out now. Yup, that's our sign. Let me go look outside," Joey said.

Joey was right back. "Yup, our sign's gone. How in the blue blazes did it get all the way up to y'all in North Carolina?"

You could hear other folks laughing and talking about the sign in Grandaddy Mimm's place.

"Well, seems the wind storms might have sailed it up our way. That's what we're thinkin' here."

"Sounds like a good explanation," Joey agreed.

"So, just where is your place? We're about thirty miles northwest of Boone in the Blue Ridge."

"We're in the upper northeastern corner of Georgia. real close to Kentucky and South Carolina in the Blue Ridge. Guess that makes us cousins a few times removed."

"Sure does," Miss Cora hollered. Folks laughed at this.

"Well, what would you like us to do with your sign? This here is Ted," Ted asked.

"Hey Ted, and everyone else. I tell ya' what I'm thinking. This here is Billy Townsend, grandson to Tommy Townsend who sort of took over the business my great grandaddy Mimm started during the Depression. As for the sign, well, I guess it would be really expensive to get it back here. So, how about this? Y'all can keep it as a reminder of today's storms. Sure did travel a long ways and it looks real good. Take a bunch more pictures of it, some with y'all, too, and send them along. I'm feelin' a story comin' on about that sign. We'll put a picture of it up here at the distillery and add it to the history of the place. How's that sound?"

"Hey Billy, this is Michael here. We love the whole idea. We'll get busy and send our story along with the pictures and all."

"Great! What a crazy day for sure. Y'all take care now," Laura Ann said.

"We will. Y'all do the same. Nice talking to everyone," Michael as he hung up.

Folks set a spell on the porch talking about the sign and the day. It was getting close to supper and some folks got take-out and some folks stayed.

The folks in Blairsville shared a sip or two of shine while they were talking about their sign ending up in The Creek.

Ethan and Finn showed up as folks were heading home with their take-out.

"Hey, Michael. See we have a new sign on the road." Ethan said as he headed up to the dining area.

"We sure do. All the way from Blairsville, GA. Seems the wind delivered it a little while ago," Ted said as he headed back into the kitchen.

"Does it have a story?" Finn asked as he joined Ethan at the table.

The group in The Store filled Ethan and Finn in on the details of the sign.

"That's really wild," Finn said laughing along with everyone.

"Hey, how about I make a kind of frame for it? The guys and I will set about makin' sure it's secure in the ground and all," Ethan offered.

"Sounds great."

"Good idea."

"Good thinkin', Ethan."

"I think, to start, it should be set back a ways from the road, just in case someone decides to drive off-road, if ya' get my drift," Finn offered.

"Now, that's right smart thinkin' Finn," Miss Cora said as she joined them.

"Hey, Miss Cora," both Finn and Ethan said at the same time.

"Boys. I like your ideas. Sound thinkin'. How about some supper Ted?"

"Yes, Ma'am. Anything you'd like. Just let me know. You two, too," Ted replied.

They gave Ted their orders and settled in.

Ted came back in a few minutes with everyone's dinner. The place was crowded as is usual after any kind of unexpected event in The Creek. Emily, Kendra and Katelyn were already seated when Ethan and Finn arrived. Finn sat down between Katelyn and Emily.

"Hey Katelyn. Crazy day," Finn said as he nodded to everyone else.

"Sure has been and I'd be mighty happy if it never happened again," Katelyn responded as others agreed.

"Ted, this is delicious as always," Miss Cora said.

"Thanks, Ma'am. Y'all know how much I love to cook," Ted said.

"Anyone have any damage to their places today?" Ethan asked.

"None here," Michael replied.

"I'll have to check the farm when I get home," Emily said.

"I spoke with Jonah a bit ago. He says Jordan's place is okay. A few small sticks were blown around earlier today and the stables are good at your place. No damage at my place, either," Ethan said.

"Well, I do believe this storm thing was nothin' like I've seen before," Miss Cora added.

"Wonder if climate change had anything to do with it?" Jenna offered.

"Well, that's a possibility for sure. I wonder if this all had somethin' to do with The Magic around here." Katelyn said. "I'm learnin' real fast about how things happen here that don't happen other places. So, I just wonder if it has to do with The Magic in The Creek."

"Now, Katelyn, I do believe you've got somethin' there," Kendra agreed with Katelyn.

"Wow! I never thought of that," Jenna said. "I called Matthews and he says everything is good at his place."

"Looks like folks are checkin' in with each other. That's a good thing," Miss Cora said.

Cell phones began to buzz while others called to check on folks. After a bit, word was that there was no damage in The Creek or anywhere around the area. The flatscreens were on in the main part of The Store and reports were comin' in from all around the Blue Ridge.

"Hey, everyone, I'm gonna' turn this on in here even though we usually don't have it on. But, ya' gotta' see these reports. They're unbelievable," Michael said as he turned on the flatscreens in the dining area. Folks set their chairs so they could watch the reports.

They watched report after report about the damage to towns all across the Blue Ridge.

"This is so sad. All those people killed by the weather," Jenna said as the reports finally ended and Michael turned off the flatscreens.

"We hear about such things from a storm or two once in a while, but not all at once like this and all over the place. Not just one place. This is tragic," Katelyn added.

"Well, I'd better be getting home. I think we should all say a prayer or two for those folks and be thankful we have been protected this time. Night all," Miss Cora said as Ethan walked her out to her truck.

"Ethan, ya' know this was all caused by The Dark, don't 'cha?" Miss Cora said as she sat in her truck.

"I do believe it was, Miss Cora and that scares me. Just what is The Dark up to this time? Seems it's unusually angry about somethin'. And, I do believe that accident of Jordan's was by The Dark as well. We need to figure this out right away before anyone or anywhere gets hurt or killed."

"You're right Ethan. I think I'll spend some time tomorrow thinkin' about all this. I'll get back to ya' when I know anything. Now, take care and be real careful. Okay?"

"Yes, Ma'am," Ethan said as he leaned in and kissed Miss Cora's cheek. "So glad we have you here in The Creek with us. You are loved and appreciated."

"Why, thanks Ethan. Bye-bye," Miss Cora said as she drove away.

Others were taking their leave from The Store as well and good-byes were hollered out.

"Katelyn, how about you come over for a chat in a few minutes?" Kendra suggested as the two of them walked across the road waving to Ted and Michael.

"Sure. I'd like that. See you in a few," Katelyn replied.

As Katelyn and Kendra settled on the porch, Katelyn began the chat with, "So, what gives? What the hell was today all about? And, I know it was all the doing of The Dark. I could feel the raw hate from early afternoon until it stopped over The Creek."

"Well, I guess I don't need to ease into this conversation. You're right. It was The Dark. Every bit of it. Seems somethin' is brewin' and it looks like The Dark is targeting The Creek again. Just when one battle ends, we think we can relax and breathe. But, no! The Dark is unrelenting in trying to take The Magic for itself."

"Nasty bastard!" Katelyn said.

"Indeed. So, this is going to be a shorter evening than I thought. So glad you're workin' on your Gifts. You've come a long way in a short time. Now, about Jordan's accident," Kendra began.

"Oh my God! I wanted to tell ya' what I saw when we were at the site but everything was so bad and Jordan needed to get to the hospital and all," Katelyn interrupted Kendra. "Sorry, you were sayin'?"

"No. Go right ahead, please," Kendra said with a laugh.

"Okay then. Well, when they were cutting the truck apart and liftin' Jordan from the wreck, I thought I saw somethin' movin' around the backside of the truck. I looked and saw a dark shadowy thing hoverin' over the truck like it was tryin' to block the rescue workers from getting Jordan out. I knew it was evil so I called on The White Light to surround us all and that shadowy thing just popped into a million pieces and disappeared. Gone. It was The Dark, right?"

"Yes, Katelyn, it was. Good call and great job calling for help. Well done. I saw it, too, and was about to do what you did, but you beat me to it."

"Whew. So glad I didn't second guess myself. After that basement monster Jenna and I were attacked by, I decided that if I ever got the feelin' that evil was around, I would just call out for help and think about it all later."

"I like your game plan. So, I know you went to see Jordan this morning. Ethan told me. How is he?"

"Well, he got the breathin' tube out just before I arrived. They do things real early there. Anyway, he was trin' to talk a bit. His voice was a bit raspy when he finally did say hey. I teased him sayin' I liked his raspy sexy voice. He smiled. We talked just a little 'cause I could tell he was hurtin'. I told him the farm was in great shape and he said Jonah had been by when he was still a mess and he heard him say so. I told Jordan I'd come by tomorrow and check in on him. He liked that and said to say thanks to everyone for sending the love and that he could feel waves of it goin' through him."

"I'll let everyone know what you said. Now, why Jordan? Why did The Dark attack Jordan?"

"Damn good question. I know we're all connected to The Magic in The Creek even if we don't have any Gifts. But I can't come up with any reason The Dark would want to kill Jordan. Oh no. No way! Say it ain't so Kendra."

"I can see from the look on your face that you've figured it out already. Jordan has a strong connection with The Magic around here for sure. I'm not sure he has any Gifts. So, I'm thinkin' it must be the land he's on."

"Wow! I never thought it out that far. Wonder if the eagles setting up their nest in his barn has anything to do with it? Maybe they're there as a protection thing."

"Could be. And, why we're on the subject of his land, I bet 'cha those crystals have somethin' to do with all this, too."

"Oh my God! I know you're right. They didn't even start to show up until he bought the land. Then, wham! He's got a bunch of them. And, they showed up like someone had just set them on the ground, waiting to be found by Jordan. This is all startin' to make some sense," Katelyn offered.

They sat there thinking for a minute or two.

Then Katelyn said, "I wonder if Jordan has any idea about all this Magic stuff on his place?"

"Oh, Katie girl, I do know Jordan is aware of The Magic in The Creek. He knows that those crystals were no accident, too. I bet he's been wonderin' what they're all about as much as the rest of us."

"Probably so. Just wonderin' about the land, though. What could be so special about the land?"

"Well, the Blue Ridge do hold most of The Magic here on the earth. There must be special spots that have a direct connection to all the universes. I know you weren't here for the battle in The Holler, but The Dark chose that spot to hold its dark energy while it tried to take The Magic. Didn't work as you know. The White Light sent it into the spaces between the dimensions to be blocked for all time, so to speak."

"I agree. My folks told me a bit about that day and Finn has been fillin' me in on more of it as well as Emily and Miss Cora. Seems The Dark will do anything to take The Magic for itself. Fat chance! I keep thinkin' about Jordan's farm. All kinds of thoughts."

"Like what" Kendra asked as she leaned towards Katelyn.

"Well, could it be because it's a place where Magic gathers and kinda' waits until it's needed? Or, could it be because it's always been there through the millions of years since the earth was created like it is now? Or, maybe, it's a vortex that gathers The Magic to send it out as it's needed when the earth plane is damaged and people need its energy? I don't know. Just a bunch of thoughts."

"I've been thinkin' some of those exacts thoughts as well. Like the one about it always being in that place. Maybe it picked Jordan to live there 'cause he's a good guy and will protect the earth and all that live on it as a way of protecting The Magic."

Just then, a huge sunbeam shone directly on the porch. It was beautiful.

"Well, I think we got a sign from The White Light on our thoughts. Wicked cool!" Katelyn said as they watched the sunlight move around the porch and all.

"Agreed," Kendra said. "Now, how can we help Jordan stay safe and protect the earth and all?"

"Let's tell Miss Cora and Emily our thoughts and then set up a protection grid on the land with Jordan's approval, of course."

"Great idea. I'll call Emily and Miss Cora know on a group chat. How about you and I go out there tomorrow evenin' and set up the grid? You ask Jordan if it's okay tomorrow when you visit him. I'll get the things we'll need."

"Love this plan. Alright, I'll get along home now. I've got some things to do for tomorrow. Thanks for the talk," Katelyn said as they hugged and she went on home across the yard.

Kendra told Emily and Miss Cora their plan. They liked all the things Katelyn and Kendra had been talking about and agreed about Jordan's place. They would join the two of them the next evening to place the protection grid around the property.

Kendra next called Ethan to ask if she could borrow his gator to get them around on the property.

"Sure, Kendra. What's up?" Ethan asked.

"Well, Katelyn and I have been talkin' and thinkin' about why Jordan was targeted. I spoke with Miss Cora and Emily and they agree with what Katie and I have come up with. We believe there is powerful Magic on Jordan's farm and he's been chosen to protect the land and critters and all. So, tomorrow evening, the four of us are going to set up a protection grid around the edges of the property and your gator will help us get around."

"Great idea and I agree about The Magic in Jordan's land and all. I'll bring it over around six-thirty. Sound good?"

"Yes, it does. Katelyn is going to talk to Jordan in the morning to get his okay. Thanks Ethan."

"Y'all are very welcome. Let me know if I can do anything else."

"We will be performing a sacred ceremony so no need for you to stay unless you want to watch. Please don't tell anyone else though. I don't want a big group around just in case The Dark tries to keep us from completing the grid. It's been known to happen."

"No worries. I think I will stay with y'all just to help if things get crazy."

"Love the way ya' take care of us, Ethan," Kendra said.

"Gotta'. We need to take care of each other. See ya' tomorrow evenin'," Ethan said as he hung up.

"Same here, "Kendra replied.

The Creek settled in for the night as the stars shone brightly. This night was quiet.

CHAPTER 15

The next day found folks talking about the reports about the damage from the storms as they went about their daily business. Katelyn joined Kendra around six o'clock and they gathered the things they would need at Jordan's place. Jordan had readily agreed to the plan Katelyn told him about. He was thankful that folks were taking care of his place and all.

Kendra and Katelyn arrived just as Ethan pulled in. Miss Cora and Emily followed a few minutes later.

They all went into the barn to have a look at the eagles and offer a prayer of thanks for the eagle's living there.

When they were finished, Kendra explained how the ceremony would take place. They would start at the farthest eastern boundary, perform the sacred prayers and the giving back to Mother Earth of her quartz crystals. They would then proceed to the southern-most boundary, repeating the ceremony. Then the western-most boundary, repeating the ceremony with the last ceremony being at the northern-most boundary.

Kendra cautioned them all. "As we begin, there may be a slight breeze or rumbling sound as we put the crystals back into the earth. This will most likely increase as we set the next two areas. It's the northern boundary that may have the strongest reaction."

"How's that?" Ethan asked.

"Well, Ethan," Miss Cora explained. "The Dark doesn't like us to put up barriers that they can't cross no matter what. And, this protection grid is one of the strongest barriers The White Light has created. It covers all the earth deep to the core and a ways above the property as well. Each time we place the crystals they connect the energy. The more we place, the stronger the energy becomes as we connect from one direction to the next."

"I see," Ethan said. "Well, let's get busy then."

And, so, they started the protection grid ceremony.

As soon as they arrived at the eastern-most boundary of Jordan's property, a slight breeze came along. They all looked at each other as they began the chants and prayers. Ethan stood a bit away from the women out of respect for The Magic and all. As the crystals were placed back into the earth, the wind increased a lot and the sky began to get cloudy.

"Well, looks like The Dark knows just what we're up to," Miss Cora said as they got into the gator and headed for the next site.

They arrived at the southern-most boundary and began the ceremony. The sky continued to darken and when the crystals were placed into the earth, the ground shook a bit and a low growl was heard.

"Does that usually happen?" Ethan asked as they drove over to the western-most boundary.

"Yes, and it's about to get more intense," Kendra answered.

As they got out of the gator, the sky became pitch black, shooting lightning everywhere. The wind became stronger, blowing stuff around on the ground. The women had put hats on knowing this would happen. They didn't want anything to interfere with the sacred ceremony. Just as they dug the whole for the crystals, the ground shook violently, catching everyone off balance. They grabbed onto each other as Ethan stepped over to help them stay upright.

The growling became louder and as the crystals were placed this time, the wind screamed and continued to strengthen.

"Let's get to the last site as safely as possible," Kendra said. It took them an extra few minutes 'cause stuff was blowing all over the place. Twigs, branches, leaves and whatever wasn't tied down went swirling in the air.

Once again, as they stepped onto Mother Earth, the ground shook as if an earthquake was taking place. A strong one at that. They had to bend forward into the wind to keep their balance to get to the northern-most place.

As they had been placing the crystals at each of the other three boundaries, the power of the grid connected with each other and you could hear a low buzzing and see the what looked like electricity running back and forth between each direction.

As the prayers began, the wind screamed even louder and The Dark sent demons to try to scare the women and push them away. They all called on The White Light for protection and power and the women and Ethan were immediately engulfed in a brilliant white and purple kind of fog. As they continued the chants and prayers, The Dark tried everything to stop them from completing the grid. The demons it sent were horrible but they couldn't penetrate the fog. This made The Dark even madder. It sent an earthquake that should have toppled the whole area into a giant chasm, killing them all. But just at the quake was at its worst, the women, having to crawl to the opening they had made in Mother Earth to place the crystals, dropped their crystals and finished the chant all at the same time.

You could see the power connection of the grid become complete. A strong white light rope connected all the four directions, sending protection deep within the earth to far off into space.

The Dark was furious. It tried to kill them but it was stopped as if a roof of protection surrounded the place. The Dark sent bolts of lightning and flames but they were stopped by the grid.

They all stood there, regaining their balance and watching the light show. The Dark finally gave up and disappeared howling like a wounded animal. A very large wounded animal. The wind stopped and settled into the usual slight breeze of the night. The stars began to show as the dark clouds faded away and the quiet of the night came upon them.

"Ladies, I think we need to sit down for a bit," Ethan started to say as the women sat right down on the ground.

"Ethan, will ya' get us the water from the gator? We all need it right now," Kendra said.

Ethan was back in a second and they all drank a full bottle of water, each one of them. Kendra began calling on Reiki energy to heal them and everyone sat quiet for a bit.

Ethan was the first to speak. "Holy shit, Ma'am," he said as he nodded towards Miss Cora. "That was somethin' fierce."

"Yes, Ethan, it was. The Dark is a poor looser," Miss Cora replied.

"The property and anyone on the property are now all protected from The Dark. Period." Kendra explained.

"This is unbelievable. What a battle for sure," Katelyn said looking around the meadow. "Is it always this hard to place a protection grid?"

"Yes, usually. Sometimes it's even worse," Kendra answered.

"Boy, have I got a lot to learn," Katelyn replied as they heard a truck approaching.

It drove right over the meadow, stopped, and Finn jumped out.

"What the hell was all that?" he asked. "Sorry, Ma'am," he added as he saw Miss Cora.

"Thanks, Finn. No worries. It was a bit of a tug-of-war with The Dark. We set a protection grid and The Dark didn't like it. It had a bit of a temper tantrum."

"Well, I hope it's gone from here," Finn added looking at Kendra then Katelyn. She looked a bit shook up.

"It's gone for now," Kendra said as Finn walked over to Katelyn.

"You okay? You look a bit shook up," Finn said as he sat down next to her.

"I'm doin' alright. Really. It was just so intense," Katelyn said looking at the others then laughing a bit.

The others laughed along with her.

"That's one way to put it," Ethan agreed. They all sat there for a bit as the night deepened and the quiet surrounded them.

"Well, looks like it's getting late," Miss Cora said.

"I guess so. It's well onto ten o'clock," Kendra said.

"Ten o'clock? Really? I didn't realize we had been at it that long," Katelyn said in astonishment.

"Time seems to have a way of vanishing when we are in The Magic," Emily said.

"I guess so. Are we ready to get along?" Miss Cora asked.

They all agreed it was time to get home.

"Katelyn, how about I take you home? Ya' look a bit frazzled."

"Why thanks Finn. I'd like that," Katelyn replied.

They all said their good-nights and went on their way.

Katelyn and Finn walked into the kitchen and Katelyn went straight for the frig.

"I'm starvin'! That Magic stuff is hard work."

"I can see that. You still look a bit unsettled." Finn said as he walked up to her.

Katelyn set her food on the counter and turned to Finn. "I am. That was wicked scary."

Finn pulled Katelyn into his arms and held her close for the longest time. She melted right into him and sighed.

She finally pulled away apologizing with, "I sure do like the way you hold me, Finn. But I am really hungry. Help yourself."

Finn laughed and raided the frig while Katelyn warmed up her food and set at the table. He joined her a few minutes later.

They talked about The Creek while they ate, sharing stories of their work and family and friends.

As they finished cleaning up, Finn took Katelyn by the hand and led her to the couch.

"I do believe you need more holdin'," Finn said as he wrapped his arms around her and began to kiss her.

"I do, Mr. Finn" Katelyn replied as she kissed him back.

While their kisses deepened Finn began to explore Katelyn starting slowly by stroking her back ever so softly. She moaned and he moved to her sides and ran his fingers along her breasts. She responded by kissing Finn more deeply, exploring his mouth with her tongue.

141

Finn nodded towards the couch. Katelyn moved them to her bed.

Shoes and shirts came off as they tumbled onto the bed.

"I do like the way you move me," Finn said as he ran his fingertips along the lace of her bra.

"I do like the way you explore me," Katelyn said as she closed her eyes and moved into Finn.

Finn got the message as he bent and licked the mound of her breasts. She released the front clasp and Finn got busy exploring by running his tongue along her breast and, finally, the nipples.

Katelyn moaned in ecstasy and pushed Finn's mouth onto her breasts.

Finn quietly laughed as her took her lead and pulled her breast into his mouth and began sucking her.

She stroked his hair and ran her hands along his back again and again until she couldn't stand it anymore. He moved to her waist and undressed her the rest of the way. She did the same to him.

As soon as he was free of his clothes, she grabbed his dick and began stroking it ever so lightly. It grew and throbbed at her every touch. Finn lay there enjoying her touch until he was about to explode.

He ran his hand down to her wet spot and began to stroke her clit. She opened for him and he stroked faster and faster bringing her to her first climax. She fully enjoyed herself and as she began to relax, Finn moved to her breasts once again.

After a bit, she pushed him aside and rolled onto him, straddling his dick. She leaned forward so Finn could have her breasts as she began taking him into her. She rocked back and forth as she took him in deeper and deeper. She felt him getting bigger and he started to rock with her.

She moaned as she said, "I love the way you make me feel. Push harder. Push harder."

Finn grabbed her ass and pushed harder and harder feeling her close to her climax.

She reached her climax just as Finn pushed her hard and she rocked him even faster as he joined her. They soared for the longest time before coming back to the present. They collapsed and slept for a bit, holding tightly to each other.

It was somewhere in the night when they began to wake up. Finn watched her sleep for a minute before she awoke. She saw him smiling at her.

"Hmmm, delicious Mr. Finn," Katelyn said with a smile.

"You, too, Miss Katie girl," Finn replied as he gently kissed her on the lips.

"Now that's what I call first-class dessert," Katelyn said.

"I agree," Finn said as well.

"Hm, talkin' about food has made me realize I'm starvin' again. What do you think we should do about that?" Katelyn asked.

"Well, since I saw chocolate chip cookies on the counter, I say we raid the kitchen. Again," Finn answered.

"Agreed! Now, if I can only find my clothes," Katelyn said as she crawled out of bed. She grabbed her robe and found one for Finn.

"Try this on. I think it'll fit," Katelyn said as she handed the robe to Finn.

"Thanks. Fits fine," Finn said. "Not too sure about the colors though. I don't think shades of pink and purple work for me."

Katelyn laughed as she said, "I think it's a great match."

They wandered into the kitchen, found the cookies and got drinks. They settled at the table for a bit.

"So, I guess you really are my girlfriend now," Finn said with a smirk on his face.

"Why, Finn, I'd be happy to be your girl," Katelyn said with a laugh.

"Deal!" Finn said as he reached out for her hand. They shook and laughed and ate more cookies.

Finn looked at the kitchen clock. It was midnight on the dot.

"Well, my Katie girl, looks like I should be headin' home. I do so appreciate the evening and I think we should do it again real soon," Finn said as he kissed her on the top of her head.

"I agree," Katelyn said as she walked with him back to her room. Finn found his clothes, dressed and they walked to the door.

"Goodnight my Katie girl," Finn said.

"Goodnight my Finn," Katie replied as they shared a long and soulful kiss before Finn drove off.

Katelyn went back inside and crawled back into bed thinking about how great the night had turned out. Her last thought as she floated off into sleep was how much she liked Finn and what a great lover he had been. She was smiling as she fell into a deep, deep sleep.

The Creek slept as well.

CHAPTER 16

E than had told Katelyn not to come in to work until around 12-noon or so. After what he had watched at Jordan's place, he saw how worn out all the ladies were.

Katelyn arrived just a bit past noon, having slept until close to ten o'clock. She figured it was a combination of the ceremony and her hours with Finn. She didn't even know she was smiling when she walked into the shop. The new addition was close to being finished and that's where she found Ethan and Ian.

"Hi guys," she said as she walked into the new space. "Hey, this is really comin' along. Looks great."

"Hey Katie girl," they both said at the same time.

"What do ya' think, Katelyn? Take a look in your office and let me know if ya' want anything changed or added to the layout," Ian suggested.

Katelyn walked into her office and was stunned at what she found. The walls were finished and she had a digital wall like the one in the main area.

"Wow! This is so, so…I don't know what, but it is," Katelyn said in amazement as she looked all around. Her desk was set between two full-length windows and her architect table faced the windows with special lighting above it.

"You haven't missed a thing, Ian. And, you've surely spoiled me from taking any other job 'cause no one's gonna' have all this futuristic stuff like y'all do."

"That's the idea. We don't wanna' lose you ever," Ethan said smiling at Katelyn.

"Not a chance of that ever happenin' for sure," Katelyn said as she walked all over her space and marveled at everything.

"How soon do you think before we get the occupancy permit for the new space?" Katelyn asked Ethan.

"We have a small punch list to complete, but I scheduled the inspection for tomorrow. You and Finn could be in your new offices tomorrow afternoon if the rest of the furniture arrives today like it's supposed to."

"Fantastic! Ian, what's planned for this afternoon? I'd like to get stuff ready for moving day, if ya' get my drift." Katelyn said laughing and winking at Ian.

"We have a couple of folks stopping by to look at the second set of plans for their homes and then the rest of the day is all yours," Ian replied laughing.

"Great. So, when is the first appointment?"

"In about twenty minutes. Let's get ready," Ian said.

"I've got site visits to make. I'm meeting with Finn at that new build with all the thermal and wind energy stuff so I think we'll be there from about mid-afternoon until we finish. Let me know if we have any significant changes from these two clients. Later," Ethan said as he left.

Ian and Katelyn spent the afternoon with clients getting their ideas set into their building plans.

Katelyn had called the hospital as soon as she woke up and spoke with Jordan for a few minutes. He told her they were moving him into the med-surg unit because he was mending faster than they anticipated. The docs thought he might come home in about four days. Katelyn said she would let The Creek know so everything would be ready for him. She said the guys had moved his bedroom into the first-floor guest room so he wouldn't have to worry about that. She asked him to have the doctors call her so she could get all the instructions and be ready for him. He said the Boone Visiting Nurse Group would be coming home with him and would be with him for about a week, round-the-clock, to help him adjust to getting around and all. And, he would have physical therapy coming in as well.

Katelyn said she was thrilled that everything was being taken care of for him. She said The Creek would be feeding him so not to worry. He loved that idea sayin', ''cause you know how much I love everyone's cookin and all!'

Katelyn called Emily on her way to the shop and told Emily everything. Emily said she would take care of the details and start a phone tree.

Word got around fast as Ian mentioned how he and Ethan were gonna' build a ramp for Jordan the next day so he wouldn't have to worry about the stairs for a long while. Once he was healed, they'd take the ramp away.

As The Creek went about their day, The Dark was so wicked pissed it was causing havoc in other galaxies and universes. It made a star go nova before it's time. And when The Dark finally did settle down, it began to think of all kinds of ways to get back at The White Light for stopping it from getting The Magic from the Blue Ridge and The Creek, most of all.

It had lost a lot of power in the Blue Ridge weather fiasco so it needed the time to grow more. That's why it was attacking everything it could other than the earth. And, it worked. The Dark was gaining a great deal of new power and it wouldn't be long before it was ready to get back at The White Light.

The shape shifters were hard at work, too. Greg was especially pissed off that the accident he had caused hadn't killed Jordan. The plan had been that The Dark would send a 'new' person to buy Jordan's farm and The Dark would take possession of the land. The Dark wanted that land really bad. Seems there was some special Magic and power in that place. Now that Jordan had lived, Greg was put in charge of a way, or ways, to get to that Magic.

He decided to take a trip over to Jordan's farm while Jordan was in the hospital figuring no one would be around to bother him. He planned to walk the whole place to find where The Magic Power was hiding.

It was now the first week of August and summer was in all its glory.

Greg decided to go to the farm the same day Katelyn learned that Jordan was being moved to a new room. He tried to turn down the road but was stopped rather abruptly like he had run into a brick wall. He thought something was wrong with his truck, so he put it in reverse, backed up a bit, and tried again. He was stopped again as he ran into an invisible wall. He hit the steering wheel 'cause he didn't wear a seatbelt. It hurt.

"What the fuck?" he yelled at no one in particular.

All of a sudden, a shape appeared in his truck. A familiar shape. It was ugly and gross, but loved by some many demons and bad guys.

"Madman, what the fuck are you doing here?" Greg asked. "And, could ya' change into something that doesn't smell like centuries old dead alien?"

Madman shape shifted into a rather handsome man.

"Cute!" Greg laughed at him. "What the hell is going on here? Why can't I get on the road to the farm?"

"So glad to see you again, old friend. Well, seems the folks here are figuring things out and put a protection grid around the place. We can't get in there. No way. No how."

"Shit! Just as I thought. This place is filled with The Magic Power The Dark wants. How we gonna' take it if we can't get near it?"

"Well, old friend, that is for you to figure out. And, don't take your time. The Dark is growing impatient as it gathers new power from a whole mess of destruction it's causing. It's really shit pissed. I've only seen The Dark like this once before when The White Light Paladins beat him at The Holler. Great battle. Lots of destruction and all until The White Light vanquished The Dark to the nether regions of all existence. Some of it is still trapped there. And, The Dark is still beyond angry about that. So, if we don't find a way to get this Magic, we're all gonna' suffer."

"Fuck! Okay. Thanks for the info. I'll work with the others and maybe you can send a few of your kind here to work with us as well. Just make sure they're in human form though. We've got enough to deal with as it is."

"You've got shit to deal with. Not me. And, yes, I'll send three of my best monsters your way. They're busy assisting The Dark in gaining new power. As soon as they're finished, they're all yours."

"Thanks. And, as they say around here, much obliged," Greg sneered. Madman growled in response as he vanished.

Greg sat there for a few minutes, then realized he needed to get away as fast as possible. He didn't want anyone to know he was at Jordan's place.

Greg sent out a telepathic message to all the other shape shifters to meet him in the place in Boone in three days. That would give him time to try to start to come up with ideas about getting onto Jordan's place and taking The Magic Power.

Jordan was healing faster than anyone thought he would. He told Katelyn when she visited a few days after the protection grid was placed that he would be sent home on the next Sunday, the second Sunday of August. Emily and everyone had been busy getting everything ready. The frig was stocked with food and drink and there was a schedule for meals for at least a month. Folks would be around to clean and freshen the place up as well. Jonah had rounded up folks to take care of the building and yard needs with Ethan and Ian's help. Jordan only had the eagle family living in the barn so there wasn't much to take care of. The apartment above the barn was almost complete. Ethan had taken care of that. Folks stopped by every evening to watch the sun shine on the crystal by the front door. They said no matter how many times they watched, it was always a new bunch of colors that shown all over the place.

Katelyn went over on Saturday, late in the evening, for a walk around the place. She was drawn to the land for some unknown reason. A few folks came by to watch the sun shine on the crystal. She joined them and they marveled at the whole thing. Once the sun was below the trees, everyone left, except for Katelyn. The house lights were on a timing system and Ian had the security company they used install cameras around the place for twenty-four-hour security.

As Katelyn began to walk towards the barn, she smiled and waved at one of the cameras. They were hidden well, but Ian had told her where they were just in case anything should happen. As she walked into the barn, she watched the eagles begin to settle for the night. The female flew in just then, circled around Katelyn, then settled in the nest with the family.

Katelyn nodded her head in response and walked out the back door of the barn. It was usually left open so the eagles could come and go at will.

She found herself wandering just a bit behind the barn. It was getting onto dusk and she hadn't brought a flashlight with her. She found herself standing and starring out across the field, looking towards the small rise in the hill. This was where the cave entrance was. As the evening gave way to night, she saw a shape appear over the small rise. It looked like it could be a hawk or owl. It circled the hill, then flew away past the hill.

She didn't know how long she stood there after the night had arrived. She finally came back from wherever her mind had wandered off to and realized it was really night time. She gave herself a little shake and walked back to her SUV. She thought she caught sight of that big shadowy thing flying just past her vision again. Maybe not. It had been a crazy few days for sure with setting the protection grid, Finn and all, and her work with Ethan and Ian. That part of her life was fabulous. She loved designing buildings and interiors for people to help them see their dreams come to life.

Katelyn set out for home and was all set for the night a little bit later.

Kendra saw Katelyn pull in and smiled. She knew something was up in The Creek and Katelyn had something to do with it. Katelyn was about to learn about more of her Gifts. It had to do with Jordan and his place. Time enough for that later.

Miss Cora had been over to Emily's for supper that night and they were busy talking about Jordan's place, Katelyn, and The Magic in The Creek.

As they settled on the porch to look out over the mountains, Trouble, Emily's dog, decided to chase butterflies in the yard. This kept the women laughing for quite a while. Trouble finally gave up and plopped himself on the porch after a long drink of cold water. He was snoring in no time.

"I do declare, Trouble sure knows how to have a good time," Miss Cora said laughing.

"He sure does. And, he knows how to fall asleep just like most men do," Emily agreed laughing along with Miss Cora.

"Ya' sure have settled into a nice place here, Emily. It does have a peaceful energy about it. I like settin' here on the porch with you after such a great meal."

"Thanks, Miss Cora. Ethan surely built the home, farm, of my dreams. I can't imagine it any other way."

"Thanks for taking care of the details for Jordan's return home tomorrow. I know it's a lot of work, but you're just the one to take care of the details."

"I wouldn't have it any other way. Jordan's one of us now and we take care of our own. Besides, lots of folks have been helpin' out and will keep takin' care of him until he can run us off the place," Emily said with a smile.

"Ya' know, Emily, there's somethin' unsettling around here. Again."

"I know. I just haven't been able to get an idea of what. You?"

"Same here. We know it has somethin' to do with Jordan's place. Just not sure what. We'll keep our eyes peeled for anythin' off. It's so beautiful here in the Blue Ridge. Just look at how the sun is startin' to slowly drift down to the trees?"

The two of them sat there watching the sun dip below the trees, then through them and, finally, disappear below the horizon. Miss Cora set out for home and Emily and Trouble went about settling the chickens and all before they turned in themselves.

Sunday morning found The Creek busy as usual for a summer Sunday. The Creek was taking care of last-minute stuff for Jordan's return in a few hours. Tourists were wandering into The Store for last minute things for their day in the mountains. Greg walked in late morning just as Matthews was walking over to Jenna. She was helping Michael and Ted on account of the busy summer tourist thing.

"Hey, Jenna. Didn't hear ya' leave this mornin'," Matthews said as he kissed her cheek.

"I was bein' especially quiet on account of our late night. I know you needed your beauty sleep," Jenna replied laughing softly.

Just then, Greg made his way over to them to look for something on the shelf.

"Greg, may I help you find somethin'?" Jenna asked.

She got a chill that Matthews noticed. He stepped in front of her and said, "What can I help you with Greg?"

Ted scurried right over when he saw the look on Jenna's face. "How can we all help ya' Greg?" Ted said as he stood next to Matthews, blocking Greg's view of Jenna.

"Oh, nothin' special. Just lookin' things over to see if anything piques my interest," Greg replied as he tried to look directly at Jenna.

Ted took Greg by the shoulder and turned him away from Jenna. "Well, what'd ya' have in mind?"

"Oh, just somethin' to have in the cupboard in case I got a hankerin' for somethin' sweet," Greg replied trying to turn back towards Jenna.

Matthews joined the two men and firmly moved Greg over to the shelves with cookies and sweets. "Here's a mess of sweet stuff. Maybe you'd like to take a dessert home as well?" Ted suggested.

Greg realized he was being blocked and moved away from Jenna so he backed off with, "I think these cookies will be the perfect thing and a slice of your chocolate cake, Ted," Greg replied.

"Excellent choice. I'll get the cake and meet ya' at the register. Michael, add a piece of cake to Greg's bill, will ya'?"

Greg walked over to the register with Matthews a few steps behind. "Thanks, Ted. How much?"

Ted came back with the cake all wrapped up and Greg paid for his things.

"Have a nice day now," Ted said as they watched him walk out of the store.

Matthews walked over to Jenna. She looked a bit ruffled.

"Jenna, you alright?" Matthews asked.

"I am now that Greg's gone. I got a not good feelin' about him for the first time. I gotta' call Emily and tell her and Kendra, too." Jenna took her phone out to call Emily as Kendra walked in.

"Where's Jenna?" she asked.

"She's up in the kitchen about to call Emily. Why?" Michael asked.

"I got a weird feelin' just now when I thought about her. Not good," Kendra replied as she stepped up into the dining area and saw Jenna on the phone.

Jenna waved and finished the call. "I was on with Emily. Weird stuff just now."

"I know. I felt it, too. Let's sit and have somethin' to drink," Kendra said as she looked at Matthews.

I'll get 'cha both a sweet tea," Matthews said as he reached into the cooler and grabbed two bottles of sweet tea.

"Thanks," Jenna said as she took a long drink.

"Same here, Matthews," Kendra said.

Jenna began to settle down and her color returned.

"What the hell was that?" Jenna finally said in a rather pissed off tone.

"That, my sweet Jenna, was a demon of The Dark tryin' to damage you. You're new to all this Magic Stuff and The Dark knows it. What The Dark doesn't, or didn't, know until a few minutes ago, is that you walk in The White Light and are very well protected. Demon Greg was tryin' to steal your power. No way that was gonna' happen."

"Sweet Jesus! So, can we vanquish him or somethin'?" Jenna asked seriously.

"Not in those words. But we can make life really uncomfortable for him and force him to leave. I suspect he's gonna' give his notice today for an abrupt departure. As a matter of fact, I'll be right back," Kendra said as she took another gulp of her sweet tea and walked out the door.

Greg was just walking over to her house when she said, "Hey, Greg. Lookin' for me?"

"Why, yes, I am, Kendra. I've been called back to the regional office in Boone. Seems that storm the other day damaged some of the sub-stations and they need help getting them back online. Here's cash for the next month's rent since I won't be givin' ya' any notice. Thanks for the place and all," Greg said as he handed the money to Kendra.

She immediately cleansed it and a small puff of smoke rose from her hand. Greg saw this and got into his truck rather quickly and drove away.

Kendra laughed as she counted the cash and saw that it was for three month's rent. She put the money in her pocket and went back to The Store.

"He's gone, just like I said he would be. And, he paid for three month's rent in advance. Ted, would ya' put this in the community box for whatever or whomever may need it?" Kendra said as she gave most of the money to Ted.

Michael snatched the money right outta' Ted's hand as he said, "Thanks Kendra. That's mighty generous of you. I'll record the gift and take care of it."

Matthews and Jenna laughed at Ted's expression as they all sat down at the table.

"Well, I guess we know who's in charge of the money around here, don't we?" Jenna said.

"Yes. Me," Michael replied making a face at Ted.

Everyone laughed at their antics and settled into talking about The Creek.

Emily breezed in to grab a few things and saw the group at the table.

"Hey, y'all. You alright now?" Emily asked as she sat down next to Jenn.

"Hey yourself. Yes. We're just hangin' out for a while," Jenna replied with a wink.

"Right! Ted, you look like someone deflated your balloon," Emily said with a laugh at the face Ted made looking at Kendra and Michael.

Kendra filled Emily in on the antics and had them all laughing again.

"Well, I guess Michael would know Ted best. Love ya, Ted," Emily said blowing a kiss Ted's way.

"Gee, thanks, Miss Emily. At least someone around here shows me some lovin'," Ted said.

"What news brings you in in the middle of the day, Emily?" Michael sked from the front of the store.

"Well, I have some fun news. Ya' know the Redstone clan up past Laine and Mo's place a ways to the north-east? Well, they just called to let me know that they're gonna' open The Meadow to everyone for a picnic thing this

Saturday. Ya' know how we all bring our picnic baskets and coolers and some fun outdoor games and stuff? Well, they said to tell everyone in The Creek as they love us all, and said it's about time for a fun day any ways."

"Yahoo!," Ted hollered dancing around the place.

"Love it when they open The Meadow," Michael added.

"What's this all about?" Jenna asked as Hal and Finn walked in the door.

"What's all the hollerin' about?" Hal asked as the two of them joined the group.

"The Redstone's are opening The Meadow for a picnic and games day on Saturday," Emily said.

"I love that place. The picnic day is always so much fun," Hal said.

"It's been a while since they opened The Meadow for a picnic. Wonder why?" Finn added.

"Well, I've been thinkin' about that. Seems The Meadow is a real special place to them and they take real good care of it and protect it at all costs. So, I was thinkin' it's been a few years and we have some new family here in The Creek. So, maybe it's time for us all to come together again. I'm gonna' call Miss Cora right now. Hold on everyone," Emily said as she dialed Miss Cora.

"Hey, Miss Cora, it's Emily. I'm here at The Store with folks tellin' them, and you, that the Redstone clan is opening The Meadow for a picnic and games day next Saturday. We were wonderin' if you knew why it's been a long while since they had the picnic and all?"

"Hey, Miss Emily, and everyone. I love this whole phone thing 'cause I can see y'all while I talk. Well, it's been about five years since the Redstone clan had a gatherin'. They don't usually have one every year. I think this one has to do with the new members of The Creek family and all. They're real special people for sure. And, even if they live outside The Creek, there surely is some Magic up their way. They've been around the Blue Ridge for as long as anyone can remember. I do believe they came here just a few years after the first settlers. The Meadow has some Magic in it for sure. Ya' say the picnic is this Saturday?"

"Yes, Ma'am," everyone replied.

"Well, I'll be sure to be there. Always a great time and the food is the best around. Emily, how about we plan on goin' together?"

"I like that idea. I'll pick you up a bit after noon and we can drive on over and visit a bit with the Redstone's before everyone else gets there."

"Great idea. See y'all later," Miss Cora said as she and Emily finished the call.

"I think Miss Cora is really liking her cell phone," Michael said. "She sure has figured out how to use it. She called the other day to ask about the specials and placed her order before getting here."

"I remember those picnics at The Meadow," Hal began. "I remember one particular day when I was a few years younger. The games had just ended and we were all getting ready to set out our food for everyone to sample when an eagle flew over, dropping a feather. We all stood around lookin' at it 'cause, as most of us know, ya' never touch an eagle feather unless you're a chief or shaman. Well, it dropped right in front of Chief Running Bear. He chanted somethin' in his native tongue, offered tobacco in thanks, then, and only then, did he pick up the feather. As he did, the eagle flew over again, circled around twice, gave a holler then flew off into the bright blue sky over the mountain. We all stood real quiet for the longest time as the chiefs offered a song chant. Then, a blessing was offered, and we began eatin'. It was a real special picnic for sure."

"Well, it's been years for sure for me. I remember the games and all. It's always fun watchin the young ones in the potato sack races. I'm thinkin' I'll bring my frisbees with me. Should prove to be a fun time for sure 'cause I'm not that good with the darn things," Michael added.

"They should have a cook-off for best burgers. I'd definitely enter that contest," Ted offered.

"Maybe I'll give Seth a call and suggest a burger cook-off," Michael said thinking out loud.

"Now, that's a great idea," Ted replied.

"Sounds like fun to me," Matthews said. "Do we get to sample the burgers after the winner is announced?"

"I'll offer that to Seth as well. I'll call him right now," Michael said as he grabbed his phone and placed the call.

"Hey, Seth, Michael here. Doin' great. How about all of you up there?" Michael paused as he listened to Seth's reply. "Seth says hey to everyone. So, Seth, Ted had an idea for the picnic. He was wondering if you'd consider a burger cook-off as one of the games?"

Michael paused again and then smiled. "I think it's a great idea. And, Mathews, one of the newer Creek family members, was wonderin' if we could sample all the burgers after the winner is announced? Okay. I'll give them the news. Seth, I just want to say thanks so much for opening The Meadow for the picnic and all. It's mighty kind and generous of y'all to do this for everyone. Take care. We'll see ya' this Saturday around two. Bye."

Michael paused for a minute smiling then said, "Ted, he loves the idea and said it's a deal. All of it with Matthews' idea as well. Guess we all know what Ted's gonna' be doin' for the next few days."

Everyone laughed and began talking at once. It was a while before things quieted down and folks began to leave.

"See y'all later," Hal said as he took his leave.

"I better get back to the animals. So thankful Jonah's around. He sure is Magic with those critters," Emily said as she paid for her things and left.

Matthews and Jenna looked at each other than Ted and Michael for a minute.

"That man was evil," Jenna said. "So glad he's gone."

"I'm gonna' keep track of him for a while to make sure he doesn't try anything crazy with us around here," Kendra said.

"We'll keep an eye out, too," Michael added.

"Well, time to get along. I have some graphic designs to work on," Jenna said as she and Matthews made their way to the front door.

"Later, all," Matthews said as they went on their way.

Ted and Michael waved to everyone then got back to work running The Store It wasn't long before Michael could smell Ted's cooking. He was probably working on a recipe for the burger cook-off. Michael smiled just thinking how happy Ted was when he was cooking for folks. That Ted sure was a great guy, Michael was thinking as he went about his chores.

Kendra sat for a few minutes in her kitchen thinking about the Greg problem. There was something about him that just didn't sit right with her. She gathered her thoughts and focused on her Guides for a bit. They confirmed that Greg was a problem and firmly connected with The Dark. Kendra knew that something was a'brewin' in The Creek for sure now. She'd stay vigilant and connected with Miss Cora about it. Always something going on around The Creek.

Word got around about the picnic in no time and folks were making plans. Katelyn was excited 'cause she hadn't been to a picnic in The Meadow in forever. She was just thinking about it that Sunday evening when she got a ping on her phone. It was Sami.

'It's about time girl. Where you been?" Katelyn said as she answered the call.

"Me? Where have you been?" Sami replied back.

"Well, I've been busy with my new job with Ethan and Ian and, wait for it, Finn." Katelyn answered.

"Finn? The Finn? He works with the guys?

"Yup. I knew he did some jobs for them, but didn't know he was there full-time. So cool," Katelyn said.

"He's a hunk for sure," Sami replied with a laugh.

"Why, yes he is," Katelyn started as she was interrupted by Sami.

"You two got together, didn't ya'?" Sami squealed.

"Yup. The angels wept," Katelyn replied.

"Damn! It's about time," Sami yelled. "No wonder ya' haven't been in touch."

"No, that's not the specific reason. We have a ton of clients and it's been really crazy around here. Jordan was attacked by The Dark and was in the hospital for about a week and some. He came home this afternoon and The Creek is takin' care of him. Emily, Kendra, Miss Cora, and I set a protection grid over his place 'cause it was a demon of The Dark that caused his accident. Seems the land he now owns is real special. Ethan came along with his gator to get us around the property."

"Wow! You have been busy!" Sami exclaimed.

"Hey, let's do a live chat. Here's the meeting link. See ya' in a minute," Katelyn said,

"God, you look great Sami! Been outside a lot?" Katelyn asked as soon as they were live.

"Yup. And, oh my God, Katie, that whole underground railroad thing is getting outta' control." Sami replied.

"How's that? I thought you were done in Maine for now."

"I am. I've moved onto the Boston area and there's more underground railroad houses and tunnels and all. This whole thing is blowin' up into a huge new part of the project. My bosses love the whole thing and have assigned two assistants to me for research both online and on the ground. And, let me tell ya' somethin', they are awesome! Paul and Gloria. I swear they were made from the same mold and, yet, they each have a special thing about them. They're out tracking down some of the tunnel entrances this week in Boston. They've found some of the hiding houses in and around the Boston area. We're gonna' put together a 3-dimensional map online tomorrow with all the info they've gathered and see what turns up. I never would have imagined any of this when I took this job. So cool."

"Sami, that's truly awesome. I'd love to see the 3-D map as you work on it. It will almost be like I'm there with you. I miss you so much, my Sami."

"I miss you so much, too, my Katie girl. At least you've got your Finn there. Good thing I don't have a special someone. I wouldn't have time for her."

"I hear ya', Sami. I gotta' tell ya' somethin' and I know I can, no matter how weird it sounds."

"What's the matter, Katelyn? What's goin' on?"

"Well, at first, I just chocked it up to the way things go. But recently, there seems to be some very subtle differences around here that all of a sudden appeared. It's like one minute was how everything has always been, then the next, some things changed. I mean really changed."

"Like what?"

"Well, Emily and Ethan have been a set couple for as long as they've known each other. But one day, I learned that they weren't a couple at all. Never had been. And, there are a few other differences Like the stuff on the shelves at The Store. One morning they were there and the next afternoon, all different stuff showed up. When I mentioned it to Michael, he kinda' looked at me funny and said that that stuff had always been there. I came back with somethin' about being so busy I must have gotten stuff mixed up. But, Sami, I didn't. There's somethin' goin on around here that just doesn't measure up."

"Wow! Emily and Ethan have been solid for quite a while. This is some weird shit for sure. What 'cha gonna' do about it?"

"Well, I'm bein' careful about what I say and watching everything, and I mean everything, I keep watchin' to see if anything has changed. It's a weird feelin'."

"I'll bet it is. Don't know what I'd do in your place. Keep a journal about all the changed stuff. Maybe you'll see a pattern."

"Good idea. I knew you'd have somethin' to help me with this. Now, about Jordan's place. The eagles have settled in. They really are awesome. The young ones are flyin' around a bit. Fun to watch. I was over there the other afternoon, a few days before we set the grid and I felt like I was called out to the field. I walked around until I was near the hill. I stood there for the longest time. I didn't even realize I was just standin' there until the sun dipped below the hills and evenin' came on. I think I was out there for about three hours or so. Just standin' there. It was as if I was called to be there. I felt at peace and safe. And, remember that huge shadowy thing that flew over my house one night in Alabama? Well, I saw it again. It flew over me, circled the hill, and then flew off into the night. And, Sami, it was huge. I mean beyond huge. Bigger than any bird I've ever seen. If I didn't know better, I'd say it was one of those birds from the dinosaur era. It had a long tail, too. So much stuff happenin' around Jordan and his place. There must be Magic out there. Real strong Magic for sure."

"Jesus, Katie. Sounds like you've got Magic on steroids and I've got the underground railroad showin' up everywhere. I wonder if there's any underground railroad connections up your way? I'm gonna' look into that myself."

"So cool, Sami. I'll take a look, too, and we can compare notes. How about we video chat again Sunday morning?"

"Yes. Ten o'clock. You send me the link."

"Okay. Oh, and one more thing. That Greg guy I told you about before. He's the one that tried to kill Jordan. Kendra told me he tried to get to Jenna earlier today and Matthews and Ted blocked him. He left the store and headed over to Kendra's to say he was leaving and gave her three month's rent for no advance notice. She said he got real scared when he handed her the money and smoke rose from it when it was in her hands. She blew the smoke away to cleanse it and he jumped into his truck and drove off like a bat outta' hell. She just laughed and went over to The Store and gave most of it to Michael for the community fund. I don't like all this stuff goin' on. It seems like somethin' bad is gonna' happen. I know I'm new to all this Magic stuff, but I've learned to listen to my hunches and this one is a big one. What do ya' think, Sami?"

"Shit! How's Jordan? You said he came home today. Is he gonna' recover alright?"

"Yes. When we found him in his rolled over truck a ways off the road, Emily sent out word to get Reiki goin' and it hasn't stopped. The docs say he's way ahead of the usual healing schedule and he will make a full recovery. He's pissed about the accident. He never hurt anyone and this is the second time he's been targeted by The Dark."

"When was the first time?"

"Oh, yeah, back just before the battle in the Sacred Rock Meadow with Emily. The Dark used him to try to get him to kill someone and he wouldn't do it. They hurt him then, too. But not like this time. Makes me kinda' wonder about his connection to The Magic and all. I wonder if he's gonna' be a warrior or somethin'? Hmmm."

"Geez. I wonder about that, too. Well, for now, so glad Emily's got everyone takin' care of him. Give him my love and all, even if I haven't met him yet."

"I will. Oh, and one more thing. Kind of a fun thing. Ya' know about those storms that blew through here the other day? Well, they were sent by The Dark. Miss Cora told us they were so we know they were. Anyways, after we all came up from the basement in The Store, we found a sign set into the ground across the way like it had always been there. It was from Granddaddy Mimm's Moonshine Distillery in Blairsville, Georgia. It's the coolest thing. Michael called them and told them about the sign and sent a few pictures. The folks at Granddaddy Mimm's thought it was the coolest thing and said to keep the sign as it would cost too much to ship it back. So, Ethan and Finn are gonna' design a frame-like thing to go around it and reset it back aways from the road. A few of the folks are gonna' get together to write up a piece about how it got here and all. Ted and Michael said they'd hang it in The Store for all to see. How cool is that?"

"Now that is cool. Send me a picture or two. Love when good things happen along after bad stuff. I'll bet your story even makes it into the news media. Someone should get ahold of the media folks and tell them about your story after Ethan and Finn fix up the sign."

"That's a great idea. I'll send word around. Thanks. Hey, it's getting late and we both have to work tomorrow although it doesn't really feel like work. I love what I do and I know you do, too. So, let's get some rest so we can play tomorrow"

"Well said. Love ya' my Katie girl, always and forever."

"Love ya,' my Sami girl, always and forever. Until Sunday morning, signing off," Katelyn said as they ended the chat.

Sami fell sound asleep in her Boston hotel and Katie fell sound asleep in The Creek. And, all of The Creek slept well that night. Including that big shadowy flying thing.

CHAPTER 17

Monday found Jordan getting settled in his new bedroom in the guestroom on his first floor. The physical therapist approved his guest bed with the addition of an overhead frame so he could pull himself up and swing his legs around to the side of his bed. He had recovered enough from his spleen surgery to be able to use his gut muscles without harming the stitches from the surgery. He was learning all kinds of new ways to move around without damaging his broken body. It took a while but he was getting the hang of it.

This morning, the visiting nurse and physical therapist arrived around eight o'clock. Thing is, some of The Creek folks were already there fixing breakfast and lunch, helping Jordan move around a bit, and making sure he had everything he needed right at his side.

Jordan was busy most of that Monday and was wiped out tired by supper time.

Katelyn and Finn were meeting with clients all day at the shop. New clients and those with their projects under way. Ethan and Ian were in and out all day.

The Store was a buzz about the picnic in The Meadow for Saturday. Folks gathered around in waves throughout the day sharing memories and thoughts about this new picnic. Miss Cora stopped by around noon and decided to have lunch. Folks stopped by and everyone talked about the picnic.

"I remember the last one about five years back. Hal and Jonah had paired up for the egg tossing contest. They kept things goin' for quite some time. Then, it happened. Jonah caught Hal's toss just so and it exploded all over his head. Folks were laughin' for quite some time. Jonah had to go take a quick shower of sorts and change his shirt. The kids had a grand time and the rest of us brought our crochetin' and such to keep us busy as we watched and gossiped. It was a great day for sure," Miss Cora remembered.

"I remember that egg toss," Ted replied. "Jonah did get a face full. He was a real good sport about it, too."

Lunch came and went and the day moved along.

Greg was working hard at trying to come up with a plan to get back at The Creek. The Dark was wicked mad about the protection grid and demanded that something be done. Greg and his fellow shapeshifters went about their regular day so as no one would think anything was amiss. At night, they spent hours remembering other plots and plans that might help them complete their assignment.

Kendra was keeping a quiet eye on The Creek along with Emily and Miss Cora. The three of them knew something was coming especially after that storm thing and the fight they had to complete the protection grid.

Kendra also knew about Katelyn. She suspected Katelyn was beginning to question the changes around The Creek. Kendra knew she had noticed a lot of them. She was gonna' let Katelyn go about it until she had to tell her all about the weird changes she was finding.

Katelyn and Finn called it a day around six and said so long as they drove off. Katelyn was stopping by Jordan's place to check in on him.

When she arrived, she saw two other cars parked near the barn. She knew they were the folks that were gonna' stay with Jordan throughout the night.

As she walked into the kitchen from the back door she heard, "Hey, Katelyn. Nice to see ya'," from both Sherry and Kevin.

"Hey, guys," Katelyn replied. "Where's Jordan?"

"He's in the bedroom. We worked him hard today and I think he's about to fall asleep even before supper is ready." Kevin said.

"I'll go take a look. Smells great in here. Barbeque chicken and beans?"

"Yup. My specialty," Sherry replied. "You're welcome to stay. I think I fixed enough for ten people. And, cornbread, of course."

"That did it. I'm stayin'," Katelyn said as she left the kitchen.

Katelyn found Jordan lying back against a mountain of pillows trying to put a pillow under his cast leg.

"Hey, Jordan, looks like you could use a little help here. May I?"

"Of course, Katie. Thanks. Never thought I'd be so helpless in my life," Jordan said as Katelyn placed the pillow under the knee part of the cast then put another against the foot.

Jordan sighed as he relaxed back against his pillows. "Thanks Katie, that's just perfect. It smells fabulous in here. Not sure I can stay awake for supper though."

"Jordan, you close your eyes and when you wake up, you can devour Sherry's delicious supper."

Jordan smiled at Katelyn as he closed his eyes. He was asleep instantly. That's how Shery found him with Katelyn holding his hand.

Sherry whispered, "That's just what he needed. Sleep and someone to hold his hand. Makes a body feel safe when someone is there for them. Supper's ready when you are."

Katelyn nodded her head and held onto Jordan for a few more minutes until he was breathing softly and quietly.

Katelyn joined the others in the kitchen and they talked and ate for a while. Just as they finished, they heard Jordan.

"Hey guys, sure hope you saved some of that for me. I'm starvin'," Jordan hollered. A minute later he showed up in the kitchen on his crutches.

"These things take a lot a work. Good thing my therapist has me doin' arm exercises. I thought I was strong haulin' all those packages and stuff. But, Jesus, I'm no wheres near ready for all this stuff," Jordan said laughing as he sat in a chair at the table.

Kevin came around and helped him with the table on wheels that Hal had made just for this type of thing. Jordan couldn't put his leg under the table just yet. Sherry dished up his food, warmed it in the microwave, and set in front of him.

"Sherry, I swear you're an angle directly from heaven. This smells amazin'," Jordan said as he reached for his spoon and grabbed some of the baked beans. "Hmmmm, so good," Jordan said as he continued to sample everything.

"Do ya' think I should give him some of your cornbread, Sherry? He might just inhale it all in one piece," Kevin said as they watched Jordan enjoy the feast.

"Ya' mean there's some left? Really? I've been told how much Katelyn loves cornbread. Thought she might have eatin' it all."

"No chance. I saved some for you. We need you to get strong and healthy so you can get back to work around here. There's still a lot to do mister," Katelyn replied.

"I know. I haven't even looked at my mail from the past couple of weeks. I'm sure there's some fun stuff in there," Jordan said as he bit into the cornbread. "Heaven, Sherry, just purely perfect."

They sat around while Jordan ate teasing and talking for quite some time.

"Well, I'm gonna' clean up here. Jordan, what do ya' wanna' do?" Sherry asked.

"Kevin, Sherry, I think I'm gonna' head for the bathroom and get ready for bed. I should be okay. Hal set up a small table by the counter so I could reach everything and I can reach the faucets just fine. Katelyn, I would like to chat for a minute after I get back into bed. Kevin, I might need your help with that. I'll holler when I'm ready. Thanks everyone. I sure do appreciate all the help."

It wasn't long before Jordan called out for Kevin. It only took a minute to get Jordan settled for the night. Kevin let Katelyn know Jordan was ready for her.

"Jordan, I'm so glad you're doin well. We, all of us, are so angry about the accident and all. I know that's what you want to talk about."

"Exactly. Have you and the others figured out just what the hell happened?"

"Yes. Kendra, Miss Cora and Emily and I have talked about this for quite a spell. It seems that Greg is not who he says he is. Or was. He works for The Dark and was ordered to kill you so he could buy the farm and take over the land. Now, don't go crazy with what I'm about to say. It's not the drugs you're on."

"I haven't taken any pain meds since this morning, although I am going to as soon as we're done here. My whole body is achin' somethin' fierce and my leg is a mess of hurt. Big hurt. But I want to wait until we're done so I can keep a clear head."

"Okay. Here we go. It seems that there is a great deal of Magic in and on your land."

"Now, I do believe that with all those crystals showin' up for no reason."

"Exactly. We're not quite sure about the details of The Magic, but we know it's concentrated here abouts. So, just before you came home, we, Miss Cora, Emily, Kendra and I, set up a protection grid over and around your property. Ethan came along with his gator so we could get from one spot to the other in quick fashion. The grid protects the physical land well underneath the surface of the earth and a ways above the earth."

"I wondered what that quiet humming was. I heard it as soon as they took me out of the ambulance. Right away I heard it. It's very quiet and soft but real."

"Yes, it is. We all heard it, hear it, too. Well, those of us that are Gifted and know about The Magic. Everyone here is protected by the grid and no Dark energy can get in. Those bad guys of Greg's and all can't even come down the driveway. You are well protected for sure."

"So, that makes me think about somethin'," Jordan began.

"Go ahead," Katelyn said.

"Well, why me? Why was I the one to buy the land? I'm not special like you others are. I don't have any special Gifts. This land did kinda' speak to me when I first saw it and walked it. It felt like home and I instantly knew this was where I would live. I do feel protective of the place. Whoa. Do you think that's why the eagles took up residency in my barn? Are they special, too?"

"Yes, Jordan. They are special. The chiefs were telling us that the eagle spirit is closely connected with the Great Spirit. The eagle is the communicator between the humans and the Great Spirit. And, eagles are known to protect sacred places. I would venture to offer that this land is a sacred place. No burial grounds on your land as you know, but there seems to be somethin' special about it. Especially with those crystals and all. Did ya' know Matthews found a large egg-shaped crystal on his land after he bought it right after that weird earthquake happened?"

"You mean the one that split the tractor path?"

"Yup. They all were walkin' down the path and saw somethin' shinin' near the creek. When they got there, it was a big, purple, egg-shaped crystal glowin' like yours do. They all took a minute to think about it, then Matthews said it was supposed to stay right where it was. Seems The Magic was talkin' to them all. So, there it sits, on the bank of the creek."

"Wow! It seems to me that somethin' is goin' on here. What do ya' think Katelyn?"

"I'm thinkin' the same thing, Jordan. Our crystals are a part of somethin' bigger than us. I'm really new to all this Magic stuff but I'm learnin' really fast. Kendra said to just hang in there and, in time, we'll all know more."

Jordan gave a big yawn and moaned as he tried to move his leg without remembering it was in a full cast.

"Damn. I keep forgetting that I've got that cast on. Now my leg is really hurtin' somethin' fierce. Would ya' hand me that bottle there? Yup, that's the one. It's painkillers. The docs said I would probably need them for the first week home. I was tryin' not to use them, but they were right. Damn!"

"Here," Katelyn said as she passed the water to Jordan.

Jordan took his meds and then settled against the pillows. "This gives me even more to think about. I gotta' sleep now, but, Katelyn, would you come back around in a few days so we can talk some more?"

"You betcha', my crystal buddy. Sleep and heal now. Your matching crystal to mine is right here next to your bed and it's glowin' like crazy. Bet it's gonna' give you some healin' energy while you sleep. Later."

Jordan waved as Katelyn left the room. He was asleep in short time. Katelyn said good-bye to Sherry and Kevin as got into her SUV and was home a few minutes later. It was around eight so she still had a little time to take care of home stuff before she nodded off to sleep herself.

The rest of the week went along as usual. Katelyn stopped in to see Jordan and he told her he was okayed to go to the picnic in The Meadow on Saturday. They made plans to hang out together with Katelyn's family for the afternoon. Katelyn was taking her tablet with her so she could live chat with Sami so Sami could be a part of the fun as well. Everyone thought that was a grand idea and couldn't wait to 'meet' Sami.

Thursday afterwork Katelyn set out for her parent's farm. They were all getting together to have dinner. A rare happening.

As soon as she got there, her twin brothers grabbed her and hugged her for the longest time.

"Where you been?" they asked at the same time?

Katelyn replied laughing, "Working with Ethan and all. It's great."

"Well, okay, if you were just workin' 'cause if you were ignoring us, we'd have to take matters into our own hands," Nathan said laughing.

Katelyn's Mom chimed in, "Boys, now leave your sister alone. Can't ya' see she's half starved? We need to feed her right now!"

They all got dinner on the table and spent the next while remembering when they were younger and all the crazy stuff they used to do as kids.

"Let's clean up here and have desert out on the porch. I made apple and blueberry pies," Katelyn's mom suggested.

"Deal!" the men said as they hurried up and cleaned up the supper stuff. They loved their Mama's pies.

Katelyn and her mom took the pies and plates and all out onto the porch. Katelyn's dad came along with the ice cream.

Everyone had a piece of both pies at the same time.

"Are these blueberries from our patch?" Katelyn asked as she took her first bite of blueberry pie.

"Yes, they are, sis. And, I picked them yesterday just for today," her brother Jeremy replied.

"These are heavenly," Katelyn sighed as she added ice cream to her spoon.

"And, the apples are from the Applewood Grove. Remember how we all harvest the orchard and share the apples around The Creek?" Jeremy asked.

"Yes, I do. And I love doin' that. Takin' care of each other. Makes me happy to be home," Katelyn said.

"Jackie, darlin', these pies are the best. You're the best pie maker I know," Joe said smiling at his wife.

"Why, thank you, honey. Sure do love to cook for my men," Jacki replied.

"You two are somethin' else," Katelyn said laughing along with her brothers.

They sat for quite some time after desert, there on the porch, just watching the evening go along.

Just as the gloaming came on them, Katelyn turned to her brothers and asked them about their houses. "So, you two decide on the size of your new houses and any details you'll be wanting in them?"

Everyone became real quiet and just stared at Katelyn.

"Well, what are ya' all lookin' at me for? As soon as I came home, the two of you told me how you were gonna' undertake building your own homes and asked for my help and ideas. What gives with the looks?"

They continued to stare at her.

Then, Nathen cleared his throat and said, "Katelyn. I think you've been workin' too hard. Jeremy and me aren't thinkin' about building anything just yet. We do talk about it, but that's for the future for sure. Don't really know what you're talkin' about."

"Very funny guys. We talked for a long time about the land and where you want to build and how you're gonna' use the geothermal energy from the underground sources and all. If this is your way of teasin' me, it really isn't that funny."

Katelyn was beginning to get that funny feeling again that something wasn't quite right.

"Seriously, Katelyn. Nathan and me haven't decided on building even a shed for the new tools and all. Are you alright? Ya' look a little pale?"

"Katie, you alright?" her dad asked as he got up to stand next to her.

"Here, drink some of your water and take a deep breath," her mom said.

Katelyn drank the water to stall for some time. She knew she had talked with her brothers about their new houses and all in great detail. They had even looked at some designs online. This was just too wrong. Something sure wasn't right and now Katelyn was sure of it. Too many things were off.

Katelyn shook herself and took a breath then spoke. "Really? We didn't talk about houses and all? I could of swore we did. That must have been one hell of a dream then. It had so much detail in it. You guys were so happy about finally deciding to build and we even walked the land one afternoon to pick the perfect spot for both of your houses. These dreams are getting way to real for sure. I must be workin' harder than I thought. Guess I better get more rest or somethin.'."

Jackie looked at Joe and then said, "You really believed you all had done the planning? Well, I guess your dream visions are comin' on strong. Maybe you should talk with Kendra or Miss Cora or Emily. Bet they can help you figure out what's happenin'."

"Mom, that's the perfect idea," Katelyn said as convincingly as she could. It worked.

"So, Katie, what kind of house do I want," Jeremy asked with true interest.

Katelyn spent the next few minutes describing the houses and where the boys and decided to build them.

"Now Katie girl, those locations are excellent for lots of reasons," her dad said.

"I agree. At least for me," Jeremy replied.

"Me, too," Nathan chimed in.

"Just might be that we should be thinkin' about our own places, bro," Nathan offered to his brother.

"Good idea. Let's talk more and see what we come up with. And, Katie, you will be needed on this for sure," Jeremy said.

They all spent the rest of the evening talking about the houses and details about the farm. It was close to ten when Joe called it a night.

"I gotta' get up early tomorrow. Lots of folks comin' to pick berries. Love ya,' my Katie girl. See ya' Saturday at The Meadow."

Joe kissed his Katelyn on the top of her head and went inside.

The others said their good nights and Katelyn was on her way home a bit later.

Katelyn knew she had had those talks with her brothers. It wasn't a dream vision at all. She saw the lights on in Kendra's house and as soon as she parked her SUV, she headed right over.

She saw Kendra on the porch and before she could say anything, Kendra, said, "I've been expecting you. Have a seat."

As Katelyn sat down, she looked right at Kendra and said, "What the fuck is goin' on around here?"

"Well, that's a direct question," Kendra replied.

"Don't give me any shit tonight. I want to know what's going on around here."

"What do ya' mean, Katelyn?"

"Don't play games with me. The Creek is different all of a sudden. It's as if I blinked my eyes and major stuff changed."

"Be patient and tell me what you see as changed."

Katelyn looked right into Kendra's eyes, took a breath and sat back in her chair.

"Well, for one thing, Emily and Ethan aren't a couple. And, there's stuff in The Store that has never been there before. I walked into the shop the other day and Ian said we needed to go to Jordan's place and talk about how to decorate it and measure stuff. We had just done that the day before. He said we hadn't and I went to pull up the measurements I know I had taken and they weren't on my phone. I remembered them and told him what they were. When we got to Jordan's barn, Ian had measured the stairs, just like I had done the day before, and the numbers were exactly the same. When we went upstairs into the apartment none of the work that had been done the day before was in place. It was as if I had walked back a day and started all over. And, just now, when I was with my family and we were having such a great time sittin' on the porch, eating mom's homemade pies and watchin' the evenin' go along, I brought up the houses my brothers and I have been working on. Ya' know, the ones they want to build on their land and all. The whole family looked at me like I was crazy. I couldn't believe they didn't know what I was talkin' about. I suddenly realized somethin' was really wrong and covered sayin' I must have a dreamed it 'cause I was so tired from the new job. My mom thought that was a good explanation and suggested I come to you about it. Well, here I am and I'm demanding to know what the fuck has happened around here. I am not goin' crazy!"

Kendra just looked at Katelyn for the longest time.

After a bit Kendra began with," So, you've noticed some things that are very different from what you know to be true. Correct?"

"Yes, No. Things are very different than what is for real. Yes, this is The Creek. Yes, I grew up here. But no. Stuff is different. It's like I'm in a deep sleep and can't wake up to the normal kind of things. I am NOT goin' crazy."

"No, you are not crazy at all. I can't say much but I want you to think about all this and try to figure out what is happening. The Magic is very real."

"No shit. And, so is the Dark stuff."

"Yes, it is very real. Why are you here now? Why have you been made aware of your Gifts and are learning stuff so fast?"

"That I don't know."

"Maybe the fact that you're learning so much so fast has somethin' to do with how you see The Creek."

"What? That's double talk. One thing has to do with the other that has to do with the first thing."

"That's about it in a nut shell. Now, don't throw that plant at me. I'm just the messenger," Kendra said as Katelyn grabbed the small plant on the table between them and raised it up high.

Katelyn looked at the plant, not realizing she had even picked it up. She put it back on the table, got up and began to pace on and off the porch without saying a word.

It was quite a while later that she sat back down in the chair on the porch feeling somewhat defeated.

"Jesus fuckin' Christ. I don't even know where to start tryin' to figure this all out."

"I figured as much. I'm surprised you didn't show up sooner," Kendra said with a smile.

"Just validate that things are different than normal," Katelyn said.

"That is where the problem begins. What's normal for one may be different for another."

"Really? That's all ya got?" Katelyn said with a look of frustration on her face.

"It's the start to understanding all this that involves you and your Gifts."

"Holy crap. This is more than I can handle right now," Katelyn said as tears fell down her cheeks.

"Katelyn, it's okay to be lost with all this. Know this. This is all real right now. Very real. Jordan's accident caused by The Dark. The protection grid we did. Your Gifts. All real right this instant. Hold onto that. Listen as I talk with your Guides. I call upon Katelyn's Guides and Guardians to come to this space. Please give her a break, will ya?"

Katelyn smiled at Kendra. She always used the direct approach whenever possible.

"She needs some time here to get comfortable and accepting of all that is happening in this sacred place. Please give her healing energy and grace as she works at figuring things out. Thank you everyone," Kendra ended her chat with The Other Side.

The air seemed to calm and a cooling breeze blew through The Creek. Katelyn looked at Kendra and nodded as she wiped away the tears.

"This has been so overwhelming all of a sudden. Thanks for askin' for help for me. I am much obliged," Katelyn said as she got up and hugged Kendra.

"Well, now. Go get some rest. There is still a lot of Magic work to be done, but you get a few days off, so to speak. We'll talk again soon, for real. We've got the picnic at The Meadow comin' up. Gotta' be all rested for that for sure."

"Yes, we do and I will be rested and ready for a day full of fun. Jordan got the go-ahead from his docs to come so Ethan and Finn are gonna' get him there and he's hangin' with my family. We got a set up for him so he will be comfy and cozy all day and night long."

"That's wonderful. I'll bring a few things myself and join y'all."

"Great. Now, I am so suddenly drop-dead tired. Gotta' get up enough energy to walk those few steps home," Katelyn said as she yawned and stepped off the porch. She felt like someone was almost carrying her home. She smiled at Kendra and was in bed without remembering it like when you were a little kid having a blast one minute and feeling tired then waking up all cozy in your bed the next mornin. Katelyn was smiling with those memories as she fell into a deep, deep sleep. She was gonna' need all the rest she could get. Something was brewing in The Creek.

Friday brought the beginning of a fun few days for Katelyn. She and Finn left Ethan's around six. Finn was following Katelyn home so she could change into something more casual and leave her SUV there. Finn had brought a change of clothes with him and was gonna' change at Katelyn's place before they headed out on their dinner date.

As soon as they drove in, Finn heard his name being called from across the road. Seems Michael needed him for a minute.

"I'll be right back," Finn said as he walked across to The Store.

"Hey, Michael, what's up? Katelyn and I have a date for the diner tonight. Make it quick," Finn said as they walked into the store.

"Well, I wondered about the recliner y'all made for Jordan? Do ya' need some cushions and all so he'll be comfy?"

"Well, Michael, we put some padding all over the thing, but I'll take whatever ya' got. We want him to be comfy while he enjoys the day."

"Great. Here they are. I'll help ya' carry then across the road. Hey, Ted, watch things for a minute while I help Finn with the cushions."

"Okay," Ted replied as he walked down to the front of the store.

Finn and Michael put the cushions in the back of Finn's truck.

"See ya' tomorrow, Finn," Michael said.

"Thanks for the cushions. They look real comfy," Finn said as Michael walked back to The Store.

"Have fun tonight," Ted hollered from the porch.

"Thanks. We will," Finn said as he stepped up onto Katelyn's porch waving at the guys.

Finn found Katelyn all dressed and ready for their date.

"I'll just be a minute," Finn said as he began to undress on his way to the bathroom. Katelyn heard the shower and a few minutes later, Finn appeared fresh and clean.

"I do like a freshly dressed man," Katelyn said as she leaned up to kiss Finn softly on the lips.

"And, I like a girl who appreciates my efforts," Finn said returning the soft kiss.

"Let's go. I'm getting really hungry for diner food," Katelyn said as they locked up the house and got into Finn's truck.

Kendra was on the front porch and waved at them. "Have a great time. Eat a few fries for me," she said as they drove off.

Katelyn and Finn waved as they went on their way.

The diner was busy and they had to wait about a half hour. They decided to stay outside and walk along main street a bit. They remembered times when they were young and all the fun and mischief they had created.

"Remember when you and Jay decided to see who could jump the creek behind The Store? You must have been about fifteen. The two of you dared each other and a bunch of us decided to watch. The two of you picked the narrowest part of the creek. Thing was, it was also the fastest runnin' part of the creek in that place. It was summer and the two of you had on slacks and t-shirts. You went first and barely made it, fallin' on the other edge of the creek. Jay didn't make it and fell right into the creek and was carried down about a quarter mile. We all ran along to make sure he was alive. He was tryin' to swim along until the water slowed down. When he finally made it to shore, he was a mess with scrapes and bruises already showin'. We all laughed our heads off at you two. You changed into the dry clothes you had and we went back to The Store for munchies and drinks. Folks laughed about that crazy stunt for weeks."

"I do remember. I had so much mud on me, I thought I'd been in a mud bath. Jay was a mess with twigs and mud and the like all over him. He even said he swore some of it ended up inside his clothes, if ya' get my drift,"

Katelyn laughed along with Finn as they wandered back in the direction of the diner.

"He sure was a fun guy," Katelyn said as she got lost in thoughts of Jay.

"What do ya' mean was? He still is, just not as wild as when we were teenagers, so to speak," Finn said lookin' at Katelyn.

"So to speak," Katelyn covered herself. She could of swore Finn was talkin' as if Jay were still alive. "I guess we finally got wise and decided to calm down in our older age of twenty-somethin. Must have been the college influence although I do believe I heard about some college antics that could be compared to the stuff you all did around here."

"Yes, indeed. We carried our dare-devil ways to college for sure. What about you? Did you get into any mischief yourself when you left The Creek? Hmm?" Ethan smiled at Katelyn waiting for her answer.

"As a matter of fact, I did. Sami and I have had quite a few adventures, shall we say, since we met and there have been a few that would be right up there with the one you and Jay and your suite-mates pulled your third year in undergrad school. If I do remember correctly, you all decided to take the rowing team's boats out for a spin and got caught in a current that made it impossible to get back to shore. And, if I remember your Mama's tellin' of the story, y'all had to have shore patrol come and tow ya' back. And, then, ya' got a tongue lashin' and were put on community service for two weekends." Katelyn was laughing so hard she had to stop talking for a few minutes.

Finn was laughing right along with her. "Yup," he finally said after he caught his breath, "We sure did get into trouble for that one. But it was lots of fun and no one got hurt and the boats were not damaged. Just really wet. We laid low for a few weeks after that."

"I bet ya' did," Katelyn started to say when Finn's name was called and they were seated at the diner.

They ordered a bunch of stuff and then looked around to see who was there. Some of their childhood friends were there and they all started to get caught up on their lives.

"Hey, Katelyn, I hear you're quite the designer according to Ian. He loves your work," Dana said.

"Thanks, Dana. I do love my work and Ian and Ethan are great to work with. What are y'all up to these days?"

Folks continued to share their stories as they all ordered, ate and ate some more. The diner had slowed down by the time Katelyn and Fin were eating so there wasn't a need for their table. It was full nighttime when they all wandered back onto the sidewalk. They stood around teasing and talking for the longest time until someone started to yawn and they realized it was getting rather late.

"Hey, y'all, time to get along. We got the picnic tomorrow and I most surely do not want to be tired for that," Finn said.

Good-byes were said and he and Katelyn wandered back to his truck a couple of blocks away on a side street.

"Sure was fun tonight. Loved seein' everyone and getting caught up. But, holy cow, I'm all of a sudden really tired."

"Just set back and be cozy as I drive us back to The Creek," Finn said as they set out for home.

Katelyn didn't fall asleep like she thought she would. As they were just passing the road to Ethan's and Matthews' she saw a twinkling of lights in the field to their right.

"Stop! Look!" Katelyn yelled at Finn. He pulled over, stopped the truck, and looked where Katelyn was pointing. They both saw the field full of twinkling lights all above the field.

"What is that? It looks awesome'," Katelyn said as she got out of the truck to walk a couple of steps towards the field.

"Looks like a firefly convention," Finn replied.

They watched for a bit then the lights changed colors.

"Whoa! Did ya' see that? I've never saw fireflies do that before." Finn said.

"I think we're watchin' some Magic here, Finn."

"I do believe you're right," Finn said as he put an arm around Katelyn. The light show kept on for about ten minutes then slowly faded away.

"Wow! So cool," Finn said in awe.

"Thanks everyone for the light show. It really was special to be able to see it. So beautiful and a great way to end a fun night," Katelyn said softly.

"Oh, yeah, thanks," Finn added in awe. They stood there in the quiet for few minutes before getting back in the truck.

"I wonder if those are the same faerie lights that Matthews and Jenna saw last fall? Ya' know? When Matthews was showin' Jenna his property for the first time?" Katelyn wondered out loud.

"I wonder, too. Could be. There's so much Magic around here. And, they weren't that far from Jordan's farm, as the crow, or I should say, the eagle flies. Wonder if Jordan's place has anything to do with it, too?"

"Good thought. We'll have to give the idea some thought and ask Miss Cora about it," Katelyn said as they pulled into her driveway.

Finn leaned over and pulled Katelyn into his arms and they spent a few minutes saying goodnight in that special way that lovers do,

"Until tomorrow, my Finn," Katelyn said as she got out.

"Until tomorrow, my Katie girl," Finn said as he watched her go into her house. She blinked the porch light and he drove off home.

Katelyn got ready for bed and was thinking about Finn and the faerie lights as she fell into a restful sleep. All her dreams had faerie lights in them that night.

The Creek slept while the faeries went about their Magical ways.

CHAPTER 18

Saturday dawned as perfect as it could get. The Creek was a buzz with getting ready for the picnic in The Meadow.

Now, The Meadow wasn't in The Creek proper, but as long as anyone could remember it was considered a part of The Creek. The clan had been there since the beginning of time it seemed just like a lot of the families in the Blue Ridge. So, when the clan said they were having a picnic and all, The Creek was expected to be there with food, fun, and stories for everyone.

Ethan and Finn were taking care of getting Jordan to the picnic. Emily was cooking up a storm of deserts. Matthews and Jenna were getting their picnic basket ready and Jenna had some prints she had made of folks around The Creek she was gonna' give away. Mathews had done a security check, again, on Greg, and found that he was still listed working with the electric energy company just like before. He requested a deeper probe into his identity and was waiting for the results. This kind of investigation could take up to a week to get back.

Katelyn's family was bringing blueberry deserts of all kinds. Miss Cora was being picked up by Emily. Ted and Michael had a surprise for everyone. Seems Ted had been experimenting in the kitchen again and had sworn Michael to secrecy. Those two sure were a lot of fun.

Two o'clock found folks arriving at The Meadow and parking along the creek that ran along the west side. The clan had built a couple of footbridges across the creek. They looked like old-fashioned foot bridges from a time long gone bye. The creek they crossed ran a ways then flowed into the Crab Apple Creek. It was a lively thing and the sound was soothing and beautiful like a symphony. Folks began to set up under the shade of ancient trees along the other side of the creek. Ethan and Finn had set up a kind of recliner they had made just for Jordan. It had cushions and side tables for his stuff. It was adjustable as well.

Jordan gave a holler of joy when he saw the chair set-up. "You guys are amazin'. This looks to be just about perfect. Let's see how it works."

Finn moved Jordan's wheelchair next to the recliner and helped him stand up. Folks applauded this event as Jordan hadn't been using his crutches much on account of his stitches in his side. He bowed to all and they laughed and encouraged him along.

He set down in the recliner and was comfy in no time.

"Guys, this is great. It feels just right, too. It must of took ya' a while to build the thing."

"Oh, it did. We had a few adjustments to make along the way but we made it fine," Ethan said.

"Adjustments my ass. We made some great mistakes a couple of times and had to start over," Finn added laughing.

They filled Jordan and the folks close by in on the details and had everyone laughing for a while.

That's how Katelyn's family found them. They set up next to the guys and Katelyn and Kendra joined them a few minutes later.

Emily and Miss Cora set up along with the growing group and before long, there was a mess of folks set up along the creek. It was great how the creek curved around The Meadow so all could see each other and the open part of the field.

The games were being set up and the kids were getting excited. They loved this part of the picnic. Not much later, the head of the Redstone clan called everyone to attention.

"Howdy everyone. Great to see y'all here," Seth called out.

Everyone answered him back. The Redstone clan was scattered all around everyone else so it took a few minutes to get settled again.

"I see we have a few more folks wanderin' in. Come on and pick your-selves a spot. We've got plenty of room for everyone. We were just sayin' how it's been quite some time since we had a picnic so we decided to have this one and got the word out right away. I see word still gets around rather quickly as always."

Folks laughed and commented on this.

"As some of ya' know, our own great grandpappy has crossed over to that beautiful home in the sky. He was one-hundred and three years old and drinkin' his own shine right up to a few days before he took flight. So, the clan thought we should include him in this celebration as is only fittin'. Grand-pappy Redstone, we love ya' and miss ya' and welcome you here always."

Folks offered their support for a bit.

"Thanks, y'all. Some of ya' knew about his passin' and have been sharin' the love and we are much obliged. Now, Grandpappy Redstone would say enough about all that. Time to get this picnic goin'. The kid's games are ready to go over yonder. So, kids, off ya' go and have a lot a fun. The adult games will commence a bit later. Time to visit and all for now."

The crowd applauded and laughed as the kids ran over The Meadow to the area where the games were ready to go. The next hour and some saw kids winning and laughing and having a grand time.

While the kid's games were taking place a few late arrivals showed up. Katelyn had just connected with Sami and was saying hey as she moved around the place so folks could say hey as well.

"Sami, looks like you're outside today. You in a park or somethin?" Katelyn asked as she stood still for a minute.

"You could say that. I'd say I was at a picnic in The Meadow," Sami replied as she tapped Katelyn on the shoulder from behind her.

Katelyn whirled around and screamed an instant before she grabbed onto Sami. They hugged each other, laughing and crying and talking at the same time.

"What are ya' doin' here? Why didn't ya' tell me you were comin'?" Katelyn demanded as they finally stepped apart.

Folks were watching and laughing and some were even tearing up a bit 'cause they knew how much the two meant to each other and how much they had been missin' one another.

"I wanted to surprise ya'. I couldn't stand to be apart another second so I asked my bosses if I could take a long, long weekend and come visit y'all. I left early yesterday mornin' and got a room last night in Boone and here I am."

"For how long?" Katelyn asked.

"I need to be back a week from Monday," Sami said. "I'll be doin' some work while I'm here online of course."

Katelyn hollered something fierce. "Hot damn! Now that's what I call a surprise. Let's go meet everyone."

Katelyn dragged Sami to meet her parents first then everyone else. They finally ended up back at their picnic spot to meet Emily and Miss Cora.

"Nice to meet ya', Miss Cora. Emily," Sami said as she nodded her head at Miss Cora and got a hug from Emily.

"Really great to meet ya'," Emily replied.

"Ya' really surprised our Katelyn. Good job. She can figure out a surprise in a heartbeat. Glad you're here," Miss Cora said.

"So am I. I've missed her somethin' fierce. We both love our new lives but it doesn't take the place of the connection we've been growin' all these years. And, this place is beautiful. I loved the drive down yesterday once

I left all the city stuff behind. I can feel the Magic in these Blue Ridge mountains for sure."

Miss Cora looked right at Sami a minute, then replied, "I do believe ya' can."

They took to talking and sharing stories along with the rest of the folks at the picnic. It wasn't long before someone asked about The Meadow.

"Miss Cora, we all are aware of the special place The Creek is and all. And, we know there's a sweetness about The Meadow, like it was from a different time and place. Would ya' take a few minutes to tell us about this place? Seth, you, too, if ya' wouldn't mind."

Folks heard that Miss Cora and Seth were gonna' tell the tale about The Meadow and, soon everyone had gathered around. They all encouraged Seth and Miss Cora to tell the stories about The Meadow and settled down to listen.

Seth offered Miss Cora to begin. She accepted.

"Well, most of ya' know about The Magic in these here parts. Sami, I think you might have experienced some of the Magic as soon as you drove into the foothills."

Sami nodded her head in response.

"Thought so. It is a special place for sure. We here in the Blue Ridge, and especially in The Creek, are very protective of The Magic that lives here."

Folks agreed with Miss Cora.

"Now, as most of you know, my folks have been around here for hundreds of years, since the first folks arrived from Scotland and England. Most of your kin came over shortly after mine and Seth's did. I've been on our land since the beginning. The original cabin is long gone but the chimney stones from the original fireplace make up a good part of my own. Ya' gotta keep the history alive. My clan tells the story about findin' the Magic, or noticin' the Magic, right after they arrived. It was late in the summer and the air was beginning to get cool at night. They had to build a cabin and shelter for the animals as quick as they could. They spent every wakin' minute cutting, haulin', and shapin' logs for the cabin. They had it weather tight by late October. Good thing. Ya' know how it can get real cold that time of the year. The animal shelter was only just started and they felt a change in the air. Seems one of those surprise winter storms was on its way. Now, there weren't any folks nearby to help like now so my ancestors just kept working as hard as they could. The night the storm started they had only half-finished the shelter. They prayed that God would keep the animals safe and hunkered down for the storm.

"It lasted three whole days and on the fourth morning, they looked out the door and were met with a great surprise. Almost as great as Sami showin' up. They looked towards the shelter and saw that a whole barn had taken shape. A real, whole barn. They were stunned. They cleared a path right quick and when they walked into the barn, all the stalls were filled with hay and straw and such for the animals. Even the water buckets were full. They fell to their knees and thanked God for the miracle. Just as they were about to leave the most amazin' thing happened.

A brilliant light shown through the open door and then a figure appeared. It seemed to be floatin' in the air. They heard it talk to them tellin' them that the Other Worldly beings were very happy that my ancestors had listened to their dream visions and left Scotland to come to this place. It had been waiting for them for a long while. Seems my family was always meant to protect The Magic here just like in the highlands of Scotland. So, the great beings made sure my kin had everything they needed to survive and live on.

"Now, as far as The Meadow goes, we walked the land the next summer and found this place. It was so peaceful and calm. The Meadow seemed to glow as if it were beckonin' us to walk here. So, my kin did. And, when they did, they felt a slight tremor and then the mists came upon The Meadow. It was a sunny day so they couldn't figure out what was happenin'. The mists would part a bit and my kin say they thought they could see the faint shapes of mountains and valleys and lakes and such. They even thought they saw a woman. She was wavy and had flowin' hair and clothes. She smiled at them then vanished. She was only there for a second or two. Every summer, this apparition would appear for a few seconds then vanish. Seth can fill ya' in on more."

"Thanks, Miss Cora. Like Miss Cora said, this Meadow is Magical. My kin came here a couple of years after Miss Cora's. We rode the land and walked a great distance until we found this Meadow. Now, mind ya', we hadn't come upon Miss Cora's kin yet. This was, and still is, a big mountain. It was mid-summer when we found The Meadow and knew instantly that this was where we were to settle down. There were about twenty folks in the original group. They took to asking a blessin' on the land, including this Meadow. Then they all decided where to build their cabins. There were six to be built. We still have the original two-hundred acres and those cabins are still in use. We keep repairin' them as needed. My kin always told each generation about findin' this place and that under no circumstances was anything to be built here, in The Meadow. Each generation has followed this directive. One thing, though, was that my kin saw the apparition just like Miss Cora's kin.

"The first time was the next summer after we got here. My greats grandpappy happen to be walkin' along the creek and saw someone standin' just about where we are today. By the way, y'all know the name of the creek, right? No? Well, it's called the Whispering Creek 'cause it always sounds like someone is talkin' in a quiet voice. Anyways, my greats grandpappy saw this person standing here and walked over to him. It was Miss Cora's greats grandpappy. They introduced themselves and then Miss Cora's kin shushed my kin and pointed to the middle of The Meadow. Just then, the apparition began to appear. My kin was stunned by it all. Miss Cora's kin had to take a hold of my kin's arm 'cause he thought the fella' was gonna' collapse. He smiled at him and they both kept watchin' for the longest time until the sun started to settle over the trees and the apparition vanished.

"Story goes they both stood there mesmerized until it was full dark then came back to their senses. That's when the friendship between our two clans got started and how it got started."

Folks started talking about this and kept it up for a few minutes until Seth brought them back around.

"Now, over the centuries, this apparition seems to keep appearing most summers. Not all of them, but most of them. We haven't seen it yet this year. But, one thing my kin did say was that the harmony of the land needed to be kept in balance. Seems whenever they had folks around for a gatherin' here, their land flourished in every way. Animals seemed to be plentiful. The plants and all seemed to grow more and more and furnish all the livin' creatures with food and such. So, the Redstone clan has continued the tradition of gatherin's for centuries. Not gonna' stop somethin' that helps everyone out. So, let's get to enjoyin' each other and this beautiful place. We have a new event that's about to start. It's a burger cook-off. Ted and Michael are in charge, kind of. Go on over and get cookin', 'cause we're all gonna' taste them to decide who's the winner."

Folks thanked Miss Cora and Seth for the storytelling and went about visiting with each other. The kids' games had just ended and kids were running all around showing their folks the ribbons and prizes and crafts they had won and made.

The next bit of a while found the burger cook-off a grand event. Everyone that tasted the burgers voted and their vote was placed in a hat. Once the votes were counted, Seth announced the winner.

"Well, folks, these were some tasty burgers and y'all have picked a winner. It's George's bacon, cheddar, jalapeno burger. Congratulations George. We'll have the burger-shaped trophy for ya' in a few weeks, as soon as it's finished. It'll have your name on it, of course. Now, let's get to all the fun games and such."

Folks wandered over to that area of The Meadow for the next few hours having a grand time.

As the games ended, a dinner triangle was sounded and folks brought their dish-to-pass to the common area and all commenced to eating.

Katelyn and Sami found a spot on one of the blankets their family had spread out and started in on their dinner.

"This is fabulous, Katie. This food is so delicious. I think I'm gonna' need seconds and thirds," Sami mumbled with a mouth full.

Folks close by laughed at Sami and agreed with her.

"Hey, Ethan, is Jordan all set?" Katelyn asked.

"Yes, Ma'am, he is. Finn filled his plate full and then some. Look at him. He's about as happy as anyone can get. And, he didn't have to walk over there and get it."

Ethan laughed at the faces Jordan was making while trying to eat.

"This food is so heavenly. I love livin' in The Creek. Hey, anybody know who made the three-bean baked bean dish? It has molasses in it," Jordan asked.

"I did," a voice was heard to say. It was Clara Redstone, Seth's wife.

"Well, ma'am, these are the best I think I've tasted in a long while. Thanks for fixin' them and all," Jordan offered.

"Thank you, Jordan. Those are mighty kind words. Wouldn't be a picnic without 'em," was Clara's reply said with a smile.

Folks ate and gathered more and kept on eating until evening started to show.

As the food was packed away, a fiddle could be heard tuning up. Then a guitar and a mandolin and a harmonica joined in.

The Redstone clan was known for their music all over the Blue Ridge and the crowd was in for a treat. Lanterns were lit and hung around the edge of The Meadow and the music took hold. Old tunes from the old countries were played. Current tunes were added in. They played a few tunes for dancing and all. Folks jumped right up to dance. A while after the night came on, the fiddler began an old ballad that most folks knew and the singing that came about was sweeter and more beautiful than any had heard in a long while. The ballad was a long one and when it was finished, there was a hush around The Meadow as folks just sat and remembered things.

Seth eventually stepped forward. "Folks, thanks so much for joinin' us here in The Meadow for the picnic. I see some of the little ones are already dreamin' about today. It's time to gather our things and say so long until the next time we meet. We love y'all so much. Take care of yourselves."

Folks offered farewells and hugs were given and received. Miss Cora went over to Seth for a little chat.

"Seth, this was just perfect as always. Ya' gonna' stay behind a bit?"

"Yes, Miss Cora, my kin and I are gonna' stay behind like always. You?"

"Yes, Seth," Miss Cora answered and walked on over to the middle of The Meadow as the last folks were driving away.

Seth, his kin, and Miss Cora stood silent in the middle of The Meadow, offering thanks to the White Light and all.

A short time later, they were greeted with three spirits that appeared right in front of them.

The Spirits spoke. "We know this is different than usual. You are all aware that a great evil is trying to take this place from you. Stay strong. It will be a different kind of battle. You have always taken great care of The Magic and this sacred space and we thank you. Miss Cora, place a protection grid here just like you did at Jordan's farm. Get Emily, Kendra and Katelyn to assist and Ethan, too. Just like you did before. Do it tomorrow. It will make a big difference and protect this place. We thank you for your continued vigilance. Blessed be."

The three spirits floated away and the apparition that had always appeared here came to life. The group watched as they had always done. The apparition only stayed for a brief few minutes then vanished as always.

"Well, that was different," Miss Cora said as they walked over to the footbridge.

"Yes, it was. But I'm not surprised," Seth replied. "Somethin' is afoot here and we best be prepared."

"Agreed. I'll get in touch with the girls first thing tomorrow and we'll come set the grid as soon as possible. Thanks, Seth. This was real special as always," Miss Cora said sharing a hug with Seth and his kin.

They all waved as they drove off.

"I don't think I've ever been to a picnic like this before. This was fabulous!" Sami said as they got ready to drive away from The Meadow.

"I still can't believe you're really here. This is the coolest thing," Katelyn replied." Let's get home so we can talk and talk,' Katelyn said.

They drove off and were home a little bit later.

"Oh my God Katelyn! Finn is gorgeous! I could just stare at him forever," Sami said as they went up onto the porch.

"Yup. And he's all mine," Katelyn said laughing as they went into the house.

"I guess when you decided to come home, it was the right thing to do. You seem so happy and at ease. And, Finn is an extra bonus."

"You are correct on all counts. I'm glad I came home, too. It feels so right. The work with Ethan and his gang is a blast. Not really work at all. And havin' Finn there every day is what I call a fringe benefit."

"I can see that. It's quite apparent he adores you with the way he's always lookin' at you and makin' sure you have everything you could want and need. And, what a guy to help out with Jordan all day."

"Well, Sami, that's what we do here in The Creek. We do take care of each other. It's a natural kind a thing."

"I can see that. Those two mountain men you call Bubba and Earl, well, I met them and they were real polite and all. I was told by a few that they make the best moonshine in the Blue Ridge. They offered me a taste. I took a little sip and, for sure, that stuff is pure alcohol. Whew!"

"You actually had some shine? I haven't even done that yet. Don't really like the hard stuff but a cold brew on a hot day is great!"

"Oh, I agree. I always wanted to see what it would taste like. I handed the cup back to Earl and he laughed a bit at the face I made. He said he understood and thought I was a real sport for tryin' it. He said I belong to The Creek family now and all."

"Well, I could have told ya' that. As soon as The Creek heard about you, they adopted you 'cause you're my BFF."

"Well, I accept and would be proud to be called one of The Creek's own."

"So glad you're here. So much to tell you and show you. But, first thing is we have to get you settled. Here, take your stuff and we'll do that right now,"

Sami looked through the window across the road and saw The Store. "So, I take it that's the famous Bend in The Road Country Store?"

"Yes, it is and we love Ted and Michael and everything they have and do. Their food is famous all over the Blue Ridge. Some folks take a drive just to eat here."

"You were tellin' me about their breakfast bagels. I gotta' get me one tomorrow. For now, I think I'm ready for that settlin' in you mentioned."

Katelyn got Sami all settled and was sitting on the bed with her a few minutes later.

Sami looked across the way and saw Kendra's light on.

"That's Kendra next door, right? She sounds so sweet. I can't wait to talk with her," Sami said with a big yawn.

"Time for sleep. More of The Creek tomorrow. So glad you surprised me with you today. Love ya' forever and always, my Sami," Katelyn said as they hugged good night.

"Love you forever and always, my Katie girl.' Sami said in return.

A few minutes later the lights in both houses were off.

The Creek and The Meadow slept. The Magic was safe.

CHAPTER 19

unday morning dawned in its usual way. Sami and Katelyn found their way to The Store around nine and met up with a few others.

"Hey, Ted, Michael. I would like you to meet, again, my best friend in the world, Sami," Katelyn said making the introduction.

"Sami, this here is Ted and this here is Michael."

"Nice to meet you both, again," Sami said.

"It's our pleasure. Katelyn's been talkin' about you ever since she came home so we kinda' have a knowin' about ya' and it's all good," Ted said.

"Great to finally meet you in person," Michael added.

"Well, Sami has heard me talk about your delicious breakfast bagels for so long that she is demanding to have one this morning," Katelyn said as they walked up into the dining room.

"This is really cool, guys," Sami said lookin all around. "I know I've never seen anything like this before. It really suits the place."

"Thanks, Sami. We love it as well. Now, what can I get you two for breakfast?" Ted asked.

"I'll have an onion bagel with egg, sausage and cheese, please," Sami replied.

"And you, Katelyn. The usual?" Ted said laughing.

"Yes, indeedy, Ted," Katelyn replied. "We'll get our drinks and have a seat if that's okay with y'all?"

"Sure thing, Miss Katelyn," Hal said standing up and making a place for the two of them.

"Hal, not sure if ya' met Sami yesterday and all," Katelyn said.

182

"Yes, we did," Sami replied. "Nice to see ya' again, Hal. Thanks for making some space here for us."

"Of course," Hal said.

The table was full of folks and they talked about the picnic as Ted brought order after order out from the kitchen.

Sami bit into her bagel and moaned. "Oh God! This is truly paradise. I don't think I can ever leave."

Folks laughed at her comments and everyone enjoyed Ted's creations for a bit.

Some folks left and more arrived. Katelyn's cell buzzed and she excused herself from the table to talk in the front of The Store.

"Okay, Miss Cora. I'll be ready about two. Thanks for callin'," Katelyn said ending the call.

"Everything okay, Katelyn?" Michael asked rather concerned.

"Oh, sure. We're just gonna' go up to The Meadow and set a protection grid there. Seems Seth and Miss Cora were talkin' and it seemed the right thing to do."

"That would mean somethin's probably about to happen around here," Michael said rather quietly.

"I do believe you're right, Michael. I'm still really new to all this, but from what y'all have told me about the other stuff that's happened in the past, I would say you're right about that thought. Let's keep it quiet for now. I really don't want folks to worry."

"I agree. You be careful up there. All of you," Michael said as Katelyn put her phone away and went back to the table.

"Everything okay?" Sami asked.

"Yup. Just the usual stuff goin' on around here. Let's get on back to the house and bother Kendra. She needs to be invaded on this beautiful day. And, I don't think I could eat another bite. Ted, great as usual," Katelyn said as she and Sami headed to the front to pay Michael.

They paid their bill and headed outside. They walked over to Kendra's house. She was on the porch with a cup of her favorite tea as was the custom on a summer Sunday morning.

"Mornin', you two. I see you've been to Ted for breakfast. How was it, Sami?"

"Beyond delicious. I think I may have to stay in The Creek. I know I've only had one, but with yesterday's food and that bagel breakfast, I don't think I could be happy anywhere else."

"Oh, oh, Katelyn. Our secret is out. It's Ted's creations that keep folks in The Creek," Kendra said laughing with them as they sat down.

"Kendra, I wanted to include Sami in on today's agenda, if you get my drift," Katelyn started.

"I agree," Kendra replied.

"What's goin' on here?" Sami asked.

"Well, that phone call I had in The Store was Miss Cora. Seems the White Light wants us to place a protection grid around The Meadow right now, today. It's imperative we do it immediately.," Katelyn explained.

"That hunch we had the other day, Katelyn, about somethin goin' on here? I do believe we were right in that hunch. If the White Light has asked us to set a grid, it means The Dark is really on the war path. Not sure why The Meadow, though. It does hold Magic and all, but I heard an urgency in Miss Cora's voice that I've not heard before. I suspect The Meadow holds a lot more of The Magic than anyone around here has seen and knows about."

"Really? That means it's gonna' be a tough one today, right Kendra?" Katelyn offered.

"I suspect so. Miss Cora said Ethan will pick us up a bit before two. In the meantime, why don't the two of you enjoy this beautiful day. Get Sami caught up on all the stuff about The Creek. Ya' might want to set up a visit with Emily and then with Laine and Mo. Ya' gotta' go to their farms to get the full jest of their specialness"

"That's what I was thinkin'," Katelyn said. "Come on, Sami. Let's make some calls."

Sami and Katelyn waved at Kendra as they talked and walked back over to Katelyn's porch. A few minutes later all was set.

"Emily says any time and Laine and Mo are lookin' forward to Tuesday evenin' for supper," Katelyn told Sami.

"Great. I liked visitin' with them all yesterday. They seem to be real special folks. And that Emily, wow, with all you've told me about how she got here, I am lookin' forward to meetin' her for sure."

"What do ya' mean, how she got here? I told you she had kin that left the land to her and how she built the farm and all. Remember?"

Sami took only a split second to realize what she had said. "That's what I meant. Ya' know, the way she got the farm and all. I can't wait to see the covered bridge. It sounds so cool."

"It is. It's the coolest thing. I've never seen anyone have one on their farm."

"Well, let's drive down the Pine Ridge Road and I can show ya' some of the stuff Ethan's been buildin' and we can check in on Jordan. I've got a few hours before I have to meet with the others," Katelyn suggested.

"I'd love to. Can't wait to see all of The Creek," Sami replied as they got their stuff and piled into Katelyn's SUV and were off.

"There's the sign I told ya' about that landed here in the storm. Finn and Ethan made that frame and all and all of The Creek showed up to see it set a ways back off the road. We had lots of pictures taken with it. Michael framed the best one in a big portrait frame and then made a frame just for a bunch of the other pictures. He sent the big portrait off just a few days ago and the folks in Georgia set up a video chat with The Creek thankin' everyone. We're gonna' take pictures for all the seasons and holidays and share them with the Georgia clan."

"It looks even better in person. I love the whole story," Sami said as they went down the road.

They arrived at Jordan's a bit later. Katelyn took Sami to the barn to have a look at the eagles.

"They are magnificent. The babies don't look much like babies anymore," Sami said as one of them poked its head over the edge of the nest.

"And, they all fly really well, now, too. I wonder when they're gonna' leave the nest for good? We've been told by the chiefs that it shouldn't' be long now. They'll make their home somewhere in the area and probably come by from time to time as eagles do."

"So cool," Sami said in a hushed voice.

"Let's go check on Jordan. I know he has folks in all the time, but I still feel connected to him with those special crystals and all," Katelyn said as they walked to the back porch where they found Jordan.

"Hey, Jordan. Looks like you're getting around more and more. How's the pain?" Katelyn asked as they stepped up onto the porch.

"Hey, Katelyn, Sami. Mighty nice of y'all to come visitin'. Not much pain anymore. More like a soreness and muscle fatigue. My physical therapist is workin' me hard even with the leg still in the cast. It's been about two weeks now. Doc says another cast change this week and four to six more weeks in different casts. He wants to make sure my leg heals right the first time."

"I like this doctor of yours. Glad to hear the pain is mostly gone. You look pretty good on those crutches, too," Katelyn said.

"Hey, Jordan. I sure am sorry for all this trouble that fell on ya'. It just doesn't seem right for a good guy to suffer like this," Sami said.

"Why thanks much, Sami. I appreciate your worryin' about me. I really enjoyed our talkin' at the picnic yesterday. I want to hear more about the underground railroad thing you've discovered. Will ya' keep me posted along with Katelyn?" Jordan asked.

"I would be happy to, Jordan," Sami replied.

They visited for a short while then were on their way.

Katelyn showed Sami where she worked and where Matthews and Jenna lived. Sami knew all the stories that went with everyone in The Creek.

"This is great. Now, I have the real picture of where everything is," Sami said as they headed back to the house.

"I've gotta 'go along in about an hour so, so let me know if there's anything ya' need, Sami," Katelyn said as the settled around the house.

"Well, ya' know how you're always sayin' how things work out just like they're supposed to? And, ya' know I believe that and always have?"

"Yeah, and," Katelyn said smiling at Sami.

"Well, it just so happens that the manager of the Boston site would like to video meet this afternoon. He asked about it this mornin' and I said I'd get back to him. So, when you told me about the grid, I texted him back and we're gonna' do a video meeting at two-thirty. Probably take a good hour and some. He's got a lot of questions and so do I."

"Love when it all works out," Katelyn said as they talked and walked around the house.

Ethan pulled in just before two and Katelyn and Kendra were ready.

"You take care now," Sami said as they pulled away.

"We will. No worries," Kendra said seriously.

Ethan waved and Sami watched them as they went around the bend in the road on their way to pick up Miss Cora.

Miss Cora had been on the phone with all of them that morning and each one was ready. Miss Cora was standing outside when Ethan drove in.

"Hey, Miss Cora," Ethan said as she got into the truck.

"Hey, y'all. Got everything ready? Crystals cleansed?" Miss Cora asked.

"Yes, Ma'am," Katelyn and Kendra replied.

"Alright then. Let's go, Ethan. And, thanks for getting us there," Miss Cora said.

"Always anything you need, Miss Cora," Ethan replied as they drove north towards The Meadow.

When they arrived, they found Seth and Emily waiting for them Seth had his gator ready for them.

"I though ya 'might need the big gator, so I brought this one," Seth said.

"Mighty kind of ya' to think of us, Seth," Miss Cora said as the tools and things the women would need were placed in the gator.

"Ready?" Seth asked, then they were off to the eastern-most border of The Meadow.

"Y'all hear that? Sounds like The Meadow is hummin'," Katelyn said.

"I do believe you're right, Katelyn. It seems The Magic is showin its strength today. I suspect this is gonna' be more powerful than Jordan's was," Emily said.

"For sure," Kendra said as they came to a stop.

"The eastern-most border is at those two giant pines. They set on our land, but beyond them is the national forest area," Seth offered.

"Thanks, Seth. Ladies, let's get busy," Kendra said as the women gathered their things and headed over to the pines.

"Should we go with them in case they need protectin' or something?" Seth asked of Ethan.

"Seth, you're about to see how The Magic takes care of the special ones around here. It is somethin' to behold. Can't find the words to tell ya' about it. Ya' really just have to watch and feel everything that's happenin'. Don't worry, we'll all be okay," Ethan explained as they stood and watched the women.

They placed the crystals into Mother Earth at the eastern border. A slight breeze came up just like at Jordan's farm.

They moved along to the southern border and even before they got out of the gator, the breeze became a strong wind.

"This is gonna' be somethin' to remember," Miss Cora said as she gathered her crystal and Kendra started to dig the hole. The sky began to cloud over as the prayers were said. As each crystal was placed, the wind became stronger and the sky became darker.

When they arrived at the western boundary, the wind was strong enough that they had to bend into it to get to the place for the crystals. Emily began digging the hole and the wind screamed at them.

"Stay strong," Kendra said as she placed her crystal in the hole.

As Emily bent to place her crystal, she was knocked over by a sudden gust of wind. She rolled back to the hole and dropped her crystal. The sky turned red.

Miss Cora bent and walked to the hole and as she extended her arm, she was pushed back. She stood tall and yelled, "You have no power over me. I walk in The White Light!"

She moved to the hole and as the wind howled, she placed her crystal.

Katelyn was the last one. She stared to take the step she would need and found she couldn't move forward.

"It's as if there's a wall here," she yelled as the wind was screaming and howling non-stop.

The other women stood next to her, linked arms and moved the one step closer and bent with Katelyn as she dropped her crystal in the hole.

Lightening flew all around as the wind intensified.

"Let's get to the northern boundary. This is gonna' be a doozy," Miss Cora said as they set out in the gator.

Stuff was flyin' all around them. They hunched over to stay safe. It took a few extra minutes to get to the northern boundary.

Miss Cora motioned to them to look at The Meadow. The grid was active on all the three directions. It shown like brilliant blue lightning.

"We need to stay touching each other for this. Keep chanting for White Light protection," Miss Cora instructed the women.

As soon as they touched the ground, they locked arms. Good thing. The Dark was about to throw all it had at them. Seems The Meadow held a lot more than just Magic and The Dark wanted control of it, whatever it was.

The women walked the few steps to the site. Seth had parked as close as he could to the place for the crystals.

The full assault on the women began as soon as Miss Cora touched the earth with the shovel.

The earth shook. The women were still linked together and they kept Miss Cora upright as she dug the hole. The Dark caused an earthquake that should have pulverized the mountains but the women were chanting for White Light protection and help from everyone on The Oher Side.

As Kendra dropped her crystal, the earth shook and the wind became a cyclone.

As Emily dropped her crystal, the cyclone came right at them.

As Katelyn dropped her crystal, the cyclone struck with lightning bolts of fire.

The women had to lay flat on the ground to keep from being killed by The Dark.

As Miss Cora reached over the earth to place the last crystal that would connect the protection grid, the women were pulled from the earth by a mighty force. Miss Cora took one look at the hole and dropped her crystal as they were twirled around, about to be thrown into the sky.

The next thing they knew, they were all on the ground, the earth was still and the cyclone and all were gone.

It was eerily quiet as they lay there catching their breath.

Seth and Ethan had been thrown to the ground as well.

As they all began to stand up, Miss Cora said, "Well, I guess my aim was perfect."

The others started to laugh and nod their heads.

"Sure was," Emily said as she brushed stuff off her like the others were doing.

"Whew! That was somethin' else," Seth said as he looked at the women. "You do this all the time?"

"Well, no. Only when needed," Kendra said.

"You women are powerful for sure. So glad we're on the same side," Seth said as he shook his head in wonder.

"Me, too," Ethan agreed.

"Now, let's get that water we brought. I need a drink somethin' fierce," Miss Cora said as she swayed a bit.

"Here, Miss Cora, you just sit down right here in the gator. Here's the water," Katelyn said as she handed a bottle to Miss Cora.

They all took a long drink and sat quiet for a bit.

"Well, I guess this place is real special. I've never had that kind of struggle with The Dark when I've set a protection grid," Miss Cora said. "Jordan's was a bit fierce, too. But not like this."

"I've been a part of two grids and I must say I couldn't even have imagined any of this no matter how creative I am," Katelyn added.

"Same here," Emily said. "This will go down in my history book as somethin' truly unexplainable."

"I've always known about The Magic around here and that The Meadow is special with The Magic. Just didn't know The Dark wanted it at all. And, now, as badly as it does. Guess this means it's not gonna' get it, right?" Seth asked the women.

"Not now, with the grid in place. It's there forever," Kendra replied.

"Good. I wouldn't want to have to cancel the picnics, ya' know?" Seth said with a wink and a smile.

"Agreed," Ethan said.

"Don't really know all about The Magic and all, but if there's anything I can do to protect it, I will," Seth promised.

"We know, Seth. And, The White Light knows and that's all that matters. You and your kin have been and are still doin' your part and we all thank ya' for that," Miss Cora told Seth.

"Our privilege. Always."

Kendra stood up and stretched a bit. "Well, I guess we better be getting back. I think we've been out here for hours. Must be nigh onto five o'clock or so."

"Well, Kendra, it's only about half past three. Ya' know how time gets wonky when we're workin' with The Magic. That's one thing I've learned really well," Katelyn said.

"Really? I guess you're right. I always get lost in time when workin' with The Magic, too. Anyway, let's get on home, y'all," Kendra replied.

They got back into the gator and Seth drove them to the footbridge.

"I think I'm gonna' need a nap and all," Seth and Ethan said at the same time.

They all laughed as they said good-bye and headed home.

The Creek spent the rest of Sunday having fun and visiting around. Evening found most everyone home and getting ready for the week.

That is most everyone. Greg and his fellow demons were working on a plan they liked. They were in the apartment in Boone and were busy with the details.

They knew they couldn't get to Jordan and his land because of the protection grid. However, they had come up with a way of trying to kill him.

"I like this plan," Greg said as he walked around the table with the map of The Creek and the surrounding areas. It was a geological map that had the geothermal springs and creeks that flowed from the springs on it. They had circled the springs and high-lighted the streams that flowed from them.

They were concentrating on the two streams that flowed beneath Jordan's far edge of the land, near the eastern/southeastern border. Finn had tapped into these streams and their geothermal power for Jordan's farm. They supplied all the heat and water he would need. He had those new solar panels that Laine and Mo had designed on his barn and house roofs for electricity. He was still connected to the electrical grid for a while just in case something didn't work well. The new glass solar panes that really looked like windows were being tested on Jordan's farm for the first time. The girls had been using them on their green houses, but that was a much smaller scale project. Jordan's farm was the first big structure test in place. Everyone was excited about how it would work and could hardly wait for a year to go by to look at the results. If these solar panels worked, the whole of The Creek was gonna' add them to their buildings and lower, if not completely wipe out, their electric bills.

Well, Greg and The Dark were working on a plan that would change the power in the streams to Dark Energy, which they then would control and be able to kill Jordan and have someone buy his land. A demon imposter like Greg. A shapeshifter. They just had to figure out how the Dark energy was gonna' do its worst.

And that's what they were talking about on that Sunday evening. Outta' nowhere, Madman appeared. He was as disgusting as always.

"Madman! Please, change yourself," Greg yelled. "You're even more gross than usual."

Madman changed into a human as he said, "Why thank you, Greg, for the complement. I was just killin' a few creatures on the planet Zaeton 'cause they were tryin' to cheat me out of my reward."

"Rightly so you were. What brings you here, Madman?" Greg asked.

Madman looked around at the others in human form. Some of them were looking scared of him.

"You should be afraid of me. If you don't do your job, I will torture you for eternity," Madman said with a sinister laugh.

"Understood," they all replied at the same time.

"To answer your question, Greg, I'm here to give you some news. Those White Lighters from The Creek set a protection grid over The Meadow. The Dark is not happy at all. He's on the war path. He's blowin' up stars and all again just like after the storm thing. He thought he had The White Light fooled about takin' The Meadow. He was just about to take it when he saw those humans settin' up the grid. The Dark sent earthquakes and cyclones with fire bolts to kill them but they called upon The White Light for protection and finished the grid."

"I felt a powerful surge a while ago and wondered what it was. It was Dark energy just didn't know why it was around. Now what?"

"Well, you got any ideas how to get Jordan's land?"

"Yes, we are just figurin' out the details," Greg answered.

"Tell me," Madman demanded.

Greg hurriedly explained their idea. Madman like it and asked for details.

"We were just startin' to figure those out when you stopped by," Greg said. "Got any ideas we could use? You've done this stuff a hell of a lot more than us. We could use your expert advice."

"Yes, I have. Let's see," Madman said as he walked over to the map and took a few minutes to study it.

"Well, let's see. One, you could stop the flow of water to the farm, but they'd just dig a well. You could turn the water cold, but that wouldn't work, either."

"How about putting Dark Energy in the stream? We could charge it with the ability to destroy stuff? Remember, we're just thinkin' here."

"I like that idea. Now, how can we charge it so it would destroy stuff?"

No one said anything for the longest time until one of the newer demons began to speak.

"I know I'm new at this, but I'm just remembering a tv show I saw as a kid. The evil guy made water turn into like, an energy bolt, when it got near its target and it was blowin' things up and killin' people all over the place," the new demon said.

Madman looked right at this new demon. "Now, that's not a bad idea. I like that. Good thinkin'. I know just how to charge the water. Now to figure out how to get it to target Jordan and anyone else who is on his land. Humans. That's the special thing we need to target. Keep thinkin'. I'm gonna' check in with a few of the other upper-class demons and see what we can come up with. Good job everyone. At least you will all live a while longer," Madman said as he transformed back to his usual gross self. "Later," he said and he was gone in an instant.

Greg looked at the others then said, "Good job rememberin' stuff, new demon. Keep it up. That's enough for tonight. Back to your fake selves for tomorrow. I'll call a meeting in a day or two. You get a hold of me if you come up with anything. And I mean anything. We don't want to disappoint The Dark now, do we?"

The all disappeared and Greg was left alone. He was working on a plan of his own to get back at The Creek for getting in his way when he was about to take Jenna's artistic gift from her in The Store that one afternoon. He was pissed at being stopped from having a little fun killing an earthling. They were useless to him so why not kill some for fun?

The Dark's anger was building.

CHAPTER 20

Tuesday found Katelyn and Sami at Lanie and Mo's for supper.

"So glad we could do this. I love it when ya' come over Katelyn and, now, ya' got your Sami here as well," Laine said as they walked around the farm, showing everything to Sami.

"Well, I'm really glad to be here after hearin' about all your special farmin' techniques and such," Sami said.

"We've been real busy this summer. We finalized the new glass solar panels that look like regular glass by adding a transition chemical so when the batteries are full, the glass looks like it's one big sunglass lens. That way, there is no over-charging of the batteries and they last longer. Jordan's been tryin' them out on his place and they are working perfectly."

"So perfect", Mo added, "that Ethan's customer down the road from Jordan is having them installed on his house and barn and such. We love this whole thing. We've had a bunch of companies try to buy us out, but we keep sayin' no. Hope they get the message soon."

"Katelyn told me about them and I just had to see for myself. Where do y'all make them?" Sami asked as they walked out behind the barn and found a new greenhouse.

"This is where we make them. It's really easy since we got the chemical formula for attracting the solar rays and all. Glass is easy to make. We mix a batch up, pour it into the molds and wait about three days for it to cure. Then we try a few of the panes out on our test roof up there. If they collect energy at a specific rate, they're good to go."

"You two are fantastic!" Katelyn said as she looked around.

They walked over to the marijuana greenhouse to show Sami how the glass solar panels were working. They were clear and that meant that they were collecting energy and sending it to the storage batteries.

"We've got four different varieties here as you can tell from the separate rooms. We're gonna' be seeding the late fall grow this week."

"Wow! You really know what you're doin'," Sami said as she wandered from doorway to doorway. "Some look like they're about ready to cut."

"You're right. We think about Thursday. We check a couple of times a day at this point of growth."

"Where do y'all dry them?"

"In the greenhouse behind this one. It's a dryin' shed, so to speak," Mo explained. "It's empty right now so we're cleanin' it up for the new crop. It has to be completely cleaned of dust and stuff so it won't damage the buds. We turned the dehumidifier system on two days ago. Should be ready right on time."

They walked through the rest of the greenhouses with the veggies and fruits and such and finally settled on the porch. A special blend was passed around with cold brews and the girls thoroughly enjoyed themselves.

"Now this is what I'm talkin' about…vacation time," Sami said as she laughed.

"Agreed," Katelyn said.

It was well into the night when the buzz fell away and the girls figured it was time to leave.

"Thanks, Laine and Mo, for this special visit. Loved it all so much," Sami said.

"I love ya 'both. Ya' know that," Katelyn said as they hugged and promised to meet again soon.

After the girls left, Laine looked at Mo and said, "I'm getting that feelin' again, Mo."

"Me, too," Mo said. "Wonder what The Dark wants this time?"

"Always The Magic, Mo. Always," Laine said as they turned off the lights and headed up to their rooms.

"I'm thinkin' there's somethin' more this time. Somethin' none of us really know about, except maybe our Miss Cora. We'll see. Sleep well," Laine said as they went their separate ways.

Friday afternoon found Jordan restless. He'd been home almost two weeks and had been making great progress. He had just gotten a new cast on. It was made of fiberglass and had waterproof on the inside so he could sit in the tub and shower. It was now set just below his knee to his toes. And, he had already had one physical therapy session on how to begin to bend his leg without damaging it.

He wanted to get out and around the place. He asked Kevin if he would take him around in his golf cart.

A few minutes later, they were headed to the barn to look at the eagles.

"Wow! These guys have really grown a lot in the past three weeks," Jordan started to say when the two babies took to flying around the barn and then outside. "Holy cow! They can fly. So cool!"

Kevin drove Jordan outside and they went behind the barn to watch the eaglets. Jordan felt a sudden urge to go over near the cave.

"Kevin, can we take a ride over the field to a place I know about? I'll show ya' how to get there."

"Sure. Lead on," Kevin said as Jordan directed him over the field to just before the cave entrance. He didn't want Kevin to know about the cave. Or anyone, for that matter. Jordan instinctively knew that no one besides Katelyn and he were to know about the cave.

"Okay. Stop here. This will do. I'll just take a few steps around. No worries, this new cast is so light, it makes it easier to move."

Kevin stayed with the golf cart as he watched Jordan walk a few steps away. Jordan was in front of the cave entrance. Ya' still couldn't tell there was a cave here 'cause of the bushes in front, but Jordan was very protective of the cave and didn't want to take any chances. He looked down and there was another crystal just setting on the ground. It looked like a miniature pineapple. It was yellow with blue and white spikes off the top. It was about a quarter the size of a real pineapple. As he bent to pick it up, he all of a sudden knew it was for Sami. He put it into his pocket and walked back to the golf cart.

"Hey Kevin, look," Jordan said as he took the crystal out of his shirt pocket and showed it to Kevin.

"Wow! Now, that's beautiful. Looks like a little pineapple," Kevin said as he looked at the crystal.

"Yup. Just what I was thinkin,'" Jordan said as he settled into the cart.

"Looks like someone is givin' you a sign that all is okay around here," Kevin said as they drove back to the house.

"I do believe you're right about that, Kevin," Jordan said.

Once Jordan was settled back on the porch, he held the new crystal in his hand for the longest time. He could hear it humming and it glowed softly. He made a silent promise to get it to Sami the next day.

Katelyn and Sami went over to Emily's the next Saturday. Sami loved riding and hadn't done any in a long time. Emily was getting her on a horse and taking her around the meadow.

"Well, how do I look?" Sami said after they got on the horses.

"Ya' look like you belong there," Emily said. "Let's start out real slow and easy."

They went out to Emily's Meadow and walked the horses around for a bit.

"Ya' look like you remember how to ride," Emily offered.

"It's all comin' back to me. I love this," Sami said.

"Let's go on up to The Sacred Rock Meadow the long way around. Should take about a half hour to get there."

"Sounds good to me," Katelyn said.

They set out by going down by the pond and out of Emily's Meadow on the southwest side then up through the forest. There were natural trails there and they fully enjoyed them.

They arrived at The Sacred Rock Meadow about a half hour later. They had stopped to look at the forest and mountains along the trail.

They dismounted and tied the horses to a post near a small natural pond. They walked the few yards to the opening in the meadow.

Sami just stared at the place for the longest time. "I don't know what to say. Beautiful. Magnificent. Indescribable. The energy here is like nothin' I've ever felt before."

"Let's go inside for just a few minutes," Emily said.

They walked inside The Meadow and all three of them heard the humming at the same time.

"Just like always," Emily said.

They watched as the lights came and played on the stones and the birds flew all around. An eagle appeared, as was the usual thing, and set down on the center alter stone. Katelyn and Emily bowed to it as Sami watched. It bobbed its head back at them then took flight.

Sami was in total shock and amazement. She just kept looking at everything without sayin a word.

"I think Sami might be close to overload. Let's step out of the meadow," Emily said as she guided Sami out past the boundary.

Sami blinked her eyes a few times and shook herself. "Never have I ever been a part of anything so magnificent."

"It truly is," Katelyn agreed.

"Let's get our water and sit for a minute or two," Emily said as they walked over to the horses then found a shady spot and sat down.

Katelyn was glad to see that The Sacred Rock Meadow was still the same. At least something was.

"That is the most peaceful and beautiful place I've ever seen," Sami said. "Do you go there often, Emily?"

"It all depends. If there's trouble with The Dark I go there for information and energy. Otherwise, I leave it alone," Emily said.

"Katelyn, have you ever been here before?" Sami asked.

"Yes. Just once. It was, oh, I don't even know how to describe it. But it was that," Katelyn replied.

"Let's get back to the house. I'm starvin'," Emily said and in just a few minutes they were back in the stables, settling the horses.

They went into the kitchen and grabbed the fixin's for sandwiches and such and took everything out onto the front porch.

"You got yourself one awesome porch. I hear Ethan built this for you," Sami said between bites.

"Yup. It sure is something special. I love it," Emily replied. "I come out here every chance I get and, as you can see, so does Trouble"

"Your dog is such fun. I love the way he chases butterflies out in the meadow. He looks like he's on a mission," Katelyn said laughing at Trouble. He was doing just that.

"How'd ya' find him?"

"Well, Ethan was workin' here one day and he just wandered in. He didn't have any tags. We asked all of The Creek if they knew him. No one did. We looked online for a missing dog report all the way to Tennessee and Boone. Nothin'. So, he stayed with us. It wasn't long before Ethan named him for one very obvious reason. He found the pond the day he arrived and immediately fell in. He was a mess. The more he tried to get out the muddier he got. Ethan and one of his crew had to get into the row boat and rescue him. They were all a mess when they got back here. Good thing the outdoor shower was finished. Trouble and Ethan went in mud-covered and came out fresh as could be. The other guy did the same."

"That's hilarious. I can just see them covered in mud. What'd Trouble do after he was clean.?" Sami asked.

"Well, he found himself a sunny spot in front of where the porch was bein' built and promptly fell sound asleep. Snorin' like a wood saw. I took pictures and there's one hangin' in the front hall. Go take a look if ya' like," Emily offered.

Sami went inside and came out laughing. There were two pictures side-by-side. One of trouble and Ethan covered in mud and the other of Trouble sound asleep in the meadow.

"Sure looks angelic sound asleep," Sami said as she sat on the swing.

They sat and talked for quite a while until it was time to leave.

"Thanks so much, Emily, for havin' us over," Katelyn said as they all hugged each other.

"This place is so special. I can't wait until I can get back here again," Sami added.

"Any time. Katelyn knows y'all are always welcome here without callin' first," Emily offered.

Trouble decided to come by and give his paw to Katelyn and Sami.

"Love this dog," Sami said as she gave Trouble some lovin'.

"He loves to soak up the love," Emily said as she watched Katelyn and Sami get into the SUV.

"Have a safe trip back to Boston, Sami," Emily hollered as they drove away.

"Thanks. I will," Sami hollered back as they went down the drive to the covered bridge.

Katelyn stopped on the bridge for just a moment. "There's somethin' about this bridge and this place I can't quite put my finger on, but it beckons to me and it's real peaceful when you're just standin' here for a minute."

They sat quiet for a few minutes.

"I can feel it and it is real special," Sami said with a sigh.

They got going again and pulled into the drive a short time later.

It was late Sunday afternoon and they were headed to Katelyn's family's farm for a farewell cookout a bit later.

"Katelyn, Jordan asked me to stop by today for just a few minutes. I think we have time before we need to head over to your folk's place. I'll drive on over now and see what's up," Sami said.

"Good idea. I've got a few things to get ready for tonight. Give Jordan my love."

"I will. See ya' soon," Sami said as she left.

Sami was at Jordan's a few minutes later and found him on the back porch just hangin' out.

"Hey, Jordan, got another one of those?" Sami asked.

"Yup. In the frig. Help yourself. There's some chips on the counter."

"Thanks," Sami said as she grabbed a beer and joined Jordan. "You seem to be getting around a bit better."

"New cast. Made of fiberglass. So much lighter and its below my knee. Easier to move around."

"Great. So, here I am. What can I help ya' with?"

"Nothin'. It's I who can help you. I found this out in the meadow yesterday. It was callin' to me and when I picked it up, I just knew it was meant for you," Jordan explained as he handed the crystal to Sami.

"Wow! This is beautiful. It looks just like a little pineapple," Sami said as she picked it up. "I think it's kind a hummin' or somethin'." She held the crystal to her ear. "Yup, it's hummin' real quiet-like and it feels like its vibrating."

"Exactly. That's what I heard and felt when I picked it up off the ground. Not sure why you need this just know ya' do. I'm learnin' not to question the findin' of the crystals and who they should be with or where they should go."

"Katelyn showed me the one she has that's a twin to yours and told me how you two found them. I know about Magic and all but I've never seen it so' in-your-face' like I have in the few days I've been in The Creek. This place truly is a place out of time."

"I do believe you're right about that. So, you leavin' in the mornin?"

"Yeah, after breakfast at The Store. Just gotta' have me one more of Ted's breakfast bagels before I hit the road," Sami said laughing along with Jordan.

"I love those things, too. That Ted sure is a gifted chef. Love that he's ours."

"Just one of many reasons to get back here as soon as possible," Sami added.

They talked for a few more minutes before Sami had to leave.

"Time to get back. Katelyn's folks are giving a farewell cookout and I'd better move along."

"I know. I was invited, but I'm getting tired by supper time so I thought I'd better stay home."

"Good idea. Thanks for the friendship, the beer, and the crystal," Sami said laughing as she hugged Jordan.

"Any time. And, Sami, make sure we text and live chat a lot. I want to make sure our Katelyn is okay. And, I love the whole underground railroad project you've got goin'. I've always been a history buff and when Katelyn was tellin' us about your discovery in Maine, it really got my attention. I'd love to help you with any research you gotta' do. I'm not goin' anywhere for a long time, especially back to work. Doc says he thinks it's gonna' be at least six months before I can drive one of the big trucks again. I need somethin' to do to keep me from goin 'crazy."

"I love the idea. I'll tell my bosses that I've hired a history researcher for the underground railroad thing. We've dubbed it the URR. I'll have HR get in touch for all the payroll stuff."

"Oh my God, Sami. I didn't mean for pay. I was offerin' so I wouldn't go crazy."

"No worries. I've needed a researcher and they already approved it. I do believe your salary will be around the 75-80K area. Sound good?"

"Sounds fabulous. I might never go back to bein' a delivery guy. It only paid about 60K. Deal," Jordan said as they shook hands. "A crystal for you and a new job for me without even thinkin' about it. I do love the way things work out around here. Now, off ya' go and tell everyone about your new employee."

"I will. So glad you mentioned the URR. I can't wait to get ya' goin'," Sami said as they hugged again and Jordan walked with her to the door, watching Sami get into her SUV and drive off.

"Hot Damn! This is truly a great day for sure. Thanks everyone," Jordan said to the spirits he knew must be around him. It was The Magic that had made all this happen. He was smiling as he walked into the living room and settled on the couch to watch a movie.

Sami was thrilled with being able to hire Jordan. She had a good feeling about him. She told Katelyn all about it as soon as she walked in the door.

"That's totally awesome! Love it so much," Katelyn said when she heard the details.

"I know. This is so cool. I gotta' text my bosses right know so they can get things rollin'. I got Jordan's info so things should move along real quick. Absolutely love this place," Sami yelled as she texted her bosses and got an immediate reply. They were happy, too, that Sami had found someone without even trying.

"Let's get goin'. Ya' got everything ya' need?" Katelyn said as they loaded the SUV.

'Yup. Ready to roll and eat way too much more fabulous food," Sami said as they pulled onto the road and headed to the farm.

The cookout was a blast. Stories were told and a lot of teasing was dished out. Miss Cora, Emily, Kendra, Ethan, and Finn had shown up and they added to the stories. Ted and Michael had sent desert with Kendra as they couldn't close The Store. And, Laine and Mo were busy with the harvesting of their special plants. They sent a little something for Sami with Emily. Emily gave it to her in a quiet moment before the cookout ended.

"I'm gonna' say it again and again, Sami, that was the best kept secret I've seen played out in a long time," Miss Cora said as they all gathered to say goodnight.

"Miss Cora, I had to keep tight control on myself so many times 'cause I wanted to tell Katie I was comin'. But then I thought about how surprised she would be if I just showed up. That's what kept me from spillin' the beans," Sami replied laughing.

"I would not have been able to do that at all," Katelyn's mom said. Others agreed with her

"We're glad ya' showed up. So great to finally meet ya' after all Katie's been tellin' us about ya' for the past few years," Katelyn's dad said.

Good luck was heard as folks took their leave. Katelyn and Sami were the last to leave.

"You are officially part of this family now. So, stay in touch," Katelyn's mom and dad said as they hugged Sami good-bye.

"I promise," Sami replied as she was hugged by her 'new' brothers.

"Here's a little somethin' to keep ya' happy while you're drivin' back to Beane Town," Nathan said as he handed Sami a container with fresh picked blueberries.

"Great. I love your berries. Thanks bros," Sami offered.

"Come on back real soon," everyone said as Katelyn and Sami got into the SUV.

"I will. I promise," Sami said hanging out of the window as Katelyn drove away.

"Oh, Sami," Katelyn said as she saw that Sami had tears running done her cheeks.

"I'm just overwhelmed at all the love I've been given in such a short time. I can't believe you stayed away for all those years. But I'm glad you did. Otherwise, we wouldn't be the friends we are."

"I agree. Time for some sleep so you'll be good for your drive tomorrow," Katelyn said as they got home and settled for the rest of the night.

"Oh, by the way, Laine and Mo sent along a little gift from their greenhouses," Sami said laughing.

"They sure do know how to take care of us," Katelyn laughed along with Sami.

Monday morning found Katelyn and Sami at The Store for one more bagel breakfast.

"Here ya' go, Sami. Just the way ya' like it," Ted said as he presented Sami with her breakfast bagel with a flourish of his kitchen towel.

"Well, I do feel so privileged by all the fuss. Thanks, Ted," Sami commented.

Katelyn and Sami enjoyed their breakfast as some of the regulars came by for their breakfast as well.

Hal stopped by just as Sami and Katelyn were getting ready to leave.

"Sami, great to meet ya'. You come back home real soon," Hal said.

"I will, Hal. And, thanks for the kind words," Sami replied.

Michael came up into the dining area as Ted came from the kitchen.

"Now, Sami, Ted and I have put together a survival basket for your trip back to Boston. Hope you enjoy every bite," Michael said as he handed the basket to Sami.

"You two are the best. And, I will enjoy every bite and every pound I gain from your fabulous basket," Sami said as she hugged them both.

Jenna and Matthews stopped in just then to say farewell.

So-longs were offered by all and Sami and Katelyn finally left The Store.

A few minutes later, Sami had her SUV all packed and she and Katelyn were standing by the driver's door.

Both were crying a bit.

"I hate this whole so long thing," Sami said.

"Me, too," Katelyn said.

"But, we gotta' do this so I can come back real soon."

"Well, when ya' put it that way, I guess that makes it a bit better. Love ya' forever and always, my Sami.

"Love ya' forever and always, my Katie girl."

They hugged for an extra-long time then finally pulled apart.

Sami got into her SUV and started it up.

"Make sure ya' let me know when you get to your hotel for the night." Katelyn said.

"I will," Sami replied as she backed out of the drive and sent off down the Pine Ridge Road with a honking of her horn.

Katelyn went back inside and cried for a bit then got busy with some chores. Sami was crying a bit as she drove away but that ended as soon as she saw the moonshine sign. Now that whole thing was purely magical for sure. She just shook her head and smiled as she rounded the curve and left The Creek.

The summer was coming to a close as it was mid-August and the dog days of summer were upon The Creek and all of the Blue Ridge. Folks took time off during these last two weeks of August just to enjoy the last of the summer.

Matthews was still waiting for the detailed report he had requested on Greg. He was kept busy checking on all the new folks that showed up to hike around the area.

Jenna was wicked busy with her new studio and new clients. She had a few murals she was working on. One of them was for a children's playroom and they wanted a magical mural showing faeries and rainbows and gardens of magical flowers. She knew just what to draw and was busy working on it. She was gonna' send them a sketch in a few days.

Jonah was kept busy with Emily's horses and all. She now had eight borders and her own two to take care of. She had a great morning routine that Trouble knew by heart and did his best to mess up given half a chance. Trouble knew just when Jonah would arrive and set about telling everyone around when he got there.

Time flew by. The protection grids were keeping Jordan and The Meadow safe. Jordan was using his crutches all the time now. He had had a few cast changes lately and was in a half leg cast now. He still couldn't put any weight on his leg and his was doing his physical therapy just like he was shown. His side was all healed from the spleen surgery although he was still a little sore on account of the crutches. Finn's mom heard about this problem and made a special pad he could wear to keep his side protected. It had Velcro straps that went around his belly and across his shoulders. It worked like a charm. And, Finn's mom used a soft flannel print that showed trees and tonka trucks. The humor wasn't lost on anyone and Jordan took a bit of kidding about it.

Finn and Katelyn stopped over to Matthews' one evening a few days after Sami left. There were only a few days left to August. Finn had asked Matthews if he and Katelyn could stop by for a visit. Matthews and Jenna were thrilled. They all gathered out on the big back deck off the barn, of all places, and set to grilling all kinds of stuff. Seems Jenna liked to experiment. She was grilling lime chicken and it smelled yummy.

"Hey, Jenna, Matthews tells me you like this whole grillin' thing," Katelyn said as she brought the plates and stuff to the table.

"I do. I found this recipe and thought it would be fun to fix for tonight. It has lime and cilantro in the glaze. I fixed potatoes with garlic and onions in foil with a touch of parmesan cheese. Matthews made the veggie dip, so dig in."

Matthews and Jenna brought the rest of the food to the table and they all got busy sampling everything.

"This chicken is fabulous. I need the recipe for sure," Katelyn said with a mouth full.

Finn and Matthews agreed as they kept eating. They chatted a bit but ate more until they were more than full.

"I don't think I'm gonna' need to eat until tomorrow night. This is so good!" Jenna said as Matthews laughed at her.

"That means I get the leftovers," Mathews said.

"No leftovers. I'm taken' it all with me," Finn said making as if to grab all the food.

"Oh, no you don't, mister. I made lots extra so Matthews and I would have leftovers for tomorrow. I might be willin' to part with some for the two of you. After all, I did fix enough for an army," Jenna replied laughing.

"Sounds good to me," Katelyn said setting back and smiling. "I am content for the moment."

They all sat back and chatted for a bit.

"So, Matthews, Katelyn and I wanted to share somethin' with you and Jenna that you might be interested in. The Friday before the picnic in The Meadow, we went to the diner in Pine Ridge. Is there any other diner we love? Anyhow, we had a great time and we all walked away around nine or so. On our way back, Katelyn saw something in the field across the main road from your road. You tell them."

"Well, if I can bring myself out of this food-induced coma," Katelyn said laughing. "We were just passing your road when I saw some lights out in the field to my right. To the east. We pulled over and got out and watched them. There were so many. Too many to be all lightnin' bugs. And, then they all changed colors. Gorgeous colors just blinkin' and twinkling for about ten minutes. Then they softly faded away. We just stood there real quiet. I said a thank you and we got back into the truck and headed home. We thought they might be faerie lights like you and Jenna saw that time before you began your build and all. What do ya' think?"

Matthews and Jenna looked at each other than at Katelyn and Finn.

"Holy cow! That's so cool," Jenna said.

"Really cool. Our lights didn't change colors," Matthews added.

Katelyn and Finn looked at the two of them. "That's all ya' got, Matthews?" Finn asked laughing.

"Well, for the minute, yeah" Mathews answered.

"What about you Jenna?" Katelyn asked.

"Me? I got nothin'. Absolutely nothin'. Yet," Jenna said.

"Really? Ya' need some time to think about this?" Finn asked throwing a plastic cup at Matthews.

"Finn, I don't really know much about all this magic stuff. I only know about what's been happenin' here and a bit about around The Creek. I am definitely a baby at this stuff. I would think, though, that if y'all saw those twinklin' faerie lights, ya' must have done somethin' right as far as The Magic goes with the land and the animals and all. I think there is a strong connection between the little ones and the land and the animals that live on the land not including humans. We seem to be able to take care of ourselves just fine. That's what comes to mind."

"Well, that's a great start for sure and I think you may have somethin' there, Matthews," Katelyn replied. "It would seem that may be the case. Finn and I have been workin' with the geothermal springs and solar energy at Jordan's as a kind of test site to see how it all works out.

"We've even got a client, well Ethan does, that's set up to use the same power sources as Jordan. He definitely does not want to be on the energy grid at any cost. I agree. Matthews and I have been talkin' about doin' the same thing here if it all works out at Jordan's place."

"And, I've been commissioned to create a mural of magic for a family. They want it for their kid's play room." Jenna added. "I've included faeries and little folks and the earth and rainbows, of course. So, I like the way y'all are thinkin' about this. It makes perfect sense to me. Look how Mother Earth took care of the damage The Dark did here with the earthquake and all. There's that big purple crystal settin' on the creek bank and the island that was created. It's all so beautiful. We should be able to see the rays from the crystal in a little bit as the sun hits it before it starts to fall below the tree tops."

They kept talking and coming up with ideas about the faerie lights they all had seen. It wasn't long before Matthews pointed towards the creek and they saw the rays shining from the egg-shaped crystal on the creek bank. The rays were thrown all over the place from the field to the treetops and everything in between. A few even landed on them as they sat on the barn deck. They only lasted a minute then were gone.

"Now, that's what I call a private light show," Jenna said.

"Indeed," Katelyn agreed.

Once the sun had almost set, they cleared everything and brought the dinner things back into the house. They all helped clean up then sat in the living room for a bit.

"This has been a great evenin', y'all," Finn said. "Thanks so much for havin' us over."

"We are definitely doing this again. I love this whole getting together with you two thing," Matthews said.

"Me, too," Katelyn added.

After a while, it was deemed time to end the evening. They all walked out to Finn's truck and as they were saying good night, Jenna happened to see something near the east side of the barn.

"Look," she said softly pointing to the barn.

As they all turned to look, a flash of colored lights met their gaze. It was the faeries showing their love for just a minute or two.

"Well, I guess we got our answer," Katelyn said as they all said thank you to the faeries. A swift twinkle told them they were right.

"Now this will give me a lot to think about," Finn said as he and Katelyn got in the truck.

"Me, too," Matthews and Jenna said together.

"Night, y'all. Sleep well," they said to each other as the truck drove away.

Katelyn was in bed a few minutes later and Finn was headed for his bed. They were both thinking about the faerie lights as they fell asleep.

Magic sure was beautiful.

CHAPTER 21

G reg and his cronies had come up with a plan. Good thing. Madman showed up for an update and he wasn't taking any prisoners.

"What do ya' have?" Madman asked changing into a human.

Greg looked at the others. It was well past midnight the last day of August.

"We went to work on the idea the new demon had about sending energy through the water. We got to thinkin' and figured out a way to blow Jordan and his place to hell without damaging The Magic."

"Good plan. Sure it's gonna' work?" Madman asked.

"Well, we're gonna' test it out on a different place before we send it to Jordan's place. It's set to go off tomorrow. I know you'll be watching," Greg said.

"Yes, I will. Good luck. If it doesn't work, you'll all be destroyed," Madman warned. Then he vanished.

Greg looked at the others and they weren't saying a word.

"Let's get this set up for tomorrow. It should go off at noon."

They worked throughout the rest of the night, setting the explosion for 12-noon that day. They had targeted Ethan's new build a ways from Jordan's with all the thermal energy power. They figured they'd kill all the work crew at the site as a bonus that would make The Dark happy.

The day before the bad guys were working on their evil plan, Jordan called Katelyn and asked if she could stop by after work.

Katelyn arrived just a bit after six. She had her twin crystal in her hand as she knocked on the back porch door.

"Hey, Katelyn. Come on in," Jordan said. He was sitting at the island. "How's about a cold drink? You've probably been wicked busy today and it's hot out. Love this weather," Jordan said as he passed her a sweet tea.

"Thanks, Jordan. Just what I needed," Katelyn said as she took a sip and smiled.

"How's the job goin'?" Jordan asked as Katelyn settled on a bar stool.

"Great. I love designing stuff and working with Ethan and Ian and everyone. And, I'm home."

"It shows. You seem to be happy and full of energy," Jordan replied.

"How are you comin' along?"

"Well, I saw the surgeons today. The belly's healin' just perfectly although I don't think I'm gonna' be playin' any football this fall. The leg has another new cast on it. Same place. Just clean and fresh. About four more weeks. That's okay. I've learned how to get around with it and all now. Still can't drive, of course. But I can use the gator with my other foot. I drove around the barn a few times to get used to it. The visiting nurses were dismissed today. No need for them anymore and the physical therapists are gonna' be here three times a week for the next 4 weeks to get me ready to start walking with the crutches and no cast. They said it kind of feels off balance at first. I can get around so much better. I don't need anyone here anymore either. So, I thanked Emily and everyone and they showed up with enough food for the next month any way."

"I can see that," Katelyn said as she walked over to the frig and counter and looked at everything. "These are top-notch goodies for sure."

"Yes, they are. Hey, how about stayin' for some supper? We can sample some of 'em together?"

"Great idea. Thanks. How about I set the table and you pick out the food? We'll get it heated and ready in no time."

"Done," Jordan said as he figured out what they would eat.

A few minutes they were sitting at the table enjoying the efforts and gifts from the folks in The Creek.

"This has gotta' be Miss Cora's cornbread," Katelyn said moaning as she took a big bite.

"I do believe it is. And, this has gotta' be Jenna's barbeque chicken pot pie. I swear no one makes it quite like she does."

"Agreed," Katelyn said.

They ate and talked for quite a while.

As they finished, Jordan said, "Katelyn, I asked ya' here 'cause I keep havin' this dream with you in it and we're both holding our twin crystals. Not sure what it means but thought I'd better tell ya' and, maybe, we could figure it out."

206

"Sounds interesting. I haven't had that dream that I know of. But, yeah, let's talk about it. I brought my twin with me. Here it is," Katelyn said as she took it out of her bag.

Jordan picked his up at the same time and it happened.

They looked at each other and saw each other as very different people. Jordan saw Katelyn as if she were from an ancient time dressed in a full-length dress cut low in the front. She had on a robe of some sort and she was in a cave working next to him.

Katelyn saw Jordan as if he were from an ancient time. He had a full long beard and was dressed in robes of some sort. He was standing at a crude table working with some stuff over a low fire. He kept adding things to the pot and writing stuff down. He looked at Katelyn and smiled.

They both dropped their crystals onto the table at the same time and just starred at each other as the vision disappeared.

Finally, Katelyn looked at Jordan and said, "What the hell was that?"

"That's my question," Jordan replied. "What the hell WAS that?"

They just sat there and starred at each other and their crystals for the longest time.

"We were in a cave," Katelyn started.

"And, we were dressed in clothes from a long time ago. Maybe an ancient time,' Jordan added.

"And, you were mixin' something over a fire," Katelyn said.

"I know. I know. I don't know what all that stuff was. I looked wicked old, too. And, where was that?"

"I had on a long dress without much on the top. What was that all about?" Katelyn said.

Jordan smiled a bit at Katelyn as he said, "Ya' looked good like that."

Katelyn threw an apple at him and hit him square in the chest.

"Hey! Nice throw," He replied as he set the apple on the table. "Just sayin' the truth."

"Cute, old man. Real cute," Katelyn sassed back.

"So, you're gonna' play the old man card, huh?" Jordan replied trying to look hurt.

"Yup! It's what I saw," Katelyn said laughing along with him.

"So. What the hell was that? Where did it come from? What does it all mean?" Jordan asked in rapid-fire succession. He tried to pace, but it was a bit difficult with the cast and all. He threw the crutches across the room in confusion.

"Well, at least I know now that ya' have a bit of a temper," Katelyn said.

"Look," Jordan started as he tried to hop over to the crutches. Katelyn grabbed them and gave them to him. "Thanks. This whole injured thing gets old real fast sometimes."

"No need to apologize. I don't know how I'd act if any of that whole thing happened to me. Jesus!"

Jordan nodded his head at Katelyn then said, "Any ways, I'm feelin' so totally lost with all this Magic stuff. It was The Dark that tried to kill me. Why? I'm a nice enough guy. I try not to hurt anyone. That whole thing with the Sacred Rock Meadow thing wasn't me. I was bein' controlled. That's how Miss Cora and Emily explained it to me. Then, there's the accident. Why me? Y'all had to put a protection grid around the farm and all. Why? I'm not a magical person. I don't have any Gifts like you and some of the others do. Why me? What the HELL IS GOIN' ON?" Jordan hollered out to the universe.

Katelyn remained quiet for a bit as they sat there.

"Well, at least I got that off my chest along with the apple," Jordan said smiling a little.

"Well said," Katelyn agreed. "As for why you? Well, we've been doin' some thinkin' about that very thing. Miss Cora, and Emily and Kendra and a few others seem to think that it's not exactly you all together. It's your land. The farm. Seems there's a whole lot a Magic here that needs protectin' and you were chosen by The White Light and The Magic to be the keeper of that very special Magic."

"Me? This place? Really?" Jordan replied looking lost. "Why me?"

Katelyn just shrugged her shoulders and shook her head as she said, "We don't know except maybe 'cause you are such a nice guy. Really."

"Really? I'm a nice guy?"

"And," Katelyn said cautiously, "because you were a protector of The Magic in a past life."

"Oh, no! Don't bring that on me. No way. Past life? Holy shit!" Jordan said shaking his head.

"That's what we've been thinkin'. Don't know for sure but it does make sense. What I don't get is why were the two of us in that vision thing. What the hell does that mean?"

"You're askin' me? Me? How the hell should I know? I don't even know anything about anything about The Magic. Just what I've seen and heard about it from everyone in The Creek and that adds up to maybe a little bit of a little bit of a miniscule bit of nothin'."

Katelyn and Jordan laughed at his description. "Well, now, that you put it that way, I get it. NOT!"

They sat there laughing for quite a bit making wise-ass comments about everything. After they finally settled down, they talked about the vision some more.

"All of this has to do with the crystals you've been findin' around here. That I'm sure of," Katelyn offered.

"I agree," Jordan said. "These crystals and the one on Matthews' land are special. They have somethin' to do with The Magic in The Creek. Now, why here? Why me? Why was I drawn to this land and all?"

"I believe it has to do with the crystals, with you bein' the one to find them," Katelyn offered. "There seems to be a connection with all this. Just don't know what it is, yet."

"Okay. I'll agree with that. But that vision thing. God! What was that all about?"

"I don't have a clue. I haven't had any dreams about any of that. Have you?"

"No," Jordan answered. "I've been a bit preoccupied with getting better and all."

"Okay. Accepted. Just don't know. Guess we'll be doin' some thinkin' on this for a while," Katelyn offered.

"Yup. Hey, I'm hungry again. How about you?"

"Sure thing. Let's check out the deserts. I think I saw a blueberry pie on the counter and ice cream in the frig." Katelyn said going over to the counter. "Yup. Right here. Want some?"

"Yes, I do," Jordan said as Katelyn got their pie, warmed it up, then added a healthy scoop of vanilla bean ice cream.

"Now this is what I call first class service," Jordan said as he bit into the pie. "Gotta' be from your mom. She knows how to bake a pie. Come to think of it, so does Finn and Jay's Mom. Those guys are pie hounds."

Katelyn began to tear up but caught herself. "That's for sure. No matter what time of the day or night, they had, always have, room for pie!"

"Yes, they do," Jordan agreed.

They enjoyed the pie as the sun began to touch the tree tops.

"Let's watch the crystal by the door," Jordan said.

They walked through the house and found a few folks doing just that.

"Hey, y'all. Looks amazin'," Jordan said as they all stood there in silence watching the light show the sun and the crystal put on for them. As the sun went below the trees, the crystal settled down to a quiet shine. Folks went on their way with thanks.

"Well, time for me to go on as well. After all this, I got a lot to think about," Katelyn said as they went back into the kitchen and she grabbed her crystal. It was a bit warm and glowed like always. "At least it's behaving right now."

"Good thing. Mine, too," Jordan said as he picked his up.

"You be careful around here and call if ya' need anything," Katelyn said as they hugged so long.

"I will. I'll let ya' know if I come up with any thoughts about all of this," Jordan said as Katelyn got into her SUV. Jordan stayed on the porch as she drove down the drive and around the curve to the road.

Both of them spent the rest of the evening thinking about that vision.

The last day of August was busy for many. Folks were getting their kids ready to go back to school. Last minute vacationers were having a blast. Ethan's business was beyond busy. They had builds scheduled for the next two years.

Katelyn's brothers were taking care of the berry patches, getting them ready for the fall and winter. They had a pumpkin patch to attend to as well as a field of popcorn for the first time.

They were experimenting with a few new things. Always trying new stuff.

Laine and Mo were busy with their late summer harvest. Lots of veggies to sell and their marijuana was looking fabulous. The drying shed was working perfectly and the latest crop growing would be ready for harvest around November and Thanksgiving.

Bubba and Earl loved their new cabins. They felt like they were living in paradise. Ethan had finished with everything and had replanted the road to look just like the forest. Ya' had to look real hard to be able to tell it had ever been a road.

Matthews had finally gotten the detailed report on Greg and his hunch was confirmed. The person with that name and birth date had died in the 1940s. Greg was an imposter. Matthews had reported this to the local sheriff's department and they were going to give the information to the electric company. Hopefully, that would end the existence of Greg around The Creek. And the Blue Ridge.

Jenna's art business was keeping her busy. She loved the new studio and she had just gotten a commission to create a mural for one of the old buildings in Boone. It would be outside and the owners wanted it to depict the Blue Ridge from before it was settled by the Europeans. Jenna liked the whole idea and was busy coming up with sketches and ideas non-stop, or so it seemed.

So, on this last day of August, it seemed as if everything was going along just fine.

It happened at noon. High noon to be exact. An explosion that rocked The Creek and the area around The Creek for miles.

Folks ran outside and looked in every direction. They began to see smoke rising from south of The Creek, past Jordan's place.

Ethan and Ian knew right away where it was. The new build using all the earth energy southeast of Jordan's place about ten miles down the Pine Ridge Road. The drive was a good mile into the property. They ran to their trucks and headed to the site along with Finn. Ethan called the fire department. They were already on their way.

The folks in The Store all ran outside and watched as the smoke got darker and the smoke cloud grew.

"I bet that's Ethan's energy build," Hal offered.

"I agree," said some of the folks standing there.

"This doesn't feel good. I wonder if evil's got somethin' to do with it?" Michael said out loud.

"I'm just wondering the same thing," Hal said looking right at Michael.

"Did I say that out loud? Shit!" Michael replied.

"Looks like Miss Cora's on her way," Ted said reading a text from her. "She just sent a text. Should be here in a few minutes. I'm gonna' get her some tea."

More folks arrived over the next few minutes and they were all standing outside The Store. Some parked across the way. Kendra came over just when Miss Cora arrived.

"Kendra, Folks. Let's get to talkin'. We can sit right out here," Miss Cora suggested. A rocking chair was set up for Miss Cora next to one of the cracker barrels and Ted brought the tea he had fixed for her.

"Why, thanks, Ted. Just what I was needin'," Miss Cora said. "And some lunch. Let's get our food ordered and we can commence to talkin' while Ted gets it ready."

Orders were place and Ted went back inside to prepare them. Everyone looked at Miss Cora. She was quiet for a few minutes and ready to start when Emily and Jonah arrived.

Heys were shared and folks set to listening.

"Well, this is not good. Not good at all," Miss Cora began. Just then Michael got a text from Ethan.

"Pardon me, Miss Cora. I got this text from Ethan. He says no one was hurt 'cause they all had the day off on account of the need for two inspections set for later today and some supplies that are needed and will be arriving tomorrow. Thank God."

All agreed with Michael.

"Well, that's great news. No one was hurt or killed. What the hell happened out there?" Emily said.

"I'll tell ya' what I think," Miss Cora began. "I think The Dark is getting ready to strike. Again. I think it wants somethin' up there on Jordan's farm. Maybe the place where all those crystals are comin' from. If they're comin' from the earth. I think they've been placed there by The Magic for Jordan to find. There's somethin' special about that land. Anyone get a hold of Jordan yet to make sure he's alright?"

211

"I just got a text. The explosion threw him to the ground, but it didn't hurt him or his cast. He said he stayed there for a while to make sure nothin' else happened that could hurt him. He says the smoke is real black and the fire services are at the build. Some of the trucks are at his place. He gave them permission to drive over the field to the far boundary. They want to make sure the fire doesn't spread. He told them not to go over the little hill on account he doesn't know if it's solid or not."

"Good thinkin,'" Hal said.

Ted brough everyone's lunch out and folks helped Ted hand it around. Some went in to get drinks for everyone.

Once they were all settled eating, Miss Cora continued.

"I think this is a warnin'. I think there's gonna' be somethin' worse real soon now. The Dark doesn't just blow stuff up. I'm thinkin' it thought lots of folks would be there and they all would be killed. Since no one was there, The Dark is gonna' be really angry. We better be on alert for anything and anyone that doesn't fit in around here no matter how nice they are. Let's get the word out to all of The Creek and the Redstone clan as well. I just don't like the feel of things. Not good. Not good at all."

Miss Cora ate her lunch and they all talked a bit waiting for news from Ethan or Finn or anyone at the explosion site.

It was about an hour later that Matthews showed up. He looked around at everyone then said, "We're not sure about anything yet. We do know an explosive was used with a kind of detonation timer and signaler. The FBI bomb squad is on their way from DC. Ethan called it in when he saw the damage. He knew it wasn't from a normal kind of combustion. The squad should be here by this evening. We are all to stay away from there. I ordered extra protection for The Creek, especially Jordan's place as it's the closest to the bomb site. We need to set up a check-in system with each other. We need to know where everyone is all the time. One of my men will be stationed here at The Store. Emily, can ya' help with all the contact info?"

"We've already got an alert goin' around The Creek. We can add whatever you want into the message. We're sendin' it by text and email and callin' folks as well."

"Great thinkin.' You're gonna' make that part of my job so much easier. Looks like everyone's been enjoyin' Ted's creations again."

"Yes, they have. Ya' need anythin', Matthews?" Ted asked as he gathered empty plates and all.

"Yes, I do. How about one of those bar-be-que chicken sandwiches with all the fixin's? Not sure when I'm gonna' have a chance to eat again. Might as well enjoy the best while I can," Matthews replied.

Jenna came flyin' in just then. She ran to Matthews and looked at everyone. "Did anyone get hurt out there?" she asked frightened.

"No. No one was workin' today. And when Ethan and the rest of them got there, they stayed away from the fire until the fire services came," Hal explained to Jenna.

"Oh God! Oh my God! The explosion threw me off my chair in the studio. I was just getting ready to send emails to clients and then, WHAM! I was on the floor. Some of my supplies fell off the shelves and a few jars broke. Nothin' special. Just mason jars. I'm not hurt," Jenna said as Matthews began to look her over. "Really. Not one scratch."

"Okay. Just makin' sure. I thought you had already left for Pine Ridge a while ago," Matthews said still looking her over.

"I was headed that way then got involved in doin' one little thing then another. Then I had a great idea for the outdoor mural and was sketchin' that for a bit. I had just finished when I sat down at my laptop and ended up on the floor."

"Okay. You look okay. Good." Matthews was interrupted by his phone. He talked for a minute then hung up. "My team has arrived. Kendra, can we use your porch?"

"Sure," Kendra replied.

Matthews directed his seven-man team over to Kendra's and was there when Ted brought his lunch out.

Ted hollered over to Matthews. "Matthews, your lunch is ready."

"We'll be right over," Matthews said as his team crossed the road. They all ordered lunch and talked with everyone about The Creek waiting for their food.

Meanwhile, Ethan, Ian, and Finn were in shock at the destruction of the build. Every building was on fire and the fields around the build were on fire, too. When Ethan called 911, he told them the fields were on fire as well. The fire department called in the National Park Fire Service. Trucks and equipment began to arrive just a few minutes later. Rigs from Pine Ridge arrived first, then from Boone and the fire service a few minutes after that. Ethan and the guys watched from a safe distance so the crews could do their work. A couple more explosions happened when the gasoline cans that had been left on the site exploded. They were on the backside of the barn.

Ethan kept saying he was sure nothing explosive had been left on the site except the two one-gallon gas cans that were mostly empty. Finn was saying the same thing. Ethan was a stickler for following safety rules. Finn just stared at the whole thing.

Ian looked at the other two, then said, "I'm gonna' say what we're all thinkin'. This was done on purpose. This was intentional. Someone doesn't want us to be buildin' like this using wind, solar and geothermal energy is what I'm thinkin.'"

"I was thinkin' the same thing. Only thing is, it doesn't take any big amount of money away from the power companies. Electricity and natural gas. One house isn't worth the effort," Ethan said.

"Well, when you say it out loud, it does make more sense. But why would anyone do this? It was intentional. Arson for sure." Ian replied.

"I'm with you on that, Ian. I just spoke with Katelyn and she's headed to The Store. Folks will be gatherin' there," Finn said. "Katelyn sent out messages through a group email to our customers and suppliers tellin' them no one was hurt in the explosion and to please stay away from the area so the fire crews can do their work. She spoke with the client and tried to calm him down. She reassured him that everything was covered by insurance and he wouldn't be charged any more than the contract. She told him she would keep him informed when she learned more stuff. She locked the place up and should be at The Store by now."

"God. I hadn't even thought of all that. Remind me to thank her when I see her," Ethan said. Ian agreed.

Greg and the other demons were havin' a grand time. Madman had joined them and he was okay with the explosion. He wasn't happy that no one had been killed. But, knowin' that the method to deliver the Dark Energy had worked made him happy any ways. Now they had a way to kill Jordan and take the special Magic from the land. He allowed all of them to celebrate for a long, long while. They would be very busy soon enough putting the real plan together.

Katelyn arrived at The Store about the same time as Matthews. She ordered lunch and joined the group on the porch. They exchanged information and waited to hear more.

Jordan called Katelyn while she was waiting for her lunch.

"Oh my God! You alright?" she hollered into the phone. It was on speaker mode.

"Katelyn. Calm down. Yes, I'm good. Matthews sent a team and they have arrived," Jordan explained.

Folks were thrilled to hear this news.

"You hurt at all?" Katelyn asked in a quieter voice.

"Nope. I fell down and stayed down for a while. The guys are helpin' me stay put. They're all over the place. Fire service trucks drove into the back field to make sure nothing catches on fire with the wind and all. I think I'm gonna' have another beautiful bruise on my ass from the fall. And, no, no one can have a look at it."

This made everyone laugh and make some colorful comments on Jordan's behalf.

"Take me off speaker please," Jordan said.

Katelyn changed the mode and kept talking to him. She walked a few steps from the porch.

"Katelyn, my crystals, all of them, have been shinin' like a laser was on them. Everyone has to keep their sunglasses on even in the house. Our twin crystal is bright as all get out. Take yours outta' your pocket and look at it with your sunglasses on."

Katelyn took her twin crystal out of her pocket and it was hot and shining like Jordan said his was. She had to hold it off to her side so she wouldn't get blinded.

As soon as folks saw this, they all started to talk.

"I can tell it's bright and hot, too. I think someone or somethin' is tryin' to get to the land here and all my crystals. You're not on speaker phone, right?"

"Right. What 'cha thinkin', Jordan?"

"I think that Dark Energy is trying to get to the cave out back where all those crystals are."

"Oh my God! I know you're right. There must be some kind of powerful Magic in that cave. So, that's what all this bad stuff is about. The Dark is tryin' to get to your cave. Hmm. Like that's never gonna' happen. Never. The White Light won't let it. Don't say anythin' to anyone. I'm gonna' see if anyone can make the connection with the crystals and your land. Then we'll talk again. You stay safe."

"Good idea. You stay safe, too." Jordan said.

Katelyn returned to her chair and finished her lunch.

Ethan, Ian, and Finn just stood back and watched as the fire crews got control of the fire and put it out. It took them about an hour to get the main part of each fire under control.

The fire chief came over to talk to Ethan.

"Ethan Sutherland?" the chief asked.

"Yes, sir. I'm Ethan. This here is my brother Ian and our energy expert Finn," Ethan answered shaking hands with the chief.

"Any idea how this could have started?"

"No sir. There weren't any combustibles on site. Only the gasoline in the two small containers set apart from the back of the barn. If we use any others, they are transported back to the shop and stored according to state law."

"We didn't see any signatures from those either. As a matter of fact, we haven't been able to trace the start to any one spot yet. Even with the fire still going a bit, we can usually tell how it got started. This time we haven't been able to do that yet."

"Ethan and I were the last to leave the site yesterday. We'd gotten it ready for a few inspections. Our new shipment of supplies was delayed a day so we gave the crew the day off with pay. We made sure every single thing was stored correctly. This is an energy build. There are no electric lines and no natural gas lines set here. We use our generators for power. You can see there are no generators here. The crew takes them home every night for safe keeping," Finn explained.

"I wondered why there wasn't a natural gas line on the site map and I didn't see any electrical service either. Very interesting. What kind of power are you tapping into?" the chief asked.

Ian explained about the geothermal springs and creeks and the solar panels.

"I don't see any solar panel debris, though," the chief said.

"We're using a new solar panel technology. Glass panels that are made similar to everyday glass window panes. They were invented by a couple of folks in The Creek. Patented and trademarked. This build was the first full build that was not tapping into the commercial energy grids," Ian explained further.

"Makes me wonder if it was arson by someone from the commercial world. We'll look into it but, I'm not confident we'll find any traces of explosive materials. It's like they don't exist. We can usually smell somethin' or see some trace at a site. Not this one. I truly am puzzled," the chief confided to the guys.

"We are, too," Ethan added.

They all stood there a bit until the chief was called away. The fires were out about an hour after that. Only hot spots remained and the chief explained that some of the crew would remain on the site until they were cooled. He instructed Ethan to take pictures of every building and from every angle possible for insurance purposes.

"I've already notified the insurance company. They're sending a crew over right now. Should be here in just a bit. I told them to wait until you cleared the site for them," Ethan said.

"I'll let the sheriff know so he can let them come up the drive," the chief said as he got on the radio.

"I'm not worried about the insurance. We've got that covered. I want to know what the hell happened here. It was arson but I'm thinkin' it was The Dark that did this. I gotta' talk with Miss Cora and the folks at The Store as soon as possible," Ethan said quietly to Finn and Ian. "I'm gonna' stay until the fire chief and insurance guys don't need me anymore. Then I'm headed to The Store. I'm gonna' call Michael right now and ask him to ask Miss Cora, Emily, and Kendra to stick around until I get there."

"Good idea. Finn and I will stick around until it's safe to leave. Send some food and water over, will ya'?" Ian said

"Will do," Ethan said as he was talking with Michael. When he finished, he told the guys food and water were on the way. Ted had put a care package together and Hal was delivering the goods. Ethan told the sheriff to let Hal up the drive.

The Store was crazy busy. Folks kept coming from all over The Creek and then some. Seth and Clara Redstone showed up as well.

"Hey, Miss Cora," Clara and Seth said at the same time.

"Wondered if the two of you were gonna' come by. We got us a mess here," Miss Cora said. "Sit yourselves down and let's talk."

Seth got chairs for the two of them and Clara went inside to get drinks.

"Now, Miss Cora, Clara and I have been talkin' about this whole thing. When we saw the smoke all the way from the site to our place, we knew somethin' wasn't right."

"That's for sure," Miss Cora said.

"We got to thinkin' and wonderin' and the more we thought about it, it began to feel like somethin' sinister was at hand," Clara added.

Folks nearby nodded their heads in agreement.

"I've heard from Ethan and he says the fire chief and the arson crew haven't been able to find any bomb stuff or anything that would cause such a huge explosion. So, I got to wonderin' like others and it is my opinion that there is evil at work here. I do believe you're right Clara," Miss Cora agreed.

"But why target a building site? It seems a bit off unless The Dark is only practicin'." Seth offered.

"Exactly right, again. That's what I'm thinkin' myself," Miss Cora said in response to Seth.

"Now, folks, don't get all scared just yet. We haven't figured out what The Dark is after. It's always after The Magic here, but this time it feels different. What are y'all's thoughts?"

"Well, it does seem to be kind of striking whenever and wherever. The storms in just the Blue Ridge and then the building site and nothin' much in between," Emily said.

"And, I wonder if that guy who died in his basement that Jenna and Katelyn were gonna' do some work for was a part of all this?" Kendra added.

"I forgot about that," Jenna said. "Could be. Or, it was just a coincidence. Oh, wait, there are no coincidences. Probably connected. Then, if Katelyn and I were targeted, who else is in harm's way?"

"No one at the site is Gifted like some of us," Miss Cora said. "The folks who bought the land are driven to take care of it but they're not Gifted."

"Well," Clara thought out loud, "maybe it's about the land. Maybe the site was just a warnin' and all. Maybe The Dark is after sacred places on the earth. We know there are some that hold special Magic." Clara was looking right at Seth and Miss Cora.

"Yes, we do know that. Just like up at The Holler last spring. Now, that was some battle," Kendra said.

So," Emily said, "I wonder if the land at the site was special?"

"I checked in with The Other Side and they weren't sayin' much, although all the earth in and around The Creek has some kind of Magic in and on it," Kendra explained. "But it would seem that the building site, like a lot of y'all have offered, was just a practice run. I'm thinkin' The Dark's demons thought they'd be killin' a lot of people so they picked that site. But I'm now thinkin' it has somethin' to do with some land around here."

"I agree," Miss Cora said. "We'll have to do some more thinkin' on that."

Emily put her hand up as she looked at her phone. It was Ethan calling.

"Hey, Ethan, you all okay up there? No one got hurt fightin' the fire?"

"No one got hurt. And, they all said to say thanks to Ted for the sandwiches and all. They were really hungry. Some of them have left but a good-sized crew is stayin' until the site is cold, as the chief put it. I'm headin' your way in a few minutes. Finn's goin' back to the shop to take care of phone calls and such. Ian's stayin' here. See y'all in a bit."

"Okay. We're here," Emily said as they finished the call.

"Well, I guess I'll go meet up with Finn and handle the customer calls and emails and all. I'm sure there are lot of folks scared and worried out there." Katelyn said as she stood to leave. "Let me know if ya' figure anything more. Nice to see ya' again, Seth and Clara."

"Take care," Clara said as Katelyn went on home to get into her SUV and head to the shop.

The Pine Ridge Road was smothered in emergency vehicles. There were sheriff's trucks, rescue rigs, more fire trucks and mountain fire service trucks as well. Katelyn was stopped by a sheriff's deputy asking where she was headed. She gave him her license and her business card showing she was with Ethan's group. She told the deputy she was headed to the shop to do some damage control. He sent he on her way, radioing the others about her vehicle and all.

She arrived at the shop a few minutes later and saw that Finn was already there.

"Hey," Katelyn said as she walked through the door. "How bad is it in here? Lots of calls and emails?"

"Yup. I've got the phone messages under control. How about you attack the emails. We can compare notes after we get a list of who contacted us. I'll bet some of them called and emailed both," Finn said.

"Great idea. I'm on it," Katelyn said as she began to take down customer names.

About an hour later, they had compared their lists and noticed that clients had, indeed, both called and left emails. They came up with an email to send to everyone explaining how no one was injured and they didn't think any of the other projects were in danger. The fire arson squad and the sheriff's department were looking at all angles to make sure all the projects were safe. Once they finished composing the email, they sent it to Ethan and Ian for approval. It was approved in record time and Katelyn got busy sending it to all their clients and vendors.

Finn took care of contacting the suppliers for the burn site, explaining that they would begin rebuilding within a few weeks and would appreciate it if the vendors could procure the same amount of stuff they had already sent and be ready to send again.

Katelyn and Finn finished at about the same time. Katelyn got bottles of juice for both for them and they were just setting down to drink and talk when they heard the shop door open.

Katelyn turned to see who it was as Finn said, "Hey, bro. I'm okay. Really"

Katelyn stood up and starred. Right there in front of her was Jay, Finn's twin brother. He had died about two years ago. There was no way he was alive.

The next thing Katelyn remembered was waking up on the floor with Finn holding her head in his lap.

"Katelyn. Katelyn. Wake up," Finn said looking at her.

Jay was on the other side pressing a cold washcloth to her forehead.

She opened her eyes and saw Finn. Then she felt someone pressing something cold on her face and turned and saw Jay again.

She moaned and closed her eyes, passing out again.

"We better call 911. Somethin' is very wrong here," Finn said.

"Wait a few minutes, Finn. It seems she's troubled when she sees me. Look, she's comin' around again."

Katelyn took a deep breath and looked at Finn. "Is that really Jay next to me?"

"Yes. Is that a problem?" Finn asked.

Katelyn shook her head no then said, "I swear he was dead. I remember the call from my parents when he died. This is all a nightmare. Did the energy site just burn down? Was that real?"

"Yes, it was. No, I'm not dead. I know my brother wishes I was sometimes, but, really, I'm in the flesh," Jay said to Katelyn as she just stared at him.

"Whoa. Hold on. Take a deep breath and then just sit here for a bit," Finn said as Katelyn tried to sit up.

She sat up and then a few minutes later, the boys walked her to the couch.

"This is the most hellish day. I swear you died. I know dreams can feel very real and all. But I haven't seen ya' since I moved back almost two months ago. Where ya' been?"

"Finn, didn't ya' tell her I was workin' on a job in Tennessee and I was only home some weekends?"

"Ah, no. I forgot," Finn replied as Jay punched him a hard one in the arm.

"Okay. I deserve that," Finn said rubbing his arm.

"Boys, really? Really? This is just too bizarre. Just too strange. How about ya' get me some more juice. I think the one I had spilled all over the place," Katelyn suggested.

Jay grabbed another juice and handed it to Katelyn.

Katelyn pinched Jay. Jay hollered. "What was that for?"

"Just needed to make sure you were for real," Katelyn said laughing.

"I do like your style," Finn said laughin at Jay.

"Ya', know, this is gonna' leave a bruise. How do I explain that to mom and dad?"

"Just tell them a girl did it," Katelyn said laughing even more.

"Very funny," Jay replied.

Katelyn was tryin' not to lose it again. She knew Jay had died in that terrible accident two years ago. Almost to the day if truth be told. It was great seein' him again and all. But, Katelyn knew, beyond a shadow of a doubt, that this Creek wasn't her own. She needed to see Kendra right away.

"Well, I do feel so much better. Did all the emails go out?" she asked Finn.

"Yes. And, Ian says the media has begun to show up and the sheriff won't let any of them up the drive. He thinks they're all gonna' come over here and try to get information from us. Ethan said to leave and make sure everything is locked tight and the security lights and all are on."

"Okay. Let's go then," Katelyn said as she slowly got up, took a breath to show the boys she was good, and grabbed her bag and laptop.

They were just driving down to the Pine Ridge Road when the first news van passed them. They had left a note on the door informing the media that Ethan Sutherland would get in touch with them when there was news to share.

Katelyn waved to the boys and headed home. The boys were headed back to the build site to meet up with Ian and get the latest news. Ethan was at The Store talking with Miss Cora, Emily, and Kendra in a small private group.

Jordan had company. The fire service had a tank truck and crew on the back of his property. The fire had not spread that far but embers were still flying all around. They sprayed the area to be safe and would stay there until the all clear was given by the fire chief.

The sheriff's department had sent two deputies to block Jordan's driveway from anyone trying to get in to look around.

Miss Cora had sent Kevin over to make sure Jordan had someone with him just in case Jordan needed anything he didn't already have.

Katelyn headed home first. She needed to sit down. The shock of seein' Jay was really too much to handle. She knew things were a bit different and had tried to make sense of it all. Now, the fact that this wasn't her Crab Apple Creek was more than she could handle. Alone. More than she could handle alone. She needed some answers and explanations of what the hell was going on and why she was a part of whatever it was. She knew Kendra was at The Store with the others and they were talking to Ethan. She felt light-headed and a bit sick to her stomach. She made some calming tea and sipped it while just sitting at the kitchen table for the longest time.

She heard voices and went to the front door to see folks leaving The Store. Ethan was headed to his truck and Kendra was coming across the road. It was now or never.

"Hey, Kendra, could ya' come over here, please?" Katelyn said.

Kendra immediately knew what was happening.

"Let's just sit a spell on the porch. Shall we?" Katelyn said as she sat down.

"You feelin okay?" Kendra asked rather quietly.

"NO!" Katelyn yelled. "And, you know why. Explain all this shit."

"Take a breath, Katelyn. I've been waitin' for you to ask for answers."

"Well, isn't that precious? Why haven't you explained all this before when I asked?"

"I was told not to. The Other Side said you had to experience some stuff first. You have, haven't you?"

"Fuck yes! I saw Jay a little while ago at the shop. I passed out. What the fuck is goin' on? I know he's dead. And Emily and Ethan NOT being together is wrong, too. I know I talked with my brothers about their new houses and all. In great detail. And all the other things that just don't seem to be right. So, don't try any crappy explanations. I want the truth. Now!"

"Jesus, girl. You sure can get angry," Kendra said as Katelyn looked around for something to throw at her.

"Ya' better be thankful I'm not throwin' the plants at ya'."

"Oh, I am," Kendra said seriously.

"Explain all this and don't keep anything out," Katelyn demanded.

"Okay. We think you can handle it all now. If not, we're gonna' make sure you'll be alright. Well, first things first. Remember when we were talkin' back in July and you mentioned how some of the stuff on the shelves of The Store were quite different from the day before?"

"Yes, I do." Katelyn replied.

"Do you remember what you were doin' the day before that, in the afternoon?"

"Ah, yes. I had been doin' some stuff around here then went over to Jordan's place. I wandered over to the hill in the meadow."

"I know all about the cave and the crystals," Kendra said.

"Why am I not surprised?" Katelyn replied sarcastically.

"Wise ass. Well, you remember walkin' into the cave and seein' all those amazin' crystals and all?"

"Yes," Katelyn.

"Tell me what happened when you walked into the center of the space there," Kendra said.

"Nothin,' really. I just walked into the middle of the place lookin' all around. That cave is beyond words," Katelyn said.

"What happened when you walked into the center of the space? Take a moment and think about it," Kendra instructed Katelyn.

Katelyn thought for a few minutes, closing her eyes and kind of going back to that exact moment.

"As I walked into the center space, I felt a wave of somethin' go through me. Or, it was like I walked through a wave of energy or somethin'. Nothin' changed in the cave," Katelyn explained a few minutes later.

"That's exactly what happened. You walked through a wave of energy. We call it an interdimensional portal," Kendra replied, then waited for Katelyn to take it all in.

All of a sudden Katelyn jumped up and yelled, "A portal? Like a time-warp? Ya' mean I'm in a different time and place? Holy shit!"

"Katelyn, calm yourself and sit down. Folks will think you've gone batty or somethin'," Kendra got up to help Katelyn sit back down.

"Breathe, Katelyn. You're in The Creek for sure. It's just a different dimension. Not a different time. Now, here, drink some of your tea before ya' pass out again."

Katelyn took a big gulp of her tea and just starred at Kendra for the longest time.

A bit later, Katelyn said, "What the fuck?! A portal? Travel through a portal to a different dimension not a different time. How does that happen?"

"Well, not sure about the science of it all," Kendra started when Katelyn interrupted her.

"Kendra, don't even think ya' can go there. It's all about The Magic. It's that simple," Katelyn said.

"Yes, it is, Katie girl. I don't know how it all works, for real. I just know it does. There are portals in all dimensions in all places so we can travel in the blink of an eye. Sometimes The Other Side needs a Gifted person to go into a parallel dimension to do something so the other dimensions will be safe.

222

It usually has to do with defeating The Dark in some manner. The Dark can travel through the portals, too."

"Bastards. All of them. Evil fuckin' bastards!" Katelyn hissed.

"Yes, indeed," Kendra agreed. She gave Katelyn some time to take in the new information.

"So, why me? Why did I go through the portal thing?" Katelyn asked.

"Well, then. You accept all that I've told you?" Kendra asked softly.

"Guess so. It does make sense of all the changes I've seen," Katelyn answered.

"Okay then. I, ah, think I'll go grab a couple of waters or somethin' for us. Be right back," Kendra said quickly going into the frig and coming back with two bottles of water. "Here ya' go."

"Thanks. Why do I need this? Oh no. You're gonna' say somethin' even more bizarre than the portal thing."

"Yup," Kendra said as she motioned to Katelyn to take a drink.

"Well, here goes. The reason you were the one to come through the portal was to be a part of a much bigger project."

"What? Like what?" Katelyn demanded.

"Like a battle the likes no one has ever been a part of yet. No one," Kendra said plain as she could.

"Me? Part of a battle? You're nuts," Katelyn said rocking back and forth real fast.

"Hard to understand. I know. I'm not even sure how it's all gonna' play out yet. Never am until it happens."

"What? I'm not gonna' know what to do until it happens? How am I supposed to get ready for it? Tell me that!" Katelyn hollered.

"Katie, calm down, please," Kendra said as she walked over to her and stopped the chair. "I think you're about to go into orbit."

Katelyn looked at Kendra and realized she had been rocking really fast.

"Most likely," Katelyn said laughing a little. "If there's anything else I should know, you should tell me know. I don't think I can take anymore news."

"No. Really. Just take a bit to think about all this. I'm stayin' right here," Kendra said.

"Why? Is somethin' gonna' happen right now?" Katelyn asked.

"No. Just that we need to do some more talkin.' I think you need some time to take in all that I've said so far. We'll pick up the conversation in a bit," Kendra answered.

Katelyn got up and began to walk around the porch, then inside the house, then around the yard. All the while, Kendra stayed sitting on the porch just watching her.

Eventually, Katelyn came back to the porch and sat down.

"This is a lot to take in right now. Is this real? All of it? Emily and Ethan? My brothers? Jordan?" Katelyn asked.

"Yes, in this dimension," Kendra replied.

"But not in the real one. My real one," Katelyn said.

"That's right. Not in the one you were born into," Kendra.

"Are you the same in my real place?"

"Yes," Kendra answered.

"How can that be?" Katelyn asked lookin at Kendra.

"I knew you were gonna' ask that question. I gotta' tell ya' the truth but I think it's gonna' push you into overload."

"Overload? How much crazier can it be? Unless you're tellin' me that you're an ET or somethin'." Katelyn said laughing.

Kendra took a breath and just looked at Katelyn for a minute before saying, "Well, yes. That's exactly it."

"Right. You're an ET. Please," Katelyn said in disbelief.

"Katelyn, come with me," Kendra said as she walked the two of them into Katelyn's house so no one outside could hear and see them.

"Why are we inside?" Katelyn asked as Kendra pusher her onto a kitchen chair.

"I'm going to prove to you that I really am an alien. An ET," Kendra said as Katelyn sat down with a thump.

As Katelyn watched, Kendra shape shifted into a man.

"Whoa! No way!" Katelyn yelled not believing her eyes.

Then Kendra shape shifted into her own ET self. It was a strange creature, not scary. Just different.

"What the hell is that?" Katelyn yelled again.

"This is my original shape," Kendra replied in the voice everyone was used to hearing. "I can shape shift as needed depending on the place I'm in or on."

"Overload doesn't begin to explain all this shit," Katelyn said just staring at Kendra. "Does anyone else know about you?"

"Yes. Emily and Miss Cora in both dimensions. Miss Cora and I were there when Emily was battling The Dark in The Sacred Rock Meadow. I shifted into my real self to help protect the others from The Dark. It worked. As soon as the battle was over, I shifted back to my Kendra self."

"And you can go between dimensions like I did?"

"Yes, I can go between dimensions but not in the way you did. I'm able to move between dimensions using energy as my source. Humans need a physical place to cross dimensions like crossing the road. My group, shall we call them, is able to use the energy around us to just disappear into another dimension."

"Now, that's really cool," Katelyn said in a daze. "So, why am I here? Why did I walk through that portal? You said somethin' about a battle."

"Yes, The Dark is trying, once again, to take The Magic from here. But, this time, there's a twist. Seems it want's Jordan's land. That's why we placed the protection grid."

"I remember. So, it wasn't just to protect Jordan then. Why the land?"

"I've been tryin 'to figure that out. Miss Cora and Emily are tryin' to figure it out, too. So far, we've come up with nothin'."

"I think it has somethin' to do with the crystals that keep showin' up," Katelyn said.

"That's a great thought. I bet it does. How's the one that you and Jordan found together? You call it your twin crystals."

"It's been glowin' and warm ever since just before the explosion. I was over at Jordan's and we both were holdin' onto our crystals at the same time and we saw a strange vision. Ever since, they've been glowin' like crazy and warm and hummin' non-stop."

"May I see yours?"

"Sure," Katelyn said as she took it out of her pocket. It was glowing and all.

"Wow. It's really active. Must have somethin' to do with the explosion down the way from Jordan. I wonder if it's in sync with the cave crystals?" Kendra said.

"I'll bet a million dollars it is. I'll bet 'cha the cave is glowing like crazy right now, too."

"I'm gonna' call Jordan and ask if his crystal is acting like yours," Kendra said hitting the button for Jordan's phone.

"Hey, Kendra," Jordan said answering the call.

"Hey, Jordan. Katelyn and I are in her kitchen and her crystal is glowin' and all like crazy. Just wondering if yours is doin' the same thing?"

"Why, yes, it is, Kendra. I was wondering the same about Katelyn's. Bet it has to do with the explosion down the road."

"That's just what we were thinkin'. We also thought the cave might be 'alive' shall we say."

"I'll bet it is," Jordan replied. "There's somethin' special about that cave. I'll bet The Magic is protecting it from whatever started the fire. That explosion wasn't a normal one."

"Most of us think that, too. As a matter of fact, Jordan, a bunch of us think it was an attack by The Dark. A kind of practice attack. We're all tryin' to think of how it happened. Got any ideas?"

"Not yet. I'm not really sure how all The Magic stuff works but I'll think about it and let ya' know if I come up with anything."

"Okay Thanks. Stay safe," Kendra said as they hung up.

"Well, ya' heard the whole thing. And, I know there's somethin' that needs your Gifts to make sure The Dark doesn't get what it wants."

"Great. That's all I got," Katelyn said.

"I know. Me, too. We'll all keep thinkin' about this and I'm sure we'll come up with the real reason The Dark wants that land. It has to do with the cave for sure."

"Agreed," Katelyn said. "Now, it's way past supper time and I'm headin' over to The Store. I feel like I haven't eaten in days," Katelyn said as she stood up.

"I know exactly how ya' feel. Let's go," Kendra said as they moved towards the front door. "Katelyn, I'm kind of sorry to dump all this on you like this, but we don't have much time left."

"It's okay. I get it. Just need food and a little time to process it all," Katelyn said as they stepped outside.

As they walked outside, they were greeted with a wild scene. It looked like almost every soul that lived in and around The Creek had shown up. Tables and chairs had been set up outside to accommodate everyone and it looked like a party was goin' on. It wasn't a party. The fire crews had come by for supper along with everyone else. Folks were talkin' about the fire and such as they ate their supper. Jenna and Matthews were helpin' Ted serve everyone.

Katelyn and Kendra were greeted by all and a place was found for them. Jenna took their order and Katelyn went inside to grab drinks and such.

"Hey, Katie," Miss Cora said as Katelyn stepped into the dining room to get drinks from the cooler.

"Hey, Miss Cora," Katelyn replied as she went over and kissed her cheek.

"I see you've been talkin' with Kendra," Miss Cora offered.

"Yes. I know about her," Katelyn whispered into Miss Cora's ear.

Miss Cora gave Katelyn a hug to show she understood. "You'll be alright, Katie."

"I know. It's just a lot of stuff," Katelyn said as she stood up.

"Get your drinks and get back outside with everyone. I'll come along in a bit," Miss Cora said.

"Yes, Ma'am," Katelyn said with a smile.

The rest of the evening was spent with everyone talking about the explosion, eating Ted's fantastic food, and catching up on everything else going on. Kevin had come by for dinner for himself and Jordan. He told folks that Jordan was just fine. Frustrated about not being able to help and get around very quickly, but he was behaving and all. Folks sent their love to Jordan.

It was well into the night when things finally started to quiet down around The Store. It usually closed around nine, but not tonight. Everyone helped Ted clean up and get the kitchen ready for the morning. Michael had help restocking the shelves as well.

It was well after ten when only Ted, Michael, Katelyn and Kendra were left in The Store. They were sitting in the dining room comparing notes to make sure everything had been completed.

"Well, I guess we're all set for tomorrow. I called in an extra order for food supplies around six, telling the supplier about the fire and all. They said they'd have it here by eight tomorrow mornin'. I need to get me some sleep. So glad no one was hurt from the explosion and fightin' the fires," Ted said as he got up from the table.

"Me, too. Sleep well, ladies," Michael said as Kendra and Katelyn said their goodnights walking out the side door.

Katelyn and Kendra were silent as they crossed the road. Katelyn looked up at the night sky and sighed.

Kendra looked up as well and sighed, too. They waived at each other and went into their houses. Both were asleep a few minutes later.

The Creek slept. The Dark did not.

CHAPTER 22

The next day The Creek was back to mostly normal. Ethan had everyone, including all the crews, show up at the shop at seven sharp. He explained what was going to happen at the explosion site and how everyone who worked at the site from the excavation crew up to the day before the explosion would be interviewed by the fire arson team and the Sheriff's dept. It was all protocol. No one expected anyone working with Sutherland had anything to do with it. It was just that it was such a strange fire, that no stone was gonna' go unturned in trying to figure out the cause.

Ian explained that the build would begin again after the site was released by the authorities and clean-up was complete. The client had approved the new plan. Of course, they weren't happy about the explosion, but very relieved that no one had been hurt or killed. And, they understood about the time it would take to get it all in place.

After the crews were sent back to work, Ethan and Ian sat with Katelyn and Finn. The sheriff had sent two deputies over to block the media from bothering them.

"Katelyn, thanks for your excellent work in sending those emails. Ian and I haven't had time to do any of that. Finn, great job with the phone and setting a new answering message. Today, we get back to normal with all the projects except the energy build. There's gonna' be an ongoing investigation for quite some time. The fire chief and sheriff will release the site as soon as they can. I told them to take all the time they'd need."

"And, Finn, you and I will be working on the re-build. I think I have a new idea for the solar panels. Somethin' the fire chief said about not seeing any solar debris. I've already talked with Laine and Mo. They're gonna come

228

by in a week or so to talk about my idea. They're a bit busy right now with all their stuff."

"Good. So glad no one was hurt. But, I gotta' tell ya', it seems The Dark is responsible for this" Finn said.

"We all agree and know the arson squad isn't gonna' find a direct cause," Ethan said.

"So, what now?" Katelyn asked.

"We don't really know," Ethan replied. "I've been talkin' with Miss Cora and the others. They think somethin' is about to happen that has to do with Jordan's land. I have no idea why. When it comes to The Magic around here, I listen to the experts."

"Me, too," Ian said.

They talked about the other projects then got busy with their day.

Miss Cora and Kendra had no doubt about Jordan's land holding some special Magic. They had been talking with each other and had come up with some ideas of how the explosion had happened. Kendra was gonna' talk with Finn this afternoon about her idea.

The Dark was happy with the explosion. It had discovered a new way to damage The Creek. Madman was sent to be in charge of the attack on The Creek. Greg was told he was still needed and Madman let him handle the other demons.

"We're ready to attack Jordan's place and take the powerful Magic now that we have a way of getting in without being detected. We're gonna' charge the stream that flows from those thermal hot springs just like we did on that first site. We'll start at about the same place. The Dark has given me special powers to charge the water with enough explosive energy to blow the whole place into space."

Everyone cheered at the news.

"This is gonna' be even better that before," Greg said as he looked at Madman. "What do ya' need me and the others to do to get ready?"

"Well, you, Greg, need to make sure there is nothin' blocking the flow. You'll have to morph into a bird to get a good view of the place. Once you report back, then we can plan the last phase. The Attack!" Madman laughed maniacally at his choice of words.

The others joined in and began to come up with ideas on how to make everything happen.

"Okay. I see you've all come up with some great ideas. First things first. Greg, drive over to Pine Ridge and park somewhere no one will notice. Then, morph into a hawk and fly over the stream."

"Ah, Madman, we can't change into a hawk. The White Light holds that energy along with the eagle. How about a crow? No one will think it's out of place. Should be good."

"Okay. Damn that White Light! No matter. We'll soon have so much Magic energy we should be able to damage The White Light into nothin' permanently."

Cheers went up for this idea.

"I'm outta' here," Greg said as he left and set out for Pine Ridge. They were still using the apartment in Boone that was the upstairs of a warehouse that wasn't used anymore. No one was ever around.

Greg found a parking lot on the north side of Pine Ridge. He got out of the truck and headed towards the building. As soon as he walked behind the building, he saw that no one was around and changed into a crow. He flew off to The Creek.

He knew he couldn't fly over Jordan's place because of the protection grid. It went a long ways up into the air. Too high for a bird to survive. He decided to fly along the Pine Ridge Road to just past Jordan's place. Then he would fly over the stream to see if the place they wanted to use to send The Dark energy into the stream was open and free of debris.

Jordan was in the barn when Greg flew down the road past his place. All of a sudden, the adult eagles set up a cry and took off faster than lightspeed. Jordan only saw a blur of them as they left the barn. He hobbled out the back door and saw them flying north.

The juvenile eagles took off as well. They were just a bit behind their parents. The site of four eagles flying together was magnificent. Jordan knew better. Something was wrong. He grabbed his phone and called Miss Cora.

"Hey, Jordan," Miss Cora said as she answered the phone.

"Miss Cora, the eagles just flew outta' here at lightspeed headed north. All of them. I got a bad feelin' about this."

"Thanks for callin'. I'm getting a bad feelin' as well. You're safe there. Stay put. I'll see what I can find out. I'll call ya' back," Miss Cora said ending the call.

As soon as the eagles cleared the protection grid, they flew right at the crow attacking him with their wing tips. Greg wasn't prepared. He fell down a long ways but managed to regain his balance before he smashed into the ground. He was close to the spot he needed to see. As soon as he got above the tree tops, the eagles attacked again. This time from all four directions. They managed to push him away from the stream and drive him straight into the sun's rays. Greg was blinded. He couldn't see a thing. The eagles kept moving him into the path of the sun. He completely lost the ability to see. The eagles were counting on this and moved him into an area of closely grown hardwood trees. He hit the first one and fell sideways. He managed to flap his wings a few more times before he flew straight into an older tree head on. He was killed instantly.

The eagles flew close by for a few more minutes making sure he was dead. As he drew his last breath, Greg morphed into his original alien self. He vanished into thin air as dead demons will do. The eagles set out to return to the barn.

Jordan was standing in the field behind the barn. He had managed to get there on his crutches. It hadn't been easy. All of a sudden, he saw the eagles coming back. They flew around him a few times, then, one-by-one, they returned to the nest.

Jordan got back into the barn and looked at them. They were all lined up in the nest looking over the edge at him as if to say, 'All is safe now.' That's how Jordan felt and thought he heard them say. He bowed his head at them and they settled into the nest.

Jordan called Miss Cora back and told her what had happened.

"Good news, Jordan. I think they attacked something just north of your place. Looks like that something was a demon in disguise. I felt the evil energy and concentrated on the sky. The White Light showed me a black bird tryin' to get a look at the stream that flows from the hot springs to your place. My Guides are tellin' me right his minute that the stream is where The Dark sent the explosion through. I'm gonna' need to concentrate for a bit. You're alright. Rest and eat. Later," Miss Cora said before she could give Jordan a chance to say anything. She needed to concentrate right there and then as her Guides were giving her important information about how the building site was attacked.

Jordan was so shocked at all this, he sat right down on the floor of the barn. One of the young eagles looked over the edge of the nest at him and gave a quiet squawk. Jordan looked up at him and smiled. The eagle bobbed his head a few times and kept looking at Jordan.

"Well, George. I think that's what I'm gonna' call you. Okay with you?" Jordan asked.

The eagle bobbed his head again and Jordan took that as a 'yes.'

"Alright, then, George. Thanks to you and your family for chasing after that black crow thing. Miss Cora says you drove it away from the stream into a bunch of trees where it flew head on into a tree and died. Thanks so much for protecting everything. Much obliged."

George flew right over to Jordan and stood in front of him. He bobbed his head a few times and Jordan nodded back. George returned to the nest and settled in.

Jordan smiled and shook his head a bit as he grabbed his crutches and stood up, got his balance, and went on into the house. This surely had been a strange day. So far.

Miss Cora had gotten just the information she needed. She set up a conference call with Emily and Kendra.

"Girls, I know what's been happenin'. My guides have filled me in on the details. Seems we were right about the powerful Magic on Jordan's land. That explosion was a practice run just like we thought. Just now, a demon that looked like a black crow was flyin' over the stream north of Jordan's place. Jordan called me to tell me that the eagles took off like all get out from the barn and headed north. I felt a shift of evil energy just then so I hung up and concentrated on my Guides. They told me that the fake black crow was a demon in disguise and was tryin' to get a look at the hot springs stream that flows into Jordan's meadow and all. Seems The Dark has figured out a way to send Dark Energy through the water. That's what caused the explosion. At Ethan's building site. And, I'm thinkin' that's just what the Dark is planning to do at Jordan's place."

"That's wild. A demon morphed into a black crow to get a look at the stream. Jesus! What will they think of next?" Emily said.

"Don't ask," Kendra replied. "We got ourselves a mess of trouble here. What else is The Dark gonna' throw at us to get to Jordan's place?

"That's exactly what I'm thinkin'," Miss Cora replied.

"How can we protect every one, everything, and the earth all at the same time?" Emily said out loud in a worried tone.

"Exactly," Miss Cora and Kendra said at the same time.

"Now, girls, we all know the connections we have with The Other Side and The White Light. Let's take a little bit of time to see what we can do and think of to try to protect The Creek. All of The Creek."

They agreed with Miss Cora and ended the call. Each one of them set to connecting with The Other Side for help and ideas.

Katelyn and Finn were busy at the shop when all this was happening. Katelyn felt a shiver go through her about the time the demon alien bird thing died. She shivered and Finn saw it.

"Katelyn, you okay?" Finn said going over to her desk.

"Not sure. Just felt a chill go over me. I'm okay now," Katelyn replied as she shook herself and settled back to work.

"Let me know if ya' need anything," Finn said returning to his desk.

Katelyn felt unsettled. She couldn't really concentrate so she decided to walk around the grounds for a bit.

"I'm gonna' take a walk around. Wanna' come with me?" she asked Finn.

"Yes, I do. I don't wanna' let you out of my sight," Finn said as they walked out the door. The Sheriff's deputies were still there. One was walking around the grounds and the other was at the entrance to the driveway keeping the media out. Their radios were on but in a rather quiet mode.

Madman was pissed. He felt Greg's death the instant it happened. He howled and blew up two demons he was so mad. The others ran out of the apartment and hid. Madman called some of his fellow crazy ETs to come to him. They showed up almost instantly. They were as hideous as Madman in their own form.

"I got a job for you. We need to take some land that has super powerful Magic that The Dark wants. We know how to get Dark energy to it. One of your own had morphed into a bird to fly over the stream we need to use and get a good look at it when he was attacked by The White Light and flew into a tree and was killed. We still need that information. Got any ideas how we can get it? Oh, yeah, the land has a protection grid around it so that's why we can't just go there and destroy it."

"Fuck The White Light," one of the monster aliens said. The others howled in agreement.

"Settle down. I need some ideas," Madman said.

"How about we morph into humans and drive over to the place to get a look," another said.

"Nope. The Creek is protected by The White Light. They're all on alert for strangers comin' by."

"Damn!"

"We could morph into clouds and sail by," someone else said.

"Like a thunderstorm." The first monster alien added.

"Now, that's a good idea. You just gave me an idea. How about if we wait until nightfall and become rain or storm clouds and sail over the place?"

"No one would even see us or, if they did, they'd just think the clouds were normal," someone replied.

"You're right about that. Good. Whose gonna' be the cloud?" Madman asked.

The first monster alien replied, "I'll go. No problem. I've done this before."

"Let's say around 11pm. That way everyone should be asleep. As soon as we get the information, we can plan the final attack. Hey, you scaredy cats, get back here," Madman demanded of the others that had run away.

The others returned instantly. The plan was finished and all was ready to go by nightfall.

Mathews was on the phone with the sheriff.

"One of the reasons I wanted to talk with you was because I got a report back that shows that one of the electric company guys who was staying in The Creek until last week was an imposter. He used the identification of a man that had died a long time ago. I've had some of the Boone crew looking out for him. Seems he was last seen there two days ago at a local bar. He goes by the name of Greg. I sent you a picture of him a few minutes ago on the secure website."

"I just pulled it up. I've seen this guy around here driving a company truck. Thing is, he was always alone and not at any specific job site. Makes sense now. I'm sending an alert out to the county and local agencies with his picture. Hold on a second," the sheriff said.

"All set," the sheriff replied when he finished. "We'll keep an eye out. Anything else?"

"No. That's all for now. I'll check in later," Matthews said as he ended the call.

Jenna walked into Matthews' home office just then.

"Hey, Matthews, I got a weird feelin' a few minutes ago like somethin' wasn't right," she said.

"I just got off the phone with the sheriff tellin' him about the fake Greg. How do ya' mean not right?"

"Well, it was like everything was goin' along fine, then, it was like a wave of energy came by and changed the flow of things. That's the only way I can explain it. Like there was a bright sunny day then it was a bit cloudy-like."

"I get it. Think somethin's gonna' happen again?"

"I don't know. I really don't know how The Magic works, just that it does," Jenna said rather hesitantly.

"Maybe you should get a hold of Emily and talk with her. She may have felt the same thing," Matthews suggested.

"Good idea. I'll call her now," Jenna said as she punched Emily's number into the phone while walking out of Matthews' office.

"Hey, Jenna," Emily said answering the phone.

"Hey, Emily. I've got somethin' to ask you. I was goin' along just a few minutes ago workin' on a sketch and, all of a sudden, I felt like the energy changed. Kinda' like a cloud rolled by," Jenna explained.

"Good call. Something evil did happen just a bit ago," Emily said. She then explained what she and Kendra had been talking about.

"Holy shit!" Jenna yelled loud enough to get Matthews out of his office. "That's really bad. No one was hurt right?"

"No. No one just the bad demon," Emily replied as Jenna put the call on speaker phone.

"The bad guys really tried to get a look at the stream that runs over Jordan's land?" Matthews asked.

"Hey, Matthews. Yes, that's what Miss Cora has figured out. She says The Dark wants some kind of Magic that is in Jordan's land," Emily explained.

"I wonder if that bad demon was the guy named Greg?" Matthews said out loud.

"I don't know. Why?" Emily asked.

"Oh, just thinkin' out loud. That's all," Matthews convincingly replied. "So, I guess we're in for some trouble with The Dark again," Matthews added.

"Looks that way," Emily replied. "I'll let ya' know if Miss Cora comes up with anything else."

"Okay. Thanks. By," Matthews and Jenna said.

Matthews and Jenna just looked at each other for a minute.

"Matthews, is this gonna' be bad?" Jenna asked.

"How the hell should I know? I'm not a Magic person. I hope not," Matthews said as he gathered Jenna in his arms. He began to stroke her back and she pushed into him.

"I like the way we comfort each other," Jenna said as they climbed the stairs leaving a trail of clothes.

They fell onto the bed and Matthews moved between Jenna's legs, spreading them apart and finding her hot spot with his tongue. He licked her into ecstasy and just before she came, he entered her. She grabbed his ass and pushed him into her and responded with a moan. She moved hard and fast and as she reached her climax, she thrust against him so he would push harder and faster. He brought her to her pinnacle as she brought him with her. They soared into that place of indescribable pleasure for the longest time.

Finally, they came back to the present time and space, both sighing.

"Why, Miss Jenna, I do like the way you show your appreciation for your protector," Matthews said.

"Why, Mr. Matthews, I do appreciate your efforts to protect and serve me," Jenna replied.

They both laughed as they went to gather their clothes.

"I do like this little mid-day recess thing," Jenna said as she finished dressing.

" Me, too," Matthews replied in kind. "Now, food!"

They ran to the kitchen and raided the frig and enjoyed themselves.

Katelyn and Finn were walking out into the woods and came upon a faerie circle. She saw the circle and stopped before stepping into it.

"This is a very special and sacred place," Katelyn said as she looked at Finn.

He smiled and nodded his head. They stood there for a few minutes wrapped in the energy of Mother Earth.

"Let's get back," Finn said quietly as he turned them around and they headed back towards the shop.

"I've seen faerie circles before. Did you know this one was here?" Katelyn asked.

"No. But I'm not surprised. Ethan and Ian are tryin' their best to protect as much of the earth as possible with balancing the needs of the creatures and the humans. I think their doin' a great job and it looks like Mother Earth thinks so, too."

"I agree and am thrilled to be a small part of all this. It surely is a special place here in the Blue Ridge," Katelyn replied as they went back into the shop.

"Yes, it is," Finn said as they went back to work.

The end of the day found everyone a little apprehensive about the strange energy shift that had happened when Greg killed himself. Most folks weren't aware that anything was happening more than usual. But for those few who were specially Gifted, they knew something was gonna' happen and happen right soon now.

The energy of The Creek was a bit unsettled that night as folks drifted off into sleep

CHAPTER 23

The monster aliens were jazzed and ready to put their plan into action. As the night wore on, they began.

The alien monster that was gonna' be the cloud transported himself to the woods about a mile northwest of the stream spot they wanted to see. He became a gray cloud and began to move through the sky at a slow steady pace.

Miss Cora had stayed awake figuring that The Dark would try to get to the stream again. She didn't feel that an attack was underway, just that The Dark wanted something from the stream. She stepped outside a little bit before eleven and saw a clear night sky. It was beautiful. Millions of starts shining like crazy.

As she watched the sky, she saw a cloud coming from the northwest. That was a strange direction for a cloud to come from as it was summer and most clouds came from the west and southwest. It began to change to a darker gray color as it picked up a bit of speed.

All of a sudden, she knew it was no normal cloud. It was The Dark tryin' to get to the stream again.

"I call upon my ancestors and The White Light Guardians to stop that cloud from getting to the stream. Please help us."

Another cloud formed in front of the dark gray cloud. It was pure white and it created a strong wind that pushed against the gray cloud.

Miss Cora watched in amazement as the white cloud struck with bolts of energy at the dark gray cloud. Bolts of energy kept striking the dark gray cloud until a mighty scream was heard and the alien monster that was the dark gray cloud was forced to morph back into itself and fall from the sky. It splattered onto a group of boulders and was killed instantly.

A mighty roar was heard and Miss Cora was wrapped in protective energy as Madman tried to kill her. The White Light Guardians pulsed and stabbed Madman with energy bolts of all colors until he was forced into the space between the dimensions to exist there for all eternity.

The roaring noise awoke Emily, Kendra and Katelyn from sound sleep.

They knew something bad was happening and Kendra tried to call Miss Cora. All of a sudden, the roaring noise was gone and the night was quiet again.

The group called Miss Cora and this time she answered.

"You alright, Miss Cora?" Kendra asked.

"Well, I am now. The Dark sent another morphed alien to get to the stream. I woke up and saw a dark gray cloud comin' from the northwest and knew right away somethin' was wrong. I asked for help from The Other Side and they sent a pure white cloud. It attacked the gray one so much that the alien morphed back into its original form and fell onto a pile of boulders. It was killed instantly. Then, some other Dark Energy Alien started to attack me and The White Light wrapped me up and then sent the bad alien far, far away. He won't be botherin' anyone ever again."

"Holy shit, ah, cow, Miss Cora. You're really alright?" Emily and Katelyn asked at the same time.

"Yes, girls, I am perfectly alright. Just tired. We'll meet at The Store at sunrise to talk. Sleep well now," Miss Cora said as they hung up.

They set their phones for a bit before sunrise and went back to sleep.

Just as the sun was peaking over the mountains, Katelyn, Kendra, Emily, and Miss Cora arrived, all at the same time, at The Store. It was around five a.m. but Ted had awoken Michael earlier and said he felt like they should open right away. Michael knew Ted got hunches about strange stuff, so he didn't question Ted about this request.

The Store was open and Ted was in the kitchen making coffee and such and Michael was putting the porch furniture out.

"Mornin', Michael," Miss Cora said as she stepped up onto the porch.

"I knew Ted was right when he woke me up and said we should open early. Mornin', Miss Cora, ladies. I do believe Ted has your tea ready inside, Miss Cora."

"Thanks, Michael," Miss Cora said as they all walked into The Store and up the steps into the dining room.

"There you are, Miss Cora," Ted said placing her tea on the table at the place where she always sat.

"Thanks, Ted. Just what I need at this moment," Miss Cora replied sipping her tea.

"Hey, Ted. How about a sesame bagel with bacon, egg and cheese for me?" Katelyn said.

"Me, too, please," Emily chimed in.

"My pleasure, ladies, Anything for you Miss Cora?" Ted asked.

"Well, now that the subject has been brought up, how about some scrambled eggs, wheat toast, and grits and gravy?"

"Great choice," Ted said as he disappeared back into the kitchen.

Michael was busy in the front and outside so the ladies got busy talking.

"I guess I don't have to say the obvious. We're in for a fight here," Miss Cora started. "The Dark wants Jordan's land and it looks like it will not stop at anything. So, we have to come up with a plan."

"We agree," Kendra said. "We were talkin' while Emily was drivin' over. Hands free, Miss Cora. The grid should protect Jordan and the land, right?"

"That's what's been botherin' me. The Dark knows it can't get inside a protection grid. I wonder why it thinks it can send Dark Energy through the water? I think we better be prepared for a diversion or some kind of attack that would cause one of the protection grid crystal sites to be dug up."

"How could that happen? I thought the animals could sense the energy spots and leave them alone?" Katelyn asked.

"You're right, Katelyn," Emily answered. "We know that for sure. I think The Dark energy might be tryin' to use the water to disrupt the north or east spots."

"I was thinkin' the same thing," Kendra said quietly.

"But wouldn't Mother Earth protect her crystals?" Katelyn asked again.

"Yes, she would and does. But when a storm of great energy comes along, like a tornado, hurricane, or flood, she doesn't always interfere. Sometimes, those storms are sent to kinda' rebalance things down here. If The Dark can create a flood of that magnitude, then chances are it would be allowed to go forward and all," Miss Cora explained.

"Well, Miss Cora, I've been thinkin' about all that. I don't think a flood is what The Dark is all about. It seems that the new build was attacked by a massive energy bolt or somethin'. I wonder if The Dark is gonna' try that same thing at Jordan's?" Katelyn offered.

"Keep talkin'," Miss Cora said.

"Well, I think all this has somethin' to do with those crystals. Seems they have some kinda' special power or Magic and The Dark knows and wants the Magic. It's always after power. I've been thinkin' that there may be more crystals on or in Jordan's land that we don't know about and The Dark thinks there might some power, too. Makes sense to me."

"Now, that's good thinkin'," Miss Cora replied. "I think Katelyn has somethin' here."

Ted came out from the kitchen at that point to serve the ladies their breakfasts and they stopped talking.

"Thanks, Ted," they all said together as they began to eat.

"Tastes wonderful," Katelyn hollered with her mouth full.

"Thanks, Katie," Ted said laughing as he went back into the kitchen.

They ate their breakfast and talked about the upcoming Labor Day holiday activities.

"Let's hope this whole Dark Energy thing is over by Labor Day," Emily said.

"I think it will be," Miss Cora said. "As a matter of fact, I think it's gonna' start right now. Let's go outside."

As soon as they got outside, they all stood in awe at the orange-red sky that greeted them. Michael was standing so still, ya' would have thought he was a statue.

"Oh my God!" Emily said as the sky kept changing the orange and red hues.

"Looks like we got ourselves a problem," Hal said as he walked up onto the porch.

No one had seen him arrive.

"Hey, Hal," they all said as they continued to stare at the sky.

"Ya' ever see anything like this before?" Hal asked no one in particular.

They all shook their heads 'no' and continued to watch the sky.

"Look at that," Miss Cora said pointing to the east at the sun. It looked like a huge red/orange fireball, shooting flames from its core.

"Oh shit!" Kendra hollered as a bolt of orange lightening hit the earth near where The Dark had been tryin' to get to the stream.

"Miss Cora, you and Katelyn go over to her house and start chanting and connecting with The White Light Warriors. Emily, you head over to Ethan's place and tell him what's happened. I'm gonna' see what I can do," Kendra said as everyone headed out.

Kendra entered her house and immediately shape shifted into her original alien form calling on her Ancestors and alien family for help.

"The Dark has finally found a way to charge the stream with Dark Energy. I need help in fighting The Dark this time. I'm gonna' go over to Jordan's and try to stop the Dark Energy. I need your help," Kendra said as they all appeared one after the other, filling up her little house.

"You got it. Let's go," one of her alien family said.

'Thanks, Al," Kendra replied as they all made themselves vanish and flew over to the north end of the protection grid over Jordan's place.

When they got there, they could see the orange water boiling its way towards the grid. They all hovered in their invisible shape over the grid near the where the stream passed into the grid zone. It would only be a minute or two until the Dark Energy hit the boundary of the grid.

Emily got to Ethan's in record time. She burst into the shop to find Ethan, Ian, and Finn working on a project or something. They were there earlier than expected.

"Emily, what the hell is the matter?" Ethan asked as he walked over to her and brought her to the couch.

"I know some of you will find what I'm about to say insane, but I swear it's the truth. The Dark is tryin' to get to Jordan's land just like it blew up your energy build site thing," Emily said.

Ian gave Emily a bottle of water as he asked," How's that?"

"Well," Emily said pausing to take a gulp of water, "The Dark has charged the stream that flows from the hot springs to Jordan's place with Dark Energy."

"What?" Finn exclaimed.

"For real, Finn. Kendra, Katelyn, Miss Cora and I met at The Store just at sunrise to talk about something that happened around eleven last night. When we walked outside, the sky was orange-red just like it is now."

Emily was interrupted as the guys ran out of the shop to look at the sky.

Ian was the first to speak. "Now, that's just wrong as wrong can be."

Finn nodded his head in agreement sayin, "What the hell is goin' on here?"

Ethan replied with, "Not sure, but, I gotta' bad feelin' somethin' horrible is about to happen just like at The Holler."

"That's what I'm tryin' to tell ya," Emily said as they stood there staring at the sky. Just like at The Store, the sky kept changing hues of the red-orange colors. "Miss Cora and Katelyn are at Katelyn's working with The White Light sending positive energy to Jordan's place. Kendra is workin' on somethin', too. I'm here to tell ya' about the thing, which I have."

"Now what do we do?" Finn asked.

"Maybe we should go over to Jordan's to make sure he's safe?" Ian said.

"I like that idea. Someone should stay here, though, to make sure we stay okay," Ethan said.

"I'll stay," Ian replied.

"Okay. Finn, you, me and Emily are goin' to Jordan's right now," Ethan said.

They all went back inside so Ethan and Finn could grab their stuff. Just as they were about to get into Ethan's truck, the ground began to shake and tremble.

"Earthquake!" Finn said as they all fell to the ground.

Miss Cora and Katelyn were sittin' on the porch chanting and sending energy to Jordan's when the quake started.

"Oh boy," Katelyn said as they were rocked around in their rocking chairs.

"It's The Dark tryin' to shake the protection grid crystals loose from Mother Earth. Let's send our energy to the four spots right now," Miss Cora said.

"Okay. Here's goes," Katelyn said as she started chanting out loud and moving her hands in waves towards Jordan's place.

The folks at The Store felt the quake. Some of the ones standing up found themselves on the floor. While those sitting at the table found themselves shaken up. Ted was comin' through the kitchen door with his hands full and fell against one of the coolers. He lost a couple of breakfast bagels but managed to hold onto the rest. Michael was at the register and grabbed onto the counter before he fell to the floor.

Kendra and her group saw what was happening and sent energy to Mother Earth to calm her down. Kendra communicated with Mother Earth telling her The Dark was causing the earthquake to hurt her precious children, the crystals. As soon as Mother Earth got the message from Kendra, the quake stopped.

The quake stopped all of a sudden and Ethan, Finn, and Emily cautiously began to stand up.

"Y'all okay?" Ethan hollered.

"Yes," they both replied as they stood up and saw each other, brushing stuff of themselves.

"Alright then. Let's get over to Jordan's real fast," Ethan said as he started the truck up and put it into reverse before Finn and Emily could close the doors.

"Hey," Finn yelled as Ethan began to turn the truck.

Emily and Finn closed their doors really fast as Ethan peeled outta' the drive. They were at Jordan's in record time.

Katelyn and Miss Cora just looked at each other for only a second before they began another chant to protect The Creek and Jordan and the land.

Jordan was online with Sami working on his first URR research project when the earthquake hit.

"What the fuck is this?" Jordan yelled as the quake intensified.

"What's wrong Jordan?" Sami asked alarmed.

"It's an earthquake. I'm bein' shaken all over the place. Can't keep my chair in one place. Stuff's fallin' off the shelves in the kitchen."

"Get off the chair and onto the floor. Go under the desk if ya' can," Sami replied.

Jordan was on the floor a second later, half falling and half putting himself there. He moved under the desk and called Sami on his phone.

"You okay?" Sami asked when she answered.

"I think so. I'm under my desk. I kind of fell onto the floor as I was tryin' to get down to the floor."

"Does your leg hurt at all? Is the cast still intact?"

"It does ache some like I was tryin' too hard to exercise. The cast is still in one piece. I felt around the back with my hands."

"Okay Good for now. We can get you to the ER for a check-up once this all stops."

"Good idea. It's still shakin' here. Real bad. Jesus! A lamp just fell off the table near my desk and shattered into a zillion pieces."

"Stay put. Breathe."

"I think I know what's happenin'. Seems The Dark wants somethin' on my land. Katelyn was tellin' me that it might try to attack me here. I'm pretty sure that's exactly what's happenin'. Hey, the quake just stopped."

"Hold on a minute to make sure nothin' else falls on ya' before you crawl out from under the desk. Remember, everything can be replaced," Sami advised Jordan.

"That's exactly what I'm gonna' do."

"I can see stuff all over the place. Your laptop is still on the desk and the WIFI is still on. It doesn't look too bad."

"Good. I'm gonna' crawl out and keep the phone on. Here goes," Jordan said as he half crawled, half pulled himself out from under the desk.

"I'm out from under the desk. It's gonna' take a bit to try to stand up," Jordan said as he heard his backdoor open and Ethan call his name.

"I'm in my office, Ethan," Jordan replied as he stayed on the floor.

"Holy fuck! You okay?" Ethan said as he looked down at Jordan.

"As a matter of fact, I think I am. I could use some help getting off the floor and back into my chair. Where the hell is it?"

They looked around and found his chair in the kitchen.

"Hope it had a good time travelin'," Jordan said as Finn held the chair still and Emily and Ethan helped Jordan stand up then sit into his chair.

"Alright. Stay safe everyone," Sami said.

"Here, Jordan, put your leg on this," Emily said as she moved the waste basket near Jordan and put a pillow on it.

"I locked the chair into place," Finn said. "It came with locks. That's really cool."

"Thanks, y'all," Jordan started to say when they heard a loud thundering sound come from outside. It rattled the house.

"Stay here. I'll take a look through the kitchen window. No one go outside," Ethan ordered.

Jordan happened to look at his twin crystal. It was pulsing laser beams of light all over the place and it was changing colors real fast.

"Jesus! Would ya' look at that?" Jordan said as he pointed to his crystal on the desk next to his laptop.

"Hey, y'all," Sami said.

They looked at Jordan's laptop and saw Sami waving at them.

"Hey, Sami. How's things your way?" Finn asked.

"Good. Everything's good here," Sami replied. "Can ya' turn the laptop so I can see the crystal please?"

"Sure," Emily said as she repositioned the laptop so Sami could see the crystal.

"Wow! That's amazin'. Have ya' looked at any of the other crystals yet?"

"Nope. We will now. Hey Jordan, I'll push you in your office chair. Ready?" Finn asked.

"Yup. Thanks," Jordan replied as he pointed to the living room.

The crystal on the mantel was acting just like the twin crystal.

"Jesus! It's doin' the same thing," Jordan said. "Let's look out the front door. Betcha' all my crystals are acting the same."

They opened the front door to look out and were almost blinded by the light from the crystal.

"Yup. I knew it. Let's go to the back porch. I need to take a look outside," Jordan said. "Hey, Sami," Jordan said as he stopped at his desk for a minute. "The crystals are all glowing and sending beams everywhere. I'll get back to ya' when things calm down here."

"Alright. Stay safe everyone," Sami said as they ended the video chat.

As soon they got onto the porch, they heard a piercing scream.

"What was that?" Finn asked as they all looked around.

The sky was still a mesmerizing kaleidoscope of orange and red colors and, now, some yellow was streaking through. But, that's not what Ethan was staring at this time. It was the eagles, or what he thought were eagles, flying high over the land. They were a ways up in the sky. Thing is they had brightly colored wings of brilliant blues, purples and streaks of bright green from wing tip to wing tip. There was a silver streak like lighting zig-zagging from head-to-tail along their back feathers. They were bigger than the eagles in the barn. But, as they all watched, another eagle flew out of the barn and changed into one of the colored birds. And, birds seemed a small name for these magnificent flying creatures. As they flew lower and neared the barn, they reminded Finn of another type of creature.

"I swear those kinda' remind me of pterodactyls. Sort of. No, not quite but something as ancient," Finn said out loud.

"Yeah, I know. They remind me of somethin' else, too. Just can't quite put my finger on it. Look, another one's coming outta' the barn. It's one of the young ones," Emily said.

"Hey, George," Jordan hollered out to the bird. As it flew back to fly a circle around Jordan, it changed into the same bright colored creature as the ones in the sky.

"Holy shit! Would ya' look at that?" Jordan said as a bright purple feather fell at his feet as George flew off to join the others.

"Emily, would you please pick that up and give it to me?" Jordan asked rather quietly.

Emily did just that and as soon as she handed it to Jordan it began to glow like the crystals.

Jordan was speechless as he looked at the feather. It was a big feather as well. All of a sudden, he knew where it belonged.

"Emily, would ya' please get my twin crystal and bring it out here? Finn, would ya' grab that barrel over there and turn it upside down?" Jordan asked of them.

They both did as Jordan asked and as soon as he had the crystal in his hand, he was pushed in his chair over to the barrel and placed it on the barrel then set the feather next to it, just touching a bit of the edge of the feather to the crystal.

They all heard a humming sound then the crystal and feather sent a beam of light up into the top of the grid. It illuminated the whole of the grid like it was a tent over the land.

They heard the piercing scream again and saw it was coming from the flying creatures.

"They seem to be happy about that beam of light," Finn offered.

"Yup," Ethan replied. They all sat down to keep watching the sky. Ethan had phoned Ted to let everyone know Jordan wasn't alone and he was okay. They were all okay. Ted told Ethan that everyone who had been in The Store when the quake hit was alright, too. Some were helping take care of the stuff that had fallen off the shelves and all.

Just then the Dark Energy hit the grid wall and an explosion like no one had ever heard before shook The Creek. Bolts of orange-red energy flew out from the grid wall like solar flares. The heat was intense and the ground around the stream was instantly pulverized. The Dark Energy tried again to flow past the gird wall and, again, it was stopped and exploded.

The Dark was beyond angry. It had counted on The Dark Energy being able to flow in the water without being detected. It wanted Jordan's land at any cost. It began attacking the grid at every conceivable point it could get to.

Kendra and her group were ready. Every time The Dark sent a bolt of black energy to pierce the grid, they blocked it and sent it back into the great abyss of space. They were still invisible and this made The Dark really mad because it couldn't figure out what was happening. It sent more energy bolts at the grid where the four directions held the crystals. Again, it was blocked before the energy bolts could get anywhere near these sacred areas.

The sky shook with thunder that rattled the ground and lightning that struck out in every direction. Kendra's group was kept busy but they managed to block all of this. It wasn't until The Dark materialized into hundreds of flying demons that were throwing lightning bolts at everything on the earth that Kendra called for more help.

Miss Cora heard the cry and told Katelyn to keep chanting.

"Katelyn, I know where ya' came from and why. You're gonna' have to go to Jordan's in a little bit and get to the cave. It won't be easy. Matter of fact, it may be the hardest thing you've ever had to do. No matter what, get to that cave. We're all countin' on you. There's somethin' ya' have to do in there. Then ya' gotta' go back to the other Crab Apple Creek. Wait about five minutes then go!"

Katelyn just looked Miss Cora. She knew Miss Cora was right.

'How long have ya' know about me?" Katelyn asked.

"It don't matter. Just do your work like you're supposed to. We'll all be grateful," Miss Cora replied.

Miss Cora got into her truck without sayin' another word and headed for the Applewood Grove. Katelyn sat there thinkin' about everything that had happened to her in this place.

She looked at her watch and saw that she needed to get to Jordan's place right away. She jumped into her SUV and set out. It took a few extra minutes cause there was stuff in the road. She had to stop all together at one spot to move a large branch out of the way.

As she tried to turn into Jordan's driveway, a bolt of lightning hit the road next to her and moved her SUV past his driveway. She backed up and turned into the drive quickly as another bolt came close to hitting her. Once she was on his driveway, she was under the protection of the grid. She sighed as she drove right past the barn to the edge of the field.

She got out and looked at everyone on the back porch as she set out across the field.

"Wonder where she's goin'?" Finn said as he started to leave the porch.

"Ya' gotta' stay here, Finn. Katelyn's got somethin' to do and she needs to be by herself," Emily said as she laid a hand on Finn's arm.

Finn looked at Emily as he said, "Really? She gonna' be okay?"

Emily just looked at Finn then out at the sky.

The energy strikes kept coming and the earth all around the grid was being destroyed.

Miss Cora pulled off the road onto the two-track that led to The Applewood Grove. She got out and took her offering with her. She entered The Grove and went straight to the middle where a flat stone sat as if waiting for her. She placed her offering of lavender and a pure quartz crystal on the stone. Then stepped back, bowed and walked to the northern edge of the Grove where she spoke out loud.

"I call upon the protectors of The Creek. We are in need of your help. The battle for The Special Magic is underway and we can't defeat The Dark by ourselves. Kendra has already called on her own kind to help and they are above the protection grid, invisible from The Dark for now. But not for much longer. It has taken all their energy and strength to fight The Dark. I know I can always call upon y'all to help and I haven't much over the dimensions. But now, I need y'all. The Creek needs y'all and all the dimensions of existence need y'all. Thanks for listenin'."

Miss Cora bowed her head and said a prayer of thanks. It was only a few minutes later when she heard a soft whirling sound. She looked up and there it was. The silver disk she had called upon. It set down right next to The Grove and as Miss Cora watched, ETs began coming out of the disk and going into The Grove, over to the stone table.

There must have been at least fifty of them or more. Miss Cora couldn't really tell as they filled up The Grove and five more ships arrived and set down all around the outside of The Applewood Grove.

As the last ones entered The Grove, one of them approached Miss Cora. It beckoned her to follow it to the center where the stone table sat. She joined it and the others moved in around them.

They were the true gray aliens and looked just like what people had been saying all along. The one with Miss Cora spoke.

"We have answered your call for help. The Dark Force is, indeed, overpowering Kendra and her kind. They have done a great job holding the grid safe. Now, we shall help to keep the Special Magic in its place here with you guardians of The Creek."

"Thanks for comin'. I didn't know what else to do. I greatly appreciate your assistance and will continue to serve you as well," Miss Cora replied.

"You are a true guardian and we are pleased with your work here. Now, let's take care of The Dark and get this place back to its peaceful self."

Not one word was said, but all the ETs knew exactly what each one of them had to do. They vanished right before Miss Cora's eyes as the leader said, "Miss Cora, you go join the others at Jordan's place and we'll be there shortly."

"Thank you," Miss Cora said bowing to the leader. He immediately vanished and she was alone in The Grove. The ships were still there, but they became invisible as she watched. Good idea. Ya' just didn't want anyone to come across them right now.

Miss Cora headed out to Jordan's arriving a bit later. She, too, had trouble getting to the driveway, but as soon as an energy bolt was sent her way, it was blocked in mid-air. It took her three times to get onto the driveway and safety. She parked near the barn and joined the group on the porch.

"Oh, Miss Cora, this is horrible. So much destruction. We keep seeing the earth flyin' all over the place on the other side of the grid," Emily said hugging Miss Cora.

"I know. Keep watchin'. I think things are about to change in our favor," Miss Cora replied and looked towards the top of the grid.

"Katelyn's here. She set out across the field. She gonna' be okay?" Finn asked.

"She's doin' her job," Miss Cora replied.

"And what is that?" Finn asked.

"Sorry Finn. Can't tell ya'," Miss Cora said waving her hand at Finn to stop any more questions about Katelyn.

"Look there," Emily said pointing to the top of the grid near the barn. "What is that?"

Miss Cora looked and said, "Help."

Kendra and her kind had materialized into their alien selves.

"They're here to help keep The Special Magic in its rightful place," Miss Cora said. "Let's all send them lots of positive energy and love."

They all sat down and each one, in their own way, started to do just what Miss Cora suggested.

Kendra and her group were being attacked by The Dark. As soon as they materialized, The Dark sent monster demons to attack them. For every alien in Kendra's group, The Dark attacked with two of its monster demons.

Kendra's shape shifters kept morphing into other shapes and the monster demons had to look for them time and time again. Kendra's group was getting tired and worn out. Miss Cora sent a message to Kendra to tell her help was only a few seconds away. Kendra passed the message along and her group gathered its energy to keep fighting the monster demons.

As the group on the porch watched, a great noise was heard and a lot of shapes appeared above the grid. There must have been hundreds of them. They attacked the monster demons throwing White Light energy spears at them. When one hit its target, it blew it up into millions of pieces of black energy. The pieces were further blown to smithereens and scattered throughout the universes, never to form again.

Every hit was like watching a hundred years' worth of July fourth fireworks all at the same time. The Dark fought back by sending more monster demons to kill the new arrivals but the new guys kept killing the monster demons in so many ways it was hard to figure out how they were doing it all.

Then, The Dark decided to throw its best shot at Kendra's group. It sent shape shifter demons that morphed into looking just like the folks in The Creek. They were identical in every way, except they had demon powers.

Kendra just looked at one of them as she approached her. It looked just like Miss Cora.

"Oh, no ya' don't. You're not Miss Cora," Kendra said as the demon shape shifter tried to throw a flaming fireball at Kendra. One of The Applewood Grove ETs created a bat and swung at the fireball. It hit the fireball and sent it back at the demon where it destroyed the shaper shifter demon.

Ethan and Finn appeared right next to Kendra and tried to grab her from both sides. A few of The Applewood grove ETs grabbed their arms. Kendra moved back as the demon shape shifters tried to swing their arms at her and hit each other instead. Once again, they were destroyed into a million pieces of red and yellow leftovers.

As the group on Jordan's porch watched, they saw their eagle creatures fly up against the inside of the grid. As The Dark sent laser bolts to the top of the grid, the eagle creatures would wave their wings. This sent energy through the grid to the laser bolts and sent them right back at The Dark demons. It was amazing to watch. The eagle creatures flew all along the grid from the earth to the top of the grid sending bad energy back at The Dark and destroying the monster demons.

The sound of this battle was hard to describe, folks would say, when they talked about it for years to come. It was like the roaring of a train and a tornado and a hurricane all together with screams and piercing cries heard throughout. The sky was still red and orange but it was beginning to fade.

"Hey, look," Ethan said pointing to the sky. "It looks like it's fadin' some."

The others agreed and kept the positive energy flowing.

Kendra was battling with Ted and Michael demons at the same time. She kept laughing at them and they kept getting madder by the second.

"What's the matter Ted? Can't find the right food to throw at me? Oh, and Michael, your aim is way off. Good thing ya' don't play professional baseball," Kendra said as she grabbed the mirror one of her group had instantaneously created and put it in front of her to reflect the food energy ball the Ted monster had thrown at her. It hit the mirror and burst into pieces sending bad energy all over the place, killing many demon monsters at the same time.

The Applewood Grove ETs had begun to disintegrate the shape shifter demon monsters and it wasn't long until they were all gone. The only demon monsters left were three that had morphed into shapes the size of the universe. They were hideous and huge.

They were trying to surround the protection grid while sending those energy bolts to every point on the grid. The ground shook so hard it was difficult to stand up. The gang on the porch had retreated into the house and was sitting around the kitchen island just listening and watching the explosions through the windows. It was like fireworks were exploding right outside the house.

Katelyn was trying her hardest to get to the cave. She knew she was safe from the Dark Energy but every few steps she was tossed to the ground. She was only half way and that had taken five times as long as usual. She decided to kinda' hunch over and try to keep her balance. This worked better and she was making good progress. She could see the hill that was the top of the cave and the bushes in front of the entrance. Just a little more to go and she would be inside.

That's when The Dark saw her. It knew she was the key to this whole thing. If they could keep her from getting to where she was headed, it didn't know just where that was, then The Dark had a better chance of taking the power. It sent a thunderous shock wave through the air. It bounced off the grid alright but it hit the ground around the grid and the shock waves moved through to where Katelyn was trying to walk. She was thrown down so hard, the wind was knocked out of her leaving her gasping for air. She just lay there trying to breathe for what seemed a very long time. She finally got her breath back and was breathing good again. She tried to get into a crawling position and that worked.

She began to crawl to the cave and was only a few feet away when The Dark struck again. It sent a deafening noise that hurt her ears. She fell to the ground again and grabbed her ears, covering them from the noise. She didn't even know she was crying until she felt tears dripping off her chin. The noise would not stop and became even worse.

Katelyn cried out to The White Light for help and her ears were surrounded with a soft something. Almost like a length of cotton balls. The sound was still there but it was greatly muffled and Katelyn began to crawl as fast as she could towards the cave entrance.

The Dark was beyond pissed off. It sent horrible sound waves that Katelyn could hear even with the protection around her head. It wasn't as loud as before but it did make her head throb. It sent shock waves that made the ground tremble and shake harder than it had before making it near impossible for Katelyn to take that last couple of steps to the cave entrance.

Miss Cora had told her it would be the hardest thing she would ever do in her life. She was right. Katelyn lay there on the ground trying to move. It was as if she was being held down by a mighty force. She had a quick thought. What if she stopped trying to move? Maybe she could fool The Dark into thinking she had given up. So, she stopped trying to move. She lay there as relaxed as she could. She slowed her breathing and hoped The Dark would ease up on holding her down. She didn't know how The Dark could do that, but figured it had something to do with the noise energy.

Her trick worked. The Dark stopped the noise assault and the pressure on her was gone. She lay there for just a minute more, then gathered her strength and raised up and bolted to the cave entrance. She was one step inside when the noise assault began again. It took all her strength to pull herself the last step into the cave. She felt like her head was gonna' explode. When she was inside, she fell to the ground shaking and crying. It was silent inside the cave. The ground was still. She sat up and leaned against the wall for a few minutes. She felt safe inside. She could still hear the battle outside, but, in the cave, there was no battle. It was safe and quiet. The protection grid was working quite well.

Kendra instinctively knew that Katelyn was inside the cave. Now was the time for her and all the others to finish and destroy The Dark Energy. She sent instructions to the others and they came up with a plan almost instantly through their telepathic abilities. The all knew that, for The Special Magic to be protected, they must destroy the last of The Dark's forces.

The Applewood Grove ETs had suggested they surround The Dark Energy on all sides like you would place a net at the farthest boundaries to catch fish. ETs were sent in their invisible forms out into the universe to surround The Dark Energy. Once they were all in place, they began to move in on the three demon monsters. They threw energy bolts and laser points from every angle and had done a great deal of damage before The Dark knew what was happening. It tried to get the three demon monsters to fight back, but they were surrounded on all points. Every time the demon monsters sent a fireball at the good guys, one of the ETs blocked it and sent it right back, destroying part of the monster blob. This happened again and again and the three huge demon monsters were down to about the size of a baseball diamond. The Dark was so angry it didn't know what to do. The White Light Warriors were counting on this.

Meanwhile, Katelyn stood up and started to walk down the small hallway tunnel into the great room with all those amazing crystals. As soon as she got there, she heard someone tell her what to do. She looked around but no one was there. She went to a corner of the room and found the pink crystal with the long point the color of every sunset you've ever seen. It was breathtakingly beautiful beyond description. She bent down and picked it up. It was a bit heavy but she managed. The voice instructed her to place it on a crystal ledge beyond the main room. She had never been to this part of the cave before. It took her a few minutes to figure out where the path was before she could go further into the cave.

Once she found it, she walked down it a step of two but didn't see any ledges anywhere. She took a breath and walked a few more steps. She came to an opening like an entry way with a tall ceiling. It was a small space. The walls were all crystals. Most were shining and shooting beams all around. It really was a beautiful thing to see and feel. She took a few more steps walking out of the little entrance-like space and found three large tunnels. Just where the tunnels began, she found the ledge. She knew, deep within her soul, that this is where the crystal was to be set.

Katelyn set the crystal on the ledge in a space that looked like it had been made especially for this very crystal. She stepped back from the ledge and the tunnels lit up like someone had thrown a switch. They were each a different rainbow of colors. As she looked into each one, she thought she saw something in the last one she looked into. It was the tunnel on the right and it was every shade of purple and then some. As she looked into the tunnel again, she could have sworn something winked at her. It looked like an eye. A big eye. It didn't feel malevolent or evil. It was almost as if it was saying 'thank you for setting the crystal in its place'. She looked at the other tunnels again and then back at the one on her right. The eye was gone. It could have just been her imagination which was running on overload. She felt the need to return to the main room. So, she walked back through the little entrance room and down the pathway back to the main room. The crystals were not only shining like the world's best laser light show, they were humming as well. The sound made Katelyn cry it was so beautiful.

As soon as Katelyn set the crystal in its place on the ledge, the point of the crystal sent a beam of energy upward through the cave roof out into the universe. The ETs, Kendra and her shape shifter aliens and The White Light Warriors saw this energy and knew they had won. They all gave one last mighty pulse of energy at the remaining three tiny demon monsters along with the crystal energy pulse and exploded each one into so many zillions of pieces, it looked like the sky was alive with super novas. It was seen all around The Creek. It brought people out of The Store, out of Jordan's house, and out of every building all around. It lasted about ten minutes and was enjoyed by all who saw it. This was gonna' be one of those things that was talked about for generations. Stories were gonna' be told for sure.

As soon as the crystal laser beam was seen by The Dark and The Dark Energy monsters were destroyed, The Dark screamed one last time. It wasn't heard because the light show had its own sound track. The Dark pulled away from The Creek and the earth and went deep into a universe far, far away to recover and plan its next attack.

Katelyn felt the energy shift as soon as the demon monsters were destroyed and The Dark left The Creek. She was standing across the crystal room from the entrance near the far wall. She didn't quite know why she needed to cross the room; she just knew she did. She saw the wavy energy a few seconds before she passed through it. When she walked through to the other side of the wavy energy, she noticed the crystals were no longer shining so brightly. They were shining for sure. And, they were just as beautiful as before. She took a moment to look at them before she headed for the tunnel back to the entrance.

As she walked outside, everything looked like it always had. The sky was a beautiful blue and the field was full of the usual stuff you find in a field. There wasn't anything out of place.

Katelyn walked along the field to the barn. She walked inside to look at the eagles and saw that they were in their nest. The young ones looked a little smaller than she remembered. Hmm. No biggie. She proceeded through the barn to her SUV. It didn't look like Jordan was home. She felt really hungry and looked at her watch. It was past five. She could have sworn she had only been there about an hour or so.

Anyway, she set out for home, stopping at The Store for take-out. She was really tired and looking forward to some great food, which she got, a hot shower, which felt like heaven, and finally, bed.

She slept as if she hadn't slept in days.

The Creek slept as well. Her Creek.

CHAPTER 24

Katelyn woke up rested and ready to go to work. She was going to be extra cautious about what she said until she knew she was back home in her dimension of The Creek.

She knew she was home when she saw Ethan and Emily kissing at the door of the shop when she arrived.

"Hey, you two," Katelyn said smiling.

"Hey, Katelyn," they both replied ending the kiss.

"I better get goin'," Emily said. "Thanks for the stuff for the barn shelves."

"See ya' tonight," Ethan said as Emily left.

"What's she up to now? Another project to keep ya' busy?" Katelyn asked as she laughed and walked into her office.

"Kind of. I built her a couple of shelves in the barn for stuff and she needed a few pieces of lumber longer than the ones I made. So, I just cut them for her. She's gonna' finish them this morning and probably have stuff on them by the weekend."

"Always somethin' to do, isn't there?" Finn added as he walked into the shop.

"Yup," Katelyn and Ethan said at the same time.

Ian was already in his office and the four of them got busy planning their day.

Katelyn was off in another world for a while. She was remembering the other Crab Apple Creek. Jordan wasn't hurt here. She needed to get busy planning her brother's new homes. And, she really liked the fact that in the other dimension, Jordan had started to help Sami with research on the URR.

Katelyn was just thinking how she could approach that idea with Sami when her phone rang and she saw that it was Sami.

"Hey, Sami, what's new?" Katelyn said answering the phone.

"Hey, Katie girl, some really cool stuff. Ya' know how the owners of the hotel group said I could look into more underground railroad stuff at their other sites?"

"Yes, and I love the idea even if I may say so myself" Katelyn said.

"Cute. Real Cute. Well, I've found so much stuff that I need someone to help me. I wondered if you had any ideas about who that could be."

Katelyn smiled and laughed out loud. "I know just the person. Jordan Jackson. You know the delivery truck driver that has the farm with all those crystals I've been tellin' you about?"

"Yeah," Sami replied.

"I've heard him say how he loves to look into the history of places learning all he can find out about them. How about I talk with him and get back to you?"

"I love the idea. Maybe we could do a digital meeting or something," Sami replied.

"Great idea my Sami. I'll call him in a few and see about setting something up asap."

"I knew all I needed to do was talk to you. You always have great ideas."

They chatted for a little while longer before hanging up.

Katelyn called Jordan right there and then.

"Hey, Katelyn," Jordan said.

"Hey, Jordan. Ya 'got a minute to talk? I don't want to interrupt your drivin' and all."

"Sure. I'm just sittin' in my truck getting ready to move along to the next stop. What's up?"

"Well, ya' know my best friend Sami? The one I talk about all the time?"

"Yes," Jordan replied.

"Well, I think I told you about her discovering that tunnel under the hotel in Maine and how they figured out it was part of the underground railroad system," Katelyn said.

"Yes, you did. And, I love the whole thing and all. I love to learn about the history of stuff."

"I know you do. That's why I'm calling. Sami got the go-ahead from the hotel group and her bosses to investigate the history of the underground railroad at all the hotels she's gonna' be workin' on. We call it the URR project. Anyway, she just called and asked if I knew of anyone who might be interested in working with her on the historical research side of the remodel project. I told her I thought you might be."

"I definitely am. What else can ya' tell me about it?"

"Well, Sami said how about we set up a digital meeting asap and I said I would call you."

"Great. I'm free tonight any time after six."

"Me, too. I'll let Sami know and we'll chat with her tonight. She'll send us the link."

"Okay. How about you come over to the farm for the meeting?"

"I like that idea. See ya' tonight."

"Thanks for thinkin' of me Katelyn. I love the whole idea of the history of the URR," Jordan said just before they hung up.

Kendra knew the instant Katelyn was back and was just waiting for her to stop by. They had a few things to talk about.

The afternoon went by quickly for everyone in The Creek. It was late July and summer was in full swing as usual. The Store was busy and Ted and Michael had corralled Jenna to help them in the afternoons. She had her art work to do but she loved those two and would do almost anything for them. Coming home had been the right thing to do for sure. She was glad she listened to her hunches. They were always right.

Miss Cora was busy in her garden. Folks would stop by if they saw her outside and chat for a bit. She had a bunch of veggies just picked and wouldn't be able to eat them all herself before they spoiled. She had a table out near the road and she walked over to it and set them down. Two trucks of folks stopped by a minute later and took some of the veggies while Miss Cora was still standing there. They gave her a few dollars even though she said it wasn't needed but thanked them anyway. By the time she was back on her porch, a few more folks had stopped by and the veggies were all gone. She got a text from one of them that told her to go out to the table. They had left a little something for her. She found an envelope under one of the rocks on the table and drawings from some of the kids. She would put the art work around the house. The envelope had cash in it. It would come in handy for sure. The Creek folks took great care of Miss Cora. They loved her very much.

Miss Cora had the feeling that something was gonna' happen in The Creek before long. It was just a very distant thought which she had learned to pay attention to when she was a young girl. Nothing right now. But she knew it wouldn't be long. She sighed as she got herself a cold tea and sat in her rocker on the porch. She would enjoy the peace and quiet while it lasted.

Sami had texted both Katelyn and Jordan about the online meeting. It was set for seven. Katelyn texted Jordan to say she'd be there a bit before so they could get set up.

Ethan and Ian would be in the shop late tonight as their projects were in motion and inspections, supply deliveries and permits were scheduled in rapid succession over the next week and some.

Finn headed home around six. His family had some relatives from Tennessee stopping by for supper and a visit.

Emily was taking care of the horses with Jonah. Trouble was trying to herd the chickens. They would have not of it. They kept cackling and running around as if they knew they were giving Trouble a hard time. Emily and Jonah watched for a few minutes laughing and commenting on the whole silly thing.

Katelyn's brothers were sitting at the table with sketch pads jotting down ideas about what they wanted their new homes to look like. They were teasing each other about their lack of drawing ability.

"That's why I'm writing down detailed notes so I'll remember and maybe Katie will be able to make the sketches the way I want things to look," Nathan said sticking his tongue out at his brother.

"Oh really? Very mature," Jeremy said as he threw a pencil at Nathan.

"Boys! I know y'all are never gonna' grow up but could ya' at least not throw stuff around my kitchen? Go outside and do that," their mother said laughing.

"He started it," Jeremy said making a face at Nathan.

"You started it," Nathan said to Jeremy making a face back at him.

Their mom was laughing when their dad came through the kitchen door.

"At it again, are they?" their dad said shaking his head.

"Always," their mom replied.

"Workin' on your ideas for your houses?" their dad asked as he looked at the drawings.

"Yup. Katie said to get busy and try to draw something and make lists of every little thing we want in them. She said to look at each room one-by-one and write everything down we wanted and didn't want in them," Nathan replied.

"And, to try to show her the shape of the house which I cannot do. I'm not good at drawing anything except plants," Jeremy said laughing.

"Well, maybe your house should look like a bright red overgrown strawberry," Nathan suggested.

The craziness went into overdrive with their mom and dad going right along with the silliness. They had a fine time talking about their houses and all.

Katelyn and Jordan had just connected with Sami for their meeting.

"Hey y'all," Sami said greeting them.

Hey, Sami," Katelyn and Jordan said at the same time.

"So, Jordan, I hear ya' like history," Sami said.

"I love history and learning how things got to the way they are now. I'd love to work with you on the URR project."

"Did ya' have time to look at the stuff I've done so far?" Sami asked.

"Yes, I have. And it looks fabulous. I especially like the mural sketch with the past changing into the present."

"Thanks. I need a bit more history on the area. That's where you're work would need to be done. Interested?"

"Absolutely! Just tell me where and when I can start," Jordan answered.

"Well, Jordan, since Katelyn told me I'd be a fool not to hire you, you're hired. How does $85 thousand in salary as a start sound?"

"Fabulous! I accept. I'll send my two-week notice to my boss as soon as we finish here. I can start on a few things right away. I have a lot of vacation time coming and if I can use it for the two-week notice, I can start right away."

"Now that sounds great. How about we say you start tomorrow and we'll work on hours later? Ya' have to do all that new-hire paperwork first and then you can start getting caught up on the Boston project."

"It sounds great! I love this whole thing. And, I get to work from home," Jordan hollered out.

"Yes, you do. And, you can keep an eye on your eagles this way," Katelyn added. "They seem very protective of you."

"Oh, and, Jordan, the company will be sending you some new computers and laptops as well. You'll have the same ones I have for design work. And, a new cell phone for company use."

"Yahoo! This is gonna' be great. I'm gonna' have to get a new desk and stuff just to accommodate the new stuff," Jordan said thinking out loud.

"Send me the receipts and the company will reimburse you for every little thing, including office supplies, ink cartridges and all."

"Okay, boss. Will do," Jordan said.

"Katie, I gotta' hand it to you. You always have the greatest ideas for me. I like the feel of this already and we haven't even begun," Sami said to Katelyn.

"You are very welcome," Katelyn replied bowing a bit.

"The company HR folks will be sending out a bunch of stuff for you to complete. Keep an eye out for it. Damn! This is so great. I don't have to worry about this stuff anymore. I can keep goin' with the sketches and all. Jordan, welcome to the design family."

"This is so great. I was kinda' getting' tired of the delivery thing. I had begun to look for other work just a few days ago. I love how all this stuff happens."

"So do we," Katelyn said.

"Well, I gotta' get goin'. I've got a few things to take care of before I crash for the night. Thanks for accepting the offer, Jordan. Workin' with you is gonna' be great. Bless your lil' ol' pea-pickin' heart, Katie, for thinkin' of this," Sami said.

"Same here. Thanks, Sami. Sleep well," Jordan replied.

"Love ya', my Sami," Katelyn said as the ended the meeting.

"Katelyn," Jordan said, "I am overwhelmed at all this. It's so cool. I don't think I'm gonna' sleep much tonight with all this great new stuff. Thanks for thinkin' of me. I am much obliged."

"You deserve every bit of this Jordan. I gotta' get along home, too. Say goodnight to the eagles from me," Katelyn said as she headed out the door to her SUV.

"I will. Sleep well, too," Jordan said as he watched her drive off.

He looked in on the eagles and gave them Katelyn's message. They all bobbed their heads as if replying likewise.

Jordan sent his two-week notice asking if he could use his vacation time and was immediately approved. He would need to finish the week though. He agreed.

He finally fell asleep somewhere after midnight with a big ol' smile on his face.

It was well onto nine when Ethan finally drove over the bridge at Emily's place. He was tired but thrilled with all the work he and Ian had accomplished. They were set for the next few days of craziness. They had grabbed take-out from The Store around six and kept going until all the details were in place.

Ethan saw the soft lights from the house shining through the windows onto the porch. The moon was coming up in a clear sky and a million stars shown like diamonds. Trouble came out and greeted Ethan as he got out of his truck. They walked into the house through the back door and found Emily just finishing up with muffins and cookies. She was always baking something.

"Mmmm, smells heavenly," Ethan said as he bit into a blueberry muffin still warm and all gooey.

"Glad you like 'em," Emily said as she set the last of the cookies on a cooling rack. "I'll just put this stuff in the dishwasher for tomorrow. I am officially done in the kitchen."

"Good," Ethan said as he ran his hand up her back and around to her breast, brushing her nipple ever so softly.

"Let's go look at the moonrise from the porch, shall we?" Emily suggested as she took Ethan's hand and they walked out onto the porch.

"I like the way you think," Ethan said as he sat them down on the long couch and reached for Emily's shirt.

Emily pulled Ethan's shirt off at the same time. She didn't have a thing on underneath.

"Oh my, Miss Emily. Looks like you could use some tender lovin' care," Ethan said as he pulled her to him and began caressing her breasts.

Emily moaned as Ethan began to circle her nipple while his other hand trailed down to her shorts and tugged on them to take them off. Emily raised up a bit and the shorts were gone in an instant. She didn't have anything on under her shorts, either.

Ethan found her wet spot and began to rub her mound. Emily spread her legs apart as Ethan took her breast into his mouth and began to suck it.

She moaned as Ethan began to enter her with his hand. He rubbed her hard and brought her to her first climax. She fell against him hollering out.

As she settled from the climax, she grabbed Ethan's shorts and he dropped them to the porch floor. He was naked underneath, too.

"Seems we had the same idea tonight," Ethan said as he lay Emily back on the couch and began to run his hands all over her.

"Seems we did," Emily replied as she grabbed his hard dick and began to massage it. Ethan moaned and lay down next to Emily. She leaned over him and began to flick his dick with the tip of her tongue.

He moaned as he got harder and bigger. He let Emily lick him until he was close to his climax. He gently pushed her aside and lay her on her back, spreading her legs apart so he could repay the pleasure.

Emily came quickly as Ethan licked her mound and used his fingers inside of her. As he felt he start her climax, he pushed his hot, hard dick into her until she couldn't hold back. She came so hard she was lifted off the couch as Ethan joined her in their explosion of extasy into that other realm of immeasurable pleasure.

It was a long time before they woke up from their deep sleep, naked on the porch. Trouble was right next to them snoring away.

Ethan watched Emily as she began to wake up. "Well, I guess we should probably go up to bed."

"I do believe you're right," Emily said as they got up, gathered their clothes and Trouble and headed up to the bedroom.

They tumbled into bed and snuggled close as they fell asleep feeling pure joy with each other.

Things seemed to be going along as usual in The Creek. A few days after Katelyn's return to this dimension, Kendra and Miss Cora got together at Kendra's house for a chat. They both knew something was beginning to build in the world of Magic and they needed to think it through.

So, Friday found them in Kendra's kitchen fixing tea and muffins mid-morning and settling in for their talk.

"Now, Kendra, these muffins are delicious as always," Miss Cora said as she bit into one.

"Thanks, Miss Cora. I know how much you love your muffins," Kendra said as she, too, took a healthy bite of her muffin.

"It's time we got to talkin' about Katelyn and all that's happened. I've been feelin' somethin' comin' on for the past few days. Nothing strong just yet. But the beginning of somethin' for sure."

"Me, too," Kendra agreed. "Katelyn did a great job in the other dimension makin' sure The Dark could not get the crystals and all. I know we have to talk with her and teach her a whole bunch of stuff. But I just want to give her some time to adjust to being back here, home, as she calls it. I'm sure we're gonna' get an earful when we do sit down together."

"I agree. And, I can't blame her. Here she is home for just a few weeks getting to know about The Magic and her Gifts and she's sent through the portal to do battle with The Dark without really knowing much of anything. I know she's gonna' be upset. We'll just have to let her vent then try to help her get ready for the next time."

"That's another thing I have a few thoughts about. The next time she goes through another portal. Do ya' think this is gonna' be just too much for her to take in?"

"I hope not. She's the only one who can do this kind of thing. We've gotta' teach her everything we can if we're gonna' help this dimension of The Creek. Ya' know how The Dark can be."

"Oh, I do. Ya' don't have to remind me of that. Let's get some thoughts down on paper and sort through them and figure out just what we should teach Katie first. We really don't have all that much time."

"I agree. Let's get busy," Miss Cora said. They spent the next few hours working on their plan to teach Katelyn all she would need to know. They called The Store for take-out for lunch and kept going afterwards.

Ted and Michael were crazy busy. It seems everyone in the whole world had decided to come to the Blue Ridge at the same time and they all stopped at The Store for Ted's home cooking, provisions and the local news before they went on their way. Hal and a few of the locals had stopped by and Ted put them to work helping all over the store. It was a busy day but they all seemed to enjoy themselves. Ted and Michael treated them to supper after the rush quieted down. Ted had called the suppliers for an extra delivery for tomorrow as they went through most of the week's supplies in just that one day.

Everyone loved having supper with Ted and Michael. Stories were told, teasing was dished out and they all pitched in to clean up the kitchen and get the place ready for the next morning. Hal had offered to come by early to help with the special delivery. Ted and Michael thanked them all and Hal summed it up with, "Well, that's what friends and family are for."

Friday after work found Finn at Katelyn's door.

"Oh Katelyn?" Finn called out from the front porch.

"Why, Finn, what a nice surprise. I'll be right out," Katelyn said as she dried her hands and joined Finn on the porch. "Let's rock a bit."

Finn and Katelyn sat on the rockers next to each other.

"What brings you to my door, Sir?" Katelyn said with a mischievous smile and a wink.

"Anytime, my Katie girl. Anytime," Finn replied tipping his cap. "Right now, I'd like to know if you'd care to join me and my folks for a bit of an impromptu bar-be-que. They decided this afternoon to do this and have invited a few old friends and family that are in the area and I told them I'd come get you."

"I love the idea. I was just tryin' to decide what to eat for supper," Katelyn said.

"Great. Get yourself together and I'll hang here," Finn said with a smile. "I do believe if you need some assistance, I am ready and willing."

Katelyn got up, walked over to Finn and kissed him long and hard. "That's just a preview of what's comin' later tonight."

"Whew! I need a minute to catch my breath," Finn replied laughing. "I accept the invite for sure."

"I'll be ready in a few. I just made chocolate chip cookies. They're still warm on the counter," Katelyn said as she went inside. Finn passed her at warp speed and was eating cookies as Katelyn jumped into the shower to freshen up.

They were on their way to Finn's just a bit later with the cookies in a basket.

Hugs were shared all around and introductions made when they arrived. Diane loved the cookies that Katelyn had brought along.

"Katelyn, thanks for the cookies. We love all your baked goods. Ya' didn't have to bring them though," Diane offered.

"Well, if I had left them home, Finn would have made them disappear in no time," Katelyn replied laughing.

"You know our Finn for sure, Katelyn. He loves cookies," Hank replied.

"And, pie. Don't forget the pie," Finn said as he tried to sneak away with a fresh blueberry pie his mother had made that afternoon.

"Put it back, Finn or I'll send your cousins over to get it," Diane said laughing.

Finn was immediately attacked by a bunch of cousins of all ages trying to rescue the pie. They finally made it back to the picnic table where Finn set it down and stepped back.

"Okay. Truce! It's safe and sound for now," Finn said laughing as he fake-fought with his cousins. They had a great time teasing and harassing each other and talking about what everyone had been up to since they saw each other the last time.

The dinner triangle was rung and they all gathered around the tables.

"I just want to say how much we all love all of you and we're real happy y'all could come by on such short notice. Diane and I heard some of you takin' about Jay. Now, don't worry about us. We love to hear the stories. It honors Jay and helps us as we move along."

"He sure would have loved this food fest," Finn said. "And, he would have loved the pie, Mom. Always did. But not as much as me!"

Folks laughed at this as Diane said, "Well, I don't know Finn. I think ya' both love pie the same. Any pie. Any time. Anywhere."

"That's true, Mom. That's true for sure," Finn said as he caught site of Jay's spirit in full form leaning over the pies.

Katelyn saw it, too and it made her catch her breath. She looked at Finn and he just nodded his head. Jay tried to grab the pie and this made them both laugh out loud.

Diane and Hank looked at the two of them and saw them looking at the table. When they looked at the table, they both saw Jay trying to grab the pie. This made them laugh as well.

Folks were giving the four of them weird looks. Hank covered their laughter with," Well, folks, I think we're rememberin' the same thing. If Jay were here, he'd be tryin' to take that pie for himself."

Everyone started laughing and agreeing.

"Well, now, let's say a bit of thanks for all this and get to eatin'," Hank offered. They all took a moment and offered their thanks.

"Let the eatin' commence," Hank said and everyone began to fill their plates and talk and tell stories about Jay and Finn and their own kids for the longest time that night. It was well into the night as folks kept sharing stories. The little ones fell asleep on sleeping bags that just seemed to appear. The fire was kept going and folks sang and told stories sharing the love as family and friends do. Jay stayed close to his folks and Finn for the whole night. Finn could see him clear as day and Katelyn could make him out as well. Diane and Hank seemed to know he was there and this made them grateful for the visit. They offered silent thanks to The Other Side for this unexpected gift.

Matthews and Jenna were out walking the back pasture down near the brook as sunset came along.

"Every time I start to thinkin' about how I decided to come home to The Creek, then how we met, and how this house was built, I have to stop. It's all so overwhelming, in a great way, that I need to just take a breath at this amazing life I have with you here, in The Creek," Jenna said rather quietly as they stopped to look at the brook.

"That's exactly what I was thinking myself. About how I ended up here protecting a witness who turns out to be full of Magic and The Creek that's full of Magic. I wasn't even sure how I felt about the whole concept of Magic until I was put in charge of Emily. That was a huge shift in reality for me. I'm still processing it all although I do know Magic is real. And, then, like you said, the way we met and all this magnificent stuff. I just have to stop, and breathe, like you, and put the thoughts aside sometimes."

Matthews stood next to Jenna holding hands, as they listened and watched the water flow along the brook for the longest time. The sun was setting through the trees and the egg-shaped crystal on the bank of the brook was putting on a light show as usual. They watched as it changed colors and sent rainbows everywhere. The Magic was strong that night all around them.

Jordan was in the barn settling things for the night. He looked up at the eagles and they all were looking back at him. They nodded their heads and he nodded his in return. They settled into the nest as Jordan finished in the barn, turning out the lights and sliding the big barn door closed. Ethan had built an opening along the top of the wall along the back of the barn for the eagles to come and go whenever they chose to. They used it more often than anyone knew. Seems The Magic was alive and well in Jordan's barn as well as in the earth.

The next few days found Katelyn's brothers working on their new homes. Katelyn stopped by every day to help them decide on specifics designs. Saturday, she spent the afternoon at home with them. It took a few more hours but by late afternoon, they had finalized the shape of their houses. And, no, one was not the shape of an over-sized strawberry.

They both had numerous roof lines. They both had two full floors with a third floor they called the walk-in attic. It would be finished like the rest of the house as a full room. They'd decide on interior walls or whatever after they lived there a while. Both had wrap-around porches with railings just like Emily's house. They loved her porch and they would have porch swings as well. The style would be something like those old farm houses you saw in movies but with a modern theme. They would both have barns that looked like barns. The differences would be in the shape of the houses. Nathan liked a sprawling style house that you could walk down hallways to get to the different rooms. The living area would be separated from the kitchen by a wall that was open on the top half, framed like a window. Jeremy wanted a house that was wide and long with hallways as well. His living room and kitchen would be more of the open concept thing although there would be some kind of separation, maybe a wall of bookcases between the two.

"Well, boys, I do believe I can work with these ideas and sketches and come up with a kind of more detailed sketch over the next couple of days. You both want shutters alongside the windows on all floors. Once you decide on the colors, I'll add that in. You both want red brick chimneys for all the fireplaces. Good. You both want central air, geothermal heat and solar panels from Laine and Mo. Great! I'll get Finn on that part Monday. I think there's a stream from the hot springs up past Laine and Mo's place that we can tap into. I like that you want old fashioned looking windmills set along the center of the fields. Neat idea. How about we go walk the land before supper?"

"Great idea, sis. Let's go," Jeremy said as they all stood up.

"Don't worry mom, we'll be back in time for supper. You just ring the triangle and we'll come runnin'," Nathan added as they walked out the door and got into his Jeep.

They arrived at the area a few minutes later. They visited Nathan's site first.

"Katie, I'd like the house to face south-southwest to catch the sun all day long from different angles."

"Same here," Jeremy added.

"You got it. I was gonna' suggest that anyway," Katelyn said.

"Sure you were," Nathan teased.

"Like you can read our minds," Jeremy added.

"Always could and always will. I just choose what I'm gonna' talk about when the moment comes up," Katelyn said laughing at them.

They walked the land and looked at the stakes Nathan had set out.

"I'll take a few pictures now and then have Ethan and Ian come out next week. Same for you Jeremy," Katelyn said.

They approved. As they walked the area inside the stakes, the air became very quiet and they all stood still as statues.

Jeremy started to talk and Katelyn shushed him. She held her hands up to keep them quiet. Then she pointed to something in the sky. As they watched, an eagle flew over them and then circled back a few times, dropping a feather on the ground near them. It flew off with a screech.

Nathan bent to pick up the feather and Jeremy stopped him. "Nate, only a native shaman can pick up the feather. I'll take a picture and ask Chief Running Bear to come over and gather the feather."

"That's right, bro. Thanks for stopping me," Nathan said as Jeremy talked with the chief.

"He's just down the road. Should be here in a minute," Jeremy told them.

Chief Running Bear showed up a few minutes later driving right out to the field.

"Thanks for callin'. Jeremy, ah, yes, it is a full wing feather from an adult eagle. It's beautiful," the chief said. He spent a few minutes chanting in the language of the Catawba, offering thanks and sprinkling tobacco all around the feather, then picked it up. He showed it to the three of them.

"It's beautiful," Katelyn said looking at it.

"You said an eagle dropped it here? Tell me the whole story and why you're out here," the chief asked.

Jeremy told him all about why they were there. The chief was quiet for a minute looking out over the field.

"My ancestors tell me this is the perfect place for your home, Nathan. They are happy you have chosen this place and sent the eagle as a messenger to let you know that by offering this feather."

"Wow! That's really awesome," Nathan said rather quietly. "I am humbled and honored by their approval and your presence, Chief Running Bear."

"We all are," Katelyn said as Jeremy nodded his head.

"So, Jeremy, are you building around here as well?" the chief asked.

"Yes I am. As a matter of fact, we were about to go over to my field when the eagle came by. Let's go there now."

"Let's go," the chief said and they all drove over to the other side of the family's property to where Jeremy would build his home.

As soon as they walked into the staked-out area, a second eagle flew by, circled them, dropped a second feather, then screeched as it flew away.

"Now, that's just wicked cool Magic for sure," Nathan said as they all looked at the feather.

The chief chanted again, circled the feather with tobacco in thanks, then picked up this feather. It had a slight blue tinge to the tips of the feather.

"This is beautiful with that blue tinge," Katelyn said pointing to the tip of the feather.

"It sure is. I'll set them near the fire circle tonight when we have sacred ceremony."

"Thanks chief. I guess we're okay to get busy building our homes, Jeremy," Nathan said as he put an arm around his brother.

"Yes, I do believe you're right. Now if Katelyn does her job as well as we think she will, we'll both have the homes of our dreams."

"Always the best for my brothers," Katelyn said as she and the chief looked out over the field. They spent some time there talking about the life of the fields where their houses would be built, remembering all the trouble they had gotten into as kids when they went out on the ponds near their fields and fell in up to their wastes 'cause the ponds weren't frozen all the way through yet.

"Good thing Dad followed us both times," Jeremy said laughing.

"Sure was 'cause we were freezing cold when he pulled us out and Mom was pissed as hell," Nathan added.

"I remember that day. Y'all must have been about eight or ten years old or so. Boy, were your folks mad. You never tried that trick again after the second time," the chief said.

"You guys were grounded for the rest of the winter I think," Katelyn said as they returned to their trucks.

"Well, it sure seemed like it," Jeremy said.

"Boys, I'd like to come by before you do any diggin' and all and bless these sites. I'm sure Chief Soaring Eagle will be joinin' me. Okay with you?"

"Absolutely, chief. That would be fantastic. Let us know a good time for you and we'll meet y'all at Nathan's first then come over here. Let us know if we need to bring anything," Jeremy replied.

"I'll be in touch, time to get along. I think that's your mom's dinner triangle ringin'," the chief said.

"Sure is. Thanks for comin' right over chief. See you soon," they all said.

As soon as they got inside the house, they all started talking at once while trying to wash up.

"Hold it everyone. One at a time. You, Katelyn, tell us what happened," their dad said as they came to the table.

Katelyn told the story with help from her brothers, of course. Their folks were thrilled with all that had happened and couldn't wait for the ceremony to bless the land. The spent the rest of the evening talkin about the houses, the eagles, and how there must be Magic in the land. Had to be. This was The Creek, after all.

Monday morning dawned bright and beautiful. The Creek was busy as usual with work and visitors and all. It was a perfect summer day. Katelyn's dad Joe was getting ready to head out to the blackberry fields to help with the day's harvest.

"Here, Joe," Jackie said as she handed him a cooler full of frozen water bottles and juices. "Now you make sure you drink all this stuff."

"Jackie, I would miss it if ya' didn't say that every mornin'. I love ya', too," Joe replied with a sweet kiss for his wife.

"Love the way we communicate," Jackie said as Joe headed out to the berry buggy. That's what they fondly called the four-wheeler that they had equipped with all the stuff ya' need for berry picking including a canopy. Jackie had made it special with material that had all kinds of berries on it. That's how it got its name.

The blackberry patch was in about the middle of all the berry fields. It was a few acres in size but they all called it the blackberry patch anyway.

Joe was just coming around the stand of trees that were set between the fields. They had been planted years back as a wind break to preserve the soil and all. As soon as he cleared the bend and the trees he came to a sudden stop. In front of him was a hill or a rise about thirty-five feet tall and about fifty feet in diameter at the center. It was mostly round. Most importantly, it hadn't been there the day before. And, there was something shining near the top.

Joe just sat there for a long while staring at the thing. He finally came back around and radioed Jeremy, Nathan and Jackie.

"Y'all need to come to the blackberry patch right away. Something has happened out here."

"What?" Jackie said.

"Just get here right away," Joe replied.

They all arrived about ten minutes later and got out of their trucks and just stood their staring at The Rise. Not a word was said for the longest time.

Joe was the first to speak. "I came around the bend in the tree line and here it was. Is. What is it?"

"It's huge!" Nathan said.

"I haven't the foggiest," Jeremy replied.

They all looked at Jackie.

"What 'cha all lookin' at me for? I don't know how it got here," Jackie said as she started to walk over to it.

The boys and Joe followed her until they were at the edge.

"Well, it's big," Jackie said.

"Yup," they all replied.

Jeremy began to walk a ways around it when he said, "Hey, come over here. Looks like there's steps or stairs here."

"Sure does," Nathan replied. "Let's climb them and see where they lead."

"I'll go first just in case somethin' happens," Joe said as he began to climb the steps.

It took the four of them about ten minutes to get to the top. The stairs were in a diagonal pattern that took them right to the top of The Rise. It was flat on top.

"Wow! This is wild. You can see all over The Creek from up here," Nathan said as they all turned around looking in all directions.

"Hey, what's that," Jeremy said as he spotted something shiny near the middle of The Rise.

He walked over and found a crystal the size of an egg. It was clear and had colored beams shooting out of it. "Would ya' look at this?"

"Don't touch it. Let it be. I'm gonna' call Miss Cora right now and see if she can come right over," Jackie said.

"She said she'll meet one of you at the house. Joe, take the berry buggy and go fetch Miss Cora. The boys and I will stay right here," Jackie explained to them.

Joe went back down and took off in the berry buggy. He was back about twenty minutes later.

While he was gone, Jeremy, Nathan, and Jackie explored the top of The Rise. There were a few more crystals poking up through the earth. They were all different colors and shapes and seemed to be sending beams of light everywhere. They were soft beams of light so you could look at them.

"Hey, Miss Cora, thanks for comin' right over," Jackie said as Joe stopped the berry buggy and he and Miss Cora walked over to the steps in The Rise.

Miss Cora was the first to appear then Joe. He was staying close to Miss Cora in case she needed some help.

"Much obliged for your help, Joe," Miss Cora said as she walked over to the others in the center of The Rise.

"This is magnificent. Truly amazin'," Miss Cora said as she looked out across The Rise and all around The Creek.

"Ya' can see a lot from up here. Look, there's Emily's covered bridge," she said as she pointed to the northwest. The bridge was easy to see.

"Yup, that's the bridge. It's so cool," Nathan said.

"One of the best things I think Ethan and his crew have ever come up with," Joe said.

They all agreed and spent a few minutes looking at everything from the top of The Rise.

"Well, I kinda' think ya' got me here 'cause maybe you think I know what this is all about," Miss Cora started with.

"You were the first person I could think of that might have some idea about all this," Jackie said. Nathan and Jeremy had gone down to the berry buggy and grabbed chairs for them all. They sat down to talk about this new phenomenon.

"Well, thanks for thinkin' of me. I haven't ever seen anything like this happen before. Never. I must say it is, well, I don't know what, but it is for sure," Miss Cora said.

"The only thing I could come up with was it might have somethin' to do with The Magic in The Creek. That's why I thought you might have some thoughts on it," Jackie replied.

"Well, I do believe you're right about that. Magic is the only explanation I can come up with as well. We didn't have an earthquake last night strong enough to do all this. And, those crystals that are pokin' up all around tell me that it has somethin' to do with The Magic for sure. Now, we need to be thinkin' about why it's here and why now. That's what I'm thinkin'," Miss Cora said.

Joe had been looking around while Miss Cora was talking. "Would ya' look at that? Some of the berry plants are still here. There's about four patches of 'em."

They all looked around and saw the four patches.

"They seem to be placed in the four directions," Jeremy said. Pointing to them he added, "North, south, east and west. It's gotta' be The Magic. I think The Magic is thankin' the native's ancestors for somethin'."

"I do believe you've got somethin' there, Jeremy," Miss Cora agreed. "I think we should get the chiefs over here to take a look at this. Once word gets out, folks will be comin' from all around to have a look."

"Now that's kinda' weird," Nathan said.

"Why's that, Nathan?" Miss Cora asked.

"Well, Jeremy, Katelyn, and I were out here lookin' at the places we're gonna' build our homes Saturday and an eagle flew over both sites and dropped a feather. We called Chief Running Bear and he came right over, blessed the feathers, and offered thanks for the eagle and the feathers. He and Chief Soaring Eagle are comin' over soon to bless our home sites. I think ya' got somethin there, Miss Cora. I think we need to get them over here as soon as possible to see this spectacular addition to the landscape."

"I agree," Joe said.

They all agreed. Miss Cora made the call.

"They said they'd come over after lunch, about one o'clock. In the meantime, I think we'd better keep this quiet until the chiefs have a glance at it. You can tell Katelyn. I think she should be here. I'll get Kendra and Emily here as well. But, don't tell anyone else just yet. We need to keep quiet until we know why this has appeared. I think ya' can pick the berries now boys," Miss Cora said with a chuckle.

"Good idea," Nathan said as he and Jeremy did just that. They picked four quarts and gave one of them to Miss Cora.

"I'm gonna' leave one here for the critters and birds and all. Kind of a thanks for The Rise and the crystals and all," Jeremy said as he spread a quart of blackberries in the center of the rise.

"That was kind and thoughtful. Now, let's get on our way and leave The Rise alone for a while," Jacki said.

They all walked down the steps and put their things in the berry buggy.

"Joe, I'll come back a bit before one and meet ya' at your house," Miss Cora said as they got into the berry buggy.

"Good idea. We'll all meet at the house just before one. We all got things to do so let's get goin'," Joe said.

As they left The Rise, Miss Cora glanced back and saw an eagle swoop down and take a berry from the offering. She smiled as they returned to the house. She'd bet anyone that there was an eagle feather in the center now.

Miss Cora wasted no time in telling Emily and Kendra about the early morning discovery. They said they'd be there. Jackie called Katelyn and told her what had happened.

"No way!" Katelyn yelled into the phone. She was alone in the shop for the minute. "Really? That's fuckin' amazin'. Oh, sorry mom."

"No worries. You're all grown up now. Anyways, Miss Cora thought you should be over here with the rest of us this afternoon. We're meeting at the house a bit before one. Can ya' make it?"

"Sure. I'm on my own today traveling around looking at projects. I'll take my lunch then. I'll pick somethin' up from The Store. Any excuse to get some of Ted's creations is a good excuse."

"Alright. You do that. I'll see ya' later. And, Katelyn, not a word to anyone. We don't want any damage to The Rise."

"Got it, mom. Not a word. Later," Katelyn said as they hung up.

The rest of the morning seemed to fly by and before anyone could say 'boo', they were all arriving at the MacDonald's farm house.

"Hey, y'all," Joe greeted everyone. "This is the strangest thing I've ever seen in all my born days. And that's saying a lot. Not sure why The Rise is here, but maybe the chiefs and Miss Cora can shed some light on all this."

Joe nodded to Miss Cora and the chiefs.

"Well, Joe, everyone, I'm not sure about the specifics, but I'll hazard a guess that it's got somethin' to do with The Magic we protect here."

Chief Soaring Eagle looked at Chief Running Bear as he added, "I agree, Miss Cora. We've been talkin' all mornin' about this. Neither of us has ever seen anything like this on the earth plain before. And, as for our own vision quests, we can't tell ya' about those, but some special things have been observed."

"Alright then. Let's get goin'," Joe said.

They piled into the berry buggy and a few of the trucks and set out for The Rise.

As they came around the bend in the tree line, you could hear gasps from those that had not seen The Rise yet.

"Holy cow!" Katelyn said as she saw The Rise. "That thing is huge."

"You said it," Emily and Kendra added.

"And, look. It doesn't even look like it just pushed through the earth. All the ground is grown in with berry plants and such as if it's been here all along," Kendra added.

"You got that right," Jackie said pointing to the base of the rise. "It does look like it's been here for a long time."

"I'll have to remember to pick those berries at the base, too," Nathan said.

They all got out of the vehicles and stood near the steps.

"Chiefs, I think you should go up first. The rest of us will follow just in case there's something y'all need to do before we set foot on the top," Joe offered.

They started up the steps with Chief Running Bear in the lead followed by Chief Soaring Eagle then Miss Cora and everyone else.

As the Chiefs topped the rise, they both stood stock still at what they saw in the center. In the place where the berry offering had been made, they saw three large eagle feathers standing up as if they had been pushed into the earth by hand. The tips were pointing outward toward the sky.

"Wow! Would ya' look at that!" Chief Running Bear finally said as Chief Soaring Eagle gave him a nudge.

"Whoa! Now, that is wicked awesome!" Chief Soaring Eagle said as he stepped onto The Rise.

Miss Cora stood next to the chiefs just looking at the feathers. "Don't know what to say," she said as the others joined them in awe.

"This is surely Magic at work here," Kendra said as she and Emily saw the feathers.

"They weren't here when we left," Jeremy said looking at Nathan.

"This whole thing is unbelievable," Katelyn said looking all around.

"I agree," Jackie said.

They all stood there looking at the center for a few minutes in complete silence.

"Well, I think we should offer thanks for sure," Chief Soaring Eagle suggested.

"Let's walk over and stand around the center and we can offer our own kind of thanks silently first. Then, Chief Soaring Eagle and I will offer our kind of thanks for all to hear."

They agreed and walked over to the center. Another surprise met them as they looked at the feathers. Another brilliant white crystal was sitting in the middle of the feathers glowing like crazy. It was the size of a grapefruit. The smaller one was next to it glowing as well.

"Would ya' look at that?!"

"Where'd that come from?"

"It's beautiful!"

"So bright!"

"More crystals. Gotta' be The Magic for sure," Miss Cora added.

"I do believe you're right about that," Kendra said in amazement.

"There's sure somethin' goin on here. The Magic doesn't just put on a show this big just because," Katelyn said. "Or, that's what I'm thinkin'. I'm kinda' new at all this stuff. But, one thing I have learned is that The Magic knows just what's its doin' and if it's showin' us somethin' big, then somethin's about to happen."

"You're right about that, Katelyn," Miss Cora replied. "I've been feelin' it for a little bit."

"So, is this somethin' good or somethin' bad?" Jackie asked looking at Miss Cora.

"Well, if The Magic is workin' hard, it usually means The Dark is gonna' try to take The Magic. So, I guess we'll need to be on the lookout for anything strange goin' on in The Creek."

"And, everywhere else," Kendra added.

"I agree. I'm kinda' new at this stuff, too, Katelyn. I have learned that The Dark will attack other places on the earth just 'cause it can," Emily said.

"Now, Nathan and Jeremy, ya' look kinda' pale. Sit down and take a few deep breaths," Miss Cora ordered them. Joe pushed the boys to the ground and Jackie went to help them. "When you're ready, we'll do what the Chief's said to do."

A little bit later, Nathan and Jeremy seemed to be much improved.

"So, this magic stuff is really real," Jeremy said as he looked over at Nathan across the circle.

"I've always heard about magic but didn't give it much thought until now. This is all so surreal," Nathan added.

"Boys, I've always talked about The Magic in The Creek since you were born. Did ya' just think I was bein' weird or somethin'?" Jackie asked her boys.

"Well, you're our mom. Of course, you're gonna' tell us lots of things including legends and stories. We just thought the talk about magic was a kid's thing," Jeremy said.

"We both can see that it's for real. Really real," Jeremy added bowing his head in reverence towards the feathers and crystal.

"Thanks for sayin' that, Jeremy. It shows respect for our ancestors and The Magic here in The Creek," Chief Soaring Eagle said.

"Shall we get started?" Joe offered as they all settled to watch and offer thanks.

"Let's begin by offering our own personal thanks for all that's happened in this short while," Chief Running Bear said.

They stood silent for a few minutes as they all offered their own prayers of thanks.

Next, the chiefs took out their own feather wands and herbs and tobacco and began their prayers of thanks in their native language. They circled the outer rim of the group sprinkling lavender over each person. Then, they leaned into the center circle and offered lavender and tobacco into the feather circle onto the crystal. As the offerings touched the crystal, they were burned into ash and the smoke rose straight up into the sky.

The chiefs continued to chant as they stepped back from the feather circle for a few minutes. As they ended, Emily looked up and saw not one, but four eagles coming towards them.

"Look," Emily said quietly as she pointed toward the eagles. Everyone turned and watched as the eagles circled The Rise four times then came to land in the circle. They morphed into native ancestors facing into the four directions.

Each one offered a chant in an unknown language that sounded like the music of a babbling brook.

The group was in total awe and amazement at this unbelievable site. The chiefs bowed in reverence while their ancestors chanted. As they ended their chants, they turned to the chiefs, bowed and held out their hands to the chiefs. Each ancestor had a pipe in their hand. As the chiefs accepted the pipe and drew smoke from it, they were immediately changed in to their ceremonial garb.

The chiefs were invited into the circle to dance and chant for a little while. The others found themselves seated on the ground a little ways from the center. The chiefs and eagle ancestors danced around the circle chanting in that unknown language for what seemed a long while.

As the dancing came to an end, one of the eagle ancestors began to speak.

"You have all answered the call to come here and witness this Ancient Rise. It is made of Magic. Just like The Magic in The Creek, it is a sacred place. It will stay here now for eternity. You are the guardians of The Rise for you have been shown the sacred dance with the chiefs. Keep the secret and protect this sacred place. Others will be curious but will not be able to climb onto The Rise as the steps are only shown to the guardians. Others will come to look at The Rise and leave offerings. We accept them and their gifts and bless those who honor this place. You will always remember today. It is now a part of your Spirit. You will be called here from time to time to learn things and take those lessons with you to help keep The Creek and all The Magic within The Creek safe. We thank you for being here and send abundance in all that you do while on the earth plane."

The four eagles gathered once again in the center of The Rise and, as everyone watched, they morphed back into the eagle birds they were. As they took flight, they circled each person on The Rise and left an eagle feather on the ground next to them.

Then the eagles were gone.

No one spoke for a minute then they all started talking at once. Once they calmed down a bit, Emily said, "I do believe these feathers are for each one of us. Is that right, chiefs?"

"Yes, Emily, it is," Chief Soaring Eagle replied. "You each may pick up your feather and take it with you. This is a deeply sacred gift from our ancestors and the Keepers of the Spirit."

Each one of them leaned down and carefully lifted the feather that lay at their feet. They held them gently next to their hearts.

"Well, this has been an unexpected day," Jackie said.

"I do believe we now have some idea as to why The Rise is here. Seems my family has become guardians of this place. It always did feel special to me since I was a boy. Didn't know why than, but now I do," Joe explained to the group.

"Wow Dad. This is so, so, I don't know what but it surely is," Nathan said as he looked all around then down at his feather.

Katelyn was speechless with tears running down her face. Emily was crying, too.

"Hey, look at that," Jeremy said pointing to a blue crystal that lay a ways away. "It's shiny and all and it looks different than most crystals."

Jeremy walked over to the crystal near the southern point of The Rise. The crystal was shaped like a zodiac symbol.

"It looks like a constellation like one of the zodiac symbols," Katelyn said as she bent to look at it.

The others gathered around looking at the crystal.

"It looks like the constellation and zodiac symbol for Pisces," Nathan said.

"How do you know that?" Jeremy asked his brother.

"I've always watched the stars and the sky since I can remember," Nathan replied.

"That's true, Jeremy. Your brother has always been infatuated with the sky since he could walk and talk." Joe said.

"I remember that. You were always spouting off facts about planets, and stars and the constellations every time someone would listen," Katelyn said.

"And, Nathan always did projects for school about the sky and all. He always got 'As' for those projects come to think about it," Jackie added.

"Well, I guess all that knowledge is gonna' come in handy now, isn't it Nathan?" Miss Cora said smiling

"Yes, Ma'am, it surely is," Nathan replied.

"Well, I guess we all have a lot to think about. And, this crystal, should we leave it here or take it with us?" Chief Running Bear offered.

"My gut is tellin' me that Nathan should take it with him. He knows just what to do with it and where it should be placed until his house is built. Katelyn, you are planning a special space in the third-floor attic area, aren't you?" Chief Soaring Eagle asked.

"Why, yes I am chief. How did you know about the third-floor space?"

"Just saw a picture of it in my mind. And, you, too, Jeremy. Keep that space opened up until you know just exactly what it's for," Chief Soaring Eagle suggested.

"I will. Thanks chief," Jeremy said tipping his hat at the chief.

"Me, too, chief. Thanks," Nathan said doing likewise.

"Well, I think we should get back to the house and have somethin' to eat and drink. I feel like I haven't eaten in days," Jackie said.

"I agree. I don't think I can take anymore new Magic stuff at this moment," Emily said.

They all agreed and took a moment to stand at the center of The Rise and offer thanks for all that had happened that afternoon.

They returned to the farm house and Jackie and the boys got the food and drinks out for everyone. Joe helped get stuff to the picnic tables under the awning and they all settled into eating and talking about all that had happened.

As they settled back from their mid-afternoon snack, Joe offered, "I know it's only three o'clock but it feels like a whole day has gone by. I was thinkin' about the berries all around The Rise. I'm thinkin' we should leave them there for the critters and birds and all as a sort of offering. I'm gonna' make a path to The Rise through the patch so we don't trample all the plants."

"That's good thinkin', Joe," Miss Cora agreed.

The others agreed, too.

"And, speakin' of berries, I guess we all better get busy. I know I have a field full of blackberries ready to pick and Jackie, here, is itchin' to make a couple of pies," Joe added winking at his wife.

"I get it, Joe. You bring the berries home and I'll make the pies," Jackie said laughing. "And, I'll be the first to eat some," Nathan stated but was interrupted by Katelyn.

"I'll stop by after I check on one more project and help ya' Mom. I'll even go get those berries from dad. That way, I get the first piece," Katelyn said.

"She's got ya' there, bro," Jeremy said laughing at his brother.

"Yup. She's got ya', Nate," Joe said laughing along with the others.

"I'll make one for you, too, Miss Cora, just the way ya' like it. Small and tasty," Katelyn offered.

"And, I'll be obliged to accept," Miss Cora replied.

"Let's take a while to think about all the stuff that happened today. I'm sure we'll all have a question or two. How about we send emails to each other as a group so we can stay on top of this thing?" Chief Soaring Eagle suggested.

"Great idea. I'll manage the email group if y'all are okay with it?" Chief Running Bear offered.

They all agreed with this plan.

"Well, I've got things to do," Joe said as he stood up from the table.

"Thanks for the snacks, Jackie. Most yummy as always," Kendra said as the others got up as well.

They all took their leave and left Jackie and Joe alone in the kitchen.

"Jackie, I knew bein' married to you was gonna' be great. But I never, in all my wildest thoughts, came up with anything like today. I knew you had The Magic around ya', but, holy cow, honey, today has been unbelievable. Sure glad we're a family," Joe said as he gathered Jackie in his arms and kissed her ever so sweetly.

"Same here, my Joe," Jackie answered with a sweet kiss of her own for Joe.

Joe sighed. "Time to get back to the berries. I can hear them callin' me."

Jackie laughed as Joe left. She found herself alone for quite some time, thinking about the day. She had to pick up her pace to get the pie crusts ready for those berries Katelyn was bringing by.

The week went along its way. Late Thursday afternoon found folks coming into The Store for take-out. Kendra was on her porch so folks decided to stop by and chat for a bit. Before long, there was an impromptu picnic taking place at Kendra's. Folks put up a few pop-up tents and chairs were gathered under them.

It was well onto late afternoon when a few folks started to share some of their summer stories with each other.

Kendra called on one of them to tell her story. "Hey, Betty. How about you tell the folks here about the ponies that showed up at your place the other day?"

"Sure thing, Kendra," Betty replied. "Well, I was just workin' on a few things in the house when I saw somethin' movin' by one of the front windows. I walked outside and there they were. About a half dozen or so beautiful young ponies. Couldn't have been more than four months old or so. I counted about six of them. They were munchin' on the clover in the yard. I got a few buckets of water for them and they seemed to like that. They wandered about for a bit then came to stand in front of the porch lookin' at me. They just stood there watchin' me. I talked with them a bit askin' where their mommas were. They just nodded their heads and kept lookin' at me. I wasn't sure just what to do."

Folks laughed a bit.

"Did ya know who they belonged to?" someone asked.

"Well, I didn't at first. I remember something about a few new colts along the road a ways up from me, but wasn't sure. I know Jonah had a few new colts over at the Two Moons Stables but that's a fair ways away for these young ponies to be walkin'. As I sat there for a bit just talkin' to them, one of the boys from the Kirkland farm drove in with a horse trailer. Seems they had a few ponies missing from their farm."

"Now, that's a might closer to you and all," Hal said. Others agreed with him.

"Yes, Hal it sure is. Well, Ben got out and walked over to the ponies givin' them a hug as he talked with them.

'Alright you guys. What have y'all been up to wonderin' off like that? Seems you had a hankerin' for visitin' Miss Betty here.'

'I was thinkin' the same thing, Ben,' I said to Ben. He smiled, tipped his hat and talked some more with the ponies.

'Well, y'all need to come along into the trailer and get along home with me. Your mommas are lookin' for ya'. It's feedin' time.' Well, those ponies must have known what feedin' time meant 'cause they all turned at the same time and followed Ben, one by one, into the trailer. He hooked them up safe and all, closed the back gate and came back to the porch.

'Well, Miss Betty. Looks like you've made six new lifelong friends. Just give us a call if any of them come by for another visit. We'll come fetch them home.' I told Ben I would do just that. I walked out onto the drive and watched Ben and the ponies drive away. They haven't returned. Yet," Betty said ending the story.

"Animals know who loves them. That's for sure," one of the group offered.

They agreed and talked a bit more.

Katelyn showed up with Finn as the others were talking about Miss Betty and her new friends.

"Hey, Katelyn. Finn. Join us for a bit," Hal offered as he gave his chair to Katelyn.

"I'll grab a few chairs from my truck," Finn said as he and Hal walked across the road to get them. They returned and set them up and the afternoon continued on.

"Hey, Finn, you remember the story you were tellin' us the other day at the job site about how you and Jay went fishin' one day and caught more than you reckoned on catchin'?"

"Sure do. Why?" Finn replied.

"How about you tellin' us all about that day? Sure was a good story."

Folks encouraged Finn and he agreed. Hank and Diane showed up just then and they were welcomed and settled into the group.

"Finn's gonna' tell us a fish story about him and Jay," Kendra told them.

This got Hank and Diane laughing some.

"You go right ahead, son," Hank said laughing. "It's a good one for sure."

Finn stood up and smiled at everyone. "Well, I was just tellin' the gang about this the other day. We were talkin' about stuff we like to do and fishing, of course, came up. Jay and I used to go fishin' any time we could. We must have been in our teens when this whole thing happened."

Finn looked up and saw Jay standing there pointing at him and pretending to cast his fishing pole into the pond. Finn nodded his head and smiled a bit. Diane saw him do this and looked where Finn was looking. She saw Jay and smiled as well.

"Well, one Saturday around mid-mornin', Jay and I decided we'd done enough chores and grabbed our fishin' gear and took off in that old pick-up truck Grandad Fred had given to us. It was a sight but we kept it runnin' throughout our teen years and it got us all around."

"And, into a mess of trouble as well," Hank added.

"Boys will be boys," was heard from someone sitting there.

"We lived up to that for sure," Finn agreed. "We headed for the pond up beyond the caves west of Emily's place. We took the fire road off the main road then walked the rest of the way. We settled in and started catching little ones which we threw back. We talked and some for quite a while then decided to set the poles down and eat the lunch we had brought with us. Now, mind you, the critters were havin' fun with us. As soon as I set my pole against a tree trunk, a couple of squirrels decided it was part of an obstacle course and began running over it, around it and even ran up it once or twice."

This brought laughter from the crowd.

"The more I tried to shoo them away, the more fun they were havin'. Then Jay sets his pole down to try to help me and a couple of rabbits come along and were tryin' to figure out if Jay's pole was edible. He goes back to his pole, takin' it from the bunnies and they hop on over towards our lunch. Well, you never saw two boys move so fast in your life. We hollered at the bunnies and squirrels as we rescued our lunch. We saved it, of course, and set our poles closer to us while we finished eatin'."

Folks kept on laughing at the story.

Finn was laughing real hard 'cause Jay was clowning around as if he was chasing the critters. Diane saw this and was laughing and crying so hard she could hardly breath. Kendra looked around and saw Jay and his antics and this made her laugh real hard as well. Jay saw that Kendra had seen him and he winked at her.

"Diane, you really like this story, don't you?" Hank said looking at her. She whispered in his ear, "Jay's over there."

Hank took a look in the direction where she had nodded her head and saw Jay being a wise guy. Hank started laughing as well.

Folks were enjoying watching Hank, Diane and Finn laughing and carrying on some.

Finn finally calmed down enough to go on with the story.

"We finished our lunch and set to catchin' fish again. We had us a grand time that afternoon. Just as we decided to call it quits, Jay had a big pull on his line. He hollered at me to help him. Now, y'all know there's nothin' real big in that pond so we couldn't figure out what was causing the problem. We'd heard a few tales from y'all tellin' us about a big fish that folks had seen but no one had caught yet. We figured this must be that fish. So, we kept pullin' and reeling it in. It must have been about a half hour or so when we finally got it close to shore. I walked out into the pond just a bit cause, if y'all remember, it cuts off to really deep only a few steps in.

"Well, we kept pullin' and finally brought it to shore. That's when we saw what it was. We just stood there laughin' and cussin' some for the longest time."

"Well, what was it ya 'caught?"

"Was it the big one?"

Finn happened to look at Jay just then and couldn't control himself. He burst out laughin' along with his folks. They saw Jay, too. He was acting like he was reeling in the biggest fish in the world. He was having a grand time makin' faces and prancing around to make his family laugh out loud.

"Ya 'know, if Jay were here, he'd be actin' this whole thing out," Finn managed to say when he could get a breath.

That's all it took for some of the folks to pretend they were Jay reeling in the big one. This made everyone laugh and play along for the longest time. Jay kept looking at Finn making rude jesters when his folks weren't watching. Finn managed to reply with a few gestures of his own once or twice.

Finally, Jay calmed down and the folks at the gathering calmed down, too, and Finn took to telling the end of the story.

"Now, that was a blast. Thanks for the entertainment," Finn said to everyone looking right at Jay. Jay bowed and tipped his hat at Finn and their folks.

"When we finally stopped laughin' and such, we saw that we had pulled in the top of an old windmill. An old metal windmill."

This brought even more laughter, comments. and antics.

"Well, we just couldn't leave it there. So, we brought it home for the folks to see as we told the story. Ya' see, we were in a mess of trouble for not finishin' our chores and all and not leavin' a note to tell them where we had gone. I think grounded-for-life was heard from our mom a few times. That is until we told them the same story I just told you. They were laughing like y'all and when we showed them the top of the windmill, they really got to laughin'."

Hank and Diane nodded their heads in agreement as they laughed along with Finn and Jay's ghost.

"Dad took a long look at the windmill top. It was in excellent shape. All the parts were there and it didn't look too old for havin' been in the pond. You tell 'em dad."

"Finn's right," Hank said. "It was in pretty good shape. I was thinkin' about where it could have come from. I know we used to use windmills in the open fields around The Creek but it was a long time ago and I didn't rightly know who it could have belonged to and why it was in the pond. We took it outta' the back of the truck and set it down next to the shed. It stayed there for just a little while."

"Dad said he'd ask around about the windmill and see if anyone knew anything about it," Finn said. "It must have been about a month later when dad told us that it had belonged to a family that had farmed down the Pine Ridge Road near Pine Ridge about a hundred years ago. They had lost the top of one of their windmills in a mighty wind storm and never found it. It must have been some storm to take it all the way up to the pond. Dad got a hold of the family that owns the land now and they're kin to the old farmers. He told them about the windmill top.

"They came out to see it and told dad we could keep if we kept the story going along. We kept it and if you've been by our place, you've seen it sittin' on its own stand near our mom's veggie garden. It's about ten feet high. Dad cleaned it up and it looks really nice, especially when it's spinnin' around."

"I remember hearing stories when I was a kid about how that windmill got torn apart from way back when. I'll stop by and take a look at that windmill for sure," Hal said.

"Still, I would have loved to see the two of you reelin' that thing in," someone else said and the laughter and antics started up again. Jay kept his family and Kendra entertained for the longest time.

Folks eventually gathered their things and went on their way. Promises of visiting the windmill were made and thanks for the fun were offered.

Kendra found herself alone with Jay a bit later and she and Jay visited for a bit.

"Jay, what a great gift to spend some time with you," Kendra offered.

"It sure is a gift for me, too. I miss my family like I can't even say. These little visits with them make my new life more bearable. I love being back in Spirit again, but I still mess y'all."

"We miss you more than words can say, too." Kendra said as a tear fell done her cheek.

"Now Miss Kendra, please don't cry. I didn't mean to upset ya'," Jay said as he sat rocking next to her.

"Now, Jay, if ya' keep rockin' like that someone's gonna' know there's a ghost out here," Kendra said looking at Jay and sticking her tongue out at him.

"That's exactly why I'm doin' it," Jay said laughing at Kendra. " That was a great thing this afternoon happenin' just like that. I love when that used to happen. So much fun and all."

"It sure was and always is," Kendra agreed. She looked at Jay for a minute then said, "I know somethin's getting ready to begin. Miss Cora and I have been feelin' it for a while now. We know it involves Katelyn and her moving between the dimensions."

"I know. I don't have anything to do with this particular event but I'm gonna' stay real close to The Creek from now on until whatever takes place is finished. And, yes, it does have to do with Katelyn. What a way to be welcomed home."

"For sure. She's done so well with it and all. She just got back from her recent visit to one of the other Crab Apple Creek dimensions. She seems to be takin' it all in okay. She's comin' over soon so we can talk more. I'd like you to be here for that if that's okay with everyone."

"They're giving me the okay. I'll be here. She won't be able to see me. I'll behave anyway," Jay said.

"Okay. I'm gonna' hold ya' to that. I guess it's time for you to leave," Kendra said.

"It is. I'll be around," Jay said.

"Thanks for the fun this afternoon, wise guy. Thanks to the Divine for this special time," Kendra offered.

Jay slowly faded away and Kendra was left alone on her porch. The sun had started its slow dip towards the trees. The Store was busy as it always was around supper time and early evening. Kendra got some iced tea and leftovers and brought them out to the porch so she could watch the evening go by. It was a mostly peaceful time. There was that little bit of something on the wind that she knew only too well. Enjoy this moment she said to herself. Things are gonna' change real soon.

The evenin' gave way to night as it will and The Creek settled into slumber.

CHAPTER 25

Saturday morning dawned clear and beautiful. Sami and Katelyn had set up a video chat for nine and they were talking away.

"I'm really glad Jordan is working out for you," Katelyn was saying.

"Oh, Katie! He's just what I needed. He really likes history and has a knack for finding little details that could be missed. He's been researching the slave trade and found a bunch of documents that show not only African people were enslaved, but Native Americans, and even a lot of Europeans and Asian folks as well into the 20th century. It's so horrible what we've done to each other."

"Agreed. Jordan loves that he gets to stay home and work now. He said he misses the clients he used to deliver to but does not miss the driving all over the place. And, he showed me some of your ideas for murals and displays for some of the hotels you're workin' on."

"Having him onboard has given me more time to create that stuff. The mural at the Maine hotel is done and they love it. The manager says people from all over have been comin' in just to see it and learn about how the slave trade impacted that area. He said the major news networks are planning on visiting when they can safely go down into the tunnels and have a look around."

"This is amazing. Who would have thought all this was waiting for us when we met all those years ago?" Katelyn said.

"So, Katie girl, how's Finn?" Sami asked with a sly look on her face.

"Do ya' really need to ask? He's wonderful!"

"I'll bet he is. He's so gorgeous!"

"You can look all ya' want my Sami," Katelyn said pointing at Sami. "But keep your hands to yourself."

They both laughed at this and kept talking for a while.

"Sami, ya' know how I was tellin' you about going through that portal thing in the cave on Jordan's land?"

"Yeah. Anything new?" Sami asked.

"I've been thinkin 'about it and all. It still seems like it was a dream or somethin' but then I know it was for real. It just seems that there's more out there. And, get this! Dad was goin' to the blackberry patch and found a rise in the middle of the field. Just sittin' there. It wasn't there the day before. He called all of us and Miss Cora, the chiefs and Kendra to come and look. Which we all did. It's about thirty-five to forty feet high and about fifty feet around. It has stairs to climb to the top, which we all did. The chiefs had a ceremony and eagles came and left all of us a feather. It seems The Rise, as we now call it, is pure Magic and my family are the guardians. It had a zodiac crystal of Pisces on the top just lying there. Nate took it home and will place it in his third-floor room when the house is finished. What do ya' think of that?"

"Oh my God! It just appeared one day out of nowhere?"

"Yup. Just showed up and the ground around it looked like it hadn't even been moved."

"Wow! So much Magic at your place. I gotta' come for a visit soon. As a matter of fact, I'm due in Boone next week for about a month"

"Yes! You can stay with me whenever ya' want."

"I'm gonna' do just that. I'll have a suite here for work and all but I think I'm gonna' be with you most nights and all the weekends for sure."

"When next week?"

"I'll arrive at the hotel on Friday night kind of late. So, I'll get settled there and come your way early Saturday morning. One week from today."

"I can't wait to see you again and I'm gonna' tell everyone today. Ya' know how much they love ya'!"

"Yes, I do and I love them right back."

Sami and Katelyn spent a little more time planning Sami's visit and talking about everything in The Creek. They hung up around ten and both got busy with their day.

Katelyn set out for Kendra's. It was time to find out what the hell was going on!

Kendra knew Katelyn was on her way. She set the table for tea and muffins as Katelyn came charging through the door.

"Mornin', Katelyn" Kendra began.

"Hey, Kendra. Time we talked. What the hell is going on here? Why didn't you tell me about the portal thing before I went through it? Why wasn't

I better prepared for all that shit that happened? I almost lost my life!" Katelyn yelled out.

"True! All of it. Now, take a breath and sit down," Kendra ordered Katelyn in a quiet low-toned voice pointing to the chair. "Tea and food first. Then I'll explain things with Miss Cora."

Miss Cora came through the door at that moment.

"Hey, Miss Cora," Kendra said setting the tea pot on the table.

"Hey, Kendra, Katelyn," Mis Cora replied. "Katelyn, ya' have every right to be upset. Kendra and I are gonna' explain things to ya' in a bit. Eat."

Katelyn looked at Miss Cora then Kendra. She calmed down some and they set to their tea drinking and eating.

When they finished, Miss Cora looked at Katelyn and said, "I know you're upset and angry with us and ya' have a right to be. Everything has been happenin' so fast, we haven't had time to explain things and teach ya' new stuff. The Other Side needed you to go through that portal just when ya 'did and set things right."

"You call 'almost getting killed 'setting things right?" Katelyn said.

"Well, it does happen like that sometimes. Not very comfortin'," Miss Cora replied looking at Kendra.

"Katelyn, just hear us out and I think you'll begin to understand what's happening around here," Kendra pleaded with Katelyn.

"Okay. Get on with it," Katelyn.

Kendra and Miss Cora looked at Katelyn for a minute.

Then Miss Cora began. "Katelyn, you've always known about The Magic here and how special it is. Your momma told you lots of things while you were growin' up and ya' took them as true. Now, before you came home you had a lot of dreams and visions about comin' home. Some of them seemed down right real. And, when ya' got here, it felt very right. True?"

"Yes, Ma'am. All true. I get that part of it and accept it," Katelyn replied.

"Okay. Now, let's get going on the now and the future," Kendra stated.

"The now and the future? You mean we're not finished?" Katelyn asked.

"Yes, Katelyn. The battle between The White Light and The Dark never ends. It just quiets down from time to time like right now. You remember when you and Jenna were attacked?"

"Yes, Miss Cora."

"Well, that was just a bit of a fuss from The Dark. There's always more. Emily, Kendra, and I have been feelin' a bit of an unsettled energy for a few days now. Kendra and I learned a long while back that it's a bit of a signal that The Dark's gonna' try to take The Magic again. Not today, but in the near future. Emily's just beginnin' to get the hang of it so she's still learnin' just like you."

"I see. So, what next? Will it be as bad at the other Crab Apple Creek thing was? Is someone gonna' get hurt bad like Jordan?"

"Ya' can't compare the events. They're each awful in their own way," Miss Cora answered looking at Kendra.

"Miss Cora's right. Each happening is truly different. And, we don't know if anyone's gonna' get hurt. Or even die. God, I hope not," Kendra explained. "Now, Katie, it's time for us to teach you some new skills and explain more stuff to do to protect The Magic. Mostly, we want 'cha to know we're here for you all the time. You ready to learn some new stuff?"

Katelyn looked at both of them for the longest time before saying, "I don't have to do any of this right? I can leave my Gifts and walk away, right?" Katelyn said rather softly.

"Yes, you can, Katelyn," Miss Cora answered just as softly.

"It's always your choice," Kendra added in a whisper.

"I'm gonna' need some time. I'm still so scared and shaky and horrified from the event in the other dimension that I don't rightly know if I can handle anything more. I need some me time to think about this."

There was a silence for quite some time before Miss Cora said, "Katelyn, you can choose your own path. If you're not sure right now, it's good ya' know that. Take a few days to think about all this then get back to us. What I think you need is a bit of a vacation and some fun."

Kendra nodded her head in agreement. "Amen to that."

"Well, it just so happens that Sami is arriving in Boone Friday evening to get started on the hotel renovation project there. She's gonna' come over first thing Saturday mornin' and stay with me as much as possible. Ya' know what? She's just what I need. Maybe we could all have a picnic for her at The Store Saturday suppertime."

"Great news for sure. And, yes. We'll put together somethin' at The Store for Saturday evenin.' I'll tell Emily and Miss Cora can tell Ted and Michael today."

"I most certainly will tell them. I'm glad Sami's comin' along now. I do believe she's just what ya' need. Do some fun things like you used to do and have a grand time," Miss Cora said.

"Oh, we will for sure. Once we get started, there's no stopping. Oh, can I take her to The Rise? I think she should see it," Katelyn asked.

Kendra and Miss Cora looked at each other again and then nodded in agreement.

"Yes, you may. I think she'll connect with it and all those crystals up there," Miss Cora replied.

"Miss Cora. Kendra. I'm not ignoring my Gifts. I'm just totally overwhelmed with all that's happened in the few weeks since I've come home and need some down-time to process it all. I'll make a decision after I talk with Sami and all. Thanks for understandin'," Katelyn said.

"Thanks for not givin' up yet. All this magic stuff is overwhelming even for us seasoned ones. Ask anything you want any time and we'll do our best to answer," Kendra said.

"Well, I do believe it's time for me to get along. I'll go over to The Store and tell Ted and Michael about Sami's visit and all and maybe take home some goodies," Miss Cora said as she stood up and stretched.

Hugs were exchanged. Katelyn went back home and Miss Cora crossed the road to The Store. Kendra cleaned up and settled in the living room with one of her real estate projects.

"Hey, Miss Cora," was heard before Miss Cora was even all the way through the door.

"Hey, y'all. How are ya'?" Miss Cora replied looking for Ted. Michael was at the register with a couple of customers. Emily was at the table in the dining area.

Miss Cora went on into the dining area and sat down to talk with Emily.

"Miss Emily, have ya' seen Ted?"

"Yup, Miss Cora. He's in the kitchen creating something with chicken. It smells divine," Emily answered inhaling deeply and smiling.

"It most certainly does. Hey, Ted," Mis Cora hollered at the kitchen door.

Ted peeked out with a grin and said, "Hey yourself, Miss Cora. What's new?"

"Ted, that smells heavenly. Can ya' spare a taste or two yet?"

"As a matter of fact, I was just gonna' bring a sample dish out. Hold on,' Ted replied disappearing back into the kitchen.

He came through the door carrying a small tray with three small bowls on it.

"Here ya' go, ladies. Try this and be honest," Ted said as Michael came up the steps. "This one's for you."

They all took a couple of bites then smiled and sighed.

"This is heavenly as always. It's got a touch of rosemary in it," Miss Cora said.

"And, I detect some kind of pepper something. Not hot, just enough to taste it," Michael said.

"I like the idea of the rice blend and the gravy. Gravy is always a must," Emily added.

"Good. I'm glad ya' like it. I'm putting it on the menu for tonight," Ted said.

"And, I'll be the first order to go whenever I leave," Miss Cora said. "Oh, Michael, stay here for a minute, will ya'? Katelyn just told me that her Sami is comin' to Boone to work on the hotel there next Friday night. She's gonna' come here Saturday mornin' and stay with Katelyn as much as possible. Katelyn wanted to know if we could have a picnic thing here Saturday evenin' so folks could stop by and visit and all. Ya' think you could put somethin' together for Sami?"

"Of course we can," Michael replied lookin at Ted.

"We'd be thrilled to host a picnic," Ted added.

"Now, I think folks will be more than happy to bring a little somethin' from home. Maybe we can ask them to bring a desert. Y'all know how much we all love sweets around here," Emily offered.

"Great idea Emily. That's just what we'll do. I'll get a group email out with the details and folks can tell me what they're bringin'. I'll handle the picnic food and, maybe, ask the chiefs to bring some of their special bar-be-que. One does the chicken and one does the pork kind," Ted said.

"Great! Looks like y'all have it well under control. I've passed the message along and can't wait to sample everything."

They continued to talk about the picnic as folks came and went and soon The Creek was busy making plans for Sami's picnic. Emily texted Ethan and he said he'd get folks to bring pop-up tents, tables and chairs. Emily went on back home to tend to her chores. It was nigh onto supper time when Miss Cora headed home with some of Ted's latest chicken creation, cornbread, and carrot cake.

There were other plans being made as well. These were the bad kind. The Dark had been licking its wounds since the failed attack on Jordan's farm in the other dimension. The Dark needed to destroy The Creek in all dimensions to able to grab and keep the powerful Magic that lived in the earth. Once it had the earth Magic, the rest of the universe would be easily destroyed. That's how special The Magic in Jordan's land was and always had been.

The Dark had planned on taking The Magic easily in the other dimension. It hadn't counted on Katelyn being there. It didn't even know about Katelyn and her special Gifts. It knew The White Light would try to stop it but it had planned a special surprise attack without any other warnings. Well, that failed big time. It had done everything it could think of to get The Magic but Cora, Kendra, and, now, Katelyn were guarding it with everything they could think of. And, that's why The Dark was so angry. It had missed its chance in that dimension.

So now, it was planning on attacking another dimension. One that none of the others would be in. Or so it thought. Seems Miss Cora and Kendra were in all The Creek dimensions. The Dark knew how to handle them and get rid of them. So, the plan was to figure out which dimension to target next. That's what The Dark was planning while The Creek was getting ready for Sami's picnic. This made The Dark a bit less angry 'cause if figured it would take an alternate dimension with little to no resistance.

Sunday found the MacDonald family and the others gathered at the site for Nathan's home mid-morning. The chiefs were ready to offer the sacred blessings and Nathan had brought something along to offer in thanks as well. It was a crystal he had found in this exact spot when he was a little kid of about eight years old. It was no special shape and it had yellow, orange and pink colors that shone brightly when the sun shined on it. The others didn't know he still had it.

"We all ready?" Chief Soaring Eagle asked as they formed a circle around the middle of the property.

"Let's begin. I'll offer my blessing, then Chief Running Bear will do his. Then y'all can offer your own special blessings silently or out loud."

Chief Soaring performed the blessing followed by Chief Running Bear. Nathan then stepped into the middle of the circle, laid his crystal on the ground and offered his thanks. The crystal shot a beam of bright yellow light skyward as Nathan finished and kept on glowin'. The others offered silent thanks then nodded to the chiefs to let them know they were finished.

"Nathan, where'd that crystal come from?" Katelyn asked.

"I found it out here when I was a little kid. It looked so cool. So, I brought it home and set it on my window sill. It's been there ever since. Until today. It just seemed the right thing to bring it out here and give it back."

"Now, that's wicked cool," Jackie said.

"Let's go over to Jeremy's place now," Joe suggested.

They all drove over to Jeremy's site and gathered in a circle in the center. The Chiefs offered the sacred blessings, then Jeremy laid a handful of wildflowers in the center and offered his thanks. The others offered theirs as well. As they all watched, the wild flowers took root and grew tall and increased as they blossomed.

"Now, that's truly a blessing," Chief Running Bear said.

"Only thing is, we gotta' dig deep there and I don't want to kill those wildflowers. Should I dig them up first?" Jeremy asked the chiefs.

Before anyone could say a word, the wildflowers were transported to the edge of the field where they were planted once again and grew and bloomed right before everyone's eyes.

"Well," Katelyn said in awe, "I guess that answers your question."

"So cool," Jeremy said. "Thanks for transplanting them. I'll be sure to set up a little fence or something around them so they don't get bothered while we build."

An eagle flew by and circled them all as if in reply.

"Well, I guess y'all got the best blessing anyone could get about building your homes out here. How about we get back to the house and all?" Jackie suggested.

They all piled into their vehicles and returned to the house. Drinks and snacks were served and folks talked for a bit.

"This has been truly spiritual. Thanks for comin' over chiefs and blessing the land. We do so appreciate y'all," Nathan said as he and Jeremy shook hands with the chiefs.

"It's our pleasure. Can't wait to see those houses. Ethan and Ian's build are spectacular," Chief Running Bear said.

"Take a look. I've got the new sketches with me. Still need y'all to choose the outside colors though. I put some on them but you two need to make the final choices," Katelyn said as she placed the sketches on the picnic table.

"Wow! This is so cool, sis," Jeremy said looking at them.

"This is just exactly the shape I had in my mind," Nathan said as he pulled his to the side.

"And, mine is almost perfect. I'd like to change the garage roof line to have its own shape different than the house please."

"Okay. I'll do something like this," Katelyn said as she quickly drew a separate garage outline alongside the original one.

"That's it. Perfect! It gives a whole different dimension to the shape and all," Jeremy said as he hugged his sister.

"My pleasure," Katelyn said. "Now, how about the colors? I was thinking for you, Nathan, maybe a hunter's green on the front of the house and garage with dark gray or charcoal gray shutters on all the windows? And, for you, Jeremy, how about a burgundy with black shutters all around?"

"I love the colors," Nathan said. "Get me some paint chips and I'll take a look."

"I was thinkin' more of a not-so-navy blue with burgundy shutters, sis," Jeremy said. "Ya' know, a darker blue than normal but not so navy 'cause real navy almost looks black."

"Oh, great idea," Joe said.

"You got it. I'll get some paint squares over tomorrow or Tuesday. I think no one else is using them right now. I know y'all want full basements. Finn and Ian said that's not a problem. Finn has been looking over the geo-thermal thing and will have a report for you two later this week. Ethan always installs underground utilities for electric and all. Ian's trying to figure how to get county water out to y'all. It might be expensive. Septic will be tanks and we'll figure out the best system to preserve the fields and all. That's it for now. Ian and I will be meeting with each of you in a couple of weeks to begin the long process of choosing floors, bathroom designs, and fixtures for everything. Evenings would be the best time so y'all can take care of the berries."

"Holy cow! I never even thought of all that stuff. This is gonna' take a while," Nathan said. Jeremy was nodding his head in agreement.

"You boys may not be pounding nails on your homes, but you will still be required to be hands-on all along the way," Joe offered.

"Your dad's right, boys. I'd cancel those long party nights if I were you," Chief Running Bear said laughing.

They all joined in teasing the boys for a bit.

"Time to get along. Lots to do today. Thanks for the snacks," Chief Soaring Eagle said.

"Same here," Chief Running Bear added as they shook hands, hugged, and took their leave.

"Time for me to get home, too. I've got lots to do to get ready for Sami," Katelyn said as she gathered her sketches and all.

"That's right, Sami's comin' next Saturday. Can't wait to have her here," Jackie said.

"Me, either. I miss her so much. We're gonna' have a blast," Katelyn said as she walked over to her SUV.

Hugs were exchanged and Katelyn went along. The boys and their folks talked about the houses as Jackie got Sunday dinner under way.

The week seemed to fly by at warp speed. Katelyn dropped off the paint squares for her brothers to look at. Ian and Finn were busy with the geo-thermal preliminary design stuff and had been talking with Laine and Mo about the solar panels. The Creek was busy with summer stuff and Friday found them making deserts for Sami's picnic the next day.

Miss Cora had begun to feel a change in the air. It seemed The Dark was getting closer to causing trouble. Emily had called Kendra about feeling that same change in the energy around The Creek. The three of them kept in close touch with each other.

Before Katelyn knew it, Sami called to say she was in Boone. It was Friday night already.

"Oh my God! I can't believe you're already here. It was just Monday morning a minute ago," Katelyn said.

"I know the feelin'," Sami replied. "I'm wicked tired. I left Portland, Maine yesterday and stopped somewhere about half-way to look at a side-project for the firm. I think it was in the northern part of Virginia. I left around ten and a couple of stops later, here I am. I'm gonna' crash in a few minutes so I can be at your place first thing."

"That sounds like a good idea. It's well past nine. Sleep well, my Sami. Love ya' forever and always."

"You, too, my Katie girl. Love you forever and always," Sami said as they hung up.

The Dark had made its decision on the dimension it would attack. Time to get busy with the details. It wouldn't be long now.

Katelyn was so excited about Sami that she woke up with the chickens. That means she was awake around four-thirty-five-o'clock in the morning. Sami must have been excited, too, 'cause she pulled into the driveway around eight.

Katelyn came flying through the door and grabbed Sami as soon as she got out of her SUV.

"You feel so good," they both said at the same time laughing and crying.

"You look super," Sami said when they finally stepped away from each other. "I do believe bein' back home and that Finn guy are good for you!"

"Look at you! You seem so happy," Katelyn replied.

"I am. This URR project is absolutely awesome. Some much goin' on with it. Jordan and I are gonna' get together Monday at his place and spend some time goin' over everything. The plans for each hotel are comin' along so easily. None of the managers are giving me a hard time about designs, murals, and stuff. As a matter of fact, they have some cool ideas as well."

"Let's get your stuff inside then we can eat. I'm starvin'," Katelyn said as she grabbed a couple of Sami's bags.

"Me, too. Let's go," Sami agreed as they went into the house and got Sami settled into her room.

"This place is so cool. Kendra must really like you to let ya' stay here and all," Sami said as she wandered around the house.

"Oh, she is. And, I love her for all she's been doin' for me. Learnin' about my Gifts has been truly overwhelming. We gotta' talk about that later for sure. I need your take on everything."

"I'm always here for ya'," Sammi said as she threw a couch pillow at Katelyn.

"Oh. So that's how this is gonna' be," Katelyn said as she threw it back. They ended up outside and Katelyn turned the hose on. She was aiming at Sami when she got blasted herself.

"What the fuck?"

"All's fair in a water fight," Kendra said as she handed her hose to Sami.

The water fight lasted a few minutes until all three of them were soaked through. Folks at The Store stopped to watch and applauded them when it was over.

"Nice to have ya' here, Sami," Hal said. "I see you've been officially welcomed."

"Thanks Hal. Nice to finally be here," Sami said laughing and wringing out her shirt.

Others added a few comments as they went on their way. The girls decided to sit on Kendra's back patio to dry in the sun a bit before they went inside.

"Hey, Sami. Welcome home," Kendra said laughing.

"Great welcome girls," Sami said laughing along with them. "So much for the shower I took this morning. Guess I'll need another one later to freshen up a bit."

"Nah. You look great with all that curly hair gleamin' in the sunshine," Katelyn said.

"Right!" Sami replied sticking her tongue out at Katelyn.

"I don't think I've had a more fun water fight in years. Thanks girls," Kendra said.

"Any time, Kendra. Any time," Sami offered.

"Remember those super soaker water guns we used to have? I loved those things. They could shoot a stream of water really far. That's how I usually got even with my brothers," Katelyn said remembering past water fights.

"Those were the greatest. We'd fill them up down home and use them to shoot at each other to cool off. That's what we always said. However, there were a few times I used mine to blast a few pain-in-the-ass boys and girlfriends, too. We had so much fun," Sami said.

"I loved those, too. Only problem was we used to hide them from each other before we attacked. I finally figured out that I could use the hose to get back at them. It was great! They had no idea what hit them the first time I did it," Kendra said laughing at the memory.

"Ah hah! That's why you were so quick to give Sami the hose. I'll remember that for a long time," Katelyn said.

"I'll get the iced tea," Kendra said as she went into the house.

"Sami, that was a blast," Katelyn said.

"Sure was. I don't think I could've planned a better welcome," Sami replied as Kendra returned with tea and muffins.

"I don't know about you two, but that water fight has made me super hungry. Enjoy," Kendra said as they went about devouring the muffins and laughing and telling more stories.

It wasn't long before they were dry again and the muffins were gone.

"This was fun. Thanks for the yummies and the water fight, Kendra," Sami said as they stood up.

"Great to have ya' home, even if it's the first time here. It's home," Kendra replied as she gathered the stuff and headed for the house. "Don't be a stranger."

"I won't. I promise," Sami replied as she and Katelyn crossed over to Katelyn's back porch.

"I guess I'd better unpack and all. Come on, enough for both of us to do. Besides, I want to hear all the Finn details," Sami said with a snicker.

They spent the rest of the afternoon catching up on everything they could think of. Katelyn hinted at the other dimension thing and they decided to save it for Sunday morning. It was gonna' take a while to explain.

It must have been late afternoon when Sami noticed pop-up tents going up across the way and in their yard as well.

"Katelyn? What's goin' on out here?" Sami asked as she pointed out the window.

"Well, my Sami, this is the way The Creek's welcomin' ya here, home, even if it's the first time you've been here. I've been talkin' about you so much that they figure this is now your home. It's a welcome home picnic and all," Katelyn said as she gave Sami a squeeze across her shoulders.

Katelyn saw that Sami has tears in her eyes as she said, "Wow! I'm overwhelmed at their kindness."

"They love ya', my Sami, and sharin' food and stories is how they're letting ya' know."

"Well," Sami said as she wiped the tears off her cheeks, "I guess we better get along and let them know how much they all mean to me."

Sami and Katelyn spent a few minutes getting ready. They really needed to change out of the water fight clothes.

Ethan saw them as they came out of the house. "Hey, Sami. Welcome home. Great to finally see ya' in person."

"You, too, Ethan. And, thanks to y'all for this great surprise," Sami said as she and Katelyn crossed the road and stepped up onto The Store porch.

Greetings and hugs were shared for the longest time while Ted and Michael got the food ready. Jenna and Matthews were helping out as well. Hal was in charge of the drink's coolers on the porch and Miss Cora was directing folks with their deserts to the big table in the dining area. Michael had suggested they set up the food tables across the front porch under the windows and folks were helping with that as well. Some of the kids and all were playing frisbee and whiffle ball and such over in front of to the houses across the road.

The chiefs and MacDonald's showed up about the same time as the Redstone's and more greetings were exchanged. It was close to six-thirty when it seemed like the whole of The Creek was assembled ready to eat.

Ted asked the chiefs to say the blessing and they did. Then it was chow time. And, what a feast it was.

"Hey, Finn," Sami said as she and Finn got in line at the same time.

"Hey, Sami. Welcome home. Katelyn's been counting the seconds up to this morning."

"And, so have I. It's great to finally be here and I get to stay for at least a month this time," Sami agreed.

"Now, that's what's made our Katie girl so happy. She gets you for a whole month in person," Finn said.

"And, I get her as well," Sami replied as Finn handed her a plate.

"Eat up. Looks like there's enough food here for a week."

They filled their plates and joined Katelyn and her family under one of the pop-ups on the lawn across the road.

"Oh God! This is what I miss the most, besides Katelyn. Homemade food. Some of the managers bring stuff in for us all. But this, this is heaven on a plate. Speaking of my plate, I need more," Sami said as she got up.

"Me, too," Katelyn replied. "Let's go attack the tables."

The two of them joined a bunch of folks ready to sample more yummy food.

"Hey, Sami," Laine said as she and Sami met at the food tables.

"Hey, Laine. How are you two? I hear your solar panels are a huge hit with Ethan and all. Katelyn said she's gonna' use them on her brother's houses."

"Thanks, Sami. Yes, they are and Mo and I have decided NOT to let anyone else make them. We're keeping the technology secret. It's all patented and copyrighted so no one can duplicate it if they ever figure it out. You're welcome to them if ya' ever decide to build a house."

"Oh my! Thanks, Laine. I will definitely take ya' up on that offer. So glad y'all have created somethin' so special. And, even more happy that the land around here is owned by private individuals and the forest service so no one can come in and build a development. Your secret is safe with me."

"Stop by our table in a bit. There's someone I want 'cha to meet. Bring Katelyn with ya'," Laine said as they left the porch with loaded plates.

"Will do if I can move after all this food," Sami said laughing.

"Katelyn, I was talkin' with Laine at the food tables and she wants you and me to come over in a bit for a chat. I said of course if we can even move by then."

Everyone laughed at this as they were on their way for more food as well.

"Hey Ted," someone called out as Ted came down the porch steps with a plate full. "This here new chicken dish is great. Keep makin' it."

"Thanks. I will," Ted replied as he joined some of the folks settin' near The Store porch. He didn't want to be too far away in case someone needed something.

A while later found Katelyn and Sami headed over to Laine and Mo's table. Earl and Bubba we there and they stood up as the girls came by.

"Hey Bubba, Hey, Earl. You two are such gentlemen," Katelyn said offering a curtsy to them.

"Thanks Miss Katelyn. Welcome home, Sami. Nice to have ya' here," Earl offered as the girls sat down. Only then did Bubba and Earl take their seats again.

"I must say I do appreciate the respect you southern gentlemen have shown us tonight," Katelyn said as she got comfy.

"Hey Katelyn. Good to see ya' again," Clara Redstone said as Seth tipped his hat as he sat down.

"It's always a pleasure to see you as well," Katelyn said.

"We asked Laine to ask ya' over 'cause we heard Sami's working on an Underground Railroad project in the hotels she's renovatin'," Seth began.

"That's right, Seth. It's become such a big project that I hired Jordan to help me," Sami said as Jordan walked over.

"Hey, everyone," Jordan said as he sat down. Replies were offered.

"Well, I wanted to tell ya' about a place here in The Creek that was an unofficial part of the escape route for the slaves. It wasn't on the route that was used regularly. But some knew about it and used it when the regular route seemed to be overflowin' with bounty hunters."

"Really? I never knew about that. It's not in any of the stuff I've looked into," Jordan said leaning forward. "Do tell us Seth. I can't wait to hear all about it."

"Me, either," Sami said as she leaned forward to hear more.

Others had heard a bit of the conversation and word had gotten around and folks came by with their chairs and blankets and all and settled in to hear the story.

"Looks like y'all are interested in this bit of history. Miss Cora, ya' ever hear about this?" Clara asked.

"Well, Clara, not much more than a passing word or two. Nothin' detailed. So, tell us everything," Miss Cora replied as she was set up front to listen with everyone else.

"Well, my granddaddy always told the story he heard from his great-granddaddy and great-grandma. They were alive during the late 1800's. Matter of fact, my great-grandaddy was born in 1874. That was nine years after the civil war ended. It was his daddy who told him the story. And that makes it when slavery was still goin on.

"We all know the horror stories about slavery of the Africans, the Native peoples, the Irish and all the other Europeans and Asians that were kidnapped into slavery or sold their services for a trip to America and found out when they got here that they were indentured slaves with no hope of ever bein' free. I still get real angry and sad thinkin' about what we all did to each other back then. Deplorable," Seth said wiping tears from his eyes.

"It's okay honey. We know and feel the same way," Clara said as she stood to give her husband a little hug.

"Well," Seth cleared his throat and continued. "It was during the time when the slaves began to take control of their lives and plan to escape to Canada. It seems that ya' couldn't just run to another state 'cause the law said ya' could be caught in any state and returned to the state ya' run away from. So, they all took to planning to make it to Canada. Canada welcomed them with open arms and helped them get jobs and homes and all. Canada refused to return those to the United States that made it to Canada.

"My family, my kin, has always been against slavery of any kind. Although my boys might beg to differ with me. They say I made them work like slaves when they were young for no pay what-so-ever."

Folks laughed at this as some of the Redstone boys and grandboys were there and they all said they're daddies made them work for nothing.

"Sure, made an honest man of ya', didn't it?" Bubba asked looking at them smiling.

"It sure did, Bubba. It sure did. Wouldn't have had it any other way. We love ya', dad," one of the Redstone boys replied. The others agreed.

"Good to know," Seth responded with a chuckle. "Now, oh yeah. So, when my kin heard about the slaves tryin' to run away and hide, they decided to help out. Y'all know we have those two really big red barns a ways back from the farmhouse, right? Well, my kin decided to build rooms under the second barn. The one farthest from the house. So, they went about diggin' and making rooms and tunnels under that barn with strong framework that's still there today. We use some of that space to store crops for the winter.

"It took them the better part of a year to get it ready. They listened to folks here at The Store and out and about to learn who was helpin' the slaves. They finally got a hold of the preacher of the Baptist church for the Blacks. Things wasn't so nice back then. My kin took a few meetings to ask if there was anyone who would know how to let the Underground Railroad know about their hiding place. The preacher went over to the farm and walked the barn with my kin. They did this in the deep of night so no one would see them. Ya' had to be real careful back then. Some of the folks in North Carolina were sympathizers with the slave owners and would do anything to get their hands on the runaway slaves. Seems the money for returning a slave was pretty good.

"My kin took the preacher down into the tunnels and rooms. They had tables and chairs and beds and food stored away for them runaways. And clothes that looked like everyone else's clothes. The preacher fell to his knees cryin' and thankin' God and my kin for their kindness. The preacher and my kin got to talking about other things that would help the runaways. The preacher told my kin that tunnels were dug that led into the deep woods so the folks wouldn't be seen movin' on. So, my kin said they'd take care of that, too.

"And they did. They dug two tunnels that led deep into the Blue Ridge. Remember, things weren't so built up back then like they are today. One of the tunnels came up at the north end of the property that was in the forest. So, that was helpful. There were animal paths that folks followed to their next stop. No one knew about them except the few of us up in these hills. The other tunnel was special. It led right up into The Meadow where we have gatherings once every few years."

Folks gasped at this news 'cause no one knew a thing about it.

"Yup. All these years and ya' didn't know you was on top of one of the Underground Railroad tunnels."

"That's fantastic, Seth. Ya' never told anyone,' Hal said in astonishment.

"We never thought about tellin' anyone 'cause we always kept our kin's secret and the secret of those runaways that came by. The tunnels are still there and in great shape. I keep tellin' Clara ya' never know when I might need to escape for a spell," Seth said laughing.

"I hear ya', Seth," Jed hollered out as his wife whacked him upside the head in fun. "Wish I'd known about them the other day. I forgot to pick up a few things and the wife wasn't happy with me. I could a used that tunnel for a few hours."

Folks laughed at Jed. He was quite the storyteller for sure. They settled down a few minutes later and Seth continued.

"My kin kept track of the names of the folks that came through our farm. There weren't many as we weren't on the main Underground Railroad line. But my kin did see quite a few over the years. We got the names all written down and in a protective book if any of ya' would like to see them. I know Ceceilia's been by. Seems her kin used our place on their way to Canada. Her family's been over a few times to tell us their story and look around. We love them dearly."

"We love all the Redstone's. Past and present and any others that may be comin' along," Ceceilia called out.

Folks talked about this news for a bit.

"Well, I got to thinkin' about all this when I heard about Sami and her URR project. That's the nickname for the thing. So, I thought I'd tell ya' all about it today seein' we're all gathered and such. How about Sami and Jordan come over one day soon and I'll take ya' on a tour?"

"On my God! Seth! This is beyond belief. I absolutely accept and am so appreciative of the offer," Sami said as she came forward and shook hands with Seth and Clara.

"This is fantastic. I can actually see the real thing," Jordan said. "Oh, ah, Seth. Should we keep this a secret from the outside world? If this gets out, the world will want to see it all."

"Now, that's right smart thinkin,' Jordan. Let's keep this as a secret for The Creek for now. I'm not sure if I want a whole bunch of strangers trampling the place and The Meadow. The Meadow is real special to us."

Everyone agreed to keep this news a secret from the outside world. Sami and Jordan wouldn't mention any of it in their work. They were thrilled to be invited to go down and walk the tunnels and see the rooms and all.

Sami was thinking how this new development would add another layer of reality to the project for her and Jordan. This was an amazing homecoming.

Evening gave way to night and folks were still talking about the Redstone's farm. Stories were told and you could hear laughter coming from one group then another. Supper had been cleared and the deserts were sampled by everyone so much that there weren't any leftovers when all was said and done.

It was a clear, warm, and starry night as folks began to pack up and get ready to head home.

"Folks," Sami called out. "I just want to say bless all your little ol' pea pickin' hearts for showin' me the love."

Sami went on to thank each and every one of them for their kindness and love welcoming her home to The Creek. It was as if she had belonged here forever.

Ted, Michael, Sami, Finn, and Katelyn finished up getting things in order in The Store. There wasn't much to do. Folks always helped out so Ted and Michael could take it easy.

"Now, that's what I call the best-ever welcome home gatherin'," Sami said as she leaned against the cash register counter.

"It certainly was," Finn replied as he put an arm around Katelyn.

"As always, you boys were all first class with everything," Katelyn said.

"Ya' know how we love takin' care of our own," Michael said.

"Yes, we do," Ted added.

"And, the Redstone's story was out of this world. I couldn't even imagine anything like that around here with this being the 'South' and all," Sami added.

"Agreed. It sure was incredible that they've known all about this for decades and never said a word. Oh, I agree with keepin' it secret and all for sure. I wouldn't want the world crashin' down on The Creek," Finn said.

"Time for bed. I'm so tired I can hardly keep my eyes open," Katelyn said covering a yawn.

"Me, too. It's been an A-1 day and I thank y'all," Sami said bowing a bit. "Come on sleepy head. Home with the two of us," Sami said as she took ahold of Katelyn's hand and started for the door.

"Come on, you two. I'll walk ya' home. By guys. See ya' soon. Thanks again," Finn said as the three of them stepped out the door.

"Later," Ted said as he locked the door after them. Michael set the lights and they both wandered upstairs.

"You are a gentleman for walkin' us home," Katelyn said.

"I'll let you two say a proper good night. Thanks for the fun, Finn," Sami said as she went inside.

Katelyn smiled as Finn gathered her into his arms. "I do like the way we say goodnight."

"Me, too," Finn said as he covered Katelyn's mouth with his. The kiss was deep and long and seemed to last forever

When they did finally part, Katelyn said," If I wasn't so tired, we could keep this goin' for a long while. But I think I'm gonna' end up sleepin' on the porch if I don't go in right this minute."

"I can see that. Good night my Katie girl," Finn said kissing the top of her head.

"Good night, my sweet Finn," Katelyn replied as she caressed his cheek and stepped inside.

Katelyn looked in on Sami. She was sound asleep with a smile on her face. Katelyn fell into bed and was asleep in no time.

The Creek slept deep that night.

CHAPTER 26

Sunday found Katelyn and Sami talking about more stuff. It was mid-morning when Katelyn began to tell Sami about her talk with Kendra. She explained everything that had happened since she came home. Some Sami already knew about but the portal thing was new.

"A portal in a cave on Jordan's land? Wow!" Sami said. "And nobody knows about it except you and Kendra and Miss Cora?"

"Right. And, Jordan hasn't even gone past the main room yet. That's what they tell me. I am so overwhelmed about all this I told Kendra and Miss Cora I needed time to think about everything. So much has happened I don't even know if I can handle any more," Katelyn said.

"I don't blame ya.' Have you been thinkin' about all this?"

"Yes. All week long when I wasn't workin' or thinkin' about you comin' here. I just need to say everything out loud and need your thoughts."

"That's what I'm here for. Start talkin'," Sami said settling back in her chair at the kitchen table.

"Well, I've always known about The Magic here. My mom told us stories and I've seen a few things growin' up that had to be linked to The Magic. Nothin' big but some things that couldn't be explained any other way. Really cool stuff. Once, when I was about twelve years old, my brothers and I were walkin' through the strawberry field at sunset and all of a sudden, the plants started to twinkle like they had teeny tiny lights in them. It was wicked cool. The whole field was glowin'. We stopped walkin' and just watched the light show. It lasted about ten minutes, then the lights were gone. We didn't say much. Didn't know what to say except it was awesome. I said thanks to whatever made the lights twinkle and a few blinked real quick. It was like they wanted us to know they saw us and heard us.

"When we got home, we told our folks about it and they smiled and said it must have been some Magic in the fields. Remember when I picked up that shocked crystal at the fair in Alabama right before I moved here? That was some strong Magic for sure."

"Yes, it was. How is that crystal?" Sami asked.

Katelyn went into the living room and grabbed it from the window sill where it sat.

"Here it is, glowing like it always does. It sits in the window on the west side of the house. Seems to like it there," Katelyn said setting the crystal on the table.

"Looks just like it did when ya' found it. Beautiful," Sami said. "Keep goin' now."

"After I got home things were quiet for a few days. I kept feelin' like I needed to talk with Kendra and that's when she told me I had special Gifts from The White Light gang, as I call them, with all due respect. Well, that was a surprise and a half. I chose to walk in The White Light and then things really began to happen. I became a Reiki practitioner and began learning how to use my Gifts, or powers, as some would call them. It wasn't until Jenna and I went to that guy's house to look at the basement that the real bad stuff began to happen. Remember, he was possessed by The Dark and tried to get me down the stairs and all? Well, I called for help from The White Light and they saved Jenna and me and the bad guy was blown to pieces. That was more than I could handle alone. Good thing Jenna was with me. She's Gifted, too. Seems she uses her connections to create art work for her clients that's real special for them. I've seen some of it and it sure is magnificent."

"I got to talk with her last night for a bit. She invited me, and you, to come over to her studio to look around," Sami said.

"Now that's cool. Well, Laine and Mo said to come by as well for a visit. They are two of the most special people I know," Katelyn added.

"Great! We'll visit with everyone," Sami said laughing a bit.

"That means you're gonna' have to stay here for a few months," Katelyn said laughing as well.

"I love this place," Sami said. "Now, keep goin' with all this stuff."

"Well, it wasn't too long after the bad guy exploding thing that I first found the cave. It's filled with crystals and Magic. The second time I went to the cave is when I went through that portal thing and found myself in the other Crab Apple Creek. I didn't know it right away. I kept seeing and hearin' things that didn't make sense. When I walked into The Store a little while after bein' in the cave, and now I know, going through the portal, I noticed some stuff on the shelves that hadn't been there before. Ever. I found that strange but figured Michael was tryin' out some new merchandise.

"The one thing that began to get my attention was that Emily and Ethan were not a couple. Just friends. I figured somethin' was very wrong and kept a closer eye on things. But the thing that finally proved I wasn't in my Crab Apple Creek was when I saw Jay. I passed out. And when I came to, I saw him again and passed out again. I knew somethin' was very different. When I got a few minutes to myself, I flew into Kendra's house and demanded to know what the hell was goin' on. Ya' see, she's all Magic and goes between the dimensions with little effort. That's one of the things I learned that afternoon."

"Whoa! Oh my God! That would be enough to push me over the edge into insanity," Sami said.

"Oh, it was. I was hollerin' and stompin' around for quite some time. Kendra finally got me to calm down enough to sit and listen to her. Seems the good guys have chosen me to fight for The Magic in Jordan's land and all of The Creek. Seems The Magic has always been here and is protected by a few of us. Miss Cora's one of us as well. There's somethin' special about Jordan's place. I haven't been told what or anything about it except it seems I'm supposed to protect it. Me! Me! Do I look like a warrior? No! But they chose me anyway.

"Well, there was a battle with The Dark and they tried to take The Magic from Jordan's land. They couldn't because Kendra, Emily, Miss Cora, and I set up a protection grid from deep within the earth to outer space somewhere. The Dark tried to send a wave of bad energy through the creek that goes through the field but it was stopped at the edge of the protection grid. Miss Cora came to me and told me I had to save The Creek and to go back to cave and I'd know what to do when I got there. She said it would be the hardest thing I ever did. She was right. I thought I was gonna' die a couple of times. The closer I got to the cave, the more The Dark sent sound bombs that hurt my head and threw me to the ground. I only had a couple of feet to go to get into the cave. So, I called on The White Light to help. It wrapped my head in some kind of somethin' like cotton and the noise was less. I had to play dead to get The Dark to stop pressing me to the ground. It finally eased up and I darted for the cave. As soon as I got in, all the bad stuff stopped. My head stopped pounding and I could breathe again."

"Katelyn, why haven't you told me about this yet?"

"Jesus Christ, Sami, I'm still processing it all. I think I've lost my mind most of the time I think about it all. It's been a bit overwhelming," Katelyn said.

"Oh, Katie, I'm sorry. I can't even imagine your terror and confusion and everything. Let's get some tea before you tell me the rest."

"Good idea," Katelyn said as they fixed the tea and settled at the table once more.

"This tea was a good idea. I do feel calmer and stronger," Katelyn said.

"Good! So, tell me the rest," Sami said.

Katelyn took a deep breath, relaxed her shoulders and continued with her story. "Well, when I was in the cave, I had to take a special crystal down a little tunnel to a place with a shelf made just for the crystal. There were three places to set it and I felt it belonged in one of them and placed it there. I looked down the three tunnels in front of me and I swear I saw a big eye lookin' at me in the purple tunnel on my right. I know I saw an eye. When I looked back the eye was gone. I know I saw a great big eye lookin' at me. I left that place and went back to the main room. Those crystals were shinin' somethin' fierce. I felt that I had done my job and walked back across the room. I saw that wavy energy thing just before I passed through it but didn't think anything of it. As soon as I walked through it, the crystals weren't shinin' so bright. I noticed it but didn't think much about it.

"When I left the cave, the battle was over. Everything was back to normal like it was before I went through the portal. I went on to The Store, got some take out, ate, showered and crashed. When I got to work the next day, I saw Ethan and Emily kissing in the doorway to the shop. I knew I was back here, in my Crab Apple Creek."

"So glad you're okay after all that stuff. How long were you gone?"

"Well, it seemed like three or four weeks, but when I came back through the portal it was the same day I had gone into the cave in the first place. Only a couple of hours had passed. Talk about bein' confused. Whew!"

"Holy shit! No way! Only a couple of hours for real? I don't think I could wrap my head around all that for a very long time. No wonder you're overwhelmed and confused. And angry. I would be, too," Sami said.

"Really!" Katelyn replied. "Food. I need some food. This magic stuff always makes me hungry. I made some cookies the other day and Finn has not eaten all them all for a change. Here."

"Oh God, Katie. I remember these chocolate chip cookies of yours. They are somethin' special for sure. I am so in heaven right now."

"So glad I warmed them up. They are yummy," Katelyn said biting into one.

"That's a lot to live with Katie. How do ya' want to go forward with it all?"

"That's not all of it. This next part is beyond belief. So, Saturday afternoon after we talked, I stormed into Kendra's place and demanded to know what the hell was goin' on. Well, Miss Cora showed up and what they told me was this: the battle between The White Light and The Dark never ends. It just has a few breaks now and again. I was chosen to save The Magic in Jordan's field. I had to go to the other dimension so this one wouldn't be blasted into nothingness. And, there's always gonna' be more. This is the part I just can't fathom. Everything that's happened has been more than I can take. And, now, Miss Cora says there's more coming right soon. Holy fuck! What am I supposed to do? I just can't handle all this."

"I, ah, I don't know what to say either. Breathe for now. We'll come up with a plan to handle everything that's happened so far. How about we write it down in order and then set it aside for a bit?"

"I told Kendra and Miss Cora that I was gonna' put my Gifts or powers on hold for a bit while I try to sort all this out. They said I always have the choice whether to accept them and use them or not. I told them and The White Light I wasn't gonna' use them for a while. Everything's on hold. This is just too much to handle," Katelyn said as tears fell from her cheeks.

Sami got up and put her arms around Katelyn and she held her for the longest time.

"Oh, Sami. I really needed to tell someone about all this and you're the only one I can. Nobody else is here to talk to about The Magic and everything. And, I don't think most of them would believe me any way."

"Oh, Katie. I am so sorry I wasn't here earlier. Ya' could have called and said it was an emergency. I would have come right over."

"I know. I thought I could handle it a little at a time, but it didn't work. That's why I stormed into Kendra's and fell apart. They are so sweet to understand me. I do love them bunches."

"I know. I may not have known them long, but I am quite fond of the folks around here, too."

Katelyn broke their silence a bit later. "Well, I do feel better tellin' ya' all about it. And, I need more food as usual. How about we table this for a bit and whip up some of those leftovers from the picnic? I seem to remember there's some bar-be-que in the frig."

"Oh, yes there is. Me first," Sami said as she ran to the frig a second ahead of Katelyn and grabbed the packages of leftovers.

The girls had a grand time eating and remembering the picnic and that made them remember fun times from college and their Alabama days. Katelyn felt calmer after telling all to Sami. Maybe now they could work on all that had happened and make some sense of it. The biggest question Katelyn had was 'Why her?' She knew Sami was just who she needed to help her out.

Monday found everyone going about their usual business. Bubba and Earl were thrilled with their new cabins that Emily had built for them Ethan had used geothermal energy to keep them off the grid and hidden. They had a few of Laine and Mo's new solar panels on their roofs. Thing is they weren't reflective so they wouldn't been seen by anyone. The road Ethan had cleared for the build was almost completely grown in. It was only a foot path now. The boys were very happy about that. They needed to remain hidden with their moonshine and all.

Ethan, Finn, and Ian were over at Laine and Mo's that morning. They were discussing the need for solar panels. Seems every new client wanted those panels and to be off the energy grid if at all possible. Laine and Mo were thrilled. They had built a surplus of the latest style of panels and would be able to supply Ethan with all that he needed. Ethan was thrilled to hear the news. He left Finn and Ian to work out the details for the next six builds. He headed for one of those builds to let his crew know that the solar panels would be used.

Miss Cora was busy with her gardens but she was very aware of the energy changes coming along. She knew it wouldn't be long before The Creek would need to defend The Magic. She hoped Katelyn would have a decision for her in the next few days.

Jordan was busy with the new information they had learned about at the picnic. He was writing notes so they could be used without identifying the location. It was late morning and he kept getting the feeling that he should go across the field to the cave with all the crystals. He hadn't been there in a while but he kept feeling a pull to drop what he was doing and go out there. So, he did just that.

He took the gator and was near the entrance in a few minutes. He never parked close 'cause he didn't want anyone to know about the cave. Katelyn knew and that was okay. He looked around before he pushed the bushes aside and walked into the entrance. He was a tall guy and had to bend over to get to the main room. The crystals were glowin' some and it took his breath away. It was stunning. They sent beams of colored light all over the cave. Ya' couldn't even tell it was an earth cave.

He stood at the entrance to the room for a bit just looking at everything and feeling the peace and calm there. He almost felt like he'd been there before. That's before he bought the farm. A long time ago it seemed. It was like a distant memory that creeps up just enough to get your attention then stops before you can figure it all out. It was a peaceful feeling so he wasn't concerned.

He eventually walked around the edge of the room and looked at all the nooks and spaces. He hadn't been aware of them the other times he had been there. He got to a spot along the far wall and found another tunnel. He decided to walk down the tunnel and explore things. It was tall enough so he didn't have to bend down. It led to another room with three more tunnels leading off the room. Each tunnel was a different color. The one on the right was purple. It had crystals all over the walls and floor and there was every shade of purple you could imagine and then some. The tunnel in the middle was bright yellow and the tunnel on the left was deep red like royal robes. They were beautiful.

Jordan looked into the burgundy tunnel and thought he heard some kind of singing. Faint but definitely singing. He looked into the yellow tunnel. It had a welcoming feeling He then looked into the purple tunnel and was stunned to see two big huge eyes looking back at him. And I mean they were huge! They were quite a ways back into the tunnel and they just kept looking at Jordan. He took a minute to see if they were really there. They blinked slowly. They were there. He was about to turn around and run when he felt like he heard someone telling him he was safe. He looked around but no one was there. He heard the voice again. It was soft and whispery but it was for real. He stayed still looking at those eyes for the longest time. He didn't feel anything bad so he stayed right there.

Then the eyes were gone. They blinked at him one more time and vanished. Gone. He looked for a few more minutes than felt like it was time to leave. He walked back to the main room, looked around, and headed for the entrance tunnel. Just as he stepped into the tunnel, a crystal the same color purple as the tunnel and shaped like an eye appeared at his feet. He smiled and picked it up.

"Not too sure what this is all about, but I do thank you for the visit and this gift. It surely means somethin' special to me," Jordan said as he held the crystal.

He walked down the short entrance tunnel and looked for anyone about before he pushed the bushes aside and walked out of his crystal cave.

Now where'd that come from he thought? His crystal cave. Felt right. Sounded right. Guess that's what it was then. Jordan's crystal cave. He got into the gator and returned to the barn. The eagles flew in right after him and George settled on the floor in front of him. They did this every day. It was their customary greeting. George nodded his head a few times at Jordan and Jordan nodded his in reply while talking to George.

"Hey, George. How ya' doin' today? It's great to see you again," Jordan said as he bobbed his head at George.

George gave a little screech in answer. They stood there for a few more minutes than George took flight back up into the family nest. He poked his head over the edge as he always did to let Jordan know he was all safe and sound.

Jordan waved at George, closed the barn and headed for the kitchen. He was starvin'. He looked at the clock and saw it was already well past noon. He'd been out there for a good hour and some. He always seemed to lose track of time the few times he was in his cave. Jordan's crystal cave.

He kept seeing those eyes in the purple tunnel while he ate and all afternoon as he worked on the URR project. He was researching the Boone,

NC connection with the URR. It seems there were more sympathizers than most folks thought. This project kept getting more and more interesting and sad. All those people held against their will and some forced to leave behind tribal teachings and become 'civilized' like the new Americans. Just so wrong.

Well, with Sami's bringing attention to the URR and the whole slavery history maybe some facts would be learned and some respect would be paid to those that had suffered. Time didn't matter. Dignity and respect did.

It was well after supper time and Emily and Trouble had just rounded up the chickens and gotten them into the inner coup when she felt a wave of energy go through her. It wasn't good. She had goosebumps all over. She stood still for a minute and tuned into the space around her. There was definitely a change in the air and it wasn't the weather. Kendra and Miss Cora had felt the beginnings of this change a few days back and this was the largest wave so far. The Dark was finally on the move. It wasn't anywhere near The Creek yet, but this was a warning that something malevolent was coming.

She offered light and love to the universe and all then she called out to Trouble, who was trying to round up the meadow birds. He really thought he was a shepherd. Too funny. The birds were used to him and they played with him every evening at this time.

She finally got Trouble onto the porch and as she looked out over the meadow and the mountains, she saw something flying over the far mountains. It was really big for her to be able to see any part of it from her place. It swooped around and down into a hollow or two then went back up over the mountain tops and was gone. It had a familiar shape. Maybe an eagle or turkey buzzard. Thing is, it was huge. It had to be something else to be able to be seen from such a far- away distance. Maybe the setting sun was playing a trick on her with the light and the blue mist in the mountains and all. Oh well, it sure was different. She'd think about it later after she had supper and got Trouble settled for the night. Ethan would not be home tonight. He was sleeping at his house for a change. He had supplies being delivered to work sites beginning at six in the morning and always stayed at his place for these early morning deliveries and such.

Katelyn was settling in after supper. Sami had a long day and evening of meetings and planning sessions and would stay in Boone tonight. Sami told Katelyn it was always like this when she started at a new location. Crazy for about the first two weeks, then things settled some when the work actually started.

Katelyn was letting her mind wander as she listened to folks coming and going at The Store. She found herself remembering Seth's URR story about The Meadow. Then she remembered how she had seen it from the top of The Rise. It looked like it always had. There was no way you could tell there were tunnels under it. Sami had texted her to let her know that she and

Jordan were going over to the Redstone's Tuesday after supper to have a look at the tunnels and rooms.

Her mind kept focusing on The Meadow and she began to see it with people in it. She thought they were from the last gathering they had had there a few years ago. But something wasn't right. It almost looked like the people were scared or something and had come together. She thought she heard them crying and talking about how the recent storm had damaged a lot of folk's homes. The whole of The Creek was there. Her family was there along with Ethan and Ian and Miss Cora and Ted and Michael. She couldn't really hear many details or see things clearly. It was all a bit hazy and muffled. But something was definitely wrong. She kept trying to hear more but the vision started to diminish and then was completely gone.

Katelyn didn't realize she had had a vision until she came back to the evening and saw that it was dark out. She had been somewhere else for at least a couple of hours. It all seemed like only a few minutes.

Then she got mad. "Hey, White Light guys, I said I was putting my Gifts on hold. How dare you interfere with and disregard my decision."

Katelyn saw a mist begin to form in front of her. Good thing she was inside. It only took a few seconds to form. It was a female in lavender and white flowing garments with long flowing black hair and beautiful blue eyes.

"Katelyn, please don't be alarmed. I am sent to you by those White Light guys you just yelled at," the vison said with a smile.

"Oh, for goodness' sake. What the hell is going on here? I don't want to be bothered right now. Too much to process. Please, leave me alone."

"We know this has been beyond overwhelming for you. We wish it didn't need to be like this. But, remember this: You agreed to all this before you came down into a physical body. You knew you would be on overload. You asked for our help when all this was going to happen and here we are. I'm the only one you can see right now. But, believe you me, there are countless numbers of us here to help you through all this. We're really surprised you haven't asked for help before now."

"I never thought about asking for help. I thought I was supposed to process all this with Miss Cora and Kendra's help," Katelyn replied.

"We know. That's why I was sent to you. Ask me anything you want. And, I mean anything. If I can give you an answer, I will."

"That's the part I don't like. I'll only get the answers you want me to have at this time."

"Yup."

"That's it? Yup?" Katelyn said laughing at the vision.

"Yup," the vision replied laughing along with Katelyn.

"Well, that's really funny when ya' think about it. Y'all existing on the human level of thought."

"I agree. It's really kind of fun for a change," the vision answered back.

"Okay. So, I have a few questions. The why me one is mostly answered. How am I supposed to know what to do with all this stuff? How am I supposed to know what powers to use and how do I get them? Let's start with those questions."

"These are great questions Katelyn. Miss Cora and Kendra are ready to teach you the new stuff to help you when the next thing happens. And, no, you don't get to know ahead of time what the next thing is. I can tell you it's coming along right quick. They will teach you how to protect yourself and others when the time comes. They will teach you how to call on the White Light Paladins for help. They will help you try out those knew Gifts and powers so you are ready to use them when the time comes. How's that for answers?"

"Good answers. All of them. Does this all have to do with going through another portal thing?"

The vision held up her hand for a minute as if she were talking with someone then answered Katelyn.

"I have been given the okay to tell you it will involve another dimension. That's all. The next time you travel between the dimensions you will know almost immediately that you have gone through another portal. No guessing like the first time. That's all I can tell you."

"Fair enough," Katelyn said. "Fair enough. I do feel a lot better talking with you. I will remember all of this after you leave, right?"

"Yes, Katelyn, every word. And you can tell Sami all about our chat as well. She's a good soul and can be trusted to keep our secret."

"Now, that makes me feel really good about Sami. She's the best friend anyone could ever have."

"We agree. Any more questions for us?"

"Yes. It's more of a thing, though. I'm feeling so overwhelmed with all that's happened since I picked up that shocked crystal in Alabama. It seems I haven't had time to think about each thing and process them and be okay with it all. My head is goin' in so many directions I don't know what to think and feel."

"We can see that. I'm going to give you some Reiki right now to help even things out. Ready?"

"Yes, Ma'am," Katelyn replied as the vision stepped next to her and held her hands over Katelyn's head. The energy that entered her was calming and warm and beautiful. It lasted a good few minutes then the vision stepped back.

"Wow! That was great. I should have remembered to do Reiki on myself. Thanks so much," Katelyn said.

"Katelyn, you have been hit with so much stuff that we are not surprised you didn't remember about the Reiki. We're gonna' be sending you Reiki continually from now on so you can better balance things and not feel so overwhelmed and desperate for peace."

"Thanks to everyone. I do feel much lighter. My thoughts aren't goin' all over the place. I do feel okay with my Gifts and all. I still need a day or two to settle into this new space. I am humbled and honored by these Gifts from The Divine to help me carry on with my journey."

"We accept your thanks and await your final decision in a day or two. Things are beginning to move forward and we need your decision to better prepare for the next assault from The Dark."

"I understand and will have that decision by tomorrow evening," Katelyn promised.

"Thanks Katelyn. Rest easy now. I leave you in the light and love of The Divine," the vision said as she vanished.

Katelyn sat there for a few minutes thinking about all that had happened. Oh shoot. She forgot to ask about the vision she had had before the Spirit showed up. Well, she thought, I guess I'll get an answer to that real soon.

Katelyn got ready for bed and was soon asleep. No dreams that night. The Creek settled in as well. There was a mist over the stars that night.

CHAPTER 27

Tuesday afternoon found Katelyn leaving work a bit early. She was making supper for Sami, Miss Cora, and Kendra. She had made her decision about being involved with The Magic in The Creek and was gonna' tell them all at supper.

Sami got there first and was greeted by the smell of bar-be-que and roasting potatoes coming from the back porch.

Miss Cora arrived a minute later, carrying something for supper. Kendra walked out of her house carrying a large bowl of something.

"Hey, everyone," Katelyn said as they all set their food on the table in the screened-in porch. "Chicken and taters will be ready in a few. There's lemonade and ice tea next to the table. Help yourselves."

Bar-be que chicken and roasted potatoes were placed in the middle of the table and they all commenced to filling their plates and eating.

"This is heavenly," Sami said through a mouthful. "I haven't had your roasted grilled taters in forever."

"Same here," Miss Cora and Kendra said at the same time.

"Thanks, ladies. I was of a mind to eat some myself. Enjoy," Katelyn said.

They ate and talked and ate some more for a while.

"Well, now that we're finished stuffin' our faces for a bit, I asked y'all here 'cause I've made my decision about all this magic stuff," Katelyn said looking at each one of them.

"I figured you had," Miss Cora commented.

"Well, tell us your thoughts," Kendra added.

"I spent a lot of time talkin' with Sami about this and it helped some. Always does talkin' to you. Then, last evenin', while I was kinda' day dreamin' in the kitchen, a spirit came to me and we had a conversation. She was beautiful and had a sense of humor. She explained a lot of things to me about my bein' here and all. I won't go into detail. Then she said if I chose to continue helpin' to keep The Magic safe here, Miss Cora and Kendra would know just what to teach me and explain to me so I would be better prepared for the next time. She told me, just like you did, Miss Cora, that the struggle never ends."

"That's true, Katelyn," Miss Cora said.

"Well, with that and some other things just for me to know about, I spent last night thinkin' about all this. The Spirit did apologize for everything that's happened so fast without me being ready and agreed with sayin' she'd be scared to keep goin', too. This is still more than I can possibly manage by myself and she reminded me that all I ever need to do is ask for help from The White Light guys. She said I am never alone and to remember that. So, I've decided to keep goin' forward with my Gifts and try my best to help keep The Magic safe."

A moment of quiet followed.

"Well, Katelyn, I am so thankful to hear this," Kendra said.

"Me, too," Sami added. "Ya' know I'm always here for ya'."

"Miss Katelyn, you've made a huge decision and your life will be forever changed. I am glad ya' decided to keep helpin' out. Kendra and I are gonna' be teachin' you stuff every night startin' tomorrow after supper. Sorry, Sami. Ya' can't be here for these sessions."

"I understand and was gonna' tell Katelyn that I'm gonna' be needed at the hotel around the clock for the rest of the week. We got the go ahead with the renovation plans and the crews are gonna' start with the third-floor tomorrow mornin' and work until about eight o'clock every night until the 3rd floor is finished. Then, they'll start on the 2nd floor. The first floor they do always has a few extra surprises so I stay around for that project."

"Well, that works out quite well although I'm gonna' miss ya' not bein' here until Friday," Katelyn said.

"Oh, I'll be back Friday for sure. But late. Probably after ten. I need y'all to keep me grounded and fed," Sami replied.

They laughed at this as Miss Cora said, "Let's get my desert I brought out. Time for somethin' sweet."

They sampled the chocolate desert Miss Cora had made. It was a flourless chocolate cake with chocolate cream cheese frosting. Just what they needed at that moment.

The evening ended shortly after desert and Sami and Katelyn just stood there looking at each other.

"Well, that was a huge decision," Sami said. "I guess you're gonna' need my help."

"Oh, yes I am. I can't tell ya' the stuff I learned about but I will be in need of you. Just because."

"Let's go set on the porch for a bit and watch whatever's goin' on out there," Sami suggested.

They set out on the porch for quite a while. The Store was its usual busy self and a few of the kids were playing ball in the field south of Kendra's houses. Evening gave way to night and that stopped the ballgame. The kids set down on The Store porch waiting for their folks to finish inside.

The girls waved to everyone who drove by and stopped at the store. Eventually, The Store became quiet and Ted and Michael came outside to bring some things inside for the night.

"Evenin' girls. Enjoin' the peace and quiet?" Michael called out to them.

"We sure are. It's wonderful," Katelyn replied.

Ted came across the road with a take-out container in each hand.

"Now girls, I was just cleanin' up and had a few leftovers so I put sample plates together for ya' both. Enjoy." He handed them the containers and waved as he went back across the road.

"Thanks, Ted. We love your sample plates. Hey, they're still warm. And, look. Forks. You think of everything Ted," Sami said as she opened her container.

"Oh, this is gonna' be fun," Katelyn said as she took a bite of the goodies.

"Sure is," Sami said.

They sampled the leftovers and didn't leave a crumb behind.

"I think I'm gonna' need a nap before I go inside and get ready for bed," Sami said laughing.

"Me, too. This was such a great treat. I love Ted's creations," Katelyn said.

"Time to call it a night. It's been a busy day for both of us," Sami said as she held the door for Katelyn.

Katelyn turned and looked out over The Creek for just a second. She knew this peaceful time was short lived.

"Night, my Katie girl. Sleep well," Sami said as she went into her bedroom.

"Night, my Sami. You, too," Katelyn replied as she stepped into her room. Her crystals were glowing softly and humming. Seems they were happy with her decision, too.

The rest of the week went by rather quickly. Katelyn and Finn were working with new clients on their energy needs and floor plans. Ethan and Ian were busy with inspections and permits. Emily had her hands full with Trouble and the chickens. Jonah was taking care of the horses and their owners. Miss Cora and Kendra met with Katelyn for three nights in a row teaching her new skills and giving her information about how and when to use them.

Sami was busy at the hotel and Jordan was busy with the research. They had to change their visit with the Redstone's to next week on account of Sami's schedule. They set the next Tuesday evening for the visit.

Ethan was at a new job site just over the Tennessee line. He was meeting with the excavators and the building inspector before any work was done.

The site had been researched and approved by the county for the new home build. The new owners had bought twenty acres that abutted the national forest and were thrilled that Ethan was able to be their builder. His reputation was well known all over the Blue Ridge.

The owners had met a few times with Ian and Ethan about the exact spot they wanted their home built on. It would be about a half mile into their forested land. The EPA had okayed the project and given the go-ahead.

Ethan, his crew chief for this project, Karl who owned the excavation company, and the building inspector were standing along the road talking about the project.

"Hey, Karl," the building inspector said shaking hands, "Nice to see you're on this build. I can always rest easy when I know you're in charge."

"Thanks Bob. My pleasure to be a part of a Sutherland build."

"Thanks, guys. Now," Ethan said, "How about we walk and tag the trees to be taken down for the road which will be the driveway when we're finished. The owners like the idea of a winding road so no need to keep things straight."

"I love this idea. Only thing is, there's a creek that crosses the area. Looks like we'll have to plan a bridge and all to protect it." Karl said.

"I looked at your arial shots. Great pictures. And, yes, that creek is all across the property. I asked the conservation folks about it and they said it tends to swell in the spring from the winter snow run-off. The highest they've seen it at in the last one-hundred years is about six feet over the banks," Bob said.

"Okay. So, we'll take a look when we get there. Ready?" Ethan asked.

They stepped into the forest and followed an animal path for a bit. Just as it ended, they could hear the water in the creek. They walked a couple more yards and were at the banks of the creek.

"Looks like we found the creek. Yup. It's gonna' take some work to build a bridge over this and put in the right kind of flow guides so as not to interrupt the flow much," Ethan said.

"And, I don't think we can walk through it right now. It does look quite deep in the middle. It seems to be about forty feet wide here. It looks to be the same all along this area," Karl said.

"What are ya' thinkin' Karl?" Ethan asked.

"I'm thinkin' we should walk back along the animal path and mark trees and stake road boundaries so we can get busy. At least we can clear up to the creek. My crew will build a temporary bridge structure so we can continue the walk through to the build site. We should be able to have it done by Monday, next week."

"I'm gonna' get the drone airborne so we can get a good look at things when we get back to the road," Bob said.

"Great idea. Let's go," Ethan said as they got busy walking, tagging trees and staking road boundaries all the way back to the main road.

"This is a beautiful spot those folks bought. It's way off the main road so no noise or traffic and the road they're on is paved with utilities. They gonna' need the utilities, Ethan?" Bob asked.

"Now, Bob, that's a great question. We're definitely gonna' install Laine and Mo's solar panels on the house and they just told us they want a barn, too. So, panels on the barn as well. Finn's working on the geothermal aspect of things. He thinks, because the stream is so strong and full even in the summer, that there must be a natural feed close by. He's hoping there's a geothermal feed nearby as well. He's working with the geologists and volcanologist from Appalachia State University to figure things out," Ethan explained.

"Here goes the drone. Let's watch," Bob said as he set the laptop on top of his truck so they all could see the pictures sent back from the drone.

Bob had the drone look over the path and creek, then up to the building site. The drive way would be winding for sure. There was a swampy part just to the left after you cross the creek so the driveway would have to angle to the right a ways to stay clear of the wetland.

"This is so cool," Ethan said. "We use drones, too, so our clients can get a good look at their property from the air. Folks tend to change their plans once they see how things are from the air."

"We use 'em, too," Karl added. "Especially when we can't get to a place we need to just like this site. Bob, this is great. You just saved me a half-day's work. Can ya' send me the link so my crew can work from these pictures?"

"Be glad to, Karl," Bob replied. "Just sent them to you. Have fun!"

"Ya' know, with all this digital technology, our work has been cut back when it comes to planning the excavations and road building. I'd say it's cut time down by about three to four weeks anyway," Karl said.

"I agree. It's made things easier for all of us and that means better cost control and all," Ethan said.

"It sure has," Mike said. "It really makes a difference when we can get a bird's eye view as we build." Mike was one of Bob's assistants.

As they continued to look at the drone footage, a rumble went through the place.

"Did ya' feel that?" Karl asked.

"Sure did," they others answered.

"What the hell was that?" Mike asked out loud.

Another rumble was felt and this one was stronger.

"Is this an earthquake?" Bob asked as they all grabbed onto something to steady themselves.

"Hell if I know," Karl replied.

As they watched the area across the road from where they were parked, they felt a stronger shaking and saw a few trees fall down.

"Oh no," Bob said as they watched a part of the hillside collapse.

"It's a landslide and it looks like its headed right at us. Get out of the way," Ethan yelled as they jumped into their trucks and drove to safety. They stopped and got out of their trucks just in time to watch the hillside across from the property collapse and fall into the road. It blocked the entire road and even flowed a bit onto the build property.

"What the hell was that all about?" Karl hollered.

"Holy shit!" Bob said.

"I've never seen a landslide in person," Mike added.

"This just isn't right," Ethan thought out loud.

Bob was talking to the highway patrol guys. Karl called his office and Ethan texted Ian and Finn and Emily about the landslide.

Mike just stood there in shock.

"Hey, Mike. You okay?" Ethan asked as he gave Mike a shake.

"Oh, ah, yeah. I think so. This is just so huge. All that land in the road. And, we were in its path," Mike replied.

"I was just thinkin' the same thing," Bob said. "The forest service and sheriff's patrol are on their way. They're gonna' set up detour signs and get some heavy equipment in here to start clearing the rubble. The forest guys said they have to look at the hill area to make sure nothing more will collapse when they clean up. It's gonna' take a few days. They said it's really strange for a landslide to occur out here. There haven't been any heavy, prolonged rain events to loosen the ground. He got the geologists at the university on it right away. He said they should have a report in a few hours. Jesus!"

"So, I guess we can't start until next week sometime," Karl said. "I'll keep y'all updated. We might have to set the opening for the driveway at a different place. It all depends on the results of the geologists and the road crew. I let them know about the property here and they promised to remove the rubble instead of just pushing it onto the property. I also told them I would stake the property lines all along the road. Care to help?"

They all took stakes and flags and had the property identified in no time as far as they could.

"I'll go around to the other side on my way back to the shop and place the rest of the stakes," Karl offered.

"Thanks, Karl. Here comes the forest service now. Let' see what they have to say," Mike said pointing to a truck coming their way.

The green truck was followed by two sheriff's cars and then a truck towing a trailer with a front-end loader on it.

"You guys don't waste any time," Bob said greeting the forest service crew.

"Wow! Would ya' look at that?" Lyle said. "I haven't seen a landslide like that all the time I've been here and that's over ten years."

"It sure was a surprise," Mike said.

"Did ya' hear any blasting or such before it happened?" one of the sheriff's deputies asked.

"Nope. Just a few rumbles like heavy trucks passin' by," Ethan said.

"Then, whoosh. The hillside began to slide down. We got our trucks out of the way just in time," Bob added.

"Well, the geologists are comin' out in a bit to look at things. Hope they can shed some light on this," Lyle said.

"We'd better get out of your way. If ya' need any of us, ya' know where we are," Karl said.

"Thanks guys," the sheriff's deputies said at the same time.

Ethan and everyone left the scene to the officials. Ethan and Mike drove around to the approach on the other side of the landslide and set the property stakes.

"This just seems so eerie," Mike said.

"I hear ya', Mike. No warning except a couple of rumbles. It's like someone was trying to stop this build," Ethan said.

"Oh, I agree. I worked out on the California coast for a while. Remember? And, when there's a landslide, warnings go out ahead of time so people can get out of the way. And, there's usually a lot of rain for days before they do happen. I've never seen a landslide just happen like this before."

"I remember you tellin' us about them. It sure is weird. I think those geologists will have an answer before long whatever it is," Ethan said as they left. Ethan drove back to the shop. He could hardly wait to talk to Emily about this.

Emily was the only one in The Creek who knew about the landslide. So far. Word would get around quick enough.

As the afternoon wore on, clouds began to gather. It looked like a good old-fashioned thunderstorm was building.

Folks got their kids, animals and things in place before it started. The wind began to pick up and then the first flash of lighting was seen.

"Looks like that thunder boomer finally made it here," Ted said as he looked out the window.

And then the rain came. A few big drops at first, then the skies opened. The lightning flashed and the thunder boomed for about a half hour. The wind got a bit strong as well. Then, just as it had started, it ended. Everything was freshly washed and the sun came through the last bit of the rain creating a double rainbow bright as day.

Folks ran outside to see it taking pictures and texting each other. It sure was a beautiful site.

"Well, would ya' look at that?" Ian said as everyone in the shop was outside looking at the rainbow.

"And, after that landslide and all, this is sure a great way to end the afternoon," Ethan said.

"Landslide? What landslide?" Katelyn asked. She had gotten to the shop just as the rain started.

Ethan looked at them all then explained about the landslide. When he was finished, they all just kept looking at him.

"Well, now, that's a fine how-do-ya' do," Ian said. "Anyone get hurt?"

"Nope. We heard a couple low rumbles and Bob just happened to look at the hill across the road from the property we were marking and he saw the hill begin to give way. We all got into our trucks and drove a ways down the road. When we got out, the hill just disappeared into a massive wave and slid across the road. It went onto the property just a little. No real damage there."

"Then what?" Ian asked.

"Then we got on the line with the forestry service and the sheriff's department and they sent folks and equipment to begin the clean-up. They're taking care of the road closing and all and getting the word to the media. The forestry folks are gonna' keep in touch with Bob and Karl and let them know when we can get in there to begin clearing for the road and all."

"A landslide?" Katelyn asked. "Y'all know if there's ever been one like that around here before?"

"Can't say as I've ever heard of one," Finn said. "With all the research I've been doin' for the energy builds, ya' think there would be mention of one. But, no. Nothin'."

"Me, either," Ian said.

"I'm think I gotta' say it then. Seems like somethin' evil is tryin' to bother us," Katelyn said.

"Yeah, that's just what I was thinkin', too. I'll talk to Emily and see what she thinks. But I think the thunderstorm was just a thunderstorm. Nothin' evil there,"

"Me, too," Ian added. "It was a regular mountain storm for sure."

"Well, we all got things to do to finish the day. Let's get to them," Ethan suggested as he went into his office and the others got busy.

It was after supper when Ethan and Emily talked about the landslide. Emily got right on the phone and had a long talk with Miss Cora.

"Well, Miss Cora thinks it's the Dark, too. She says she's been feeling a bit uneasy for a while now and isn't surprised," Emily told Ethan as they were rounding up the chickens and getting the farm set for the night.

"Here we go again." Ethan sighed.

"Yeah, here we go again," Emily agreed as she brushed his arm as she walked into the stables.

Miss Cora was thinkin' about all that Emily had told her when Kendra picked her up for Katelyn's nightly sessions.

As they walked into Katelyn's house, they were talking about the landslide.

"So weird. So glad no one was hurt," Katelyn said as they sat down at the kitchen table.

"Seems to me," Miss Cora began, "That The Dark is playin' around. Doin' whatever it likes to scare folks. I think it would be right to say things are gonna' get crazy around here again before long."

"I agree," Kendra said as she gathered the things they would need tonight. "Ready Katelyn? Lots to learn tonight as promised."

Katelyn smiled at the both of them. "Yes, I am. Bring it on."

During the next couple of hours, Katelyn learned ways to block The Dark, keep folks safe, call upon The White Light Paladins. She even met a few of those Paladins right there in her kitchen. They told her that Finn was one of them and she could call him by name anytime she felt threatened by The Dark for whatever reason. She thanked them and kept going.

As the evening wore on into night, Miss Cora called an end to the session.

"Katelyn, you've learned a lot tonight," Miss Cora said.

"I gotta' say I'm not surprised about Finn. There's always been somethin' special about him. So glad he's on our side."

"And, that he's gorgeous and sweet on you, doesn't hurt, either" Kendra said teasing Katelyn.

"So true, Kendra. So true," Katelyn replied blushing a bit.

"Kendra's right. He's sweet on you for sure. What are ya' blushin' for? Bein' in love is a splendid thing. I can remember a few times I was in love myself. It was glorious."

"Okay. Yes, we are in love and it's a blast," Katelyn said laughing.

"Well, with those memories floatin' around in my head, it's time Kendra took me home. Sleep well Katelyn. We love ya' for doin' all this."

Katelyn gave Miss Cora a kiss on the cheek and a hug as she said, "I love ya' both, too. And, I'm honored to be a part of keepin' The Magic safe."

Katelyn cleaned up and was getting ready for bed when she heard her name called. She looked around and saw Jay standin' in the living room.

"Well, look who's here," Katelyn said when she saw him.

"So, ya' found out about Finn tonight. That's awesome. By the way, I'm for real. Human. And, I'd like a hug from you," Jay said as he walked over to her.

"Really? Oh, my God! How awesome!" Katelyn exclaimed as they hugged each other.

"So, I do believe this is how Finn got through your death and all, isn't it?"

"Yes, it is, Katelyn. I was with him the whole time and was teachin' him about bein' a White Light Paladin. It was so horrible with me bein' dead for the both of us and our folks. When the Divine allowed me to be 'real' it was such a great thing. It helped Finn go on with livin'. Our folks have seen me 'real' a few times and that's been, well, the best thing ever."

"I'll say it is. When I saw you in the other Crab Apple Creek, I thought I was goin' crazy. Now that I know about all that other dimension stuff, I get it. So, why are you 'real' for me right now? Not that I'm complainin' or anything."

"I have a question before I explain this. Got any pie?" Jay said walking into the kitchen and going straight to the counter for the pie plate sitting there.

"Wondered why my mom brough this blackberry pie over today. Now I know another reason. I love blackberry pie and so do you. I'll get the ice cream," Katelyn said gathering things and dishing out the pie. She put both pieces in the microwave for a few seconds then added a healthy scoop of ice cream.

Just as she was setting the plates on the table, Finn walked through the door, saw Jay, and gave a holler grabbing him.

"Damn! This is such a surprise," Finn said. "Hey, why are you at Katelyn's? Don't even think you can take my girl from me."

"She's all yours. Not that I wouldn't be interested. She is a cutie! I came for the pie. Get your own,' Jay said as Finn tried to take his away from him.

"Take this one. I'll get another piece," Katelyn said laughing at the two of them.

Moans and groans were heard from the boys as they bit into the pie and ice cream.

"Oh, Katelyn, tell your momma this is an amazin' pie," Jay said. "Oh, tell her Finn said so."

"Right. I got that," Katelyn said as she sat down and bit into her piece.

"Oh, my momma sure does know how to fashion a pie," Katelyn said as she took another bite.

They enjoyed the pie for some time before Jay got to the point of his visit.

"Hey, Finn, so glad ya' got my quick message to come over here," Jay said.

"I am, too. This pie is heavenly," Finn replied.

"Wise ass. Always the wise ass," Jay said punching Finn in the shoulder.

"Oh, so that's how this is gonna' go," Finn said punching him back.

"Damn! You've been buildin' up your muscles," Jay said pretending to rub his sore arm.

"Yeah, right you whimp," Finn said laughing. "Yes, I got your message and am ready to show Katelyn what we look like as White Light Paladins. You ready?"

"Yes. Now Katelyn, just breathe and try to stay calm. We're ready," Jay called out to no one or so it seemed if you didn't know about The Magic.

A bright light began to shine in the room and a flash of silver shown. As Katelyn watched, the boys were transformed from regular guys into warriors all in white with silver swords and knifes at their waists. Their hair was silver, too. And, they glowed.

"Holy shit! Oh, sorry, ah, cow!" Katelyn said in amazement. "If I wasn't turned on with you before, Finn, this surely would do the job."

"Thanks, Ma'am," Finn said bowing a little.

"So, I guess all those super hero comics and sci-fi guys are for real. And, girls, too." Katelyn said.

"Well, let's just say, the ones who created all that stuff are highly gifted and connected with The Other Side in many different ways. That's a given," Finn explained.

"Katelyn, we were told to show you how we look when we're protecting The Magic, or, fighting the bad guys, so you'd know who we were. Sometimes The Dark tries to take the shape of the White Light fighters so they won't kill them. Thing is, The Dark cannot take the shape of those of us that walk in the Light. Be aware of this," Jay explained to Katelyn.

"This is so cool," Katelyn said walking over to the guys touching their hair and clothes and all. "Really cool. I don't feel so alone now like I did when I was tryin' to get to the cave. This does make a lot of difference. Thanks to everybody for takin' care of me."

"We are honored as well, to be allowed to take care of you. It is what we were born to do. It's our way to protect those that protect The Magic here in The Creek," Finn said.

"In every dimension?" Katelyn asked.

"No. Good question. Every dimension has its own story. You saw that I was alive in the other Crab Apple Creek. I'm not a White Lighter in that dimension and neither is Finn. That's just the way things evolved," Jay explained.

"Okay, 'cause if I end up in other dimensions, I'll be better prepared to know some of what's goin' on I think," Katelyn said.

"Miss Cora and Kendra are teaching you a lot of stuff. Don't worry that you won't remember it all. You'll have the information just when you need it if you let The White Light work with you."

"Oh, I will. I most certainly will," Katelyn said with conviction.

"Well, you ready to change back, bro?" Finn asked.

"Yup. Here we go," Jay said as the light came back into the room and returned them to their usual selves.

"That is the coolest thing," Katelyn said looking at and touching the guys again. "Really cool!"

They tousled her hair and teased her a bit, "Now, Katie girl," Jay said, "We're thrilled ya' like us in our fightin' gear. It's great to have a groupie."

"So glad ya' like my outfit. Maybe ya' can show me how much later?" Finn whispered in her ear.

"Behave yourself, Finn. You're makin' Katelyn blush," Jay said which made Katelyn blush even more.

"Stop it, you two. Now, behave your selves for a minute," Katelyn said laughing and sitting back down.

The all sat down and they talked for a while longer.

Jay stood up and grabbed his brother in a big hug. "Time for me to go back to my ghostly self."

Katelyn joined in the hug. "This has been so cool. Hope you get to do it again soon. It gives a whole new meaning to crossing over. Thanks for the gift of Jay here in the flesh. It's been incredible. And I like the super hero White Light Paladins for sure."

Jay took a step back, winked at Katelyn, smiled at Finn, pointed to the pie and slowly morphed back into a ghost.

They waved at him one more time as he vanished into thin air.

"Now, that was super amazin'," Katelyn said as Finn gathered her into his arms.

"Yes, it was. And I thank the Divine for the gift of my brother here tonight. Sure was a great surprise."

"I didn't even know you could do that. It really does make leaving the body, dying, easier to accept."

"It surely does. Now how about a little more of that pie? It is an amazin' thing for sure, too." Finn suggested.

"Okay by me," Katelyn said as they ate a bit more.

"Stay for a bit," Katelyn said quietly as Finn began to get ready to leave.

Finn turned off the kitchen light, locked the doors and followed Katelyn into the bedroom.

"I sure do love my super hero. Got anything super fantastic to show me?" Katelyn said as she dropped her clothes one piece at a time.

"I'd be more than happy to accommodate your request," Finn replied as he undressed.

They fell onto the bed and spent the next while enjoying Finn's super powers that were matched by Katelyn's move for move. And, yes, the angels wept for joy at their love making.

The rest of the week was very busy. The geologists from the university could not tell what had caused the land to slip. They called in the United States Geological Survey, the USGS, in Charlotte to come have a look. They were quite interested and had a crew there the next day.

The forest service and the county road crews had to wait for the USGS to figure out if moving the earth on the road would cause any more landslides. It was Friday by the time the USGS had come up with two things. First, they couldn't figure out why the landslide had taken place. Nothing in the geology of that part of the side of the mountain had any chance of a landslide forming. There hadn't been torrential, long-term rain activity. There weren't any active fault lines anywhere near the area. Although there were some geothermal springs in the area, none of them were in the immediate vicinity of the landslide. The geologists from the university and the USGS couldn't figure out why it had happened. They were definitely gonna' stay on top of it. They ran some scenarios concerned with the moving of the debris and calculated that little to no more earth would be released. They suggested that the debris, especially the larger tree trunks and rocks, be pushed back into the trench at the base of the landslide to act like a barrier kind of thing. The forestry service was going to salvage as much of the timber from the downed trees as possible to give to the local sawmill owners. The road crews worked all weekend to move as much debris as possible.

The forestry service kept Karl and Bob updated on their progress. It looked like Karl might be able to get back on track around Tuesday or Wednesday of the next week. He told Ethan and Ethan informed the landowners of the time change. He also told them that the USGS did not expect another landslide for any reason and their land would be safe and sound.

Miss Cora and Kendra kept Katelyn busy learning new things.

Sami and Jordan went over to the Redstone's on Wednesday evening for a walk through the barn and tunnels and rooms that had been created for the runaway slaves. The barn farthest from the house is where the tunnels were first dug. The Redstone kin dug the tunnel a ways down before it headed north-northwest. They made the first two rooms just a couple of yards after the turn. They made a second tunnel to the barn floor directly from the rooms for safety and a possible fast way to get to the rooms just in case anyone was being chased.

Seth and Clara met Sami and Jordan when they arrived.

"We wanted ya' to see somethin'," Seth said as Clara set three large old record books in front of them.

"Please use these gloves to protect the pages. They are over a hundred and fifty years old and fragile. We keep them in a special safe that is air controlled."

Clara gave them each a pair of cotton gloves.

"This here is the oldest one and I've set page markers for the oldest names and all," Clara said.

"Clara is the family historian here. She has a degree in library science and genealogy. So, we keep her busy takin' care of all this stuff."

"I love taking care of these things and all the history of the family from back when they first settled here," Clara said.

Sami and Jordan were listening as they looked at the pages with the names and dates of when the first runaways came to the farm. The name of the slave owner, the town or county and the state where they had lived was listed as well. And, the name of the plantation, if that's where they had run from, was here, too.

"This is incredible!" Jordan said as he kept reading the entries. "So much detail. I'll bet you could connect these folks with their living kin."

"Yes, we probably could. But we don't want to bring attention to this place and The Creek. We were thinkin' of findin' a way to get this information to the Underground Railroad Historical Society so they could make the connections. We just can't seem to think of how to do that without giving our secret away."

"I have an idea," Sami said all of a sudden. "Clara, have you created a spreadsheet or chart or somethin' on the computer with all this information?"

"Why, yes, I have. I just completed it a few weeks ago. I'm goin' over the details right now to make sure I didn't leave anything out."

"Now, I'm just brainstormin here, but, what if you printed it out and mailed it to the society? That wouldn't leave a trail especially if you mailed it from a different state or somethin'."

"Yeah, and you could send them a letter with it informing them that you don't want to be identified for safety reasons, or somethin' like that," Jordan added.

"Now, that's some good ideas. We'll think on that a bit and let ya' know. We may just come up with somethin' to connect folks with their ancestors and the story of where they came from." Clara said.

"I like that idea," Seth said.

"The story of these people makes me sad and happy. Sad that they suffered like that and happy that they found the inner strength to run away," Jordan said.

"I know. Me, too," Seth said. "Well, let's get out to the barn and take a look at the tunnels and rooms and all. You comin' with us, Clara?"

"No, not this time, Seth. I'm feelin' that I should stay here. I'm gonna' put these away safe and sound. I've got my evenin' chores to do. I'll see you two when Seth brings ya' back here."

"Thanks, Clara, for keeping the history and showin' us these records. We are much obliged," Sami said.

They followed Seth out to the far barn. He closed the doors after they got inside. This was a special barn. It was weather tight and had blackout curtains across the windows.

"Before we go down, I just want ya' to know I sometimes hear voices and see wavy things in the air. Don't be alarmed. I've never felt scared," Seth told them as he handed out LED flashlights and helmets with lights on them. "We need to be safe here."

"We agree. Thanks for the equipment," Sami said.

"I put a light at the opening pointing down so we can see the ladder and the floor. I'll go first to make sure everything is in good shape. My kin really knew how to build a tunnel," Seth said as he opened the hidden door in the barn floor.

"I didn't even see that door there. It blends in with the floor like nothin' was different," Jordan said.

Seth went down first, then Sami and, finally, Jordan. What they saw made them gasp. The tunnel was made perfectly as if it had been made that day. It was a splendid work of art. No wonder it had never collapsed or rotted. The air was dry and relatively cool. There was plenty of room for a body to walk upright even for a man as tall as seven feet.

"We added lights along the tunnels and into the rooms. Easier and all. Follow me. I'll take ya' to the first room," Seth said as he set out down the tunnel.

They walked a short distance and Seth stopped at an opening. "This here is the first place the runaways came to. They were given a place to bath and change into clothes that looked more like farmers. The next room is where

326

they ate and slept. My folks cooked for them and made sure they had the foods they liked and were used to. Some of the runaways took to cooking with my kin," Seth said as they walked down the tunnel to the second room.

"This room is really three rooms. A common room then two rooms for sleepin'. There are beds for about six people in each room. The record books show us that no more than ten people were here at any one time on account of keeping the numbers low for easier movin' from place to place."

"Seth, this is so surreal. It feels like people are here right now," Sami said looking around.

"I'm just gonna' take a look in each room," Jordan said as he walked around.

They stayed and talked in these rooms for quite some time.

"I can't even imagine how these folks felt. It's just so unbelievable that we could do this to each other," Jordan kept saying.

"I know, Jordan," Seth said placing a hand on Jordan's shoulder.

"Look," Sami said pointing to a shadowy area in the common room.

"Yup. That's what I see sometimes. I think it's a ghost of someone who came through here," Seth said pointing to the shadowy air that was beginning to take shape.

As they watched, the air morphed into a man. It nodded at Seth, then, morphed again, into a full human ghost. You could see the wrinkles on his face. As they were looking at the man ghost, a few more formed in front of them.

And, if this weren't amazing in itself, the older man became a physical person.

"Now, don't get all scared. We don't mean no harm. We've been tryin to find a way to thank you and your kin, Seth, for takin' care of us all and helpin' us get to freedom. These folks here are my family. My wife and six children. You'll find my name in the book Clara has. I'm Will Banks. I was given my owner's last name when I was sold to him as a child."

"Holy Hanna!" Seth said looking at Will and his family.

"I know Magic is all around but this beats all," Jordan said.

"Well, I'm honored to meet ya', Will. Truly honored," Sami said stepping forward and offering her hand. They shook hands and all offered their greetings to each other.

"I've been given my body for a short time to help y'all understand what happened to us and got us here and such. Let's all sit down and I'll tell my story so you can add it to the book. Oh, and to make things easier, the story is gonna' be put in writing in Clara's notes. She will be surprised, but when ya' tell her about this, she'll understand."

They all sat at the table and Will began his story.

"I was stolen from my village in Africa on the Gambia river and taken aboard a slave ship when I was six years old. There were hundreds of us and lots of folks died on the passage over. We landed at Charleston, South Carolina where I was immediately sold. I was taken to a plantation in Alabama and that's where I grew up and found my wife, Beth. We were married secretly because slaves weren't supposed to marry. The ceremony was performed in my tribal tradition and that's what meant the most to all of us. I was eighteen and Beth was sixteen when we married. I arrived here in 1830 and we got married in 1842.

"The one thing we knew we were gonna' do was escape. The men in our group had been watching and tracking the movements of the plantation owner and his foremen for years. We knew there was gonna' be a special week of celebration for the plantation and the foreman that was in charge of us slaves, there were about sixty of us, was told to take us to the farthest end of the plantation and keep us there for about a week. We weren't to work the fields or go anywhere near the main house and buildings because the owner didn't want any of us to be seen. That was the best thing we had heard in a long time. We didn't have anything to stay in. We just put up some material between the trees for tents and that's where we stayed. The Foreman came once a day with food. There was a stream nearby for water. We were treated horribly."

Sami was crying and Jordan was noticeably moved. Seth just kept clearing his throat.

"Beth wants me to tell you all that you shouldn't be sad for us. You gave us back our freedom and dignity and that meant the world to us. You validated our humanity."

"Well, my folks always taught us that we should respect all mankind. And, that's just what they were doin'. Tryin' to show love and respect for you all," Seth stated.

"And, you all did," Will replied. "Well, is was in the middle of the celebration that we decided to leave. It was October 12, 1848. I'll never forget that date. All of us had made the right connections and the oldest would leave first. They had been acting sickly for about a week to get ready to leave. There were about twelve of them. They left on the Wednesday right after sundown. We dug twelve graves on the edge of the woods so the foreman wouldn't get suspicious. We buried animal carcasses so the graves would stink. That was a great idea from one of the womenfolk. She was a smart one, that Sara," Will said smiling.

"Well, when the foreman came, we were cryin' and sad. We told him about the twelve folks that had died and showed him the graves with the crosses on them. The plantation owner demanded we become Christian. We did, but it was all fake. So, the crosses were a great touch. He offered his condolences then told us he wouldn't be back until Sunday and he was leavin' food for the next three days. We thanked him and he left. This was great news. It meant that the rest of us could leave that night and no one would miss us for two days and three nights. We would be able to make good progress before word got out that we had run away.

"It was a silent celebration for us all. We had endured years of beatings and most of the women had been raped. Some gave birth to the children of the plantation owner and his men. Some lost the child before it was born. Others died in childbirth. It was a silent celebration as we prepared to run for our freedom.

"It was a new moon and a bit cloudy that night. As soon as night was upon us, our guides showed up. We told them about the foreman not returnin' until Sunday mornin' and they were happy with this news. They said we should be able to get to North Carolina before we were missed. We left that corner of northeast Alabama for the last time that night.

"We walked for about an hour then came upon some wagons. We were split up into four groups. My wife and six children, we had two sets of twins, were in a group with two other young people. The young folks helped with the children and they passed through here as well. We were the only ones from that place that came here.

"Well, we were set in the wagons and were covered with tarps and old furniture and such to make it look like the folks drivin' the wagon were movin' along. We stopped a few times to eat and such, but we kept goin'. It was fall and the air was a bit cool so the tarps kept us warm. We saw the sun come up, set and come up again. Just as it was setting on Saturday night, we stopped.

"We were told we had reached our first safe house. It was in the middle of nowhere set back from a field full of corn ready to be harvested. We were taken to the barn and settled for the night. The farmer and his family told us that we'd be leavin' before dawn to be taken to the next safe place. They fed us hot food and gave us blankets and told us we could bed down on the straw in the loft. We fell right to sleep and it was about an hour before dawn when we were woken up.

"It seems a patrol of bounty hunters was about an hour away and the farmer said we needed to leave immediately. They gave us some food and water to eat later and told us to follow the path at the back of the property. It was marked by wooden planks with a cross on them and the words Jesus is Lord. It would be about a ten-mile hike through the forest until we came to the next place where folks would be waiting with wagons once again.

"It was a long walk as the little ones got tired and had to be carried. We stopped a couple of time to eat and rest. We had to go back a little way a few times because we saw some men on the trail ahead. We had a scout go ahead to look for any trouble. It wasn't until that Sunday night that the scout saw the wagons ahead. They had the sign of the cross and words painted on the sides. That is exactly what the farmer told us to look for. He said the man's name was Benjamin and he would be singing a song about Benjamin.

"That's exactly what we heard and saw when we were about to clear the woods. He couldn't see us yet. Good thing. Turns out he was a fake. There were others there with rifles just waiting for runaways. We happen to hear one of them say they figured no runaways were comin' and the information they had been given by their spy was false. They waited another two hours then finally left. We retreated way back down the trail and our scout stayed where he could hear and see them. The little one's fell sound asleep and so did some of the rest of us.

"The plantation owner now knew we had all runaway. It would take a day or two for word to travel north to the bounty hunters that tracked slaves. We had, maybe, one more day before they would be looking for us.

"The scout came back and said everyone had left and he had waited a third hour to make sure they weren't waiting down the road. He had walked a far stretch in both directions to make sure they were gone. Just as he was about to come back down the trail, another wagon came to a stop and the man started to sing an old song the scout knew. It was in his native language and no one would know that song from the Americas. He called out to the man in his native language and the man turned and looked at him. It was his brother. They had been separated when they landed in Charleston and had not seen each other for years.

"They were joyful to see each other. They were cryin' and huggin' and talkin' all at once. The older brother with the wagon pushed apart from his brother and told him to get the folks really quickly 'cause the bounty hunters were on the road that night.

"The scout came back to us and we got into that wagon in no time. We traveled on that road for only a few minutes then turned onto a track of sorts. It was rutted and a mess and a few times we had to get out and free the wagon from a few deep ruts. It was just beginin' to come onto sunrise when we got to the second safe house. We got down and were led into another barn. We settled in the loft again. We ate and slept most of the day. This farm was so far off the main road that not one soul came along all the day long.

"Nightfall came and we gathered again. It was Monday night and we knew they would be lookin' for us by mornin'. This time we were covered again and the wagon kept to the main road for a long while. The driver kept us informed about where we were. He said he was headin' to a safe house in the Blue Ridge that was off the regular route. It was used once in a while and the folks there were wonderful.

"We arrived here a couple of hours after sunrise on that Tuesday. As we got out of the wagon, we were greeted by your kin with hot food and such.

We were outside and enjoyed the beautiful scenery. The trees had started to turn colors and the sight was a wonder to behold.

"Your kin assured us that we were safe and could stay outside for quite a spell. They gave us clean clothes and showed us where we could bath in hot water. We all took turns and by late day we were dressed in fresh clothes and had plenty of food to eat. The little ones had a great time playin' outside with the barn cats and all.

"Your kin told us we would be stayin' here for a couple of weeks as new plans were bein' made for us to get to Canada on as straight a trek as possible. They showed us the tunnels and rooms and we settled in. We all pitched in with the harvest and chores. The women took to cookin' and sharin' recipes and stories and the little ones were taught their letters and numbers and all. Most of us had learned to read in secret and your kin taught us so much more that we were pretty good at it when we finally did move on.

"There was only one thing that seemed strange while we were here. Now, none of us had ever experienced an earthquake in our lives. But the night before we were supposed to move on, an earthquake struck. It was a rather strong one and it hit at sundown. We were all sittin' outside after supper just watchin' the land and the sky as the sun dipped below the trees. One of your kin had a fiddle and was playin' it some. Some of us took to dancin' with your kin and the kids were havin a grand time. All of a sudden, the earth trembled a bit. We all stopped and looked around and stood stock still.

"Your name's sake Seth said he had felt a little somethin' a few days before we came but didn't think much about it. This one was a lot stronger he was just saying when the big quake struck. We were thrown to the grown and heard stuff crashin down in the house. We watched as a few trees were toppled at the far edge of the field. And, then, right before our eyes, the earth opened up not fifty yards from us in a long trench. Must have been about twenty-five yards long. We watched as it opened up. Then the quake stopped. We all sat still for a bit not sure what to do. When we did finally get up, the women and kids went into the house to look at the damage and the men folk went over to the trench. It wasn't more than twenty feet deep. A few trees had fallen in and there were some big boulders showin' on the bottom. But the strangest thing about that trench was the crystals lyin' all over it. Some were small and some were quite big. The largest one looked to be the size of a wagon. They were every color of the rainbow. We hollered for the others to come over and when they saw them, they were as amazed as the rest of us.

"We just stood there looking into that trench until the sun finally set below the horizon and the light went away. We walked back to the barn and house talkin' and wonderin' why that quake had happened. Most of us prayed on it in our own fashion and fell sound asleep.

"Next mornin,' the trench was closed, but a whole mess of crystals were on the ground where the trench had been. We talked about taking a crystal for each of us and thought we'd better pray on it for a minute. When we opened our eyes, these crystals were glowing like crazy and they hadn't been before. So, we took that as a sign and each one of us took a crystal and we handed them down to our own through the years. If ya' find our families these days, I know those crystals will be with some of them."

"Wow! Crystals again," Jordan exclaimed.

"What do ya' mean by that, young man?" Will asked Jordan.

"Well, Will, y'all, I bought some land south of The Store and crystals have been showin' up since the day I decided to buy the land. My friend Katelyn, has a crystal from the meteorite sight in Alabama. It's called a shocked crystal. And, she's been given crystals from my field as well. Gifts from the earth, ya' might say."

"Well, Jordan, the crystals my kin gathered that day are in the house for y'all to see. Except this one," Seth said as he pointed to a shelf in the room that held a rather large crystal. It was the size of a baseball and was shining bright green.

"It's only glowed one other time when I was down here and I thought I saw a wavy kind of ghost thing then."

"You did. It was me. I was tryin' to get your attention but I was told by my Guides that it wasn't time to talk to you. Today it is. So, I'll finish my story.

"We got word the next day that the route to Canada was all set for us. We were leaving that night and should be in Canada in about ten days or so. We had a special picnic that day and by night fall the wagons to take us north had arrived. My family would be in one and the young couple would be in the other. They were taken by a different route but we would meet up again in Quebec in about two months. Goodbyes were said and tears fell as your kin sent us on our way. We did arrive in Canada about two weeks later. There was one incident with a couple of bounty hunters that tried to take us but the locals killed both of them. We were in New York near the Canadian border by then. Our guardians took us to a different safe house about a days' ride out of the way just to be sure no one would come lookin' for us when they found out the two bounty hunters were nowhere to be found. The locals cremated their bodies just to be sure no one could find a hint of them. Ya' don't want to mess with New York folks. They are firm in their beliefs and slavery is not somethin' they believe in.

"We settled outside of Quebec on some land given to us and we farmed and grew our family for the longest time. I do believe there are kin on that land today. They bought about fifty acres all told after we passed away. They had offers to sell but refused. Seems they cherish all that happened to us to get there and have vowed never to sell the land. Some of them are craftsmen wood carvers and they're work is known all over the world.

"I wanted to come back in the physical world to tell you thank you for all your kin did to keep us safe. We love y'all to this day and always will."

Seth cleared his throat and spoke first, "Will, Beth and y'all here today, I am honored to be able to hear your story. It sure answers a lot of questions. Did y'all keep the last name of Banks?"

"No, we created one of our own. Our last name is Northington for travelin' north to freedom.," Wille said.

"Great name," Sami said.

"It sure is," Jordan added. "It will make it easier to find your kin in Canada and tell them your story about getting here."

They heard a noise and saw Clara as she came into the room. As soon as she looked up and saw Will and all of them, she said, "I knew it. I knew somethin' was happenin' down here. Pages of new information are being keyed up on my computer and the crystals in the window sills are glowin' like all get out."

"Hi, Miss Clara. I'm Will Northington. My family came through here back in the late 1840's. We were tellin' our story and sayin' thanks to all your kin for helpin' us to freedom."

Clara replied with, "It's an honor to meet you all and amazin' to be able to see and hear ya'."

They all talked for a while more before Will said," Folks, it's time for me and my family to leave. Thanks for listenin' to our story and everything today. Sami and Jordan, thanks for bringin this shameful time to light. All slaves everywhere are grateful that you're tellin' our story and all."

"I am humbled and honored to be able to be a part of this revealin' history," Sami said bowing to Will.

"Same here, Will. I am never gonna' forget today. Thanks for the gift," Jordan said bowing his head a bit as well.

"Seth, any time ya' want, just call out and one of us will come along. I'm sure those crystals have stories of their own to tell," Will added.

"I sure will. Thanks for bein' here," Set said as they began to fade away.

They were gone a bit before anyone tried to talk.

"I, ah, think we need to finish walkin' the tunnels and then get upstairs for some drinks or food or somethin'," Seth offered.

Sami and Jordan stood up and the four of them finished walking the tunnels to the far side of The Meadow. Seth took them up the ladder and outside.

"Wow! I didn't realize the tunnels were that long. We must have walked about three miles anyway," Sami said.

"Well, we cut across a lot of land in a rather straight line. The Meadow isn't that far from the farm as the crow flies," Clara said.

"Right. Now, how do we get back to the farm?" Jordan asked looking all around.

"The golf cart's over here," Seth said as he walked a bit into the woods and drove the cart out to them.

"Good thinkin', Seth," Sami said as they all got in and drove back to the house.

They spent a while eating and drinking and talking about all that had happened in the underground room.

"It must be well past midnight," Jordan said looking at his phone. "No way! It's only nine o'clock. How can that be?"

"One word, Jordan," Sami said. "Magic"

Seth and Clara looked at them and they all laughed.

"I swear it seemed like hours that we were listenin' to Will's story. It sure is incredible. I'm glad The Divine keyed it up into your computer Clara. I think I would have missed some of the details if I was writin' it down," Jordan said.

"Me, too, on all counts," Clara agreed.

"Well, it may only be nine but I feel like I've been busy all night. Time to get goin'," Sami said.

"Thanks for everything, Seth, and Clara. This has been a very special night. It's gonna' take some time to process it all but it's been a great thing for sure. I'm so glad I was a part of it," Sami offered.

"Me, too. What Sami said," Jordan said. "Clara, once the computer is finished typing that story, I'd appreciate it if you could email it to me."

Before Clara could reply, Jordon's email notification buzzed and he saw the story there.

"Wow! I love how The Magic works around here. Thanks," Jordan said lookin upward with a wink.

"Okay then. I guess my work is done except for the dishes and they can wait for tomorrow," Clara said laughing.

Seth and Clara walked them out to their cars and waved them off.

As Seth and Clara walked back into the house, Seth mentioned, "Ya' know, Clara, and I know ya' know this, but I gotta' say it."

"Go ahead, honey," Clara said as she turned off lights on their way upstairs.

"The Africans weren't the only slaves that came through here. We had Native Americans, Italians, and other newly arrived Europeans that were held in bondage. So glad our ancestors helped them all."

"Yes, indeed, Seth, yes, indeed," Clara said as she closed her eyes and drifted off to sleep. Seth followed a minute later.

The Creek slept.

CHAPTER 28

The next day found Ethan over at the Kirkland's nursery. He was ordering his next group of trees. He and Ian planted a sugar maple, a dogwood, and a yellow birch on all their private home builds. It was a way of giving back to the Blue Ridge for them. Their clients loved the surprise as well.

Katelyn was scheduled to go to a couple of the home sites today with one being near the Redstone's farm. Sami had told her about the visit last night and Katelyn really wanted to go to The Meadow and look at the place where the tunnel came up into the edge of The Meadow.

She had to drop off her latest sketches to her brothers. This was her final stop. She found her mom in the house and they talked for a minute. She left the sketches on the kitchen table for her brothers. As she walked back outside, she felt the need to go to The Rise. She drove and parked near the tree line. She climbed to the top and felt an immense peace and calm.

As she looked out over the land, she recognized The Meadow. It looked so much smaller from up here as did most of The Creek. She looked at other landmarks but kept being drawn back to The Meadow. She focused in on it to see if she could make out where the tunnel exit was located. Nope. You couldn't see any differences in the land. As she climbed back down, she grabbed a handful of blackberries for a snack. They sure were delicious.

She was getting into her SUV when she decided to go over to The Meadow and have a look around. She followed Sami's directions and came to the spot where the outlet was supposed to be. She couldn't see any spot that looked like a door. She stood there for a bit then started to walk around. She spotted some crushed wild grass and followed it to where it ended just inside the woods. She moved the plants around a bit and then saw a faint outline of a square in the earth. So, this is where the tunnel came out. She wasn't gonna' bother the earth. It sure looked like it was protecting that tunnel exit.

She felt a pull to walk into The Meadow. She stood at the edge with the creek running to her right and The Meadow laid out before her. She looked for and found The Rise. It looked like it had always been there. She started to walk into The Meadow and thought she heard someone call out to her. She stopped and looked around but saw no one.

Katelyn decided to walk through the middle on her way to the other side. It was a nice walk. Just as she reached the southern edge, she thought she saw something in the air in front of her. It was a hot day and the air sometimes played tricks on you.

She turned and looked at The Meadow from this perspective. It looked pretty much the same. She decided not to cross the field again and, instead, walked over to the creek and followed it back to the footbridge. She looked around for a minute then crossed the footbridge to get to her SUV.

The air seemed to change as she set foot off the bridge. It looked a bit hazy and it wasn't moving at all. Maybe that was because she was in the shade and it was well onto suppertime. She got in her SUV and drove home.

As soon as she got out of her SUV, she knew something was different. The Store was busy as always but some of the folks were hollering at each other. As she turned to watch, a couple of strangers came through the door fighting about how much stuff cost. Their license plate put them from out west. Maybe things cost less in their hometown. They saw her watching them and stopped yelling, got into their car, and drove off down the Pine Ridge Road.

Katelyn took her things inside and walked over to The Store for take-out. She was tired and didn't even want to think about what to fix for supper.

"Hey, Michael," Katelyn said as she walked in.

"Hey, Katelyn. How was your day?" Michael replied.

"Busy. Looks like your day has been interesting," Katelyn said as she stopped to chat.

"It sure has. I always wonder about folks that complain about the cost of stuff. If they can't afford to go on vacation, maybe they should stay home. Makes sense to me."

"I hear ya'. What's Ted got cookin' back there?"

"Great stuff as always," Michael replied as Katelyn headed back to the dining room.

"Hey, Ted. Smells delicious in here," Katelyn said as she read the daily specials sign.

"Hey, Katie girl. What's new with you?" Ted replied as he put more plasticware in the dispensers.

"Just dropped off my brother's sketches for their homes. I think we've just about got it right."

"Really? They must be thrilled. It's been about a year since they started talkin' about buildin' their own homes. Too bad Ethan can't do the builds with all the problems he's had," Ted said as he went back into the kitchen.

Katelyn stared at the door. Ethan's got problems? Now this was like déjà vu all over again. Ethan and Ian did not have any major problems at all She should know. She worked for them.

Ted came back out still talking about Ethan. "He's such a great guy. It's been horrible how those last three builds collapsed on him. Well, not ON him. But, ya' know, collapsed. The owners sued and he sued the wood supplier for inferior product. The case has been movin' right along, but, in the meanwhile, his business has really slowed down. It's beginnin' to pick up again now that the truth about the materials is out and it wasn't his fault. But, still, it really is a sad thing. Good thing you've got your job. Solid and strong as ever. How's it feel to own your own design firm?"

"Well," Katelyn said trying to figure out what to say. "It really has been a wild ride but I love my work and anytime I can design something someone loves is a good thing."

What she said was all true. But she didn't own her own business. She needed to get her supper and get home to figure things out.

She placed her order and Ted had it for her just a bit later.

"Here ya go, Katelyn. Now, don't stay up too late workin' tonight Ya' need your rest," Ted said as Katelyn took the package he offered.

"Thanks, Ted. I promise to get a good night's rest," Katelyn said smiling at Ted.

'Here ya go, Michael," Katelyn said as she paid her bill. "See ya' later."

"Take care," Michael said as she left.

As soon as she got into her house, she sat down.

No! Oh no! Not again! She sat there shaking for a long while. She kept trying to focus her thoughts then realized she needed to eat. It had been hours since lunch and that handful of blackberries didn't really count.

She heated her supper and ate without even realizing it. She knew what had happened and she didn't want to believe it.

She'd gone through another portal. This time it was on the footbridge next to The Meadow. She knew it. She knew for certain. The air had changed as soon as she set foot off the bridge. She was in another Crab Apple Creek. Fuck!

At least she knew right away. Not like the last time when it took a few weeks to figure things out. One thing was for certain, this dimension was very different. It felt weird. Off somehow like it wasn't a regular Crab Apple Creek.

Katelyn sat for a few more minutes getting her thoughts together.

First, she decided, she needed to know about her business. She looked around for files, pictures or something. She logged onto the computer using her regular password. She found her client files and spent a couple of hours learning them and what she needed to do for the clients. She had three meetings the next day. All here in her kitchen/office. She cleaned house and got things ready for tomorrow. The first meeting was at nine-thirty. She'd grab muffins from The Store for that one. The other two were at one and three in the afternoon. Plenty of time to prep for them tomorrow after the morning meeting.

Now, time to sleep if that was even possible. She called on The White Light to help her sleep and didn't even remember falling asleep.

She woke up at six the next morning and got things going. The meetings went well and by the time the day was over, she knew a whole lot more about this dimension.

Katelyn had learned from her morning clients that Ethan and Ian's business was in a great deal of trouble. Seems one of the major lumber suppliers they used had intentionally given them sub-par, poor-grade, lumber. They weren't aware of it until three houses collapsed all in the same week a few months ago. A few of the workers were injured and one was still out with a broken leg. The client's immediately filed law suits against Sutherland Construction and half of the remaining clients canceled their contracts. Some had already had foundations laid.

Ethan and Ian's attorneys investigated the lumber company and discovered they had other law suits in place for poor-grade lumber. Further research showed they knew they were selling poor-grade lumber and charging for the first-rate stuff. Ethan's attorney's filed lawsuits on behalf of the company siting multiple complaints.

Katelyn was told some of this by her morning clients as they informed her that they had canceled their contract with Ethan when the collapses happened. After they learned from the Sutherland attorneys about the real problem, they had turned around and re-hired Ethan's company just yesterday. They had already been working with Katelyn on the design and wanted her to continue. Ethan told them he would revise the contract to show the removal of the design services fee and informed them he would be very happy to work with Katelyn on their home.

Katelyn was taking a break and looking out her front door just after they left when she saw Jordan in his delivery clothes. She drove right down to where his farm was in her Crab Apple Creek and found it was just an open field. Well, that explained that. She wondered if the cave was there. She would talk to Kendra and find out who owned the land and see if she could walk the field.

Katelyn had lunch and met with her other clients throughout the afternoon. She wondered if she and Finn were together in this dimension. Just then her cell rang.

"Hey, Ethan, how are ya today?" Katelyn said.

"Well, things are improving a bit. We got some of the clients back now that they know what really happened. And that's why I'm callin'."

"Yup. Thought so. I met with the Howard's today and they told me they hired you back. When do ya 'want to get together?"

"How about tomorrow around ten?"

"Good time for me. I don't have any client meetings tomorrow. Your place?"

"Yes, that would work best. I'm gonna' have Ian in the meeting so we can work out whatever details they want. I love your work so I don't think this is gonna' take much effort."

"Thanks for that. I appreciate it. Your place at ten tomorrow. So glad your business is getting back towards normal. Was that lumber used in any other builds?"

"Yes. Just one. We had started framing when the collapses happened and we stopped work on the framing job. When my attorneys found out about the bad lumber, we tore everything down and started over with lumber from a supplier in Boone. They were happy to supply us with all that we need going forward. For clients like yours, we are not increasing the costs for the lumber, but we are including it in the legal stuff. Bastards."

"Exactly. Sorry to hear about the guy with the broken leg though. That's really hard when you're out of work for months."

"We've got him covered. We're supplementing his worker's comp pay to make up the difference and other costs that come along. It's what needed to be done."

"Oh Ethan, that's wonderful of you guys. Well, until tomorrow," Katelyn said.

"Later," Ethan said as he hung up.

She ate supper than went over to Kendra's. She needed to find out what was happening around here and why she was here.

"Hey, Kendra," Katelyn said as she stepped up onto the front porch.

"Hey, Katelyn. Have a seat," Kendra said pointing to the rocker next to her. "Miss Cora will be here any minute."

"Ya' know why I'm here?" Katelyn said as Miss Cora drove into the driveway.

"Hey, Miss Cora," Katelyn and Kendra said as Miss Cora came up onto the porch.

"Katelyn. Kendra," Miss Cora replied looking at each of them.

"Yes, Katelyn, we know why you're here. We knew the minute you arrived, shall we say?" Kendra answered.

"Well, why am I here?" Katelyn asked.

"We aren't sure of the exact details, but we do know The Dark is getting ready to attack. It's been building for some time. "

"Is that why those folks at The Store last night were fighting? I can't recall a time I heard such hollerin'," Katelyn asked.

"Yes," Kendra answered. "Seems there's been a build-up of negative energy all around the Blue Ridge with folks fightin', houses collapsing, just a general discontent felt all around for the last few weeks. It's a rather subtle build-up of negative energy."

"I agree," Miss Cora said. "It seems that instead of causin' damage to things, The Dark has targeted people and their emotional state of mind. Hal was just talkin' about that a couple of days ago when he came over to repair a window frame."

"I've been feelin' it, too," Kendra said. "So has Emily. Oh, she and Ethan are together this time. Let me bring up up-to-date about things around here. Jordan doesn't own the farm. He never will. Jay is dead and his mom has not used her gifts since he died. She's mad at the Divine for not healin' him. Ted and Michael are about the same although there seems to be a bit of more than the usual tension between them. Matthews has not met Jenna because Jenna has not come back to The Creek. Matthews did buy the old farm and all and has built his home and such just without Jenna. There was an earthquake on his land and the creek there did change its course but there's no egg-shaped crystal on the banks."

"I did see Jordan deliverin' stuff across the road yesterday and drove right over to the farm and saw it wasn't built up or anything. So, I figured he hadn't bought it. I was gonna' ask you who owns it 'cause I want to walk the field and all."

"That shouldn't be a problem. The last owners gave it in conservation to The Creek. We all own it. Walk around all ya' want. Ya' lookin' for somethin special?" Miss Cora asked.

"Yes, and you both know what it is," Katelyn replied.

"It's there although now one's been in it for centuries. I do know you're supposed to go find it. The reason for all this will be known once you spend some time in it," Miss Cora explained.

"Oaky, Thanks for that. Now, what about Finn and me? Are we together?" Katelyn asked.

Miss Cora smiled. "Yes, Katelyn you most certainly are and have been since you got back home same time as your 'real' Crab Apple Creek. And, he still loves your chocolate chip cookies."

"Great! Well, at least I know how to act around him. Does he work for Ethan and Ian?"

"Not just yet although they have been talkin' about adding other energy sources for some of their new builds. One of the returning clients wants to be off the grid completely. Ethan and Ian have been tryin' to work that out. They mentioned it to Emily one day and she asked if they had talked with Finn since he has his advanced degrees in that kind of thing. They got ahold of Finn a couple of weeks ago and have been talkin' about the geothermal energy from the hot springs. Emily said she thought Ethan was about to ask Finn to come work with them any day now."

"That would be wonderful. He loves the whole energy thing. Have Laine and Mo created their special solar panels yet?" Katelyn asked.

"No. Not in this dimension although they are playing around with solar panels on their special greenhouse."

"Good to know. I don't want to talk about things that aren't here yet," Katelyn said. "And, what about the me from this dimension? Where did she go?"

"Well, that's a good question," Kendra said. "The Divine has transplanted our Katelyn, shall we say, into the Light while you're here. She's doin' just fine. She's reconnecting with lots of other energies she hasn't seen for a long while. The Divine will return her when you leave. And, she'll remember everything she's done while you're here and everything you did while you were here in her place."

"Well, that's an incredible thing. More Magic for sure. Good to know how it's all workin' out," Katelyn said. "Now, about those collapses. Do ya' think The Dark did it?" Katelyn asked.

"That is all The Dark's doin'," Kendra replied. Miss Cora nodded her head for Kendra to continue. "That was the first real physical thing we could identify that told us The Dark was beginnin' the attack here. It took everyone by surprise. Miss Cora, Emily, and I had no idea it was comin'. We sent protective energy to everyone as soon as we heard the noise from the first collapse. It was a very quiet night and the breeze sent the noise this way. It was awful."

"Okay. So, at least I know I'm not home. Just wonder why I'm here," Katelyn said.

"We know that if you're here, there's gonna' be an attack on The Creek and The Magic here. We've been puzzling over this for some time now," Miss Cora said.

"I think I'd better go find that cave tomorrow afternoon. I have a meeting at Ethan's with him and Ian at ten and some work to complete afterwards back here. I should be free around two o'clock. I'll let ya' know what I find out, if anything. Especially if I find the cave," Katelyn offered.

"Sounds good," Kendra said. "Now how about some sweet tea and we just sit a spell and enjoy the evenin'?"

Kendra brought our sweet tea and cookies and they watched the evening go along. Nothing out of the ordinary happened.

Miss Cora left just as evening was melting into night. Katelyn went on her way, too.

Most folks had no idea trouble was brewing in The Creek.

The Dark was planning its next strike as The Creek slept. The house collapses were child's play for The Dark. It so enjoyed destroying the physical world. And, it had managed to strike without anyone knowing it was coming. The next attack would be a bit more devastating.

The Dark decided to blow up two things. First, it would blow up the Pine Ridge Road just as it entered Pine Ridge. And, at the busiest time of the morning. That way, maximum damage and death would occur. And, no one would be able to get into and out of The Creek. The Dark planned this attack for the day Katelyn was gonna' go walk the field.

The Dark sent a bolt of energy to the middle of the Pine Ridge Road, just where it enters Pine Ridge, around eight o'clock that next morning. It was a busy time and vehicles and people were blasted into oblivion. The energy ripple flew out about a mile from the blast center. Buildings nearby were destroyed into piles of rubble. Most folks hit by the blast died instantly. And, more died in the surrounding areas as vehicles crashed into each other and buildings fell. The whole place looked like a war zone.

The blast was felt from Boone to The Creek and beyond. You could hear sirens and there were emergency reports on all the news stations. Folks gathered at The Store to find out what was happening. They gathered around the flat screens and were silent as the event unfolded. The sky began to show clouds of smoke coming from Pine Ridge.

Miss Cora knew the instant it happened that it was The Dark striking again. She went straight to The Store and was one of the first to arrive.

Emily was at Ethan's shop getting ready to go down the road to the Two Moon Stables to pick up some special feed for one of the horses. Jonah said the horse wasn't feeling right and knew the blend of herbs was just what they needed. Emily offered to pick them up as she needed to talk to Ethan about something for the barn.

The explosion shook the shop so hard that Ethan and Emily had to grab hold of the furniture to keep from falling over. Ian was in his office at his desk when it happened.

"Holy shit! What the hell was that?" Ethan yelled as they all tried to walk out of the shop and look around.

They managed to get outside and look all around the place but didn't see anything that had exploded or fallen down except a few big branches from a few of the trees around the place.

"Look!" Emily yelled as smoke began to fill the sky south of them. Ian's cell phone began to sound alarms he had set for emergency notifications in the area.

"Oh my God! Seems something blew up in the middle of the road just at the town line. This is bad. Really bad," Ian said as his phone continued to buzz. Ethan's had started to do the same thing.

"Ethan, here," he said as he answered a call. "Shit! Anyone hurt? No? Good. Stop working and get clear of the build until we know what caused that blast. I'm sending out a text to everyone right now. Stay clear of the build!"

Ethan sent a group text to all his employees telling them to stay clear of the build they were on until further notice. Get to a safe place and sit still. He would send further information as he received it.

Ian was in touch with his clients as well telling them he would send an update about their new builds as soon as he could safely travel to each one of them. He told them he thought most of the damage was in Pine Ridge at the moment according to his emergency notifications from the county emergency management folks. He asked of everyone to be patient and stay safe. The most important thing was that no one was injured and dead from the blast. Everything else could be taken care of.

Both Ethan and Ian's phones calmed down as soon as the texts were sent. They received okay texts from everyone.

Ethan had gotten a couple of chain saws and he and a couple of the crew went to work cutting up the big branches that had fallen and blocked the drive. Some were leaning against the buildings as well. No damage was done to the buildings. There was a huge branch that had landed on the top of the barn. Ian started to laugh when he saw it and Ethan and Emily looked up to where he was pointing. It looked like someone was doing a cartwheel and was in the upside-down position right on the top of the roof. They all took pictures before the crew got a couple of cherry pickers and worked at removing the branch without damaging anything.

"Well, out of the chaos a bit of humor," Emily said. "I'm sending this to everyone so they can take a moment and laugh as well."

"Me, too," Ethan and Ian said at the same time.

Funny and wise ass comments started to come in to them all and they laughed as well. They went into the shop to see if they could get anything on the web.

The local stations were down due to a massive power outage in the Pine Ridge area. Seems The Creek was affected as well as folks in parts of Boone and over the state line in Tennessee. The digital news was still on as they had their own power sources and such.

Pictures of the destruction started to flood people's phones as friends and family in the areas of Pine Ridge that had been damaged were taking them and sending them to everyone including the news media folks.

A state of emergency was put in place by the governor as emergency management people started to arrive on scene. The first thing they declared was that the Pine Ridge Road to The Creek from Pine Ridge was completely destroyed and blocked and probably wouldn't be reopened for weeks. Folks would have to go north of The Creek and then drive south to get to Boone and then back northwest to get to The Creek and Pine Ridge. Pine Ridge was put on emergency status and the citizens were directed to stay away from the blast area. American Red Cross support had arrived and was coordinating the names of the missing with the sheriff's department. Local healthcare offices canceled patient appointments and opened for emergency care. The hospital in Boone was put into emergency mode – trauma level 1. And, since most folks couldn't help with the whole thing, they began to coordinate food service for the crews and the folks that had lost their homes. The diner was the central meeting place as it was on the edge of the blast zone and folks could get to it without getting in the way of the officials.

Emily went over to get the herbs and head back home about a half hour after the blast happened. There were branches in the road but she managed to get around them. She informed Ethan and since his crew at the shop was waiting for the okay to travel to their work sites, they decided to clear the road.

Emily drove to her place and left the herbs with Jonah. He said she should get to The Store right away. There were a few small branches and such in the road but nothing big. As soon as she got there, she went straight to Miss Cora, Kendra, and Katelyn. They looked at each other and knew what had caused the blast without saying a word.

They held each other close for a minute then set down at the dining room table. Ted brough tea out for everyone.

"We got us a real bad problem here, folks," Miss Cora began. "This was no ordinary blast. My friend Connie says she was lookin' out her kitchen window when the blast struck. She lives the other side of Pine Ridge on the way to Boone so she's okay. She said the lightning or whatever it was, was so bright her eyes hurt and are still hurting her. She put her sunglasses on right away and that seems to be helpin' a lot. She said the bolt was brighter than anything you could even imagine. I sent her healin' energy and ask for y'all to do the same for a while for all those folks down there. The ones that were killed and hurt and the rescue folks."

Folks nodded their heads and said they would do just that. Emily started a Reiki circle online right there at the table and asked for others to forward the request so that Reiki from around the globe would be sent.

"It's the bad guys tryin' to steal The Magic again, isn't it, Miss Cora?" Victoria asked.

"Yes, it is and we gotta' get ready to protect it." Miss Cora replied. "Now, for those of you who aren't gifted with special energy, just start sending light and love to The Creek and every livin' thing in and around us. Your prayers will help keep us safe."

Folks gathered on the porch and commenced to sending positive energy all around. The Reiki circle was in full force. That left Miss Cora, Emily, Kendra, and Katelyn at the table.

"This isn't gonna' be easy. We gotta' come up with a plan right now to protect us," Miss Cora began.

"We should put a protection grid over The Creek first thing," Emily offered.

"That's a good idea, Emily. Thing is, we can't get to all the points we need to 'cause of the terrain. We can put grids over our own places and all, but that's gonna' take a lot of time. We need somethin' right now," Miss Cora replied.

"I think my going to the field is the next step while y'all place grids everywhere ya' can starting with The Store. There's somethin' about that cave that's callin' me," Katelyn said.

"I do believe you're right about that," Kendra said. "Do you think you can get there right now with all this goin' on?"

Katelyn sat quiet for a minute then said, "I do believe I can. The authorities aren't here yet so I should be able to get there without any problems. Emily said the road is pretty clear except for a few leaves and sticks and all. I'm gonna' get a few things then set out."

"We'll surround you with The White Light right now. Be safe," Miss Cora said.

Katelyn went back home and grabbed a backpack. She filled it with her LED flashlight, water and some food. And, her set of crystals that happened to be here just like in her Crab Apple Creek. She put the twin to Jordan's in her pocket even if he didn't own the land here.

She set out and was at the field in just a few minutes. She drove as far into the field as she could. The field road ran along the north side of the field.

She left her SUV and set across the field, headed for the where the cave should be. It was just a few minutes later that she saw the little hill in front of her.

She went to the where the bushes were and found the entrance. The bushes were a lot bigger than in the other dimension. She had to force them aside a couple of times to find the exact entrance. And, there it was, just like it was supposed to be.

She pushed through the bushes and walked into the entrance tunnel. It was just like before. She emerged into the crystal room. It was magnificent. Those crystals began to glow something fierce as soon as she walked into the room as if they were just waiting for her. The light increased so much that she considered putting her sunglasses back on. She didn't though. It seemed the crystals knew they were very bright and toned down just a bit.

She called out to the powers that be saying, "Now, don't put that portal in place here. I don't think I'm supposed to go through it in here right now," Katelyn said.

She walked around the edge of the room looking at everything. She saw the tunnel that leads to the other tunnels. She circled the room one time then stepped into the middle as if she had been instructed to. She stood very still in the quiet of the room.

As she looked across the room towards the far wall, one particular crystal began to glow more than the others. It was the size of a baseball but more oval shaped. It was every shade of blue and purple you could imagine and it shot beams of color all over the place as was usual.

Katelyn walked over to it and picked it up. It was a bit heavy but not too much. She held it in both hands then turned to face the middle of the room. The room seemed to change. It was as if there was a big movie theatre screen in the middle of the room. It began to show pictures like a movie.

It began with the creation of the universes and galaxies. The stars and planets began to form. Next, she saw the earth take shape and go through its many changes with volcanoes erupting and land masses moving and glaciers moving around. She saw Pangea form and separate into the way the earth looked today. She saw the moment, the instant, that The Magic was placed in the Appalachia's especially the Blue Ridge mountains. She saw the people come to the Blue Ridge and learn to protect The Magic over millennia.

Then, she was shown the many times since The Magic was placed here that The Dark had tried to destroy it. It was horrible. Millions of people were killed and the earth was severely damaged all because of the greed of The Dark.

Katelyn found herself weeping and sat down on the floor of the cave. She must have sat there for a long time because as she calmed herself, the movie was gone and the cave had returned to its beautiful self. She took a deep breath and stood up slowly. She felt tired and weak.

She remembered the stuff in her backpack and took out the food and water and ate and drank. She felt a lot better when she finished.

The whole time she was eating she felt as if people were talking to her. It was very quiet but she could understand every word. She looked around a few times and didn't see anyone. She figured the guardians of the cave were speaking to her.

Katelyn learned that this cave could never be touched by The Dark. Ever. A special kind of Magic and Power were held here. The Dark had been trying since The Magic had been placed here to take it for itself. It would never succeed. There were other types of Magic all around the Blue Ridge, and, especially in The Creek, that The Dark could take if it wasn't well protected. That's what was happening right now. The Dark wanted some of the other Magic and was going to keep attacking until it got The Magic or it was defeated. That's what the explosion on the Pine Ridge Road was all about. The Dark figured that if it took all The Magic from around the cave it would then be able to get The Magic in the cave. It didn't even know the Special Magic and Powers were in the cave let alone know there was a cave in the field. Well, nice thinking but it would never happen. The Divine would relocate that Special Magic and Powers from the cave before The Dark could ever take it. No need to relocate because The Dark would never get that Magic.

Katelyn realized she was still holding the new crystal. She felt a warmth from her pocket and took out her twin crystal. As those two crystals touched, there was a shot of light sent around the room and the two crystals began to hum. It was easily heard and other crystals joined in. The music was beyond beautiful and Katelyn listened with a smile on her face.

As the music stopped and the glowing crystals began to calm down, she knew it was time to leave. She looked at the new crystal and knew it was to go with her. It was to be taken to its new home by Katelyn later on. She didn't know where that new home was to be nor when to take it there but she knew that was her job.

She left the cave expecting to find it nighttime as she figured she'd been in there for a few hours. It was bight and hazy. Seems the smoke from the explosion and consequent fires was moving over The Creek. She looked at her phone and saw that only two hours had passed. It was so weird how that time thing happened when The Magic was in charge.

She put on her sunglasses and walked the field to her SUV. She was surprised to find an eagle feather with a note. It read, 'This is for Katelyn. It is a gift from the eagle spirit for all you've done to protect The Magic. We thank you. Keep this feather close to you at all times and it will bring messages to you from The Other Side.'

Katelyn was humbled by this gift as she knew eagle feathers were only for the native shaman to handle and use. She bowed towards the feather and thanked the eagle for the gift. A soft breeze blew by just at that minute and Katelyn knew it was in response to her thanks.

Katelyn passed Ethan and his crew clearing the road to The Store on her way back home. She left her backpack in the house then headed across the road to get the latest news on the explosion and talk with Miss Cora.

Ethan and the crew had cleared the property and their road all the way past the Two Moon Stables. It wasn't difficult work. The sheriff's department had not given the okay for folks to get back on the road so everyone was staying close to home or The Store. Ethan had sent a group text to The Creek telling folks to take pictures of their property and the road for the emergency response folks so they could figure out all that had happened and how far the damage of any kind from the explosion had reached.

Miss Cora and Kendra were at the table waiting to hear from Katelyn.

"Well, that was an educational experience for sure," Katelyn said as she grabbed a soda from the cooler. "I can't go into detail but the most important thing I gotta' tell ya' is this: The Dark will never get The Special Magic and Powers in that cave. Ever. It will keep tryin' to take all The Magic it can from The Creek to grow more powerful. That's why we need to protect The Creek."

"Well, I wondered about that cave. It looks like we got our hands full. Emily went back to her place to help Jonah with the animals. They seem to have sensed the energy change and are a bit restless. Kendra and I put protection grids around The Store and her houses so far."

"Good. It does feel calmer in here. What's the latest news?"

"Not good. The body count is at forty-two so far. Lots of folks were injured and were being treated at the local offices. They set up an emergency medical tent to triage folks and have sent another twenty or so to Boone for care. They were injured more seriously. The emergency management folks have turned off electricity to most of Pine Ridge and shut off the natural gas supply to all of Pine Ridge until they can assess how far the damage extends. They don't want any sparks to start more fires. They've got the two big ones under control with help from the forest service and the Boone fire department. No one has any idea what caused that explosion especially in the middle of the road," Kendra explained.

"Well, we know what happened," Miss Cora said. "We'll let the professionals take care of Pine Ridge and we'll do what we can around here. I suspect The Dark won't strike again for a few days. In the meantime, we've got lots to talk about. Ted, can ya' bring us somethin' to eat? I'm starvin','" Miss Cora said.

"Sure can. What would ya' like? I got the supper specials ready early and there's plenty to go around. I figured folks would gather here real soon now." Ted replied.

"That's for sure, Ted. I'll take the lasagna this time with everything," Miss Cora said.

Katelyn and Kendra placed there orders as well and before Ted could bring their dinner out to them folks began to come through the door.

Ethan and his crew showed up a bit later and ordered dinner as well. Spots were made around the table and extra tables were set up around the place. No one wanted to sit outside on account of the smokey air and all.

"Ethan, that was a fine thing ya' did clearin' the roads," Miss Cora said.

"Thank you, Miss Cora. Just seemed the right thing to do even if the road is gonna' be closed for a long time."

"Do ya' know how long yet?" Ted asked. "My delivery guys are already planning new routes to get stuff here. It's gonna' take an extra hour each way,"

"No, Ted. The sheriff said for at least two weeks while the investigation's takin' place. I suggested once that was over, maybe a dirt road could be cut around the damaged area so folks could at least get through if needed. The sheriff liked that idea and was talkin' with the county about doin' somethin like that. But, it's still gonna' take about a month to get that done. They're gonna' bury the utilities when they remake the road and bring that all the way up to here. No more overhead lines and all."

"Well, that's a great idea," Michael said as he came into the room.

Folks talked about this and the temporary dirt road for some time. Ian had stayed at the shop to make sure everything was okay. The power had been turned off up to the shop so he was running the generator and wanted to make sure someone was there the whole time it was on.

Finn was just setting out to meet with Ethan and Ian at the shop when the blast occurred. He was only a few yards down the road and turned right around to get back home. His dad was in Boone on business and his mom was in the kitchen making pies.

Within seconds of the blast the FBI called Matthews and put him on high alert. He was told to check in with the sheriff and the Boone FBI immediately. He did just that and they both told him to work from home investigating a list of persons of interest that they knew were in the area. Matthews knew it was The Dark. He just knew but he began running the inquiries knowing none of them were responsible for the blast. Sometimes, one investigation turned up someone the FBI was looking for. Maybe that would happen this time.

As soon as Matthews got the inquiries running, he decided to walk the farm to see if any major damage had occurred. He started at the road and noticed it was clear. Someone had been busy. He walked around the barn and didn't see any damage. No one was doing cartwheels on the roof. He then walked along the tractor path to the brook. He noticed a few large tree limbs along the bank on both sides and would take care of those in a few days. He didn't think they'd interfere with the flow pattern but wanted to make sure. They looked to be hardwoods so he'd take them back to the barn to dry and use over the winter in the house.

Matthews saw a message from Ethan. He wanted to know if there was any damage to his place.

Matthews called Ethan to report what he'd found. "No damage to the buildings. Just some big limbs down along the banks of the stream. They look to be hardwood. I was gonna' cut them up and store them in the barn for next winter."

"Tell ya' what, Matthews. My crews won't be workin' much over the next couple of days so how about I send some of them to do the cleanup for you? I suspect you're gonna' be busy for a while."

"Ethan, that's a great idea. Send them over whenever it's best for y'all. I'm already busy," Matthews said.

"Great. At least it'll keep them outta' trouble," Ethan said laughing.

"Just let me know the bill and I'll send it along," Matthews replied.

"No charge, Matthews. Remember, we take care of our own around here," Ethan said.

"Okay then. I accept your generous offer. That's my hot line, Gotta' go," Matthews said as his FBI phone was going crazy.

Matthews was told that two wanted federal criminals were in the area of Pine Ridge and had been identified by undercover agents. The FBI was gonna' arrest them and wanted Matthews there for the questioning phase. He told them he'd be there in about an hour or two all depending on the road conditions from Boone to Pine Ridge. His SUV was FBI equipped so he'd be using all the lights and sirens as he got into traffic. No need for that stuff as he left The Creek.

Michael saw him as he slowed down passing The Store. They waved and Matthews sped away. Michael told the folks in The Store that he'd just seen Matthews and it looked like he was on official business as he was dressed in a tie and all. They all sent good energy to Matthews to keep him safe.

It was evening by the time the news media had new information. Seems the fires were all out. They had identified those that had died and the officials were contacting family members. Everyone had been accounted for and that was a relief. The injured had been treated and released although some of them would be in the hospital in Boone for a while. Electricity and natural gas had been turned back on in most of Pine Ridge except the area around the blast. Not one building was left standing in a half-mile radius. The authorities put up flood lights to keep folks safe and the sheriff's department along with the state troopers and FBI. They had armed sentries every few feet.

The power came back on in the area south of The Store and Ian had turned the generator off, secured the shop and went on home.

Most folks left The Store after this news report. Emily had come back a little while earlier. Ethan sent his crew home and told them not to come in until ten o'clock the next morning They were gonna' go over to Matthews and clear those fallen limbs. The rest of the crews were told to report to the shop by eight. Safety inspections had to be conducted before any more work could be done at the build sites. Ethan had a procedure in place for this very thing and a qualified and certified safety person on every site.

"What a day," Ted said as he finished clearing the table.

'It sure has been. Time for me to get along home. Thanks for the good food, Ted," Miss Cora said.

"You are always welcome, Miss Cora. No need to pay for anything. Now, get along home," Michael said as Miss Cora tried to pay for her meal.

"Why, I do thank you kindly, boys. I am ready to get home and settle in for the night. Sleep well, y'all," Miss Cora said as she walked out the door.

Ethan and Emily left soon after Miss Cora with promises of keeping Ted and Michael up-to-date on anything and everything.

Kendra and Katelyn helped Ted finish cleaning up then went on their way.

As they crossed the road, they looked up at the sky. The sun was just setting and the sky looked a bit orange and red and still smelled of smoke from the fires.

"Now, that just looks so ominous," Katelyn said as they walked across the lawn.

"It sure does. Was there anything else you wanted to tell me about?" Kendra asked.

"Just this. This is gonna' be a really bad fight this time. I learned so much in the cave. The Dark has always tried to get The Magic from this place. The cave is a special place that's safe for The Special Magic and Powers and anyone who can get there. I'm gonna' be processing all the things I've learned for quite some time. Right now, we gotta' stay alert for any little thing that is strange and weird no matter how little it seems. That's what we need to re-member."

"Thanks, Katelyn. I'll let Miss Cora and Emily know. Time for us to get some sleep. I'm dog-tired tonight," Kendra said as they went up onto their own porches and through their front doors.

The Creek slept fitfully that night. Folks just didn't feel right and were concerned something like the blast would happen to them.

CHAPTER 29

The next week found everyone following the progress on the road and all in Pine Ridge. Most folks in The Creek knew the authorities would never find anyone involved in the blast because the evil demons were responsible. Folks went about their business concentrating on sending positive energy all around the place. Kendra, Katelyn, and Miss Cora had met a few times at Emily's place to discuss things. They weren't too sure what else they could do.

Miss Cora went to the Applewood Grove. She called upon the ETs to visit her as she had a few questions for them. They showed up that night after dark and Miss Cora was waiting for them.

"Thanks for answering my call so quickly," Miss Cora said as they met in the middle of The Grove. Only one ship had come with the ancients onboard.

"We are gravely concerned with all that has happened. The Dark can do serious damage to The Creek even though it can't get The Special Magic from the cave."

"I understand. We aren't sure what more we can do to protect things here. Can ya' help us?"

The ET bowed his head and said, "Miss Cora, you have served us well. You have only called upon us when things were getting out of control. This is one of those times. This time, we cannot interfere. We have sent the one who can make a difference. Keep teaching her about her special powers. She is the one to save The Creek."

Miss Cora bowed her head in response. "I thank you for your wisdom and assistance each and every time I've asked for it. You have given to us again in tellin' us Katelyn is the one. I will teach her now about her special powers. Blessed be."

The ET reached out his hand to Miss Cora. This had never happened before. She took his hand as offered. They looked at each other and Miss Cora was filled with knowledge and a new set of special powers for herself.

The ET stepped back and boarded his ship and, in a flash, he was gone.

Miss Cora felt empowered and sad at the same time. She knew she had to get Katelyn trained right away so she gathered her thoughts and headed home. Once home, she called Katelyn and they agreed on getting together the next evening after work.

Katelyn spent the next two evenings with Miss Cora. She learned about her special powers. She learned to throw energy balls and how to block such being thrown at her. She learned to channel her thoughts and send them out to destroy negative energy from The Dark. She learned to identify the many different ways The Dark could attack. She practiced her new powers for hours then went home and fell into a deep sleep.

On the third evening she met with Kendra and was taught how to call out for help.

"You taught me that already," Katelyn said,

"I did teach you some of the basic ways to call for help. Now, I'm gonna teach you how to call upon The White Light Paladins. It's a long-held secret only a chosen few get to learn. Ready?"

"I am," Katelyn said.

Kendra proceeded to teach Katelyn the special way to call upon these very powerful warriors and a number of other ways to get help when fighting The Dark.

On the next evening, she was told to report to Emily at her farm.

"Hey Emily and Trouble," Katelyn said as she was greeted by Trouble the second she stepped out of her SUV.

"He sure is happy to see ya'," Emily said laughing at the way the two of them were playing around.

"He's such a lovable dog. How could ya' not want to play with him?" Katelyn replied.

"Come on in and we'll have supper. We have somethin' very special to do tonight," Emily said as they walked over to the house and into the kitchen.

"Miss Cora just said to show up right after work and not even eat. Just get here. So, I did," Katelyn said as she helped bring food to the kitchen table.

"And we're mighty happy ya' did just that. Enjoy," Emily said as they ate their supper.

Katelyn sat back and smiled. "I do declare, there's no place like The Creek for good home cookin'. Thanks for makin' my favorite cornbread. It was fantastic!"

"Any time, Katie. Any time. Now, let's tidy up and get busy with you," Emily said.

A few minutes later, Emily led Katelyn out to the front porch.

"Katelyn, there's a special place here I know you've heard of. Now is the time for you to go there. Follow me," Emily said as she stepped down off the porch and headed to The Sacred Rock Meadow. Trouble was right at her side.

As they came to the edge, Emily stopped and looked at Katelyn. "You will remember everything you experience here today and learn a great deal as well. Please follow me," Emily instructed her.

The instant they stepped into the meadow past the rock wall border, things began to change.

Katelyn felt the energy shift and began to see wavy air. She watched as animals and birds of all species filled the place. The wavy air seemed to begin to take shape. She watched as a native warrior formed into a physical man right in front of her.

The warrior extended his hand to Katelyn to follow him. Katelyn looked at Emily to see if it was okay to follow and was amazed at what she saw. Emily had been transformed into an ethereal vision. She had on flowing garments of blue and purple just like the crystal Katelyn had found in the cave. It was Emily for sure. But a very different Emily. Emily nodded her head at Katelyn and Katelyn followed the warrior into the center of the meadow.

An eagle flew in and landed on the alter table across from where Katelyn was standing. It bowed its head at her then morphed into a human being. It was a woman with long flowing golden hair wearing white garments with gold ribbons hanging from the shoulders.

Katelyn stared at her for a few minutes then smiled.

"Katelyn, thank you for coming through the portal on the footbridge in The Meadow," the woman said.

"Ah, you are very welcome," Katelyn replied quietly.

The warrior pointed to a stone chair and Katelyn sat down.

"We know this is a lot to take in right now, but we need you to learn some things about The Magic here and in all dimensions of The Creek," the woman said.

Emily came over to Katelyn and placed her hand on Katelyn's shoulder. "This is all real, Katelyn. This is not a dream or a vision. This is really happening in the meadow next to my farm."

"Okay, Emily. I believe you. I just don't know why I'm here. That's all," Katelyn replied looking around at everything.

"We know and will explain it all to you," Emily said sitting next to Katelyn. "Time to listen to the story of The Magic that lives here in the Blue Ridge."

They turned their attention to the woman spirit as she began to speak.

"Thank you, Emily. Katelyn, there are only a few human beings that get to know this story. You are one of them. There is light and dark in all of creation. There are powers and such that most humans don't know about because they wouldn't know what to do with the information. So, The Divine created a way to protect all Magic from The Dark. The Divine created the earth and the universe that the earth exists in and placed The Magic in the Appalachia mountains even before they were the Appalachia's. Over the millennia during which the earth was formed and reformed, The Magic was safe from The Dark. It was so very deep in the core of the earth; The Dark couldn't tell where it was. As the earth finally took the form it now has, after what you know as Pangea, The Magic settled here in the Appalachia Mountains in the Blue Ridge range.

"Once the earth had cooled and began to form life and grow, The Dark was able to sense where The Magic lived. Throughout the time of mankind, The Magic was safe until humans came to this continent and began to live here. That's when The Dark was able to sense the exact location of The Magic. The people of Crab Apple Creek were sent here to protect it. Most of them are descendants of the original protectors. Some of them know they have special gifts, but a lot of them don't. We keep an eye on everyone here in many ways."

The woman spirit paused and looked at Katelyn.

"I understand and find this all fascinating," Katelyn said.

"Good. You have recently become aware that there are parallel dimensions of existence as you passed through the portals. You saved Crab Appl Creek in the first dimension you traveled through. I know things were very confusing and frustrating and we thank you for hanging on and getting to the cave. You saved that Crab Apple Creek and The Magic by placing the crystal in its place in the cave."

"I wondered if everything turned out okay. Thanks for telling me," Katelyn offered.

"Now, you have come through another portal into another parallel Crab Apple Creek. The Dark is causing a great deal of destruction and death trying to get The Magic from here. It won't give up this time. It will destroy all of The Creek if it has to. It will never get The Special Magic and Powers that are protected in the cave. This is where we need your help."

Katelyn looked at Emily and Emily gave her a hug. "This is gonna' sound crazy so just listen first. We'll talk about it all later."

Katelyn nodded her head at the woman spirt and the spirit continued. "Katelyn, we need you to take the blue and purple crystal you found and place it in the middle of The Meadow. This won't be easy. The Dark doesn't know you have it yet but it will the minute you take it out of the satchel you have placed it in. The effort needed is beyond human. That's why Miss Cora and Kendra have been teaching you so much these past few days. The Dark is ready to strike as we meet here so you need to be ready to get to The Meadow in an instant."

"How will I know when that time is?" Katelyn asked.

"Take a moment and search within yourself now. Then tell me what you feel," the woman spirit instructed Katelyn to do.

Katelyn closed her eyes and began to breathe slowly and calmly. She cleared her head and allowed the energy to surround her. She saw the different dimensions of The Creek as if they were sitting side-by-side. All of them looked the same. Then she saw some differences. The Store was burned down in one of them. Kendra's houses weren't there in another and in another one everything looked like it did in her Crab Apple Creek.

She took a deep breath and slowly exhaled as she cleared her mind again. Then she saw it. The black cloud of The Dark engulfing all the dimensions of The Creek. She saw the battle she had been a part of and how it had saved that dimension. Her dimension was saved. But the one she was in was completely destroyed, blasted off the face of the earth. She shuddered and Emily put her arms around Katelyn's shoulders.

"Katelyn, come back to us," Emily whispered in her ear.

Katelyn opened her eyes and looked around. The creatures were watching her as she stood up and faced the alter table and the woman spirit.

"I saw this dimension completely obliterated by The Dark. Gone from the face of the earth and The Dark madder than mad because it didn't get the Special Magic and all. It was horrible. Everyone was killed," Katelyn said crying.

"That is exactly what will happen now. I am sorry we had to show you this tragedy. You need to see why it is so important for you to continue to use your gifts. We know about your decision to continue and we thank you so much. We know this was a difficult and scary decision to make. With that decision, there is hope for this dimension. We don't have much time at all. That blasting of the road is the beginning of the attacks. Are you ready to help us again?'"

"Yes, I am," Katelyn replied standing tall. "I have learned to call for help from many sources and I know that is how I will be able to help save this dimension."

"You are right. But, Katelyn, things are going to happen so fast, that you won't have time to think, just react."

"Thanks for telling me that," Katelyn said.

"Please approach the altar," the woman spirit said to Katelyn.

As Katelyn stepped to the alter, the creatures all gathered around her forming a circle. Emily and the warrior each took their place at the ends of the alter. The woman spirit stood across the alter from Katelyn

As Katelyn watched, the woman spirit placed a cloth of pure white across her head. It cascaded down behind her touching the earth. Next, the woman spirit handed Katelyn a bouquet of wild flowers. She held these in her arms across the front of her body.

And, lastly, the creatures began to sing as they do. The sound was beautiful and as Katelyn watched, the flowers she was holding morphed into a small wand with a small blue crystal at one end and a small purple crystal at the other end. It was about twelve inches long and very light to hold. As she looked at it, she instantly knew what it was for.

She looked at the woman spirit and nodded her head.

"I accept and thank you," Katelyn said.

"It is time for us to leave this sacred place. Go now and prepare," the woman spirit said as it morphed back into the eagle. The eagle took to flight and circled the meadow three times then flew up into the sky until it disappeared. The warrior walked over to Katelyn and bowed to her. She bowed in return and he vanished. The creatures left the meadow one by one until only Emily, Katelyn and Trouble were there.

Emily took Katelyn's hand and led her out of The Sacred Rock Meadow. As Katelyn turned and looked, the meadow was once again the way it was when they arrived. She looked at Emily and Emily had her regular clothes on and all. Thing was, Katelyn was still holding the wand and the white material was still draped over her head and flowing behind her.

"That was incredible. And, look at this wand. Beautiful. And, what about this?" Katelyn said as she touched the white material. It fell into her hands and as soon as it touched her hand, it morphed into a whole bunch of rainbow-colored butterflies and they flew away across the land.

"Wow! This is wicked cool," Katelyn said watching the butterflies.

"It sure is. Never saw anything like that before," Emily said as they watched Trouble trying to catch those butterflies.

They laughed at Trouble's antics as long as the butterflies were around, which was only a few minutes. He came back to them and they walked back to the house and straight into the kitchen. Trouble had a long drink then collapsed onto his bed and was snoring a minute later.

Emily got juice for her and Katelyn as they laughed at Trouble and settled down at the kitchen table.

"I remember everything. It was amazing," Katelyn said as Emily watched her.

"Yes, it was. That meadow is a very special place. I fought my first battle there just after my house was finished. It's more than a body could ever imagine," Emily replied.

"Yes, it is. Miss Cora and Kendra have seen all this, too?" Katelyn asked.

"Yes, they have," Emily replied.

"Well, this wand is incredible. It has the same crystals as the one I found in the cave the other day. I know they're linked and I know I have to keep it on me all the time," Katelyn said. "The spirit said the attack had already started. Guess we better be on the lookout for more stuff," Katelyn offered.

"I agree. Let's have a snack before you head home," Emily suggested.

"What time is it anyway. It's still light out. How can that be? We must have been in the meadow for hours," Katelyn said looking at the kitchen clock. "No way. It says it's eight o'clock. That means we were only there for about an hour. That's not possible. We must have been there for at least five or six hours. So much happened."

"Crazy, huh? It always seems like a lot of time has passed and I mean a lot of time like you said. But The Magic has no time and things happen as needed. You needed to experience a lot of stuff tonight and in our own time it probably would have taken five or six hours. But, when we are in the realm of Magic, time doesn't exist. It kind of stands still."

"Now that's just wicked cool and somethin' I can understand," Katelyn replied.

They talked a bit more then Katelyn said, "Time for me to head home. I got a lot to think about and tomorrow the weekend will be comin'. Thanks for everything."

Emily walked her out to her SUV. "Looks like we finally tired Trouble out. He's sleepin' like he's been goin' for hours," Emily said.

"Give him a love for me when he does wake up," Katelyn said as she got underway. She waved as she went down the driveway and paused on the covered bridge. She got out and walked to the end and looked back at The Sacred Rock Meadow. She saw a mini light show for a minute or two, smiled, and got back in her SUV and was home a short time later.

She got ready for bed and fell asleep holding the crystal wand.

The Creek slept that night. It would be the last night of peace for a long while.

CHAPTER 30

The attack had indeed started and The Dark struck the next day. It started when some folks turned on their water faucets and saw something red flowing out. It stank and the more they looked at it, they realized it was blood. Gross. Someone texted Miss Cora and she told them what to do to get rid of the blood. They said the prayer and smudged with sage all over the house. The water came back and The Dark was pissed.

Word got around and folks all checked their water. It was all water now. Katelyn got the text at the same time as Kendra and Emily. They responded to each other and became very vigilant about their surroundings.

The next day, two days after Katelyn was in The Sacred Rock Meadow, a number of people went to open their doors and found snakes surrounding their homes. Poisonous snakes. They slammed the doors closed and got a hold of Miss Cora. She called upon the earth children to remove the snakes and put them in a place far away. The earth children responded and all the homes that The Dark had surrounded with snakes were cleared up instantly.

The third day after Katelyn's visit with Emily, people reported looking in the mirror while getting ready for their day and finding demons reaching out for them. One woman was grabbed and had all she could do to stay out of the mirror. At the last minute she remembered a prayer from her childhood and began reciting it. This made the demon mad and the more she shouted it out over and over again, the weaker the demon became until it suddenly let go of the woman and vanished back into the mirror. The woman got up and put sage on the sink and the whole mirror cleared up and was normal again. She sat there and cried for a while then called Miss Cora and told her what had happened. Miss Cora surrounded her with healing energy and the woman said she felt better right away.

Miss Cora sent healing energy all around The Creek and other folks began to report the same thing happening to them. Just not being grabbed or anything physical.

The damaged road was coming along. The investigation was still under way so the county couldn't begin to cut a dirt road out of the woods just yet. People were healing and those whose businesses and homes had been destroyed were being taken care of by the community. All except one guy. Seems he was very angry about everything and was bad-mouthing the recovery efforts. He made threats about blowing up other homes and businesses because his had been destroyed and he didn't have any place to live and any work to do. He was offered a shelter place for as long as he needed it but said he wasn't gonna' live like a dog. He deserved the best. He demanded the county put him up in a four-star hotel and pay the bills until they built him a new home and business building. The county refused of course and the man was even angrier than before. The same day the blood showed up in the water in The Creek, the man was found, that night, with explosives in a bag he was carrying. He was walking through a neighborhood in the southern part of Pine Ridge quite a ways from the blast site. People reported a stranger walking the streets late at night. The police and sheriff's deputies responded to the complaint as they suspected it might be the very angry man they had a watch on. Sure enough, it was him. It was just before midnight when they spotted him walking up a driveway and going around the side of a house. The authorities encircled the house then turned on their lights and saw him placing explosives along the foundation of the house. The house belonged to one of the county administrators that had denied the request for the hotel thing.

He was apprehended and thrown to the ground before he could finish wiring the explosives. He yelled and screamed and put up a strong fight. He kicked a few of the officers in the face and was trying to get up when they all stepped back and he was tasered. He fell to the ground and as soon as the electricity stopped flowing, he was picked up, hand cuffed and taken away.

All the while visitors to the Blue Ridge made it to The Creek the long way around. The Creek was a great stopping point to gather supplies before they took the road into Tennessee to explore the mountains.

Most folks were kind but a few started complaining about the cost of supplies and the long detour they had taken to get to The Creek. Most folks ignored them. There was one woman who just wouldn't stop complaining the whole time she was in The Store.

Finally, Michael asked her if he could help her with anything. She started yelling something fierce at him about whatever came to her mind. This brought Ted out of the kitchen and Matthews from the dining area.

Michael and Ted were trying to calm her down but she would not have any of it.

Matthews stepped in saying, "Ma'am, may I help you with something?"

"You? No. You hicks out here think you can jack up the prices of everything 'cause you're the only store around. Well, I'm not gonna' pay these prices," the woman hollered at Matthews.

"Ma'am, you have every right to leave here without buying a thing," Matthews said.

"Leave without anything? You must be mad. I need some food but I'm not gonna' pay these prices. I'll give ya' what I think it should be and that's that," she said as she laid a twenty-dollar bill on the register. The total was more than sixty dollars.

She tried to step away and leave but Ted and Matthews blocked her way.

"Ma'am, you're going to have to pay the full price or leave the food here and leave this place," Matthews explained to her.

"You set one finger on me and I'll holler rape," she threatened as she tried to leave again.

Michael and Ted watched along with folks on the outside of The Store.

"One more time, Ma'am. You need to pay the full price or leave the food here," Matthews said again.

"Who's gonna' make me? You and what army?" she demanded.

Matthews took out his ID and moved his jacket aside so she could see his weapon. "I, am, Ma'am. I'm an FBI special agent and will take you into custody if you don't pay the full bill or return the food to the owners and leave quietly."

"Nice try, asshole. You think you can threaten me with a fake badge and gun? Wrong," the woman screamed as she back-handed Ted, sending him into a chair. She turned to run out the door but didn't get very far.

The door was blocked by the folks outside and Matthews grabbed her by the arm and put her into very painful hold. She screamed as he grabbed her other arm and hand cuffed her. He pushed her into a chair and called for assistance from the sheriff's detail down the Pine Ridge Road. They arrived a few minutes later lights and sirens blazing.

Matthews had taken her purse and found her license. He ran her number and found out there were five outstanding arrest warrants for her in three different states. Add North Carolina and that made it four states. She was escorted out of The Store and put into the sheriff's SUV and driven away. The sheriff's department would process her with written statements from Matthews, Michael, Ted, and the others that had watched the whole thing.

Matthews had the paramedics stationed at the Pine Ridge Road work site on this side of the blast come take a look at Ted. They said it didn't appear as if any of his facial bones where broken. They cleaned up the cut lip he had and suggested if anything else appeared or the pain didn't lessen over the next two days that he should go to the emergency room in Boone for a follow-up.

Michael thanked the paramedics and gave them lunch for their efforts. A couple of the folks at The Store tended to Ted. They told him to stay in the chair for at least an hour. He agreed. They replaced the ice pack when it warmed with one from the kitchen. The bleeding from his lip had stopped and they changed the bandage for him.

He thanked everyone and managed to say, "Thanks y'all. Good thing I had supper all made. It just needs to be warmed up later."

Katelyn and Kendra had come in when they saw the paramedics show up.

"Ted, Katelyn and I will handle food service for the rest of the day. How about the guys help you up to your bed so you can rest? Ya' must have a hell of a headache and all," Kendra said.

Ted nodded his head and a couple of the guys got him upstairs and settled. Michael came up and checked on him while the guys and Kendra watched the cash register.

"Oh, my sweet Teddie. That woman was pure evil. How dare she attack you?" Michael said as he fussed over Ted.

"I know. She was vicious. So glad we live in The Creek. You sure had a great idea all those years ago to create this store for us. I love ya' for it forever," Ted said grabbing hold of Michael's hand.

"And, I love ya' forever too, my Teddie. Now rest. Ya' want one of those painkillers we still have?"

"Yes, I do. This lip hurts somethin' fierce and my back feels like it's on fire from hitting that chair so hard. That woman sure was strong and I'm no whimp," Ted said as Michael got him the pill.

Ted swallowed it and settled back against the pillows with the ice packs in place. Michael leaned over him and kissed him on the head ever so lightly.

"Sleep and rest. Kendra said she's got folks sending you Reiki already," Michael said as Ted closed his eyes.

"Tell her thanks," Ted replied as he settled into his bed.

One of the guys was gonna' stay with Ted the rest of the day to make sure nothing else showed up from being attacked. Sometimes other injuries came to light a while later.

Michael went downstairs and told everyone Ted was resting and had taken a pain pill. He thanked them all for helping out and the day got busy as usual. Folks stopped in just to hear how Ted was doing.

Miss Cora showed up a while later asking for Ted.

"He's asleep right now, Miss Cora. Thanks for askin'," Michael said ringing up an order.

She waited for the customers to be finished then said, "I'm gonna' go set at the table for a spell."

"Kendra and Katelyn are running the kitchen so I know you'll be well taken care of," Michael replied as Miss Cora went up the steps.

"Hey, Miss Cora. How about a sweet tea this warm summer day?" Katelyn asked as she got Miss Cora settled.

"I would surely appreciate that, Katelyn. Got any cookies or somethin' back there?"

"Why, yes I do. Good timing. I just finished bakin' a big batch of my oatmeal chocolate chips cookies. They're still warm. I'll fetch ya' some."

"Thanks, Katie," Miss Cora replied.

Katelyn came back a minute later with warm cookies and sweet tea for them both.

"Now, Miss Cora, I know ya' didn't just come over here for a mid-afternoon snack. It's about all the crazy things happenin' around here, isn't it?" Katelyn said quietly so no one in the front would hear her.

"That's it exactly and to see how Ted's doin'," Miss Cora said biting into a cookie. "These are delicious. Thanks."

"You are always welcome to my cookies no matter where we are," Katelyn replied taking a bite of hers.

They talked a bit as they enjoyed the cookies. Kendra joined them a few minutes later just as Emily came through the door.

"Hey, Michael. What the fuck?! How's our Ted?" Emily asked.

"Well, he's upstairs resting. He looks like he was in a fight for sure. And, only thing is he never got a throw in. He was the punching bag. He's gonna' be in a mess a hurt for a few days and he's gonna' look real pretty when all those bruises stat showin' up," Michael replied, smilin a bit.

"Poor baby. I got Reiki goin' all around. Let me know if I can do anything else," Emily said as she went into the dining area.

"I'll be sure to tell him you were askin' about him," Michael said as he turned his attention to his customers.

"Well, Emily, so glad ya' could come by. The animals are all okay?" Miss Cora asked.

"Yes, they are, Miss Cora. Jonah is takin' care of them as we speak. I truly love that man," Emily replied as she reached for a cookie. "These are heavenly, Katelyn."

"Glad you're enjoin' them so much," Katelyn said laughing.

"Well now, Katelyn, ya' know why we're all here?" Miss Cora said.

"Yes, I do. Seems the attack is well under way with all the crazy stuff goin' on with that guy tryin' to blow up the house and Ted getting beatin' up and all. This is just what we were told to watch for, isn't it?" Katelyn replied.

"Yes, it is," Kendra answered. "The attack is under way. The Dark is getting closer to The Creek. I suspect the next hit will be in The Creek somewhere and we need, you, Katelyn, to be ready to take control just like we've all been teaching you."

"I know. I've been practicin' and all and goin' through make believe scenarios just to be better prepared. I know how to call for help and I think that's gonna' be a key factor in all this."

"I believe you're right," Miss Cora said. "I don't like this feelin' of not knowin' what's next. Bothers me some."

"Me, too," said Katelyn and Kendra at the same time.

"Well, then I guess the only thing I can say is let's keep in touch like we've been doin' and keep sending positive and protective energy around the place," Miss Cora offered. "I'm gonna' get back home. My garden needs some harvestin' and all. See ya' later," Miss Cora said as she walked back down to the front area. "Michael, my love to you and Ted."

"Thanks, Miss Cora. We love ya', too," Michael replied as Miss Cora left.

Everyone went about the business of taking care of The Store. Miss Cora called Michael and told him she had a mess of fresh veggies for him. He sent one of the kids over to pick them up.

Suppertime was wicked busy as everyone came to see how Ted was and either stayed for supper or ordered to go. It was well past nine when Michael was finally able to close the place. Kendra and Katelyn were just finishing up in the kitchen and dining room. They had sent supper up to Ted and his caregiver and some of Katelyn's cookies. They were well liked.

"Ladies, I have locked the front door and set the lights for the night," Michael said as he plopped down in a chair.

"You must be exhausted with work and worryin' about Ted," Kendra said as she laid a hand on Michael's shoulder and gave it a squeeze.

Michael covered her hand with his and returned the gesture. "You got that right. I don't know what I would have done without you two. Thanks," Michael said his eyes tearing up a bit.

"Now, Michael. We got folks comin' in for the next few days to manage the kitchen until Ted feels better. He's not to come down here tomorrow for any reason," Kendra said as she sat down.

"I don't think that's gonna' be a problem. He's hurtin' really bad and will be happy to stay put tomorrow. I called his doc and she's gonna' stop by sometime tomorrow morning to check up on him."

"That's fantastic," Katelyn said. "She must be a great gal."

"That she is. She was concerned about the blow he took to his face. She said sometimes other things can show up a day or so later."

"Good thinkin'," Kendra said. "Well, things are all set for tomorrow mornin' just like Ted does it. Time for us to mosey across the road and call it a day."

Kendra and Katelyn left by the side door and Michael locked it behind them.

They each went right home, showered, and were in bed a little while later. Katelyn's last thoughts were of the experience in The Sacred Rock Meadow. It was a beautiful place.

It was well past midnight when The Creek was awakened by a blast really close to their homes.

The Dark was beyond pissed by all the ways Miss Cora had blocked its attacks. It had a little something special planned for her. Once she was out of the way, The Dark would take all The Magic and blow The Creek into nothingness once and for all.

Katelyn, Kendra, and Emily knew what it was. The Dark had begun the final assault.

Katelyn was on her porch in a flash and so was Kendra. They saw the smoke and flames north of them.

"Oh my God. It looks to be close to Miss Cora's place. Let's go!" Kendra said as Katelyn jumped into Kendra's SUV and they took off.

Sirens were heard as they were getting closer. As soon as Kendra came around the curve in the road, they knew it was Miss Cora's cabin.

"No! No! No!" Katelyn yelled getting out of the SUV before Kendra had a chance to stop on the side of the road. A fire truck came from the other direction and turned into the driveway.

You could feel the heat all the way to the road. The whole place was one giant fireball. The gardens were on fire as well. The firetruck had to stop at the end of the drive things were so bad.

A second and third truck showed up and parked right in the road. Katelyn and Kendra stood out of the way sobbing and holding each other. They knew instantly that Miss Cora had been killed.

"I thought she put a protection grid around her place," Katelyn said.

"She got most of the places set up and was gonna' do hers tomorrow. Damn The Dark," Kendra cried out shaking her fist at the fire.

Matthews walked over to the girls and asked them about Miss Cora.

"She was inside, Matthews. I know she's gone. I can feel the emptiness," Katelyn said crying.

"Same here, Matthews. Looks like The Dark blasted her place the same way if blasted the road. Nothing's gonna' be left but ashes."

"Holy shit! You girls need to move back. Looks like you're getting a bit hot," Matthews said.

They followed Matthews a bit down the road away from the fire trucks.

"This is wrong. So wrong," Katelyn said. "She never did anything to hurt anyone. She's one of the special ones here protectin' The Magic all her life."

"You're right about that, Katelyn. Looks like The Darks stepped things up some. Maybe it's time for you to take control, if ya' know what I mean.," Kendra whispered into Katelyn's ear so no one would hear her.

"Oh my God! Kendra, you're right. I gotta' do what I was sent here to do. Send me all the protection you can. Let's get me home so I can gather my things," Katelyn said.

"Matthews, we're gonna' go back home. We can't do anything here. We've sent protection to the firefighters and all of ya' and we'll keep it going as long as it's needed. We'll tell everyone the sad news."

"Okay, Kendra. But I think they already know. This is so sad," Matthews said as he watched the girls walk down the road to where Kendra had stopped her SUV.

As soon as they got back, Katelyn said, "Kendra thanks for all your help teachin' me stuff and all. I don't think I'll see you again in this space and time. Love ya."

Love ya, too," Kendra replied as Katelyn ran home.

Katelyn ran into the house, slammed the door shut and fell on the floor. She sobbed for the longest time over the murder of Miss Cora. That was wrong. So very wrong.

As she started to calm down, she began to think about things. Well, first, she thought, I should get up off this floor, splash some water on my face, and sit quietly to figure out what to do next.

The Dark was on a rampage. She had the key to stop it. She thought for a minute then knew exactly what she had to do. She grabbed her backpack and put a bottle of water in it. Not to drink. She got the feeling she would need this for something else. Next, she put her twin crystal in her shirt pocket close to her heart. It felt good there. She took the new crystal, the blue and purple one, and put in the backpack. She grabbed the wand from where she had left it on the floor and held it close. This she would keep in her hand from now on no matter what happened. She took a minute to slow her thoughts. Then she saw a picture of The Meadow. That's where she must go right away.

"Okay, all you guys on the Other Side, I need your help to get to The Meadow. Here we go," she said out loud as she got into her SUV and pulled out of the driveway. There were lots of people at The Store already. Kendra must have gotten the word out about Miss Cora. Her eyes began to fill with tears again and she made it stop. She needed to focus right now. Time for tears later.

She headed north to the first turn off to get to The Meadow. She passed all the firetrucks at Miss Cora's place. She looked straight ahead. She made the next turn and passed the Redstone's farm. Good. Only two more roads and she'd be at The Meadow. As soon as she turned down the third road, things began to fall into the road. She kept going and got onto the third road before real trouble began. Just as she turned a giant boulder came crashing down the hillside. She sped up and it barely missed her. She kept going and could see the parking place at The Meadow. Only a couple more minutes. That's when three giant trees fell across the road in front of her. She hit the brakes and bumped into the one closest to her. They were huge. No way around them. She started to get out of the SUV and a swarm of hornets attacked her. She got back inside with only one sting. She sat there for a minute. She figured The Dark knew what she was about to do and was trying to keep her from getting to The Meadow.

The hornets were finally gone and she got out of the SUV again. This time, the earth shook so hard she fell down and more trees came crashing down all around. She got back into the SUV and it only took her a minute to make a decision. Before anything else could happen, she put the SUV into reverse and backed up as fast as she could down the road, back to the second road. She turned around and headed back to the first road. The wind had picked up so much that stuff was flying around.

As soon as she saw the Redstone's farm she knew how to get to The Meadow. She pulled in and ran to the door yelling for Seth and Clara.

Clara came to the door and Katelyn rushed inside.

"Sorry for the sudden intrusion, but I need y'all's help," Katelyn said.

"We heard about Miss Cora. Horrible," Seth said standing next to Clara. "How can we help ya', Katelyn?"

"Now, don't ask how I now about this, but I need y'all to take me to the underground railroad tunnels under the far barn and get me to where they come out at the top of The Meadow."

"No one knows about those tunnels. We've kept that secret for a long time," Clara said.

"I know. Know this. Magic is at work here. The Magic y'all know about here in The Creek even if no one else knows you are aware of it. That's how I know. I need your help so evil can't hurt anyone else here. Will y'all help me?"

Seth looked at Clara and they nodded to each other.

"Yes, Katelyn, we'll take ya' there now. Ready?" Seth said.

"Great Seth, and thanks for believing in what I've said. Much obliged," Katelyn replied as they left the house by the back door and set out for the far barn.

The wind increased so much that they had to bend over to keep from being blown over. As they entered the barn, the wind blew so hard it shook the barn from top to bottom.

"That's no ordinary windstorm," Seth said as he cleared a space on the floor and reached for the handle to open the door that led into the tunnels.

Clara had gathered the lights and all and was the first to go down. As soon as Katelyn set her foot on the ladder, the ground shook hard enough to make Seth fall down

"Keep goin'," Seth yelled as he rolled over to the ladder. Katelyn was in the tunnel and Seth was halfway down the ladder when the next quake hit. It was bigger than the first one and shook the tunnel some.

"We need some help here," Katelyn called out into thin air.

The quake immediately stopped and they all stood there making sure their equipment was in place.

"Thanks," Katelyn said as they looked at each other. "Don't ask, just say thanks."

Seth and Clara offered thanks and then Seth said, "Let's get movin.' It's a fair walk to the other end. Let me know if ya' need to stop for any reason."

"Okay, Thanks Seth. I'm ready," Katelyn said.

They set out and were about half-way down the tunnel when the first spider web appeared. It covered the whole of the tunnel.

"Would ya' look at that?" Clara said. "It's the biggest web I've ever seen."

"Sure is. Wonder how it got here? It wasn't here this morning when I was checking on things."

"I know how it got here," Katelyn said. 'Evil. Pure evil."

Katelyn took her wand and held it out in front of her. She then waved it from the top of the web to the bottom and then side-to-side. When she finished, the web disintegrated into nothing.

It was gone. As they took a few steps forward, a giant spider with glowing bright yellow and red eyes appeared in front of them. It shot webs at them. They all ducked and backed up.

"What the hell is that?" Seth hollered. "You're as ugly as shit!"

"I got this," Katelyn said as she pointed her wand at the spider and shook it as if she were firing it like a weapon. Laser beams flew from the blue crystal end and hit the spider between the eyes.

She pointed and sent another laser beam at the spider hitting it at the top of one leg. The beam seemed to ricocheted from one leg to the other and in just a few seconds, the spider's legs were destroyed. Only the body with the face remained.

"You think you've killed me but you're wrong. I and indestructible," the spider hissed at them.

Katelyn pointed the purple crystal end at the spider and aimed for the center of its body. With one well-placed zap, the spider was hit and blew up into zillions of tiny pieces that then vanished altogether.

"What is that?" Seth asked pointing at the wand.

"A new toy," Katelyn said smiling. "Let's get a move on."

"I like that toy. Can I have one?" Clara said laughing as they moved along.

A few minutes later Seth said, "Just a few more yards than we'll be there."

No sooner had he said this than a man appeared in front of them.

"You can't go this way. The floor is all rotted out and the timbers have fallen. It's a dead end. You're gonna' have to go back," the man said.

Seth, Clara, and Katelyn looked at each other than turned to the man.

"Who are you and why are you in my tunnel?" Seth said.

"I'm here on an inspection detail. We always inspect the tunnels for the runaways," the man replied.

"Liar!" Clara yelled at the man. "You're a ghost. Not real. And, you're pure evil."

"Sir, I do believe your wife is delusional," the man replied holding his ground.

"You, sir, are the one who's delusional," Katelyn replied.

"You aren't going to listen to this witch, are you?" the man asked Seth. "All she does is lie about everything just to get her way."

"I don't know who you are but I agree with my wife. You are pure evil. I command you to leave this place for all time."

"Not gonna' happen, Seth. It's time for the three of you to die," the man said as he brought his hands forward and threw an energy wave at them.

"Not today," Katelyn said as she blocked his energy throw and sent it back into him. It ripped him into shreds.

Katelyn sent another energy pulse from her hands and the evil man was gone.

They ran to the end of the tunnel and Seth climbed the stairs and opened the door. It was quiet outside.

"Come on, Katelyn. It seems to be quiet right now," Seth said as he gave her a hand when she reached the top.

She stepped onto the land and saw that she was just a few steps from the edge of The Meadow. She instantly knew that Seth and Clara needed to go back home as fast as they could.

"Clara, stay down there. Listen. The two of you need to go back through the tunnels home as fast as you can. Nothing is gonna' block you. You just need to get there and be safe right away. I thank you both for getting me here. I must take care of the rest myself," Katelyn said hugging Seth.

"I know this. I don't know how I do, but I do. Take care, Katelyn. We love ya'," Seth said as he went back down the ladder into the tunnel and closed the door. The earth moved things around so you couldn't tell there was a door there. Wicked cool, Katelyn thought as she stepped into The Meadow.

The Dark was waiting for her. It sent an energy wave through the ground to knock her down and stop her from getting to the middle. She rode the wave like an accomplished surfer. She never let go of the wand and her backpack helped her maintain her balance. When the wave ended, she took to running as quickly as she could.

The Dark put a wall up in front of her. She saw it and slowed down enough to only bump into it. It was all electricity and she was jolted for a second. It hurt for sure. She took a step back then had an idea. The one thing that would stop the electricity was interrupting the flow. How could she do that? She had an idea from a sci-fi show she had watched as a kid. She found some small branches and took an old piece of wire she had found on the ground the other day out of her backpack. She had meant to through it away. Good thing she hadn't. She tied the wire to the branches using the bark and then she threw it at the wall. It hit the wall and the wall exploded. It began to burn and she sent a wall of water at it. The whole thing fizzled out and the wall was gone. She kept going.

She was almost there when evil demonic soldiers appeared lined up from one side of The Meadow to the other. This was gonna' be quite the battle. Time to call for help.

Just as the first demonic soldier sent an arrow of energy at her, she called out for help.

"I call upon The White Light Warriors to help me get to the middle of The Meadow." She then sent an energy pulse at the arrow and it went back to the soldier who sent it and blew him up. Demon after demon sent those arrows and Katelyn kept deflecting them.

Then the demon soldiers morphed into one giant demon soldier with several arms. Just as it was getting ready to send multiple energy balls at Katelyn, The White Light Warriors flew in and wrapped the demon soldier monster in black energy bands. As soon as the monster threw the energy balls, the bands blocked them from going anywhere and destroyed the demon soldier monster.

Katelyn ran the last few steps to the center of the Meadow. The White Light Warriors encircled her to protect her. She took the blue and purple crystal from her backpack and was about to place it on the ground when a wall of darkness encircled The Meadow.

She tried to set the crystal down but was blocked from doing so.

A deep and growly voice spoke through the darkness. "You have lost this battle for I now control this meadow and the air around it. You cannot put that crystal on the ground no matter how hard you try. Give up and I'll kill you instantly instead of slowly as I was going to. I love to watch people suffer."

"You have no control over me and The Meadow. It is of The White Light. You can try to persuade me to think you have control but we both know different," Katelyn replied.

"You're a feisty one. But, no worry. You know I'm right," the voice said.

"I know you're wrong. The White Light Warriors surround me here and protect me even if I cannot see them," Katelyn said.

"Are you sure about that? Look," the voice said.

Katelyn looked up without moving away from the center spot. She was shown a meadow that looked like this one. It was surrounded by The Dark and as she watched, The Dark destroyed The White Light Warriors.

"Nice try. Not The Meadow. Just one that looks like it," Katelyn said.

"Are you sure of that?"

"Yes."

"I see. Because you refuse to surrender, watch your friends at The Store die," the voice said as he flashed a picture of The Store blowing up and everyone inside dying.

Katelyn felt the wave of energy from the blast but did not pick up on anyone's spirit crossing over.

She took a deep breath and said, "Nice try with the energy thing and all. Fake. All of it. Not one soul crossed back into The Light. You lose again."

Katelyn was getting very tired from holding her position. She remembered how she faked The Dark out when she was trying to get into the cave. She decided to try it again. She sent a message to the White Light Warriors about what she was gonna' do and they responded immediately with their approval. They would be waiting for that moment when The Dark thought it had won then blast it to hell and some.

'Here we go' she said through her mind to the White Light Warriors. She relaxed some to show how tired she was. Then she almost fell over. It was enough for The Dark to think she had given up.

"So, you're finally giving up. Good thing. You really don't have the strength to stay in that position another minute. I have decided to kill you ever so slowly so I can have a great time watching you suffer. You've taken up enough of my energy and all. Now you're mine," the voice cried out.

Just as The Dark was stretching out an energy hand to kill Katelyn, she took that tiny bit of a second and placed the crystal on The Meadow then touched it with her wand. This caused a blinding light to shatter the darkness.

The Dark was so shocked at what had happened that it screamed out and shook the universe with its anger. The White Light Warriors destroyed the darkness into oblivion and The Meadow was returned to its normal self.

The crystal was sitting in the middle sending beams of light all around. The wand lay next to it shining as well. Katelyn had fallen onto the ground and lay there. She was listening to the birds and all. She saw the White Light Warriors come to the earth and stand around her.

She sat up and looked at them. "Thanks y'all for helping with this. I'm so glad I learned about you and all the things I was taught. I think we saved The Magic but The Creek is a mess. So sad about Miss Cora and everyone else."

"We're glad we could help. Remember to call on us whenever you need us," one of them said as they took to the air and vanished.

Katelyn stood up. She looked at the crystal and the wand and watched them vanish as well. It was as if they were made just for this moment.

She picked up her backpack and didn't really know what to do next.

"Katelyn," she heard someone call her name. She turned and saw Miss Cora. Not a human one, but a spirit Miss Cora.

"Oh, Miss Cora. I'm so sorry for what happened to you," Katelyn said as she ran to the spirit and cried.

"Now Katie girl, stop those tears. You did exactly what you were supposed to do here in this dimension. Same for me. I was supposed to die like that. I'm free know to help The Creek recover from all this horrible destruction and help them keep protecting The Magic," Miss Cora said.

"I know, but still, it's been horrible," Katelyn said drying her tears.

"I know it has for a lot of folks. Ted's gonna' recover just fine, by the way. I'm gonna' stay close to him for a spell."

"Oh, good. I figured he would but it's good to hear it from you. What do I do now, Miss Cora?"

"Well, Katelyn, you've fulfilled your destiny here. Time to go back," Miss Cora said.

"I thought so. It seems like everything's gonna' be good now. I watched that crystal and wand vanish. Now, that was some Magic goin' on," Katelyn said as she approached the edge of the footbridge.

She looked at Miss Cora's spirit for a minute then said, "Thanks for everything, Miss Cora. I'm much obliged."

"You're very welcome, Katie girl. Now through the portal you go," Miss Cora replied.

Just as Katelyn set her foot off the bridge into the portal, she heard Miss Cora say, "See you on the other side."

Katelyn was smiling like crazy as she walked into her own dimension. Her SUV was right where she had left it. She got in and drove right over to Miss Cora's place. She jumped out and ran to the door just as Miss Cora was opening it. She flew into Miss Cora's arms crying tears of joy.

"Nice to see you, Katie girl," Miss Cora said hugging Katelyn.

"So great to see you, Miss Cora."

"Katelyn, I suspect you have lots to tell me but I want ya' to get home and rest for a bit," Miss Cora said.

"I agree. I need some time to think about all that's happened and what needs to be done here. I love ya', Miss Cora,' Katelyn said kissing her on the cheek.

"I know. And, I love ya' right back," Miss Cora said giving Katelyn a little nudge sending her on her way home.

Katelyn got home and sat on her couch thinking about all that had happened. She didn't remember falling asleep but laughed when she woke up the next day still on the couch.

Katelyn's Creek slept well that night.

CHAPTER 31

hen Katelyn emptied her backpack the next day, she saw the blue and purple crystal and her wand tumble onto the bed. Holy cow! This was great!

"Thanks everyone for the gifts," she offered out loud.

Katelyn had a long day ahead of herself. She was in the shop all morning meeting clients and discussing fixtures and layouts. The afternoon had her with Ian meeting a new vendor in Boone. They were going to look at the inventory and discuss possible pricing and such.

Finn met Katelyn in Boone and the two of them went to a build site south of Boone to meet with the new land owners. The property had just been signed over three days ago and now it was okay for the new owners to plan where they wanted their new home and the type of energy supply needed. Finn and Katelyn spent almost two hours with the owners walking the more than ten acres of land. Finn had already done the preliminary survey for underground water sources and possible problems that might arise for the foundation. Katelyn had met with them the first time in the shop for a brief visit when they signed the contract for Ethan to build their new home.

By the time everyone left, it was well past six.

"Hey, Finn. How about we go to the diner for supper? I'm starvin' and I don't relish that drive home then havin' to fix supper," Katelyn suggested as they walked over to their vehicles.

"Great idea. See ya' there," Finn said kissing her.

"Mmmm. I like the appetizer," Katelyn said getting into her SUV.

They arrived at the diner a while later and saw that Ethan, Ian and Ian's family were there.

"Hey, y'all," Finn and Katelyn said as they walked in.

"Hey, Finn. Katelyn. Come sit next to us so we can talk and all," Ian said pointing to a table next to Ethan and Ian's booths.

They sat down and the waitress came by.

"Hey, y'all. How's everyone this evenin'? You kids thirsty?" Carrie asked.

"Yes, Ma'am, we are," Ian's son Caleb answered.

"Well, what would ya' like?" Carrie said.

"Carrie, would ya' put everything on one bill? The business will take care of things tonight," Ethan said.

"Thanks, boss," Katelyn replied raising her water glass in a salute.

"Same here," Finn said.

"Thanks Uncle Ethan," Nessie and Caleb replied.

"Y'all are very welcome. It isn't often my favorite people get together so tonight's deemed a special night," Ethan replied.

Everyone placed their orders for drinks and food and got to talking.

They spent the next couple of hours teasing and laughing with each other. Friends came by and talk moved along to old times, current times, and future plans. There was even a bit of a French fry food fight between Ian's kids, Ethan, and Finn. The rest of them egged each other on and fries were flyin' for some time.

It was well past eight when things started to wind down. Errant fries had been collected and thrown away. The kids were still talking about the food fight as friends stopped by to say so long.

Once outside hugs and kisses were exchanged and promises of gathering again soon were made.

Carrie stepped outside just as they were going their separate ways.

"Hay, y'all, ya' left a lot of money on the table," Carrie said.

"Yes, we did. It's all for you in thanks for your excellent service," Ian said.

Carrie looked at them all and placed her hand on her heart. "Bless all your little ol' pea pickin' hearts for showin' me the love."

They waved at her as she went back inside.

"See you at the shop tomorrow," Katelyn said as she and Finn headed to their cars.

"Make it an eight o'clock start. Lots to talk about," Ian said.

"Yes, sir," Finn said saluting Ian.

"By uncle Ethan. Thanks for supper and the food fight," Caleb said acting like he was throwing food at Ethan.

"Ya 'missed, buddy. Good try though," Ethan said throwing imaginary food back.

"I got ya'," Nessie said as she smeared an imaginary French fry all over Ethan's arm.

"Oh, Nessie. I'll remember this for a long time," Ethan said as he messed up her hair. "Love you two."

"Love you more," Nessie and Caleb said at the same time.

Finn and Katelyn spent a few minutes enjoying each other before they went their separate ways.

"Appetizers and desert I could get used to," Katelyn said as they stepped apart.

"I could get use to servin' you as well," Finn said. "This sure was a great idea of yours, Katie girl. Loved how it all turned out."

"Me, too. Ethan's niece and nephew are a blast. I hadn't seen them yet. Ian must be so happy bein' a dad."

"He is and Melissa is thrilled to be a mom. She loves staying at home and takin' care of everyone. She does some side jobs as an editor for one of the big publishing houses once in a while."

"Has Ian said anything about building a house for them yet?"

"Yes, just yesterday. He wants to be completely off the grid. I'm gonna' take a look at his land and see what it offers. It's down the road about a mile from the shop. Most of the hot spring's streams flow on the east side of The Creek. But Ian said he found one about a ten-minute walk west of his place in the national forest close to the Tennessee line. I'll be workin' on that tomorrow along with the new clients and all. When did he tell you?"

"Just when I started workin' with y'all. He swore me to secrecy. We've had a few planning sessions and both of them like what I've come up with so far. There's still a lot more to do before anything can be ready for staking the land."

"Well, you can really keep a secret. Should I be worried?"

"Not one bit. I gotta' get goin'. I'm tired and we got an early start tomorrow."

"Katie girl, I got just one more thing to say. You are very dear and special to me. Stay safe okay? I know somethin's brewin' around here and it feels bad."

"You're right about that. I'm in good hands with Miss Cora and the others. And, you're just as dear and special to me, too, my Finn."

Finn kissed her again slow and deep to seal his words.

"Bye, my Finn," Katelyn said as she got into her SUV.

"Bye, my Katie girl," Finn replied.

As Katelyn was walking to her front door, she heard a loud crack then felt the ground shake. She ran around to the back just as Kendra was running out of her house.

They saw a full-grown sugar maple lying on the ground. They walked over to it to have a look.

"It doesn't look sick or anything," Kendra said.

Hal joined them along with a couple of folks that had been across the road.

"It looks like it was cut off down here near the base," Katelyn said pointing to the bottom of the tree.

"This is a perfectly healthy sugar maple. How in the world did it fall down?" Hal asked looking at the leaves and the bark.

They all heard a sizzling sound and stepped way back from the tree. A bolt of lightning hit it and cut it right down the center from bottom to top.

Katelyn and Kendra looked at each, held their arms out and said together, "White Light surround and protect us now!"

The lightning disappeared instantly.

Folks looked at the two of them for an explanation of what had just happened.

"Well, y'all, that's just a little somethin' I learned from Miss Cora. She said to say that if I ever felt like somethin' bad was around. Well, I do and I said it and now that bad energy is gone and we're safe," Kendra explained to them.

"Well, thanks for doin' that," George said. "I never heard of that before but I do like the way it works. Can anyone use it?"

"Yes, George, you can. Just be sure to say thanks when you're done," Kendra said as she and Katelyn offered a thank you looking upwards.

The others said thank you, too.

"Well, I do declare. That energy thing cut this tree perfectly in half. Now, Miss Kendra, I know this is your tree, but I'm wonderin' if I could take it with me? I'll get it to the sawmill up past the caves north of Emily's place and have them cut it so I can fashion a table or two from it. Is that okay with you?"

"Why, yes, Hal. That's a great idea. Do ya' know of anyone who needs a table or stand or whatever?"

"Yes, I do. I'm gonna' do the work as a gift. Ya' know how much I love makin' furniture and things."

"Alright, Hal. It's yours. Ya' gonna' let it sit here for a week or so?"

"Yes, Ma'am. It needs to dry for just a bit and the critters and birds and all can take the sap for food."

"This is great. I love when a tragedy turns out for good," Katelyn said looking right at Kendra.

"Me, too," Kendra.

Michael came over saying, "Anyone get hurt?"

"No, Michael, just the tree and Hal can tell ya' all about how it's gonna' be put to good use. Hal, I'd like some of the wood ya' can't use for my fireplace. Should be ready by winter time," Kendra added.

"Oh, me, too, if there's enough left over," Katelyn said.

"Oh, there will be. I'll tell ya' what. Once I start cutting the branches off, I'll leave them here and y'all can take what ya' want. I'll cut them into small lengths so they fit in your fireplaces."

"Another great idea, Hal. Get the word out so others can have some as well," Kendra said.

"I'll post a note on the front door today," Michael said. "Gotta' get back over there and let everyone know no one's hurt and all. By."

Folks kept looking at the tree and Kendra and Katelyn found the place The Dark had cut the base. It was a clean cut and rather high, about three feet from the ground. They figured the tree would sprout again in the next year or two.

The Dark was not happy with how all this had worked out. It struck again around midnight, downing a tree along the Pine Ridge Road. One of the delivery companies that made early morning deliveries to The Store found the first tree. He radioed the sheriff's department and they sent a cruiser right over. It parked behind the delivery truck and they looked at the tree. It was an old oak about ten feet in diameter. The deputy radioed dispatch and asked them to contact the highway department to get a crew out right away. The sheriff's department sent a couple of cruisers and deputies down the road to stop traffic and turn them around.

The second tree was found when Jonah tried to get to Emily's place. It was just north of The Store around the second bend in the road. It was an old oak as well. Jonah called the sheriff's department with the information and was told they were at the scene of a downed tree south of The Creek. The dispatcher told Jonah he would contact the highway folks again about the second tree. The dispatcher also said not to wait. It would take quite a while to get someone there.

Jonah called Emily and told her about the trees. She didn't like the sound of it at all. She texted Miss Cora, Kendra, and Katelyn. They said they would meet at The Store as soon as the trees were cleared.

That was gonna' be a long while. The Dark had a plan to carry out.

Just as the first tree was cleared, there was a great splintering sound and a huge maple fell not fifty feet north from the old oak the highway crew had just cleared. The maple landed along the yellow line on the road like someone had placed it there on purpose. It was about sixty feet tall like the one on Kendra's land. The crown of the tree was pointing towards The Creek.

The crew just looked at each other before they ran for their trucks. They weren't sure if it was safe outside right now. And, that's just what The

Dark wanted them to think. The crew chief got a hold of the supervisor informing him of the new development. The supervisor told them to hang on. He was gonna' contact the USGS and ask if there were any quakes in the area. He was gonna' contact the weather service at NOAA and ask about any strange lightning in the area, too.

Word got around The Creek about the maple tree and Miss Cora set up a video conference for the four of them.

"We got a problem here," Miss Cora began. "Katelyn, can ya' tell us about your latest adventure. Did it turn out well?

"Yes, Miss Cora. The Magic was saved and is safe and sound back there. But The Creek is a mess. Lots of destruction and many people were crossed over. It's gonna' be a long time before The Creek is recovered. I learned that I needed to save The Magic in that dimension so it could be saved here. And, that's gonna' need to be done real soon."

"Yes, Katelyn, it is. Thanks for the information. Now, Emily, what have you learned this morning?"

"Miss Cora, girls, I was told to prepare for a great battle. It will start right soon like Katelyn said. It's gonna' be a wicked crazy battle 'cause The Dark thinks if it completely destroys The Creek, and I mean not just the people and buildings, but the land and all, it can take the Special Magic and Powers from the cave."

"That's the message I got this morning as well," Kendra said.

"The one thing I learned from y'all and my time in the other dimensions is that I need to call for help as soon as I think I'm gonna' need it. I thank y'all for all the things you've taught me and the powers I've been given. But the one thing I found out recently is that ya' can't do this job all by yourself."

"Well, amen to that," Miss Cora said nodding her head. "It does take help from The Other Side."

"Yes, it does. Just like all the help I got up in The Sacred Rock Meadow," Emily added.

"That place is amazing," Katelyn said in awe.

They all looked at Katelyn and smiled.

"It truly is," Kendra said.

"Is there anything y'all don't know about this place?" Katelyn said smiling.

"No, not really, except maybe Emily. She's new to all this like you," Kendra said.

"I figured. So, now what?" Katelyn said.

"Katelyn," Miss Cora said. "Tell them what happened to me in the other dimension."

Katelyn took a breath then said, "The Dark blew Miss Cora and her house to smithereens."

"Oh, Katelyn. I'm so sorry ya' had to experience that. How awful," Emily said.

"It was horrible. As soon as I got back, I went right over to Miss Cora's and gave her the biggest hug I could for the longest time. Things are much better now."

"Good. Now, we've got some work to do," Kendra.

Kendra's phone buzzed at the same time as Emily's, Miss Cora's and Katelyn's.

The looked at the message then at each other.

"Oh my God! Not Tracey's farm," Kendra said. "Another tree fell into their barn and took out half of it along with two cows and a goat. This is really bad. The Dark is on a rampage."

"Sounds like it. That's the fourth tree this morning. That makes five altogether," Katelyn said.

"And, the road crews are on hold until the reports come back from the USGS and NOAA. Ethan said he'd get back to me when he finds out anything," Emily said.

"Let's get a positive energy thing goin' around the whole area outside The Creek as well as in The Creek. Maybe we can stop The Dark right now," Miss Cora suggested.

"I'm on it," Emily said as they heard her working on her laptop for the next few minutes.

"Folks are responding and sending that energy around right now," Emily told them.

No sooner had she said this when she got a text from Ethan saying the crews were back at clearing the trees. "Seems the USGS and NOAA reported no activity in the area. The supervisor said he felt a breeze pass over them and knew they'd all be safe clearing the trees. It shouldn't be long now. They know about the one up this way. Folks that can get to Tracey's place are on their way to help with the barn and animals and all. Now, that's just pure evil to kill those animals."

"I agree," Miss Cora said. "Well, we've got the positive energy thing going on. Let's get some Reiki around us, too."

"I'll send that request as well to my global contacts," Emily said.

"I do believe you are the computer email wizard Emily," Katelyn said laughing.

"I do believe she is. She's good at this kind of thing," Miss Cora said.

"Done," Emily said as she finished. "Let's see if this gives us a few more hours to plan how to be ready for The Dark's attack. I feel it's gonna' be any time now."

"Me, too," Miss Cora agreed. "Katelyn, looks like this is gonna' be your battle. What are ya' thinkin'?"

"I'm thinkin' I'm scared first of all. I know lots of stuff but I'm wonderin' how I will know what to do and where to go?"

"Remember how ya' kind of tuned in in the last dimension and then knew exactly where to go and what to do?" Miss Cora asked Katelyn.

"Yes, Ma'am, I do remember all that. I guess that's just what I'm gonna' have to do this time, too. Good thing I've had a little practice."

"Okay, then. For now, let's keep our eyes and ears open for anything else that may happen," Kendra suggested.

All agreed and the video chat ended. Word got around that the maple tree had been cleared and folks could pick up the wood from both trees later on. The crews had left the wood by the road so folks could use it. They set out for the tree up near Emily's place.

The crew stopped at The Store for lunch and water and a well-deserved rest. The Creek took good care of them and they were back on the road an hour later. It was early afternoon when they started to clear the next tree. They had heard about the tree falling into the barn and all and felt sad for the family.

The last tree, the sixth tree, fell on a house just north of The Creek around three o'clock that Thursday afternoon. The family was inside and the tree landed smack dab in the middle of the house. All the family members were killed instantly. The ground shaking alerted someone passing by the driveway and they turned down the driveway to see what had happened.

They immediately called 911 and the paramedics, fire trucks and sheriff's department responded right away. They had to come from the north as the road wasn't cleared yet. It wouldn't have mattered. The family was killed instantly by the double-trunked oak.

This was gonna' be a sad clean-up. The first thing that was done was the sheriff's deputy got the utility guys to come and shut off the electricity and natural gas to the house. Next, they sent a drone up to inspect the top of the house and the lay of the tree. They decided to get the crew up on the tree to cut it into about four huge pieces then a crane would be brought in to lift the pieces off the house. Only then could they get to the bodies.

The crew members they sent were mountain rescue trained. They had to use lines and climbing gear to be safe. The ladder truck was set up against the house to be a base for the safety lines and the crew walked out on the ladder and were suspended from the ladder to get to the tree. It was close to six o'clock when they started to cut up the tree. It took four hours and flood lights and all were brought in. Relief crews were brought in as well. As each chunk of tree was freed, it was pulled up by the crane and placed behind the house. The last piece came away easily and the inside of the house was revealed. The family lay across the kitchen floor crushed to death.

The crews had to take a few minutes to compose themselves. The scene was gruesome. The medical examiner's crew had arrived a little while earlier and was ready to do their part. It took them a few hours before the bodies could be removed and placed in the van. Folks were crying because most of them knew the family.

It was the Baker family. They had three children all under ten years old. They had moved here about a year ago and everyone liked them. When word got out just after it happened, folks got together on video chats and set up a fund for the family. Their kin had been contacted by the Kentucky State Troopers. It was a real sad day all around.

The Dark was pleased with the tree thing. It was happy as a kid at Christmas. It decided the time was right to begin the big attack to take The Special Magic and Powers by destroying everyone and everything in The Creek. It was giddy with its plan. It decided to cripple The Creek over several days so it wouldn't be able to protect The Magic when the final strike took place.

Folks were very quiet around The Creek that Friday. They grieved for Tracey's farm and the Baker family. They were scared that something else would happen and they might be killed. Miss Cora had called a community meeting at The Store for Friday evening Folks gathered for supper then the meeting got started.

"My dear sweet family here in The Creek, it's been a horrible few days for us. We've all been cryin' these past days. I called this meeting so we could share our grief and set up a plan to protect each other and The Creek," Miss Cora started.

"Whether you're gifted or not, most of ya' know how special The Creek is. We were put here to protect The Magic. We always have and we will continue to do just that. The Baker kin have been in touch with me and Kendra and they said to give away anything that was useful to anyone who needed it. Hal's gonna head up that group. The family wants to sell the property so Kendra's handlin' that aspect of things. Ethan was asked to pull down the house and all and clear the land and he agreed to do that. Some of us have been talkin' about what to do with the tree. Well, Ian's wife thought we could make tables from it and place them in the schools around the county. They're always in need. And, I suggested we take a piece of the trunk in the whole and make a plaque that honors the family and place it somewhere here in The Creek."

"Miss Cora, Ted and I have been talkin' about that and we'd like to offer a place on one of the outside walls of The Store. A place where we could see it and remember how precious our time on this earth really is," Michael said.

"Well, that's a mighty kind offer. What do y'all think? Should we do that? Who says yes?" Miss Cora asked.

Everyone raised their hands and the idea was set.

"Let's have Melissa decide what should be carved on the plaque. She's got a way with words and all," someone said.

"Sounds good to me. Let's get that project over to her as soon as we can. The guys cutting up the tree can decide which piece would be the best," Miss Cora said. "Next we gotta' talk about all this bad stuff goin' on. We need to come together and decide how we're gonna' stay safe. Kendra, how about you tell them about what we came up with?"

"Yes, Miss Cora," Kendra said. "Well, it seems The Dark is tryin' to take our Magic again. I would like to offer that instead of taking about how bad things are around here, that we talk about how special this place is and all the great times we've had. Evil likes negative talk and will bring down everyone involved in that kind of talk. The tragedies are for real and they are bad. And, we're feelin' sad about them. That's a part of grievin' and I wouldn't for one minute tell ya' to forget about that. Keep it real and understand it and place it where it needs to be so you can move forward. Let's think about that for a minute and see what we can come up with to support each other."

Folks began to think about what Kendra said and before long, they were talking in groups about how to move forward in positive energy remembering the recent past and learning from it.

Kendra called for order a while later. "I like what I've been hearin' from y'all. I've been cryin' a lot myself about things and I know that's okay. But I've come up with an idea about how we can keep goin' as a community and make some good things happen.

"I was thinkin' we could collect some pictures of things that y'all remember and love from whenever in your time here and make a big collage to hang in The Store. That way, we'd always see it and it would help us remember that bad stuff doesn't always have control of our lives. That there are wonderful things that happen and we should remember them and take comfort in them."

Folks really liked this idea and spent more time talking about it.

"I've offered to oversee this project. So, if ya' have any pictures ya' want to put in the collage, get them to me and I'll make copies so you can always have the originals. You can leave them here with Michael if I'm not around," Jenna said.

"Now that's a great idea, Jenna. Thank you," Miss Cora said. "Now, for somethin' a little more serious. I know you were asked to send positive energy and Reiki around the place when the tree thing was happenin'. Now, I'm gonna' ask you to keep that goin' and to add Light and Love along with it. We need all the positive energy we can get. I feel we're gonna' be seein' some more evil doings around here right soon. Leave all that to those of us who know how to handle it. The rest of ya' keep sending that energy stuff as much as ya' can. And, Miss Emily said, if ya' get to feelin' really sad, be sure to reach out to someone and talk about it. That way, the sadness gets easier and less of a burden to bear."

Folks talked for a bit before the meeting ended.

"Well, I think that's about it for tonight," Miss Cora said. "Take care everyone. Sleep well."

Most everyone went on their way right after the meeting. Ted and Michael were talking with Jenna about the collage project. Miss Cora and Emily had left together and talked for a minute outside before going on their separate ways. Katelyn and Kendra walked across the road together saying goodnight as they walked into their own houses.

The Creek settled in for the night with a lot to think about.

CHAPTER 32

Sami had gotten back to The Creek late Friday night and she and Katelyn talked well into the night about all the stuff that had happened since Katelyn had come back through the portal Tuesday afternoon. They finally fell asleep around two and slept a bit later than usual.

"How about we grab breakfast across the road since it's almost ten. We can call it brunch," Sami said as she yawned again.

"Great idea," Katelyn said as she yawned back at Sami.

"We sure are a sight to see. Tired for sure," Sami said as they walked across the road.

"Hey Sami. Katelyn," Ted said from the dining room. "You two look like you've been up all night."

"Hey, guys," Katelyn replied. "Only until about two. It's brunch time."

"Sounds good to me," Jordan said as he joined them at the table.

"Hey, Jordan. You look better than a body should," Sami said teasing him.

"Why, thank you, Sami. I appreciate that," Jordan said laughing with Katelyn and Ted.

"Tell y'all what. I'm gonna' fix you a special brunch thing. You just get whatever you want to drink and I'll be back in a bit," Ted said as he walked into the kitchen.

Katelyn was laughing as she said, "We must look a sight, Sami, for Ted to decide what we need. You, Jordan, look great."

"You do look like you didn't get much sleep last night. Partying or talking?" Jordan said.

"Talkin' into the wee hours," Sami said as she covered a yawn.

"I worked into the evenin but did get to bed at a decent time. I'm fascinated with the Redstone's barn and all the history that goes with it. Lots to learn about. Clara is reaching out to one of the URR historical societies about the names she has. She's being very careful about what she talks about to whom."

"I'm glad she's gonna' get those names out so the folks can find their ancestors and add more to their histories. This is one of the best ideas you ever had, Sami. And, you've had quite a few," Katelyn said.

"I think one of the most fun projects I ever had was the one about the water works department in Montgomery. Remember how the old pipes were buried under the current ones. Only thing was, no one told the road maintenance guys about the new pipes. When they were diggin' up the road to run the utilities underground, they broke into a number of the new pipes all over town and water flooded the streets and no one had any water for a long time. It was in the middle of summer so the kids had a blast with the flooded streets. It took the water department and the highway guys about four weeks to fix the new pipes. In the meantime, they brought bottled water in for everyone. Some of the folks saved rain water for flushing and washing dishes."

"How was that fun for you?" Jordan asked.

"Well, I was redesigning an office suite for the city's water works department when that rupture happened. We went into the basement to see if the problem was down there somewhere and came upon some murals from a long time ago. Seems the first water works department had gotten someone to paint the outline of the city on the basement walls. None of the subsequent building occupants had since paid any attention to them. I started looking at them and realized they were maps of the city's water pipe design. They showed where all the old pipes were laid. I informed the building owners and they came and had a look the same day.

"The owners got the historical society involved and they took a lot of pictures and magazines and newspapers wrote a lot of stories about them. The owners asked me to renovate the basement as a kind of museum. It was great. I learned so much about Montgomery from that project and fell in love with the history. Some of it was horrible and there were a few murals that depicted the slavery element. But, one of the funniest murals showed water shooting out of the fire hydrants caused when the pressure had been increased by mistake. The kids had a blast and the streets were flooded for the day. Sound familiar?"

"That's really funny, Sami" Jordan said as Ted came through the kitchen door with a big tray full of dishes.

"I made y'all a good old fashioned southern breakfast. Enjoy," Ted said as he set down the serving dishes full of every imaginary southern breakfast food you could think of. There were biscuits and gravy, grits, bacon, sausage, ham slices, scrambled eggs, eggs benedict, fruit cups and cornbread muffins. Butter, honey and jams showed up a few seconds later.

"Holy cow, Ted! We look that deprived?" Katelyn said laughing along with Sami and Jordan.

"In a word, yes! Now eat!" Ted said laughing as well.

"I guess I walked in at the right time," Jordan said as they put food on their plates.

"I'd say ya' did," Sami said.

They enjoyed the feast and laughed and talked more until most of the food was gone. Michael came by for a few bites as well as Ted. It was a fun morning.

"I may well be tired most of the day, but there's no way I'm gonna' be hungry for quite a while. Ted, you've outdone yourself once again and I thank you," Katelyn said.

"Ditto," Sami said.

"Same here," Jordan said.

"So, Jordan, Katelyn's been fillin' me in on all the crazy stuff that happened this week. Anything happen out your way?" Sami asked.

"No. Everything seems to be okay. Those trees crashin' down was just evil. I could feel it in my bones. Pure evil," Jordan answered.

"I agree," Sami said. "It feels like somethin's building up around here. Isn't that right Katelyn?"

"I think so, too. I'm quite new at all this Magic stuff. But I have learned to pay attention to my hunches and they are on high alert. Miss Cora says to watch for anything out of the ordinary."

"Good advice. I was at the town meeting last night and I like what I heard and saw. Folks are tryin' to move forward from the tragedies, taking little steps at a time and working at protecting things around here," Jordan said.

"Katelyn told me about the meeting. I agree with you, Jordan. What is it you call it Katelyn? The Dark? That's a good name for evil energy for sure."

"It most certainly is. Jordan, any weird stuff happening at your place?" Katelyn asked.

"Well, now that I'm thinkin' about it, there were some strange noises comin' across the field at sunset a couple of nights ago. Almost like screeching of some kind. I figured it was just some animals being hunted. Never heard it before or since. It was eerie."

"I'll let Miss Cora know. We're trying to keep track of anything not usual and that sounds not usual to me."

Kendra came by as they were talking.

"Hey, Jordan. I just heard what you said. I'll make a note of it," Kendra said.

"How about some leftovers? Ted thought Sami and I looked deprived," Katelyn said pointing to the table.

"Ooo, yes. I'll fix some up and zap em," Kendra said. "Breakfast was a long time ago."

Kendra came right back and began tasting the goodies. "Ted's outdone himself again."

"Always," Sami said. "Hey, Kendra, what's your take on all the weird stuff happenin' around here? Evil?"

Kendra nodded her head. "Absolutely. Y'all know about The Magic around here. Well, it's been my experience The Dark will do anything it can to get control of it. No matter how many times we win a battle, it eventually comes back around."

"The Magic here is really special. Especially The Magic in the cave," Sami said.

Katelyn and Jordan looked at Sami at the same time. "What do ya' mean, Sami?" Katelyn said.

Sami quickly looked at Kendra. She knew she had made a mistake mentioning The Special Magic in the cave. She wasn't supposed to know about it.

"Did you happen to mention it last night when y'all were talkin'? Sometimes, secrets get told to those we trust the most," Kendra said trying to cover Sami's error.

"Did I? I could have. We talked really late about everything. I may well have told Sami about that specific thing. Sami, please keep this secret. There are only five, now six, people, who know about that cave."

"Magic in my cave? I knew it. I just knew it. That explains everything," Jordan said quietly.

"Oh, boy. Keep the secret you two," Kendra said firmly and quietly.

"Kept," Sami said.

"Promise," Jordan said. "Katelyn, we gotta' talk later."

"I can't tell ya' anything else, Jordan. So, don't ask," Katelyn told him.

"Really? How about George, my baby eagle? He seems connected to me and me to him," Jordan said.

"That's okay. We all have animal guides and protectors. Looks like George is yours. He is a show off and rather funny,' Katelyn said.

"Yes, he is. I was out there last week and as soon as Jordan and I walked into the barn, he came swooping down and stood in front of Jordan. He was talkin' and bobbin' his head like they were havin' a full-on conversation,' Kendra said laughing.

"That's how we communicate. Every mornin' and every evenin'. He is a bit sassy," Jordan said.

"Oh, I gotta' meet your George," Sami said.

"Sure. Come on over when ya' get a bit of time. If he's out flyin' around he seems to know when I'm lookin' for him. He'll come by," Jordan said.

"Well, I've got some real estate stuff to do. The Baker kin said to sell the place when it's ready. The land won't be ready to show for a long while yet. They're just beginning the clean-up. Ethan said it would take a good month to demo the house and foundation and put fill in the ground. Once that's done, Miss Cora and I are gonna' have a ceremony freeing any spirits that may be lingering and offering love and light to the earth. The chiefs are gonna' cleanse it like they do. I think then it will be ready to show. Time to work," Kendra said as she left the dining room.

"Time for me to get along, too," Jordan said. "I think I'll visit my cave and bring an offering showing respect and thanks. The chiefs have taught me some stuff so I have what's needed. Thanks for the info," Jordan said as he left.

"Girl, we gotta' get home and get our chores done. Let's go," Katelyn said pulling Sami up by her arm.

"Agreed. Let's go pay the bill," Sami said as they stopped at the register. They paid Michael and thanked Ted again for the special brunch.

"Well, ya' look more awake then ya' did when ya' got here. Later," Ted said as they waved good-by and walked back home.

A while later, Sami was shaking a few rugs out on the back porch when Kendra called her name.

"Hey, Sami. Could ya' come over here for a minute, please?" Kendra said.

"Sure," Sami replied and left the rugs hanging over the railing.

"So, ya' know about the cave and The Special Magic in it," Kendra said.

"Yeah. I didn't know about it before last night though. I think Katelyn must have said somethin' about it for sure," Sami said. "It makes sense that it has Magic with all those crystals she and Jordan have been collecting."

"Yes, it does. Just promise me you won't say a word to anyone else. Please," Kendra said.

"I do so promise not to breath a word of it to anyone. I won't even talk about it to you and Katelyn. I'll act as if I don't know a thing," Sami promised crossing her heart.

"Okay then. Thanks. We gotta' protect that special place," Kendra said. "If Jordan offers you a chance to visit it, please decline."

"I will. Good idea,' Sami said. "I gotta' get back before Katelyn misses me. Later."

Sami ran back to the back porch and grabbed the rugs just as Katelyn came looking for her.

"I asked ya' to shake them, not remake them. Come on," Katelyn said laughing at the faces Sami was making.

"I kinda' got lost looking into the woods. I saw where that big tree came down. It leaves a space for sure."

"Kendra thinks the tree will regrow 'cause a three-foot stump was left. She said trees have been known to regenerate when a long stump is left."

"That would be great. You're gonna' have to let me know," Sami said.

"Let's get the rest of the tidying done. I'm really tired from last might. Or should I say this morning?" Katelyn said throwing a pillow at Sami.

Yup. You guessed it. A pillow fight ensued for a bit. The girls did finish their chores and grabbed cold drinks and retired to the front porch to watch the world go by.

Sunday morning Emily was in the stables feeding the horses when Trouble began to act weird. He was turning in circles and whining at one of Emily's horses' stall gates. She walked over to take a look.

"Hey Trouble, you hurt or somethin'?" she said as she looked him over and began to feel his body to see if something was wrong.

Trouble nudged her hand in the direction of the gate and she looked into the stall. Her horse was lying down and her breathing was irregular.

"Oh my God! Thanks for getting my attention, Trouble. I gotta' call Jonah right now," Emily said as she took out her cell phone.

"I'm right here, Miss Emily. What's up?" Jonah said as he walked over to her.

"She's not doin' well, Jonah," Emily said pointing to her horse.

"She most certainly is not," Jonah said as he walked into the stall and knelt down by the horse. Free Spirit lifted her head a bit to acknowledge Jonah.

Emily watched as Jonah placed his hands on her flank then moved them all over the horse.

"I know just what's ailin' Free Spirit," Jonah said as he stood up. "I'm gonna' need some sage and lavender. It's in the tack room. You know where. Now go get it for me, please"

Emily flew to the tack room, grabbed the herbs and was right back. Trouble had settled down along Free Spirit's back. Jonah took the herbs and sprinkled some lavender over Free Spirit and around the edges of the stall.

Next, he placed pieces of the sage leaves at the four corners of the stall and across the gate. He then put sage around Free Spirit. He stood at Free Spirit's head and began to chant in a language Emily had never heard before.

As he finished chanting, he moved to the back of the stall and began waving the sage from side-to-side and demanded the evil spirits leave the stall, the barn, and the earth all around Emily's Meadow.

When Jonah was at Free Spirit's side Emily saw a bunch of dark gray shadowy figures leave her body and fly to the gate. The sage stopped them and held them there. Jonah saged all of Free Spirit's body and more dark gray shadowy figures flew to the gate. When he finished with Free Spirit, he saged the space up to the gate.

At the gate he threw the shadowy gray figures into the spaces between the dimensions to remain there for eternity. When this was completed, he sprinkled lavender across the gate opening.

Free Spirit stood up, gave a whiny and a shake and looked great. Trouble came around to stand in front of her and she leaned down and gave him a nudge.

"Mr. Jonah, how did you know it was The Dark that had possessed Free Spirit? That was amazing!" Emily said as she stood next to him.

"I've always known about evil spirits. That's why I'm here this time, to take care of the critters Miss Emily. The Magic is everywhere," Jonah said looking right at her. She placed her hand on his shoulder.

"I kind of wondered about you and all. I'm so happy to know about you. It all makes perfect sense. Thank so much for sharin' the love and light of The Divine," Emily said.

"My pleasure, Miss Emily," Jonah said as he walked out of the stall. "Let's leave Free Spirit here for awhile more as she gets used to being okay. I'll get her fed and watered then Trouble can help me walk her in the paddock," Jonah said.

"Great idea. Thanks," Emily said as they went about their day.

Although the rest of the day seemed to be as normal as always, some folks were a bit uneasy. They could feel ripples of strange energy go through The Creek a few times that day. They kept a look out for trouble.

The rest of the week was totally normal. No bad energy ripples. They were gone. No trouble with anyone or anything. Visitors were pleasant and happy to be in the Blue Ridge. Everything was going along just fine.

Jordan decided to visit his cave that Friday afternoon. It was a hot summer day with a clear blue sky. As he set out George flew by and kept him company on his walk. George had a few things to say and Jordan laughed at his antics.

When they arrived at the cave, Jordan moved the bushes aside and looked at George. He had landed right next to Jordan. Jordan had a thought and moved aside to let George enter. George walked into the cave like he belonged there. He strutted right into the crystal room and stood there waiting for Jordan.

"Well, George. I guess you know about this place," Jordan said as he came to stand next to George on the edge of the room. George bobbed his head a couple of times in response.

"This sure is a beautiful place and knowing that The Special Magic lives here makes perfect sense with how I feel when I'm here," Jordan said to George as if George could answer him.

George gave a soft squawk as he stepped into the middle of the room. He looked back at Jordan and Jordan could have sworn George winked at him as if he had a secret. The air began to change and swirl around the room in a gentle motion. The crystals began to glow brightly and George spread his wings as if to feel the energy all around.

Jordan knew something magical was about to happen. He could feel it. As he watched, the air began to swirl closely around George. A cloud of color enveloped George for just a split second. Then it happened.

George morphed into a man. He was taller than Jordan and looked ageless. Not old or young but no particular age. His hair was blond and he had eyes the color of gold.

"Hi Jordan. George here," he said as Jordan stood staring in utter amazement. "Well, aren't ya' gonna' say anything?" George laughed at the look on Jordan's face.

"If you could only see the look on your face. Oh, wait a minute, you can," George said as he walked over to Jordan and put a mirror in front of his face.

Jordan looked at himself, took a breath, then laughed. "I sure to look dumb struck. Hello George."

"Jordan. Just one thing about the name. George? Really? Couldn't you have named me something more dignified like Jameson or Stuart?"

"No. George works for me," Jordan replied. "I can't believe I'm standing here talking to my eagle that just changed into a human man. I shouldn't be surprised knowing how special this cave is, but I am."

"Let's sit for a bit and you can ask any questions you want. I may not be able to answer them all but you can still ask them." George suggested as he led Jordan to a table and chairs made of pure clear quartz crystal that materialized out of nowhere. They were set in the middle of the room where George had been standing. Mugs full of some kind of beverage and plates of food appeared. Everything was made of different colored crystals. Everything was beautiful.

"This place is beyond magnificent," Jordan said as they sat down.

They ate and drank for a bit then Jordan started asking questions.

"So, why me? Why are you here with me?" Jordan asked.

"First of all, we want to thank you for following all the signs and things and buying this land."

"You're welcome. Who's 'we'?" Jordan asked.

"We are the keepers of The Magic. A part of The White Light. We have been protecting The Magic since time immortal."

"Okay. I get that. But why are you talkin' to me?"

"Because you own the cave," George said in a matter-of-fact tone.

"Oh. So, what if someone else owned the land like the last owners?"

"They chose not to believe in magic and all other forms of non-physical life. We tried to contact them one afternoon and they freaked out. They left the next day and sold the property which you bought. They thought something demonic was happening. Oh well."

"I remember Kendra telling me about them. Hope they're okay now."

"Yes, they are. We removed that memory from them and relocated them to a different place that they are very pleased with. They love the land and are doing some gardening and they love they're new jobs. We didn't want them to suffer from the experience of seeing a magical entity."

"I can understand that. I am keeping this place secret like the others asked me to. Don't know what else I'm supposed to do now."

"We left you some presents. Did you get them?" George said smiling.

"Yes, I did. Thank you. Those crystals are so beautiful. The one by the front door acts like a beacon every evening when the sun hits it. People stop by every evening to watch it shine and glow."

"It is a great one. Katelyn has a few crystals, too. She knows about this place as well."

"Yes, she does. We love our twin crystals. That's what we call the ones you gave to us a while back when we were walking out here."

"Good name for them. Have you placed them next to each other yet?"

"No. Why?"

"How about you call her over tomorrow and tell her to bring her twin. Place them next to each other out behind the barn. You're gonna' love what happens."

"Now you've got me curious," Jordan said laughing.

"I'll be here watching as always," George said.

"Well, I have a few more questions," Jordan said.

"Go ahead."

"I was walking around this room the other day and found that short tunnel that led to those three other caves. When I looked down the purple one on the right, I swear I saw two big eyes lookin' back at me. They blinked and then they were gone. Is there something alive in that cave?"

George took a moment to thing before he spoke. "Jordan, I am being told I can't talk about that. Period."

"Okay. Fair enough. I know what I saw though. There's a lot going on in this cave that I don't know about. I do know it's all good stuff. So, whatever is down there must be magical as well."

"Good thinking, Jordan." George said. His eyes were glowing brightly.

"Your eyes tell the truth. I'm gonna' remember that," Jordan said.

"You figured that out very quickly. Sooner than we thought you would. No matter," George said. "Let's take a walk to those tunnels. I want to show you something."

"Okay," Jordan said as they walked across the room to the short tunnel.

"I gotta' tell ya' George. This seems so surreal. I'm lovin' every second of this."

George just smiled at Jordan as they entered the short tunnel.

"Look here," George said as he passed his hand across the wall. A small room appeared. They walked into it and looked all around.

There were stalagmites and stalactites all over the place. All made of crystals. Extraordinary. Every one of them. Every color and shade of the rainbow and then some.

"George. This is so cool!"

"Yes, it is. Please walk around. The crystals will make room for you."

"Huh?"

"Go ahead and take a few steps and watch what happens."

Jordan took a hesitant step into the room and the crystals right in front of him cleared a path for him. They moved out of the way.

"Wow!"

"Really wow!" George replied. "No matter how many times I've seen this it still takes my breath away to watch."

Jordan continued to walk around the small room and the crystals continued to move around him. He stopped near a very long crystal hanging from the ceiling.

"This one is humming," Jordan said.

"Touch it and see what happens," George said.

Jordan placed his hand on the crystal and it came loose from the ceiling and changed its shape into a sword made of a deep red color. The hilt was silver, the blade the deep red and there was a purple crystal that covered the top of the hilt.

Jordan held the sword out in front of himself for a minute then said, "It doesn't weigh much at all. I thought it would be heavy when it first came loose from the ceiling. But it's very easy to hold. What should I do with it now?"

"Ask it," George said.

"Okay. Sword, what shall I do with you now?"

A voice answered Jordan. "This sword is for you to take with you. You will know what to do with it when the time comes."

"Whoa! That voice came from the air," Jordan said as he brought the sword to his side.

"Yup. Magic at its best."

"I'll say it is. So, I guess I take this home with me and wait to see what happens."

"That's exactly what you're supposed to do. Time to leave this magical place," George said as he stepped back into the tunnel.

Jordan followed and when he turned around to look at the room, it was gone. The wall was back in its place.

"Jordan, time to return to the crystal room," George said as they walked back into the crystal room.

George stepped into the middle of the room again. "It's time for me to morph back into my eagle self. Thing is, from now on, you will hear me talking just like this in my eagle form. No one else will. They'll just hear me squawking as usual. Be careful what you say to me when others are around. They might think you've gone batty," George said with a laugh.

"Funny, George. Thanks for bringing George to me everyone. I am much obliged for today. The sword is magnificent and I will listen and be ready when it's time to give it to the right person," Jordan said.

"Take care, Jordan. Until the next time," George said and, in an instant, he was back to his eagle self.

"George, what do ya' mean 'the next time'?" Jordan said looking at George.

George just bobbed his head and walked back through the room, into the entry tunnel and waited for Jordan to move the bushes aside.

Once outside, George said, "Time to fly my friend." He took to the sky, circled around a few times then flew off over the trees on the edge of the field.

Jordan stood there for a bit looking at the sword and thinking about all that had just happened. This was one of the most incredible things that had ever happened to him. He smiled and set out walking across the field back home.

Once he got home, he placed the sword in his bedroom across a shelf in the closet. He felt the need to protect it from others. It felt like the right thing to do.

Rain had been forecast for Saturday morning and it showed up as expected. It was supposed to clear later in the afternoon. It didn't. It got heavier and became torrential by supper time. Flashflood warnings went out for The Creek and surrounding areas as stream beds and ponds began to take on a lot of water. There were little streams running down the roads.

Right in front of The Store, the water started on one side of the road just north of The Store, crossed to the other side of the road in front of The Store, then began to pool on the land south of Katelyn's house. A pond began to form out of nowhere.

The weather service had no idea where the rain was coming from. It was only over that specific area of the Blue Ridge encompassing an area about 30 miles in diameter with The Creek right in the middle. Miss Cora knew what it was right away. She texted Emily, Katelyn, and Kendra to meet her at The Store immediately.

Miss Cora was the first to arrive. Katelyn and Kendra were trying to figure out how to get across the road. They decided to walk a few yards up from The Store on their side of the road, then cross. When they started to cross, the small stream that had formed on the side of the road suddenly got bigger and stronger. Kendra called out for some help and a tree was set across the water for the two of them to walk on. As soon as they were over the water, the tree disappeared.

"I knew it," Katelyn said.

"Me, too," Kendra replied as they got to the porch of The Store.

Emily pulled alongside of The Store on account of the front area being completely under water. She came through the side door dripping wet.

"Now I know what a mermaid feels like," Emily said as she took off her rain jacket standing there dripping all over the place.

"Here, sweetie," Ted said handing her a towel. "I'll hang your jacket up in the mudroom off the kitchen."

"Thanks, Ted. You are a true southern gentleman," Emily replied.

"Hope so. That's how my mama raised me."

Emily joined the group at the dining room table.

"There may a drought in some parts of the country, but there isn't any around here," Emily said as she got herself something to drink and sat down.

"Hey Ethan," Michael was heard to say.

"Hey, Michael. I would like to set up a command station here. Some of the folks are becoming stranded with the water cutting them off from the road and other folk's homes are beginning to fill up with water. The sheriff's department is trying to get to them and bring them to a safe place."

"Sure thing. How about I put up a table right here in the front so folks can get to you?"

"Great. The sheriff's sending a deputy over and the Red Cross is tryin' to determine if they need to set up a shelter."

"Okay. Here ya' go," Michael said as he set up a folding table for Ethan by the stove.

The deputy arrived just then and he and Ethan got busy. They had two-way radios and were in touch with county officials. Seems the rest of the county was dry.

"I didn't see any rain until I crossed the line into The Creek. Then holy hell broke loose," Rick said. "It's really weird how that happens. Dry than wet. Like a line had been drawn."

"I know. Really weird," Ethan said agreeing with Rick.

"Miss Cora, your place is up a bit, isn't it?" Ethan called back.

"Yes, it's good, Ethan. I'm liking the pond across the road. Katelyn, ya' can probably get a boat and paddle around later."

"That's what I was thinkin', Miss Cora," Katelyn replied smiling.

Reports started to come in on the people stranded. The sheriff's deputies were driving around trying to get those folks to safety. They had their flat-bottomed boats at two different locations. The rain just kept coming down. It was so torrential that it looked like a wall of white water, not rain water, falling from the sky.

"Hey, y'all, look out here," someone hollered from the front of the store.

Folks gathered by the windows on the west side and the back and saw the strangest site. There was a new stream flowing not far from the back of the store and another coming down from the path that led to the hot springs. It looked like it was gonna' hit The Store any minute. It did. A wall of water smashed into The Store. Nothing was broken but it kept coming.

The pond across the road was growing bigger by the minute. It would reach Katelyn's house before long.

Jonah called from Emily's place. "Emily, your pond has breached the bridge. It's flowin' all over the place. The bridge is completely under water and there's a new stream flowing between the house and the barn. It's moving fast, too. I got the chickens inside and all the others are safe. Me and Trouble are in the stables keepin' an eye on things. I never seen anything like this before."

"Thanks, Jonah You stay safe." Emily replied.

"Well, I think we're gonna' need some help here," Miss Cora was saying when Ethan came into the dining room.

"I'm sorry to have to tell ya' this, Miss Cora, but your house just floated away down a new river that formed a few minutes ago. One of the sheriff's guys was checking on it and he said he couldn't believe his eyes when a wall of water came outta' nowhere and just pushed your house from its foundation. It's floatin' along in the new river right now, going through the woods crashing into trees and all. So sorry, Ma'am."

"Thank you, Ethan. It's not the kind of news I wanted to hear. But, I'm safe here and that's all that really matters," Miss Coral replied. "Ethan, would ya' keep folks from comin' up here for a bit. You'll know when it's okay to let them come in again."

"Yes, Ma'am," Ethan replied as he went back to the front table.

"We need some help right now. Hold hands ladies and let's get callin' for that help," Miss Cora said.

Kendra started. "I call upon The White Light to help us here."

Katelyn was next. "I ask for help from all the guardians of The Creek."

Emily continued with, "I call upon The Ancients to help keep us and all here in The Creek stay safe."

Miss Cora took over. "And, now, I call upon those that protect The Magic from the other realm to stop this assault from The Dark. Father Sky, I ask ya' to stop the rain. Mother Earth, I ask ya 'to accept the rain and keep all us critters safe. And, we thank ya' all for your help. Start chanting and don't stop no matter what happens. Got it?"

"Yes, Ma'am," they answered as one.

The chanting was low and quiet, but it could be heard by all in The Store.

The rain began to slow and The Dark was pissed. It sent a bolt of lightning at The Store. Father Sky stopped it. The Dark sent an earthquake to swallow The Creek. Mother Earth stopped it.

The rain continued to slow down to nothing more than a drizzle. The Dark was beyond angry. It sent a wall of water to destroy The Creek. The ancients blocked it. They needed The Creek to keep protecting The Magic.

Then the strangest thing happened. The sun came out while it was raining. The sky was filled with black clouds but the sun broke through long enough to heat up the water and turn everything to steam. It wasn't fog in the air, but steam. The Ancients focused this steam into a bolt of energy and directed it at the blackest cloud in the sky. It blew the cloud apart and a ripple of energy shredded the rest of the black sky. The sun shinned brightly through the now cleared blue sky and sent rainbows everywhere. Little ones and big ones. Sunbeams bouncing off rooftops and the pond and streams that had formed from the rain vanished almost instantly.

Folks ran outside to look at things and saw those sunbeams and rainbows. Sad thing was, Ethan reported that one old man died in the flooding of his land. He was known as old man Noah. Folks would take care of him and his place.

The sheriff's deputies sent up a few drones to survey the land that had been damaged. They looked for Miss Cora's house and saw it was setting on her land as always. They couldn't believe their eyes. Weird stuff was surely happening around here.

"Miss Cora, your house is back where it should be," Ethan said shaking his head. "I don't even want to know."

Miss Cora laughed out loud. "Thanks, Ethan."

The storm was over. It was well past eight and Ted said supper would be out in a minute. Folks came in with food as well and everyone had stories to tell while they ate. They were very thankful that The Creek was safe once again.

They went outside to watch the sky as the sun dipped below the trees. It was shades of purple, gold and pink. Beautiful.

Jordan's farm had some water flowing around the field where it shouldn't have been. Jordan went out into the barn after the rain stopped and George flew in.

"Everything look okay, George?" Jordan asked.

"Yes, Jordan. That water was lookin' for the cave. Never found it, of course. All's safe," George replied.

"Thanks for checking on things. I do like the fact that you can fly all over the place and see so much in a flash. Wicked cool."

"I agree. There are advantages to being an eagle."

"Time for me to call it a day. I'm tired from all the cool stuff that has happened today and the URR project. Time to sleep."

"Sleep well, Jordan."

Jordan returned to the house just as the sun was setting below the trees. The sky was beautiful shades of purple, gold, and pink shining all over the place.

The Dark was angry. His plan had been thwarted by The White Light. It was time to attack in a big way. No more pussy footing around. Time for The Creek to be destroyed and The Dark to gather all The Magic for itself. Especially The Special Magic and Powers, wherever they were hiding.

CHAPTER 33

The Creek spent the next couple of days drying out. Branches had to be cleared around the properties. The Pond that had been created by Katelyn's house may have disappeared, but the stuff left behind needed to be cleaned up. Kendra started cleaning the area the second afternoon when she was finished with her real estate work. Katelyn got home a bit earlier than usual and she pitched in.

They found stuff one would expect to find. Stones, branches, leaves, even an old newspaper still rolled up. When they got to the bottom of the stuff they stood back and smiled. Staring back at them was a bunch of small crystals all covered in dirt. They picked them up and put them in a basket.

Once they had moved all the debris, minus the newspaper, to the edge of the woods, they brought the stones to Kendal's back porch and set them on the steps. They gently hosed them off and watched as they began to shine a bit.

"Let's take them to the front porch and put them on the railing," Katelyn suggested.

They gathered them again and when they had placed them on the railing, the late day sun shone right on them and they came to life.

"Kendra. Katelyn," they heard from across the road. "I found some crystals alongside our driveway after everything was cleared, too," Jackie said coming across the road.

"Hey, mom," Katelyn said as she hugged her mom.

"Hey, Katie girl. Were these in the pond area?"

"Yes, they were," Kendra replied.

"Your dad and I found these this morning," Jackie said as she took a few small crystals out of her pocket.

"They're beautiful. Here, put them next to these," Kendra suggested.

Once they were on the railing, the crystals began to throw rainbows onto the house.

"Would ya' look at that?" Miss Cora said as she joined them. "Beautiful. I found some at my place, too. Right up against the front and back steps like someone had laid them there."

They watched the rainbows dance along the house as the sun began to move closer to the trees. Others saw the lights and came by to enjoy the show.

Miss Cora went on her way saying she had things to take care of.

"I wonder if there were crystals all over The Creek? Wouldn't surprise me none," Diane said. "Hank and Finn found them lined up along the driveway like runway lights. They cleaned them up some, too, then put them right back in place. I'll bet they're shinin' like all get out right now, too."

Pictures were taken and texts sent all around. Soon others were sending texts to show the crystals they had found. Seems The White Light had given a bit of love to everyone. They were all small but lit up like crazy.

"Hey, everybody, come to the back of The Store and look at what happened back here," Michael said waving his arms.

They walked over to the back and found the coolest thing. Seems The White Light had a great sense of humor among other things. The crystals had been laid out to spell, "Hi Ted and Michael'. Underneath the message were two little 'stick' figures made of crystals to look like the guys. Ted had on an apron and Michael was holding a dollar sign.

Everyone burst out laughing at this making comments and wise ass remarks. Someone suggested Ted and Michael stand at each side of the figures for pictures. The guys graciously agreed and posed and made funny faces as well.

Ted and Michael went back inside to take care of customers while folks stayed out back talking and laughing and taking pictures of themselves next to the message and figures for the longest time. Every time a new person walked into The Store, they were told to go out back and take a look at the new landscape design. This kept up through supper and well into the evening.

Miss Cora came by after she received a group text. She was laughing when she saw the new landscape design.

"Now, I'd say that was a clever and artistic way to get a message around," Miss Cora said laughing. "They got those two boys pegged for sure."

The evening turned into a fun kind of thing and everyone who came by had a grand time.

Jordan was heard to say, "Well, I guess Katelyn and I aren't that special anymore with everyone getting some crystals. This place is gonna' be shinin' so bright, NASA's gonna' wonder what's goin' on down here."

Hal added, "I'll bet the aviation folks are gonna' have to include The Creek on a map of bright light places."

More and more comments were made as the evening went along. It was close to dark when the last folks went on home. Ted and Michael came outside one more time to look at their special message and offered prayers of thanks and love.

"This is really awesome, Michael," Ted said as they stood hand-in-hand looking at their gift from The White Light.

"Sure is, Ted. Let's finish up and get settled for the night. Good night all you special crystals. Thanks Mother Earth for sharin' some of your children with us."

A few of the crystals blinked back at them.

The Creek slept with sweet memories that night.

Folks got back to work the next day. Gardens needed picking and weeding. Lawns needed mowing. Farm work was going along as usual. Katelyn decided it was the perfect time to place the new crystal on top of The Rise the next Saturday. Sami had to go back to the hotel to take care of some things for the day so Katelyn was free to get things done.

Katelyn set out mid-morning stopping at the house first.

Hey, y'all," she said as she walked into the kitchen. Her mom and dad were the only ones there.

"Hey Katie girl," her dad said as he gave her a big hug.

"I love your hugs, dad," Katelyn replied squishing into him.

"So do I," Jackie said smiling at Katelyn.

"What brings you here on this beautiful day?" Jackie said

"I thought I'd go over to The Rise. I love looking out over everything from the top. Kind of puts things into perspective."

"I can understand that. I've got some equipment to clean and repair. Have a grand time. Take a few containers with you. Ya' might want to pick a few berries for yourself," her dad suggested.

"I'll do just that. Good idea. I just may make a pie later today," Katelyn said kissing her dad on the cheek. He left through the kitchen door.

"You want some of those berries mom? I don't mind gathering some for you," Katelyn asked.

"If you want to. You know how much your brothers and dad love berry pie. I might just mix them with some of the strawberries I froze earlier. That would make a really yummy pie."

"I like that idea. I'll be sure to bring ya' some. I'd like a bag of those strawberries if you can spare one. A mixed berry pie sounds right nice."

"Find me when you get back. I'll grab a bag for you then. Have a nice time on The Rise."

"Thanks mom. I will."

Katelyn left with four berry boxes and drove out to the berry field near The Rise. She picked the berries first. It didn't take more than twenty minutes. The plants were still full of them. She set them on the floor of her SUV out of the sun. She grabbed her backpack and headed for The Rise.

It was such a beautiful thing to see. She stood still for a minute a ways back from The Rise. It did look like it had always been there. It felt like it should have always been there as well. She walked to the edge of the stairs and paused. The air was still and peaceful almost as if The Rise was waiting for her.

She climbed the stairs and reached the top. She stood looking at the top for a minute. Then she walked to the middle. The eagle feathers were there but the crystal that had been there from the first day was gone. Room had been made for the crystal she had been given.

She took the crystal from her backpack and gently placed it in the middle of the circle. As soon as it touched the ground, she saw a ring of energy go out from the crystal to the edges of The Rise. It almost looked like an energy fence. The energy was blue like the blue in the crystal. She noticed the crystals that were partially showing on the ground were now gently glowing. There were little pockets of light all over the ground as if tiny Christmas lights had been placed there. It was really pretty. She stepped back from the center to look out over the land.

The view was magnificent. She could see The Meadow with the secret tunnels underneath. She could see The Store and smiled as she remembered the new landscape feature in the back. She could see Jordan's farm and felt a powerful connection to the cave. She could see where her brother's homes would be. The land had been cleared for the excavation to begin. She saw where The Creek ended and the Pine Ridge Road kept going towards Pine Ridge. She looked to the northeast and remembered the archeological dig up that way. She turned a bit and could make out the fields that would eventually give way to Boone.

She felt privileged and blessed to be standing here looking out over the place she loved and called home. She wasn't sure how long she stood there remembering the past years of her life. She suddenly felt hungry and thirsty. She must have been up here quite a while. She laughed at herself for getting lost in memories and daydreams. Time to return to now and get those berries to her mom and pick up the strawberries for her pie. She turned to look at the center once more and saw that the blue and purple crystal was glowing like crazy. She bowed to it giving silent thanks for its energy. It twinkled back at her.

She descended and walked to her SUV. She was at the house a few minutes later.

"Hey, mom. Here's the berries. You in here?" Katelyn called out.

Her mom walked in the back door. "I was hangin' the blankets I washed on the line. I love the way they smell when they've been sun dried."

"Me, too," Katelyn said as she drank a bottle of cold water from the fridge.

"Did ya' have a good visit with The Rise?"

"Yes, I did. Thanks for askin'. There's somethin' about that place that gets me to forgetting about today and takes me back to other times and places."

"I know the feelin'. I walked up there before the rain and felt the same way. Here are the strawberries for your pie. Have fun makin it and eating it."

"Oh, I will. I was gonna' invite Finn over for desert tonight. I know how much he loves pie," Katelyn said smiling and laughing.

"I hear ya'. Enjoy them both," her mom said as she walked Katelyn outside. She waved at her as she drove off.

Ian was in Boone meeting with a new supplier for plumbing supplies. He had finished his meeting and stopped at a gas station to fill up his truck when he heard his name called out.

"Hey, Ian," he heard a guy say.

Ian looked around and saw one of his long-time friends waving to him from across the gas pumps.

"Hey, Gerry. How the hell are ya'? They really let you drive around by yourself?" Ian answered as he hung up the pump handle and walked over.

"No. But I do sneak away some times like today. The whole band and crew are off for the next two weeks and most of us came back home here. I'm headed to my place just west of Pine Ridge. You built it. Remember?"

"You bet I do. This is great. How come you don't have all your body guards around ya'?"

"I ordered them to go on ahead to the house and leave me alone for a few hours. I need some free time and space."

"I can understand that. It's lunch time. Join me for a bite?"

"Ah, that might be a little difficult around here," Gerry answered.

"I was just thinkin' that. How about we go to The Store in The Creek? When was the last time you were there?"

"Ian, it's been more than a year. I'll follow you," Gerry said as he put the pump handle back on the pump.

Ian led the way and about a half-hour or so later they parked on the side of The Store and walked in by the side entrance.

Ted was in the dining area when he heard the door slam.

"Hey, Ian. Oh my God! Is it really you, Gerry? Where the hell have you been?" Ted called out as he gave Gerry a big hug.

"On tour and recording in the studio in Nashville. Got a new album comin' our in a few weeks. Damn, Ted, ya' look great."

Michael came running up the stairs and grabbed Gerry into a huge hug.

"Gerry, you old son of a son. I can't believe it's really you!" Michael said as he stepped back and looked Gerry over.

"Don't tell anyone he's here. He wants to remain unnoticed," Ian said.

"No problem. No one's here right now but they will be. We'll ask them to keep your secret," Ted said.

"Thanks guys. I've really missed this place and you two. Ya' helped me when I was just tellin' folks I was gay and my career was bein' launched. I love ya' both so much."

"We love ya', too, Gerry. Forever. Now, I suspect you're in need of some of Ted's creations?" Michael said.

"Yes, I am in desperate need of Ted's creations. Saw Ian at the gas station in Boone and he suggested we come here to avoid the public."

"Good thinkin', Ian," Ted said.

"Well, let me look over the special's board and try to make up my mind," Gerry said laughing.

"Y'all know the routine," Ted said as he went back into the kitchen and Michael went back out front.

A few minutes later, Ethan walked in and went right up to the dining area.

"Hot damn! Look's who's finally home?" Ethan hollered as he and Gerry hugged each other.

"Don't tell anyone," Ian said.

"No worries here about that," Ethan replied. "Gerry, when did ya' get here and how long are ya' gonna' be around?"

"Got into Boone late last night. Stayed at a local house and was just headin' home when Ian and I saw each other at the gas station. And, here we are. I'll be around for quite a while. Can't wait to see everyone again. I miss y'all so much. You're my family. Always have been and always will be."

"We all feel the same," Ethan said. "I gotta' tell ya' that Emily is about to come through the door. She relocated here about a year and some ago. She loves your music so she's probably gonna' be a little star struck."

"Thanks for the warnin'. You two an item?"

"Yes, they are," Ted hollered from the kitchen.

"That man can hear for miles," Ethan said laughing and nodding his head

Just then Emily came into The Store and headed up the stairs. She stopped in her tracks when she saw Gerry.

"Oh, my stars!" she said looking at Gerry then Ethan. "You two know each other?"

"Ever since we were little dudes," Gerry said offering his hand to Emily. "Hi, I'm Gerry Bailey. I grew up around here."

"Hi. I'm Emily Henshaw. I moved here a while back. I love your music by the way."

"Thanks, Ma'am. Sure do appreciate that," Gerry said.

"Ethan, we really need to work on our communication. I didn't know ya' knew Gerry Bailey," Emily said whacking Ethan in the arm.

"I do have a few secrets I've kept from ya'," Ethan said.

"Oh, mister, we're gonna' have to talk for sure," Emily said laughing. "Well, I came in for some lunch with Ethan. I guess it's gonna' be four of us now."

"Yes, it is," Ian said.

They settled with their lunch and the questions began.

"So, Ethan, Ian, and Gerry, how did y'all get to know each other?" Emily asked.

"Well," Ian started, "We grew up together. Gerry was adopted by his family when he was about six, right?"

"Yup. I remember havin' my sixth birthday with my new family right after I was adopted. They invited a lot of the kids from around here. That's when I met Ethan and Ian. Ethan was a bit older but Ian and I were the same age. We hit it off right from the start and have stayed close all these years," Gerry said.

"Yes, we have and I'm so glad we did," Ian said.

"Do ya' have a place around here, Gerry?" Emily asked. "Oh, don't worry, your bein' here is safe with me. I'm not gonna' tell anyone. We keep all kinds of secrets here in The Creek."

"I know y'all do. These two built me a fantastic home just west of here. And, they built me a separate recording studio a ways back from the main house. We have a guest house, too. And, Ian suggested I build a smaller studio in the main house so I could record my voice overs while the band was busy in the outside studio. It's worked out really well."

"So, you have a Sutherland build. I love mine. I even have a covered bridge over a pond as part of my driveway," Emily said.

"Really? Whose idea was that?" Gerry asked looking at Ethan and Ian.

"It was Karl's. The same guy who did your excavation and suggested we add that gradual slope to the far reaches of the property for better drainage," Ian replied.

"I love that guy. He's so gifted with his ideas and all. It seems he can see things in his mind long before any work is done," Gerry replied.

"I agree. I love my bridge," Emily agreed.

Gerry's phone buzzed. "That's Tommy. I texted him to come over but he said he was busy at the house. Ted, Michael, did ya' get his email yesterday?"

"Yes, we did, and we said yes to everything," Michael replied as he joined the group.

"Said yes to what?" Ian asked.

"Ian, my sweet friend, Tommy thought we should have a family reunion since we haven't been home in a long time for more than a day or two. We're here for two weeks of rest and fun. Then, the band and producers and all will join us here to record our next album. That means we'll be around for a few months on top of everything else. We start our new tour in February so we've got time to be home," Gerry explained.

"That's fantastic," Ian replied. "So, when we gonna' has this shindig?"

"Well, it's gonna' be next Saturday. Ted, Michael, and Tommy have been planning the food thing. We've got everyone's email addresses and Tommy's gonna' send a group email out today. I just wanted a little bit of time to myself and y'all. You're so special to me. Y'all are the brothers I never had. Emily, my new family had four girls. So, I have all the sisters I'll ever need, but I do believe I may just need one more. You available?"

"Oh my God, Gerry. Of course, I am. I'm thrilled," Emily said laughing and smiling like crazy.

"Good. Ya' never can have too much family," Gerry said.

Folks were beginning to come in for lunch and all so the group left by the side door and talked a few minutes more outside.

"Alright then. Next Saturday at my place. Can't wait," Gerry said shaking hands all around.

"So great to have ya' home, bro," Ethan said.

"I'm honored to be your new sister," Emily said.

"I'm blessed to have such a beautiful new sister. Later, y'all," Gerry said as they got into their trucks and headed off to work and home.

Katelyn was outside the shop when she felt a cool breeze blow by. It was colder than usual. She looked around and saw a dark shadow over by Finn's truck.

She immediately walked over and told it lo leave.

"Leave? Me? I'm gonna' blow this thing up," the shadow laughed at her.

Katelyn surrounded herself with White Light and began to pulse at the shadow. It began to waver a bit.

"You have no power over me. I am with The Dark force."

"This place is protected by The White Light. Now, be gone to the spaces between the dimensions," Katelyn demanded.

She threw her hands out in front of her pushing the dark shadow away from the truck. It was thrown into the sky screaming at her.

"You can't harm The Dark. It will take The Special Magic and Powers from this place and rule all existence."

"Be gone!" Katelyn said as she threw a White Light energy ball at the dark shadow. It blew up into a million pieces then was taken into the spaces between the dimensions as if sucked up by a huge vacuum.

"Katelyn, what's goin' on out here? I heard you yellin' at somethin'," Finn said as he walked over to her.

"Oh, it was a Dark Force shadow tryin' to blow up your truck. I stopped it and threw it into the spaces between the dimensions. Your truck's all set now," Katelyn said matter-of-fact like.

Finn laughed at her shaking his head. "Really? No big deal?"

"Yup. All set," Katelyn said looking at him.

"You are surely a force to be reckoned with. Ready to look at the blue prints for the next build?"

"Yup. Let's go," Katelyn said as they went back into the shop.

The Dark was trying to worry people. This time it had backfired. The Dark would try harder next time and that would be more sooner than later.

Tommy's email went out and The Creek got busy making plans for the family reunion. The Dark got busy making plans to take The Special Magic and destroy The Creek.

Miss Cora was suspicious of the quiet going on. She knew the Dark was getting ready for a major battle but it had been too quiet since the flood episode. She loved the whole family reunion thing but kept her senses sharp for anything out of the ordinary. Katelyn had called and told her about the dark shadow by Ethan's truck and how she had gotten rid of it rather easily. Miss Cora said that was a good thing that Katelyn was comfortable with her powers to jump right in and take care of business.

It was Monday and Ethan and all his crews were busy at build sites all over the Blue Ridge. It happened around eleven when a wave of energy seemed to flow through the Blue Ridge like a wave of water does onto the beach. It knocked some things over and a few people were slightly injured. The crew bosses radioed each other and reported that all was okay.

Emily and Jonah were in the paddock with the horses when it came through. The horses didn't like the wave and acted out. It took Jonah a few minutes to quiet them. The chickens sent up a bunch of noise as well.

Miss Cora was picking her veggies and was knocked over. She was okay. She sat there for a minute concentrating on the energy and sent it far away from the Blue Ridge. She got up, brushed herself off, and went back to her garden.

Jordan was working in his office when it went through. A few things rolled around in the house a bit. He went right out to the barn to look for George and George came flying in like a bolt of lightning.

"George, did ya' feel that? What the hell was that all about?" Jordan said as George stood in front of him.

"That, my dear Jordan, was The Dark sending a bit if a calling card to let ya' know it's still around."

"Fuck that! The flood was enough of a calling card," Jordan yelled.

"Fuck that is right!" George yelled. "It's not like we'd be able to forget about The Dark. Jesus!"

"I do like the way you get pissed off, George," Jordan said laughing.

"Just because I'm an eagle right now doesn't mean my brain isn't functioning like a human. It is!"

"Good to know for future stuff," Jordan said.

"Well, I think I'll take to the sky and do a bit of a fly over the general area. I'll get back to you later."

"Bye George. Thanks for zoomin' right in," Jordan said as George took off.

The digital world was going crazy. Folks were texting, calling, emailing not only all over The Creek but all over the Blue Ridge and then some. Police and sheriff's phones were exploding as well as fire and rescue stations. Folks were reporting the energy wave every which way they could.

The police and other authorities were contacting the military. No one had any idea what that thing was. It set radar and sonar alarms off all over the place. The air force was the first to be made aware of the energy wave as it triggered an alarm at their base in Goldsboro, NC. They had sensors all over the mountains and some of the Blue Ridge sensors went off.

The internet went crazy as posts were made on all social media pages asking and speculating just what and where that energy wave came from.

Most knew it wasn't an earthquake because the wave was along the ground at ground-level up to about four feet. Some thought it reminded them of the wave that goes out from a bomb blast. The media was trying not to alarm folks but was speculating on the air as well. They said it wasn't an earthquake and it wasn't the sound barrier being broken. Anyone's guess was as good as the next guys.

There were some who knew exactly what it was. Miss Cora, Katelyn, Kendra, Emily, and Jordan knew it was The Dark working at scaring people just because it could. And, if a few people died, great!

Miss Cora sent a group text out to The Creek telling people to stay calm and ask the White Light to surround the whole Blue Ridge area. Folks did just that and things began to calm down a bit. She also told folks to turn off their TVs and ignore the news. The media didn't have a clue and would only scare people with their false words.

Jenna had an idea about it being The Dark. She sent word across the internet asking for Reiki and all kinds of healing energy be sent to The Creek and the Blue Ridge. The request went viral and in just a few minutes wave after wave of healing energy was going through the Blue Ridge. The calls slowed way down and folks felt better.

This made The Dark angry so it sent another energy wave across the Blue Ridge. This one was stronger and caused damage to the land, structures, and people.

The USGS said it registered as a 4.0 on the earthquake scale and it wasn't even in the ground. People went crazy at first. The ones who were sending healing energy just doubled their efforts. The media was in a panic as they had reporters in the Blue Ridge and some of them were injured from falling equipment and trees and such.

Most places in The Creek were already protected so there wasn't any real damage anywhere. Outside The Creek was a different story.

Buildings collapsed. Vehicles crashed into each other and folks were thrown around. Fire hydrants blew up and there were water falls from these all over the place. The kids loved them and played in them for quite a while. Police, fire and rescue crews were kept busy all over the Blue Ridge for most of the day. The hospitals were on trauma alert for twelve hours as they tended to the injured. There were a couple of fires in Boone but they were contained quickly and didn't spread any further than the buildings they were in.

All in all, no one died. A few buildings were lost. There was damage to a few areas of the national forest as some trees were thrown down. A couple of roads were blocked for a few hours and some folks had to clear their property where trees fell across their driveways and along the houses. A bit of panic and chaos got hold of folks at the beginning of the event but once the authorities took charge things settled down and folks calmed down as well.

The Dark was not happy with this result. It decided to bide its time before it tried again.

The week went by with folks working and playing as always. Saturday dawned with great expectations of a grand time at the family reunion at Gerry's house.

It was set to begin mid-afternoon and that's exactly what happened. It seemed as if everyone had the same idea at the same time. The field down from the house had been mowed so folks could park easily. The place filled quickly as they all arrived at the same time.

A line of people and their stuff proceeded to Gerry's place as if a parade had been rehearsed.

"Hey, Gerry," Miss Cora said as she was dropped off at the house by Emily and Ethan.

"Hey, Miss Cora," Gerry said as he gave her a big hug. "It sure is great to see you again and have ya' here. It wouldn't be right if you weren't here."

"Thanks, Gerry. I will say I agree with you. Just don't tell anyone I said that," Miss Cora said as Gerry walked her around the house to the back area.

"Ya' done yourself proud here, Gerry. Looks great," Miss Cora said as she stopped alongside the pool. "I do love the flower gardens and all."

"I planted some veggies, too. Really, me, when I was home for a couple of days the first week of June. Tommy's been takin' care of them and cookin' with them, too. He loves fresh veggies."

"Good. I'll bring some by in a day or two. I've always got more than I need."

"Why, I'd appreciate that, Miss Cora. Now, let's get you settled. You pick the spot," Gerry said.

Miss Cora chose a table with a big umbrella a little ways from the pool. She said she didn't want to get splashed much.

Folks wandered in and found places to sit. Some grabbed tables and some took to setting up under the pop ups that were dotted around the place. Kids were in the pool in no time with their folks following them.

There was a volleyball net set up at the edge of the lawn and a basketball court a few steps away. These areas were busy in no time as well. The grills had been set up on the west side of the patio away from the pool and you could hear food sizzling already.

"Hey, Ethan," Finn said motioning for him and Emily to join his family. They were set up under a pop-up tent and had brought chairs and a small table. The guys put up another pop up next to the first one and they all got settled right well.

Katelyn's family had brought their own pop-up tent and set it up the other side of Finn's family.

"Now, here's a mess of trouble just waitin' to happen," Tommy said as he walked over to say hello.

"Hey, Tommy. Us guys? Trouble? I don't think so," Finn said.

This made everyone laugh.

"Just make sure I'm included," Gerry said as he joined Tommy. "So glad y'all came. This is gonna' make today real special with all of The Creek here. Has anyone seen Kendra yet?"

"She's pickin' up Jordan. We've got places for them here with this motley crew," Joe said.

"Great. Well, help yourselves to everything," Gerry said as he and Tommy wandered off to visit with the others.

411

Folks hollered out to each other. The Kirkland's were setting up opposite from the MacDonald's. Laine, Mo, Earl, and Bubba set up next to the Kirkland's. Ted and Michael had closed The Store for the rest of the day. They arrived and drove right up to the house. Tommy's friends unloaded the food the guys had brought and set it up on the patio near the pool. That's where the food tables were. They were under awnings hanging from the house. The chiefs and their families arrived. Gerry had reserved a place for them between the MacDonald's and the Kirkland's.

Everything looked great and folks were having a great time. The weather was perfect. The afternoon wore on without anyone noticing the time. Gerry called for attention for a minute around supper time to tell folks the grills were loaded with food ready to be enjoyed. Kids were pulled from the pool under protest with promises of going back in a bit after they ate.

Feasting began and went on for a long, long time. A few errant frisbees made their way into folks' areas with hollers and laughter and a few were sent back to who knows where. Miss Cora took a hand at throwing a frisbee and folks laughed along with her as she tried to get it somewhere near where it was supposed to land. She turned out to be pretty good at it. She took a bow when she finished to applause and comments.

Finn was walking with Katelyn near the pool's edge when one of his childhood friends decided he needed to cool off. He was summarily pushed into the deep end to cheers from the crowd. Katelyn took a hefty step away from the pool's edge. She didn't feel like swimming at that moment.

Folks brought a dish to pass and these were sampled and enjoyed and soon they were all eaten. Deserts were to be put out a bit later.

"So, Gerry," Katelyn asked, "Is that the studio over there?"

"Yes, it is. We, that's Ian and Ethan, suggested we build it quite a ways from the house so the noise wouldn't bother anyone. It's a professional studio with excellent soundproofing and all. We just felt we needed to separate it from the house so folks wouldn't feel worried about bothering anyone. Some of us tend to keep really late hours and all."

"I get it. That's good thinkin' for sure. It looks really great. I love Ethan and Ian's builds. They just aren't like anyone else's builds."

"That's for sure. And, now that you're a part of the team, I'll bet your stuff is quite unique as well."

"I do believe it is if I may say so myself," Katelyn replied laughing.

"From what I've heard from the guys, you're really special when it comes to design work. I may just have ya' take a look around here for some ideas for the guest house."

"I'd love to. Just let me know when and we'll see what we can do," Katelyn said.

Folks were called to gather in the middle of the lawn.

"It is time for the first annual tug-o-war for the kids first, then the grown-ups. The pits are located across from the driveway. One is sawdust for the kids. However, we have a much more interesting one for the adults. Follow me," Gerry said as he set off around the house to the areas across from the driveway.

As soon as folks saw the pits, they began to laugh and holler.

"So, that's for the grown-ups, is it? This is gonna' be great."

"No way I'm gonna' be a part of that."

"Hey, Finn, hope ya' brought a change of clothes."

The other pit was a huge mud puddle made especially for the tug-o-war.

"Let's get started with the kids. First up are kids ages 4-7. Then 8-12. And, finally 13-17," Tommy explained.

The games commenced and each group had a blast working really hard to win. Prizes were handed out to everyone and this made the kids really happy.

"Okay, now, all you adults, pick your teams. Mix em up. No all boy and all girl teams," Tommy shouted.

It took a few minutes, but, finally, the teams were set. There were ten people on each side of the puddle. The whistle blew and the tug was on.

Jordan was the captain of the north-side team and Jenna was the captain of the south-side team. First one side would gain a few feet then the other side would take it back. Once the teams got going the real fun began. The first three people on each team were pulled into the puddle amongst laughter and hollering.

The teams kept losing folks until it was down to Jordan, Kendra, and Hal on one team and Ethan, Ian and Jenna on the other. They were trying hard to pull each other into the mud puddle. Ethan slipped and the other team was able to pull the other three right into the mud. Ethan, Ian, and Jenna landed with a splat while the other team dropped the rope and cheered for themselves. Folks were applauding and cheering right along with them. Ethan crawled out of the puddle and grabbed Hal and pulled him in. Kendra stepped way back and was saved from the mud bath. Jordan wasn't so lucky. Jenna sneaked up behind him and pushed him into the puddle. As Jordan looked up from the puddle, he saw George flying around at tree top level. One of the kids pointed this out to the group and they watched as George circled the gathering a few times then flew off. Only Jordan knew it was George. He was following Jordan everywhere he went ever since they had met in the crystal cave.

The mud-covered folks used the outdoor showers to rinse off before changing their clothes. The desert buffet showed up and folks enjoyed the creations as always. A stage had been set up during the tug-o-war so folks knew that Gerry and his band, The Moonshine Country Gang, was gonna' perform.

The sun was just beginning to reach for the tree tops as the band took to the stage.

"Hey, y'all. Thanks so much for comin' over today. This is just what we all needed. It's so great to be back home with my family and all. That tug-o-war is gonna' be remembered for a long time. Especially since we got so many pictures of it. I'll have my photo guy set up a bunch online and y'all can order the ones ya' want. We thought we'd play some old tunes and some of the new ones we're working on and recording these days. They won't be released for a while yet, so let us know what ya' think about them. Here we go."

Folks cheered as the band started up. Folks sang along, danced, cheered and just loved the whole show. The Dark was watching and waiting. A few tree limbs were seen to fall and then get swept away by a gust of wind. Nothing else menacing was noted.

The sun setting through the trees was spectacular throwing all kinds of sunbeams all over the place. There were outdoor lights and all, but they hadn't even been turned on yet the sun was so bright as it finally met the horizon and slipped below the mountain tops.

The band took a short break then got right back at it. They played a lot of the new stuff and folks cheered and stood up to show how much they loved the new songs.

The band played one of The Creek's favorite songs, *Will the Circle Be Unbroken,* for the last song. It went on for quite a while with folks harmonizing along with the band. Applause and hollering went on for some time, too. The band came down to talk with everyone and it was well into the night when folks began to gather their things and head to their cars. The little ones had fallen asleep and were dreaming as their mommas and daddies carried them on their shoulders.

"Now, Gerry", Miss Cora said as she was walking to the front porch to wait for her ride, "That was some family reunion. I do so love when we all get together. I'm so glad you're home for a spell. Come on by and we'll talk some."

"Thanks, Miss Cora. I will be sure to come by for a visit," Gerry said as Ethan and Emily drove up. Miss Cora was settled and they drove off waving and calling out to the others.

It was a while before the last truck pulled away. Gerry, Tommy and some of the band members were sitting along the back patio talking about the day.

"Those songs sounded really good," Tommy said.

"Your prejudice," Gerry said.

"Some. But I've told y'all when somethin' didn't sound right," Tommy replied.

"He's right, Gerry," Rick said.

"True. Alright then. Thanks. We recorded it all so we'll be able to listen and all later. Right now, I just wanna' sit here for a spell and enjoy the Blue Ridge," Gerry replied.

They talked a bit and listened to the night sounds. They heard the critters rustling in the woods at the edge of the lawn. The sky was its usual sparkling self with the moon showing up to shine brightly on the night.

"Who left the lights on in the front of the studio?" Gerry asked.

"Oh, that was me. No one's in there. I'll go turn them off," Rick said.

As he stood up, there was a mighty blast as the recording studio was blown all to hell. Rick was thrown to the ground and that's where everyone else found themselves with debris falling all over them.

They sat there stunned for a few minutes then talked all at once.

"What the hell was that?"

"How'd that happen?"

"Was it a bomb?"

"Who hates us so much?"

Gerry tried to stand up but found he was covered in large chunks of wall. The others were, too. They took a bit to push the stuff away from themselves. They had cuts and scrapes all over themselves. Tommy had a goodsized gash in his right leg. One of the band guys grabbed a pool towel and dipped it into the pool and told Tommy to put some pressure on his gash. Rick had called 911 and sirens could be heard coming in the distance.

Folks all over The Creek felt the rumble and heard the explosion. Ethan and Emily had just dropped off Miss Cora and were driving towards Emily's place when it happened. They turned around and flew back to Gerry's. They figured that's where the explosion came from.

"It was The Dark," Emily said.

"Yes, I agree. Fuckin' asshole!" Ethan said as he turned into the driveway. There was a sheriff's cruiser blocking the way.

"Hey Ethan, Emily. I can't let ya' up the drive on account of all the emergency apparatus up there. What brought ya here?" the deputy asked.

"Gerry and Tommy had a family reunion for The Creek all day and we had just left when we heard and felt the explosion. Just want to help if we can," Ethan answered.

"I'm sure Gerry could use some friends right now. The back studio exploded and they all got hurt some. Tommy's got a gash on his leg the paramedics are tending to right now. Park on the side so the rigs can get through. I'll let them know you're walkin' in."

"Thanks, much obliged," Emily said.

They parked the truck and hurried up the drive. They found everyone around back being taken care of by the paramedics.

"Ethan, Emily. So glad they let ya' in," Gerry said. "Tommy's got a good-sized gash in his leg. The paramedics said they're gonna' take him into Boone to the medical center for some stitches. The rest of us got some little cuts and scrapes but nothin' bad."

"Good to hear," Ethan said. "The studio blew up? Any idea why?"

"No! No one was in there. We were just talkin' about the light bein' left on and Rick had stood up to go turn it off when the explosion happened. He got thrown into the furniture but he's okay."

"Hey, Rick," Emily said as she waved to him.

"Hey, you two. Thanks for comin' right back over," Rick replied as one of the medics was putting bandages on his cuts.

"Gerry, can you account for everyone that was here when it happened?" the sheriff was asking.

"Yes, sir. All the band members are out here with us now. Some were settling down inside when it happened. They're all oaky. A couple windows were blown out by flyin' debris but no one was near them."

"I'll take care of getting those covered," Ethan said.

"Great. Thanks," Gerry replied.

"Ethan, you're gonna' have to wait until the bomb squad investigators give the okay. They'll be here soon and they're gonna' need to take pictures and get some samples of all the stuff that was damaged."

"No problem. I've got a couple of blue tarps in the truck I can put up as soon as they say it's okay."

"Alright. How about you and Emily stay with the group here? We moved them away from most of the debris so you can grab a couple of chairs from the lawn. Just don't move anything while you're walkin' around."

"I'll get the chairs, Emily. You go over to Gerry and all," Ethan said as he began to move carefully through the debris to get the chairs.

Ethan and Emily sat with the group for a long while. The lights that Gerry had placed around the lawn were blown to bits so the rescue guys set up a bunch of theirs.

The bomb squad investigators arrived and were looking over the debris before they walked over to what was left of the recording studio. The firefighters had put out the fire and removed their hoses from close to the area so the squad could get started.

"Gerry Baily?" someone said looking at Gerry.

"Yes, Ma'am," Gerry replied.

"I'm Rachel Simons, the bomb squad lead investigator. How ya' feelin'?"

"I'm okay ma'am. Thanks for comin' right over," Gerry replied. "Sorry I can't stand up. I'm not feelin' so great right now."

"I understand. I see your partner has been taken to Boone to be looked over and get a few stitches. We'll get him back home when the docs say he can come home."

"Thanks, Ma'am. We do appreciate that," Gerry replied.

"Gerry, can ya' tell me what happened out here?"

"Well, we were just sittin' here talkin' about the great day we'd had. Rick stood up to go turn the light off in the front area of the studio when the explosion happened. We were all thrown down and covered in debris. Rick called 911 and y'all showed up."

"Had anyone used the recording studio today?"

"Yes, Ma'am. Some of the musicians were lookin' over the stuff inside. We're supposed to start a four-month recording session in a couple of weeks and we all wanted to get used to all the new stuff."

"Who was the last person to leave the studio?"

"I don't know. I was out here and all getting things ready with my house crew."

"Ma'am," Rick said, "I'm pretty sure I was the last one to leave. I locked up right around one o'clock or so. Could have been a little later. Didn't know I left the light on so when Gerry noticed it, I said I'd go turn it off."

"Thanks, Rick. Were there any flammable chemicals in there?"

"No Ma'am! We all check when we first get in for safety issues and before we leave. The manager of my house crew makes sure we do. We have a checklist of everything that's brought in their and taken out. It's on the house computer. I'll get it for ya' when we can move around some."

"Good idea keeping a digital record," Rachel said.

The sheriff and the FBI walked over. It was Matthews and someone with him.

"Hey, Matthews. What are ya' doin' here?" Gerry asked.

"Hey, Gerry. Sorry about all this. I hear Tommy's behaving at the medical center and all. Just got an update. This here is Jack Hamilton. He's a special agent out of the Boone office. He's gonna' be the FBI investigator as I live here. I am being allowed to assist on the case."

"FBI? Ya' think someone tried to kill us?" Gerry asked.

"Not necessarily. We gotta' look at all possibilities when somethin' like this happens especially to a well-known person such as yourself."

"Oh. I didn't even think about that angle. Glad you're here," Gerry said.

They all talked for a while more than Rachel, Matthews, and Jack stepped away to talk with the fire chief. Gerry's manager had been notified when it happened and sent a lot of extra security to the place. They had the driveway blocked and some down both sides of the road. Drones had been sent up by the authorities to survey the damage well into the forest. The security company had sent drones up over the property as well as along the road to watch for possible media folks and the general public.

Rachel, Matthews, and Jack came back with a question for Gerry.

"Gerry, did you happen to have the security cameras on during the whole thing?" Jack asked.

"Of course. They're always on 24/7 whether anyone's here or not. I especially want to make sure Tommy and the house crew are safe," Gerry answered.

"We're gonna' need to see the footage," Matthews said.

"Of course. My security lead guy is in the house right now. His name's Harris. He'll give ya' anything y'all need," Gerry replied.

"Great. Let's go find Harris," Jack said to Matthews.

"Gerry, I'm gonna' go look at some of the debris. If I need you for anything else I'll come find ya'," Rachel said.

"Of course, Ma'am," Gerry replied.

After the authorities finally left Gerry and the others alone, Gerry started asking questions.

"What the hell was that all about?"

Emily looked at Ethan and they remained silent.

Gerry took one look at them and had an idea of who or what was to blame.

"Hey, guys, think we can stand up without fallin' down?" Gerry asked the others.

They all took a minute to stand up and start to move a little.

"Why don't y'all go on into the house? Get something to drink and eat and settle in your rooms or the big living room or somethin'. I don't think we need to stay out here anymore," Gerry suggested as he started to stand up.

"Whoa! This is gonna' take a minute guys," Gerry said as they all felt a bit of pain as they tried to move.

"Anyone need help getting to the house?" Gerry asked.

"We all do," they replied.

Ethan and Emily helped them one-by-one until everyone except Gerry was inside.

"Let's talk over there," Gerry pointed to a spot on the far side of the lawn where there wasn't much debris.

Emily, Ethan, and Gerry took a few minutes to walk out of the mess on the patio and move over out of ear shot of the others.

"What the hell was that?" Gerry said trying not to yell. It didn't work and a few of the paramedics looked his way.

"I'm okay, y'all. Just tryin' to figure out what the hell happened here," Gerry said waving at the medics to show he was okay.

"I saw the way the two of you looked at each other a few minutes back. This was no ordinary explosion, was it?"

Ethan took a deep breath before saying, "You got that right."

"Gerry, it was The Dark. It's been tryin' to destroy The Creek again and it's workin' hard right now to accomplish that goal."

"Fuck that!" Gerry said hissing under his breath so no one else would hear.

"Exactly," Ethan said.

"So, what do we do now?" Gerry asked waving his hand at what was left of the recording studio.

"We're gonna' rebuild as soon as the place is cleared. I already told Ian what happened and he's getting a hold of all the crews tomorrow morning to put them on alert. I know this sounds rather funny right now, but, let us know if ya' can think of anything that should be changed or added before we get started."

"Oh. That's a great idea, Ethan. It might just make the guys feel like they're doing something good from all this. I'll text them as soon as I find my phone. I think it's still in the kitchen on the counter where I left it before we all came outside to sit and talk."

"Good thinkin', Ethan" Emily said agreeing with Gerry. "Hey, Gerry, let's get you inside and comfy. I think you're gonna' start feelin' really awful soon."

"I already am, Emily," Gerry said as he reached out for Ethan's arm to steady himself as he walked back to the house.

Gerry got settled and Rachel stopped by.

"Hey, Gerry. Glad to see ya' made it in here. I'll bet you're feelin' pretty bad about now," Rachel said as she sat down on the foot stool next to Gerry.

"Oh, you bet we are. Feelin' like shit," Gerry said as he tried to move a bit.

"Gerry, the FBI crime scene folks are gonna' stay here through the night. A fresh crew will arrive at dawn with more equipment and a dumpster. We're gonna' go through everything out there and take it all back to the labs at Quantico. We're gonna' empty the pool, filter the water through one of our special filters, then drain the pool to see if there's anything left in the bottom. After we clean the pool, we'll bring a water truck in here and fill it back up. Same thing with the jacuzzi. Just wanted to let ya' know because it's gonna' get really noisy and busy around here for a bit."

"Well, thanks for the info, Ma'am. I do like the way the FBI takes care of things," Gerry said.

"We do our best," Rachel replied.

"For now, Gerry, y'all can get off to bed. Tommy hasn't been released yet. I think they're gonna' keep him for a few hours to make sure nothing else is injured. They want to make sure he doesn't have a concussion or hearing problems," Matthews explained.

"That's a good idea. I think I will go get some sleep. All of a sudden, I'm wicked tired. I was just thinkin' of a new song about being blown up when ya' least expect it. Guess I'm really tired."

"I do believe you're in shock, Gerry. The paramedics are gonna' stay for the rest of the night checkin' in on y'all so don't be surprised if ya' see them in your room. I'll let ya' know as soon as they release Tommy. We've got an agent and a deputy at his side so they'll bring him home."

"Wow. Didn't think about that side of things. This has been a bat shit crazy night," Gerry said as he slowly moved around and got up.

"I'll walk with ya' to your room," Ethan said as he offered his arm.

"Thanks bro. Really glad the two of you are here."

Emily gave Gerry a kiss on the cheek and waited for Ethan to come back.

A bit later, all the guys were settled in their rooms and Ethan returned to Emily.

"The paramedics are checking on them. I told Gerry we were leavin' and I'd be back with Ian tomorrow for a check on things. I gave the tarps to the sheriff's guys and they got the okay from the FBI lab crew to put them in place and here they come. Let's get out of their way."

Ethan and Emily checked with Matthews and the sheriff's deputy in charge letting them know they were leaving and that Ethan and Ian would be back the next day later in the morning to take a look at things.

"Holy fuck Ethan!" Emily hollered as soon as they were a ways down the road. "I'm pretty sure The Dark blew up the recording studio because it couldn't get The Magic. That's just wicked horrible."

"I'm still in shock about the whole thing. Gerry said the last truck had just left when the thing happened."

"I've sent a few group texts around The Creek letting everyone know what happened and how everyone's okay except that gash on Tommy's leg. I'm sending a last text now to let them know Tommy's had his stitches and the rest have finally gone to bed with the paramedics still there. I told everyone to stay away as this is an active investigation goin' on and they would only get in the way. Here goes," Emily said as she sent the text. She got a lot of okay replies right quick.

Ethan and Emily got home and crashed as well. Ethan's alarm went off a few hours later and he got up and got ready for the day. He told Emily to say in bed and sleep as much as she wanted to. He'd take care of the chickens and Jonah said he'd be by earlier than usual. She mumbled something then fell back to sleep. It was after ten when Emily finally woke up and got going for the day.

The next day Tommy came home and the FBI lab techs and all showed up and got busy. The Creek got busy cooking for the crews at the house and got the okay to bring the food by. A deputy would meet them at the driveway entrance and gladly accept the offers. Cooking was one of the ways The Creek could help the folks taking care of Gerry and Tommy and everyone.

The Dark wanted that Special Magic and those Special Powers that lived somewhere in The Creek. The Dark wasn't sure just where they were but it was working really hard at destroying as much as possible to narrow down the places they could be hiding.

CHAPTER 34

Sunday morning found Miss Cora on a call with Emily and Kendra. Katelyn was already at Kendra's house.

"The time has come. We gotta' be ready. That explosion was just a fun thing for The Dark," Miss Cora said.

"Fuckin' bastard," Kendra replied.

"Exactly," Katelyn and Emily replied.

"So, now what?" Emily asked no one in particular.

"Well, I think the big battle could take place any time now. But not for a few days yet. It seems The Dark is trying to scare everyone and catch us off guard," Miss Cora said.

"I agree. I can't really put my finger on it, but not quite yet. I still have one more thing to do to get ready. I'll take care of that today," Katelyn said.

"Good. Let us know when you're all set Katelyn. We got some chants to go over and such," Kendra said.

"Will do. Blessings all," Katelyn said as they ended the call.

Katelyn had had a vision that morning just before she woke up. She grabbed her three backpacks, water, and her twin crystal and headed to the cave. As soon as she drove up near the barn, Jordan came out of the house with three backpacks and water. He was waving his twin crystal to show Katelyn he had it.

"Hey Jordan, I see you had the same vision I did," Katelyn said looking at the backpacks.

"Seems so," Jordan replied. "How about we set the twins together out behind the barn? I think we're gonna' see somethin' awesome happen."

"Sure," Katelyn replied as they walked through the barn.

"Let's set our crystals right here and stand back," Jordan said as he set his crystal on the ground.

Katelyn set hers so it was touching Jordan's and stepped back. George flew in just at that moment and stood next to Jordan.

As soon as the twin crystals touched each other and the earth, a beam of pure golden light shot up into the heavens. They all watched in awe. As soon as it was gone, George gave a squawk and was hopping around like crazy. Jordan looked over towards where George was hopping around and saw something unbelievable.

He nudged Katelyn and pointed to the ground about twenty feet from the back of the barn.

They stared in amazement. Setting in front of them was the shape of a sword and shield etched into the ground like someone had designed it as a garden. It was about ten feet across and fifteen feet tall. The sword and shield were made of the tiniest crystals they had ever seen. They were silver, burgundy, dark purple, gold and royal blue and white crystals made a circle around them. Katelyn, Jordan, and George walked over to the etchings and just starred at them.

Katelyn took a breath and said, "This is what our crystals did? Holy cow! This is beyond anything I've ever been a part of with The Magic around here. Incredible!"

"No kidding," Jordan added. "I don't even know where to start thinking about this. It almost looks like something out of the old kingdom's eras and such in Europe. Absolutely whatever for sure!"

George squawked a bit as well.

"I hear ya', George," Jordan said.

"I hear ya', too, George. And, I agree with everything," Katelyn said as she began to walk around the etchings. Jordan followed her as they looked at the sight from every angle.

"I think our crystals are a lot more than just stones, if ya' get my drift," Katelyn offered.

"Oh, I agree one-hundred percent," Jordan added.

"I'm thinkin' maybe we shouldn't tell anyone, and I mean anyone, about this. Keep it for just the three of us," Katelyn said.

"Yes. Agreed," Jordan said. "How am I gonna' explain this to folks when they see it?"

At that exact moment, the etching became invisible.

"Well, I guess that answers that question. I wonder if we'll ever see it again?" Katelyn said out loud.

And, just like it had disappeared, it came back to life.

"Whoa! Wicked cool. I'm sensing that this will always be here for the three of us to see. But, if anyone else comes by, it will be made invisible so they can't see it. Right?" Jordan said as if he were listening to someone.

"I get the same message as well. Almost like it had a cloak around it. So, you and George and I have a special, what do we call it? A garden? A symbol in the earth?"

"How about a guardian symbol to protect us?" Jordan suggested.

George squawked his approval and this made Katelyn and Jordan laugh.

"Okay, then. That answers that. So cool. Just when I think I can handle all The Magic stuff around here, something else comes along. We'd better pick up our twins before your whole farm is transposed into something from another time," Katelyn said as she walked over and picked up her crystal. Jordan did the same thing then they looked at the symbol again. It was still there.

"Well, I guess we should get along to the cave now," Jordan said shaking his head and smiling.

"Jordan, I'm tellin' you, I'm thinkin' you never thought in your wildest dreams, that buyin' this farm would bring all this with it. No words to describe all this," Katelyn said.

"Exactly. No words. George, you ready to come along?" Jordan asked the eagle.

George gave a squawk and took to the air, heading for the cave.

"Let's go. Oh, George seems to follow me wherever I go these days. He's like a guardian eagle or something."

"Nice work, George. Nice to see you again, too," Katelyn said as he flew by.

"Nice to see you, too, Katelyn" George said. It sounded like a bit of a squawk to Katelyn but Jordan heard him loud and clear.

"That's eagle for agreed," Jordan said.

They didn't talk at all as they walked to the cave. Jordan held the bushes aside for Katelyn and George as they walked into the main room.

"He really does follow you everywhere. Was that you, George, at the reunion yesterday?" Katelyn asked looking right at George.

George bobbed his head at Katelyn and she laughed.

"I love the fact that George and I understand each other," Katelyn said laughing.

"He is a character for sure," Jordan said winking at George.

George bobbed his head looking right at Jordan in response.

"That is just so wicked cool," Katelyn said as they turned and looked around the room.

"Jordan, not quite sure why I'm here. Just know that I'm supposed to be," Katelyn aid.

"I'm getting the impression that we're supposed to gather a whole bunch of crystals filling our backpacks. Not big ones but more like egg sized ones and smaller," Jordan offered as he continued to stare at the crystals in the middle of the room.

Katelyn cleared her mind and began to watch the crystals all around the room. Some blinked at her when she looked at them. Others did not.

"I think I'm supposed to gather the ones that blink at me when I look directly at them," Katelyn said.

"I'm getting the same idea," Jordan said. "Let's start right here then go clockwise around the outside of the room and gather the ones that blink at us."

"Yes. The outside of the room. Let's go," Katelyn replied.

They set out and spent a good couple of hours gathering their own blinking crystals. They had filled two backpacks each and half of the third one when the came back to the starting point.

"Ya' know, these aren't as heavy as I thought they'd be. Good thing since we have to carry three backpacks," Katelyn said as she set hers down on the floor.

"Let's have some of the water we brought. I think we need to each save a bottle for somethin' else in here," Jordan.

"That's just what I was gonna' say," Katelyn said as they drank and sat quietly.

George sat next to Jordan and he poured some water in a small hollowed out space on the floor for George. George drank and flapped a wing at Jordan. Jordan smiled back.

The three of them stared across the room just looking at all the crystals.

"This place is so beautiful. It must have been here for millions of years since the earth was formed. These crystals must be that old, too. I've never seen anything like this in my life. When I lived in Alabama, Sami and I would go over to the Wetumpka Crater and walk the paths. We'd find a tiny crystal or two sometimes. We always left them there. The one I got from the artist was really cool. I have it here with me. And, we have our twin crystals, too," Katelyn said.

"Let's set the twin crystals next to each other again and see what happens, if anything, this time. I think we need to cleanse the space with the other water we brought with us." Jordan suggested.

"Okay," Katelyn replied.

They poured the water around the space just a bit into the room then placed their twin crystals next to each other. As soon as they touched, a beam of green light shot out into the center of the ceiling. The energy ricocheted off every crystal in the room. The brilliance was so bright that Jordan and Katelyn had to put their sunglasses on. George was hopping all over the place and squawking like crazy.

"I do believe George feels like you and me. What was that?" Jordan said.

George stopped squawking and just kept walking and hopping around.

"Holy cow! This is beyond belief. Magic, of course," Katelyn offered.

"Of course," Jordan agreed as they kept looking at all the crystals.

George flew a short distance into the middle of the room and came to rest next to four crystals about the size and shape of a football. They were red, blue, purple, and yellow and glowing like crazy. He turned to look at Katelyn and lifted a wing as if beaconing her to join him.

"I do believe George wants me to join him," Katelyn said looking at Jordan.

"I do believe he does. Go on over. I'll stay here," Jordan said.

As Katelyn looked for a way to get to the center of the room, the crystals moved around to make a path for her. She followed the path and stood next to George. She saw the four crystals and instantly knew they were for her to take with her.

Katelyn bent down and picked up each one offering a silent prayer of thanks for the gifts.

She looked at George and he bobbed his head as if to tell her she had done the right thing.

She walked back to Jordan and handed the crystals to him.

"You're supposed to hold these for a few minutes before we pack them with the others," Katelyn said. "Keep watching the center of the room."

As they watched, a smokey apparition appeared. It morphed into a full human shaped apparition. It stayed floating in the center of the room.

"Jordan, you have listened well and gathered all the crystals that will be needed soon. We thank you. Katelyn, you have listened well and gathered all the crystals that you will need soon. Jordan, give your crystals to Katelyn after you get home. She will know what to do with them when the time is right. Go now and remember everything you have experienced today. Do not tell anyone, including Miss Cora and the others. This time is just for the two of you."

The apparition vanished as if the wind had blown it away.

Jordan and Katelyn looked at each other for a minute not knowing what to say.

"Well, I guess we know why we're here, sort of," Katelyn said.

"Guess so," Jordan replied.

George had flown back and nudged Jordan in the leg.

"Oh, okay George. We better be on our way. Let's put these in the backpacks first," Jordan said.

They placed the four football crystals in the two backpacks with room, offered thanks for the gifts and The Magic, then quietly left the cave.

George walked around for a minute then flew off not making a sound.

Jordan and Katelyn walked back not making a sound either. They had a lot to think about.

When they got to Katelyn's SUV, they placed the six backpacks in the back and Katelyn got in.

"Katelyn, I'll always remember this special day," Jordan said.

"I will, too. We'll talk later after we have some time to think about all this," Katelyn said starting up the SUV. "Tell George I said so long."

"I will", Jordan said as he stepped back and Katelyn turned around and drove off.

George flew into the barn and landed on the floor waiting for Jordan.

"George, you are somethin' special. I do believe Katelyn could understand your noise and gestures."

"Yes, she did really well figurin' our what I was sayin'. Today has been a very special time for the both of you. Go inside and eat and rest some. I'm gonna' fly over to Gerry's place and see how things are coming along. Tommy's home and hurtin' a lot and the folks around here have made enough food for an army."

"Okay. Let me know what ya' find. Be careful, George. I'm getting quite fond of you," Jordan replied.

"Same here, my friend," George said as he flapped his wings a few times then took off.

Jordan watched him circle around the barn and head west before he went inside to eat and relax.

Katelyn got home and knew she was supposed to leave the crystals in the SUV. She went inside and ate and rested for a good part of the day as well. She got the group text about Tommy and all and was relieved that everyone was healing well. The property was gonna' be a mess for a while and that was okay. She knew Ethan and Ian would take care of the new recording studio build as soon as the FBI released the place.

And Katelyn knew the battle with The Dark was just around the corner. The more she concentrated on that the more she learned. She would need all those crystals she and Jordan had gathered today for the battle. She wasn't told where it would be yet. Her Guardians told her she would know just when she needed to.

She must have dozed off after she ate but she didn't remember feeling sleepy. It was dark when she woke up on the couch. She looked at her phone and saw that it was past ten. She laughed at herself and realized she had been awake around three and that's the last time she remembers seeing on her phone. That time in the cave must have been a lot longer than the time outside the cave. That's Magic for you.

She got herself some supper and watched a bit of tv. Nothing any good to watch so she decided to go to bed with her book. That lasted about five minutes as she fell sound asleep for the rest of the night.

The next week found everyone busy. The school season would be starting soon and folks were getting their kids all the clothes and supplies needed for the school year. The last few summer vacationers were passing through enjoying The Creek and the Blue Ridge.

Ethan and his crews were busy with their builds as some were getting close to being finished and others were moving along as well. Gerry's place was still under an active investigation although the FBI crime folks had removed all the debris and even refilled the pool. The landscaping folks had their hands full with redeveloping the whole back area as it hade been either ripped up or blown up. They told Gerry and Tommy it would take a couple of months to get things about half-way done before the cold weather hit. They'd finish in the early spring with hydroseeding again and placing new plants and all.

Ethan and Ian had met with Gerry and the band to discuss the new recording studio. The foundation had been damaged and it had been completely dug up. There was a hole just waiting for a new foundation. After a lot of talk, Gerry decided the studio needed to be bigger by half again the original size. Ethan and Ian got busy with a new design and by the end of this very busy week, Gerry had given his approval and work would begin as soon as the FBI said so.

Katelyn kept having these little nudges about the crystals she and Jordan had gathered from the cave. She had a very busy week and wasn't able to give much thought to them. Saturday morning found Katelyn and Sami taking care of their chores and talking about the tug-o-war. They had both taken a mud bath and loved every minute of it.

"I swear my skin really liked that mud. It feels smoother for sure," Sami said laughing.

"I had to wash my hair four times to get all the mud out. It sure was fun," Katelyn replied.

"Katie, I gotta' go over to Boone in a few minutes. Something about one of the suppliers didn't send all the stuff we need. Wanna' go with me?"

Katelyn thought for a minute and the crystals came right to mind. "Not this time. I've got a few boring things to take care of myself."

"Okay. I'll go be bored all alone," Sami replied laughing as she grabbed her briefcase and headed out the door.

"I should be back in about two hours. Let's have lunch at The Store when I get back," Sami hollered from the porch.

"Deal," Katelyn hollered back as she went into the utility room to put the laundry into the dryer.

Katelyn finished what she was doing and sat for a minute quietly to connect with The Other Side about the crystals. She saw what she needed to do. She didn't know why but she had learned a long time ago to follow the information.

She set out for The Rise and drove directly to it without stopping anywhere else. She grabbed the six backpacks and hauled them to the base of the stairs. She took them to the top in two trips.

When she got there, she knew just what to do with them. She was directed to a hollowed-out space south of the center and placed them all in the hollow. They were immediately taken into the earth.

'Well, okay', she thought as she stood to look around. Although the sky was clear as a bell, there was an ominous feeling in the air. She knew the battle was here. A few swirls of white cloud appeared way off to the west. They were there then they were gone. The air seemed to chill for a few seconds and the critters became quiet. As the swirls vanished, everything retuned to the way it had been before the swirls.

Katelyn kept turning around looking out over the land. She didn't like the way the air felt. Like it was holding itself before blowing into a huge storm. She offered a prayer of thanks for the crystals and the earth taking them. She left The Rise knowing things were changing right in front of her.

She drove straight home without stopping and once there, she picked up with her chores. Sami came back and they headed to The Store for lunch.

"Well, did ya' straighten things out with the supplier?" Katelyn asked as they walked across the road.

"Yes, I did. Seems someone wrote a wrong number for the quantity of paint needed for the rooms and they were about twenty gallons short. The supplier got on the phone and requested his connection get the paint to the hotel today. I dare say it's already there if not about to be."

"Good. Nothing crazier than not enough paint when you're in the middle of a project," Katelyn said.

"For real," Sami replied as they walked through the door.

"Hey, girls," Ted and Michael said at the same time.

"Hey, yourselves," Sami replied with Katelyn waving at them.

"We're here for some lunch. We'll be dining in today," Katelyn said laughing a bit as she and Sami looked over the special's board.

"Well, alright then. You know the routine," Ted said serving some of the folks already at the table.

They gave Ted their orders and got their lunch stuff and joined the group.

"What's new, Hal?" Katelyn asked as she sat down.

"Well, Tommy's healing really fast. Gerry and the others are almost back to normal," Hal was saying when Michael interrupted him.

"Whatever that is," Michael said laughing.

"That's the truth," Hal said. "And, looks like the FBI might be gone by the end of next week. Gerry sent a few pictures of the place around The Creek. It sure was torn up some. He said some of the trees lost about half of their branches on the side closest to the studio. He thinks they're gonna' have to be taken down 'cause the barks been blown off on that side. I told him I'd get a couple of my friends together and we'd come over and take a look. He seemed to like that idea."

"That's a great idea, Hal," Katelyn said. "You're such a gifted carpenter I bet you and your friends could put the lumber to good use."

"We were thinkin' the same thing. If it can be used. Some may be too narrow. That stuff will be cut up into firewood and shared around The Creek. Boy, this has been the year for salvaging damaged trees and all."

"You said it, Hal," Sami agreed. "I'm glad I came over the other evening to look at the projects you've got goin' on with those damaged trees. Hal made a bunch of frames for the pictures that are gonna' be a part of the URR display at the hotel."

"That's wicked awesome," Katelyn said as Ted brought their lunch out.

"I think so, too. What a great way to honor all those folks," Ted said.

"Thanks, Ted, this smells heavenly," Sami said as she inhaled the steam from her bar-be-que chicken sandwich.

"Hmmm, cornbread," Katelyn mumbled with a mouthful of cornbread, butter, and honey.

Folks laughed at the two of them and lunch continued in a fun mood.

"Ya' know," Hal said. "There should be a health warnin' on the front of The Store. '*Weight gain will happen if ya' eat here a lot*'."

This made everyone laugh even more.

The afternoon came on and folks went about their way. Ethan and Ian were at Gerry's place. The FBI told Gerry they would be gone by Tuesday and he could get back to rebuilding things. Sami was meeting with Jordan every morning next week to complete one of the historical write-ups for the URR in the Boone hotel. This would include the Redstone's list of people that came through their tunnels. The Redstone's would not be mentioned to keep their privacy. Katelyn's family was busy. The berry patches were changing over as the blackberries were beginning to decrease and the small pumpkin field was growing bigger than anyone would have planned. There were even a few pumpkin vines running around the base of The Rise. No one admitted to planting them so it was a mystery as to how they got there.

The brother's houses were coming along. The foundations had been poured and in a few weeks the decking would begin for the framing work.

Miss Cora was getting worried about The Dark. It had been quiet ever since it attacked Gerry's place. The authorities had no clue as to who was responsible. Matthews was going to have an unofficial talk with the sheriff about the actual cause.

Jordan kept feeling pulled to the cave on his land. He would walk up to it and just stand by the entrance. George always flew along with him and stood next to him no matter how long it took. Jordan was silent as if he was absorbing the energy and all. He would then return to the house and carry on with his day. Sometimes he didn't remember walking to the cave; just became aware he was there once he got there.

Sunday came and went as usual. It was Monday mid-day when the news began reporting a very strange occurrence in a few locations in the Blue Ridge. It seems swarms of hummingbird moths were gathering and encircling groups of people. They kept the people from moving apart and it was reported that when people would try to get inside, the moths seemed to block the entrance by creating a wall between the door and the people. When the people moved back, the moths would encircle them again. One person did manage to get inside. When they sprayed the moths with pepper spray, they instantly fell dead to the ground then disintegrated. Others saw this and did the same thing and they got inside as well. The remaining moths then moved on looking for another target.

A few people were able to record this weird activity without being in the group and they sent the videos to the news media. It was all over the internet. Folks that were able to get away would leave the building they had managed to get into one at a time. The moths did not come back to attack them. The people went straight to their cars and trucks and drove home where they stayed inside.

Katelyn and Finn had spent most of the night together at Katelyn's place. They both got back to the shop around noon after being at different build sites. They joined Ian in the kitchen for lunch and were just tuning into the mid-day news when they saw the moth report.

"That's just plain weird," Ian said. "Although I'm not surprised after what happened to Gerry's Studio."

"I hear ya', Ian," Finn said. "I wonder if it's the bad guys at work. Hummingbird moths don't swarm nor do they encircle people."

"I agree," Katelyn said as they watched the rest of the report.

It seems there had been six separate swarms in six different locations in the Blue Ridge only. No where else in the United States. Katelyn felt a wave of panic begin to rise in her gut.

"This is The Dark," she said quietly. "I can feel it in my bones. And, this is not good."

Ian and Finn looked at her and saw a look of fear on her face.

"Katelyn, what are ya' getting at?" Finn asked as he put an arm around her shoulders.

"It's just a strong feeling of trouble. Big trouble. I feel it deep within me. I gotta' call Miss Cora and all right now. Excuse me," she replied as she went to her office, closed the door, and touched the code for Miss Cora's number.

"Katelyn," Miss Cora said as she answered.

"It's here," Katelyn replied.

"Yes. It's here. Emily's on her way to get me and we're goin' to Kendra's house. Do you know what you have to do yet?"

"No. I'm just askin' now," Katelyn said then was quiet for a minute or two.

"I know now," Katelyn finally said. "I gotta' go. Be careful out there. It's gonna' get real bad real fast."

"It's definitely here. We're gonna' keep sending you energy and light and all. Know we love ya' dearly," Miss Cora said.

"I do know y'all love me and are ready to do everything and anything you can to defeat The Dark and keep me safe out there. I love y'all, too."

"Remember to take the shocked crystal from Alabama and your twin crystal with you. Keep them in the pouch that just appeared on your desk on your body no matter what," Miss Cora instructed Katelyn.

Katelyn saw the pouch appear and put her twin crystal and the shocked crystal from the Wetumpka Crater into it. She had learned to carry both of them right after she got back from her first-dimension travels. She then placed it across her body. She could feel the crystals vibrating against her skin.

"Done. Thanks. I'll see ya' when it's all over," Katelyn said.

They ended the call and Katelyn went back into the kitchen. She finished her lunch with Ian and Finn without saying a thing.

"Ian", Katelyn said as they started to get busy with business, "I've got something I need to do this afternoon. All the accounts are up-to-date in the computer files and the next set of build ideas are on my desk."

Finn and Ian looked at Katelyn for a minute. They both knew she had something to do with getting rid of The Dark.

"Take all the time you need. We're here for you," Ian said.

"Do you need me to take you anywhere?" Finn asked.

"No, thanks, Finn. And, thanks for the support, Ian. I am much obliged. I gotta' do this alone," Katelyn said.

Ian nodded and went into his office leaving Finn and Katelyn alone.

Finn walked over to Katelyn and pulled her into his arms. He held her for quite a while before stepping back.

"I love ya' my Katie girl," Finn said softly as he kissed her deeply.

"I love you, my Finn," Katie replied returning the kiss.

She walked out the door without looking back. She got into her SUV just before a huge swarm of hummingbird moths descended on the shop. She sat there for a minute staring at the whole thing. It was weird. Those moths looked like they were trying to burrow into the shop. The guys must have been surprised. It only took them a few minutes before they turned on the alarm system and bright lights. The sound of the alarms made the moths fly away. They tried to come back but the bright lights and the alarm sounds were more than they could tolerate. They left just like they had arrived. Ian and Finn sent text messages out to everyone about the swarm and to get inside right away.

Katelyn pulled out of the drive and headed to the Pine Ridge Road. She didn't have any problems until she reached The Store. Her SUV was surrounded by the moths. They were definitely not normal hummingbird moths. They were bigger and the more she looked at them the more she saw. Their beaks had serrated markings along the sides like a knife. Their wings had talons hanging from the back portion of the wing. They looked like the legs of ticks with their hooks and all. And, their eyes were glowing orange globes that shot energy rays from them at will.

She set her windshield wipers on fast and this seemed to keep them away from the windshield. Miss Cora saw what was happening from Kendra's front window. She waved to Emily and Kendra to join her. They saw Katelyn's SUV completely covered with the moths.

"I do believe those are ninja hummingbird moths," Emily offered.

"We agree. We'll call them ninja moths. Let's get them away from her," Kendra said.

The three of them surrounded Katelyn with White Light and set about chanting. Most of the moths were blown away but a few kept on trying to get inside the SUV.

"I call upon the energy of the wind to remove these moths from this place," Katelyn said.

A strong wind blew in and the rest of the moths were blown away from her. She kept going headed to her destination.

In other parts of the Blue Ridge, the ninja moths were wreaking havoc. In one small town, they had managed to break the windows on a storefront where people had run into to get away from the ninja moths. They attacked the people piercing them with their razor-edged beaks and grabbing onto some of them with their hook-like wings and legs. Once attached, they began to pierce the person over and over again. People tried to push them off, but the months stayed hooked on. One lady's face was cut up so bad, she couldn't see and she fell to the floor while the moths kept attacking her.

Three of the clerks from the store who had managed to hide in a store-room entered the main room with fire extinguishers blazing. They aimed at the people who were under attack. Once the CO_2 hit the moths they immediately disintegrated. The clerks went after the ninja moths that were swarming in the air and in just a few minutes, they had killed all of them.

Someone called 911 and the rescue folks arrived a few minutes later. There were five people needing medical help. The lady whose face had been attacked was rushed via chopper to a medical center in Virginia for trauma surgery. The rest were treated at a local hospital.

Near the small glen of Maggie, Virginia, a family was outside playing watching their toddler try to walk through the yard when a swarm of ninja moths swooped down and grabbed the child. The parents were terrified and tried to run after the boy. A neighbor, who had seen the whole thing happen, aimed his garden hose at the swarm and blasted them. The water made the swarm grow by a hundred-fold and the even bigger swarm flew off with the boy. The authorities were called and launched drones into the air to try to find the swarm. The drone footage showed no swarms of anything within a five-mile radius. A foot-search got underway to try to find the boy.

The wind the Spirit of the Wind had sent to Katelyn had calmed down as soon as the ninja moths were gone. Katelyn kept going toward her destination with little interference. But the minute she turned into the road that led to The Rise, The Dark began its direct attack on her. It sent trees crashing to the ground in front of her. The White Light removed them in an instant. The Dark sent boulders crashing onto the road. The White Light rolled them away or turned them into dust so Katelyn could keep going.

The Dark blocked the sun light and the day became solid night with impenetrable blackness everywhere. Katelyn turned on her bright lights and was only able to see a few inches in front of her. Shapes of animals appeared in her head lights and she would step on the brakes only to see they were im-ages, not real animals. She kept driving when she figured this out and drove right through those ghost images.

This made The Dark angry. She should have been destroyed by the trees and boulders and all.

Katelyn saw the landmark that told her she was at the tree line near The Rise. She drove to the spot they had all parked in when she and her family and the others had come to The Rise. She knew it was a short distance to the stairs.

As soon as she got out of her SUV, things got worse. The ninja moths returned and Katelyn immediately placed a blanket shield of protection around her as she had been taught. Every time a ninja moth would try to fly into her, it would hit the shield blanket and be destroyed. The Dark made the moths bigger and bigger but they couldn't get past the blanket shield.

As Katelyn took a few more steps getting closer to The Rise, The Dark sent creepy-crawly insect-like creatures across the field where Katelyn was walking. They tried to grab at her ankles and attack her but the shield blanket protected her again. The Dark sent a tremblor across the land. This made Katelyn fall down but she got right back up and kept going. Tremblor after tremblor was sent and each time Katelyn fell, she got right back up and took a couple more steps.

Just as she arrived at the stairs, The Dark sent spears of laser-sharp energy at her. They hit the shield causing Katelyn to stumble from the energy released. She fell again and then decided to crawl up the stairs.

This maddened The Dark even more. It sent false images of the stairs on The Rise sinking into the ground. Katelyn only paused for less than a second the first time she saw this. She knew The Rise was a part of The Magic and was protected by The White Light. She had counted the stairs every time she climbed them and knew the exact number to the top.

The Dark made more stairs appear hoping this would make Katelyn get confused and tired and decide to go back down and away from The Rise.

It didn't work. As soon as she had counted the last step to the top, she rolled across the top of The Rise and sat there for a minute. The sky was an angry black with lightning shooting all through it and hitting the ground, exploding all it touched. The air felt heavy as she stood up. It took some effort to stay standing in that heavy air. It felt like it was pressing down on her.

When she turned to walk to the center of The Rise, she heard a low-pitched growling voice.

"You are weak and worthless. You can't survive up here," the voice said.

Katelyn just smiled as she hollered out, "Fuck you! I walk in The White Light."

The voice howled long and loud and was heard throughout The Creek. The folks at The Store heard it and they all looked at each other.

"Well, I guess the bad guys are tryin' to scare us," Ted said with a smile.

"Not gonna' happen," Hal answered back.

Folks sat around and offered prayers of love to The Creek and The Divine knowing that this helped in some way. More folks came in and they had brought their crystals with them. They set them on every window sill all over The Store. Those crystals may have been small but they began to glow like they were as powerful as those search lights at a premier opening in Hollywood.

Kendra, Emily, and Miss Cora looked at each other as Miss Cora said, "I do believe our Katelyn has arrived wherever she was supposed to go. Sounds like The Dark didn't keep her away."

"Sure does," Kendra said laughing.

"I don't believe The Dark is ever gonna' learn that the folks that do battle against The Dark are well protected by The White Light."

"True. Still, their earthly bodies can be and have been known to be destroyed in these battles."

"I don't like to remember that, although I know it to be true," Kendra said.

"I didn't know that. Now, that does scare me a bit," Emily said.

"That's why our teachin' Katelyn all we know and can to prepare her for battle is so important. This is gonna' be one of the fiercest battles we've ever seen in The Creek. The Dark wants The Special Magic and Powers from a special place. It doesn't know where that place is, but it figures if it tortures Katelyn enough, she'll give up the location. And, if she doesn't, it will try to kill her and destroy all of The Creek so The Special Magic and Powers will be revealed."

"Now, that's crazy thinkin' for sure," Emily said.

"Sure is. And, it won't work," Kendra offered. "The Dark could blow the earth apart and The Special Magic and Powers will forever be protected and hidden by The White Light."

"Ya 'think The Dark would have figured that out by now, but apparently not. Ya' gotta' give it a point for being consistent in it's efforts," Miss Cora said laughing.

Ethan sent his crews home as soon as he got the text about the ninja moths from Ian. He got to the shop just as another swarm smashed into the outside of the shop. The swarm retreated and flew off to attack folks at the dig site.

The ninja moths arrived at the dig site at the same time Katelyn rolled onto the top of The Rise.

The crew at the site was busy packing up on account of the text they received from Ted at The Store. He kept in touch with everyone in the area.

One of the students shouted when she saw the swarm approach and everyone dropped what they were doing and ran for their vehicles. The ninja moths covered each vehicle and tried to break the glass. When this didn't work, they took to beating their wings faster and faster setting up a loud high pitched humming sound that made people's heads hurt.

One guy decided to turn on the windshield wipers and spray the window. He had washer fluid in the reservoir and it made the moths burst into flames and then disappear. This was texted around the site and more and more of the ninja moths were destroyed. A few students sent the text to everyone they knew and the same thing started happening all over the Blue Ridge. Some folks put their windshield washer solution into spray bottles, opened the windows and sprayed the moths that way. It worked, too.

One of the professor's was in his own car alone and he turned the windshield wipers on and sprayed the ninja moths. He only had water in the reservoir. This made the ninja moths increase in size so much that they lifted his car high into the air almost out of site then released it. It crashed into some of the trees off to the side of the dig. It burst into flames and blew up.

A second swarm destroyed one of the dig areas by blowing up the earth. You can only imagine the mess. The ninja moths finally flew off. Their numbers were greatly depleted by the windshield washer solution which made The Dark even madder than it already was.

Jordan saw the swarms go by but none had come his way. He suddenly felt a strong need to go to the cave. He thought about this for a minute or two then knew he was to go there. He grabbed the crystal sword he had been given and stepped onto the back porch where George was waiting for him. They set out together.

They didn't have any trouble until they got to the cave entrance. As Jordan looked out across the field, he saw a swarm of the hummingbird ninja moths clearing the treetops in the west aiming for him. He moved the bushes aside and pushed George in just as they arrived. They tried to attack his head but he waved the sword in a circle around his head and body and the moths were sliced into oblivion. He ducked into the cave before they could attack again.

They tried to get into the cave but couldn't no matter what they did. This made them angry. They tried to blow up the earth above the cave, but The White Light had the place protected. This made them even angrier. The flew up into the sky swirling and moving in waves over the field before they flew off. They were directed by The Dark to attack Gerry's place.

Gerry and Tommy were standing by the patio doors when they heard the buzzing sound and looked up to see the ninja moths aiming for them. They got inside safely and watched as the ninja moths tried to attack the land and buildings. They couldn't get anywhere near anything. They tried again and again then finally gave up. The flew off up the road and blew up a bunch of trees and rocks just because they were angry. Emily had set up a protection grid around the property, including the forest all around, the week before to make sure it would be safe for everyone including the new construction and landscaping work.

Jordan and George walked into the main room and saw that all the crystals were glowing in a rhythmic pattern. This was something new. It was beautiful. It brought a faint memory to Jordan he couldn't quite place. It felt very familiar to him. He knew he had seen it before. But he couldn't figure out how. He knew he had never seen it in this life. The memory stayed with him.

Just as Jordan was turning to look at George, George morphed into his human form.

"Hey, Jordan," George said smiling at Jordan.

"Hey, George. Nice to see the human you again," Jordan replied. "Something must be about to happen if you're here like this."

"Yes, Jordan, it has already begun. The Dark is trying to find and take The Special Magic and Powers from this place."

"When is The Dark ever gonna' give up? It won't ever find it," Jordan said.

"True. But, as long as it keeps trying, it can kill people and take the regular Magic from this place and other places around the globe."

"Good point, George. Why am I here? I've felt a pull to be here for the past couple of days."

"Good for you for following your instincts," George said.

"And, George, I've seen these rhythmic crystals glowing like this before. I know it hasn't been in this place and this time. It's like a soft, distant memory. But I know I've seen them like this before."

George just looked at Jordan without saying a word.

"Oh, okay. I'm not supposed to know right now. Got it. This Magic stuff sure has lots of rules," Jordan said shaking his head and laughing a bit.

"It sure does, Jordan, it sure does and there are excellent reasons for them," George replied.

"Okay then. I guess I'm gonna' have to figure out why I'm here and what I need to do," Jordan said looking out over the room.

"Yes, you are," George said. "So, be still and take in the energy of the room."

Jordan stood watching the crystals and it became mesmerizing. He felt the energy flowing over the room and began to sway with the flow. H watched as vision after vision was shown to him in the air over the center of the room. He saw a place out of time with a man and woman clothed in long robes working at a table with animals watching them. He saw the stars in the sky and saw what looked like a UFO fly by. It wasn't a shooting star. He saw this cave in a different time and space and the crystals were all there as now. He saw George as an eagle, a man, and a hawk of great importance.

Then, as he watched, he saw the eyes he had seen in the small purple tunnel looking at him. Staring at him for the longest moment and he knew those eyes were familiar to him. They slowly faded away.

The final vision was of Katelyn climbing onto the top of The Rise right at this moment that he was in the cave with George. The sky looked angry as she stood tall. She was looking over the land and had just spotted Jordan's place. She focused on the cave and smiled at Jordan and nodded her head to let him know she had seen him, too. The vision faded quickly and the room returned to its usual self.

"George, Katelyn's on top of The Rise and I know she's gonna' need help in this battle. That's why we're here in the cave. I'm supposed to help her. Not sure how though."

"You are correct, Jordan. You are going to help her but not right this minute. Very soon though. Just stay focused on the crystals and you will know when the time is right."

"Thanks, George," Jordan said as he focused on the crystals once again.

Kendra knew the instant Katelyn arrived on the top of The Rise.

"Miss Cora, I know where Katelyn is. She's on The Rise," Kendra said.

"Yes, she is. Now, lets get busy helpin' her from here with everything we've got," Miss Cora replied.

Kendra, Miss Cora, and Emily began sending wave after wave of positive energy to The Rise and Katelyn. They began chanting as well. They settled into the hypnotic chants and the here and now vanished as they worked at keeping Katelyn safe and alive.

Jonah was busy quieting Emily's horses and all. They knew when a battle was coming and they knew this was a bad one. Jonah was feeding them an herbal blend to help keep them calm. Trouble was even quieter than usual. He had taken up a spot near one of the stall doors and was lying there looking all around. Jonah gave him some of the herbal blend as well as all the critters on the farm.

Katelyn watched the sky change colors as The Dark amped up targeting places around the Blue Ridge with lightning bolts. She could see them fly out of the dark in shades of fire red, flashing orange, and bright green hitting their targets near and far. She was stunned at all the destruction.

She watched as two bolts hit close to her brother's new builds. She immediately asked for protection and the next bolt that should have blown everything to hell was blocked. She heard a growling scream come out of the clouds and figured it had to be The Dark pissed off because the bolt had been blocked.

Katelyn knew she needed to get to the center of The Rise. There was something special she felt she needed to do although she didn't know what that was. As she turned from the side of The Rise to begin to walk to the center, she was blocked from moving. It was as if there was a wall of something she couldn't see in front of her. She tried to put her hand out in front of herself but it was blocked as well. She stood there for a minute and the thought to try to slide her foot forward came to her. She tried and as long as her foot was touching the ground it moved forward.

She drew it back and stood there thinking for a minute. She remembered how she had crawled on her belly to The Cave in the first alternate dimension. She wondered if it would work here.

She decided to try it. She lay flat on the ground and began to belly crawl towards the center. It worked! As long as she kept herself touching the ground, she could move forward. It would take a while to get there because every time she forgot and lifted her knee or some other part of her body off the ground, she was blocked.

As she continued on towards the center, sharp white spears of light were flashed right in front of here eyes almost blinding her. They caused immense pain across her face.

"I call upon The White Light to protect me," Katelyn hollered out. The flashes of light must have been taken away as she could see again and felt no more pain.

As she inched forward, the air around The Rise began to blow in circles. It had been absolutely still until now. It seemed as if it was being stirred by a giant spoon ever so slowly at first. The closer to the center she got, the faster the spoon seemed to stir the air. She was only a couple of feet away when the wind picked up in intensity.

Stuff was blowing all over the place at her and around her. Small twigs, leaves, and even a few berry plants flew close by her face. She tucked her head down and kept moving towards the center. She reached out with her right arm and felt the crystal that lay in the center of The Rise. She heard a mind-numbing scream as she stood up. The Dark was totally out of control and sent a huge tremblor across The Rise. Katelyn fell down and grabbed onto the crystal in the middle of The Rise. As soon as she touched it, the tremblor stopped. She thanked the crystal and stood up once again.

"Oh, you think you have won because you have reached the center. You haven't even come close to fulfilling your purpose. Your reward for failure is that you will die a thousand deaths now each one more horrible than the last one. No one conquers The Dark. No one!"

"Don't be so sure of that. I am not finished yet," Katelyn yelled into the air which was pitch black and swirling all around in every direction possible.

She turned and focused on the crystal that lay in the middle of The Rise. It began pulsating and turning colors. She looked right at it and then saw a vision of what she needed to do. She bowed her head in acknowledgement of the message.

As she watched, the crystals she had placed on The Rise a few days before began to come up out of the earth right in front of her. She looked for the four football shaped crystals and knew just what to do with them. She was to make a medicine wheel and the four footballs were to be set in the four directions. The crystal she had placed on The Rise when she returned from her second dimensional trip was already in the center and this was to be the center of the medicine wheel.

She took hold of the yellow one and crawled to the east side of The Rise. A pattern appeared as if someone had drawn it there for her to follow. As soon as she set the crystal in its place, The Dark sent a tremblor trying to shake the crystal off its mark. It didn't work. The Dark screamed again.

Katelyn crawled back to the crystals and took the red one and set out for the southern point of the pattern. As soon as she set this crystal in its place, The Dark made hot lava burst out from the inside of The Rise. Mother Earth took care of this and the hot lava was cooled so fast that more crystals were formed right in front of Katelyn. They began to pulsate and hum. The Dark decided to increase the wind making it difficult for Katelyn to even crawl over the earth.

She did crawl back to the crystals and took handfuls of the smallest ones as she was directed to place them in an arch between the two football ones she had already set in place. As soon as they were connected, a blue energy bolt shot from The Rise and pierced a hole in the blackened sky. The Dark was not prepared for this. It sent laser bolts of fire at The Rise but they couldn't penetrate the protection that The White Light had put in place.

Katelyn knew she needed to set the other two football crystals as fast as she could. She grabbed the blue one and rolled to the western point of the circle pattern and placed it on the ground so fast The Dark didn't have time to bother her. She tried to stand, but that energy block was back. So, she went back to crawling and took more small crystals and placed them between the southern set crystal and the western set crystal. This caused a green energy bolt to shoot out and pierce the darkened sky. Now two points of light shown through. The Dark tried to destroy these two points of light but no matter what it tried; they would not go away. The sunlight shown through these points onto The Rise and showed Katelyn just what she needed to see.

The wind intensified beyond category 5 hurricane force. It made it almost impossible to breathe. She was told to lay small crystals from the eastern point to where the northern point would be. This was where the last football crystal was to be placed. She gathered more small crystals and placed them from the western and eastern points to where the last crystal would be placed on the northern point as directed. Now, she was told to lay more small crystals from each directional crystal to the original crystal that was in the center of The Rise. She completed connecting the crystals all around except for the last one. It took a bit of time but she finally finished. She was exhausted.

She tried to crawl to get the last football crystal, the purple one, but no matter how hard she tried to crawl along the ground, she was totally blocked. As she looked up, she saw the sky change shape and fiery red demons on yellow lightning bolts came riding towards The Rise. She knew she would be destroyed and all of the earth would be destroyed in an instant if she didn't come up with something to stop them. She lay there exhausted and terrified. As she tried to calm her mind, she had a flash vision of warriors all in white and silver helping her.

She suddenly remembered what Miss Cora and the others had taught her.

She called out loud to the air, "I call upon the White Light Warriors and the White Light Paladins to help save this sacred place."

In an instant she saw Finn and Jay as White Light Paladins come riding through the air on white horses. They were clothed in silver with silver crystal swords at their sides. Each sword had four small crystals in the colors of the four medicine wheel football crystals across each hilt. Right behind them, she saw countless numbers of White Light Warriors streaking through the sky. They were dressed in all the colors of the medicine wheel and rode white horses as well.

She had thought the scream and growl from The Dark she had heard before was horrendous, but the sound that came from the blackened sky was beyond description. It made her body tremble. The White Light Warriors flew right to The Rise, encircling it fighting off the energy bolts The Dark was relentlessly sending earthward. Other warriors flew across the sky intercepting other energy bolts, destroying them.

The wind was still blowing and Katelyn tried again to crawl to where the purple crystal lay. She could only move a few centimeters at a time. She cried out for more help and, as she watched, she saw forms begin to take shape just above her in the air. She couldn't believe her eyes as she saw Sami fly by her. Sami smiled and winked at Katelyn as she slashed out with her sword of brilliant blue at anything The Dark sent towards The Rise.

A second shape took form. There was no way this was for real. It was Jonah from Emily's place. He smiled at Katelyn and fought off The Dark just like Sami. They were dressed in silver cloth that showed the left shoulder and neck area. They both had some kind of tattoo or something along their shoulders. They did a great deal of damage to The Dark but the wind never stopped.

Finn and Jay encircled the medicine wheel to help Katelyn finish placing the purple crystal in the direction of the north.

Katelyn called out to the Spirit of The Wind, "Spirit of The Wind, please lessen so I can complete the medicine wheel and save The Magic of this place."

The Spirit of The Wind answered back, "You need one more special warrior to help you. Call out for him now."

Katelyn didn't have any idea who that was but she called out for him anyway.

"I call upon the special warrior The Spirit of The Wind told to me to call for. Please come and help me now."

Jordan and George were still in the cave as Katelyn called out for the special warrior to help her. They both heard her and stood looking at each other as the energy in the cave changed.

All of a sudden, Jordan was dressed all in purple. He knew he was to be transported to The Rise to help. He grabbed the crystal sword and nodded to George. Then he was gone.

A form was coming to life right in front of Katelyn as she lay on the ground. She watched as this form took the shape of a man. No way! No fucking way! She saw Jordan take shape in front of her. She lay there stunned beyond belief.

"Jordan?" Katelyn said.

"Yup, it's me. I don't know anything about all this except I'm supposed to give you this crystal sword. Here ya' go," Jordan answered as he held the sword out to Katelyn.

She tried to stand but the wind was still blowing. She took the sword while she lay on the ground.

"Point the sword at the wind," Jordan instructed her.

She did just that and the wind decreased to about half it's strength. She immediately stood up.

"I don't even know what to say. Thank you for being here. I need to get to the purple crystal and place it in the northern direction to complete the medicine wheel. This is gonna' get really bad."

"I agree. I'll try to help all I can," Jordan said as Katelyn took two steps toward where the purple football crystal lay.

Jordan spread his arms in a kind of shield as he moved in front of Katelyn. Sami flew in and stayed just above Katelyn as she worked at moving forward. Jonah was out in the sky with The White Light Warriors slaying the red demons. The Dark was sending more and more of them, then it decided to throw all it had at Katelyn. It sent disks of pure evil energy that looked like giant saw blades from all directions. Katelyn had to lash out with her crystal sword to destroy a few of them. They kept her from getting closer to the purple crystal.

"I've got one more thing to say. I call upon The Special White Light Paladins to help save this sacred place."

Finn and Jay were joined by an army of White Light Paladins. They were all in silver with purple sashes and swords. They targeted the giant demon saw blades and as soon as their purple swords made contact with the saw blade, it was blown into millions of pieces every color of the rainbow that vanished like fireworks. The sky was lit up as far as anyone could see. It looked like the best July 4th fireworks ever.

"Now, that's what I call first-class assistance. Thanks, y'all," Katelyn said as she made progress towards the purple crystal. As she looked around, she saw the tattoo thing on Sami and Jordan's left shoulders. It looked like the tail of something. Before she could think about it a second more, she felt The Rise shake so hard she thought it would collapse. She had reached the purple crystal. She bent down and grabbed it and held it close to her.

She looked at all the warriors and paladins and said, "I know I may not survive this battle, but I'm gonna' do my best."

She took one step towards the medicine wheel and felt such a deep sadness that she stopped breathing for a second. She saw her mother and father being tortured and killed in the house she grew up in. The image was so real, she threw up. She was sobbing and shaking from shock. She heard a voice say to her, "Katelyn, it's not real. The Dark is trying to keep you from getting to the medicine wheel. Don't believe it."

She looked up and realized she had stopped moving. She stood tall and squared her shoulders and took a few more steps toward the medicine wheel.

Just then, she saw a flash of orange fire in the sky above her head. When she looked, Sami was gone. Sami's body came crashing to the ground in front of Katelyn. It was all beaten up and mangled. Katelyn took one look and hollered out, "Not gonna' believe you. She's still right here above my head protecting me, you bastard."

The Dark howled and the sky shook. It sent more red demons and energy bolts aimed at Jonah, Jordan, and Sami. They destroyed every one of them with their swords.

As Katelyn took the last step and bent to place the purple crystal in its place, Sami became evil. She pushed Katelyn to the ground and began stabbing her with her sword. Katelyn instinctively knew it wasn't Sami. She raised her crystal sword above her head and pointed it at the evil Sami.

"I blast you to the spaces between the spaces for all eternity," Katelyn said crying as an energy bolt flew off the end of her crystal sword and hit Sami in the heart. The evil Sami blew into black pieces and was taken up into the outer sky to be held in the spaces between the spaces.

Katelyn, once again, bent to place the purple crystal. This time she raised her crystal sword above her and encircled herself with it and dropped the crystal. It settled into its place and a huge purple energy wave was thrown into the sky from The Rise. That energy wave looked like a nuclear explosion had taken place.

Several purple energy waves followed and as each one hit The Dark entities, they vanished and the sky began to return to its usual blue self. Katelyn stood up and looked for Sami, Jonah, and Jordan, but they were no where to be seen. It's as if they, too, had vanished as soon as the medicine wheel was complete. Katelyn heard a humming sound and turned to look at The Rise. The medicine wheel was glowing like all get-out and the crystals were humming as if they were singing a song. The football crystals had changed into signs of the zodiac with the center one being of Pisces.

The sky was instantly cleared and the night was in place. The stars shown like diamonds that had been charged with electricity and the hurricane wind had changed into a nice breeze as is normally felt in the Blue Ridge. Katelyn felt something in her hand, and when she looked down, she saw the crystal sword. It was glowing and humming right along with all the other crystals on The Rise.

As she looked around, she realized she was alone. She sent a thought of thanks to all that had helped her and realized she was exhausted. She stood looking at the medicine wheel for a long time. She didn't even know how long she stood there until she heard someone calling her name.

"Katelyn? You okay?" It was her mom. Her dad and brothers were there as well.

She looked at them and smiled, "As a matter of fact, I'm perfectly alright. Hungry as anything and tired beyond words, but, I'm alright."

"Did you see the fireworks?" Nathan asked.

"Yup. That's why I came up here. To watch them. They were the best ever," Katelyn said smiling.

"We all thought we'd do the same thing, but they were finished by the time we got here. We saw your truck and decided to climb up The Rise anyway. You know it's past midnight, right?" her dad asked her.

"Really? I honestly had no idea what time it was. It was as if time stood still."

"Would ya' look at that?" Katelyn's brothers said at the same time.

"Why, it's a medicine wheel made of crystals. And they're glowing somethin' fierce. Never saw anything like this before," Katelyn's dad said.

They all watched the crystals for a few minutes.

"I wonder if those fireworks had anything to do with this?" Katelyn's dad said.

Katelyn's mom looked right at her and Katelyn gave her a little nod, letting her know that The Magic had been at work.

"Well, let's get back to the house. I could use a late-night snack as well," Katelyn's mom offered.

They all left The Rise with Katelyn being the last to leave. She turned and looked at the medicine wheel one more time and an apparition appeared over the center of the wheel.

"Katelyn, thank you for taking on this battle. You have served The White Light well and we are all grateful for your work. We know you are injured and will heal you as you sleep tonight. The crystal sword is yours for all eternity. It will serve you well. You have saved The Special Magic and Powers in the cave and kept their home secret. You and Jordan and George are the only ones who know about this special place. Go now and know we are safe."

The apparition, all white, blue, and gold, rose up into the sky and sent a rainbow streaking across the stars.

"Look at that," Nathan hollered out and they all looked up at the rainbow as it was streaked across the heavens.

"Now, that's what I call a very special goodnight," Katelyn's mom said as she placed an arm around Katelyn as she joined the group.

They headed home and had a late-night party. Katelyn drove home and fell sound asleep holding onto her crystal sword.

The last thing she remembered was the tattoo on the shoulders of the three who fought with her. She was gonna' check that out in the morning for sure.

The Special Magic and The Powers were safe in The Cave.

And all of The Creek was safe as well.

CHAPTER 35

atelyn's phone alarm woke her up Tuesday morning. She started to get up and felt a bit stiff and sore. She remembered all about the battle and was surprised that she didn't feel worse. She stretched slowly and finally got out of bed and headed to the bathroom for her usual morning shower. As she took a quick look in the mirror she came to a sudden stop, backed up, and turned to look at herself again. No way! No fuckin' way! She walked right up to the sink and leaned into the mirror for a closer look. Her once dark blondish-light brown hair was now dark brown with silver streaks cascading from the top of her head. There were about seven in all as she turned around counting them to be sure. They were zigzagged like a lightning bolt. Holy shit!

She stood there for the longest time with the hand mirror turning this way and that to get a closer look at all of them. She was shocked. How was she gonna' explain this to everyone? Hey! Maybe they would wash out in the shower. She got in and washed her hair twice and finished in record time. She wrapped her head in a towel, got out, got dressed for the day, then went back into the bathroom and removed the towel from her head. They were still there. Holy shit! This was gonna' be an interesting day for sure.

Sami walked by Katelyn as she finished drying her hair and came to a quick stop.

"No fuckin' way! Ya' gotta' be kidding me!" Sami hollered out.

"Yes, in every fuckin' way," Katelyn replied laughing at herself and Sami's expression. "I thought they might disappear in the shower. Nope. I do believe they're here to stay."

Katelyn turned to look at Sami and saw part of the tattoo thing on her shoulder before Sami could cover it up.

"No way are you gonna' get out of tellin' me the truth about you and that tattoo thing. Jordan and Jonah have the same thing."

"Have you looked at your shoulder in the last few seconds?" Sami asked pointing to Katelyn's left shoulder.

"There's nothing there. I just got out of the shower and there wasn't a tattoo thing on my shoulder like there is on yours. Spill."

"Look again, my friend," Sami said pointing at Katelyn's shoulder again.

Katelyn whipped off her shirt and there it was. Just like Sami's.

"Holy shit! What is that and why do I now have one?" Katelyn hollered out.

They looked at each other in silence for a minute before Sami said, "Looks like we're all a part of The Special Magic around here. That's all I got right now."

"Oh, really? And when did you learn to fly? Tell me everything right now," Katelyn hollered as they walked to the kitchen.

"Sit," Sami said as Kendra walked in the door.

"Time to explain you, huh?" Kendra said.

"Yup. Food first. I'm starvin'," Sami said

"Yes, food first," Katelyn said as the three of them made a quick breakfast and sat at the kitchen table.

"I remember everything from yesterday. Especially the part where you, Jordan, and Jonah came flyin' in and fought with me. I want all the details about you Sami. Now."

"I guess we gotta' tell her don't we, Kendra?" Sami said

"Yup. It's time," Kendra said. "You go first then I'll fill in about the guys."

"I don't know why I even bother to question how you know about all this, Kendra," Katelyn said looking at Kendra and Sami.

"So glad you've figured that out. Get comfy. This is gonna' take a while," Kendra said.

"Well, to get started, I'm a shapeshifter. An alien," Sami said looking straight into Katelyn's eyes.

"Okay then. I'll believe pretty much anything after yesterday," Katelyn said. "Why haven't you told me before all this or even when we first met? Oh, wait. Don't bother. It wasn't the right time."

"Correct. At least I don't have to explain that. Remember when we first met in college? We were both having a great time."

Yes, I do. It was a great time. We became best friends almost overnight."

"Do you remember what was happening with you, personally, at the time?"

"Ah, give me a minute to think. We were doing a lot of architectural stuff. And, uh, I think that's about the time I kept having those premonitions about stuff happening. They were more than usual."

"Yes, that's it exactly."

"Now that I think of it, it seems I was seein' a lot of stuff about magic and ghosts and all."

"Yup. Anything else?"

"I seem to remember tellin' you I thought I'd seen a wavy ghost one night when I was walking to the house from my car."

"Yes, you did. Katelyn. I was sent to you at that precise time to protect you 'cause you were coming into your Gifts and you needed to be kept safe until you returned here to The Creek and we could teach you stuff."

"Really? You know about this, Kendra?"

"Yes, Katelyn. I do. You see, I'm an alien too. An ET. I'm a shapeshifter like Sami here."

"Holy shit! Really?"

"Really," Sami and Kendra answered at the same time.

"I got lots of questions now," Katelyn said. "Like, is Jonah a shapeshifter, too?"

"Yes, he is," Kendra said.

"And, Jordan?"

"No, not Jordan," Kendra answered.

"But he was flyin' around, too," Katelyn said.

"He was. But, he's a human person," Sami replied.

"No, he's not. People can't fly. Tell me what's goin' on," Katelyn said rather strongly.

"Katelyn, Jordan is a special kind of human. He's not an alien. He was given the gift of flight to get the crystal sword to you. He'll remember everything about yesterday though. And, he'll need some time to figure it out. I'm gonna' help him as best I can," Kendra explained.

"Okay. That's good. Hope he doesn't flip out over all this. He does seem to be accepting all The Magic stuff around here. Guess he'll be okay," Katelyn thought out loud. "But, what about Jonah? Has he always been a shapeshifter?"

"Yes, he has and always will be. He's here in The Creek to help keep The Magic safe and all the gifted folks safe as well. He sure loves the animals," Kendra explained.

"He sure does," Katelyn agreed. "So, now that I know about the three of you does that change things at all?"

"Well, only that you can't tell anyone else. You need to keep our secret," Kendra answered.

Before Katelyn could say another word, there was a knock on her front door.

"That's Miss Cora," Kendra said.

"Come on in. We're in the kitchen, Miss Cora," Katelyn called out.

"Mornin' Miss Cora," Sami said smiling at Miss Cora.

"So, ya' know about these two now?" Miss Cora said as she sat down.

"Yes, Ma'am, I just found out. May I fix you some tea?" Katelyn asked.

"Why, yes. Thanks Katelyn," Miss Cora answered.

"I have a question for you, Miss Cora," Katelyn began as she fixed Miss Cora's tea and placed it on the table. "Are you a shapeshifter, too, Miss Cora?"

"No, Katelyn, I'm not." Miss Cora answered.

"So, how do you know about all The Magic around here?"

"I'm a kind of guardian here. My ancestors and all have always been guardians of The Magic in The Creek ever since we first settled here."

"Well, I guess that makes sense and all, keeping it in the family," Katelyn replied.

"Each one of us was asked if we wanted the job and each one of us agreed to do the work."

"So glad y'all have," Emily said.

"Are there any more surprises I need to know about before they happen?" Katelyn said looking at the three of them.

"I think you've seen enough for a while," Miss Cora said.

"Well, I guess that will have to do for now. I know The Magic is alive and well around here and that there will probably be more stuff happening. So, I'll just keep a bit tuned in."

"That's good thinkin'," Kendra said. "Katelyn, what you did has thrown The Dark so far away from the earth that it won't be back for a long, long time. It's in a whole different place and weakened to almost nothing. It will take it a long while to even think about gaining strength. It will work at conquering other dimensions and places, not The Creek in any dimension, to get its powers back. You really offset the balance in The White Light's favor. Time for us to help those that are just waking up to their gifts and all."

"That's just what I was thinkin', Kendra," Miss Cora said.

"I accept all of that. I would like to get back to a more normal life for a while, though" Katelyn said.

"We all would," Emily agreed.

"And, so we will. There's always gonna' be the struggle between good and evil among the human race. But it will not be greatly influenced by The

450

Dark for a long, long time. It will be the more normal kind of stuff, as you call it," Miss Cora explained.

"Oh. Just one more thing. Miss Cora, the crystals on The Rise, some of the special ones, all changed into some of the signs of the zodiac as soon as a special somethin' was finished. Sorry, I can't tell ya' yet. You'll see when the time is right. I was wonderin' if you've ever seen those zodiac symbols around here before?

"Yes, Katelyn. I have. I've seen them on some of the trees in the Applewood Grove. There must be a connection for sure," Miss Cora answered in such a way that no on was to ask more about them.

"Okay, then. I love you all so dearly and thank you for all your wisdom and love. I look forward to a more normal life from this moment forward. So, do y'all like my new hair-do?" Katelyn declared.

"It's amazing what fighting The Dark with help of The White Light Paladins can do to a person," Miss Cora said.

"I like it. Wicked cool," Kendra said.

"Thanks, y'all. It's gonna' be interesting to see how everyone else reacts to it. I know, just another Magical day in The Creek," Katelyn said. "Just one more thing, can we all get back to some kind of normal for a while, please?"

"As it is so shall it be," Kendra, Emily, and Miss Cora said at the exact same time.

The four of them chatted about everyday stuff for a few more minutes than each went on their way.

Katelyn got to the shop around noon and Ethan, Ian, and Finn were waiting for her.

They all just stared at her for a minute before all talking at once.

"Would ya' look at that?"

"Holy shit, Katie girl."

"I guess that must have been some battle."

"Hi guys. And, yes, to all of it," Katelyn said as she walked up to them.

Finn reached out and touched her hair. "This happen to you yesterday?"

"Yes, it did. And, yes, I was fighting a battle with The Dark. And, yes, The White Light won as if you couldn't figure that out. The hair is here to stay."

"Those weren't fireworks, were they?" Ian asked.

"Nope," Katelyn replied.

"And, that wasn't a thunderstorm, either, was it?" Ethan asked.

"Nope," Katelyn replied.

"Ya' gonna' give us any details," Finn asked.

"Nope," Katelyn replied again, looking at the three of them.

"Well, I guess we should get busy with the business of buildin' things, then," Ethan said shaking his head and laughing. "Never thought our mild-mannered Katie would turn out to be a fierce warrior. Love all of it."

"Oh, these are muffins I made this morning. Enjoy," Katelyn said as she set them on the coffee table.

"A fierce warrior and a great cook. I love the combination," Finn said kissing the top of Katelyn's head while he grabbed a muffin.

"I kind of like the sound of that myself," Katelyn said as she went into her office and got busy.

The Creek was talking about the fireworks display all day. Some folks wondered who had set it off while others had a pretty good idea it had some-thing to do with protecting The Creek and The Magic.

Jordan kept walking around his house and farm all day. He was in awe of all that had happened. He accepted that The Magic was alive and well in The Creek. He knew his cave protected The Special Magic and The Powers and that George could take any living form he wanted to. All the rest was new to him. He was gonna' call Katelyn and have a talk with her. Just as he grabbed his phone, it rang. It was Katelyn.

"Hey, Jordan," Katelyn said.

"Great minds, Katelyn. I was just gonna' call you," Jordan answered.

"I know why. Let's get together tonight and have a long talk. I've got a few more things to finish at the shop then I'll come over around six"

"I'll fix something for supper. Oh, George says hi. He's standing on the back porch listening to this call."

"I love that George. Yes, I do. Great idea about supper. Hadn't even thought about that. Still a bit distracted I guess."

"You guess?! I'd say so for sure. I never knew I could fly," Jordan said laughing.

"Neither did I. See ya' later," Katelyn said laughing as well as they signed off.

When Katelyn arrived, George was waiting for her. He had flown to the shop and waited for her to leave then flew along with her to the farm.

"Hey, George. Thanks for the escort. You are a true gentleman or should I say a true gentle-eagle."

George bowed to Katelyn and gave a soft squawk.

"That's eagle for anytime," Jordan said as he came across the drive-way.

Jordan and Katelyn stood looking at each other for a minute then hugged and went into the house.

"This looks great," Katelyn said as she washed up at the kitchen sink. George had followed them into the kitchen. "So, George, are you a house pet now?"

George squawked and Jordan laughed. "He tries to sneak in as much as I let him. You can stay for a while George. Just don't leave any presents around the place, okay?"

George ruffled his feathers and Katelyn and Jordan laughed as they ate their supper.

George walked over to the kitchen door and Katelyn opened it for him. He bobbed at her and flew off.

"I do love that George. I swear he knows just what we're sayin'," Katelyn said as they cleaned up after supper.

They settled in the living room on the big couch and Jordan turned to Katelyn.

"What the hell was that all about? Flyin' and fightin' and all. And, look at your hair!" Jordan began.

"Jordan, I was as surprised as you about the three of you and all that you did. And my new hair thing. It's here to stay. And, what about that marc on your left shoulder? Don't tell me you haven't noticed it yet?"

"Oh, I noticed it as soon as I got home and pulled my shirt off to take a shower. What the hell is that?"

"Sami filled me in on her special thing. I asked about the three of you with the marc and she said I had one, too. I said no and she said to take a look. And, there it was. Is. See?" Katelyn said as she lowered her shirt off her left shoulder and turned so Jordan could see the marc.

"Holy shit, Katelyn! It's the same as mine right down to the little wing thing at the tip of the tail," Jordan hollered as he took his shirt off to show Katelyn his marc. "Let's go look in the big mirror."

They stood in front of the big mirror over the office bookcase and just stared at each other's shoulders. The marcs were identical. They started just to the left of the base of the neck then wove around the shoulder with the tip of the tail just on the top of the shoulder. Exactly the same.

"I wonder if that's there 'cause of the battle and all?" Jordan said as they returned to the couch.

"I don't think so. I saw that marc on the three of you: Jonah, Sami, and you, during the battle. Mine only appeared this morning. And, I like the hair thing."

"I haven't ever seen it before last night. This is really weird although I don't get a bad feelin' about it. Just not sure what it's all about."

"I don't get a bad feelin', either. Just haven't had time to ask The Other Side about it. Maybe we're not supposed to ask. I do know we'll find out when we're supposed to though."

"Oh, yeah, and, when did I learn to fly?" Jordan said jumping up and pacing.

"I did ask Miss Cora and Kendra about that. They said it was a gift for that time only so you could get the crystal sword to me. It's beautiful and I do thank you kindly."

"You are very welcome. It sure was fun flyin' although I would have preferred it during a good time, not in a battle. That was vicious and horrible. Those saw blades shootin' lasers were terrifyin'. Absolutely unimaginable."

"You're tellin' me!? I was just tryin' to get that last purple crystal in place. I was thinkin' I was surely gonna' die up there."

"I know the feelin'. And, I know I was injured a lot. Thing is, all those injuries were gone this morning. I only felt a little sore for a while. All okay now. How does all this happen?"

"Jordan, I have figured out it's best not to ask for all the details about this battle. You, me, all the others involved were chosen for special reasons and I don't even want to know those reasons. I'm just glad y'all were there to help keep The Creek and The Special Magic and The Powers safe from The Dark."

Jordan nodded his head in agreement and looked off into the air for a while. Katelyn sat quiet as she knew Jordan was working through all that they had been talking about and needed some time to begin to accept even a little of it right now.

The sun was throwing shadows across the sky and the house when Jordan seemed to come back from processing all that had happened.

"Well," Jordan sighed as he stood up. "This has been a lot to think about and it all makes sense. I'm just gonna' need a long while to think through all the details. I know we're all safe here for a long, long time. It just feels that way. And, I know we can go on with our lives in a more normal way, too. Glad for that. I thank you for your friendship and teachin' me about The Magic and all. And, that cave is spectacular. It's where I was given your sword. Now, that's gonna' be a story I tell ya' over a few beers and pizza down the road."

"I can't wait to hear all about it," Katelyn said as they walked to the front door.

"Let's watch the crystal as the sun begins to set. I feel the need to do that," Jordan said as they walked out onto the front porch and stepped into the yard.

As they turned to look at the crystal, George flew in and settled next to Jordan.

"George, I do believe you have ESP or somethin'. You seem to know just when to appear," Katelyn said softly.

George flapped a wing at Katelyn in response and looked at the crystal. The sun was just beginning to touch it and it came to life. No one else had stopped by to watch it this time. That seemed odd as folks were always coming by to watch the light and color show.

It was spectacular as always. When the sun finally dipped below the horizon, Jordan walked Katelyn to her SUV.

"Well, we are surely connected for life with the marc and all. I like that," Jordan said.

"I agree. I like that, too. And, George, of course," Katelyn said as George nudged Katelyn in the leg.

"I take that as a love tap, George, and I return the love to ya,' Katelyn said as she set her hand above his shoulders waiting for an okay to touch him. He raised up so her hand touched him and she gave him a love pat.

George sighed as he settled down.

"I'll see ya' around, Katelyn," Jordan said as they hugged good-bye.

The sky was just showing off with purple, gold, and orange sunbeams shooting out from the setting sun. They lasted only a few minutes, then the night came on in earnest and the stars showed up right on schedule. They were really shining bright tonight as if they, too, knew all The Magic was safe once again.

Katelyn drove off and Jordan and George walked up past the barn to the edge of the field. As they stood looking at the sky, a great shadow flew over them close to the earth. It was huge. It circled a few times more getting closer each time until the shape of the creature could not be dismissed.

Jordan was dumb-struck. He looked at George then at the creature again.

"Did I just see what I think I saw…a dragon? No…really?"

THE END

What's Next

The Legend of the Crystal Caves

THE LEGEND

T here's powers in those crystal caves. Strong and ancient powers guarded by a fierce creature. The creature will let some enter the caves to look around for only a minute then it scares them with fire and ice and horrible sounds until they leave: never to return.

Legend says there's a few special ones that are made to become one with The Crystal Caves. They've been around as long as The Crystal Caves. And, no one knows how long those caves have been around. Some folks found notes written about those caves and that creature from eons ago. Some found drawings of them. There are a few cave paintings in the mountains that show those caves and a strange creature standing in the middle of the crystals. Some say it's an alien. Others say it's a creature from ancient fairy tales put there to scare the kids so they won't look for The Crystal Caves.

Legend says most can't even find those caves. They are protected by strong powers. Some say it's The Ancient Magic that protects them.

Legend says those caves only become alive when their powers are needed to protect Mother Earth and Father Sky and to save The Special Magic and Special Powers.

Legends are made up of truth and speculation some would say.

The Legend of The Crystal Caves is surrounded in mystery and Magic.

About the Author

B orn and raised in the Mid-West, Karmle L. Conrad moved to New England in 1985 and built her home on Cape Cod in 1988. She completed her Doctorate in Public Health from Capella University in July 2022. Karmle has been Gifted as a Psychic Medium from birth.

The *Crab Apple Creek* set of *The Crab Apple Creek Anthology* is now complete. Karmle is working on the next 3-book set in the Anthology entitled *The Legend of The Crystal Caves.* The first book in this set is *THE CRYSTAL DRAGON.* Karmle has created a series for middle-aged kids called *The Tree-House Gang Mysteries.* The first 3 books are available on her website: www.thecapecodpsychic.com. Be sure to visit the website for more information as books and events are added.

www.ingramcontent.com/pod-product-compliance
Lightning Source LLC
Chambersburg PA
CBHW070542030726

47505CB00001B/124